THE VERITY DUOLOGY
THE VERITY: PART ONE
THE VERITY: PART TWO
MJ LAWRIE

COPYRIGHT

For the man who raised me. Who gave me my dark sense of humour. Who taught me how to be strong, independent and loyal. And who also taught me how to handle my whisky. Thank you for always being there for me and for accepting me for who I am. This book is for you, Dad. My very own Elder Eight. I wouldn't be me without you!

THE VERITY: PART ONE
MJ LAWRIE

CHAPTER ONE

A rare and welcomed gust of wind sweeps my long, auburn hair across my face. I scrape it up into a ponytail, gathering the thick mass of curls and tying it with string to keep it out of my eyes.

Crouching behind this brick barricade and keeping well out of sight is torture. Hiding, it goes against every instinct I have. My muscles twitch with the need to move and the more I think about what's coming, the harder my heart continues to beat and the more I struggle to keep from fidgeting.

I risk a sneaky peek over the barricade and have yet another scout of the area. There's not a single living tree in sight. Just their grey, brittle husks remain. The buildings are pretty much gone now. Only their bare metal frames and crumbling brickwork have been left behind. I can't remember the last time I saw a bird fly in the sky or a wild animal of any kind. I saw a dog once. I think. It ran off before I could get a proper look. Back home, we have livestock. Cows, chickens and sheep. But everything out in the wild is just... gone.

Well, almost everything.

'When are they gonna give the starting signal?' I whisper eagerly, glancing into the distance to a hill about a mile away. There, on its peak, is a large canopy with a dozen people sheltered beneath its shade. They're all watching me and the five others by my side as we remain crouching low, taking shelter behind this wall. 'I'm desperate to get out there,' I add. 'I don't know about you guys, but I can't wait!'

'Scarlett. This isn't supposed to be fun!' Tee hisses at me, jabbing her elbow into my ribs. With an enormous smirk, I murmur a less than genuine apology. 'And will you stop grinning like a lunatic!' she snaps. 'This is serious stuff. It's not a game.'

'Yeah, yeah,' I reply, rolling my eyes and wiping the beads of sweat from my brow. 'I know. I'm taking this perfectly seriously, as I always do. Keep your knickers on, Tee.'

'Never mind my knickers. Guide your concern to the mission.'

Q-Tee, my best friend. My sister, really. She swishes her long, brunette ponytail in annoyance and glares at me. She definitely has some Japanese heritage in her family tree. Of which I'm very jealous. Such a great culture.

Well, it was.

Tee usually has a smile that can make the coldest of hearts melt. Her eyes sparkle with kindness and her spirit just wraps you in love. She's a tall, slender and very elegant girl who always holds herself with grace. Even now, crouched behind a wall in this blistering heat and wearing all her leather battle gear, she does all those things. But today, her usual smile is nowhere to be seen.

Her hazel eyes are wide and dry. She hasn't blinked for far too long. She never does when she's in hostile territory. Even though I know that her heart is beating like crazy and that she's fighting the urge to throw up, she's ready to fight. Ready to kill.

The bow on her back makes her lethal. Her skills and accuracy with that thing are unreal. I once saw her use an arrow to put out the flame on a candle at one-hundred feet. Didn't even graze the wax.

Awesome.

Well, she has been using it since she was five.

I was the same age when I held my first sword.

I shot my first crossbow at six and learned to ride a horse while wielding both weapons at seven.

Our job is to kill.

We're very good at our job.

But unlike Tee, I *love* my work.

'It will be fine, Tee. Please. Blink,' I encourage with a squeeze of her shoulder. 'The way you're staring at me is making me nervous.'

'You're nervous?' she says in an uncomfortably high-pitched whine. 'You can't be nervous! You never get nervous!' She slams her hand over her eyes. 'We're all gonna die.'

'No one's gonna die. Right guys?' I look to the other four for some support in calming her down.

Flash nods far too eagerly. His eyebrows are so high, they're almost lost in his hairline and his body shakes as if he's freezing. Despite the dozens of beads of sweat trickling down his face. He's a skinny guy with extremely blonde hair who has the dullest blue eyes I've ever seen. Even duller today. Probably the result of a sleepless night. Even with no sleep behind him, he still moves faster than anyone I've ever known. Guy runs like the Devil is chasing him.

Most of the time, that's precisely what *is* chasing him.

Titan nods too, but much more confidently. He's a big guy with dark skin and short black hair. He's built like a tank and could probably crush your skull with his bare hands. But he's so gentle and sweet, he never would. He glances at Flash, careful not to show the slightest bit of the worry I know is boiling away underneath that calm exterior.

Worry. Not fear.

Because Titan's out here with the man he loves and losing Flash? Well, for Titan that would be worse than death.

He grips Flash's hand so hard, his fingers lack any colour. And Flash holds him back just as tightly.

Tee sees and gives a fretful little whimper.

Not getting any support from those two, clearly.

I look to Cass instead. A jittery archer is the last thing we need and he's always been a strong sense of reason for us all. No matter how much shit hits the fan, he never loses his cool.

'It'll be fine,' Cass agrees, as I knew he would. He places his hand on Tee's other shoulder and she relaxes ever so slightly knowing she's protected by us both. Cass's dark brown, permanently tousled hair, hangs over his grey eyes. He emanates calm. Control. Competence. But his strong jaw fails to make it into the reassuring smile I know he's trying his best to give her. She doesn't notice his disingenuous grin.

But I notice.

I also notice how his lean and muscled frame is tensed.

He's a good foot taller than me. Strong, athletic, quick and extremely lethal.

The perfect person to have by your side out here.

The perfect person full stop really.

'As long as we all do what we're supposed to do, everything will be fine,' he assures her. 'Scarlett isn't nervous. She never gets nervous. She's excited. Because she's an idiot and enjoys this madness.'

'An idiot that could kick your arse,' I remind him.

'In your dreams,' he replies, with the slightest hitch in the corner of his mouth.

'Alright. Fancy a bet?'

'What do you have in mind?'

'Whoever gets a lower kill count has to give the other a back rub.'

'Your back rubs are like slow punches along my spine,' he complains, eyebrows raised.

'Yeah,' I shrug. 'But yours are really good. And since I'll be winning anyhow, my crap back rubs are completely irrelevant.'

Cass gives a low, amused chuckle as Tee continues to glare at us both.

'We are about to face death. And you two are joking like it's any other day!' she scornfully hisses. 'Winder, will you tell th-'

'Is the sun falling to earth?' Winder groans, interrupting us and wiping the sweat from his face with the back of his hand. 'Because it really feels like the sun's getting closer. Did we miss the memo of yet another disaster trying to wipe us out, or what? I'm sweating like a pig.' His brow furrows and his eyes glaze slightly. 'Do pigs sweat? I mean, I've personally never seen a pig sweat, but people say they sweat.'

'I don't think pigs actually sweat, Winder,' I reply with a shrug and checking my dagger is secure in my leg holster. 'It's an expression. Like... raining cats and dogs.'

'Don't even get me started on that expression,' he laughs. 'What the fu-'

'Guys!' Tee pleads. 'Do you have any idea what we're about to face out there? Can you at least try and take this seriously?'

'Oh, Tee,' Winder sighs, slinging his arm over her shoulder and almost pulling her over under its weight. 'You worry about stuff way too much. Everything's gonna be fine. For sure. We've got this. We've *always* got this.' He starts scratching at his neck, picking off strands of his hair that are stuck to his skin. 'I shouldn't have cut my hair today. It's itching the hell outta me.'

'I still can't believe you shaved it all off.' I lean over and help pull out the long stray strands of ginger hair from beneath his collar. 'I can't get used to it.'

'Long hair's too much in this heatwave. Why they're insisting on doing this today is beyond me,' he complains, looking up at the spectators on top of the hill. 'Pretty damn sure it's the hottest day of the year. When are they gonna give the signal? We're gonna melt if they leave us out here for much longer. I say we just go over, clear the area and go home. It's my turn in the shower first, and I'm hungry as hell.'

'We go over when they signal. Not a second sooner,' Cass says clearly. 'And no one is having a shower until you clear up the mess you made in the bathroom. Your hair was all over the floor when we left. And the only reason you're hungry is that you lost a bet with Scarlett and had to give her your breakfast this morning. You know you can't beat her in hand to hand combat. She's too fast. You can never catch her.'

I laugh mockingly at Winder, who decides the best response is to shove his finger up my nose.

'Gross!' I hiss, slapping his hand away.

'Guys! Seriously!' Tee pleads. 'Can we focus?'

'I'm too hungry to focus.'

'You had a whole apple this morning,' I remind him.

'An apple isn't filling. It's-'

'Guys!' Tee snaps again with much more severity. 'I mean it. You focus... or... or...'

'Or?' I ask.

She narrows her eyes and crosses her arms. 'Or I'll tell the boys about the book you have stashed under your mattress.'

'Book?' I scoff. 'What book?'

'You know precisely which book I mean.'

'I have no idea-'

'Ya know... The one with all the steamy se-'

'Tee!'

'I think it's called, "*Secret diary of a call-*"'

'Alright!' I snap, feeling my cheeks redden. 'I get the point. I'm focused, okay? Totally focused. C'mon.' I smack Cass on the arm. 'Let's take another quick look. See if anything's changed.'

Together, we peer over the barricade, careful to be quiet and unseen. The top of our heads barely pokes above our cover as we scan the area.

Ahead of us is an old three-story building made of red brick. It was once an old factory of some kind. The door is boarded up with a thick piece of wood and the two windows either side of it are sealed with metal sheeting. The panelled windows above are all shattered and missing their glass, leaving behind rusty metal window frames. Unlike the rest of what surrounds us, this structure's still standing, which is precisely why this location has been chosen. There are rusted, burnt-out shells of five old lorries precisely where they were abandoned just over half a century ago.

'So...' Cass whispers in my ear, and I know he has a grin from ear to ear. 'About this book...'

'Mention it again, I'll kick you so hard between the legs, you won't be able to sit for a week.'

He's chuckling to himself as we turn back to the others.

'What does it look like out there?' Tee asks nervously.

'Well, it's still an old factory,' I reply. 'Just as it was ten minutes ago. It's still three stories high. Just as it was ten minutes ago. And it still looks completely sealed. Just as it was ten minutes ago,' I tell her, for the third time.

'I meant are there still six targets?' she asks exasperatedly, pinching the bridge of her nose and closing her eyes. 'You are such a sarcastic cow, Scarlett.'

'Yes. There are six Class Threes visible,' I laugh, nudging her with my elbow. 'Probably not part of the original assignment. More than likely, they just wandered over. The factory is our mission. We need to kill the six Class Threes first before we attack it.'

'And then?' Titan asks. 'You and Cass are up for the Red Coat positions so we're following your lead, right?' There's a pleading tone to his words. I understand why. Out here, you follow orders, or you make them. And it has to be perfectly clear who does what. Can't have people bickering about what we should or shouldn't do. Which is the purpose of this whole exercise. Deciding who will do the leading. But for the last seventeen years, Cass and I have always taken the lead. In everything. Where we go. The games we played as children. Battle formations.

And no one ever complains because without sounding big-headed, Cass and I are the best. It's life and death out here.

And a wrong call or a bad choice can end someone's life. That's a burden not many people want to bear.

But like I said, Cass and me? We're the best. And the others trust us completely. As they should.

No one's died on our watch.

Yet.

'So…' Tee says, as each one of them shuffles a little closer to Cass and me. 'What is the plan?'

'We stick to our usual formation. You two,' I point to Titan and Flash. 'You're scouts and second wave. Tee, you're our eyes and our bow. Stay up high. Me, Cass and Winder on the ground up front. Three-point formation. This is our final assignment, guys. We get one shot. We mess this up… it's over. In every sense of the word.'

'That's a crap pep talk,' Winder scoffs.

'We've been training for this since we were five. That's twelve years of experience. Twelve years of solid training. Twelve years of blood, sweat and tears. All leading us here. There's nothing else to say. Today is the day. Today will define the rest of our lives. So, we play by their rules. Show them what we can do. Earn our ranks, survive, and go home. Got it?'

'Got it,' they all agree.

'Good. How's that for a pep talk?'

'Much better,' Winder nods approvingly.

I peer over the top of the wall again. 'Titan, Tee and Flash… when Cass, Winder and I make our move, you go around the outside of those lorries. Use the vehicles as a barrier between you and the six targets. Tee, that third lorry there?' I make sure she knows exactly where I'm pointing. 'You climb up on its roof. It will give you a good vantage point. Titan and Flash, do your scout of the building and get back to us as soon as you can with what you see inside. We need to know how many targets we will be facing, and their Class. Steer clear of the six targets outside. We'll deal with those.'

'Sure thing.' Titan nods.

'Tee, how many arrows you got?' I ask.

'Twenty,' she replies. Her hand pats the quiver full of arrows at her hip. Her other rests firmly on the string of her bow across her chest.

'How many targets did you think we'd be facing?' Winder laughs.

'Well, I might miss,' she says, not taking her unblinking eyes off me as she talks to him.

'You never miss, Tee,' I remind her.

'Well, she did once,' Winder teases, jabbing my shoulder where I have a scar from one of her arrows. Tee makes a high-pitched kind of whine and chews on her lip.

'Ignore him,' I insist. 'Everything will be alright. Just stay up on that lorry. Your assignment is with your bow. That's it. Under no circumstances are you to fight with anything other than your bow.'

'I don't have anything *but* my bow,' she whispers, her cheeks flushing with embarrassment. 'Should I?'

I shake my head, but internally I'm groaning.

Why the hell didn't she bring her sword?!

I pull out the dagger from my holster and give it to her instead. 'Take this. Just in case. We all agreed, you're going for a Green Coat so they need to see your skill with a bow. That's all. They see that, you'll be put up on the wall for sure.'

'You sure you guys aren't mad?' she asks. 'Me being on the wall means I won't join your unit.'

'For the hundredth time. Of course not,' Cass insists. 'The wall needs you more than we do. You're the best archer in the army and your place is up on that wall keeping us all safe.'

As she nods and takes a deep breath, Cass settles his eyes on me.

'Thank you,' I mouth, before he flashes me a wink. Putting her up on the wall was his idea. That way, she doesn't have to be out here fighting. She can stay home and protect everyone there instead. She's capable of being on the ground. Sufficient with a blade. And brave. Stupidly so. But being out here terrifies her. And fear leads to mistakes. And mistakes can get you, and others, killed. We all care about her too damn much to let that happen.

'If you start running low on arrows, signal. I'll get more to you,' I tell her. 'We won't know what - or how many - are in that factory until Flash and Titan do their scout. Keep your eyes open and watch our backs. We have one straightforward objective. Clear the specified area quickly and efficiently of any and all targets.'

'And don't get eaten alive by them.'

'Yes... Thank you, Winder. When the six targets are down, and when we know what we're dealing with inside that factory, we head to the door and open it up just enough so a couple of them can fit through at a time,' I tell them while they all nod. 'They'll funnel out towards the light. Now remember guys, because two of us are gunning for the Red Coats, this mission will be harder. I imagine we'll be facing a few more targets than the other units have had to face. They're gonna wanna see our skills. See us prove ourselves. So please, no loud noises. No yelling. The targets will be slow as long as they're not stimulated.'

A high-pitched whistle travels through the air. We look up to the hill and see the spectators all standing in a line watching us.

'That's the signal. It's go time,' I whisper, giving Cass another whack on his arm in excitement before turning to the others. 'Tee...'

'Get to the lorry and stay there. Blink. And don't miss. Got it.' She nods.

'Flash, Titan...'

'Go peek in the windows and see what's inside the factory while you, Cass and Winder kill the six targets outside,' Titan replies. 'Understood.'

Tee gives me a kiss on the cheek. 'Love you. Be safe out there and kick arse. C'mon fellas.' She heads out, Titan and Flash following close behind.

'Six Class Threes,' Cass says as they head off. 'Piece of cake.'

'Boring.' I roll my eyes. 'I'm looking forward to seeing what's inside that factory.'

Not that I don't love the Class Threes. I mean, a target is a target, and no target should be taken lightly. But Class Threes are slow. Cumbersome. A little dull.

The group of spectators watching over us are scoring our skills with a weapon and our ability to adapt to the ever-changing environment that a post-apocalyptic world inhabited by millions of these creatures create. Today determines our rank for when we join the army in a few days' time. It's the final of sixteen tests we've had to endure this past year. Our last year of a training programme that started the day we were born and ends when the youngest member of the unit turns seventeen.

That's me. The group's baby. And today is my birthday.

'Hands in.' I hold out my hand. Cass lands his palm on top of mine. Winders lands on top of his. 'Just like any other day. No holding back. No showing off. We go in, and we all come out.'

Cass wraps his fingers around my hand and grips it tightly.

'Don't do anything stupid, Scarlett,' he tells me.

'You know me.' I grin excitedly.

'Yes. I do. So, I'll say it again. Don't do anything stupid.' His slight smile doesn't match the seriousness of his eyes. 'Killing you would really suck.'

'Please,' Winder scoffs. 'If Scar gets bitten and turns into a target... we're all screwed.'

But despite the joking, there's a heavy tension between us. People have died in these tests. And worse. Been bitten and become one of... *Them*.

'Remember our promise. We get bitten, we get put down. No hesitating. We don't wait for anyone to turn. We just do it. None of us wants to be left like that.' I nod to the creatures behind us and the boys nod in agreement. 'Death or glory.' I repeat the motto drilled into us for as long as we can remember.

Death or glory, Cadets.

Death or glory.
'Their death,' Winder adds.
Cass nods his head. 'Our glory. Let's do this.'

CHAPTER TWO

We climb up on the brick barricade and reveal ourselves.

I look down at the six putrid vermin below. Their naked, decaying bodies are slow and rotten. Their arms dangle. Their heads loll. Their feet drag behind them and their gurgling carries on and on.

They're so disgusting.

How they were ever human is beyond me.

They still have no idea we're here, even though we're all in clear view. After flashing me a quick wink, Cass walks along the wall to the left, then Winder makes his way to the right.

I stay in the middle, my full attention on Tee as she climbs up the side of the lorry to gain her high ground. Once in place, she has her bow poised and is ready to work. Her mechanically operated weapon uses pulleys and cables that help her deal with the heavy weight at a full draw. It's made from materials we salvaged from out here in the wild. The white feathers on her arrow are flush against her cheek and her eyes never stray from the six targets below.

I watch Flash and Titan silently heading around the back of the building to see what's inside.

To my right, Winder has his battle axe ready. A crescent-shaped thirty-inch long blade on one side and a square hammer on the opposite. It's heavy. Big. But he's more than strong enough to wield it and it's utterly devastating to those he swings it against.

To my left, Cass.

His weapons of choice?

His two Haladie daggers.

A pair of double-edged daggers that consists of two curved blades attached to a single hilt. Usually, there would be a third blade coming out from where his knuckles would be, but Cass replaced them with a flat, thick lump of metal so he can deliver one hell of a punch. They're a dream for stabbing and slicing while moving quickly. And the chunk of metal at his knuckles shatters skulls beautifully. Cass is a wonder to behold with them on the battlefield. It's almost like he dances as he kills.

Everyone is in position. I glance at the boys either side of me, and we all nod our readiness before pulling up our face masks. They're little more than large wrappings of black cloth. They cover our mouth and nose to ensure no blood from the targets enter our bodies, so we don't get infected and turn into the very thing we're here to kill.

Each of our masks has been decorated. They're our own version of war paint.

Winder's has the biggest grin drawn on to it, with big red lips and huge white wonky teeth. Tee's has a simple smile with comically drawn zig-zag teeth and rosy cheeks. Cass has a very realistic wolf mouth, snarling, with blood dripping from its fangs.

I drew that one. It's awesome.

And mine? Mine boasts the golden grin of a samurai with long fangs.

I'm a bit of a samurai fangirl. Ever since I was eight, after I read about them in a book I found in an abandoned library truck, I've been obsessed.

Titan and Flash refused to let us draw on their masks, fearing any backlash from our commanders back home. They have the simple army issue brown ones.

Miserable sods.

Reaching over my shoulders, I draw my weapons from my double back harness.

My two katanas.

Each one is a gorgeous, forty inches in length. Twenty-eight of which are made of the finest steel, forged into two thousand and forty-eight layers. The handles are tightly wrapped in black silk cord. The tsuba is a circular, iron beauty carved with white doves in flight. The one I hold in my right hand has a black steel knuckle-duster welded to the handle. An extra recently added by Cass, Tee and Winder in celebration of my birthday.

I love my katanas.

But what I love even more... is using them.

I give a high-pitched whistle, breaking the silence of this deserted wasteland. It echoes off the walls of the factory and draws the attention of the six Class Threes ahead of us.

'Hey, ugly!' I call over, careful not to be loud enough for whatever's inside the factory to hear me. 'Hungry?'

Slowly, they turn and look straight at me. They start chomping at the air. The gurgling of their still liquefying insides rattle in their throats as bile, pus and blood bubble from their mouths.

'That's it. We have some lovely auburn female.' I gesture to myself. 'Or perhaps you prefer some ginger-'

'Strawberry blonde!' Winder corrects me, slightly offended by my use of the G-word.

'Some strawberry blonde male. Or perhaps a bossy brunette?' I add with a nod to Cass.

'Funny,' he grumbles, twirling his haladie between his fingers.

The feet of each target drag in the dirt, and their arms sway heavily by their sides as they move. I jump down, giving my blades a playful spin in my palm and reacquainting myself with their weight.

I don't need to. I know them as if they're my own limbs.

The boys jump down too and we begin closing in on them. Whistling and calling insults to dead ears. Now the targets are distracted, Flash and Titan, along with their single swords, can get to the factory unchallenged. The small pack of six walking corpses fracture. One goes to Winder. Two to Cass. And three to me.

It's my lucky day.

'Scarlett...' Cass warns, as I start to giggle with glee. 'Don't do anything reckl-'

'WAHOO!' I run towards my marks, kicking up dust and spinning my swords as I go.

Their instincts to eat kick in and they move quicker. Louder. As I reach the first, it swipes out for me. I use an old crate and jump up high into the air, somersaulting over it and slicing my blade clear through its neck as I go. Its body falls flat and its head rolls across the dirt, but the mouth still chomps. The other two turn as I land. I spin and skid half a foot or so and wait for them to come to me.

As I wait, I stab the severed head through its temple, silencing its snapping jaws for good. As the next one reaches me, I slice through its neck with a swift swipe. But not all the way through. It stands there like an open Pez dispenser, arms still reaching out and mouth still moving. It turns so it can see me and I can't help but laugh a little at the sight of it trying to figure out if it should walk backwards or forwards in order to reach me. My fist slams into the side of its head. The iron knuckle-duster makes its skull shatter around my fist. It sways, and with a kick, I send it down, never to get back up. The third comes at me teeth first. I thrust my blade up beneath its jaw. The tip comes out the top of its skull. The target is still blinking. But stops when I pull my weapon straight through its face.

It crumples to the ground.

Three corpses of corpses surround me.

With a flick, I clean my steel of as much of their congealed blood as possible before checking on the boys. Cass ducks and weaves between his two, slicing their throats and stabbing them in their temples with grace.

Show off.

Whereas Winder uses the hammer side of his axe to slam his fat target to the floor and then brings down the curved blade executioner style, severing its head from its fat body. He then lifts his hammer and – *splat.*

'That was easy,' Winder shrugs.

'Cos that was the warm up. Where are Titan and Flash?' I ask. As if on cue, they suddenly start sprinting towards us. Flash is stumbling over his feet in his haste and Titan keeps glancing over his shoulder. 'Well... that can't be good.'

'How many?' Cass asks as they reach us.

'Dozens,' pants Titan. 'Too many to count. And the floors above have caved in, so they're all on the ground floor.'

'It's a test. I know they said it was gonna be more difficult cos we want Red Coats, but they wouldn't make it impossible for us,' I insist. 'They said fifteen at most.'

'Well I don't know what to tell you, Scar.' Titan shrugs angrily at the slightest inclination that I don't believe his words. 'I lost count after thirty. There are loads!'

'You gotta be kiddin...' Winder whispers before looking at me and Cass. 'We can't take on thirty! They'll eat us alive! *Literally!*'

But Cass and I are already preparing, wiping our blades clean with the hem of our brown leather coats, leaving a thick trail of black blood behind.

'Guys... you can't be serious?' Winder's eyebrows are raised and unsure. 'Thirty?'

'We have to. If we forfeit, we'll be reassigned to a new unit and retested,' I reply. 'If we can't pass this thing with a team we've been working with for more than a decade, we sure as hell ain't gonna do it with a bunch of other failed Cadets, are we?! We stick to the plan. But Titan *and* Flash will both work the door, and we kill whatever comes out.'

Cass nods. So does Titan and Winder.

Flash, on the other hand, looks like he's about to soil himself.

'I can't work the door, Scar. I can't.'

'You ain't got a choice,' I reply. 'Titan won't be able to hold the weight of thirty monsters pushing against it on his own, so you gotta help him. We need to make sure only a handful come through at a time so we don't get swamped. I'll tell Tee what's happening.'

'You let Tee stay out the way! Why not me?' he argues like a child.

'Tee is an archer. She's exactly where she needs to be and if we asked, she'd do the door. But your skills with a bow are not as good as they are with a sword, and you chose to specialise your training with a sword, not a bow. If I remember rightly, because *"only girls stay out of the fight and hide on high ground"*. So quit complaining and get to work. I'll tell Tee-'

'I'll tell her!' Flash insists, before turning and sprinting in her direction. I can't believe it when he starts scrambling up the side of the lorry.

'Bloody coward,' Cass mutters.

'He's scared,' Titan apologises. 'Maybe if he stays up on the lorry-'

'What? He'll poke the targets with his sword?' Cass snaps. 'For god's sake, Titan. Your boyfriend *is* a goddamn coward. Never mind he's leaving us one man down, if he stays up there, he'll fail.'

'I can work the door alone,' Titan insists. 'Flash can hang back. He can catch the stragglers that get past you guys. He'll get a score that way, and he'll be less likely to get hurt. Please?' He looks at Cass and receives no sympathy or understanding at all. So, instead, he looks at me. His big gentle eyes plead for my support. For my understanding. For me to help protect the man he loves.

'Fine,' I say, not able to cause the guy any more worry. At least this way, Titan's head will be in the game rather than worrying about Flash. 'You boys get in position. I'll get Flash down and tell him to hang back and kill the ones that might get past us. But, if that door gets too heavy, you tell us. You don't struggle and end up getting yourself killed, understand? A single whistle and we'll get to you.' He nods as I run over to the lorry where Flash is still scrambling up the side. Tee is watching him, looking utterly dumbfounded. 'Get down here!' I hiss at him angrily.

'No.' His voice is a quaking mess. He's uncoordinated, not even managing to climb the side of a simple lorry. All his training has abandoned him and terror has taken control. That's not his fault. But it still pisses me off.

I grab his ankle to try and pull him down. 'Get down here! We're being evaluated.'

'I don't care!'

I pull down my mask and look up at him. 'Flash, you can't hide from this! You refuse to fight, they will fail you! They'll punish you for cowardice and reassign you to another unit. One made up of other failures. You'll be lashed before you're sent out here with strangers to die. Do you hear me? They don't want cowards in their army, Flash. They'll find a way, any way, to get rid of you. Get down here!'

'There's too many,' he argues, kicking my hand away. 'You didn't see what I saw. We're all dead if we face them. Get off me, Scarlett! I don't wanna die!'

'Never mind the targets. Get your arse down here, or I'll bloody kill ya!' I grab his ankle and yank. He kicks at my knuckles hard but misses my hand and the sole of his boot slams into my face instead. White hot pain shoots across my nose and I see spots. I stumble back as he watches me in horror. I feel my nose and look at the tips of my fingers where a good amount of red now drips down them.

'Oh no… Scar… I'm so sorry.'

'You bloody idiot!' I bark, my insides filling with a cold fear that I rarely ever get. 'You absolute twat! Look what you've done! You've made me bleed!'

There's a hell of a high-pitched shriek from inside the factory. Inhuman and evil wouldn't even come close to describing it.

What's worse are the several others that follow. All of the targets inside the factory can smell my blood. The slightest whiff is like a hit of adrenaline for them all.

'Get on the lorry,' Tee orders in a panic, reaching down to me. 'They'll tear you apart! You're bleeding! Scarlett, get on the lorry!'

'I ain't a coward. Unlike that fool.' I turn to the others. 'BLOOD!' I yell, holding my hand up. No point being quiet now. I'm a great big bloody steak, and those human-eating monsters probably haven't eaten in years. They can smell blood for miles. They're all gonna be coming for me.

'SCARLETT!' Cass bellows, running towards me. 'GET ON THE LORRY!'

We all watch as the board of wood covering the door to the factory starts to bulge and crack. The starving creatures inside screech louder as they go mad for the smell of my blood.

'TITAN! GET AWAY FROM THE DOOR!' I bellow. He stops and starts backing away. 'NOW, TITAN! MOVE!' When it begins to splinter, he turns and sprints towards us, desperate to get as far from the entrance as possible.

'Scarlett, you have to get on the lorry!' Tee argues. I look up at her still reaching for me and shake my head.

'You may need more than your twenty arrows. Don't miss, Tee. And you...' I point to the pathetic excuse of a soldier who has finished clambering up the side. 'Keep down so the others up on the hill can't see you hiding up here. If I survive this, Flash... you and I are having a conversation. If I don't, I'll make sure I bite you first.'

Cass and Winder have run to my side to try to stop the flow of blood coming from my nose.

'It's too late!' I snap, pushing them away. 'They've smelt it. Just focus on the fight! We're being evaluated.'

'Screw the evaluation. They're all coming for *you*!' Cass barks. 'Get on the lorry!' He grabs my waist and tries to lift me up. I slap him away. 'For god's sake. You can fight from the lorry, Scarlett.'

'I'll get a bad mark if I do that. And any shot of getting a Red Coat will be gone.'

'You'll risk your life for a sodding coat?!'

'Better believe it.' I wipe my nose, pull up my mask and ready my katanas. 'I'm getting that Red Coat if it kills me. Mark my words. Boys, get in your positions. Tee, get your bow ready.'

'You keep your aim focused around her,' Cass adds sternly to Tee. 'They're gonna be going for her more than us. You keep her safe. You hear me? You protect *her.*'

'I will, Cass. I promise.'

I hold out my hand. 'Death or glory.'

'Their death,' Winder says, putting his hand on top and looking at Cass anxiously. Cass continues glaring at me, clearly considering if he could just knock me out and throw me on the lorry. But he adds his hand to the pile.

'Our glory,' he adds.

We break.

Tee gets to her feet and readies her bow. Winder takes his position to my right. And Cass leans in close, his nose almost touching mine and his angry breath landing on my skin.

'Do - not - die, Scarlett. I mean it. You die, I will bloody kill you.'

'You better.' I grin.

He tucks a stray strand of hair behind my ear. His eyes look deep into mine, and I see fear in them. A fear for me. For my life and my safety. A fear of losing me.

'Together,' he says. 'We do this together, and we come out of this together.'

'Always, Cass. Always,' I reply, resting my hand over his as it settles on my cheek. Only for a moment. Then we let each other go. And we prepare to fight for our lives.

The makeshift door holding back the undead shatters. They pour out. One after the other, all falling over themselves before scrambling up and heading this way.

It's a stampede of monsters, all bumping into each other as they head bloodthirstily towards us.

Towards me.

Their hollow shrieks go on and on. Not one of them needs to take a single breath. Their arms dangle by their side's as they run but the smell of blood has really riled them up and filled them with whatever passes for adrenaline. Their jaws are open wide. Flesh and bile are dangling from their rotten but razor-sharp teeth.

'Here they come,' Winder sings, readying his axe.

'ATTACK!'

We run straight at them, ducking and weaving between their snapping jaws and clawing hands. The air moves as they miss me. I skid. My feet slide across the dried dirt and I lean as far back as I can, dodging an outstretched hand and set of teeth. My Katana slices through its ankles, making it fall. Straightening myself, my other blade goes through its temple. But there's another. And another behind that. The boys move forwards, stopping some that are desperate to get to my blood.

But plenty get past.

As I hack, and slice, and stab, and jump around, the targets fall. And they don't get up. They never do when they taste my steel. Cass, like me, can hurl himself about. Our gymnastic and evasive techniques are our greatest weapons, and we've spent thousands of hours honing them together.

Winder uses brute strength as his main form of attack. His hammer smashes skulls and takes out legs. A whoosh passes my ear as one of Tee's arrow's goes straight between the eyes of a Class Three behind me. Before it lands in the dirt, I snatch the arrow free and tuck it into my waistband for later. The boys do the same with any that hit a target near them. The pristine white feathers make them easy to see. If she doesn't hit the right spot in the very centre of their brain, they just keep going. Destroying their brains are the only way to kill them.

But Tee is a fantastic shot, and rarely misses.

I carry on, sending one blade through a sternum and my other through a forehead. Swipe, don't retract. Destroy as much of the brain as possible.

'SCAR!' Winder bellows, pointing over my shoulder before returning to his fight. Behind me, an enormous specimen swings its thick arms at me, hitting me square in the chest and sending me flying a good six feet through the air. I slide across the floor where I land at Winder's feet with a groan. He offers his hand and yanks me up, swinging his axe, blade side first, over my head and swiftly decapitating two that were directly behind me. I plunge my blade through the gut of another approaching our side. I pull up, slicing it in two. For some, their flesh, although thick and leathery, act as nothing more than a bag to contain their liquefied insides and brittle bones. It's tough to cut through it, but with enough practice, it's possible. And I've spent my whole life practising.

We all have.

'Are you loving this?' Winder asks, bringing down the hammer edge on another target. 'Because I am *loving* this!'

'Hell yeah, I'm loving this!' I roar with laughter. He shoves his collected stash of arrows into my waiting hand and charges off, swinging that brutal weapon as he does while laughing. A target swipes for me. Its hands scratch at the air as I lunge back. Nearly too far. I thrust the tip of my katana's blade into the ground over my head and use it as leverage to push myself back up.

Swipe.

And off comes its head.

Stab.

Right between the decapitated head's eyes.

There's a path to Cass who has a fistful of arrows. I run to his outstretched hand as he offers them to me.

'Seven!' he boasts, shoving his dagger into another one's temple repeatedly. 'Make that eight! That Red Coat and your back rub are totally mine!'

'Nine. Suck it!' I brag, before I carry on running past Titan who's dealing with the odd one that manages to get past us. I reach the lorry. 'Get the hell down here now!' I order Flash. He shakes his head as he trembles all over, lying on his belly with his hands over his head. 'If you don't get down here and fight, you'll be reassigned. Is that what you want? GET DOWN HERE!'

'Oh for goodness sake,' Tee hisses, letting loose an arrow. 'Just leave the git and focus on you and the boys.'

But I try once more. 'Flash, if you don't fight for yourself, then fight for Titan. Help him!'

Nothing. So I give up.

I thrust the arrows into Tee's outstretched hand. 'How many targets left?'

'Seventeen,' she replies quickly before returning to the task at hand and letting loose a steady stream of arrows. 'Get back out there.'

Seventeen? Damn. There's no time to waste. With a quick glance to the hilltop, I spot a group heading our way. Their horses are kicking up the thick dust as they run. I get to Cass, whose hands are going so fast, he's almost a blur.

'They're sending in reinforcements,' I tell him, pointing to the incoming cavalry.

How rude.

They only ever intervene if they think we don't stand a chance.

'What? Why the hell are they-' *Stab. Slice. Kick.* 'Doing that? It will invalidate the test.' He pushes me out the way and decapitates a Class Three as I behead another coming up behind him. 'Like hell am I going through all this again!' His attention diverts to Tee. 'TEE! SEND A SHOT! TELL THEM WE GOT THIS!'

She aims her mechanical bow high, straight at the oncoming stampede of would-be saviours. She lets loose an arrow with green feathers which soars for maybe two hundred meters and lands a reasonable distance in front of them as she waves her arms in the air wildly. They slow, and thankfully, stop their approach.

They've got the message. Green means we're good. Stashed away in her quiver is an arrow with red feathers. But we won't use that. No matter what. That's a *"we need help"* arrow.

'DOWN!' Cass bellows. I land on my knees as he swipes his blade clear over me. I hear a screech followed by a thud. I reach up, taking his elbow so I can launch myself at a skinny but vicious little bastard mid-leap. It collides with me instead of Cass's back, and we land in a pile on the floor. It opens its mouth wide, but instead of my neck, it gets my steel in its mouth. I don't need to drive it through, it's that desperate to reach me it ends up decapitating itself just above the jaw. I lean to the side, avoiding its blood, and roll it off my body before getting back on my feet.

'This is so much fun,' I chirp. 'We should make them frenzied every time.'

Cass gives an eye roll and we carry on. Blades flying. Decapitating, slicing and destroying target after target as a shower of arrows fall from Tee's direction, landing exactly where they need to land. I don't know how long we fight. It feels like hours, but it's probably only been fifteen minutes or so. And as the final Class Three meets its end, I sheath my katanas, lower my mask and catch my breath.

'That was... AWESOME!' I cheer, turning to the others while laughing victoriously and wiping my still bloody nose with the back of my hand. 'Seriously! How much fun was that?'

Everyone is absolutely covered in sweat, black goo and dust as they lower their masks. Winder beams with me, Cass too, although reluctantly. We all enjoy the relief that it's done. But a low gurgling noise draws our attention to the side of the factory where one last target claws across the ground, legless and missing one arm. Its teeth are still chomping at the air.

Winder gives Cass his axe to hold and makes his way over. Looking down at it, he lifts his black boot and slams it hard into its skull before returning to us with a smug grin.

'Ten,' he boasts.

'Eleven,' Shrugs Tee with a shy smile, slinging her bow over her shoulder as she joins us all.

'Fourteen,' Cass says in triumph, wiping more of my blood from my face with his thumb.

I pat his shoulder. 'Seventeen,' I sigh happily, with a less than sympathetic grin.

'No way you got more than me!'

'Guess we'll soon find out.' I lower his hand and nod to the group heading towards us on horseback, no longer rushing, but trotting at their leisure. Elder Eight is up front. I spot Titan helping Flash off the lorry and dragging him back towards us, whispering harshly in his ear.

'Who won?' Winder calls out.

'Need you ask?' Elder Eight replies with a laugh as he approaches. I take the reins of his mare as he climbs down to give me a firm shoulder squeeze. 'Good job, Cadet 5-3-6. Kill count of seventeen. That's the highest achieved for a final test. You broke the record! Very impressive.'

As he turns to congratulate the others, I stick out my tongue to Cass who looks thoroughly pissed off.

Elder Eight is our commander. We've been with him since we were five years old after leaving the orphanage to start our training. He's in his late forties with no hair on his head, but a comical, jet black handlebar moustache. He's more muscle than man. His handshake is firm enough to make the bones in your hand grind together, and he's a wicked fighter. He uses a broad-sword. And he taught me everything I know.

'What the hell was with this one?' he asks, gesturing to Flash who lingers behind his horse. 'Scuttling up that lorry? What happened? It was a bit of a blind spot for us. We couldn't see him at all.'

'He did fine, Elder. I assure you. He killed,' I reply easily, glad that they failed to see his cowardice. 'Flash... I mean, Cadet 5-8-5, was on the lorry momentarily to try and get a head count. He remained at its base to protect Tee. I mean, Cadet 6-2-3.'

Cass furrows his brow at my blatant lie. But it's a necessary one. Those who fail or give an unsatisfactory performance are reassigned. Which means they're removed from their unit and forced to do it all again with a new unit comprised of other failures. They don't tend to survive because no one on the team seems to have a bloody clue. Imagine a group consisting of Flash's facing that lot!

'You drew blood, Cadet.' Elder Eight gestures to my throbbing nose.

'One of the targets elbowed me,' I lie.

'Careless...' he tuts. Flash avoids my stare as I lie through my teeth for him. If saving his back-side has cost me any marks... Class Threes will be the least of his problems. 'And I told you to wear your standard uniform today. We got Grey Coats here ya know. You're supposed to be makin' a good impression.'

He looks me up and down and shakes his head. But I love my outfit.

The grip on my old Nike high top shoes are still fantastic, despite them being a good fifty years old. Much better than the thick, heavy military boots the others insist on wearing. The dark red high tops and the big black tick are more than unique. They're one of a kind. Maybe the last in existence. They're one of my best finds out beyond the wall. I discovered them in what remained of a young teenage boy's bedroom. Proudly placed on a shelving unit along with a pile of video games and nudie mags.

Winder took the mags.

Above my shoes, from my ankle to my knees, are strips of thick cream leather, similar to a bandage, wrapped around my calves. A style I adopted from the great samurai of ancient Japan. They protect my skin from the monster's teeth. The brown leggings and the black tank top is standard cadet uniform. Those and the knee-length brown leather coats we all wear.

But the rest, that's all me. My style. My own version of armour.

I hacked off the sleeves of my coat years ago, much to the annoyance of Elder Eight, but I found them too constricting when fighting. Cass made me a pair of thick leather arm cuffs a few years back, which unlike the tight leather sleeves of the coats, move with me, so I'm still protected. But this morning, he surprised me with a new pair as the other ones were getting a little... well, they were falling to pieces. My new ones fit snugly from my wrist up to my elbow and give me protection against bites and scratches. He carved the word death into one, and glory into the other.

'I'm a better fighter when I'm comfortable,' I argue, defending my wardrobe choices.

'If you say so. Fantastic shooting, 6-2-3. As ever.' Elder beams at Tee, who turns pink as she accepts his compliment with a quiet giggle. 'The Green Coats will be lucky to have you, I'm sure.' That makes her smile even more. She longs for the safety of the wall. A Green Coat would make her beyond happy.

'Any chance the Red Coats would be glad to have me?' I ask.

Shaking his head and chuckling away to himself, he looks at the boys. 'And you two...' He puffs out his cheeks in appreciation for the boy's skills. 'I have to say, very impressive. Quick. Tough. Very effective.' He looks at us all in turn with a clear sense of pride in his young cadets. 'Your unit is the best I've ever seen in face to face combat. You work together like you're one organism and it's a thing of beauty. Don't ya agree, fellas?' he asks the three men who have slowly made their way towards him, still on their horses. Their black coats boast their position.

'Absolutely,' the youngest one replies with a cocky grin. He must be in his early twenties. He leans down and shakes Cass's hand. 'Your reputations precede you. I thought they were exaggerating your abilities. I was told to look out for the one that fights with two bladed weapons. They said you're the best. Congrats on breaking the record.'

'Sorry, mate.' Cass nods at me. 'You're looking for Scarlett. Not me.'

'Oh.' He looks at me like I'm something he can't figure out as Cass retracts his hand. 'I didn't have binoculars. I thought... but you're a girl.'

'That I am.' I reply.

'I was expecting a guy.'

'They usually do.' I continue to smile, my mouth filling with venom.

The Black Coat looks between Cass and me.

'So, *she* was the one that got a seventeen kill count? Not you?'

'Yep,' Cass replies, looking at me with a mixture of pride and annoyance. 'She's very enthusiastic about her work.'

I feel my face redden.

'I bet she's enthusiastic,' the Black coat says quietly with a slimy grin, looking me up and down.

'I could enthusiastically kick your teeth in if you keep undressing me with your eyes.'

'You think you could take me?' he laughs loudly.

'Better believe it.'

'I think I'd like to see you try.' His eyes linger on my chest.

'I suggest you rethink that,' Elder interjects, resting his hand on Cass's shoulder before he can go for the guy. 'She could easily kick your arse, Black Coat. You wouldn't last a minute.'

'We were just playing, right, Cadet?'

'Oh yeah,' I scoff. 'Playing.'

'You can go,' Elder orders his entourage. 'Pack up the canopy and get ready for the journey home.'

As they turn to leave, the Black coat can't resist. 'You did well. Ya know. For a girl.'

Elder pats me on the back as I watch them all leave. 'You did superbly, Kiddo. No matter what is or isn't between your legs.'

'Thanks, Elder.'

'You need to complete a sweep of the area.' He gestures to the factory. 'I suggest you and Cass head inside. Make sure it's clear.'

'We'll give you a hand,' Tee offers. But Elder stops her and shakes his head.

'No. Just them. Off you go, Cadets.'

'Alright,' I agree. 'Tee, Winder... you go around the back of the factory. Make sure it's clear. Cass and I will check inside. Flash, Titan, gather the bodies up and burn them.'

'We can help with-'

'You can do as she's told you to do, Flash,' Cass warns him, barging into his shoulder as he passes. I have to jog to catch up with him.

'Don't need to be such an arse hole, ya know,' I scorn, once out of earshot of the others. 'Flash didn't behave that way intentionally. He panicked.'

'If I were an arse hole, I would have told Elder Eight the truth. That Flash booted you in the face as he attempted to save his own skin. That he made you bleed as a stampede of the undead were a few feet away in that factory of doom. And then hid away behind Tee the whole evaluation. He's useless. Dead weight.'

'He's family.'

He scoffs as we come to the door of the factory.

'Just because he's family, don't mean I have to like the idiot.'

We peer inside. It's empty. Save for a large container with the doors bolted shut slap bang in the middle of it. Thick metal support beams are keeping the building up, but the floors above have rotted away so we can see right up to the roof which has half caved in. Rays of sunlight light up the interior.

'You were reckless today.'

'Let's check the inside of the container,' I sigh, hoping to avoid yet another telling off.

'Case and point. Why do we need to check the sealed container?'

'Because Elder Eight just sent us in here. The two-people wanting to earn a Red Coat. Chances are the Elders put the bloody thing in here as an additional test.' I go ahead as he picks up his speed to follow. 'And how exactly was I reckless?'

'Wahoo...?' He looks at me with disapproval. What's new. 'Who runs towards a group of human-eating monsters with a grin and cheers *"wahoo"*? You didn't wait for us, you just charged off. And you still stood front and centre, bleeding all over the place!'

We reach the container.

'This may come as a surprise to you, Cassius, but I'm more than capable of fighting the fight. Bleeding or not. I don't need you or anyone else to help or protect me. I may *just* be a girl, as that arrogant Black Coat just reminded everyone, but I can handle myself. Better than most.'

'You being a girl has nothing to do with it. I don't want to watch you die. That's all.'

'I ain't going nowhere.' I promise.

We draw our weapons and press our ears against the door.

'I can't hear anything. You?' I ask. He shakes his head.

'I should report you to Elder Eight,' he says gruffly, making me laugh. 'Not that he'd reprimand you. Teacher's pet.'

'Report me for what? For not being a coward? For killin' seventeen Class Threes? For leading a successful mission with you? He said I did good. Why don't you report yourself to Elder Eight for having a stick up your backside instead?'

'You know what?'

'What?'

'You're so bloody annoying.'

'Likewise.'

He gives the door a hard kick. The clang echoes within the four walls. We listen. Silence.

'Ain't nothing in there.' He concludes, turning and taking a step towards the door and back to the others. 'The test is over. C'mon. Let's finish clean up and get home. I'm knackered.'

'But there might be something useful in it,' I argue, looking up at the crate. 'It's sealed for a reason. It could be books or clothes or... or... seeds,' I add, in a desperate attempt to convince him to open it.

'Seeds?' he repeats with a disbelieving raise of his brow. 'You know there ain't seeds in there.'

I shrug. 'There could be. And it could still be part of the Red Coat test. We really should open it up.'

He folds his arms across his chest. 'You're going to open it no matter what I say. Aren't you?'

I reply with a mischievous grin I know he loves to see, despite himself. I know him way too well. The corner of his mouth twitches as he concedes.

'Fine.' He heads back. 'But you behave like this is a game. This is life and death, Scarlett. One wrong move and you could end up a target.'

'Well, if I do, then I trust that you will be there to put me out of my misery and ensure that the last words I hear will be a good old fashioned "I told ya so".'

'You think it would be that easy? For me to just kill you like that?'

'Sure... why not?' I shrug.

He shakes his head. 'You don't seem to realise that those Class Threes were once human beings. They were someone's kid. A parent. They're-'

'Boo-hoo, Cass. Whatever or whoever they were... they ain't that no more. They're soulless, human-eating beasts. And if I ever turn, I fully expect you to chop me up before I get a chance to kill you or anyone else. As far as I'm concerned, as soon as they got bit, they died.'

'That simple, huh?'

'That simple. Don't deny you don't love the fight just as much as me. I see it in your eyes. I hear it in your voice. You and me? We were made for this. And we love it. Don't we?'

He holds my gaze a little longer than necessary. 'Ready?' he asks finally, nodding towards the crate.

'Always.'

He slides the large metal bolt across the door to unlock the container and slowly opens it up, careful to keep the exit clear in case anything does decide to crawl or sprint out. It creaks as it opens. The thick rust is objecting to every bit of movement. If there were anything in there, the noise would have it coming at us. There would be screeching and scuttling. We relax. But Cass is clearly far from done with his lecture.

'I do enjoy the fight. But I also fight smart and carefully. You don't. You charge in and treat it like a game.'

'Can you just get to the point of this lecture please?'

'My point is, Scarlett. One of these days, your carelessness is gonna get your arse in a situation that requires someone to save you. And when that day comes, you better hope-'

Suddenly, the metal doors fly open. One whacks Cass in the head, knocking him down in a daze. The other, I narrowly miss, but the large bolt slams into my ribs phenomenally hard and sends me flying through the air completely winded. My katana skids across the dirt, out of reach.

As I hit the ground, I cough and gasp as the metallic taste of my own blood fills my mouth. But my attention soon shifts to what's walked out of the container.

It's no Class Three.

It's a bloody Class Two!

It stands more than six feet tall with razor-sharp teeth. Its lips have rotted off, leaving nothing behind but bone.

A Class Two target is solid muscle. It's like punching a wall. They're strong and can move twice as fast as any human and ten times faster than a Class Three. The ones we faced outside stumble and stagger about. These don't. They're focused and co-ordinated. They have some form of intelligence but zero humanity. I've faced a couple in my time, but always with the full force of my unit by my side.

Never alone.

Is this really part of the test? To kill a Class Two?

It looks down at Cass who can barely lift his head and starts to head towards him. Its fingers flex, ready to start tearing at his flesh. I spit a mouthful of blood onto the floor, hoping to lure it to me instead. It stops and sniffs the air before turning to look at me.

'Hey!' I call, desperate to get it away from the barely conscious Cass. 'You smell that?' I spit more blood. It growls and faces me. 'Come and get it. This way. That's it. Good human-eating monster.'

'S-Scarlett... run!' Cass stammers, trying to regain his senses.

'No chance.'

It sprints towards me, its mouth open in an endless hollow shriek. I try to reach for my katana over my shoulder, but the whack to my ribs has made it impossible for me to move my arm enough. It opens its mouth and goes for my neck.

'Ahhh... crap.'

I do the only thing I can think of, and shove my leather cuffed arm in its mouth.

'Try biting through that, Bitch.'

Its teeth are firmly lodged in my armour. With my free hand, I pull up my mask. I don't want anything to go in my mouth.

That would really be game over.

I thrust my forehead into its face. But that does less than nothing. I lift my legs and kick it hard in the chest. It lets go of my cuff, stumbles backwards and regains its balance before crouching low and pouncing high into the air. It reaches where the ceiling of the floor above would be if it hadn't collapsed. I roll out the way as it comes in for its landing. In a quick move, I tackle it and pin it beneath me, grunting against the pain in my ribs as I do. As it lunges at me teeth first, I grab its head as it starts clawing at my body, but it can't get through my leather coat.

They may be hot and heavy. But they really are the best type of armour against these creatures.

I slam its head into the ground again and again and again, but still it growls and snarls. Its arm swipes through the air and hits me straight across my face, knocking me onto the floor. I roll over and try to get up, but it grabs my ankle and I fall. As it claws at my leg, I kick and kick, slamming the sole of my shoe into its face over and over. With each whack, I hear a crunch and a squelch. Its fingernails hook into the leather wrappings around my leg, and it starts dragging itself up my body.

Bloody hell...

I have to get away from its teeth. I turn and claw at the ground, dragging myself away, when I see the most beautiful thing I've ever seen lying just ahead of me.

My other Katana.

I reach out. My fingernails brush it. With a growl, I push harder and wrap my fingers around its hilt, ignoring the pain in my ribs.

Now it's really over.

For it.

In a quick move, I spin round, lift the blade above me and thrust it straight through the top of its head and down its throat. With a final yell, I give every last bit of my remaining energy into one last upwards heave, showering myself with bits of skull and brain.

'Urgh. That's so gross.'

Someone starts slowly clapping. I look to the door and see Elder Eight, as well as a couple of Black Coats, standing there looking very proud. He folds his arms across his chest, gives me an approving nod, turns, and then they all leave.

I knew it. It *was* a test.

Breathless, I roll the Class Two off and lay on my back clasping my side. I pick off the bits of zombie skull from my hair and lower my mask, desperate to get some more air into my lungs. Cass stumbles to a stop beside me in a frantic panic, rubbing his head and falling to his knees.

'Oh shit. That was a Class Two! They put a bloody Class Two in a bloody container for us!'

'Seems so,' I wheeze.

'Are you okay?' he asks.

'Oh yeah...' I cough, still laying on my back and clutching my ribs. 'I'm Brilliant, Cass. Fantastic. You? How are you doing?'

'Can you get up?'

'Sure, I can.' I shrug.

'Then why are you still on the ground?'

'I'm just waiting for you to come and save me from this situation I seem to have found myself in.' I pat his arm. 'In your own time, buddy.'

He eases me up, laughing to himself. 'You're such a sarcastic cow.'

'I know. One of my many charming attributes. I have to say, thanks for my birthday present.' I gesture to the thick leather arm cuffs that just saved me. 'They came in very handy. Barely a scratch, look.'

He wraps an arm around my shoulder. 'You are very welcome. So,' he says, grinning from ear to ear. 'Seventeen kills and to top it all off, a Class Two. Tell me, have you enjoyed your seventeenth birthday, Scarlett?'

'Are you kiddin?' I smile. 'It's been the best birthday ever!'

CHAPTER THREE

Fifty years ago, the world ended.

And how it ended, well, those details have always varied depending on who you ask. Much like anything I suppose. Personally, I don't really care. I tend to live in the here and now. In my opinion, it doesn't matter what lies in the past. Today is what matters. Especially in a world where you spend your days fighting the undead and where every second could be your last.

But if I'm ever asked what I believe about how the world descended into a desolate wasteland filled with starving human-eating monsters, I repeat the story that Elder Eight told me when I was six years old, sitting on his stoop while he stitched me up after a rather messy training session with Cass and his haladies.

It all started when most of North America disappeared under the sea. Millions of lives were gone in the blink of an eye. It was the biggest wave the world had ever seen. The ice caps had melted. Global warming had reached its peak and Greenland, the U.S and half of Canada disappeared with no warning. There were no signs that this disaster was coming and no hope of survivors. Four hundred million people sank beneath the waves that day.

But that was just the beginning.

Four days later, a streak of red light illuminated the sky. And everything got very, very warm. We lost communication with the world. TV's, radios, phones and the internet just stopped working. The southern hemisphere had been hit by some kind of solar event. No one really knows what happened to them all over there. But the fact that no one saw daylight for another two weeks, because the atmosphere was too thick with ash and smoke, meant that whatever it was, it wasn't survivable. When the sun finally broke through, the radios crackled to life. Those still alive were told that South America, Africa and Australia had been destroyed.

Half the world's population had perished in a matter of days.

Three and a half billion people were just gone, leaving the rest of the world to stumble about blindly in panic and grief.

Plant life began to die. Trees became brittle. Grass became dirt. Animals withered and died.

We had made the world sick. Humanity had mined it, boiled it and raped it of everything it had. And soon, what was left of the world's human population got very hungry.

Cibus was created.

The mass-produced pill was to be taken three times a day and provided stimulants for energy, vitamins for thriving and a suppressant for that pesky hunger.

Cibus was to be humanity's saviour. You can still see it advertised on a billboard a few miles down the road from home.

But it wasn't our saviour. Not by a long shot.

Soon after the distribution of Cibus, there were reports of cannibalism, extreme violence and butchery carried out by those incapable of adjusting to life without a steady supply of food.

But no fear.

The army, or what was left of it, would fix it.

Settle down and take your pill.

But the Army wasn't prepared. No one was. How could they be when the attackers - still with flesh in their teeth - continued to charge with a chest full of bullet holes?

The streets ran red with blood.

Literally.

People were torn apart by other people... and eaten alive.

This wasn't just hunger.

It was Cibus.

The suppressants had the reverse effect and drove people mad with hunger. Hunger beyond reason or understanding.

The stimulants made their body clock stop. They didn't age. They just rotted.

Slowly.

The so-called *vitamins* attacked the blood and changed it. Cut them, shoot them, and instead of blood, a thick, black substance would ooze from their wounds, clotting almost immediately.

They stopped being people. They stopped being human. They stopped breathing.

And they just... wouldn't... die.

Unstoppable, un-killable, dead, human-eating monsters. And they were everywhere. To make it worse, their bites are contagious. If they sink their teeth into you, you become like them.

But not everyone turned when they took the pill. Certain blood types reacted differently. Some stayed human. Others turned into what we now call Class Threes. Slow but determined creatures which drag their limbs and hobble from foot to foot. Then there's the Class Twos. They became strong. Fast. Solid.

And then... Class Ones.

Although rare, Class Ones are something else entirely. Not one of them is the same. A Class One destroyed an entire town. A *whole* town! The buildings. The people. All on its own. It stood thirty feet tall, so the story goes.

I personally have never had the pleasure of facing a Class One. No one I know has. I hope one day I will. That would be a great kill under my belt.

The cities fell first. London, Manchester, Birmingham and Liverpool burnt to the ground two days after the outbreak. That was on humanity though. The army bombed them in a desperate attempt to kill the monsters.

Didn't work.

There was no evacuation either. Hard to say which side lost the most.

Survivors gathered in farmlands and small towns away from cities and tried their best to survive. To wait for someone to do something. For someone to save them.

And then the message came. It travelled over the radio for days and days.

'Come to The Haven.'

The message was followed by coordinates.

The lost and lonely travelled far to reach this so-called *"Haven"*. What they found was exactly that.

A family by the name of Sands owned a large section of land in the east of England. They'd created the one and only safe place left in the country. Humanity would have died. We would have disappeared entirely if it wasn't for them. And for one man in particular.

Harvey Sands.

He accepted everyone that turned up. No one was sent away. Everyone was fed. Clothed. Given safety.

As long as they followed his rules. He was a godly man and believed that everything that had happened was some kind of Armageddon. His town was his very own Noah's ark.

No murder. No blasphemy. No sex out of wedlock. Love thy neighbour and all that jazz.

So, unless you wanted to get kicked out and left to fend for yourself...

All hail the great Lord Sands.

To some, Harvey Sands turned into a messiah of sorts. They followed his law to a tee. And insisted that others did too. He played the part well and called himself *"God's representative on earth"*. His devout followers became known as The Grey Coats.

Grey Coats are the law keepers. They're recognisable by their grey jackets that reach their knees and boast a decorative V with wings either side, sprawled across their backs. Their coats have hoods so large, they cover their faces. We never see under the hood. We have no idea who they are or what they look like. They are the best of the best. The most highly skilled fighters we have. Most are selected at the age of ten and whisked off to be trained independently. Or as I call it, brainwashed. Grey Coats are militant in their duties. Fanatical almost. They choose you. Not the other way around. They asked me to join seven years ago when I turned ten. But I said no. Rather than fight, they dish out punishment for the slightest indiscretion anyone makes, and they take immense delight in doing so. Not the type of people you want to piss off.

The survivors needed protection, supplies and most of all hope that one day they'd reclaim their country.

So, Harvey Sands, along with the help of his faithful Grey Coats, created the Sainted Army. Back then, members of the Sainted Army were volunteers.

They started by building a fifty-foot-high and four-foot-wide wall that stretches on for twelve miles around the town dubbed *"The Haven".* Within which, the survivors built homes, cared for the land and each other. They regrew grass. Replanted trees. Looked after the animals and reproduced. All the time, following the stringent laws set forth by Harvey Sands and enforced by his Grey Coats.

But beyond the brick and metal of the high wall, was death in the form of sixty million zombies.

Harvey Sands was in his forties when all this happened. He died twenty-three years ago and his son Malakai took his place. Malakai enjoyed the devotions that diverted from his father straight to him but he wasn't happy with the small army of volunteers that helped protect him and scout for supplies. I mean, who willingly wants to go out there and get eaten alive? So, the law of Donation was created. Of course, this was instructed to the new Lord Sands direct from God and fully enforced by the growing number of Grey Coats he had at his beck and call. All happy and willing to punish anyone who dared disobey him.

Every first, third and fifth child birthed by the same woman is to be donated to the Sainted Army.

Yep, that's right. Donated!

More like torn from the hands of a sobbing woman who had spent nine months growing a baby, only to hand it over to a life of blood, sweat and eventually, a brutal and ugly death.

As soon as they're born, off they go to live in the military orphanage until they turn five. Then they're placed into a unit of six and shipped off to The Academy, where they spend everyday training together until the youngest member turned sixteen. After that, the unit undergoes a year of evaluation, demonstrating their skills so they can be assigned a rank worthy of their abilities.

And in the Sainted Army, there are four ranks.

The Canaries are recognised by a black coat with a yellow bird stitched onto their lapel. They used to search for survivors. Now they scour the country for supplies. They started as volunteers. Now, most are criminals sent out to live beyond the wall for months at a time as punishment. Most never return, which I think is probably the point.

Then there are the Green Coats.

They protect the wall and watch the borders.

Typically, they're archers. They stand guard and shoot down anything that gets too close to the wall. They tend to be female, as it's seen as one of the weaker ranks of the army by a few sexist and ignorant idiots, so most men refuse to pick up a bow unless they have to.

Black Coats go out in groups to hunt these monsters and search the surrounding area for supplies. They go out beyond the wall for a few hours at a time and never go too far. They're the foot soldiers. The real army.

Six Black Coats make up a unit.

And then there are the Red Coats.

It's the rank given to the one soldier who excels at skill, leadership, and capability. They lead all the Black coats who graduate with them.

It's the rank assigned to the best of the best. Save for the Grey Coats, of course.

The evaluations end on the youngest members seventeenth birthday.

That's me.

That's today.

And then we join the real fight.

Our mission is simple. Rid our country of every single zombie out there and keep everyone with a heartbeat, breathing.

We haven't heard anything from another country since the last ferry arrived with four hundred survivors on board over fifty years ago from Ireland.

We're all that's left now.

Two thousand and sixty-three people huddled together in the corner of Suffolk, England.

And we share our country with sixty million human-eating monsters. Otherwise known as Targets, Class Ones, Twos, or Threes, and to a few, good old-fashioned zombies is the preferred title.

Two weeks ago, Malakai died.

I heard he fell down the stairs. But if anyone asks, he was led away by an angel.

And that leaves us with Lord Noah Sands.

The twenty-one-year-old son of Malakai.

From the moment I was born, it's the one thing that has been drummed into me, into all of us, every single day.

The oldest man of the Sand's family is Gods representative on earth, and we must all follow his sacred word.

The Verity.

It's the name of our way of life. The name given to the laws we must follow. The name of the order that governs us. That Noah

Sands Governs. If we ever forget what the sacred word is, we simply pull out our Verity book. We're instructed to keep it on us at all times. The small leather-bound book we were given when we left the orphanage is similar to what some called the Bible. But this one has empty pages so that new laws can be added to it. There's a great big V on the front with elegant silver wings behind it. The same as the emblem the Grey Coats wear. Our cadet numbers are in the top right corner.

Mine has blood stains on the pages and a stab mark from a stray sword.

Plus a few doodles I drew of me decapitating targets.

Noah Sands is now in charge. He demands the same amount of respect and devotion as his father and grandfather did before him. The Grey Coats are as loyal as ever to The Verity and in turn, to Noah. But what differs now is Noah's interest in the Sainted Army. And in my personal opinion, a distinct disinterest in the religious path set forth by his predecessors. Even before his father died, he's been a constant figure and influence on the Elders on how we're trained. His family never bothered, but Noah is one hell of a skilled swordsman. I've seen him with a sword.

Very impressive.

I think he carries on the ruse of his faith only to keep order and control over the Grey Coats.

But that's just my own opinion.

Tee, Winder, Cass, Titan, Flash and I were all donated to the Sainted Army within six months of each other.

I'm the youngest. Today, I turned seventeen.

What a way to spend a birthday!

We're issued with a number when we're born. Not a name. We never learn where we come from. Never meet our parents. We live away from the civilians. We're our own family. We named each other. Care for each other. We love each other. Some more than others.

Titan and Flash are lovers. A way of life that is strictly forbidden. But in my opinion, love is love, so it doesn't bother me. It's the only thing Flash has ever been brave about. Loving another man.

Tee and I are sisters. We share a room, and clothes, and secrets. She's hands down the sweetest girl in the Sainted Army. Anyone will tell you. Which is why I chose the name I chose for her. She really is a Q-Tee.

Winder and Cass are brothers. Best friends. Comrades.

And we are all, family.

Each morning, we gather and offer silent prayers to the wellbeing of God's representative on earth.

For Noah.

For The Verity.

I personally sing, *put the lime in the coconut*, on repeat in my head and think about what I'm gonna have for breakfast.

What a load of old crap.

God does *not* exist!

No one is speaking on his behalf.

But Noah has big ideas for the Sainted Army. He's determined to win back our country. So, I'll play along. We all play along. It's hard to believe in any kind of god when you see what's happened to the world and the people that lived in it. I've not met a soldier yet that believes in god, but we all play along. Not only through the fear of the Grey Coats and their wrath, but also, to keep our place behind the safety of the wall. We lose that, we're dead.

I get to kill zombies with my friends by my side. I get to survive. So...

All Hail Lord Sands... or ya know... *"Put the lime in the coconut"*

CHAPTER FOUR

Cass reaches down and starts pulling me to my feet.

'Here,' he says, helping me to steady. 'Let me help you.' I stagger as he brushes off the dust from my legs. I spit the last of the blood from my mouth and take a deep, painful breath. 'I told you we shouldn't have opened it.'

'We were supposed to open it.' I look at the Class Two and point at what's left of it. 'They put it in here as a test. Elder Eight was watching us the whole time. Well, he was watching me kick its arse. He was watching you have a nap. Can you believe it, Cass? I killed a Class Two all on my own!'

His stern glare has little effect on me. I can't tell if he's pissed at me being right, or us almost dying. Either way, I'm pretty chuffed.

'Where are you hurt?'

'I'm fine,' I tell him, waving my hand dismissively. He lifts my top nonetheless so he can run his fingers over my ribs. I wince and hiss various swear words before batting him away. 'Will you stop pawing at me?! I said I'm fine.'

'I think one's broken.'

'I'm just bruised, Cass,' I insist. 'Like I said... I'm fi-'

'You are not fine!'

With a tut and a roll of my eyes, I step away, which makes him growl quietly under his breath. Something that always makes me laugh, and him growl even louder. 'Maybe there's something else in the container. Let's check it out.'

'What? Because one Class Two isn't enough? Are you *trying* to get yourself killed?'

'Err... no. I'm just doing my job. Maybe you should stop trying to cop a feel and do the same?'

'You wish I would cop a feel,' he scoffs. 'There's nothing else in that container. We need to get back to the others.'

'Not until we check that container,' I reply simply, shrugging my shoulders and taking a step past him.

He blocks my path. 'You're not going over there.'

'You gonna stop me?'

'Yep.'

'I'd like to see you try.'

'Okay then.' He prods my side and I double over, trying not to heave at the pain he's inflicted. The furious look I throw him as I peer up at him through my hair has him looking smug.

'You took a whack and your rib is probably broken. *I'll* check out the container.'

'I'm more than capable.'

'Yeah... perfectly capable,' he mutters, watching as I slowly ease myself up straight. He makes his way towards the large metal box, spinning his haladie in his palm. 'So, you think this was part of the test for our Red Coats?'

'Of course it was.'

'Seems a bit drastic, shoving a Class Two in a box.' He reaches the container and opens up the door fully, his haladie ready and raring. 'No more targets,' he reports, heading inside. His feet shuffle as he walks around it.

'Well?' I call over. 'Is there anything else in there?'

His head pokes out the door. 'Oh yeah... there's loads of stuff in here. Seeds, books, clothes. Scar... there's chocolate!'

'Really?!' I ask, excitement clear in my voice.

He walks out and kicks the door shut.

'No. Not really. It's empty, you daft cow.'

'You utter git,' I grumble, resting my hand on my ribs and filling with disappointment. 'You know I love chocolate.'

Still chuckling away to himself, he returns to my side, picking up my second katana from the floor on his way. 'C'mon. Let's get back to the others.' He gently returns my swords to their harness and takes a second to examine my face. I feel the warm trickle of blood still falling from my nose. With the sleeve of his leather coat, he wipes it away, letting his thumb rest on my cheek a little longer than necessary. As soon as I feel my cheeks redden, he swiftly lets go and nods to the defeated Class Two. 'I'll drag that out to the fire.'

'Damn right you're dragging it out,' I add, watching him head towards the motionless Class Two. 'Since you did sod all killin' it.'

'You're going to a doctor when we get back. Your ribs could be broken.'

'If I report an injury, I'll get marked down. So no. I won't be doin' that.'

'If I tell Elder Eight you're hurt, he'll drag you there himself. Everyone knows you're his favourite.'

'Are you threatening me?' I watch him as he grabs at the Class Two's ankle and slowly hauls it across the floor towards me.

'CADETS!' Elder Eight yells from outside. 'WHAT'S THE HOLD-UP?'

'Coming, Elder,' Cass calls back as he stops in front of me. 'A broken rib isn't something to ignore and your face is bruised and bleeding. You need medical attention.'

'I'm not risking a single mark and if I report an injury, it will affect my score. Not a word. You hear me? Or you'll be sorry, Cassius.' I jab a finger in his chest and square up to him. I have to tilt my head up and he has to lower his to meet my stare. Our noses touch and he seems to find it a little amusing. 'Real sorry,' I add in a low warning.

'Is that so?' He leans further over me, accentuating the height difference and making me crane my head back so far, my foot has to shift back so I don't fall.

'Yes. I mean it, Cass. If you tell anyone I got hurt, you'll regret it.' With a firm shove, I push him away and straighten myself up.

With a small chuckle, he carries on walking out of the warehouse with the corpse trailing behind. 'Ohhhh, I'm shaking in my boots. C'mon future Red Coat, let's go home.'

With a triumphant grin, I follow him out.

Future Red coat. I love the sound of that!

The journey back to The Haven is uncomfortable. Elder Eight, along with the three Black Coats, are riding just up ahead, leading us all home. The others who were up on the hill, various Grey Coats, Red Coats and a couple of Elders, left as soon as the assignment was over.

My stallion, Hanzo, isn't a smooth ride on his best days. Usually, it doesn't bother me. But with my ribs in this much pain, it definitely bothers me now. He's a temperamental but beautiful beast with deep, dark brown hair and a white stripe straight down his face. And no one other than me can ride him without getting bucked off.

'You doing alright?' Cass asks, trotting beside me on his stallion, Midnight. He has the deepest black coat that shines blue when the light catches it just right. Cass glances at how my hand gingerly holds my side.

'Just tired.' I brush his concern off, lowering my hand. 'I checked. Nothing's broken, now shhh. Before someone hears.'

'You're going to the doctor when we get back,' he says with that annoying matter-of-fact tone he dons so often. 'I don't care if it marks you down. Your health is more important. And then you'll-'

'I said I'm not going.'

'We can tell them that you fell *after* the evaluation.'

'I said no, Cass.'

'And I said I don't care.'

I take the reins and pull back so Hanzo stops. Cass grunts and carries on knowing all he'll find now is silence and a fair amount of eye rolling if he stays. As he usually does when he knows I won't back down. And I never back down. He simply carries on and travels beside Winder instead, and when Tee appears beside me, we trot on.

'How's it going?' I ask her.

'Great.' She beams, her eyes doing a full three-sixty of our surroundings. 'I'll be glad to get home and wash the day off me.' She brushes off the layer of dust settled on her coat and continues watching the land around us warily.

We follow what used to be the motorway to get home. Our horse's hooves clip and clop as they walk along the four-lane carriageway with cracked tarmac and abandoned husks of cars pushed to the side. The buildings around here were knocked down years ago to use for the great wall surrounding home. Anything of use inside - furniture, clothing, medical supplies - absolutely anything remotely useful, was hauled into The Haven. So now, there's nothing left for miles but a hilly wasteland and countless human-eating monsters wandering around aimlessly.

'You still planning on putting your number in for the lottery tomorrow?' I ask Tee, crossing my fingers out of sight in the hope that she's changed her mind since this morning.

She nods, a tinge of embarrassment flushing her cheeks. And I inwardly sigh and slump at the idea.

And wail.

And swear.

It's a miracle I keep my composure, but she needs my support. Nothing else.

'It's a silly thing to do. I won't get picked.' She watches me, waiting for a reaction. 'You think I'm a sell-out,' she claims when she doesn't get one. 'I want a Green Coat, which means leaving your unit to stay up on the wall. And now I want to enter the lottery so I can leave the army. You think I'm-'

'I don't think you're anything but my best friend and my sister,' I clarify. 'And I certainly don't think you're a sell-out, Tee. You're not the only girl putting their number in the lottery. I think you'll find I'm the minority here. It's completely up to you. If winning the lottery will make you happy, then I'll support it a hundred per cent. I mean... if I had it my way, you wouldn't. But that's just me being selfish. I can't imagine not seeing you every day.' I look at our hostile surroundings. The miles of dead land. The ruins of old buildings. The nothingness. 'Just think, you'll be giving up all this.'

'Will you please put your number in with me?' she asks for what must be the hundredth time.

'Tee, I've already-'

'Scar...' She reaches out and takes my hand. 'I'm begging you, please put your number in with me. If there's a shot at one of us getting out of this life-'

'I don't *want* out of this life. I love this life.'

'That's what scares me. You enjoy being out here fighting those things way too much. I'm terrified that your... er... enthusiasm-'

'Stupidity,' Cass counters.

'Will get you killed,' Tee concludes sadly.

'I am exactly where I want to be. Where I'm needed. And if anyone wants to try and take my swords from me and replace it with a ring? Let them try. I could do with a laugh.'

'I wish I were as brave as you. Every time I come out here, all I can think about is that it might be the last. I don't want to turn into one of those things.'

'Listen.' I give her hand a big squeeze and make sure she sees my eyes, because I am not messing. 'I promise you, with every fibre of my being, that you will not die. You will not turn into one of them. And if you don't win the lottery, you'll be safe up on the wall. And me and the boys will see you every evening when we have dinner in the great hall. I promise. Either way, you're going to be as safe as a soldier can be! Plus, me not putting my number in only increases your chances of winning. Less competition.'

She sighs, retaking her reigns and giving up trying to convince me to enter the lottery. Her eyes land on Winder who is digging around his backside, pulling out his underwear.

She openly sneers, 'Are you searching for gold up there, Winder? Cut it out. No one wants to be seeing that!'

The boys ahead of us chuckle to themselves before Winder turns to face us, his underwear now free of his arse.

'Do you think he was up there with the others today?' he asks.

'Who?' I reply.

'Noah Sands, obviously.'

I scoff and shake my head. 'No way. Noah is far too important to be put in harm's way like that. The Grey Coats would have been out in force if he were up there.'

'That's a shame,' Tee sighs. 'I've always wondered what he looks like. Actually, come to think of it, probably best he wasn't there today.' She glances down at her dirty and sweaty body. 'I'm not exactly looking my best.'

Winder looks to Tee. 'If Noah was up there today, he'd fix the lottery so you would win for sure, Tee. You're adorable. Even all sweaty.' She blushes as he compliments her. She always blushes when he compliments her. And he is always doing it. 'And even if Scar did put her number in and win, he would probably demand a do-over,' he adds.

'Hey!' I snap. 'What's that supposed to mean? What's wrong with me?'

'Nothing. You're fine. But you kind of have that look...'

'What look?'

Cass turns and smirks. 'The kind of look that says — say or do the wrong thing, and I'll cut your head off so I can play football with it.' They all give a small chuckle. 'Tends to put people off.'

'Could you imagine Scar being a doting wife?' Winder asks Cass.

'Hell no! She's too mean. And always covered in zombie guts. It's like her perfume. Rotting flesh and congealed blood.' Cass sniffs the air as the others laugh. 'No offence, Scarlett.'

'Oh. None bloody taken. Sod you lot. I'm a delight. And I don't smell.' I give myself a whiff and almost gag. 'Well, today doesn't count. It's a heat wave, evaluation day and we all stink. So...'

Elder gives a high-pitched whistle and points to the east where there's a Class Three stumbling towards us from behind an old building.

He turns on his horse and looks at me. 'You still bleeding?'

I wipe my hand under my nose and there is still a little wet blood there. I groan and nod, gripping Hanzo's reigns before giving him a kick.

I'm attracting the creature. So it's my duty to put it down. As I ride, my ribs cry out in pain. The sound of hooves descending on me make me turn. I expect to see Cass. But it's Elder Eight.

'You alright?' he asks, looking at my side.

'Fine, Elder.'

'Your riding is weaker on your right. You injured?'

'No, Elder.'

'Kiddo, tell me-'

I unsheathe my sword, kick Hanzo, and we take off at a gallop, leaving him in our dust. It's an easy kill. A swift swipe results in a head removal and a quick skewer stops its jaws from chomping. I return to Elder who waited patiently for me to finish. He holds up his hand and I stop. The others are continuing on, but watching us.

Elder looks pissed. 'You have an injury and you're hiding it. Why?'

'I have no injury, Elder.'

'I only saw part of the fight between you and the Class Two. Were you injured before I got there?'

'No,' I insist coolly.

'Protecting someone?' He gives a single scoff as I remain quiet. 'If I see ya claspin' your side again, you're goin' straight to the doctor when we get back. Got it?'

'They'll mark me down-'

'Then ya shouda thought about that before gettin' hurt.' After a moment's glaring, he adds, 'If it's still hurtin' ya tomorrow mornin', come see me. I'll see if I can help.'

'Will that affect my mark?'

'Not if I keep my mouth shut it won't, no.' He nods to the others. 'Go. And ride easy.'

'Thanks, Elder.'

He grumbles before riding on.

After an hour of mindless chatter and aching arses, The Wall comes into sight and we all give a collective sigh of relief.

It's really done. We've finished our final assignment and our time as Cadets is almost over.

Soon, we'll be real soldiers and we'll trade these Brown Coats in for our official army ranked colours.

Our horses all pick up their pace. They're as keen as us to get home for some rest and food. In the middle of The Wall is a large iron door which can only be opened from the inside. On each door, made of cast iron, are two gigantic V's with a set of elegant wings behind them.

The emblem of The Verity.

These doors are the one and only entrance into The Haven.

The Green Coats work the pulley system, opening the gates for us. The loud grinding of the gears puts my teeth on. We ride in and they seal behind us. We're welcomed back home by the cheery applause of the people who live here as civilians. They always gather when Cadets return from their final assignments.

Littered about are Grey Coats, patrolling the crowds. Everyone glances at them nervously, careful not to hold their gaze for too long. They're brutal bastards who seek out any criminal activity and see to it that the guilty are punished. I use the phrase "criminal activity" loosely. I've always resented the fact that we feel more paranoid than protected when we see them. After all, they're supposed to be protecting us, right? From each other. From ourselves. From the dead. But it's hard to trust a group of people whose faces we never see. Who seek out punishment more than guilt. Who wears a thick leather whip at their hip stained with blood. As they slowly walk through the crowd, those the Grey Coats pass lower their heads and keep their eyes firmly down. One wrong word. Hell, one wrong look, you'll soon feel the lash of that whip. Civilian. Cadet. Black Coat or Red Coat. It doesn't matter. The only authority they answer to is Noah. And to a certain degree, the Elders. They can't punish an Elder.

But they can – and do – punish the rest of us.

Happily.

You couldn't have two more different landscapes. Inside the wall, everything is looked after with the utmost care and devotion. There's green grass and lush trees. Flowers and berries. It's like riding through a fairy tale. Everything is sacred here. The food is grown away from the public, and it's all fiercely audited. Not a bean is grown without it going in a ledger. Nothing is wasted, and no one goes hungry. Unfortunately, it's nearly all root vegetables. Goddamn radishes are the nastiest thing I've ever eaten.

We have livestock. But we don't eat meat. All leather is from animals that died naturally or from items found out beyond the wall. It's all about healing the world and respecting nature. Which is why burning any form of fuel, or producing any kind of pollution is forbidden. Hence the horses. We see remnants of the technology that the world once had. Televisions. Computers. Machinery with hundreds of buttons and huge furnaces that would pour tons of smoke out into the atmosphere. Even enormous winged structures that used to fly and drilling rigs that went miles underground, pulling out oil!

All of it played a part in the death of the world. So now we let it rot. After we took what we needed of course.

The civilians that we pass live in the main town in the centre of our walled-in fortress, in huts and cabins. They have the babies, farm the land, collect the water, and anything else that doesn't include training and fighting the undead. Although they clap and cheer, celebrating that we've managed to survive, they avoid looking at us. Each one that holds a child's hand has donated at least one of their offspring. I could have passed my mum and dad a dozen times, and I would never know. Other than my auburn hair, I have no distinguishing characteristics that could be any sign of where I came from. Hazel eyes. Not overly tall or noticeably short. No birthmarks or abnormalities. But I'm yet to see anyone in the town to match the odd red my curly hair boasts.

They never look us in the eye. We could be theirs, and they harbour a certain degree of shame about giving us away. The life of a donated child is hard. Relentless. Brutal. Some of us don't even make it through training. Some don't make it out of the orphanage.

But I love my life. I love the fight.

I wave at the kids. They wave at me. They're too young to know what lies ahead for them. What lies beyond that gigantic wall and heavy, metal door. They don't know about the monsters as we do. They don't know that one day they'll have to donate a child of their own to a life of fighting. At least if they see us smile, wave, happy... perhaps it won't haunt them as much as it haunts their parents. So that's what we all do.

'That woman's here again,' Tee says quietly, her gaze flitting towards a tall lady with long brown hair and the same features as her. She lingers by the wall regularly when we're out, as if waiting for our return. Tee smiles and waves at the woman we all think is her mum. As ever, the woman lowers her head and disappears into the crowd, dragging a little brown-haired boy after her. Tee keeps her sweetness and waves at the kids. Her ability to maintain a brave face is inspiring. I know she would love nothing more than to throw down her bow and go dig up some potatoes. She'd be a great wife and such an amazing mum. But we don't have that choice. We can't marry until we retire. And retirement age is forty. Not many of us reach that. And even if we do, no way we'd hand over a kid to a life of this. So hardly anyone from the military marries.

This is our lot. End of.

Well... except for the lottery of course. Which is why Tee's so anxious about the whole thing. It's a girl's only way out of this life, and her one and only chance to have a family of their own without handing over a kid. Win the lottery, you're excluded from the law of donation. You get to live a domestic life with the man himself as dear husband.

Lord Noah Sands.

It would be her dream come true. It's many of the army girl's idea of a dream come true.

We follow the soldier's road, which avoids the town and leads straight from the gate to the Military Village.

No civilians are allowed down this way. We pass others training or getting ready to head out on various missions. They all acknowledge us, and we acknowledge them.

Once the horses have been fed, watered and stabled, we head back to The Academy. The building we call home. Fifty years ago, it was a great and extremely luxurious hotel, complete with indoor and outdoor pools, something called a spa, and various courts for playing racquet sports on. Now, the outdoor swimming pool is where we lift weights. The tennis court is where we practice with heavy weaponry. And the indoor pool is a gymnastics training area. This four-story, three hundred and twenty-eight bedroomed building made of dark-red brick and lead tiles, now serves as the home of five hundred Cadets all going through training.

Ten Elders spend their days passing on their specific skills to us all. Archery, swordplay, gymnastics, and a dozen other fighting techniques. The left-wing houses ages five to ten. The right-wing, ten to sixteen. And the cadets aged sixteen to seventeen live in the north wing as they undergo a whole year of evaluation.

Boys on one floor. Girls on the another.

The various Lord Sands that have been and gone in the last half century - along with the Sainted Army - extended the safe zone right up to the sea, taking in small village after small village. Now we have some good thirty-odd square miles of safety surrounded by the great wall on one side and the ocean on the other. The Academy is the centre of the Military Village. It's where we sleep, gather to eat, meet for assemblies and even witness public punishment. In the forecourt is a large stone pillar stained with blood. There's one in the civilian's village too and by all accounts, it's a lot bloodier than this one. I've never been lashed, but Cass has. After some Cadet grabbed Tee's backside, he punched him in the jaw. Knocked out two of his teeth. But that wasn't what earned him ten lashes, the scars of which still linger on his back. It was what he said.

"What the hell do you think you're doing?"

That one word – *Hell* - led to his public flogging.

Lesson learnt.

Don't swear in front of anyone you don't trust. Blasphemy is not tolerated!

But beating up a groper? Crack on.

Some of the windows of this once magnificent building have been smashed, others simply rotted out of their frames. We had to take out the revolving doors ten years ago when they jammed and no one could get in or out. The entrance is just a massive hole in the wall now. But you have to walk up a lovely flight of marble steps to get to it. So that's nice I suppose. The guttering's a mess, so the building's pretty damp and at least four of the chimneys have fallen off the roof.

But today, it looks very different. Reminds me of a pig wearing a dress.

The front forecourt outside The Academy has been tidied and decorated with blue and red bunting. The broken windows have been boarded up. The debris from years of neglect have been swept away and potted rose bushes have appeared all over the place. They even have little ribbons attached to them. Cadets pass us in droves as they carry on their work, tidying and fixing.

'Hi, Scarlett,' they greet.

'Afternoon, Scarlett,' they say.

'Well done on your final assignment, Scarlett!'

I nod and give a brief hello to them all. Every face is familiar but I wouldn't say I know all their names.

'Wow. They would crawl up your backside if they could,' Tee laughs.

'It's just my kill count they admire. Not me,' I remind her. 'Where did they find all this crap?' I laugh, looking at the stupid attempt to try and make this place look half decent. 'I asked for a new blanket last week cos mine's threadbare. I was told there wasn't one. My pillow's so flat it's like sleeping on a sheet of sodding paper. But this stuff?' I gesture to the rustic red carpet currently being rolled out the front door. 'They can find this stuff alright.' I laugh as I watch the middle-grade cadets sweep the dusty floors and wash the grime from the remaining windows. 'What a joke.'

'We have to make an effort,' Tee says simply. 'It's a big deal, this visit. I mean... *Noah Sands* himself is coming! He deserves better than this.' She gestures to the crumbling mess. It's the least looked-after building in the place cos everyone here is far too busy training to stay alive to look after it properly. And we have far too low a standard of living to give a damn anyway.

'This is our home. If it's good enough for us, it should be good enough for him.' I head over to one of the younger cadets who is at the top of a ladder. It wobbles unsteadily beneath him as he scrubs a second story window with gusto. I grip it tight and make sure it's steady so he doesn't fall and break his neck. 'Alright up there?' I call.

'Yeah. Oh! Scarlett! Please don't trouble yourself. I'm good up here. This work is beneath you.'

'Beneath us all,' I mutter, returning my attention to Tee who takes hold of the other leg. 'All this fuss. Washing windows, sweeping floors, for what?' I lower my voice and lean in so no one else can hear me. 'He ain't divine, Tee. He's no more a spokesman for God than I am. And if he weren't a good leader, a good fighter, and dedicated to defeating the targets, no one in the Sainted Army would give a damn about him. He's just a man.'

'He's not *just* a man, Scar,' she says scornfully. 'Now his dad has died, Noah Sands is the leader of The Verity! He's-'

'If you say God's representative on earth, I'll bloody slap you,' I warn.

'Of course not. You know I don't believe in all that nonsense. But, Scar, Noah and his family are the only reason we're alive.' She sighs, her eyebrows raised as if she's said this all a hundred times over. She has. As well as all the Elders. I rest my hand on my hip and let her have at it. 'They literally saved us. And Noah has singlehandedly increased food production with his new system of farming. Cadet fatalities have gone down since he added extra curriculums to our training like field medicine and evasive tactics. He deserves our respect.'

'Alright, Tee. I get it. Noah's fab-'

'And...' She ain't done. 'He just lost his dad and has been thrown into this new position of power.'

'I don't think he really minds-'

'If that wasn't enough...' Oh wow. She's really on the defensive. 'He's got to go through the process of the lottery to get a wife so he can further the Sands bloodline which is a huge responsibility on him and whoever is chosen.' She pauses and looks at me with a wrinkle on her brow. And I know exactly what's coming. 'You should really put your number in.'

'No.'

'I just think-'

'Tee, I-'

'The winner gets to have a home! Have a family! Have a real marriage! It's every girl's dream.'

'Not mine.' I shrug. 'I have a family. A home. And I'm married to my work. To my swords.'

'You're being ridiculous,' she snaps. 'And stubborn.'

'And you're being an annoying bitch!' I bark back, my voice echoing around the courtyard making her blink at me in surprise. 'I don't want to put my number in the sodding lottery. I don't want to be chosen to be Noah's sodding wife and that's the end of it! I don't get a say in much. But I get a say in this. And it is not happening. I will not be shoved into a pretty dress and used as a breeding mare.'

'Alright. Calm down. I'm sor-'

'But you keep on! You haven't stopped badgering me about this bloody lottery since we were kids and I am sick of it. You want to marry him? Crack on, Tee. Just leave me out of it. Got it?'

The cadet above us glances between us, wet sponge still in hand. Various others have all stopped to spectate too. And Tee keeps blinking at me, startled at my sudden outburst. It's very rare I lose my temper with her. And those doe eyes make me feel rotten to the core for speaking to her so harshly.

'I'm sorry,' I sigh, reaching out and taking her hand in mine. 'I shouldn't have spoken to you like that. I'm just really tired of people telling me what I should do, ya know? I just want to join the army and wear a Red Coat. Look. I'm sure Noah's nice enough. And I hear he's not bad looking either. But I want to fight. Not stay home and raise his kids. That's your dream, Tee. Not mine. I couldn't think of anything worse. To be taken away from my home and everything I know. From the fight. From-'

'Cass?' she adds with a knowing look. I narrow my eyes at her with a warning as she shows me her cheeky little grin, forgiving me for my outburst.

'I could say the same about you and Winder,' I retort.

'We get our coats before we find out who wins the lottery,' she says slowly and through her teeth, ignoring my words and scowling fiercely. Sore subject that. Clearly. But her eyes are drawn to something behind me, and her scowl disappears, only to be replaced with wide and worried eyes. 'Oh no. Scar... look.'

'What?' I turn to see what she's looking at. 'Oh bugger.'

Flash is talking to Titan, looking at me nervously as if preparing himself to come and talk to me. But it's Cass storming up to him from behind that has Tee worried.

'Cass!' I warn, letting go of the ladder and heading towards them. 'Cass, don't you dare!'

Too late. He spins Flash round by the shoulder and slams his fist straight into his face. Flash hits the ground hard, clasping his nose and looking up at him absolutely terrified.

'Cass! Stop!' I yell, running over.

Cass towers over him and points a finger in his face. 'You nearly got her killed, you selfish little bastard! What did you think you were playing at?'

'Cass, mate! Let it go!' Winder says, grabbing his elbow as he pulls it back again ready for another strike. Titan could floor Cass with ease. But he doesn't. He just kneels beside Flash and helps him to sit.

Cass pulls his arm free and tries to land another punch, but I jump between them.

'Enough!' I order. 'Stand down.'

'He almost got you killed!' he says furiously.

'You need to keep it down,' I warn in a hush, looking around the forecourt. Everyone has fallen silent and is watching us. 'He screwed up. He knows that. But it's not worth him getting reassigned over. And, he won't do it again. Will you, Flash?'

He shakes his head as he clasps his bleeding nose.

'See? It's all good.'

'It's all good?' Cass hisses. 'ALL GOOD?' he roars, shaking his head. 'Nah. It ain't good till he learns his lesson.' He charges forwards again, his furious eyes squarely on Flash still on the floor. But I stand in his way and shove him hard in the chest, making him stumble back.

'You take one more step towards him, I'll shove my foot so far up your arse you'll be tasting rubber for a week,' I warn. 'We have enough to be dealing with out there, without turning on each other in here.'

He looks me up and down and turns his anger on me instead. 'What were you doing holding up a ladder?'

'Don't you start on me.'

'Go and sort your ribs out,' he orders, pointing towards the house. '*I'll* deal with Flash.'

'What's wrong with her ribs?' Tee gasps, rushing over and fussing.

'Nothing.' I brush her off. 'I'm fine.'

'Get your backside to the doctor before I drag you there myself.'

'Just shut up, Cass. You're starting to get on my nerves.'

'SCARLETT! DO AS YOU'RE TOLD!'

'Don't you talk to me like-'

'I GAVE YOU AN ORDER!' He storms up to me, showering me with spit and towering over me so I have to lean back a little to stop his face touching mine.

'You done?' I ask calmly.

'Go. Or I will make sure Elder Eight knows exactly what happened today. Flash... that container... your injury. All of it. You'll be marked down. So go, or else. Am I making myself clear?'

'He's right. If you're hurt-' Tee takes my arm. I yank it back.

'I know that what happened with me today scared you. And that you're angry at Flash for what he did. I know you're behaving this way because you care.' I step closer to Cass, so my face is in his.

But he doesn't step back and now our noses are touching. 'But if you ever talk to me that way in front of people again... actually...' I slam my own fist into his face, and he joins Flash on the floor, clasping his bloody nose. He looks up at me furiously.

'Problem?' A Grey Coat calls over with an amused chuckle. 'Need help with the little lady, Cadet?'

'No,' Cass replies with a snarl, wiping the blood away with his sleeve. 'I think I can manage.'

I lean over him, my finger now in *his* face. 'Don't you dare talk to me that way ever again, Cassius. In private. Or in front of anyone else. Don't you *ever* threaten me or my ranking in order to get me to do what *you* want, ever again. If you do... I'll break more than your nose. Am *I* making *myself* clear?'

The courtyard is silent. Not even the Grey Coats intervene. After all, I'm not breaking any laws.

'Yeah,' he growls. 'Crystal.'

'Good. I don't need your protection. For you to defend me. Or your misogyny. I'm not a defenceless little girl that needs rescuing. It was me that saved your arse today and don't you forget it.' I turn and head inside the house. People scurry out of my way as I pass.

He's such an asshole.

I storm through the enormous entrance lobby, barging into those who don't move aside quick enough.

They glance at my swords as I pass and keep quiet.

A wise move, given my mood.

The stone floors are heavily marked and cracked from years of abuse by our military boots. The walls are peeling paint and faded floral wallpaper. Above my head - four stories high - is a huge domed ceiling with a rusty chain dangling from the centre. The crystal chandelier fell off decades ago. Killed two Cadets, according to Elder Eight. There's a small crater in the floor where it landed.

You can see each level above us. The landings are like long balconies surrounding each wall. Most of the bannisters have rotted away so you don't wanna get too close to the edge. It's a hell of a long way down if you do. There's a grand staircase straight ahead which leads up to the first floor and there are hallways, stairways and passageways leading every which way. This place is a bit of a maze. But I've lived here for as long as I can remember, so I know it all like the back of my hand.

As I walk down the halls, up several flights of stairs and through various corridors, I quietly mutter to myself about the prat I left on the floor downstairs.

Who does he think he is? How dare he talk to me that way.

Urgh.

No one gets under my skin like Cass does. And that really pisses me off. That he can make me this annoyed and angry.

Prick.

I finally reach the hallway that leads to the room I share with Tee. Our own little slice of solitude. Which we share. Joint solitary, if there is such a thing.

Room 148 on the third floor at the very front of the house. We get the sun in the morning. Lovely way to wake up. Beams of light searing into your eyeballs. We don't have curtains. Obviously.

I can't wait to wash. To get out of my clothes and into some joggers and a tank top. Something comfortable and breathable. Oh, to lay on my bed and sleep. Yes. Sleep.

No. No sleep.

Standing outside my door are two men.

Grey Coats.

Their large hoods cover their faces, as ever. Their plain black jeans and military boots are exactly the same. They stand with their arms folded across their chest, staring straight ahead. The winged V emblem sprawled across their backs.

I stop dead in my tracks. 'Ahhh... bloody hell,' I whisper. This is the last thing I need. I just want to wash and go to sleep. Not deal with this. They haven't spotted me. I back away, hoping to leave unseen.

Someone behind me clears their throat. I jump and spin to see another Grey Coat at my back.

'Oh... Mr Grey.' I nod in polite acknowledgement, clutching my chest from shock. I hate how they move so quietly. They're always sneaking up on people. Truth is, I have no idea if any of them are men or women. We never see their faces. We just call them all *"Mr Grey"* on account of their jackets.

'Language, Cadet. You know the laws against blasphemy.'

'Commander,' I reply with a small bow. 'I didn't realise it was you.' Of course, the one to catch me swearing would be the leader of the Grey Coats. 'I'm so sorry. It was a slip of the tongue, I assure you.'

'I suggest you learn better control of your tongue then, Cadet,' he says dryly.

'Is this visit about today's assessment?' I ask with forced enthusiasm. And a bit of hope. Surely, *he's* not here. Not today. Please not today. I look to the door of my room where the two men are still standing guard.

'You know why we're here.' He nudges me forwards towards my room. 'You're wanted.'

'I take it there's another *Mr Grey* in my room waiting for me then?'

The Commander just gives me another gentle nudge.

'Crap,' I whisper. 'Is he in a good mood at least?'

'He's always in a good mood,' he replies tiredly. 'Especially when he gets to see you. In you go, Cadet. He doesn't like to be kept waiting.'

I take a deep, weary breath. 'Don't I know it,' I grumble, heading towards my room.

Mine and Tee's bedroom consists of two twin beds, which are on opposite sides of the room. A large desk lies in the middle, where Tee makes her arrows. All around the room, various weapons are strewn about. Knives. Axes. Arrows and the such. No guns though. They're forbidden. Even if you are lucky enough to find one out in the wild – which no one has for over a decade – they're too noisy and too dangerous. One shot and it attracts the dead for miles. Similar to blood. And one missed shot could kill a fellow soldier. So, no guns.

There's a wardrobe where Tee and I store our selection of uniforms. We share all our clothes. We're the same size, and apart from my kicks and leather wrappings, we wear the same thing every day. Black tank top, brown leggings, our brown leather coats and joggers for our down time. There's a door to the left which leads to the bathroom. And standing by the window straight ahead, looking out at the forecourt where everyone is busy with their preparations, is another *Mr Grey*, still with his hood up. The door is closed as soon as I enter, leaving us alone. He doesn't turn. He stays looking outside with his hands cupped neatly behind his back.

'I'm amazed you let him speak to you like that,' he says, still not turning to look at me. 'Most of the Cadets here idolise you. The rest are afraid of you. Not him though. *Not Cassius.*'

'I think my right hook proved that I didn't let him speak to me like that.' I take off my harness and throw my weapons on my bed. 'How are you? I wasn't expecting to see you today-'

'What is it about him? Why are you friends with such a rude, arrogant person?'

'He's not-'

'I watch him boss you about. Who does he think he is?'

'I'm too tired for your jealousy today... *Mr Grey*. And definitely too tired for a lecture.'

'A lecture?' he scoffs. 'You're sounding a little insolent there, Cadet.'

'Apologies. I've just had a really long day. Final assignment and all that. Maybe you could come back later?'

I wait.

He stays.

I sigh.

He's not going anywhere.

'Do you mind if I clean up? Like I said. It's been a long day.' I head into the bathroom after he gives a single nod.

We have a steady water supply here. For washing anyway. It's not clean enough to drink, and it's icy. But it's more than welcome in this heat. Not so much in the winter when the pipes freeze up. I peel off my leather wrappings from my legs and shrug off my brown leather coat, wincing as I move my right side.

I lift my top to inspect my ribs. There's an impressive amount of purple and blue. I feel each rib. I'm more stiff than anything else. But it's just bruising. Nothing's broken.

He's followed me in and is leaning against the door frame, watching me.

'I heard you did really well today.'

'You did, huh?' I lower my top and turn. I rest my hands behind me on the sink as we face each other. 'What are you doing here? I thought you lot weren't supposed to arrive until tomorrow.'

'I grew impatient. Knowing I was going to see you again, I couldn't wait until tomorrow.' He strolls towards me and rests his hands on my hips.

'You should be more careful. You being here is a huge risk.'

'I'm perfectly safe.'

'For me, *Mr Grey*. It's a huge risk for me,' I remind him, looking at how he holds me. 'You won't be the one publically flogged and banished to The Canaries if caught with a man in her room, unchaperoned, with his hands on her person. And besides, I thought we agreed that this was done with. These little meetings. My training's done now.'

He lowers his hood and smiles his *oh so charming* smile. His short dark hair is perfectly groomed. His face is entirely clean-shaven and his clothes are perfectly ironed. He's clean and smells of soap, all of which makes him stick out like a sore thumb compared to the rest of us at The Academy. He tucks a few loose strands of my knotty, dust-filled hair behind my ear, rubs off some dried blood from around my nose with his thumb and looks longingly at my lips.

'*You* agreed this was done with. Not me. And for the record, I would never let anyone flog you or banish you. Ever. Have you missed me even a little bit, Cadet?' he asks.

'It's been a week since we saw each other. And I've been training like crazy. I haven't had the time to miss you.'

'But have you missed me?'

'Do you want me to have missed you?'

He laughs and firms his grip on my hips. 'You're as beautiful as ever, Cadet 5-3-6.'

Now I laugh, knowing I'm an absolute filthy mess. 'And you're ever the charmer, Noah Sands.'

CHAPTER FIVE

Noah leans in. His soft lips start working my neck and his body shifts closer.

Oh bugger.

I told him! I made it clear that the kiss we shared was a mistake. When I lay my palms flat against his chest and gently push him away, he groans.

'Take it you haven't changed your mind then. Still don't want me?' he complains.

'Noah, you're here to pick a wife. You think kissing me is the best idea right now? Your duty requires you to marry, and mine requires me to-'

'Die.'

'Fight.' I correct him. 'I need to focus on my job. And I don't want to be in the way of you and your new wife. We're friends, Noah. That kiss the other week was a-'

'Look, I know what you said, and I respect that.'

'Is that why you just helped yourself to my neck with your lips?' I ask him with raised eyebrows. 'Because you respect my decision?'

'I just wanted to talk to you.'

'Then talk without kissing. But if you don't mind, make it short. I'm exhausted. I need to wash. I'm covered in Zombie guts. My ribs are killin' me. And I ache like crazy.' As he looks to the floor sadly, I feel guilty. 'How are you doing?' I ask. 'Losing your dad and all, gotta be hard. Anything I can do to help?'

'Not really. But let me help you. Here.' He turns me and starts rubbing my shoulders. 'Purely platonic, Cadet,' he chuckles. I watch him in the little shard of mirror Tee glued to the wall when we moved into the room. He sees me looking, waiting for him to open up.

'Fine,' he sighs, avoiding my gaze. 'I'll share. I'm alright. Dad was old-fashioned, rigid, cold and firmly stuck in his ways, but losing him was harder than I thought.' He shrugs. 'But, there is something you can do to help me through this awful time of grief.' He returns his mouth to my neck and traces soft kisses all along my skin.

He's persistent if nothing else.

'I think you and your *Mr Greys* outside should get out of here before someone sees you. Tee could be back here any second.' I move a little, but he just guides me back.

'No, she won't,' he says. 'I've made sure no one can come up here.' He's not getting the hint and getting much more handsy.

'Noah... why have you come here?' I ask, gently guiding him away from me. 'Cos I've told you, that kiss was a mistake. So, if that's the only reason you came to see me, you wasted a trip.'

'Spoilsport,' he groans, backing away and fighting a smile. 'I actually came to talk to you about the lottery. I want to ask you something.'

'Oh yeah? You want the low down on all the girls who are putting their number in?' I tease.

'Are you coming to the lottery opening tomorrow?' he asks.

'I am.' I untie the string holding up my hair and let it loose. The amount of dust that comes out is surprising. As I shake free the thick mass of curls, I create a cloud of grit around me. Meanwhile, Noah's whole face has lit up with excitement. 'What are you smiling at?' I chuckle.

'You're putting your number in?'

'What? No, of course not,' I reply, laughing at how ridiculous that would be. 'Why would I?'

'Err... because we've been...'

'In all the years we've been friends, we've kissed twice. Two kisses does not a wife make, Lord Sands.' I continue ruffling my hair to try and clear it. I pull out my fingers from the nest on top of my head. Gross. There's goo in it.

'Would being married to me be so awful?' he asks shortly.

'I didn't say that. I'm sure it would be great. You'll make some girl very happy.'

'Then put your number in.' He shrugs. 'And I could make *you* very happy.'

'But that life ain't for me. I mean... could you imagine me as a wife?' I laugh at the ridiculousness of the idea and toss my brown cadet jacket in the sink. But I feel his eyes boring into my back. When I turn, he's not smiling. Far from it.

'Is it *him?*' he sneers, nodding over his shoulder to where he was standing at the window when I came in. 'Is *he* the reason you won't be with me?'

'Please tell me you're not being serious.'

'I thought we had a connection. All the time we've spent together...'

'Training. We train together. We have a laugh, and yes, we've kissed. All of two times, Noah. But you know that we're just friends.'

'I'm just asking, *Cadet.* Is it the fact that you don't want to be *a* wife? Or that you don't want to be *my* wife that's stopping you entering my lottery?'

'Both,' I tell him, taking a seat on the toilet and pulling off my kicks. I pour out the dirt I've collected into two little piles on the floor.

'I don't want you talking to Cassius anymore.'

'Excuse me?'

'You heard me.'

'He's in my unit, Noah. That would be impossible. Look. You don't see me sneaking into your mansion by the sea, demanding this that and the other. I have never once asked you for any special treatment or favours. You asked me to keep our friendship quiet, and I have. Also, Cass and I are none of your business.' I drop my shoes and look up at him leaning against the door. I've let my annoyance take control. Not a good move. Not with him.

'So, there is a you and Cass?'

'As far as we're two best friends-'

'You two kissed?'

'No. And even if we had, Noah, it would be none of your business.'

'It would be my business because I would be forced to punish you both for breaking the law. Soldiers are not permitted to be intimate.'

'*We've* kissed.' I remind him. 'You gonna punish us too? Listen, nothing is going on between Cass and me. He is *not* the reason I'm not putting my number in. If I became your wife, I'd have to leave the army. And I won't. You know that.'

'I love you,' he says plainly.

'You... you... what?' I stand and stare at him mouth open. 'No. You don't.'

'Yes. I do, and I have from the moment we met.'

'Stop it.'

'No. I thought I could just be your friend. But then we kissed. And I want more. I want to be with you. Properly.' He charges over and takes my hands in his. With a huge grin and eager eyes, he tells me, 'I choose *you* to be my wife.' He waits as I seem to misplace the ability to speak. He's acting like he's handed me a great gift. But he should know it's a gift I don't want. 'Can you stop looking at me like a fish and say something?'

'Oh my god.'

'I love you, but don't you swear at me.'

'Why are you doing this?' I pull my hands free and step back. 'What's wrong with you?'

'Why am I doing what? Giving you the life of your dreams? The chance to have a family and not spend your days fighting for your survival?' he snaps. 'I want us to be together. No one will know I've fixed the lottery for you to win.'

'Noah... I'm really sorry-'

'Don't. Don't you dare,' he warns, pointing a finger at me angrily. 'I'm giving you what every girl would kill for so don't you dare turn me down.'

'Every girl but me. You know what I want. This!' I gesture around me. 'When we met, I was crystal clear about what I wanted. I couldn't have been any clearer! You understood. You helped me train so I could be the best and earn my Red Coat.'

He's getting angrier and angrier. Like a kettle on a stove. And he's starting to whistle. This is a nightmare. An absolute nightmare. Of all the people to upset...

'Can you seriously say, that after all this time, you feel nothing for me?' he says through gritted teeth.

'As a friend and as our leader, of course I do. But as a husband?' I shake my head. 'If I'd have known you felt so strongly... I never wanted to be put into a position where I'd have to hurt you.'

'You don't have to hurt me. Just... put your number in.'

'I can't do that.'

'WHY?!' he bellows, slamming his fist into the wall making me jump and step back. I've never seen him angry. And he's left a great big hole in the wall now too. 'It's because you want *him*! *Cassius.*' I reach out and take his hands in an effort to calm him down. He swallows hard, afraid to hear some unspoken truth that simply isn't there and avoids making eye contact with me. I take his perfectly smooth and pristine face in my scarred and calloused hands. I look him right in the eye and make sure I speak as kindly as I can because hurting him is the last thing I want to do.

Or should do.

'Noah... I don't want to marry because I want to be in the army. I want to fight. I want to be a Red Coat. Cass has nothing to do with it. To be honest, *you* have nothing to do with it. It's all about the job. Please believe me, Noah. You're a great guy. You have a huge job to do yourself, and you deserve someone that will help and support you in being the great leader you are. That will devote their whole life to you in a way that I never can. You'll find a woman who will look after your heart. That will give you children and cook your meals. And while she's doing that, you'll have me to help you in the fight out there beyond the wall.'

'You could do both.'

'No. I can't. You know that. The law forbids an active soldier to marry. I can't be in the army and be a wife. Your family made that rule. If we break it, then you'll have to extend that right to everyone. Which you won't.' I run my hand down his arm as he looks to the floor. There. I think that he's accepted my choice. I turn back to the sink to finish washing up.

'I order you to put your number in.'

Slowly, I turn to gauge him. And yep, he's being deadly serious. There's a firm finality in his face. He could fix it so I'm chosen. I know it. He knows it. He could make me his wife. He could make me anything he wanted.

'A-are you being serious?'

'You will put your number in,' he says coldly. A flash of anger sparks in his eyes and the air gets colder, I'm sure. 'I will force you to put it in.'

'You'll force me?' I ask in disbelief. 'What does that mean? You *can't* force someone to marry you.'

'Is that right? And how will you stop me exactly?'

'The Elders would never allow-'

'Let me stop you right there.' He rests his finger over my lips. 'You tell anyone about us... You tell anyone that we knew each other before the lottery announcement, I will kill whoever's ears are unfortunate enough to hear your words. Do you understand me?'

'Why are you being this way?' I ask, desperation a little too clear in my voice.

'You will put your number in or else, Cadet.'

'This isn't you. You're not a cruel man.'

'Perhaps I am a cruel man,' he says slowly. 'Perhaps I've been too kind with you. Maybe a lashing would knock some sense and respect into you. Is that what you want?'

'You want to have me lashed for refusing to marry you?' I reply.

'You always tell me I'm a good man. I'm just not good enough for you, is that it?'

'No! You are a good man. You have great plans for the army. I know you'll do great things and I want to help you achieve them all. I'm your friend and your servant, Noah. Give me an order, and I'll follow it. As I always have. My sword is yours. I'm on your side.'

He rests his hand on my cheek. 'You mean that?'

'Of course,' I reply nervously.

'Then kiss me.'

I go rigid as he looks at my lips. 'W-what?'

'I'm giving you an order, Cadet. You said you would follow it. Kiss me.'

'My sword is yours,' I reply in barely a whisper. 'Not my body. I will not kiss you, Noah. Not like this.'

'I said... kiss me,' he orders through gritted teeth.

'I-I want you to leave now, please.' I back up. Desperate to get some space between us. 'I said I want you to go!'

He suddenly lunges at me, slamming his mouth onto mine and pushing me back. I try to yell, but his forceful kiss steals my voice. My lower back slams into the sink as he forces his tongue into my mouth. He takes hold of my waist, keeping me held in place. His palm rests over my bruised ribs and I groan in pain. I push against his chest, my hands finding nothing more than his immovable frame of what could be made of perfectly sculpted stone. He doesn't budge an inch and for all my skills, I panic. I've never been touched this way before. It's nothing short of a violation, I feel sick with it. I've been punched. Kicked. Shot with an arrow. I've faced monsters. But this? This has me cold on the inside. This has me scared.

I slap him hard across the face.

It gets him off. But I've just struck the most powerful man alive. And now my sense of violation shifts.

To fear.

What I've just done is a death sentence right there.

I step back, too in shock at what's happening and his sudden change in personality to think of anything to say or do. He checks his lip. There's a little blood there.

'You hit me.'

'I'm sorry,' I whisper. 'Noah, I didn't mean-'

Slap.

I get a hard-backhand right across the face and get sent down to my knees with spots in my vision. He stands over me pointing his finger in my face and such hatred in his eyes.

'If you ever raise a hand to me again, I will have you executed,' he warns, as I remain on the floor with my head down and blood dripping along my chin from my split lip. I daren't move. I daren't say a word. I stay perfectly still, not even wiping the blood away. 'How dare you,' he says in a low, menacing tone that chills me to my very core. 'How dare you strike me. I am of God. I am your leader. Your commander. Your-'

'I thought you were my friend.'

'If I didn't love you and only held you as a friend, I would have you strung up from the neck and thrown from your window this very minute for striking me.'

'I'm sorry,' I repeat quietly. 'I shouldn't have struck you. But-'

'But?' He reaches down and lifts my chin with his finger. I look up into his dark eyes. 'But what? What possible reason could you have for striking me?'

'You didn't have my permission to touch me that way,' I force myself to say. 'Just because you are who you are, doesn't mean my body is yours to touch as you please.'

'Is that right?' He grabs my arm, pulls up his hood and hauls me to my feet. 'I'll show you exactly what I can do to your body if I wish. It's time you learnt some goddamn respect.'

He pulls me out my room so fast, my feet trip over themselves. The other Grey Coats step aside and follow us as he leads me down the stairs.

In the lobby, Tee, Winder and Cass are in the middle of regaling our final assignment to a crowd of younger Cadets, all of which are watching them with awe and hanging on their every word. Cass sees me being hauled out.

'HEY!' he yells, charging after us. 'WHAT DO YOU THINK YOU'RE DOING?' He runs after us, outside, down the steps and plants his feet between me and Noah, and the lashing post. 'What's happening?' Cass demands. 'What did she do?' He looks at me with an angry frown. 'What did you do?'

Noah won't speak. His voice is too well known. So he slams his fist into Cass's face and steps over him as he falls on the floor. Noah shoves me into the arms of another Grey Coat.

'Tie her to the post,' he says quietly, his voice shaking with anger. The Grey Coat nods and leads me to the post by my elbows. I look back at Noah over my shoulder as my hands are fastened around the stone pillar so I'm hugging it. He follows and stands close.

'You do this... that's it,' I warn him. 'Me and you are done.'

He leans his face in close to mine. 'The box is opening tomorrow,' he says. 'Put your number in. And I will stop this.'

Behind him, everyone is gathering. Winder's helping Cass to his feet but it takes both Winder and Titan to hold him back. If Cass tries to stop this, my lashes get doubled and he'll receive twice more than me. We all know the rules.

I look back to Noah and my stubborn streak takes over completely. Now I'm not locked in a room alone with him, and he can't touch me intimately without my permission, I'm not so afraid.

'What will it be, Cadet? A wedding ring? Or the lash of my whip?'

'Shove your wedding ring where the sun doesn't shine. I'll take the lashes any day. I hope you enjoy this. Cos it's the last time you'll ever get to touch me.'

He grabs the back of my top and tears it right down the middle before running his fingers softly down my spine. I shudder in revulsion.

'No. It won't be. I was going to take you for a moonlight picnic on the beach tonight to celebrate your birthday. But I guess this is the gift that you have chosen.'

'Like I said. I'll take the lashes.'

Holding out his hand, he takes a few steps back and a Grey Coat hands him a brown leather whip encrusted with years of our collective blood soaked into it.

'TEN LASHES FOR DISOBEDIENCE,' The Commander calls out on behalf of Noah.

I glance around me. The Cadets stand tall and rest their hands over their hearts. A sign of respect. We all know these punishments are cruelty. Not discipline.

Tee darts through the throng of people and is swiftly grabbed by a few standers by.

'Tee, close your eyes. Cover your ears. Don't look, you hear me?'

'NOW HOLD ON A MINUTE!' Elder Eight hollers, charging towards me. Two Grey Coats block his path. 'YOU GET YOUR HANDS OFF HER.'

'Stand aside, Elder. This is Grey Coat business,' The Commander calls out dismissively.

'That's *my* Cadet!' he roars. 'I demand to know what she did. Disobedience? There's no Cadet more loyal and dedicated to the fight. How did she disobey?'

'It's okay, Elder,' I tell him, keeping my eyes firmly on him. 'It's okay. Please. Just... don't let Tee see.'

He still pushes the Grey Coat for a reason.

'Tell me what she did!'

'None of your concern,' The Commander replies. Noah unfurls the whip and slaps it against the ground. The crack it creates echoes all around us and the crowd jumps. Tee howls like a wounded animal. It hasn't even started yet.

'Elder Eight,' I plead. 'Tee. Don't let her see this!' He turns and goes to her side. His face is red with fury but he wraps his arm around her. I bury my face into my arms and get ready. Winder and Cass join Tee and Elder Eight. She buries her face in Winders chest and covers her ears as he holds her close. But everyone else looks on.

Crack.

I close my fists tight and seal my mouth shut as the whip meets my flesh.

I will not scream.

I will not whimper.

Crack.

It's a hot searing pain that throbs as soon as the whip leaves my skin.

Crack.

I peer over my arm. Cass's jaw is rigid and Elder has hold of his wrist in case he decides to try and intervene.

Crack.

Everyone flinches.

Crack.

But no one looks away.

Crack.

No one says a word.

Crack. Crack. Crack.

Noah storms up to me, clearly furious that I'm not begging or pleading for him to stop. He leans into my face, his coat pressing into my bleeding back.

'Put your number in,' he says angrily in my ear.

'You've still got one more.' My whole body is shaking. I'm in agony. But I will not let him see it. I will let no man see me buckle.

'Get on with it and get away from me. I'll take another hundred and still refuse you.'

He steps back.

Crack.

He put a lot more force into that one and I let out the slightest whimper before swallowing it down so no one can hear it.

He tosses the whip to the floor and storms off, followed swiftly by the three Grey Coats he came with.

Cass reaches me first. He unties my hands and takes my weight as I slump into his chest. Tee, Winder and Elder aren't far behind.

'What the hell did you do?' Cass asks angrily. 'You stupid idiot.'

'Enough, Cassius,' Elder scorns. 'Now's not the time. Get her to her room. I'll be there soon with some cream and medicine that will help.'

'Put your arms around my neck and wrap your legs around my waist,' Cass says, 'I'll carry you.'

I take back my weight and straighten myself up, holding the front of my t-shirt close so I don't end up half naked. Blood trickles down my skin and the pain has me dizzy.

'I can walk,' I say with a strain, wiping the tears that spilled over despite myself. 'I don't need to be carried like an infant. I'm fine.' I look at Noah who glances back at me over his shoulder before he vanishes out of sight.

Then I throw up all over the floor.

After my back was washed, dried and smothered in cream by Elder Eight and my friends, Elder hands me his *"medicine"*. A bottle of whiskey which I drink till my throat burns. It takes the edge off. I slump onto my bed topless, face down to let my back have some air. They kept asking what I'd done. I told them nothing. They kept pushing. And I kept refusing. After a while the boys leave. Elder too. Not before wishing me a solemn happy birthday.

Alone with Tee, she curls up beside me on the bed to sleep with her fingers gripping mine.

Thing is, this is no big deal. Not really. We watch someone get flogged almost daily. It's remarkable I've not been hit sooner what with my temper. Tee hasn't. Not once. She's too good. Too sweet.

As Tee snores, I can't get a wink. My ribs ache. My back throbs, but it's not bleeding much. He held back for most of it. Could have been a bloody sight worse. The Commander prides himself on his lashes. He gave Cass his scars. Noah wasn't that hard on me, except for that last one. I won't scar too bad. I'll just be sore for a few days.

It's hot and stuffy, even with the window open, but Tee's sleeping peacefully for the first time in months. Usually, she tosses and turns. The last few weeks have been the worst. The build-up to our evaluation has been hard. On all of us. But tonight, she's out like a light. The assignments are over. All tests completed. Tomorrow, she'll put her name in that box. Noah's lottery. But his threats and that nasty streak I've never seen before are playing heavily on my mind. I don't want to be his wife. Now more than ever. And I certainly don't wish Tee to be with a man like that either.

All I want is that damned Red Coat. I've earned it, Goddamn it! Noah can't force me to give it up. I won't let him. There's never been a female Red Coat. There's never been a female anything of note. They say there's no rule against a woman filling these positions. It's just that there's never been one good enough.

What a load of crap.

I roll onto my side with a deep sigh. The more I think about what happened with Noah, the angrier I get. If it were anyone else who had kissed me like that, I would have cut their hands off. But I'm the one at risk now. I was the one lashed.

Screw this.

Lying here going over it all again and again will do nothing but frustrate me. I slide away from the sleeping Tee, gingerly pull a sports bra on, some shorts and trainers, and head out the door.

I need to clear my head.

I always love the eerie quietness that the early hours provide. I walk along the Soldiers Road via the stables, checking in on Hanzo as I go. He's sound asleep. I replenish his hay and clean his water before carrying on towards the main gate at The Wall.

'Morning, Owl,' I call up to the woman above me on lookout. She peers down and waves.

'Morning, Scar. Bit early ain't it? Even for you.'

'Can't sleep.' I shrug. 'Can I come up?'

'Course!'

I head up the narrow and steep steps carved into the stone. It's the only set of stairs along the whole wall. The wall which stretches on for a total of twelve miles. At every mile, there's a guard on watch, and lengths of rope to shimmy up and down. But other than that, there's no other way to get on top of the wall.

'You alright? I heard you got punished?'

I turn and show her my exposed back. She sucks in a sharp breath through her teeth.

'I'm fine. His strike was weak. Barely made me bleed. Much going on?' I ask her, looking over the edge into the wastelands.

I've always hated that phrase. Like the world beyond our care is a waste. It's not. It needs saving. That's all.

'Nah...' she sighs, tucking her thick jet-black hair behind her ear. 'Quiet as a mouse tonight.' She leans over with me and looks out into the darkness. I can't see a thing down there. But she insists she can. 'Oh... we have a straggler.' She grabs her bow and aims an arrow down below. Her eyes narrow as she pulls it further back. And then... *whoosh*. She lets it loose. I hear a low grunt followed by a slight thump as her target hits the floor.

'Seriously?' I look at her in amazement. 'How do you see them in this light?'

'It's a gift,' she says with a wink, stashing her bow and resting her back against the wall. 'But you have your own gifts. I heard about your kill count today. That's amazing. You're gonna have cadets fighting to the death to join your unit.'

'Well, hopefully I'll be a Red Coat and in charge of lots of units.'

'Gotta dream big, huh? So, you not being able to catch some zees got anything to do with your coat? Or your girl putting her number in that box later?'

I sit on the wall, letting my feet dangle over the edge. 'Maybe. I've tried talking her out of it. But she's as determined to put it in as I am not to. What about you?' I ask. 'You putting your number in? You're eligible, right?'

'Course I'm eligible!' she replies indignantly. 'How old do I look to you?'

'I'm not familiar with the rules to be honest.'

'There ain't many, Scar. How can you not know the rules? Gotta be female. Aged sixteen to twenty-five. No Elders, Grey Coats or Red Coats are allowed.'

'Well, that's cos they're men.'

'Yeah but even if there was a woman among them, not allowed. And no physical deformities. So yeah, I'm eligible. I'm twenty. I'm hot and I'm just a humble Green Coat. But in answer to your question... no. I will not be putting my number anywhere near that box. I like my life. I like my job. And I am not giving it up to live in an old mansion with the sole purpose of popping out the next messiah,' she states.

'Wish Tee felt the same.'

'If Tee doesn't win, she'll be put up here, right? She wants a Green Coat?' She gestures to her green jacket with the wing emblem sprawled carelessly on the floor. 'She's a fantastic archer. They'd be stupid not to put her up here.'

'That's the hope.'

Owl Graduated three years ago and she spends her days sleeping, and her nights on the wall shooting the odd arrow at the rare target that manages to get past the various traps and deterrents surrounding The Haven. Her skill with a bow isn't what makes her stand out. It's how she seems to be nocturnal. Even as a kid, she would be a dozy cow all day and full of beans at night. So, when she graduated, she was put up here for the graveyard shift.

'How's the book I got you?' I ask, gesturing to the tatty old novel sticking out beneath her coat.

'Oh... it's fab!' she whispers happily, scanning the area to make sure we're alone before reaching down and scooping it up. 'It's almost finished though.'

'If I get a chance, I'll see if I can smuggle in another one.'

'You spoil me.' She tucks the book back out of sight. It's most definitely not an approved book. But Elder Eight gave it to me to read, and I thought it was terrific. Full of magic and adventures. So definitely not Verity approved. Noah would go spare if he saw it. Even more so than how he was earlier. Like me, Owl doesn't hold much stock with the religion here. But she has respect for the mission and the work. Like the majority of us really. I always think it's a lot to ask us to fight and die for a god that does neither of those things for us. But I'll do it for people.

For our people.

'You off for a run?' she asks.

'Yeah,' I reply.

'Is that wise? Cass popped up a couple of hours ago and told me to send you away if you turned up. He said you got punished and took a tumble on assignment. You sure you're up for it?'

'I'm a bit stiff, so I'll probably be a bit slower than usual. My head's a bit noisy tonight. Need some space to try and quieten it down. Ignore Cass. He's a worrier. I'm fine.' I get to my feet and do a couple of stretches as she picks up her book.

'Oh!' she says suddenly before I head off. 'Can you take this and give it to Bowzer as you pass him? He's at the fourth mile marker. If I ask the others to pass it down, it'll only get eaten before it gets to him.' She hands me a single bread roll. 'He gave me his yesterday cos I forgot mine. It's a little... hard, but I'm sure it's fine.'

'Owl... it's stale,' I tell her, looking at the rock-solid piece of bread. 'And there's a bit of mould growing on it.'

'Yeah well, he can soak it in water and scrape off the bad bits. Have a good run, yeah?' Her nose disappears in her book, and I head off.

The wall is four feet thick, so there's plenty of room to run along it. At every mile, there's a guard like Owl. All Green Coat graduates. They walk up and down, making sure that nothing unwanted lingers by our border for too long.

I run past two guards who all say a happy hello and offer the briefest bit of small talk as I pass. Mainly congratulations on my performance in the final assignment. I've been doing this almost every morning for the last three years. Not usually this early. Or late. But no matter what time I come up here, they never seem to mind. They actually seem happy to see me. They use me as a transport system down the line if they need something passed to a friend without it getting eaten or pinched on the way.

The fourth guard I pass is Bowzer. I toss him the roll and warn him of the choking hazard as I carry on. The fifth guard, Tan, a girl with the darkest suntan anyone has ever seen but who turns snow white in the winter, hands me a letter to give to Dash. A girl stationed on the fifth mile who rewards me with a sip of her water.

The sixth guard is an Elder. Elder Ten. He's in his mid-fifties and was a child when the world ended. He insists on carrying on with the watch even though he has no need to. He reached retirement age a decade ago. He has a filthy sense of humour and is very funny. He's always happy to see me and he's very good friends with Elder Eight. He jokes that the only reason he stays up here is to see me, and to make sure his best buddie's favourite cadet is okay. As I pass, he always tells me a riddle.

'What's in a man's pants, that ain't in a girl's dress?' he calls after me as I pass. I turn and run backwards as I think. He throws a green apple in the air teasingly. 'Get it right and bring me back something for my collection... you can have this!'

'You're on!' I call back before turning and running on.

The sun's just below the horizon. The dark sky is gradually getting lighter. I pick up the pace and finish the last two miles at a sprint. When I reach the end of the wall, I sit and catch my breath.

The wall was built right into the ocean. The final half mile is mostly submerged beneath the water. It's like I'm walking on the waves standing out here. Targets can't swim, they don't float and they can't climb. So there ain't no way they're getting past the wall.

The sea's calm. The sound of the waves breaking on the beach is the most relaxing sound I've ever heard. All along the shore, boats are anchored and ready to be used in case the wall is ever breached. There's enough for everyone and then some. A mile or so away, barely in view, is the main jetty and the border of Noah's mansion. Sometimes when I run out here, I find him walking along the beach. He likes to train out here and always brings an extra sword for me. Just in case I turn up. He's the best swordsman I've ever known and is the only one who I've failed to disarm. Even when I've really tried. He's just too good.

Memories of Noah and how he turned so cruel are trying desperately to swamp my thoughts. But I can't let them. He frightened me. He's never done that before. But he's not here this morning, so I watch the sunrise completely alone and relaxed. I wonder what lies beyond the ocean. What the other countries are like. I hope that there are survivors out there too. Maybe another girl is watching the sunrise over in France, wondering the same thing.

After a few minutes rest, the sun has risen enough to give me some decent light so I get to my feet.

'This is gonna hurt,' I mutter to myself, looking down at the waves. I raise both hands above my head and dive head first into the sea. The cold water is refreshing, yes. But the salt water burns the marks on my back. I emerge with a large gasp and curse loudly with a scream as the gentle waves lap over the wounds, cleaning them and washing off the dried blood. Once the pain settles, I float for a while and let my body cool down and rest.

I swim back to shore on the inside of the wall and take another few minutes to catch my breath on the beach. My clothes are already starting to dry as the heat begins to stream down once more.

I find a lovely pink and white shell to return to Elder Ten for his collection, and climb the rope signifying the final marker before running past all the same guards I did on my way down. Whereas my day is just beginning, theirs is coming to an end. They'll head back and have their dinner as we have our breakfast. When I reach Elder Ten, I hand him the shell and give him the answer to his riddle.

'Pockets,' I say a little breathlessly, holding out my hand expectantly. 'What's in a bloke's pants that ain't in a girl's dress? Pockets.'

Laughing, he hands me the apple. 'I'll stump you one of these days, Cadet.'

'You can try,' I call back as I carry on. 'See you later, Elder.'

'Take care, Scarlett. And tell that Elder of yours to come see me soon.'

'Will do.'

When I reach Owl, she's doing her hand over to Halo who nods at me politely and congratulates me on my high kill count.

'Walk back together?' Owl offers, throwing her bow over her shoulder. I lean over the wall and see three targets below being tossed into the back of a cart by three young Brown Coat Cadets. I spent a year on zombie clean up when I was fourteen. We all do. They're taken away and burnt far from here. The smell they produce as they turn to ash had us all vomiting for the first few weeks.

'Sure,' I reply, following her down the stairs. 'I'm starving.'

'ARE YOU SERIOUS?!' Cass's voice carries clear across the forecourt as Owl and I head towards The Academy. I look up and see him leaning out his bedroom window, shirtless, pointing angrily at me.

'Damn...' Owl mutters, looking up at him and chewing her lip. 'He's stunning to look at. Even when he's yelling.'

'Yeah. Shame he's a bossy and overbearing idiot. Otherwise he'd be perfect.' I look up at him. 'What have I done now?' I call back, throwing my hands in the air. 'You literally haven't seen me today. What could I possibly have done to annoy you?'

'WHAT PART OF RESTING YOUR RIBS CONFUSED YOU?' he hollers. 'RUNNING ALONG THAT WALL AIN'T RESTING! YOU WERE LASHED YESTERDAY. FOR GOODNESS SAKE!' He looks at Owl and moves his angry pointer to her instead. 'I TOLD YOU NOT TO LET HER UP THERE!'

'I AIN'T HER KEEPER, CASS,' she hollers back. 'YOU KNOW BETTER THAN ANYONE THAT TRYING TO TELL HER WHAT TO DO IS A WASTE OF BREATH!' She nudges me with her elbow, stifling a grin. 'Good luck with that, Scar,' she laughs before carrying on inside. I look back up to the third-floor window where Cass is currently leaning out with a face like thunder.

'I've told you... I'm fine!' I insist. 'Stop clucking, Cass. Your feathers will fall out.'

A couple of young cadet's giggle as they watch us. Cass narrows his eyes on them, and they stop straight away.

With an additional glare from me, they scarper.

He simply wags his finger, beckoning me inside, and then disappears.

'Eurggghhh,' I groan loudly as I head up to meet him.

Inside, Cass pulls on his black vest as I walk into his room. I look briefly at what I'm sure is the most perfect male body to exist, despite the numerous scars, before glaring at his annoyed face.

'Sit,' he orders, pointing to his bed.

I do as I'm told and sit. Only because that run has knackered me out. Winder comes out of the bathroom and throws me a wink.

'Morning, Scar. Good run?'

'How did you know I went for a run?'

'One, you stink. Two, you're covered in sweat. And three...' He nods to Cass who's currently digging through a large wooden chest in the corner of his room. 'His voice carries.'

'How did you know I went for a run, Cass?' I demand.

'Because, Scarlett. I know you.'

'Morning,' Tee says happily, walking into the room. 'How's the back?'

I toss her the apple I won from Elder Ten. 'Fine. Scabbed over and fine.'

'Ohh yummy,' she chirps. 'The apple. Not the scabs. Obviously.' She busies herself cutting it into four. 'What was it this morning?' she asks. I repeat the riddle.

'Obvious...' Winder laughs. 'A dic-'

'Pockets!' I interrupt, making Tee laugh.

She throws us each a bit of apple before taking a seat on Winder's bed. 'Winder, will you do my hair? I love the way you plait it.'

'Sure,' he says, sitting behind her and braiding it. She sits patiently as he does it. As he has for so many years. She smiles contentedly as he works. And he runs his fingers slowly through each strand with extra care and attention. He adores her. And she feels the same.

Maybe in another life...

'Right,' Cass says with a mouth full of apple and standing over me holding something in his hand. 'Let me look at you.'

'Not that thing again,' I groan.

He gets on his knees and takes a closer look at my ribs. 'Well, if you didn't keep getting injured, maybe you wouldn't need to keep wearing it.' He does a double take at my face. 'What's that?' he asks, gesturing to my lip.

'My face,' I reply with a shrug.

'Your lip wasn't cut when I last saw you. What-'

'Slipped on the wall this morning is all,' I say with a light air.

'What's wrong with her lip?' Tee asks in a worry.

As he opens his mouth to argue, I look into his eyes and silently tell him to drop it before Tee gets in a flap.

'She's fine, Tee,' he says, thankfully letting it go. 'I'm gonna check your ribs aren't broken. And then I'm gonna clean your back again.'

'I've already told you-'

'I'll give you a foot rub, in addition to the back rub I owe you,' he sighs. 'How does that sound?'

'When?'

'Your back when it's healed, and your feet? Whenever you like. But after a shower. Preferably.'

'Fine,' I sigh, lifting my arms and wincing as I do. 'But only cos your foot rubs are even better than your back rubs.'

'Eat your apple,' he laughs.

He runs his fingers over every single rib, taking his time and being as gentle as can. He leaves a trail of goose bumps in his wake but doesn't mention them. And I love watching the deep concentration on his face as he works. I could look at him doing this for hours.

Finally, he comes to the same conclusion I did.

'Nope. Not broken. Just bruised.'

'Like I said,' I mumble, as he wraps his hideous elastic belt around my chest.

'Luckily, that prat only lashed your shoulder blades so the brace won't agitate the wounds. He didn't go too hard on you. Doesn't look too bad. Tight enough?' he asks, securing the belt. I inhale and exhale.

'Perfect.'

'Here.' He hands me some folded clothes and gestures to his bathroom. 'Go get washed, and we'll head down for breakfast together. And here...' He plonks my kicks on the pile. I look at the clothes he's handed me. They're mine. He did my laundry again. 'And... I'm sorry about yesterday,' he adds. 'I would never risk your mark intentionally. I was just worried about you and I tend to say shit I don't mean when I'm angry. But I am sorry.'

I rest my hand on his chest as I make my way into the bathroom.

'You're totally forgiven. And I'm sorry I thumped you.'

'Forget it. Now, go get ready.'

'Thanks, Cass. You always look after me.'

'Someone's got to. You sure as hell don't look after yourself.'

After breakfast and morning prayers, we grab our weapons and our coats before heading down to meet Elder Eight in the courtyard out front. In the lobby, standing to the side in a small huddle are four *Mr Greys*. I look over, and one in particular watches me as I walk past them to the door.

I wonder if it's Noah.

No one bats an eye at their heavy presence this morning. After all, Noah and his group are due today, so they're checking everything is safe and to a satisfactory standard for *God's representative on earth.*

Pffft.

'Nervous?' Winder asks me quietly, glancing briefly in their direction. 'Gonna be a bit weird, him coming to-'

'Later,' I say quietly, taking his arm and leading him quickly on.

Outside, we head over to Flash and Titan who are already waiting for us along with six other units, all under the wing of Elder Eight. There are usually six members in each unit. Sadly, three of the units have lost one of their members. They were good guys. Crap fighters… but sweet enough to know as people.

We all share a courteous nod and some light-hearted conversation when we get the chance. But the only real friendships we have are with our own units.

Flash heads straight over to meet me, walking past Cass with his head down and leaving Titan behind.

'I am so sorry,' he says quietly and in a panic. 'Scar, what happened yesterday will never happen again. I was just overwhelmed.' He stumbles over his words and is visibly shaking. His skin is pale and his lips are dry.

'Are you alright?' I ask, resting my hands on his shoulders. 'You look ready to pass out!' I rest my hand on his forehead. 'Are you sick?'

He glances at Elder Eight who is busy talking to a few of the other Cadets.

'He said he's going to talk to you about my performance. Please don't get me in trouble. He wants me reassigned. Don't tell him I screwed up. I'm begging you.'

'Who the hell do you think you're talking to?' Winder snaps, shoving him hard in his shoulder. 'This girl has kept your arse safe for the last twelve years. She defended you yesterday against Cass and a well-deserved beating. You think she would screw you over now?' he barks. It's not very often I see Winder annoyed. But Flash gets under his skin. 'Man... just get back over with Titan before I slap you.' He gestures to Titan who shrugs apologetically. Flash looks pleadingly at me one last time and opens his mouth. 'Did I stutter, Flash?' Winder thunders. 'Go!' He shakes his head and leaves.

'You're too hard on him. You and Cass both.'

'Nah, you're too soft. That's the problem.' He pokes me in the chest. 'You're too soft on everyone. Prat almost got you killed.' We turn to face Elder Eight as he starts loudly clearing his throat.

'Alright you lot!' he calls, twirling the ends of his moustache between his fingers. 'It's another roaster of a day I'm afraid. So take water with you on assignment. You two...' He points to the two teams on his right. 'You're on shore duty. See if anything worthwhile has washed up and clear out the traps.'

I like shore duty. You walk up and down the coast picking up any driftwood or other goodies that may have come ashore and checking all the boats are still seaworthy. Cleaning out the traps ain't as fun. Untangling writhing corpses from barbed wire or scooping them out of the pits we dug is really, really gross.

'You two...' He gestures to the teams on his left. 'Wall breach check. Exterior. And you two...' He points at us and the unit next to us. 'Clean up the exterior. Three-mile radius. No further.' He points to Jazz, the blonde lad who tends to take charge of his team. 'North. And you...' He points at me. 'South. But before you go... a word, Cadet 5-3-6.'

'Am I in trouble?' I ask.

'No more than usual. Off you all go then,' he orders the rest.

Flash gives me another desperate glance as everyone starts to head out.

'I'll get Hanzo sorted for ya,' Winder says, giving me a kiss on the crown of my head and ruffling my hair before following Cass and Tee towards the stables.

'Alright, Kiddo?' Elder says gruffly as I reach him.

'Perfectly fine, Elder. Yourself?'

'Bloody peachy. You gonna tell me what got you strung up yesterday?'

'Disobedience. Apparently.'

'Not gonna tell me, huh?'

'It's fine. I got it handled. Was that it?'

'No. I wanted to bend your ear.'

'About what?'

He begins to walk away from the others. I follow. 'About Cadet 5-8-5,' he starts. *Oh crap*. 'Your... *Flash*. So named for his speedy retreats, I'd say.' He scoffs and shakes his head. 'Now, from what I saw, and from what I've seen, your friend prefers to stay out of the line of fire and depends on the rest of you to pick up the slack and save his skin.'

'Elder, I-'

He holds up his hand to silence me. I hold my tongue.

'I'm not asking you to betray your friend. I was like you when I was a Cadet. I protected the ones that needed protecting. But there comes a time when we have to start looking after ourselves. You're graduating in a matter of days. So is he. Beyond the wall you have to be capable. And that muppet ain't capable and I'll be damned if I allow him out there with you, only to let you down and get you killed. You all work together very well. You're a fantastic team. But when you're assigned your ranks and when you leave the training behind, you'll be out there for real. You'll all depend on each other to have each other's backs. Yesterday, you, Winder, Tee and Cassius were as one. You and Cassius particularly. You killed what was coming after him, and he killed what was coming after you. It was like a ballet.'

'A what?'

He waves his hand dismissively. 'If you were with a cadet like Flash, he would not have protected you. You know that, don't you?' He waits for me to argue. But I don't. He's right. 'Now, I think he should be reassigned-'

'I disagree, Elder,' I say firmly, folding my arms across my chest as I stop walking. He stops with me and looks curious. 'I believe he would serve better being awarded a Green Coat.'

His eyes widen in surprise before he laughs in my face.

'The Green Coat is given to archers.'

'He can use a bow. Tee taught him.'

'He can *barely* use a bow. Tee's a great teacher... she ain't a miracle worker,' he says, mimicking me and crossing his arms while smirking.

'He's a good fighter. You've seen him in controlled circum-stances. On paper, he passes every test. But when he's out there... he's afraid. That's not his fault.'

'And you ain't scared when you're out there?'

'Are you?'

He laughs a jolly laugh as he whacks my arm.

'Flash would love being a Green Coat, Elder. He would be thrilled,' I tell him.

'I couldn't give a hairy, stinkin' turd what he wants or what would make him happy, Kiddo,' he scoffs as he starts walking away. 'My priority is the unit's survival. I'm reassigning him.'

'Do it for me?' I call after him. He stops and turns back to face me. 'He'll die if you reassign him. Without us looking after him... he won't last a day out beyond the wall. Or he'll get one of us killed.' He watches me closely as I hold my nerve. 'Please, Sir. I'm asking as my personal favour.'

'Your personal favour... hmm? You know you only get one from me. Sure you wanna use it for him?'

'Please, Elder. I don't want my friend to die. Please give him a Green Coat.'

'And what about you?' he asks, still not convinced. 'Still want that Red Coat?'

'Of course.'

'Course you do,' he says proudly, his chest puffing out a little. 'I expected nothing less, and if it were my decision alone, you'd have it. I understand Cass is hoping for that too. Shame they only award one per graduating class.'

'I'm better than Cass. And if I had a penis between my legs, I'd get it no problem.'

'Part of me wondered if you were gonna accept the Grey Coats offer. I know they spoke to you a few years back and you said no. But they'd still have you like a shot.'

'And be cooped up in The Haven all day every day? No thanks.'

'What about the Canaries? If you want adventure, that's the place to find it.'

I laugh. Hard. 'I'm restless, Elder. Not suicidal.'

He laughs that deep, throaty laugh again and gives my shoulder a friendly whack making me groan as he jars my ribs.

'Glad to hear it. Now, get to work. I know you love being on clean up duty. And don't worry about Mr Flash. Whatever happens, I'll make sure he doesn't get reassigned.'

'Thank you, sir.' I call after him. 'Thank you so, so much!'

'Waste of your favour if you ask me,' he grumbles. 'Get to work, Kiddo.'

CHAPTER SIX

'It's a bit rubbish that when we graduate, we have to move to a new house,' Tee moans as we approach a still writhing Class Three, currently tangled in a spiralling barbed wire trap. I reach back and draw my Katana before driving it through its skull. It falls still and drips coagulated blood on the ground, narrowly missing my shoe. My second katana is on my back. Tee's bow across her chest. Cass has his Haladie daggers in his belt as he pushes the cart we use for shifting the killed targets. And Winder has his axe casually thrown over his shoulder. Our masks hang around our necks, and as ever, we're dressed for battle even though we're on sodding clean up duty. My wrappings are secure, the laces on my Nike kicks tied tightly and my brown coat fits as snug as ever. Not as snug as Cass's rib support though, which is making me sweat like crazy.

'I'm personally looking forward to the move. The Warren has less damp,' Cass replies, lowering the cart and heading over to help Winder untangle various limbs. 'It makes my throat scratchy.'

'The rooms have bars on the windows,' she argues.

'Well, yeah.' He shrugs. 'It was a prison, Tee. But we get our own rooms when we move, and they've made it quite nice. You know... for a prison. Man, this thing's arm is really stuck.'

'Move. I'll hack it off,' I offer. A quick swipe and the body falls free to the floor. Tee grabs its legs as I grab its head, all the while breathing through my mouth. Damn, it stinks. Cass keeps glaring at me as he picks up the severed arm. He definitely has something on his mind.

'Spit it out,' I tell him, hurling the Class Three onto the cart with the other four we've already collected. 'You'll give yourself a nose bleed, else.'

'I bet you didn't say a word to Elder Eight about what Flash did in the assignment. Did you?' he accuses, glancing over his shoulder to Flash and Titan who are out of earshot clearing another trap.

'What I did or didn't say is none of your sodding business,' I reply, as he tosses me the severed arm which I add to the cart of corpses.

'He doesn't deserve to pass,' he states, scooping up other various limbs scattered on the floor by our feet. 'He'll get someone killed out there. The bloody coward. Can you believe, he actually thought he had a chance at being a Grey Coat once upon a time?' He laughs at the idea. To be fair, it's a laughable one. 'You have one hell of a short memory. Or don't you care he almost got you killed-'

'Damn, let it go! If anyone should be pissed about what happened, it's me. Not you. Just get over it.'

'You're so... argh.' He waves his hands dramatically in exasperation, making Tee and I laugh. 'Fine. Whatever. He screws up and gets everyone rallying around him. I stick up for you, and you punch me in the face. How's that fair?' He turns and starts storming off, muttering incoherently as he goes.

'Stop acting like a baby,' I call after him, laughing at his pouting.

'I'm not acting like a baby!' he barks back.

'Yes, you are,' I chuckle.

'No, I'm not!'

I run over and jump on his back. 'Aw, Cass. Don't be pouty.' I ruffle his hair.

'Get off, you silly cow.' But he's smiling and holding me in place.

'Baby wanna bwottle?'

'Shut it.'

'What about a wittle kwiss.' He starts laughing as I kiss his cheek over and over.

'Geroff!'

'Anyway, as I was saying. A frickin prison!' Tee carries on complaining about where we'll be moving on to as she moves onto the next Class Three tangled in the next wire trap.

I look down at Cass, and he looks up at me. Both of us have a smile and he holds my legs a little firmer as I still cling to his back. But then his smile starts to slip.

'Who hit you?' he asks quietly, looking at the small cut on my lip.

'No one that matters,' I reply.

'I think that if he's still walking after laying a hand on you, he might matter just a little bit.' He blinks a couple of times and his playfulness is replaced with a solemnness. 'Do you love him?'

'Who?'

'The man you let get away with hitting you? It's gotta be love if you didn't break his neck.' I slide down his back, and he turns to face me. 'Whoever it was, you tell him that if he ever touches you like that again, I'll kill him.' He kisses my forehead before heading over to help Tee. My skin tingles at the warmth his lips leave on my skin as I watch him go.

Stop it, Scarlett. Stop looking at him like that!

I pull out my binoculars and look over at the next trap.

'Can I borrow your bow?' I ask Tee when I catch up with her. She hands it to me without hesitation as well as her quiver, and takes one of my swords instead.

'I'm gonna talk to Elder Eight later,' Cass says, still not letting it go. 'I won't have Flash put with me out there. I need people I can count on.'

'There's no need to talk to Elder Eight,' I reply, sliding Tee's bow over my head. 'Trust me, Cass. Elder knows what he needs to know, and Flash will get exactly what he deserves after graduation.' I start to head over to the next trap.

'She grassed him up?' Tee gasps.

'Where are you going?' Cass calls after me.

'To the next pit.'

'On your own?'

'Oh will you give it a rest?!'

'I'll go with her,' Winder says, jogging after me.

Together, we make our way across the dry land with the sun beaming down hard on us, past the three-story building that used to be an office block. All that remains are the metal support beams and the stubborn cement still clinging onto the bones of the building. The dry dirt leads us to tarmac as we cross a dual carriageway, weaving between the shells of deserted cars. I peer inside them. But everything's gone. They've been stripped bare. We took it all years ago.

'It was him, wasn't it?' Winder asks, walking beside me. 'Noah hit you. And he was the one that lashed you, wasn't he?'

'Yep.'

'Was I right? About the lottery?'

'Sure was,' I sigh. 'He wants me to put my number in, and he wasn't happy when I said no.'

He looks concerned. And rightly so. Noah can really mess up my life if he wanted to. Or end it. I tell Winder what happened in my room, and how I ended up tied to the pillar. Winder knows all about Noah. I admitted it all after he saw us together on the beach one morning. Obviously, it had to have been the morning we kissed that he chose to follow me out for a run. Noah has no idea he knows. If he did, I dread to think.

'What a dick. A hypocritical dick. I should tear his stomach out through his mouth for touching you like that.'

'Best not,' I laugh. 'Not unless you want to end up dead. It's just so stupid that Noah would think I'd want to get married. We kissed. Twice. In like... two years! He knows how much this life means to me. He's thick if he thinks I would ever give up a lifetime of work to sit at home and pop out kid after kid.'

'He's not thick, Scar. You would be foolish to think Noah's anything less than a very clever and cunning man. With a hell of a lot of power. He's possessive and used to getting his own way. He wants you because he can't have you.'

'And he never will.'

We reach the pit. A ten-foot by ten-foot hole in the ground where we toss a few bloody rags to lure the zombies to fall in. There are two clawing at the sides. One has no nose and no lips. The other is missing its bottom jaw completely. Their grey leathery skin hangs loosely off their bones which stick out. And they absolutely stink.

'What are you gonna do?' he asks. 'About our Lord and Master?'

'I can handle Noah.'

I let loose two arrows and hit the Class Threes right between the eyes.

'How exactly? He can easily force you to marry him, Scar.' Winder jumps in and starts tossing the corpses out. 'You said no, and he lashed you.'

'He lashed me because I hit him. I don't think he's accepted my no just yet.'

'You hit him to get him off you,' he argues. 'No man touches a woman without their permission. That's assault. Sexual assault. And if I'd have been there when he did that, I'd have introduced him to my axe.'

'Winder, please don't get involved. I can handle Noah. I don't want to start worrying about you as well as myself. If he thinks you know about us... If he thinks anyone knows about us... He'll react. Violently. Now. Can we talk about something else?'

'Did you really tell Elder Eight what happened on assignment with Flash?'

'Do you think I would?' I ask, a little offended that he thinks I'd be so heartless. He shrugs. 'Great. Thanks for that.'

'So, did you?'

I reply with the same, irritating shrug which makes him roll his eyes. I reach down so he can take my hand and climb back out. I swear and grab my ribs.

'Oh bugger, I forgot you hurt yourself. You alright?'

'Fine. I forgot too, apparently.' I straighten myself up and look to see where Cass and Tee are with the cart. They're still loading various pieces of the second target in, so we take a seat in the dirt and have a sip of water while we wait. After a cursory glance at the Class Three by my feet, something catches my attention.

'Winder?'

'Yeah?'

I shuffle closer to it. 'Something's off with this Zom.'

He shuffles closer too. It's a man. Well, it was. And he's certainly dead. But it's what he's wearing that's odd.

'He's a policeman.' Winder notices.

I flatten out his shirt.

'A German policeman,' I add, noticing the badge. 'What the hell is a German policeman, still in his uniform, doing in England fifty years after the outbreak?' We look at each other utterly confused. 'We didn't get any refugees from Germany, did we?'

'Not as far as I'm aware. How weird.'

'Are you gonna be much longer?' I call through the bathroom door. 'Tee? What are you doing in there?'

'It's open you know,' she calls back.

I open the door to find her smoothing down her long brown hair in the sad little shard of mirror we have stuck to the wall. She looks more nervous now than she does out there beyond the wall.

'You ready?' I ask. 'Ya know, it doesn't matter what you look like. It's a lottery.'

Looking in the mirror nervously, she shrugs. 'It can't hurt.'

'Are you sure about this? Once your number goes in, that's it. No taking it back.'

'It's the only chance I have of getting out of the army,' she says quietly, still smoothing down her perfect locks.

'Tee, if I asked you not to put your number in, would ya?' I ask apprehensively.

'Why would you even ask me not to when you know it's what I want? When it will save my life?'

'Because...' I sigh and slump back against the wall. I want to tell her the truth. But her knowing will put her in danger. 'I don't want to be without you. I don't want-'

'Well, not everything is about what you want!' she barks angrily. That's very unlike her. 'You know, everything you do, I support. I accept. I never tell you what to do. All your flaws, I embrace.'

'My flaws?'

'Yeah. You're rude and arrogant. You're hostile too.'

'I'm not hostile!' I snap.

'You wound up Winder all morning before the evaluation, telling him he was slow and not as good as you in hand to hand. You goaded him into a bet you knew he wasn't gonna win all because you wanted an edge.'

'What edge?' I laugh angrily, shaking my head.

'You bet his breakfast he wouldn't win and of course he didn't. More food means more energy. And for the final assignment, the more energy, the better. You got two portions and he got a tiny apple. You didn't think that him not eating enough would affect his performance, did you? And what about Flash, huh? Telling Elder Eight what happened. We have a code.'

'Hold on a minute-'

'And now you don't want me to put my number in because you don't want to be left on your own. You're selfish, Scar. Just... selfish.'

I look at her stunned. 'You really think of me like that?'

'You know how scared I am every time I go beyond the wall. You know how much I would rather stay safe, have a family, a husband, some kids. And you know that if you seriously asked me, right here, right now, not to put my number in, I wouldn't. Even though it would make me sad and resentful towards you. I wouldn't. I would live a life of fear and pain and die in the dirt because I love you and I would do anything to make you happy.'

'Tee, I-'

'And!' she snaps, cutting me off. 'Do you know that you have not once, *not once* told me you loved me? You call me your sister. You say you'd do anything for me. But you have never said that you actually love me.' She folds her arms and glares at me as I stand completely shocked and speechless at her uncharacteristic outburst. She's just scared. I know that. I'll let her vent even if it hurts my feelings, I'll take it. 'I love you, Scarlett. Say it back.' She watches me with expectant and angry eyes. 'Well? Say it!' The silence in the room is deafening.

'You know I can't say that back. You shouldn't even say it.'

'Oh what... because of the cadet curse?' she scoffs. 'That's such a cop out. Like telling someone you love them will actually curse them and they'll die. You're just scared. Say it.' She waits. But I refuse to say it. I can't. Everyone knows what happens if those words are said. Call it superstition. But I ain't risking it. Finally, she scoffs and shakes her head. 'Ask me then. Ask me not to put my number in.'

'Tee,' I hold out my hand. 'Can I come with you to enter your number?' I ask.

She sighs and nods. Clearly, she needed that. I head over and give her a hug.

'Sorry, Scar,' she whispers. 'I didn't mean that.'

'Forget it. Come on.'

'I really didn't mean it.'

'I know,' I lie. 'C'mon.'

'You still thinking about that Class Three in the German uniform?' she asks as we leave our room, keen to change the subject. And I'm keen to move on too. Her words cut far too deep.

'A bit,' I admit. 'Just seemed odd is all. How did a German zom get all the way over here?' I ask for the hundredth time. 'He was still in uniform!'

'Don't call them that, Scar. It's really disrespectful.'

'Sorry. Target. How did a German target get here?'

'He was wearing his uniform when he came over from Germany before the outbreak, obviously,' she says. 'Stop worrying about some random Class Three.' Her anxious expression has sod all to do with the policeman from Germany.

'You're right.' I reply with a forced smile, clasping her hand tightly as we walk through the halls. 'It's probably nothing. This is much more important. Are you excited?'

'I think I'm gonna pee a little.'

'Don't do that. No one wants to marry a girl that smells of wee.'

At the bottom of the main staircase, we find Winder and Cass chatting together and waiting for us.

'You sure about this?' Winder asks Tee as we join them. She just looks at him with wide eyes. All it would take would be for him to say, *"No, Tee. Don't do it."*. And she wouldn't. And there wouldn't be any of the anger she just threw my way either.

But he won't. And neither will I.

Again.

'Oh no. She ain't blinking,' Winder says. 'That's never a good sign.'

'She's fine,' I tell him. 'And she's sure. Come on.'

We all head to the open double doors which leads to the main hall. It's a massive room with a high, arched ceiling and the remnants of a beautiful painting of a night sky still visible above us. The three chandeliers were removed shortly after the Cadets went squish beneath the one in the lobby. There are four ornate fireplaces in here. In the winter, they light them all. More often than not, we all gather in here for warmth and sleep on the floor together. The winters are as brutal as the summers. Snow falls thick and fast. We collect wood all year round getting ready for it. We never cut down trees, so we only burn what we find. Which is what salvage duty is mainly for. The room is filled with odd-shaped tables with mismatched chairs and stools. At the far end of the room is a long table where all the Elders sit. But now they're all standing to the sides in deep conversation. As well as a fair amount of Grey Coats.

The sound of girls chatting excitedly and giggling incessantly is unbearable. It's my idea of hell in here. Give me the groan of a zom or the sound of my steel striking flesh over this girly crap any day. Tee's hand, which is currently squeezing the life out of mine, gets even tighter.

'Are you sure you won't do it with me?'

'Positive. C'mon.'

She glances up at me.

'Scar, being out there frightens me so much. If I ever screwed up and one of you got hurt because of my weakness, I would never forgive myself.'

'Is that why you're doing this?' I turn and face her. 'To try and protect us? Because if it is, then you're making a mistake. You have never let your fear overwhelm you. Not once! I trust you completely, Tee. We all do.'

She reaches out and rests her palm on my shoulder.

'The scar I left right here proves you wrong. I could have killed you.' She pales as she recalls the day she accidentally shot me and her head shakes swiftly from side to side as she decides, with impunity, that she will never let that happen again. 'I'm putting my number in. It's best for everyone. C'mon.'

Her legs looking a little stiff as she walks and together, we take our place in the crowd as Elder One, the head honcho of the Elders, stands at a small podium. He makes all the final decisions on what coats we end up with. He chooses who does what and when. Where Noah rules the rest of us, Elder One rules the Elders. He has short grey hair. His face is clean shaven, and he looks beyond stern. He *is* beyond stern. When I was ten, he and a grey coat caught me taking the lords name in vain. Rather than a lashing, he made me run ten miles in the middle of winter. My little legs nearly fell off. Wouldn't have been so bad if the ground hadn't have been so damn icy. I slipped and slid all over the place. Spent more time on my backside than actually running. Took hours to finish.

Utter bastard.

Think I would have preferred the lashings. But Elders don't lash. They may pass on your crime to the Grey Coats if they see fit. But normally they deal with it themselves. It's when the Grey Coats interfere you worry. My back aches just thinking about it.

Elder One clears his throat and welcomes us all in his holier than thou tone. Telling us all of the honour and responsibility that awaits the lucky lady who wins the lottery. He goes on and on about, well... Noah. And how great he is. How wonderful. And how the chosen girl will be the vessel for the next *"heavenly representative"*.

Snore.

He says all the right things. But I see the slight roll of his eyes. I sense the edge to his tone.

He thinks it's all as crap as the rest of us. But like the rest of us, he plays along. For the greater good.

Elder Six, a young man compared to the others and relatively new to his position, wheels out a large sealed box with a slit in its lid before returning to the side. He took over from a man we called Turkey. He didn't have a chin. Odd man. He died last year beyond the wall. He was a good guy. Bit strange towards the end.

I think a person can only see so many deaths before they start to lose grip on reality. And Turkey certainly lost his. He started to think that The Grey Coats were infected. Got him in a fair bit of trouble. But everyone knew he was bonkers. One day, he led a team to clear out traps, and jumped in one.

Not a good way to go.

'This is where you will put your number in,' Elder One explains to the giggling masses. 'You may only enter your number once. When you have done so, you must inform your Elder. We don't want anyone being volunteered unknowingly. We will be checking each slip put in. If you put your number in more than once, you will be disqualified. If you put your number in and do not tell your Elder, you will be disqualified. Tomorrow night we will have an assembly which you must all attend, even if you are not graduating. In this assembly, I will clarify the different roles available to you in the Army, and you do get a say to some degree in which role you would prefer. As you know, yesterday the final unit of the year completed their final assignment. There are a total of thirty-six graduates this year.' There's a round of applause. 'As well as discussing the roles available, we will also be welcoming Lord Sands and his entourage to our home. We'll be disclosing ranks the following day for the graduates and the lottery winner will be announced the next morning.' He opens his arms wide. 'Have at it, ladies. And good luck.'

The high-pitched screeches of these girls are like nails on a chalkboard. Despite that, I take Tee's hand and head towards the crowd surrounding the box. As we walk, and as they see me, they all part and let us pass. Right up to the box itself. We stand there, the room a little too quiet as the girls wait patiently for us to do what we need to do.

The paper in Tee's hand is neatly folded. Her number is written in perfect handwriting.

'I'm putting my number in.' She looks from the box to me, as if seeking my blessing. I smile reassuringly, giving it to her. She leans over, rests her paper above the slot, and with a deep intake of breath, she drops it in.

I mean, what are the chances she'll win anyway?

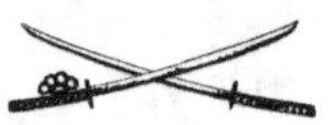

The sun is just about to disappear, and there's a pleasant breeze gently blowing as I sit beneath the trees. It's a scary time. Graduation. It's a big and sudden change after everything being the same for my entire life. I'm feeling very overwhelmed.

'Mind if I sit?'

I turn and see a *Mr Grey* behind me. I can't see his face, but the voice definitely belongs to Noah. He lowers his hood and sits opposite me right here on the ground. After a cursory glance, I know we're alone. Not even his Grey Coats are nearby.

'What can I help you with, Lord Sands?' I ask.

'Wow,' he laughs. 'That's a cold reception. Are you mad at me?'

I busy myself with a leaf and spend far too much time folding it unnecessarily again and again.

'I'll take that as a yes,' he sighs, before snatching the leaf from my hand and tossing it on the ground. 'Yesterday got out of hand and I overreacted. I made sure I didn't hurt you too much but you needed to be punished. You can't behave that way. Not with me. Hey. Look at me,' he orders. I do. Reluctantly. He sighs again, a deep and very fake sigh. 'I'm going to ask you one more time. Put your number in the lottery.'

'I can't do that,' I reply.

'You can,' he says plainly.

'I don't want to then.'

'You think you know what's best. But you don't. I do. I insist-'

'Please don't make me, Noah,' I ask desperately. 'I'm begging you. I'll do anything. Please don't force me to do this.' I hate myself for begging. But I genuinely have no other choice. 'If you make me do this, I will never forgive you. You'll have a wife that resents you. That will hate you. Is that really what you want?' With a deep breath, I compose myself quickly and sit a little straighter. But he saw my brief moment of weakness and looks a little sad himself. He rests his hand on my cheek.

'I'm also sorry that I hit you yesterday,' he says, his thumb tracing the split on my lip that still stings. 'You upset me, and I reacted badly. I promise you, it will never happen again.'

'I appreciate that. And I'm sorry I hit you too.'

'Apology accepted. So, you don't want to get married. Tell me what you do want,' he says. 'Tell me exactly what you want for yourself and your friends, Cadet. And maybe I can make it so the woman I love can be happy.'

I rest my hand on his, glad that the old Noah, the kind Noah, has come back. 'I want to be a Red Coat,' I tell him. He nods knowingly. It's of no surprise to him whatsoever. It's all I've wanted for years.

'What about your friends?'

'I want Winder, Titan and Cass to get Black Coats. I want us to stay together as a unit. And I want Tee and Flash to get a Green Coat.'

'I heard Tee put her number in tonight. Don't you want her to win my lottery?' I remain silent and try not to give anything about how I feel away. 'I get it. I wouldn't want to watch my best friend with someone I care for either.' That's not it at all. I don't want her with a bastard like him. Not now I've seen that nasty streak. But I keep my mouth shut. 'So you want the Red Coat. Your friends by your side. And you'd rather see Tee stay in the army than have the chance to leave it because you don't want her to be with me. That is incredibly selfish. Poor Tee,' he tells me, his eyebrows raised.

There's that word again. Selfish. 'Cassius wants a Red Coat too, right? But you said you want him to have Black. Very, very selfish.'

'It's not like that.' I try to defend myself, but he tuts and wraps his arm around my shoulders.

'Aw, my poor girl,' he coos, guiding me to his chest. 'This is such a hard time for you. So many choices and changes. Such threats of loss that only a warrior could ever experience.' He kisses the top of my head and rests his chin there. 'My dear sweet Cadet. You can have your Red Coat. I can ensure it. If you are certain that that's what you want.'

'You can?' I gasp, sitting up, completely taken aback.

'Of course. I love you. I want you to be happy. So, I can get you your Red Coat if that's what you really want.'

'It is! Oh, Noah... it really is!'

'But there would be conditions,' he adds.

'W-what conditions?' I ask, apprehension clear in my words.

'In exchange for your coat, I will place Flash, Titan, Tee, Winder and Cassius...' he strokes my cheek. 'In the Canaries.' He watches me as I slowly sit back, freeing myself from his gentle embrace.

'But... that would mean-'

'They would live out beyond the wall for months at a time. You would hardly see them. And as you know, the survival rate for a Canary is... bleak... at best. But you would be happy, right? With your Red Coat? Seems appropriate. What with you being a selfish bitch and all.' He watches me closely, waiting for a reaction but I'm stuck in stunned silence. 'Or...'

'Or I put my number in. Right?'

He nods. 'Be my wife. Cassius will become a Red Coat. Winder and Titan will become Black Coats. Flash can be a Green Coat and spend his days safely on the wall. And Tee will become a Grey Coat. I can have her positioned at my house. She'll never see a battle or bloodshed. She'll never have to leave The Haven. She can live in our mansion with us by the sea. You'll see Tee every day, and she'll be as safe as can be. What do you say?'

'Canaries are volunteers or criminals sentenced to time beyond the wall. My friends have done nothing wrong to warrant a conviction. And they won't volunteer for that. Everyone knows it's suicide out there.'

'I'll get them in the Canaries, Cadet. Accept my proposal, or they'll die. Mark my words.'

'Why are you doing this to me?'

'Because I love you.' He gets to his feet and looks down at me still on the floor. 'I have the power to make you and your friend's existence an enjoyable one. Or... I can make them miserable.' He pulls his hood up. 'I can make them dead. Your choice.'

'Noah.' I stand and feel my anger bubbling in my chest as he threatens my family and me. Although I can't see his face, I know he's smirking. 'If you do this, you realise that you will be forcing me to be physical with you against my will.'

'What are you on about?'

'Everyone knows what's expected of your new, young wife. In Elder One's own words, the lucky girl will be the vessel of the next holy representative.'

'Cadet... what-'

'Kids! Noah. Which means sex. If you force my hand, then the only reason I'll be sleeping with you is that you threatened to effectively kill my friends if I didn't. You know what that's called, right?'

'You're so dramatic,' he laughs.

'It's rape, Noah. You'd be raping me,' I bark in a desperate attempt to stop this from happening.

He stalks towards me, clearly enraged. Undoubtedly enraged when he grabs me by my throat and gives me a shake.

'You ever, EVER say that to me again,' he pulls down his hood and shoves his face into mine. 'You even think it... I'll have you lashed for impure and slanderous lies. You hear me?'

'You're not the man I thought you were, Noah. You're not a good man at all.'

He lets me go with a shove. 'I have always been a good man to you! I am no rapist, Scarlett. Contrary to popular belief, my life's mission is not to fornicate and breed. I have great plans for this town and the people within it. And you are the only one who can do the job that being my wife will require.'

'What do you mean by that?' I ask uneasily.

'I'll expect to hear that you have submitted your number by mid-day tomorrow.' He gives me an arrogant, lazy kind of shrug that sits well with his cocky, self-righteous half grin. 'If I haven't, well, you know what will happen. Have a lovely night, Cadet.'

He pulls up his hood and leaves me filled with a new-found hatred, showing me the winged V on his back as he saunters away.

He really has no idea who I am. He thinks he knows what I'll do.

But he's right about one thing. I am a selfish bitch.

No one... I mean *no one* will stop me doing what I was born to do.

I was born to fight. And I *will* fight.

He thinks he knows me. He thinks I'll marry him in order to save them all.

Well, he can think again.

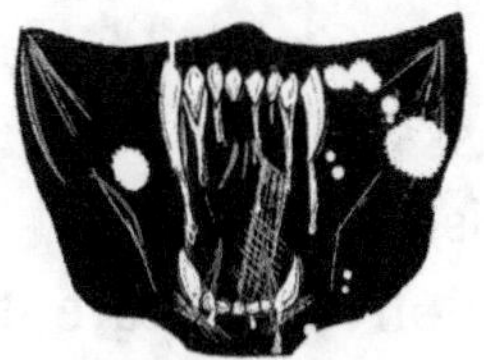

Deep in the woods, between Elder HQ and The Academy, set off the Soldiers Road by about half a mile, is a small cottage.

My favourite cottage.

Elder Eight's cottage.

No one else lives nearby so it's as quiet and peaceful as could be. He always says that after spending all day teaching a bunch of army brats, he likes the quiet. It's not what you'd expect a man like him to live in at all. But he inherited it from the man who was Elder Eight before him. And so on. And so on.

Personally, I like it. It's a three bedroom, two-story stone cottage with a slate roof and two chimney breasts. It has a little wooden porch out front with a wooden stoop and next to the white door is a rocking chair. As I head up the steps, the wood beneath my feet creaks and groans. I don't knock. I never knock. If he's up for company, he'll come out. If not, he'll tell me to sod off through the door. I sit on the steps and rest my shoulder against the wooden bannister with a sigh. Sure enough, the front door opens and he takes a seat next to me. Without saying a word, he hands me a glass filled with amber liquid. Alcohol is strictly forbidden, but Elder Eight has spent so much time working beyond the wall with his Cadets, he knows where to find the stuff and how to keep it hidden. Before he was an Elder, he was a volunteer Canary. Worked out beyond the wall on and off for five years. Then he was handed the Elder title and took over training instead. He's actually eligible for retirement. But he says he's not ready. He told me once that he'll stop fighting the fight when he's dead. And not a second sooner.

'Do you know how many Cadets I have pestering me to be put in a unit with you?' he asks.

I shrug, completely disinterested.

'Well it's a lot. They don't even care if you get the Red Coat. They want to work with you no matter what.'

'Humph.'

'You here for another book?' he asks. 'I have a great one for ya. If you fancy talking rabbits and insane men wearing stupid hats.'

'Maybe another time,' I tell him, downing the whisky.

'Wanna talk about whatever's goin' on in that noggin of yours?' he asks, downing his own drink. I shake my head and shift, resting my head on his shoulder. He wraps his arm around me and gives me a little hug.

The man taught me to read. Right here on this porch. Three nights a week, every week, for two years. He'd sit in that chair and teach me. He called it an investment. Can't have a Red Coat that can't read.

'You don't need to sit with me,' I tell him. 'I'm happy enough alone.'

'You say that. But if you meant it, you'd be with that little apple tree instead of here drinking my whiskey. Or running yourself ragged along the wall.' He taps my temple with his finger. 'Is it getting a bit loud in that old head of yours again?'

'A bit. Yeah,' I reply, looking into my glass. 'Just a lot happening. It's a bit overwhelming.'

'You don't get overwhelmed,' he says. 'Not unless that...' He taps his own head. 'And that...' He rests his hand over his heart. 'Starts to disagree. You sure you don't wanna talk about it?'

I shake my head.

'Are you in trouble?'

I give a deep sigh and settle further into his shoulder. 'I just need a safe, quiet place for a little while. And here with you on this porch is the safest place I know. Is that okay?'

'Course. My porch and my whiskey are always here when you need it, Kiddo.'

'And you, right?'

'Course,' he exhales. 'I'll sit with ya until it all quietens down a little in there and you feel ready to face whatever it is again.'

'You might be here a while in that case.'

'I have nowhere else better to be.'

'Thanks, Elder.'

'It's my pleasure.'

We sit on his porch in utter silence. And it's not uncomfortable. It's not forced.

It's home.

Has been my whole life.

It's almost midnight when I head back to the Academy. But not to my room. I go to Cass and Winder's instead. The door's slightly ajar and the last of a candle is about to burn out. As I expected, Tee is half hanging out of Winders bed fast asleep as he snores away next to her. When I'm not with her, she can't fall asleep. Winder's the next best thing, so she says. More often than not I find her in here when I'm late. Winder's hand is close to hers. Almost touching.

I'm about to leave, now that I've seen she's okay I'll head back to my room and get some sleep. But Cass pulls back his blanket and taps the empty space next to him. I linger in the door fiddling with the hem of my top.

'Scarlett... come to bed,' he whispers.

I go and slide in beside him and he sleepily puts his blanket over me.

'You alright?' he asks quietly.

'Yeah,' I whisper. 'Fine.'

'Where'd you go?'

'For a walk.'

'Did he hit you again?'

'There is no *he*, Cass. I told you. I went for a walk is all.'

He rolls onto his back and exhales deeply as he looks up at the ceiling. 'I wish you'd stop lying to me. Knowing you don't trust me hurts my goddamn feelings.'

I sit and swing my legs over the side of his bed. He sits beside me in nothing but his boxer shorts. When I go to leave, he takes my hand, keeping me sat beside him.

'What's wrong, Scarlett?'

'Nothing.'

'Please, just tell me what's going on.'

'Do you remember the night we snuck over the wall and went to the pier together a few years back?' I ask. He nods and looks at his hands, not wanting to meet my gaze. 'Can I ask you something about that night?'

'Do you have to?' he asks uncomfortably.

'Did you turn me down because I'm not a good person?'

'What? No!' he replies adamantly, careful to keep his voice low so he doesn't wake the others.

'So you just, aren't attracted to me then?'

'It's not like that.'

'Is it cos I'm selfish?' I ask.

'He called you that, did he? Your secret fella who likes to hit you?'

'Tee. Tee called me hostile, arrogant and selfish.'

He guides my face to his. Goosebumps erupt all over me as they always do with him. 'You are the best person I know,' he says with complete conviction. 'The absolute best!'

I lean in and kiss his lips thinking that right now, I have nothing to lose in trying once more to kiss him. But he dodges me.

I'm clearly not the best person he knows then. Or I would be good enough for him to kiss back.

'Sorry. I shouldn't have... Night, Cassius.'

I get to my feet and leave. And he lets me go without a word.

Well, that's definitely made up my mind.

Tomorrow, I'm requesting my coat and leaving them all behind me.

I'm better off alone anyways.

'QUIET!' Elder One hollers, raising his hands in the air. The packed-out hall falls silent. I lean against the wall with my arms folded across my chest, resenting the fact that I'm forced to be here. I know exactly what coats my family and I will be getting so this is all a waste of time. Down the very front, gathered in a protective huddle are a dozen *Mr Greys*. In the middle, the top of Noah's head is visible. He's not hiding today. He looks back briefly and his eyes land on me straight away. And he finds my hate-filled stare amusing.

'Now, before we get started, we have a guest with us today. Our Lord and Commander, Noah Sands.' Elder One gestures to Noah and the hall breaks out in enthusiastic applause. He heads up and stands before us all. He smiles so charmingly as he looks at all the faces watching him. The girls all whisper and giggle like infatuated children. Even Tee grabs my hand and squeals. I glare at him when he makes eye contact with me, lingering at the back. He starts to talk. But I can't hear him over the anger-filled blood pumping through my entire body. He's such a smooth talker. Only now does it piss me off. But he won't be that way for long. I laugh to myself at the idea of his face when he realises he hasn't got what he wants.

Despite his threats.

'Ow, Scar!' Tee hisses, snatching her hand away from my grip. 'I need that to shoot with!' She rubs her hand and returns her attention to Noah.

Someone whacks my arm. A young cadet I don't really know gestures to the door where Cass is trying to get my attention. He motions for me to come see him. But I'm even less motivated to see him than Noah. I look back to the front of the hall and again, I'm tapped by the young Cadet. With a shove, I send him flying on his arse, knocking a few other cadets off balance as he falls. A few people look at us. None more than Elder Eight who slightly shakes his head in warning. Noah continues to talk. I continue to ignore Cass, and now the others have all shuffled away from me in case I go for them next. Even though the room's crowded to capacity I have a good meter of empty space around me now.

A balled-up piece of paper smacks me in the side of my face.

Slowly, I turn my head and see Cass beckoning me over as Winder scrunches up another sheet ready for launch. I weave between the crowd leaving Tee watching Noah like a love-struck fool.

'What?!' I whisper angrily when I reach him.

'We've got the afternoon off,' Cass says quietly, grinning like a mad man. I see the excitement in his eyes and the hope that I'll let what happened between us yesterday go. 'Me, you, Winder and Tee. After this, we're free as a bird. You know what that means?' He raises his eyebrows suggestively, and I can't help but let my anger at him ease. After all, I can't get mad at him for not wanting to kiss me. Considering my dilemma with Noah, would be a tad hypocritical. Plus, we're not gonna be hanging out much in the future. Might as well enjoy the time we have left together.

'We'll make our declarations and go,' I whisper. 'I'm gonna beat you this time,' I tell Winder.

'In your dreams, loser,' he laughs.

We all turn back to Noah's speech. Noah notices Cass standing beside me. That wipes his smirk clear off his face and he continues his talk a bit colder than previously. Once finished, Elder One retakes the stand.

'You all need to find your Elder. You will sit down with him in private and discuss your preferred coat. Now, bear in mind that a lot of you will have no choice in what you receive. But some, those who have excelled, may request a preference. There are thirty-six of you joining the army this summer. And there are four positions to be issued. The Red Coat.' The crowd breaks into fierce whispering and my heart hammers at the words. 'There is only one Red Coat to be awarded. And they will be in charge of the units as a whole. By wearing the coat, they will stand out as the best of the best. The exceptional. It is the highest honour any of you could ever hope to achieve.'

Cass gives me a playful nudge.

'The real question for you all is where do you want to fight. Behind the wall? Protecting our borders and our people from the inside? If so, and if you are an archer, request a Green Coat. Or do you want to fight out there?' He points to the window. 'Do you want to chase the enemy rather than wait for it to come to you? Because if you do, request a Black Coat.' He scans the crowd for effect. He makes no attempt at all to hide the fact that he believes, like me, that we should all be out there taking back out country. But the wall and the people do need protecting. Someone's gotta do it. I know a lot of Green Coats. I think they're all brave and fantastic people.

'And, let's not forget the Canaries.' The room falls absolutely silent. There's a heavy tension as he brings up the unit no one likes to talk about.

'Now, I know that there is a big taboo around this unit. But we do still open it up for volunteers. So, if you want to join them… tell your Elder.'

'I thought the Canaries is where they put the undesirables?' Winder ponders.

'It is. But you can volunteer too,' Cass says, whispering so as not to interrupt Elder One who is still talking about things to consider when making our choice.

Choice. Ha! As if we have any choice.

'It's where they send the *"criminals"*.' Cass explains. 'You know, the soldiers who have sex out of wedlock. Or commit a crime like stealing or blasphemy. They usually get a sentence. Like three months beyond the wall or a year. Depending on what they've done. No one sane volunteers. It's suicide.'

Elder One finishes his talk with a simple statement.

'Tomorrow, you will be awarded your ranks. Once your ranks have been issued, there is no turning back. No backing out. If you do, it's desertion. And you know the consequence for desertion.'

'Yeah. Death,' Cass mumbles to himself.

We're told to go queue up outside our Elder's office. Winder goes in first. Followed swiftly by Cass. Neither takes long. They both know what they want.

I'm next.

I go in.

Elder Eight is sat in a small room behind a simple wooden desk. There's a single chair opposite and a pile of papers to his left. I assume it's the cadet's preferences.

When the door closes, I head over and sit. 'The coats are awarded before the lottery, right?' I ask him in a rush.

'Yes,' he replies suspiciously. 'Why?'

'So the ranks we all get will be guaranteed no matter what? No one can take them away or change them. Right?'

'Once they've been issued... they can't be changed,' he confirms. 'Whatever you or your friends are issued with tomorrow, that's it.' He holds out his hand for my paper. But I keep hold of it. 'You're starting to worry me, Kiddo. What's goin' on?'

'It's a bit of a long and... sensitive story.'

'Good job I ain't got anywhere else to be then. Isn't it?' He drags around his chair and places it opposite mine. 'Start talking,' he orders.

'First, I need you to promise that you will do something for me.'

'Well, that depends on what it is.'

'I need you to get Tee's number taken out of the lottery.'

His brow furrows even further.

'Why exactly?'

'If I tell you, it will put your life in danger, Elder. I will tell you if you need me to. But please keep what I tell you to yourself. If he finds out you know, he'll kill you.'

'Who?' His arms fold across his chest and he nods for me to continue as I hesitate.

'It's Noah Sands. We can't let her anywhere near him. She will be much safer on the wall as a Green Coat. Trust me.' I shudder at the idea of him hurting her and manipulating her as he has tried to do with me. 'And you better take this.' I hand him the piece of paper with the coat I'm requesting. He reads it, and slowly, his eyes drift up to me.

'Explain. Now.'

I do. I explain exactly what my actions will mean for the others and I confess everything that has happened between me and Noah Sands. All of it. Including his warnings that he would silence anyone that finds out about us.

He is not happy.

Not happy at all.

Outside, enjoying our afternoon off, all four of us race our horses along the beach, their feet splash in the waves as they go. Tee's up front, followed by Cass. Winder and I bring up the rear, running neck in neck.

'Come on, slowpokes!' Tee shouts back, laughing as she gains another foot in the lead. 'You know what the loser gets!'

'That's you, Scar!' Winder says, giving his horse another nudge to pick up the pace.

'Not this time,' I reply. 'Come on, Hanzo!' Hanzo kicks it up a notch.

Cass gives a loud, hearty laugh as I appear by his side.

'Go on, girl!' he bellows.

The horses enjoy the sprint as much as we do. Usually, we trot in a bid to conserve both our energies. But we're not on duty. Not this afternoon. I mean, we're still fully armed and dressed in our leathers and masks. But we're not looking for a fight. We're looking for fun. And when Tee reaches the Cessna 172 light aircraft that's half buried in the sand and partly submerged by the waves, she jumps off and faces us with her arms in the air.

'WINNER!' she cheers. 'Suck it... bitches! HA!' She claps her hands together and starts wiggling her arse in her usual victory dance as Cass reaches her laughing. I finally get there and turn to face Winder who's pouting as he joins us last.

'Aww. Did I beat you?' I mock, sticking out my lower lip and trying not to grin. Too much. 'Looks like you're the loser this time, Winder.'

'Shut up,' he grumbles as we jump down. He takes Hanzo for me as I join Tee in her victory wiggles before taking her hand and heading to the pier just behind the wreckage.

It's barely standing. But it's secure enough. It's a raised structure that extends out into the ocean a good thousand metres. But of course, half of it has fallen into the sea now. Most of the well-spaced pillars have rusted and crumbled into the water, taking the ornate cast-iron railings and wooden planks with them. It's spent the last fifty years being battered by extreme weather and received no care or attention whatsoever. But that's the veranda. The part we're interested in... is the amusements. That part of the building is over the beach. Not the water. So it's relatively safe to be in.

Relatively.

We climb the steps and open the heavy, arched doors to the lobby. The horses come in with us. Tee stays with them in the entrance as the boys and I head inside to check we're alone. We always lock this place up when we leave. We don't want it to get overrun with zoms. It would suck having to clean it all out again. My fingers slide in through the knuckle duster on my right-handed katana before I unsheathe it. Then, we sneak inside. The floor is a mix of yellow and blue chequers, red and white stripes, and pink and orange stars. When we first found this place all those years ago it was filled with targets that had been locked inside for decades. We had to clear it out.

Not a pleasant afternoon.

But once we did, we'd never seen anything like it. It was called an arcade. Kids used to come here and play games. They'd put money into slots and try to win toys. Or put pennies in the top in the hope that more pennies would fall out the bottom. Must have been nice. A bit different than spending your youth learning beheading techniques.

We all split up. Cass to the right. Winder to the left. And me straight through the middle. Our standard battle formation. We head past the two-player shooter. Past the whack-a-mole. Past the dance mats, fruit machines and teddy bear grabbers. All are covered in a thick layer of dust and grime. Some with dried blood.

After a few minutes, Cass calls out, 'Clear!'

'Clear,' Winder replies.

'Clear,' I agree, replacing my katana. 'Tee, you can come in.'

With the horses locked up safely in the entrance lobby, the others gather in the far corner. I slide over a service counter to the stock room, scoop up four cans of soda and pull out a sealed jar of peanut butter before heading back to the others. It's amazing this stuff is still okay to eat and drink.

Winder's already lying on his belly down the end of the bowling alley standing the pins. The single lane tucked away to the side is the cleanest and most cared for thing beyond the wall. We don't get to come here very often. Five times a year perhaps. But we've done the same thing on our afternoons off since we found this place six years ago.

Cass inspects the petrol generator we put here last year.

'It's almost out. I think this will be the last time we can use it,' he says sadly. That fits well, I think to myself. This may be the last time we all get to come here together anyway. Not that they know that of course. The image of Elder Eight losing his mind after I told him my situation sends a chill down my spine. He was so cross with me about Noah, and livid about his ultimatum. And he didn't hold back on how awful and cruel he thought my chosen path was.

But sometimes you have to do what's best for you and not everyone else. I look at them all and know that they'll be fine. They'll have each other.

'I vote we use it for Dance Revs,' Tee says enthusiastically, returning my thoughts back to our last afternoon together.

'Agreed,' I say, handing her one of the cans of soda. Winder grabs a rag and broom. He lost the race, so he has to prep the lane.

Them's the rules.

I hand him and Cass a can of soda each. We gather in a circle, open them up and raise them high.

'To surviving long enough to bowl another game,' Winder toasts.

'To surviving long enough to graduate,' Cass says.

'To refined sugar and E numbers that mean we can still eat and drink this stuff fifty years later!' Tee chuckles.

They all look at me, waiting for my toast.

'To us.'

'To us,' they all cheer, clinking my tin.

'Right!' Cass says, wiping his mouth and taking hold of his bowling ball. 'Let's bowl.'

We spend a fair few hours here. The horses rest. And we play. We bowl game after game after game. Each one is more competitive than the last. Until we get bored of Cass winning and start making trick shots. We bowl backwards. Being held up by our ankles. Blindfolded. And when we get tired of that, we fire up the generator and connect Dance Revs. There's plenty of abandoned money in here. Thousands of pounds I'd say. Completely useless now. Well, not completely. We put a load of pound coins in and fire up the dancing machine. Tee and I go first. The music kicks in and we stumble over our feet as we try to keep up with the arrows. The loser - that would be Tee - gets hauled off by Winder who attempts to defeat me.

'You ain't gonna win!' I laugh, striking every single pose. 'I'm a swordswoman. Ain't no one can move their feet better than me!'

'C'mon, man!' Cass cheers, clapping his hands to the beat as Tee dances wildly beside him. 'Kick her arse!'

'Not gonna happen!' I chuckle, moving my feet easily.

'Get off,' Cass pulls Winder off and jumps on himself. He starts leaping around, slamming his feet onto the arrows and keeping up a lot better than the others. But he still ain't a patch on me. Winder grabs Tee and starts dancing to the music, hurling her around like a ragdoll as she whoops and roars with laughter. Cass turns and faces me. Still moving his feet but not paying any attention to the game.

'Dance with me.' He takes my hand before I can give it, and we dance our own dance. Jumping around and slamming our feet down. We swap. He takes my place. I take his. He takes away all the awkwardness I felt at his rejection last night. And when he starts singing the song, we all join in.

We have another soda.

We dip our fingers in the peanut butter.

And when the generator gives out, we head to the very back of the Arcade where tucked away, is a crazy golf course. Cass throws his club over his shoulder and tosses a golf ball playfully in the air before catching it.

'Let's golf.'

We play the course. Shooting through a stationary windmill and the open jaws of a plastic shark. Winder kicks his ball in after his thirteenth attempt on a par three, and finally, we watch the golf balls roll between a clown's legs and into a basket with the others we've sent there over the years.

There's a moment of silence as we all stand around them.

Six years of games.

Six years of stolen afternoons where we could actually be what we are. Youngsters that want to have fun. But when we leave here today, we start our careers as full-time soldiers fighting an impossible war. A war that will kill us in the end. We're paving the way for the graduates yet to come. For the boys and girls who haven't been born yet. We've only just started this fight. There are decades of battles and rebuilding ahead. It's like we're all thinking the same thing.

We may never all be here together again.

Winder wraps his arm across Tee's shoulders.

'Come on, Q-Tee. Let's get the horses ready.'

'We'll come,' I tell him, picking up my coat.

Cass wraps his hand around my elbow and stops me. 'Actually, I wanted to talk to you.' He looks at the other two and then back at me. 'In private.'

Oh no.

I nod, despite filling with nerves. 'Course.' I look at the others who linger. 'Um, we'll meet you guys back at home.'

Winder leads Tee away. But not before looking back to his best buddy with a confused expression. He's not the only one. I watch them leave, and we hear the doors close.

'You kissed me,' he says as soon as they shut.

I fill with embarrassment and annoyance in equal measure. I thought he wanted to forget about it. I thought he'd want to pretend it didn't happen. Just like the last time I tried to kiss him.

'Can you look at me, please?' he asks.

'I'd rather not,' I reply. 'I'm sorry I kissed you. I shouldn't have done it and I promise I won't do it again. Okay? Can we just pretend it didn't happen?'

'Why did you kiss me?'

'Because...' I sigh and run my hands through my hair, still unable to turn and face him.

Because I thought I might not get another chance. Because I thought that if you kissed me back, it would stop me doing what I've just done with Elder Eight. And because you're the only person in the whole world I ever want to kiss.

'Because I'm an idiot.' Is my chosen answer. 'I won't do it again. I got it, Cass. You ain't interested. Let's go back home and pretend this never happened. Please?'

I make my way to the door.

'Did you kiss me so I wouldn't request a Red Coat?' he asks. 'So I'd remove myself as your competition?'

I stop and turn.

'Excuse me?'

'Well, did you?'

I storm up to him and before I can think it through, I slam my fist into his jaw. And without a word, I turn and head to the door.

'Do I take that as a no?' he calls after me, rubbing his jaw.

I'm so filled with rage. I'm shaking with it. Why does everyone think of me this way? I'm selfish? I'm hostile? Screw them! I grab one of the small stools placed beside the penny machine and hurl it at his head. He ducks and it crashes into the fruit machine behind him causing several coins to tumble to the floor.

'Because I requested the Red Coat,' he says defiantly. 'You won't manipulate me into giving up on my ambition, Scarlett. Not again!'

'Again?!' I almost screech at him. 'What the hell are you on about? I have never-'

'So, it was just a coincidence then, was it?'

'What?'

'That two years ago, I get asked to join The Grey Coats, which would have meant I would need to leave The Academy and my unit for training. And then that evening, you try to kiss me!'

'You want to join the Grey Coats? Then go and join them!' I yell. 'I couldn't give a crap if you join the sodding Grey Coats! Why the hell would I care?!'

'Because *you* have to be the best!' he argues. 'And of course I don't want to join the Grey Coats. They just hide behind the wall, tormenting everyone and wasting their unbelievable skills. That's not the point, Scarlett. My point is that you always have to be the best. And you can't bear the fact that anyone else might be better than you. Especially your friends!'

'Why would you even think that?'

'Let's look at the facts. Most recently? Winder! You took his breakfast on assignment day! I mean... how selfish can you get?'

'Because breakfast was porridge that day!' I bark. 'When he eats porridge, he gets all sluggish and gets a stitch in his side. Every single bloody time! He might be strong as an ox, but he's as stubborn as a mule and has the digestive system of a new-born baby. He wouldn't listen when I told him not to eat it. So I made a bet I knew I would win and took it from him. I went for a run early that morning specifically to win an apple from Elder Ten so I could give him that instead. Was that selfish? Doing a seven-mile run on my assignment day so my friend won't be hindered on the biggest day of his life?'

'I didn't know-'

'Was I selfish when I stayed up all night with Tee the night before her Archery exam twelve months ago? When she kept missing and lost her confidence? I stood in front of her target and made her shoot. I told her I trusted her completely. I took an arrow in the shoulder and made her shoot again. That girl hasn't missed since! Was that selfish?' I turn but only take a few steps before I spin and carry on yelling at him. 'For the record, I had no idea they approached you two years ago. That is not why I kissed you. And stopping you getting a Red Coat is not why I tried to kiss you last night either.'

'Then why-'

'Because I like you, Cass. Alright!' I bark at him. My face flushes with heat and I know I've gone scarlet as I have so often around him. Hence the name. 'I more than like you, okay? I... I...'

'Do you love me?'

'I don't love anyone. Love is a luxury we can't afford,' I snap, crossing my arms across my waist and looking at the ground. 'But if I did... ya know... ever love a man.' I give a small shrug, my gaze still firmly on the floor. 'It would be you.'

'Scarlett,' he whispers longingly. Painfully.

'But none of that matters because you clearly think very little of me. So forget it. Just,

urgh. It doesn't matter anyway.'

I turn and storm to the door. I've never, ever felt like this before. There's a pain in my chest. In my heart. And it feels like something's trying to crawl up my throat. I need to get out of here. I need to get away from him. I yank open the door.

He reaches over my shoulder and slams it shut from behind me. I spin and shove him away.

'You want to fight me?' I snarl venomously at him as he staggers back. 'Take your best shot. I'll crack open your goddamn skull-'

He moves quick, and before I can finish threatening to kill him, he kisses me. I push him off and touch my lips which are still warm. His chest is rising and falling hard and fast, as is mine.

'What the hell are you doing?' I whisper.

'Something I've wanted to do since we were kids. And I'm sick of pretending otherwise. You confuse the hell out of me, Scarlett. I have no idea why you do half the shit you do. You scare me. You make me nervous and you infuriate me. But I want to spend the rest of my life being confused, scared, nervous and infuriated by your actions and always left in awe of you. Kiss me, Scarlett. Because if you don't, I think I'll go insane. I won't go another day pretending I don't love the bloody bones of you, woman. Kiss me!'

'You... you love me?'

'Of course I love you,' he sighs. 'It's always been you. Always and forever.'

I toss my coat to the floor, and we both collide into each other. Our enthusiasm is matched only by our passion. My arms wrap around his neck as his wrap firmly around my waist, and neither one of us hold back. Our kiss is almost violent. The need we suddenly have for each other is years of yearning reached boiling point, and soon we crash to the floor an entangled mess of limbs, tearing off each other's clothes.

Right now, we're exactly where we're supposed to be. With each other. But tomorrow, everything will change.

And I know that Cass will never forgive me for what I've done.

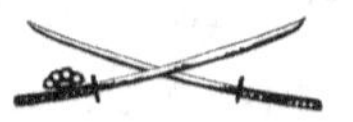

I wake when the sun rises, still wrapped in Cass's arms on the floor. He pulled his coat over us at some point in the night. As I shift, his hold on me tightens a little as he mumbles my name in his sleep.

What the hell have I done?

I'm filled with such a pang of heavy guilt it's almost crushing me. And what's even worse is that I regret it. I regret sleeping with him. It will only make what's about to happen to them all so much harder.

I take a deep breath and bury my face in my hands. Well, it's done now. Good job, Scarlett. Really well done.

I need to get out of here. I sit up and grab my clothes. My sudden movement has him bolt upright, grabbing one of his haladie daggers and looking for a threat.

'What's wrong?' he asks, scanning the room but finding nothing more than me scooping up my clothes. There's a confused furrow on his brow. 'What's the matter?'

'This shouldn't have happened,' I tell him, pulling on my top and leggings. 'This was a huge mistake.'

'A huge... what?' He jumps up and pulls on his trousers. 'What the hell does that mean?'

I avoid making eye contact as I grab my coat and walk out into the main amusements. The slam of the door hitting the wall tells me he's coming after me.

'I asked you a question! What do you mean, *a huge mistake*?' He runs after me and snatches my coat from my hand.

'Give me my coat,' I demand, spinning round and holding out my hand expectantly.

'Tell me what's wrong and I will,' he says, pulling it out of my reach as I attempt to grab it. 'You don't get to sleep with me and then storm off.'

'*Get* to sleep with you?' I snap. '*Get!* Oh well, thank you for the privilege, Cassius. I'm so honoured.'

'I didn't mean it like that and you know it. We just slept together, Scarlett. We made love-'

'I need to get out of here.' I turn and head to the door. When he grabs my arm, I shove him away from me. He staggers back, looking a mix between furious and really, really hurt.

'What did I do wrong?' he asks. 'Why are you so angry all of a sudden? Are you scared of someone finding out? Because no one will. I swear it.'

'Damn straight they won't,' I reply. 'I'm still furious with you. How could you think those things of me?'

'I... I...'

I roll my eyes and turn. He has no explanation other than that's what he really thinks.

'Later, Cass.' I get to the door and pull it open.

'I'm sorry. I thought the worst of you because I never thought for a second that you would genuinely want me.'

Hanzo lifts his head and gets to his feet when he sees me. Cass is hot on my heels.

'You're ambitious. Beautiful. Kind when you want to be. But you're so distant. The only person you seem to really care about is Tee. Her and the army. And then you try and kiss me, and I can't understand why you would risk your position in the army, risk being sentenced to the Canaries, just to kiss me. Not unless there was a reason.'

I look at him as my hand rests on the door handle. 'There are some things in this world, some people, that are worth losing everything for, Cass. Some are even worth dying for. Just because I can't show how I feel, doesn't mean I'm incapable of feeling it all together.'

'Then how do you feel towards me?' he asks. 'Because, I love you, Scarlett. Do you love me?'

'I don't believe in love, Cass. You know that.'

'Because of the stupid curse?'

'Because we're gonna die and we're gonna die bloody. I can't love *anyone* knowing that. What would be the point?'

'The... the point? The point is to live, Scarlett. To live your life with feeling and passion. For more than just killing dead things. To do more than simply exist every day, just waiting to die.'

'That's all we have, Cass. We won't live to see the world return. We're barely the start of its revival. This is it for us and I for one have accepted that. Love is unnecessary and dangerous.' I swallow hard and lower my gaze. 'And painful.'

'Do you love me?' he pushes. 'Despite the pain?'

'I'd die for you, Cass,' I tell him. 'In this life, the way I am, that's the absolute best offer I can make another person.'

'I don't want you to die for me. I want you to love me the way I love you. Scarlett. I want you to live every single day with me-'

'Well,' I sigh, looking at him one last time. 'I'm afraid it's too late for that.' I walk through the door and let it slam closed behind me. Quickly, I mount Hanzo.

He comes running out the door after me. 'What does that mean?' He grabs Hanzo's reigns and looks up at me. 'Does this have something to do with the guy you've been hanging around with in secret? Because I don't care about that. I don't! We're together now. We can be in the army and together. No one has to know. We can have it all!'

'Bye, Cass.' I lean down and kiss his lips. 'You're gonna make one hell of a Red Coat. I wish I were gonna be around to see it.' I kick Hanzo, and he sets off at a sprint, leaving Cass behind.

'SCARLETT? WHAT DOES THAT MEAN? WHAT THE HELL HAVE YOU DONE? SCARLETT... YOUR COAT!'

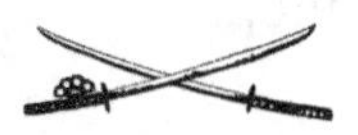

Hiding out here in the woodland alone where no one can find me, I take some time just to let myself try and relax. That is until I hear footsteps heading towards me. I jump to my feet and draw my sword.

'Easy, Cadet. It's only me,' Elder Eight says gruffly, trudging closer. 'I suppose I can't call you that anymore. You're a graduate now. Speaking of which, I come bearing gifts.' He holds up a package wrapped in brown cloth and tied together with string.

'How did you know I was out here?' I ask.

'I know more than you think,' he says, handing me the package and plonking himself on the ground. I sit beside him and cross my legs. 'Like the fact that you and your Cassius stayed beyond the wall together all night,' he concludes unexpectedly. I freeze. And he laughs. 'What? You think you're the only Cadets to act on the feelings they have for each other? I'm personally amazed you two waited this long.'

'I'm so sorry. Please don't report us. We didn't mean to. It just sort of-'

'Calm down. Don't give yourself a nose bleed. I know first-hand what living and fighting with someone in close quarters can lead to.'

'Elder...' I gasp, trying not to grin. 'You had a sweetheart?'

'Well.' He shrugs. 'That's not really your concern.' He looks at me and smiles through his thick moustache. 'She was a lot like you. Hard headed. Dedicated. Loyal. A real stunner.'

'What happened?'

'She died,' he says abruptly. 'You know they're all looking for ya, right?'

He moves on so fast, my head is still spinning.

'Did Cass make it back okay?' I ask.

'He did. Which reminds me.' He gives me a hard clip across the top of my head.

'Ow!' I complain, grabbing the spot he hit. 'What was that for?'

'Riding back without your damn coat on! What if you'd come across a target? You could have been bitten.'

'Sorry,' I grumble, rubbing my head. 'What happened today? Did you get Tee's number out of Noah's lottery?'

'Of course I did. We can't let her end up in his hands. I didn't report to Elder One that she even entered her number so if she is chosen, it won't be valid.'

'Well, that's a relief.'

'Tee and the others may be sorted, but you're still in a pickle. After Cassius knew you'd made it back inside the wall safely, he went looking for ya. When he couldn't find ya, he came and saw me.'

'And?' I ask nervously. 'What did you tell him?'

'I congratulated him on becoming the Red Coat,' he says.

I look at him and smile fondly. 'You accepted my request?'

'Of course I did, Kiddo,' he sighs. 'What other choice did I have? You would never request that Red Coat knowing what would happen to the others, and I won't allow you to be forced into marrying a man you don't want to marry.'

'Thank you,' I tell him with the deepest sincerity. I reach out and take his hand. 'Thank you, Elder.'

'I would say my pleasure, but this is far from the future I wanted for you,' he says, nodding to the brown package in my lap.

'Was he pleased?' I ask. 'Cass? Was he pleased when he found out he got the Red Coat?'

'He was thrilled. They were all very happy they got their chosen coat.'

'Did you tell them about me?' I nod to the package in my hand. 'About the coat I have?'

He shakes his head. 'I told them it was up to you to tell them. They knew your appointment was at three so they hung around. But when you didn't show, they decided to charge around the whole damn Academy yelling your name for a good hour. Last I saw, they were heading to the wall to see if you're up there. Here.

I'm assuming you haven't eaten yet.' He hands me a bread roll from inside his pocket which I eat despite the knot in my stomach. 'I took the opportunity to come and see ya. Knew you'd be out here.' He looks at the small apple tree I've been growing for the last five years. 'Looks very healthy.'

'I water it every day like you told me to. Still hasn't grown any fruit yet though.'

'It will. When it's ready. Like all things, it does what it needs to do in its own time.' He pats me on my back making me wince from the wounds Noah inflicted on me. 'You have to tell them, Scarlett. They deserve to know.'

'I can't,' I admit sadly. 'I just... I think if I see them again, I won't be able to do what I need to do.'

'Hate to break it to ya, but that ship has well and truly sailed. You've been assigned. If you wanna change your mind, the only way to do that is stick around for the lottery results tomorrow afternoon.'

'Yeah... I'd rather die.'

'And you probably will wearing that.' He jabs the package and laughs as my insides squirm. 'I'm taking command of your first mission. Before you argue and insist I'm too old,' he says, holding up his hand as I attempt to do exactly that. 'It's done. We leave at five am. I've already taken the liberty of having your bags packed. You're to meet me at the gate wearing that.' He taps the parcel in my lap. 'I'll have your horse ready. I suggest you spend the remaining time with your friends and explain what the hell you've gone and done.' He gets to his feet, but before he leaves, he looks down at me. 'Tell your man you love him if you haven't already.'

'I can't even tell Tee I love her,' I say sadly. 'Never mind Cass.'

'Take some advice from me. You regret what you don't say a hell of a lot more than what you do.'

'How long will we be gone?' I ask.

'Long enough for Noah to calm down I hope. You've done the best that you could to protect everyone. Yourself included. Staying here... you'll be forced to be in a relationship that will demand children. That's not right. The path you've chosen instead won't be easy, but it will be bearable.' He turns and heads back towards his cottage. 'And don't stay out here alone all night. You need to rest. We have a big ride ahead of us tomorrow.'

'Yes, Elder. Thank you, Elder.'

I open up the parcel and see my new coat. He's cut off the sleeves for me. Good old Elder Eight. I run my fingers along the collar, feeling the thickness and toughness of the black leather. I stand and slide it on. It reaches my knees. It's beautiful. And it fits perfectly. The small badge sewn into the lapel tightens the already impossibly tight knot in my gut.

Shit... this is really happening.

When the first glimpse of sunrise peaks over the horizon, I say goodbye to my apple tree. My one and only place of solitude.

'Grow some apples for me when you're ready. No rush, little tree,' I tell it as I put on my back harness over my new coat and stow my swords before heading towards the main gate.

It's still early. I don't see anyone as I walk through the woods. But when I reach the Soldiers Road that leads straight from The Academy to the main gate, I start to see others. As I walk, they smile at me, their eyes flick towards the badge sewn into my lapel and their smiles soon disappear. My heart is beating like the clappers. Dread and fear flow through me like never before. I've seen and done so much. I've faced zombies for god's sake, but this is the most afraid I've ever been.

'Scar?' a familiar voice calls after me. I turn and see Flash jogging up to me from the direction of The Academy. I quickly cover my badge with my hair. He looks thrilled as he gestures to his new green coat. 'I'm on wall duty this morning!' he says happily, coming to a stop as he reaches me. 'I got a Green Coat. Can you believe it?' he beams.

'That's great, Flash.' I wrap my arms around him and give him a hug. 'I'm so happy for you.'

He looks at my black coat as I let him go. 'You got Black!' he says happily. 'That's great! I mean, I know you wanted the Red, but Black's still really good. Hey... Winder and Titan got black too. Cass got Red! Tee will be with me on the wall, she got Green as well. You know everyone's been looking for you, right?'

'I heard. I just needed some space.'

'There were some Grey Coats looking for you too. Is everything okay?'

'Yeah, Flash. It's all-'

'Err... what is that?' he says suddenly. His attention firmly on my lapel. His smile goes completely, and suddenly he looks furious at me. 'What the hell is that, Scar?'

'It's none of your business,' I tell him, placing my hand uselessly over the badge. 'Listen, I have to go. But I'm really happy for you and the others.'

'Hang on a minute!' he snaps, grabbing my hand and stopping me from leaving. 'Do the others know about this? Do they know what you've done?' He glares at me showing me he does have the ability to feel something other than cowardice. He's pretty angry.

'I really have to go. I can't be late. My unit's waiting to go-'

'You're leaving now?' he says horrified. 'As in right now? I'm fetching Cass. You can't go. He won't let you.'

'He doesn't have a choice.' But he's sprinting back to The Academy before I can stop him. 'Ahh, bugger.' I turn before breaking into a sprint towards the gate.

'Morning, Kiddo,' Elder Eight calls as I approach. 'Where's the fire?' He hands me Hanzo's reigns as I skid to a stop beside him. 'He's all ready for ya, and a bag of your stuff is secured to the saddle.' I jump up on Hanzo, muttering my thanks while watching the still empty path leading back home. I have a few minutes till Flash gets to Cass and tells him. 'How did it go with the others?' he asks.

'It didn't,' I tell him, feeling very flustered. 'I stayed out all night cos I'm a coward. But Flash just saw me, and he's gone to fetch them.'

'Oh dear...' he chortles, not caring one bit I'm obviously keen to get a move on. 'Well, let me introduce you to the others.' He gestures to the two other cadets on their horses all wearing the same coat as me. I've seen them about, but never really spoken to them. 'This is Chilli.' He gestures to a man in his mid-twenties with a shaved head, light blue eyes and a very cocky smirk. 'He's usually a Black Coat. Apparently, he's good with a sword.' He gestures to the blade he has attached to his belt.

'You're not a graduate?' I ask. He shakes his head and chuckles to himself. 'What did you do?'

'He got a little hungry and helped himself to one of Elder Three's secret strawberry plants. He's been sentenced to a year of service.'

'For stealing a strawberry?' I gasp.

'Was a mighty fine strawberry.' Chilli smirks proudly.

'And what about Elder Three? What happened to him for growing an illegal strawberry plant?'

'Not a thing. That's what,' Chilli scoffs.

'Indeed,' Elder Eight sighs. 'And this is Loom,' he says, gesturing to the other guy. He has odd coloured eyes. One's blue and the other is green. He has long black hair tied back in a bun. 'He's a volunteer and an axeman.' Sure enough, strapped to his back is an axe. A double-headed thing with a steel handle.

'You volunteered?' I ask. 'Why?'

'Kinda personal,' he replies gruffly. 'I could ask you the same question. Why has the great Scarlett joined the Canaries?'

'Kinda personal too. Elder, shall we head off?' I ask hopefully, worried about what and who may very well be appearing very soon.

'Okay,' he says, looking at the gate and getting ready to order the doors open.

'WAIT!' Someone calls from behind us. 'HOLD UP, WOULD YA?'

We all turn to see a woman sprinting after us, pulling a horse alongside her and carrying half opened bags over filled with clothes.

'WAIT FOR ME!'

She approaches Elder, severely out of breath and utterly flustered.

'What do you want?' Elder asks bluntly.

'Here...' She hands him a piece of paper which he takes and reads as she catches her breath.

Elder lifts his gaze and a look of disbelief meets her.

'You're volunteering?' he asks. She nods, kneeling down and stuffing her belongings back into her luggage. 'Why?'

'Well... Let me start with telling you about when I was seven-'

'Elder,' I interrupt, glancing over my shoulder. 'I really have to go. The longer we stay, the more time others will have to try and stop me.'

He nods and stuffs Sky's paper into his pocket, gesturing for her to get on her horse.

'We're leaving now?' she asks, glancing over her shoulder. 'Don't we usually get a send-off or something?'

'Not this time.' He turns to us. 'This is Sky. She's an archer and if you ask me... a little insane.' He points to the girl with dark brown hair that reaches to her shoulders. Well, it's all brown except for two large chunks at the front which are pure white. She waves and smiles at me far too eagerly. 'She's a graduate and apparently a volunteer.' He looks at me with bemusement at her sudden appearance.

'Wasn't expecting to leave this soon,' she laughs, pulling herself onto her saddle. 'Are you sure we're supposed to leave so quick?'

'If you don't wanna come,' Elder replies. 'I can tear up your letter.'

She shakes her head and looks at me.

'No. No. I'm totally up for this! What you doing here, Scarlett?' Sky chirps. 'I had you pegged for the Red Coat. Or at least a Black. Were you naughty?' she asks, raising her eyebrows suggestively and wiping away the thick layer of sweat on her brow.

'She's a volunteer,' Elder tells them all. 'She's a dab hand-'

'She's a kick-arse swordswoman!' Chilli says. 'She fights with two mean katanas and has the highest kill count of any graduate yet. We know who she is, Elder Eight. She's a legend!' He looks back at me with an impressed expression. 'Gotta say, I feel much better knowing you're out there with us.'

'That's great. But I would really like to head off before we have company.' Either Noah or Cass.

'Right you are,' Elder says, mounting his horse which has bags and boxes attached to the saddle. I notice a crate holding pigeons, but I'm too keen to leave to ask about it. 'Suppose there's no time like the present. It's dawn. Means we can see where the hell we're goin'.'

Sky gasps and giggles wickedly. 'You swore!'

'Goddamn straight I did,' Elder grumbles. 'If I'm living out beyond the wall for a whole bloody year, you better believe I'm gonna be swearing.' He looks up to the top of the wall. 'BOWZER?'

'ELDER?' A head pops over the edge of the wall.

'READY WHEN YOU ARE.'

'YES, ELDER.'

Bowzer disappears, and the heavy doors begin to open. They grind and groan as they move. We all turn and face them. My hand settles on the little yellow bird that's been sewn onto my jacket as I take a deep, readying breath.

'Canaries!' Elder eight calls proudly. 'Say goodbye to home. We won't be back for a while.'

'Maybe ever!' Sky giggles maniacally.

I'm ready. Ready to leave. Ready to maybe never come back. If that's what it takes to keep my family safe and me out of Noah's grasp, I'll go out there to die with a smile on my face.

Then I hear it. I hear him.

Cass.

He's yelling my name in the distance. I turn and see him sprinting towards me. The others following close behind.

'SCARLETT!' he bellows. 'WAIT! STOP!'

'We can wait,' Elder says kindly. 'You should say your goodbyes.'

'SCAR!' Tee screams desperately. 'PLEASE! DON'T DO THIS! YOU'LL DIE OUT THERE!'

I feel it. The same as I did back in the arcades. Only now I know what it is. They're sobs crawling up my throat. Weird. I've never cried before. I don't like it. The pain I feel tearing up my heart. It's heartbreak.

But it's done. I couldn't change it even if I wanted to.

Yesterday, I put my number in Noah's lottery. So he awarded the guys the coats he promised. But no one, not even Noah, knew I volunteered for the Canaries. Elder kept it entirely to himself and Elder One.

If I stay, I'll have no choice but to marry Noah. And that's not an option. This way, everyone else gets their coat, and I still get to fight.

'Scarlett, say goodbye to them,' Elder Eight encourages.

'SCARLETT... WAIT!' Cass yells. 'DON'T YOU DARE DO THIS! I MEAN IT!'

I turn to the gate. 'Go.'

'You can't just-'

'PLEASE!' I yell. 'Please, Elder. Just go!'

'As you wish,' he sighs sadly.

He gives his horse a kick.

And we all follow suit.

The sound of thumping hooves slamming into the hard ground echo around us as they kick up dust. I don't look back. But Cass's final words follow me.

They follow me for months.

I dream about them every night.

Every... single... night.

'IF YOU DO THIS, I WILL NEVER FORGIVE YOU. DO YOU HEAR ME?! IF YOU ABANDON US JUST TO DIE OUT THERE, I WILL HATE YOU FOREVER!'

CHAPTER EIGHT

I hit the dirt and sigh with utter bliss.

Oh god... lying down feels good. So, so good.

The ground's hard. There's a rock in my side. And I'm pretty sure that someone has peed nearby. But it's the most comfortable I've been in days. I'm off my feet. My eyes are closed and I am gonna get some sleep!

Finally.

It's actually cold. And getting colder every day. I pull up the collar of my coat to shield my eyes from the rising sun, roll onto my side, snuggle into my arm and yawn deeply.

Finally, sleep.

'Scar... hey, Scar... you awake?' I keep my eyes closed as Sky whispers in my ear. I will not be kept awake again as she babbles on and on about the theory that the zoms might be aliens from outer space or that maybe we could develop a way to train them into doing menial tasks for us.

She'll give up. She'll leave me be. She'll-

'HEY, SCARLETT!'

'WHAT?!' I sit up and glare at her smiling face and sparkling eyes. 'What do you want?!'

'Ohh,' she giggles. 'You get so mad when you're tired. Like a big grizzly-'

'I've been up for twenty-three hours straight. I have three hours in which to get some sleep. So, this better be bloody important, Sky. Like world-ending kind of important.'

She scratches her head and her eyebrows squish together. 'But... the world has ended. How can it end again-'

I take a long and deep breath, pinch the ridge of my nose and shake my head. 'What do you want, Sky?' I ask tiredly.

She looks so excited and leans in close. 'I just thought you might like to know...'

'Know what?' I groan. 'Sky, I'm really-'

'The rules are you or Elder has to help.'

'What are you babbling about?'

'If you'd rather Elder help me-'

'Sky! Stop being so-'

'There's a Class Two out there,' she tells me teasingly.

'A Class Two?' I feel a grin creep across my lips. 'Really? We haven't seen one in weeks. You sure?'

She nods slowly. 'There it is... I love that smile. Come play, Scar. Come play. Come play...' She starts bouncing up and down like a child. In her lap is my back harness complete with katanas. 'C'mon... you're not *that* tired, are ya?' she asks, holding them out to me teasingly.

I take the harness and excitedly jump to my feet. 'Let's go.'

The structure we're currently using as a base camp was in ruins well before we screwed up the planet. Hundreds of years before, in fact. It was a circular keep. A stone fort a couple of metres thick and about eight metres high. Feeling a little like home, it forms a complete circle. Except for the one archway on the east side letting us in and out. It's in fantastic condition for... well, ruins. It fits perfectly with what we need. It's on a high mound surrounded by a deep, dry ditch. We can see about a mile in all directions before the view is obscured by hills and woodland. We're overlooking a river which we've been using for fresh water and amazingly... fish! Yeah, there are fish here. And the woodland's alive. The trees and the grass are green. We couldn't believe it when we started to see the environment change the further south we travelled.

And we've travelled a lot.

Nine months of searching towns, villages and farmlands. Of travelling through deserted train stations with the derailed carriages left to rust. Exploring long abandoned theatres, the stage now only playing to forever empty velvet seats. Of taking refuge in the old banks that are still fortresses of brick and iron, burning the former world's wealth for warmth and light. Nine months of sleeping in shifts. Of sleeping on the ground or in trees with one eye open.

Nine months of being a Canary.

We're three hundred odd miles from home, down the very end of the country. Cornwall. And it's not a wasteland like it is back home. It's recovering. Healing.

The sun has only just started to rise as Sky and I head towards the arch. I see Chilli exactly where I left him after he relieved me of watch a few moments ago, but now he's standing with a bow and arrow poised and pointed into the distance.

'Morning, Sky. Morning, Boss,' he greets cheerfully, not taking his eyes off his target.

'I've told you to stop calling me that,' I remind him, pulling out my binoculars and taking a peek at where he's looking.

'I waited like I promised. You know, I could just let this baby fly. You don't need to go down there.'

'Where's the fun in that!' Sky gasps, leaning in close and inspecting his stance. 'Lift this arm a little,' she instructs, tapping his elbow and helping him adjust. 'That's it. Top finger to the corner of your mouth... perfect.' She nods and beams very proudly as he follows her instructions.

'How are my feet?'

'Big and smelly.' She shrugs, adjusting her belt so it sits comfortably on her hips while ensuring her sword is secured to it. He takes a double glance at her.

'Damn, Sky. You look...'

'You like it?' She asks, twirling and holding out the hem of her skirt. 'I finished it last night. It was a plain black skirt but because it was all torn up, I used some other fabric-'

'That she found in that camper van with the three corpses last week,' I add, still looking through the binoculars at the target.

'Yeah, but it wasn't dirty. I checked. No blood or goo or anything.'

'But it stunk of death,' I sneer.

'Not after I aired it out.' She dismisses. 'Anyway. I used that to give it some layers and to make sure my arse is covered. And check out the buckles!' She sticks out her leg to show him how she's used the old buckles she's been collecting to bring her outfit together. Below that she's wearing black ankle boots with the slightest heel and thick, baggy socks that go over her knees. They don't stay up alone so she's hitched them up with make-shift suspenders. His eyes widen as he catches a glimpse of her thigh. I'm getting used to her odd sense of style. The way she paints the lids of her eyes to match the bright colours she adds to her various skirts and tops. How she dyes the white streaks of her hair fantastic colours with things she finds lying around. And how she makes jewellery from clock gears. She has a bracelet on her left wrist that snakes up her arm in a stunningly intricate pattern. She finds it impossible to sit still. She has to be doing something all the time.

Sky is oblivious to Chilli's stares, but notices the lack of concentration he's giving to his aim. So she smacks his arm.

'Focus, Chilli!'

'S-sorry,' he stammers, his cheeks a little redder than before. I give a slight laugh and roll my eyes.

'You set?' I ask, securing my harness. She looks me up and down very smug.

'What do you think of Scar's new and improved outfit?' she asks. 'I spent days putting it all together.'

'She looks even more terrifying than usual,' he admires.

'Watch it,' I warn, drawing my katana and twirling it quickly in my hand before pointing it at him. 'Sky says I look hot.'

'And you do,' he says with a grin. 'But in a... *look at me wrong and I'll cut you*... kind of way.'

'I can live with that,' I shrug.

My brown leggings were far from adequate out here. So they've been replaced by a pair of ribbed leather trousers Sky found and mended for me. My red Nike kicks and less-than-cream wrappings are still a firm part of my outfit but the main addition to my wardrobe is a black leather corset with buckles holding it together up the front. Beneath which is a simple black long-sleeved top made out of something Sky calls "wet look material". Over that I have my black leather Canary coat that hangs down to my knees. The sleeves still cut off and the cuffs Cass made me protect my forearms.

I have to admit, I like her style.

'I could make some awesome cuffs for your arms if you'd let me. The ones you have are-'

'Staying put,' I say simply, running my fingers over the leather cuffs. Chilli's in baggy, dark-green khaki trousers but still wearing the army issue boots he left home in. He's in a light-grey T-shirt he found in one of the old houses we slept in a week ago with the letters *"FBI"* printed on it. And underneath, the words *"Female Body Inspector"*. We're all wearing our black coats, proudly boasting our Canary status on our lapel.

'Ready?' I ask Sky.

'Yes, boss.' She pulls out her sword and gives it a cumbersome twirl.

'Sure you wouldn't rather use your bow?'

'Why? You're teaching me blade skills,' she insists. 'How better to improve than by taking on a Class Two with my instructor.'

She gives it another spin, and drops it. 'Oops.' She giggles, quickly scooping it back up.

'Chilli. Keep your aim on the target at all times. If one of us signals, you let the arrow loose.'

'Or if she drops her weapon again,' Chilli murmurs, watching Sky still attempt to spin her sword.

'Yeah. Or that.'

'I only ever dropped it once in battle,' Sky huffs.

'Three times.' Both Chilli and I correct her at the exact same time.

'Like I said. Keep an eye on the target, Chilli. Just in case. Got it?'

'Got it, boss.'

'I've told you. Stop calling me that, the pair of you.'

'Kiddo?' I turn and see Elder Eight approaching. He's stretching out his arms after an uncomfortable sleep. 'Have we got company?'

'Yes, Elder. Class Two approaching.' I report.

He stands beside Chilli and looks Sky up and down. 'What the hell are you wearing?'

'You like it?'

'No, Sky.' When her smile falters, the corner of his moustache twitches. 'I love it. Glad to see you bringing your personality into your wardrobe. I loathe the forced uniformity back home.'

'Ohh! Can I make you-'

'No!'

'It would be-'

'Go.' He points into the distance. 'Keep hold of your sword and follow her instructions, you understand?'

'Absolutely, Elder,' she says thrilled, her mind clearly made up that she's gonna create something for him anyway. 'I'll follow every word.'

'Good job. Because it's brought a posse,' Chilli tells us. I take a look through the binoculars. There are three slow and cumbersome Class Threes meandering out from the trees and making their way towards our original target.

Handing the binoculars to Elder, I pull up my mask and Sky pulls up hers too. After seeing mine, she insisted someone decorated hers. So Chilli drew a mouth that's been sewn up. Seems appropriate. She loves to talk. Even when we outright tell her to shut up.

'Where's Loom?' Elder asks.

'On watch on the other side of the fort,' Chilli replies.

'Ready, Sky?' I ask.

'Absolutely.' She nods.

'Shall I come too?' Chilli asks. 'Now there are more? I could fetch Loom to watch over-'

'The girls have it in hand,' Elder says. 'Off you go, you two. Have fun.'

'Oh, we will,' Sky giggles.

We head down the mound. Sky is close by my side as we make our way towards the Class Two which is currently facing the opposite direction and just standing there, looking into the distance.

'Remember what I told you?' I ask as we walk. 'About team work? Formation? Coordination?'

'Yes, boss.'

I wish they'd stop calling me that.

'Good. What do you want? Class Threes or the Class Two?' I ask.

'Two of course.'

I'm a little sceptical. But if that's what she wants... 'Right. It's gonna be quick and very strong.'

'I know.'

'They can jump-'

'I know! I know!'

The Class Threes slowly turn as we get closer, whereas the Class Two spins quickly. Its bloodshot eyes shine in the dull morning light as it throws back its head to let loose a high-pitched shriek that just carries on.

And on.

And on.

As the other three gurgle and groan before staggering towards us, Sky's target digs its feet into the ground and sprints straight at us full pelt. I can't see her mouth under her mask, but I know she's grinning as much as I am.

We charge forwards.

'I wanna fly!' she laughs, before falling back.

'Alright...' I carry on, her following just a little behind me. The Class Two's getting closer, closer... closer. I stop, turn and crouch down. Sky continues and leaps. When her foot lands in my cupped hands, I stand and launch her into the air. Wahooing, she somersaults over the Class Two, lands, spins, and stabs her blade through the back of its neck. I see the tip sticking out. It stops and looks down at it.

'Why would you stab? What the hell are you thinking?'

'Crap. I'm sorry. I wasn't... Crap!'

When she retracts it, it turns. She looks nervous and backs up a little as it faces her. Its leathery skin is a mix of pale-green and blue. It clings to its bones and muscles. The ribcage is half visible, and the skin from its lower jaw and down its throat is gone. And my god does it stink.

'Gross,' she mutters. 'Don't you have some Class Threes to deal with, Boss?' she snaps, annoyed when she sees me hovering. 'I got this!'

It lunges for her. She dodges and swipes her sword across its neck, and then again across its abdomen. But not deep enough.

'Class Two's skin is a lot thicker,' I call over. 'You need to-'

Whack.

It slams its arm hard into her chest and she soars backwards before landing on her back and skidding across the dew-covered grass.

'Ouch. You alright, Sky?'

She gets on her hands and knees, lifting her arm briefly with a groan. 'Fine,' she gasps, catching her breath. 'I'm fine.'

It's screeching again and digging its feet in ready to attack. She pushes herself up and gets ready for it, sword in hand and determination in her eyes.

The three Class Threes are heading straight for her too. I run forwards to intercept them, unsheathing my swords as I go. The fingers of my right-hand slide perfectly into the knuckle-dusters.

The first one has its arms outstretched. Its eyes are firmly on Sky as she fights the Class Two. The Class Three doesn't see me. Not until I jump between them. I swipe my sword and sever its outstretched limbs. It doesn't even flinch, but carries on charging forwards. I jab my second blade upwards through its skull until the hilt connects with its jaw. It falls still and silent. I use it as a shield against the second one that's right behind it, and as it tries to get through the corpse to me, I bring my second blade around, slam the knuckle-dusters into the side of its head and shatter its skull completely. When I pull my katana free, they both slump to the floor much deader than they were before.

The third one comes at me.

'SCARLETT!' Sky screams. I turn and see her Class Two charging at me as she tends to another winding it must have given her. I manage to barrel roll out the way before it reaches me, and it ploughs into the last Class Three instead. Back on its feet and looking straight at me, it screeches and then charges once more. The Class Three has no idea what happened and is slowly getting back up. The Class Two is rabid! I'd say... angry? I swipe with my left. It dodges. I have no choice but to back up as I take another swipe with my right.

It dodges.

I continue backing up. It opens its arms and hurls itself forwards. I duck and it grabs nothing but air. I thrust my sword upwards as I crouch below it. The tip of my blade pierces its side.

Holy hell, its skin is really thick! No wonder Sky barely made a scratch. I thrust upwards, pushing myself off the ground hoping to get enough momentum to make it through its body. I run at it, pushing the sword in deeper and deeper, but it's like pushing a butter knife through rubber and hardly goes anywhere. It just gets pushed back.

The remaining Class Three is coming. I crouch and with my free sword, I side swipe and cut through the Class Three's legs, just above the ankle. As it falls, the Class Two wraps its fingers around the sword I have dug into its gut and yanks it out before snatching it from my hand completely and tossing it away. It lunges and I trip over the pair of severed feet behind me, landing hard on my back. The Class Two reaches down, its mouth open wide and going for my face. I have no other move. I hold my sword tip up so it impales itself through the chest. But it keeps pushing, its body sliding down my steel. I slam my foot on its chest beside my blade and push it back up as hard as I can. Meanwhile, the legless Class Three has dragged itself next to me. Its bony and rotting fingers claw at my coat. It opens its mouth wide and slams its face into my stomach. But it finds nothing more than the leather of my corset and the metal of its buckles.

Thank-you-Sky!

It's snorting and snarling like a pig in dirt as it tries desperately to chew through my armour.

'SKY?' I yell. 'WHERE THE HELL ARE YA?'

I hear a high-pitched battle cry and then in a completely insane move, she jumps on the back of the Class Two, wraps her legs around its neck and just starts slicing and stabbing at it with her sword. All the while screeching like a nutter. It tries to grab her, but she dodges its attempts. It slides further down my sword another inch as she moves. Her weight is forcing it closer and the Class Three's pulling itself up my torso.

'GET OFF IT!' I order. 'YOU'RE TOO HEAVY!'

She's too busy being insane to pay attention to me and it slides down even further so it's less than an inch from my face.

Right, that's it!

'Get off the damn target, you idiot! AND KILL THE CLASS THREE, SKY! NOW!' She does exactly as I instruct and leaps off her original target with a flip. I slam my elbow into the Class Three's face hard a couple of times and when it's off me, I move to the side, wedging the handle of my sword into the dirt and hauling myself out from beneath the Class Two before running to where my second Katana lies abandoned. Sky grabs the footless creature and drags it away before driving her sword straight through its forehead. The Class Two has got to its feet, my sword still embedded in its chest. I snatch up my lost katana and get ready. It screeches as it runs at me. Its mouth wide. Its eyes hungry and its body nowhere near injured enough to slow it down. I hold my ground as it gets closer... closer... closer! Before it can grab me, I drop to the floor. It trips over my body and lands face down in the dirt. I launch myself up into the air, my sword above my head and the blade down, ready to strike. With the momentum of my leap behind my thrust and using every bit of my weight, I drive the tip straight through the back of its head, burying the blade not only through its skull, but also into the dirt beneath, right up to the hilt. Putting a foot each side of its head, I yank it out and severe the head completely before booting it far away for good measure.

Chilli and Elder clap and cheer up on the hill as I take a second to catch my breath before rolling the corpse over and reclaiming my other Katana. I look over to Sky who lingers by the Class Three anxiously as I wipe clean my swords.

She looks ashamed of herself. She should be. I'm not impressed by her performance.

Not. At. All.

'That was not good enough, Sky. It should never have got away from you like that.'

'I know,' she agrees. 'I'm sorry.'

'And for future reference, when there's a target on top of someone and that person is trying to push it off, don't jump on and add to the weight of it.' I flick my swords clean of the last of the goo and point the tip in her direction. 'That's really bloody stupid.'

'I didn't think. I'm sorry.'

'I know you didn't think. That's the problem with the way you fight. You don't plan ahead. You just react. You're reckless and careless and half-assed.' I take a final look around to make sure the area is clear and that everything is dead. It is. I point to the corpses with my blade.

'Get rid of them and get some sleep. No more costume making. Sleep. You clearly need it. That was absolutely pathetic.' I walk past her and snatch her sword away. 'You fight like a child. Stick to your bow from now on. You clearly don't know how to manage a sword yet.'

I leave her there telling herself off a lot worse than I ever would.

'Good work, Kiddo,' Elder says as I walk past. 'Nicely done. Get some rest. We're heading out to your next location in a few hours.'

'Yes, Elder,' I reply, trying to hide my annoyance at the mess of the fight.

'You shouldn't be so hard on her,' he adds as I pass. 'It was a difficult Class Two.'

'They're all difficult. Don't matter what Class they are. The problem wasn't them. It was her. The way she fought. Cass and I would have done that a hell of a lot cleaner.'

'Well, Cass ain't here, Kiddo.'

'Don't I know it.' I return to my spot on the floor where I curl up and close my eyes.

Don't I know it.

I wake exactly where I was when I fell asleep. I haven't moved an inch. As I sit and stretch, I notice that Sky is curled up in a ball fast asleep a few metres away. Her face is completely obscured by her hair as she hugs her bow like a teddy.

'Up already? There's some grub for ya,' Elder says gruffly from behind me. I turn and see him sitting a few metres away, nodding to some cooked fish laying in the pan by the still lit fire. 'And don't give me your usual - *"I'm not hungry, let someone else have it"*- crap. Just eat it. I cooked it specially for ya. I know it's your favourite.'

I take a seat on the grass beside him and pick at the meal. He's hunched over, scribbling away on a small strip of paper with a folded map by his foot. To his side is the cage that once contained eight birds. There are only two left now.

'Sure you couldn't try and get a bit more sleep?' he asks. I shake my head. 'Fair enough. I know not to try and make ya do something ya don't wanna do. Waste of energy and oxygen. How do you think she did earlier?' he asks, tilting his head towards the still sleeping Sky. 'Really? Now you've had a sleep and some time to calm down.'

'She did well,' I admit with a guilty sigh. 'Perhaps I was too hard on her. Her skill is getting there. But she's too reactive. Not a planner.'

He shakes his head and chuckles. 'That's Sky alright. Very reactive. She doesn't think much about what's next. Just the now. I mean, look at how she joined us in the first place! Running up to the first Canary unit she could find with only half her stuff packed and no idea what she was getting herself into.'

'She had it tough at The Haven. No one understood her, that's all. Yeah, she's a bit odd. But damn, she's loyal and sweet and hardworking. Brave and stupid in equal measure. But It can be taught,' I tell him. 'Discipline can be taught. I'm very pleased and very proud to have her in the unit.' I look over at her. 'I really like her. I really do. I like all of them.'

'That's handy, since you're stuck with 'em,' he chortles.

'Boys still on watch?'

'Yep.'

'They eaten?'

'Yep.'

I peer over his shoulder to see what he's writing. He sees me looking before covering the writing with his hand, shielding it from view.

'Tell me the information I need to enclose,' he orders, gesturing to the slip of paper.

'Another test?' I laugh. 'Alright. For lack of a better phrase... I'll bite. It's a letter back home telling them of our unit's progress which will be sent by one of the carrier pigeons. So you need to include our current location. Number of surviving members of the unit. Points of interest discovered. And any concerns we feel that they may need to know back home,' I tell him before taking another bite of the salty fish.

'So what would you put in *this* letter?'

'Well, it's our penultimate one. So, I'd tell them that we're all still alive. Where we are. That the climate here is cooler and the land greener. Much more hospitable and fertile. That we have found three locations since the last bird that they should send a unit to in order to salvage, and include the co-ordinates for those locations, as well as their risk factor.'

He nods approvingly and hands me the strip of paper as well as a folded paper map of the country.

Canary unit 63.

7/8 bird. 5 alive. S3 Current location. Fertile land.

3 salvage locations. S4. Hsp. T7. Factory. L.5. Ind est. Risk factor

3.

'What does it say?' he asks.

'That we're on the 7th bird out of eight. That will tell them that we're soon heading home. 5 alive. No one's dead.'

'Which is a miracle,' he laughs, picking up some of the food from my plate and helping himself.

'They'll look on the map they have back home and see where we are.' I pull over the map by his feet and open it up so I can point to the grid reference S3 where slap bang in the middle is our fort. 'Fertile land tells them that we're in hospitable environments. The three salvage locations are marked out in the letter.' I point to the reference locations on the map where we found a hospital, factory and industrial estate. All of which had fantastic supplies. Too many for us to carry alone. 'And telling them that the locations are a risk factor three.'

'What are the risk factors?'

'Four is little to no risk. Three is secured, but may be breached before next visit. Two is very dangerous. Not secured and large amounts of targets. One is don't even bother. Unless you have a death wish.'

He nods again, looking very pleased.

We spent a month clearing those three locations and sealing them up. They shouldn't be over-run anytime soon. So when another unit comes out to salvage, it should be clear for them. I instantly think of Cass leading his units to the hospital we found and stocking up on the bone saws, scalpels and medical supplies. There was so much stuff in these three locations. Clothes. Furniture. Weapons. Seeds. Herbs. Dry food. Metal. Plastic. We've found lots of places like that on the road. Good job too... or else we would have starved. The country is full of lifesaving and convenient supplies.

And zombies.

And destruction.

And corpses and skeletons.

The ones that died human.

So many bodies. Too many. Some were just... so small.

The loss of life that happened fifty years ago really hit home when we stumbled across a school. The teachers sealed the doors shut and they all became trapped. Everyone was hugging each other. We all saw their bones, still sharing a final embrace. I couldn't get over how small they were.

We had nightmares for weeks.

We avoided going too close to London as we travelled south. Cities are absolutely teeming with targets.

But when we passed, we soon realised there was absolutely no point in being worried about London. All we found was a crater.

There was no London. It was gone.

Plymouth was just a burnt husk buried under metres of rubble and ash. Bristol too. It was all destroyed. We found old newspapers in deserted houses with headlines telling of the horrors of the final days. Of how people were eating people. Of how cities were overrun with the dead. Of how the British government bombed their own people in a bid to try and stop the zombie population spilling out into the towns and countryside. We read that they didn't even give the survivors a chance to evacuate. That they just blew them all away.

A necessary sacrifice.

For the greater good.

And a dozen other fancy ways of telling the nation that they murdered thousands of innocent people.

I nod and pass back the paper to Elder Eight. 'It's ready to send.'

He pushes my hand away and gestures to the birds. 'You do it.'

I open the cage and scoop up one of the pigeons before securing the letter to its leg.

'You're training me to take command of this unit,' I say simply. 'Only you and I are allowed to take on a Class Two, to handle the birds, to-'

'If you're gonna continue stating obvious facts, I'm gonna get bored and fall asleep,' he tells me, gently placing some of the fish into the waiting beak of the pigeon and softly stroking the top of its head making it coo affectionately.

I finish securing the letter.

'There's never been a female Canary leader.'

'Or a female Red Coat. Or a Female Elder. Like I said, Kiddo. If you're gonna keep spouting stuff I already know-'

'Then why choose me to train up? Why not Loom? He's smart. Capable.'

'Cos you're the right person for the job. You got the brains. The sense. The skill and the level-headedness to keep not just yourself, but everyone else alive too. The others, bless 'em, are lacking some, if not all, of those skills.' He glances affectionately at Sky. 'They trust ya. The team have chosen you to lead them without any instruction from me anyway. You will make... you *do* make... a fantastic Canary Leader. Even without a penis. Isn't that right, Peggy.' he coos to the bird, chuckling away to himself.

'Why thank you,' I laugh.

'Don't thank me, Kiddo.' He lifts his gaze from the bird and focuses on me. 'Just don't die.'

I let loose the bird in my hand and it flies up high into the sky.

'I bet your people back home watch for those birds every day,' he says.

'I doubt that,' I scoff. 'The way I left things... they hate me for sure. But Tee's on the wall. So, she's safe. Winder and Cass have the coats they wanted. So they're happy. I can live with that. That's... that's enough. I'm more worried about facing Noah than them,' I admit. 'He's not gonna let what I did pass. Elder... I'm afraid of what he's gonna do when I go home.'

'Me too, Kiddo.' He taps my knee. 'Me too. But maybe we should talk about this another time.' He nods to the still sleeping Sky. 'Best no one else knows about that particular mess. The more they know, the more at risk they'll be. He's a vindictive little twerp. The more they know, the more at risk they'll be. He's a vindictive little twerp and he meant it when he said he'll kill anyone that finds out about you two, I'm sure. He won't risk losing the loyalty of his *"flock"*.'

'Of course,' I whisper. He slaps me hard on my back as he watches the bird disappear into the distance.

'Good work with the pigeon. One last mission and then we get to send the last bird. When that one finally flies...'

I watch the pigeon soar into the endless sky. 'It means we're going home...'

Bags packed, horses saddled and weapons holstered, we leave this particular camp for good. It's time to move on. And we're all a little sad about that. This place was one of the nicer homes we've made on the road. Lots of open space. A secure wall. As much fish as we could catch. A nice change from abandoned homes, ditches or the husks of old lorries.

But it's nearly time to start heading back to The Haven. Chilli's sentence is almost up and everyone is getting a little worn out. Plus, the weather is starting to turn. Seasons aren't as they used to be. There's no gradual descent into a mild winter. When it starts to get cold, it means that snow is coming. And no one stays beyond the wall when the snow falls. Not if they don't want to freeze to death that is.

But... there's just one more place we need to check out first. One final mission.

The idea of facing the mess I left back home fills me with dread.

I'd rather just carry on exploring the country. That's the coward in me talking. I'm more afraid of returning to Noah than being out here. Part of me thinks that once I return, I'll never be released. That he'll drag me down the aisle kicking and screaming.

And I know Noah will use my friends to get what he wants from me.

But you never know. Maybe he'll kill me. Maybe he's moved on. And I'll just have three furious, betrayed and unforgiving friends

– or ex friends – to worry about. Either way, the time has come to turn around. So, we agree to take a direct and known route back home. We know safe places between here and The Haven. We've secured a fair few so we can reuse them if needs be.

The plan is to ride back east and make for home.

With one detour.

And I'm seriously hoping it's worth it. Cos otherwise, I'm gonna end up with four very pissed off Canaries. And that's almost as scary as Noah.

Almost.

I'm sure it will be worth it.

As we ride, we keep our pace easy. We don't want to tire out the horses and we don't want to have to stop too often to let them rest. We're attempting to make our way back to a previous camp sixty miles east of here. It was a church once upon a time.

Still is I suppose. It offers sanctuary and protection. And peace to contemplate on ones sins and regrets.

But no one goes there to pray. Not anymore. We dragged out the bodies of the faithful who had locked themselves inside fifty years ago.

And starved to death by the looks of it.

If anyone ever needed proof that there is no god, they just need to look at what happened to his followers. To children. To the elderly. To families huddled together in a final loving embrace, knowing death was coming.

We've seen so much in such a short time. We've visited towns no living person has set foot in for half a century. Life just stopped one day. And we see that day. The plates from the final meals. The books left open and unfinished. The photo albums flicked through one final time.

Their blood still stains the ground and will never be washed clean. The ground is steeped in it. The soil drenched. Sometimes, the air stinks of death and it's almost impossible to breathe.

We all understand now why Canaries can sometimes be a littl e... off.

A zombie is one thing.

But a dead person is another entirely.

As we travel, we avoid towns and anywhere we might get cornered. It's not too difficult to be honest. There's miles and miles of nothing but farmland all around us. But of course, we still come up against plenty of targets. Not enough to cause too much trouble. Usually we don't even have to get off the horses to kill them. Sky's a very good shot. Even while riding. Just like Tee is. She just lets an arrow fly and scoops it back up as she passes. Every time I hear an arrow fly, I feel a strong sense of nostalgia for my lovely Tee.

God, I miss her.

'Alright there, Kiddo?' Elder asks as he rides beside me. 'You're looking a bit lost in thought.'

'Apart from a dead butt-cheek, I'm fine. You?'

'Both butt-cheeks are alive and kicking,' he chuckles as we lead the others along the main road. 'We're gonna have one last stop before we carry on to the church. And it's your turn to get some rest.'

'Got it,' I agree, careful not to meet the hard stare he's giving me.

'I mean it. You need to rest.'

'I said I got it!' I snap as he continues glaring.

'Don't you bark at me like a dog,' he warns gruffly.

'I'm just getting a bit sick of you guys telling me what I should and shouldn't be doing.'

'We want you to eat and sleep. Not asking for the world. You kept watch at the last stop. So you rest at this one.' Pointing up to the hill on our left, he calls back to the others, 'We're gonna stop up there for an hour.'

'About time,' Sky groans loudly. 'My arse lost feeling over two hours ago.'

We head up the small hill, at the top of which is the ruins of a little hut. All that remains are barely three walls made of large, grey stone, but the building itself is of no size at all. You couldn't even lay down in there. There's no roof anyway. None of us have a clue what the hell it was for. But it's up on a high hill and gives us a good view of the surrounding area. So, we head up and dismount. On the other side of the hill, at the very bottom, is a Class Three stumbling about. I reach for my sword to deal with it, but Elder wraps his hand around my wrist and nods to the little hut.

'I got it,' he says quietly but with a sharp edge to every word. As he withdraws his sword, he orders, 'Get in there and sleep.'

'You withdrawing your weapon for me? Or the Class Three?' I ask, snatching my hand away.

'Depends on if you head to the hut, or the target.'

I head towards the hut.

'Wise choice.'

'I'm getting real sick of this. I know when I'm tired and when I need to eat. I'm not a child.'

'Then stop behaving like one.'

The others are purposefully avoiding looking at us. Busying themselves with unsaddling the horses and unburdening the weight of their own weapons.

'Well, even if I was behaving like a child,' I yell back. 'I don't need or want you to parent me. Okay?!'

He storms up, stops me in my tracks and says with a low growl, 'I get that you're anxious about heading home. But don't lash out at the people who are just trying to look out for ya. Your shitty attitude is starting to grate and you're pushing everyone away so cut it out. Got it?'

'Got it,' I reply curtly.

'You better have.'

I head up to the remains of the little stone hut, place my hand on the wall and leap over. I sit with my legs tucked up tight and my head resting on my knees, and close my eyes. Dread fills my chest as I think of the gates back home.

But my dreams are filled with Cass's kiss as we collided in the amusements. His fingertips stroking my skin as I lay in his arms. His mouth whispering that he loves me as we make love.

And the venom in his voice as he yells that he hates me.

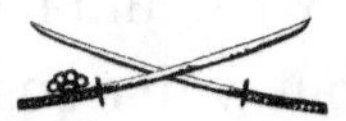

'Wakey wakey, girls.' Chilli pops his head over the wall and grins. He tosses me a flask of water and laughs at the curled-up ball beside me that is Sky. I'm amazed she even fits in here! Her face is covered by her hair and she's snoring so loud, I can't help but wonder how the hell she didn't wake me sooner. 'To someone that doesn't know that noise, they'd think there was a Class Two snarling away in here.'

I pat her head affectionately before getting to my feet. 'Let's let her get a little more rest. C'mon.'

I climb over the wall and head towards the others who are busy getting the horses ready for the next leg of our journey.

'Got some rest?' Elder asks as he tightens the straps under Hanzo's belly.

'Yep. I'm good. Sky's still asleep. Listen. I'm-'

'Never need to apologise to me, Kiddo,' he grunts, knowing that that's exactly what I was about to do. 'Just look after yourself. That's all I'm asking. Carry on breathing, and me and you will get along just fine.' He nods to the east. 'Fancy doin' a scout for us?'

'Bet your arse I do.' I beam.

'Thought you might. Have a look, see if you spot any signs of a horde. And take a few minutes to clear your head. Then get yourself back on the ground in one piece with your head in the game.'

I head over to the giant electricity pylon at the far end of the field. I love these things. I grab hold and start to climb the lattice tower. Right to the very top where a dozen or so powerlines link it to another a mile or so away. They go about sixty metres up and when you're at the top, you can see for miles. An endless canvass of hilly ground, tall untamed grass and abandoned farms. I feel like I'm on top of the world when I'm up here. Like nothing can get me. Not Noah. Not the zoms. Not even death. Unless I slip of course. The wind blows my hair across my face. The white fluffy clouds above me feel so close I wonder if I could touch them. And it's peaceful. Tranquil. I search the area with my binoculars. No sign of a horde. We've come across three in total. Mass gatherings of the undead that roam the country. I'm talking hundreds. Not sure why they do it. But they're not something you want to come up against unawares. We ended up on a roof top for two days as one passed us a few months back. Nothing seals a unit's bond like taking it in turns to use a chimney as a toilet.

I take my time up here. The wind and the height reminds me of the calmness I would feel while running along the wall back home. But it's cold. And too long up here seizes up my fingers. After a few minutes, I return to the ground and report to Elder that the path ahead is clear. Elder turns towards the hut. Putting his fingers in his mouth, he lets loose a loud sharp whistle that hurts my ears. Sky's head pops up from behind the wall. Her hair's a mess, her eyes wide, and she looks around like a confused rabbit.

'We're leavin'!' Elder calls over.

Wiping some drool from her chin, she nods and leaps over the brick and skips towards us. Her skirt flouncing around her as she does.

'For the record,' he says quietly. 'I've been looking after you for well over a decade. Just cos you're all grown up and graduated don't think for a second I'm gonna stop.'

'I don't want you to stop,' I add, flooding with affection for the old man. 'I'm just really worried about heading home is all. It wasn't personal. I just reacted. My temper seems far shorter than usual and it wasn't exactly long to start off with.'

He pats my shoulder and gives a small, sentimental nod. 'It's cos you're scared. An emotion you ain't used to.'

'Well, being scared sucks.'

'Yep. Sure does.'

We all mount up and head out. Elder and Chilli go up front. Sky and Loom in the middle. And I follow behind on my own. It's rare to get any time alone living like this. This is the most I can expect to get. Sky and Loom are talking in quiet whispers. And when they both turn to look back at me, I'm pretty damn sure they're talking about me.

'If there's something you wanna say, I suggest ya say it.'

Sky sweetly smiles and shakes her head. 'Nope. We're good.'

'Then eyes front, Canaries.'

We turn off the main road and head down a small country lane. This is something I'm not happy about. The road we took last time was further along. But the sun is setting and it's later than we thought. We need to get to the church before the sun sets completely and this shortcut Loom found will shave off an hour. The last thing you want is to be out in the open after dark. Targets don't sleep, and they prefer the dark.

The lane's thin with high verges either side. The trees that line it have grown over the road and made a canopy overhead. Beams of light from the setting sun cast a low orange hue all around us. I have to stretch out my fingers to get some feeling to return. When the hell did it start getting so cold? It wasn't this cold last night. We all have thick woolly jackets packed away. I think tonight will be the first night we have to pull them out.

Soon, the lane gets so narrow we're forced into a single line. I bring up the rear as Elder leads the way. The hooves on the tarmac echo loudly all around, and reverberates off the verges which are now higher than our heads. The trees are gone, but we're still very enclosed. We all watch the ground above us nervously. So much so, no one seems to be looking where they're going. My hand is ready to reach for my katana. Sky's just ahead of me, her hand resting on her bow. This is not a good situation to be in at all. No one can see what's above us. And we're making too much noise.

I knew we should have taken the longer and known route rather than this shortcut.

A gust of wind moves the branches. The leaves rustle and the bark creaks. A strange grinding, groaning noise travels through the air and a twig snaps. Sky moves quickly, pulling off her bow and loading an arrow. She aims it upwards, but there's no way she can see anything. A zom could literally land on our heads and there would be nothing we could do to stop it chowing down on our faces.

'Screw this,' I hiss, jumping down and fastening Hanzo's reigns to Sky's horse.

'What are you doing?' she whispers, bow and arrow still poised.

'I'm gonna walk along the top and keep watch. Last thing we need is for a horde to wander over the top and trap us in the valley of doom.' I turn and climb up the verge using the roots to pull myself up. 'Great shortcut, Loom.'

'It's another three miles to camp,' she calls after me. 'Scar, you can't walk the whole way. You need to keep your strength!'

The others have all turned to watch me. 'Yeah, well, my strength won't matter if we get caught off guard and something tumbles over the verge. Will it?' I get to the top and straighten myself up, brushing off the dirt from my climb. Another great thing about all this leather, it's so easy to wipe clean. I take a look around.

'Woah!' I mutter quietly. The field I'm in has an old wind farm in it. A dozen or so of the tall poles with three propellers still stand. Dirty and grimy. Rusted and weather beaten. A few have toppled over and lay at odd angles across the ground half submerged in long grass. Some are missing their propellers. One has landed on another and looks like one good gust would have them both down. Another has crashed through the old farm at the far end of the field. And one still turns. Slowly and begrudgingly. The groans of the gears travel through the air and echo in the vast emptiness around us with every gust of wind. That's what we heard.

'What's up there?' Loom calls.

'Nothing. Just an old wind farm.' I call back. 'It's clear. For now. But it's really crap for visibility in this terrain. I'll walk alongside you guys and keep an eye out.'

'Fine,' Elder grunts, urging his horse to continue. 'You wanna walk? Walk.'

'I don't particularly wanna walk. But I don't wanna wear a zombie as a hat either,' I reply. Chilli snorts a stifled laugh and lowers his head as Elder glares at him.

Half a mile down the road, I spot a couple of Class Threes stumbling about by a knee-high wall not too far away.

'Got a target,' I tell them all.

'How many?' Elder asks.

'Just the one,' I lie as a third head appears from beyond the wall.

'Need a hand?' Sky asks hopefully.

But I shake my head. 'Nah. I got it. Just keep going. Me dealing with it will be much quicker.'

Plus... I'm kinda bored and stressed, I add in my head. Drawing my sword, I head away from the verge and towards the wall.

'Ya know,' I say quietly as I walk. 'I think you would like to be out here with me. Sleeping under the stars. Seeing the world. What's left of it.' I pull out my second katana and give it a playful spin. 'No one telling us what to do or who we can be with.' I give a whistle to get their attention. All three turn, and as usual, their gurgling and snarling get more rampant when they see me. 'Except Elder of course. He tries to tell me what to do, as per usual. But he means well.' The first one charges at me. I swipe my right blade hard straight across its gut, just deep enough to make his insides spill out on the floor. It trips over its own intestines and lands face down in its entrails. The second one clambers over it. Its arms are stretched out and its toes squelching in guts. I cut the extended limbs off with two hard blows and then kneel so I can do the same with the feet. It lands beside the other one who is still trying to get to its feet, but getting caught up in its innards. I laugh as they stumble about, still trying hard to get to me. The third is drooling thick, stringy black goo from its mouth. It dangles all the way to its navel.

Gross.

I pull back my blade and thrust it straight through the front of its forehead. The arms fall limp. The growling stops. And the bloody phlegm detaches and sticks to its chest. I give the blade a shake, making it sway a little.

Kinda looks like it's dancing.

Then I retract my weapon and let it crumple to the floor.

'Oh Cass,' I sigh, looking down at the two still rolling about on the floor. 'I miss you.' I slam my foot down hard on one and decapitate the other. It still chomps. I stab it between its eyes and then line up a shot. I take a couple of steps back to give me a good run up and then boot it as hard as I can towards two trees on the other side of the wall. The head soars through the air spinning wildly as it travels. When it sails between the trees, I raise my hands in victory, the tips of my blades pointed high to the sky.

Gooooaaaaaaallllll!

Perfect shot.

I flick the blood clear and re-sheath my swords before turning back to the lane. Loom is standing there watching. He shakes his head looking disgusted at my behaviour before climbing back down to the others. As I approach, I hear him report that I'm fine. Just blowing off steam.

'Zombie head football?' Chilli asks.

'Yep,' Loom replies, sounding as disapproving as he looked. 'Sometimes I think there's something wrong with that girl-'

I clear my throat as I stand above them.

'Problem?'

He glances at me only briefly before urging his horse onwards. *Like I care what he thinks.*

Finally, the verge begins to drop. The lane opens up and the border of the old church comes into view. The others dismount and lead the horses off the road and up a small path towards a little wooden gate where they meet me. I open it up and let them all pass before closing it behind us. Following a small stone path through the thick blackberry bushes, we turn a bend and finally see it.

'The church,' Chilli sighs happily. 'About bloody time.'

'And *Just* in time by the looks of it,' Elder adds, looking at the sun which is now so low in the sky that in another ten minutes it will be gone altogether. 'Let's get inside, do a sweep and light a fire. It's gonna be a cold one tonight.'

He ain't wrong. I can already see my breath in the air.

The church is made of red brick with a steep slated roof. And for a building in the arse end of nowhere, it's a pretty good size. The reason why we chose this particular building as a camp was for the design of it. There are large windows all around, but they're thin, tall and a good five metres above the ground, so, apart from the main door which is made from extremely thick, heavy wood and metal hinges, there ain't no getting in. It's a gothic, solemn and foreboding structure surrounded by hundreds of weathered gravestones. On each and every corner of the building are beautifully carved stone crucifixes. And right at the very top, on the highest point at the very front and centre, is a giant, stone lady with enormous wings. Her head is bowed as she looks down to the doorway, welcoming us in.

From inside his pocket, Elder pulls out the heavy, metal key he took last time we were here and puts it in the lock. I don't know why we all watch him with bated breath, and I certainly don't know why we all breathe a collective sigh of relief when he turns it in the lock. But I certainly *feel* relieved. He turns and looks at me.

'Check the exterior?'

'On it.' I pat Hanzo as he passes and start my walk around the exterior. A single lap is all I do. And as expected it's all fine. The walls are intact. There are no zoms. So, I head inside.

Closing the door behind me and turning the key Elder left in the lock, I head inside to find the others.

Down the very middle of the building are lines of wooden benches that are bowed and rotted. The first night we stayed here a few months back, Chilli sat on one. It creaked loudly and then splintered under his weight.

Very funny.

Either side are aisles made of red and cream tiles laid out in a mosaic pattern. The walls were plaster once, but it's nearly all crumbled away now, leaving a pile of debris on the floor and the bare stone behind. But it's the ceiling I love. It's a huge cylindrical dome shape with the faintest reminder of a beautiful painting that was once there. It's faded. But I can still make out the halos of the angels and the beautiful bodies of the divine. The colours are peaceful. If a colour can be called that. My world is filled with harsh colours. Blacks. Reds. Greys. Greens. Whites. Red. The ceiling has pastel pinks. Pale blues. Subtle yellows. Even though there's not much left to see, I still think it's stunning. As I head down the aisle towards the great big wooden altar at the far end, Chilli is kicking the crap out of one of the pews, breaking the wood down and tossing it to the side. I scoop up a handful and carry it to Sky who's busy building the fire at the front.

'Here.' I hand it over and carry on past the altar and towards the large stained-glass window above it. I stand there, looking up as the last of the light shines through it. The mix of yellows and blues are pretty. But it's the pure white dove with its wings spread wide that I love. In its beak is an olive branch and for some reason, it makes me feel warm. On the inside.

'Why do you do that?' Loom asks from just behind me. I turn and see him watching me with his hands tucked into his trouser pockets.

'What? What exactly am I doing that's caused that frown on your brow?' I turn completely and fold my arms across my chest.

'It's not what you're doing now,' he replies, looking a little unsure that he should say anything at all. His eyes flick briefly to the sword over my shoulder. 'It's...'

'What?' I ask. His eyes narrow a little. He's desperate to say something. But he won't. He never does. He looks at me like this sometimes. Like I'm beyond his understanding. But he never follows through on what he's thinking. 'Loom. What's the problem?'

Everyone in the church stops what they're doing and watches us.

'It's just... I think your behaviour is... out of line.'

'My behaviour?' I ask. 'What behaviour?'

'The way you are with the... ya know... the-'

'Zombies?' I ask. He flinches at the word and his nose scrunches up in distaste. 'What? Has my behaviour put you in danger?'

'No-'

'Has my behaviour put any of our missions at risk?'

'No, Scar. But-'

'But what?' I take a step towards him. He takes one back, like I'm a threat. And that really pisses me off. 'I don't like your derisive glances and the way you're backing away from me, Loom. What exactly is it about my behaviour that you don't like? Spit it out.'

Elder's got to his feet. But he doesn't intervene. He just watches and waits. The building is so quiet we could hear a pin drop.

He raises his hand and steps back. 'Never mind. It's not important.' He turns. 'Just forget it.'

'Stop!' I order as he takes a step. He does. 'Turn around, Loom.' Again, he does. He sighs as he looks up at me. 'There's clearly something on your mind. If you have a problem with me, you need to tell me.' I look to the others too. 'This is an open forum. Everyone can speak. We won't survive for long if we start resenting or harbouring unpleasant feelings for each other so... tell me. What's up?' I lower myself down onto the step and sit. I find that when trying to confront an issue, standing above the person I'm dealing with comes off as confrontational.

'It's just... sometimes...' He's really struggling.

'Oh for god's sake, man. Just spit it out,' Elder grumbles.

'Sky... you snore,' I tell her. 'Like an animal on heat. It's unbearable. And my god, can you talk crap. Zombies are not aliens. We are not a test site. The rest of the world is not unharmed and your outfit although very pretty, is not combat effective. Plus... you're a little bit mad.' Her face falls a little. 'But I love mad. I love your optimism and unwavering joy. And your quickness to forgive is admirable.' I add. She beams. I look at Chilli. 'Dude. You need to wash more. You stink.'

'Harsh!'

'And seriously... stop pissing close to where we sleep. I know it's a pain in the arse to walk a few extra metres, especially in the dark, but if I wake up to the whiff of your piss one more time, I'm gonna punch you in the face.' He looks like he's trying to come up with an argument. But he's got nothing. 'However. You are a great laugh. And you sure can cook.'

Everyone gives a slight chuckle. But Loom still looks uncomfortable.

'Elder...'

He raises his eyebrows, daring me to say something. I grin.

'You're perfect.'

He frowns, but has a playful smile.

'Damn straight I am.'

'But you don't half moan. And just because we can't hear your farts, doesn't mean we can't smell them.'

Everyone laughs. Even Loom and Elder. So I look to him again.

'Loom. I'm short tempered and rough around the edges. I'm bossy and overbearing. I know that you don't like how I am with the targets,' I tell him. 'I know it upsets you when I-"Play with their corpses?" he finishes. 'Cutting them up and kicking their heads about? Yeah. I think it's sick.'

'But they're corpses. They're dead things. They're-'

'They were us,' he says simply. 'Scar, they were people. I saw you after we cleared out this place. The way you treated the bodies of the dead so carefully and respectfully. But with the targets, you're just plain sadistic.'

'The bodies we cleared out of here were people, Loom. Targets aren't people. They're the things that killed those people,' I tell him. 'The monsters out there? What you see walking and biting is as far from human as can be. It's death wearing a skin suit. That's all. I love your idealistic views on the world. I do. But in this respect... you're wrong.'

'If I get bitten,' he argues. 'And I turned. You would happily lop my head off and play football with it?'

Chilli raises his hand. 'For the record, if you didn't play football with my severed head, I'd be a little offended.'

With an eye roll, I return my attention back to Loom.

'It wouldn't be you. I would be killing the thing that took you away from us.'

'But if I got bit-'

'Let me be clear.' I get to my feet and look at them all watching me. 'I think the world of each and every one of you. I would, and I have, risked my life to ensure you keep yours. But, the minute one of you is bitten... You. Are. Dead. End of story. I will not hesitate in severing your head from your body and booting it as far away from us as possible because if I don't, you will kill someone else. And I will not let that happen.' The room falls quiet again. 'So, Loom, if you are bitten, I will put you down. Even before you turn. Because that's what will keep everyone else safe. And it's exactly what I would expect any of you to do to me. They are not human. They are the thing that killed the human. They are just wearing the decaying corpse of a human. That - is all - they are. They deserve no pity, nor mercy. No dignity. Because they took all those things from the person they are wearing. I am sorry if I offend you with the truth. But that's the way it is.'

'And if it was Cassius that was turned into a Class Three, would you treat him the same way?' he asks. 'Would you cut off his head and kick it about for pleasure? Would you spill his guts just to watch him slip about in them?'

I feel the all kindness I have for him slip from me in an instant. Even the others glare at him.

'Loom, Enough,' Elder says. But he pays no mind.

'What about Tee? Would you kill her before she even turns? Could you look into those big brown eyes that would be filled with fear, and kill her so heartlessly? Or is it just us that you don't care about killing.'

'You're out of line!' Chilli snaps. 'How dare you talk to her like that. They're her people. Her family. Apologise now!' He attempts to charge forward when Loom remains quiet. But when I hold up my hand he stops. I walk down the steps. My feet echo on the stone and Loom blinks at each and every one. I stop just in front of him. I can see how much of an effort it is for him to hold eye contact with me. His breathing is jagged. He's even shaking a little. And his eyes keep flicking to my hands and the hilt of my katanas.

He's afraid of me.

'I'm sorry,' he says in barely a whisper. 'I should never have said that.'

'Yeah well, you did. You think I don't imagine that? Watching the people I care for more than anything suffer? Watching them die? But you see, the question of what I would do if any of you lot got bit, is completely irrelevant,' I tell him.

'How so?'

'Because if Tee, Cass, or any of you get bit, then that would mean I would already be dead. So what I would do is completely irrelevant because I wouldn't be able to do anything.'

'I don't understand-'

'Because the only way a target would ever get close enough to bite any of you,' Elder says sounding very annoyed. 'Would be if that girl was already dead. She'd die before she let a single one of you get bit. Just as I would. If you haven't learnt that yet, you're a bigger moron than I gave you credit for.'

Sky points at me while glaring at Loom hatefully. 'She gives you her food. She takes your watch when you're too tired. She-'

'It's alright, guys. He has a right to speak his mind. He thinks I'm disrespectful. You're probably right. I've had people I care about much more than you think much worse things of me. But as long as you're breathing, I'll fight to keep you safe. But when you stop, when you start biting, I'll show no mercy, dignity or kindness. Because they never show us any. They tear us apart. They eat us alive. They kill children. They have us living in goddamn cages. So you can think I'm a bad person.' I shrug. 'I don't really care. This ain't a popularity contest. Hate me if you want. But know that I'm a damn good soldier and that I'm ready to die for the cause.' I jab him hard in the chest. 'I'm ready to die for any of you.' I take another step closer. 'And if you ever talk about Tee or Cass like that again, I'll knock your fucking teeth out. I have enough nightmares as it is from all the shit we've seen out here. And more from what I've left behind at home without you adding to it.' I barge into his shoulder and head to the door.

'I'm sorry, Scarlett. I didn't mean-'

'I'll be on watch if you need me.'

'Kiddo, you don't need to do a watch. We're perfectly safe in here.'

'Well right now, it ain't safe for Loom's face if I stay in here.'

I slam the door hard behind me and head out into the dark.

CHAPTER TEN

A few minutes after I left, Elder joined me. He's obviously rummaged through my bags because he's dug out my thick, woolly jacket and thrown it over my shoulders before plonking himself on the raised tomb beside me. I put my arms through the jacket and pull up its hood, glad for the warmth. The temperature has fallen dramatically. The weather changes quickly. Winter is around the corner. I can taste it. I can feel it biting at my skin. If we get caught out here in a snow storm, we'll freeze to death. Or starve to death. I think of the snow storms we've had in the past. Everything back home slows right down. The others and I would take our blankets down into the great hall to sleep. Along with a few hundred other Cadets all desperate for the warmth of the fire they would light in the enormous fireplace during the worst of winter, when the snow fell thick and fast. Inches of it. When it's that bad, we don't go out beyond the wall. It's far too dangerous and the horses struggle.

Many times, a snowball fight has been known to break out in the military village. Sometimes, even the Elders would join in.

Snow days are the best.

'You alright, Kiddo?' Elder asks as I quietly chuckle at the memory of a Grey Coat taking a snowball to the back of their head and throwing a hissy fit.

'You know, I'm not a kid anymore,' I sigh, stretching out my legs in front of me and leaning back on the headstone of Joseph Miller.

Whoever he was. 'I wish you'd stop calling me that. Makes me feel ten years old.'

'You'll always be my Kiddo, *Kiddo*,' he says, nudging my elbow as he laughs to himself. He leans back with me, his legs outstretched too as he lets out a deep, tired breath. 'He didn't mean what he said ya know. He doesn't think you're disrespectful. None of them do.'

'I don't really care what he thinks of me.'

He glances at me sideways with one eyebrow raised, clearly disbelieving of my words.

'What did the others call you?' he asks. '"*people I care about have called me a lot worse*", you said. Was that the reason for the late night visit you made to my porch the night before you told me you wanted to join the Canaries? Did you guys have a fight?'

'Tee and Cass said I was selfish. And Cass even thought I kissed him purely to stop him asking you for a Red Coat.' I shrug and snuggle down into my collar. The thick wool is scratchy and smells musty. 'But screw them, right?'

'Riiiggghhhht...' he says slowly. 'I assume we're taking watch?' he asks, moving swiftly on. Thankfully. 'A very unnecessary and pointless watch I might add. The church is a fortress.'

I nod and fold my arms across my chest to try and keep warm.

'I need some air and some time alone.'

'I'll sit with you,' he says, settling his hands on his lap. 'Keep you company.'

'Not really how the whole... getting some *"alone time"* works, Elder.'

'You just focus on working it out. I'll make sure you don't get eaten alive in the meantime. Just pretend I'm not here.'

'Work what out?'

'Whatever it is that's making your head noisy again and has turned you into a grumpy, insufferable git. You see, when your head gets noisy, you get careless and distracted. Always have. Ever since you were a kid. Now, when you get angry or annoyed, that's fine. You channel it and use it to your advantage. Makes you a fantastic fighter. Sometimes, Cass would wind you up before a fight to give you an edge. Not that you noticed. You just thought he was being an arse. But when you get emotional, your thoughts get noisy and drown out your senses. You don't focus. You lash out and attack the people that are just trying to help ya. So, you work it out and I will look out for you while ya do.'

'You think you know me so well.'

'I *know* I know you so well,' he huffs. 'There's no *think* about it. Besides, I like sitting outside looking up at the stars.'

'I overreacted with Loom, didn't I?'

'A tad. But to be fair, if anyone ever said anything like that about the people I care about, I'd break their nose. Putting an image of that in your head is wrong. You handled it better than I would.'

'He just mentioned the wrong people for his example. That's all. The idea of one of them being bitten...' I shudder.

'I get that. Losing the people we love is never easy.' He slumps a little and sinks into himself.

'What was she like?' I ask, looking over at him past my hood as he looks into the sky above. He moves his head to face me. 'The woman you loved. The woman who died. What was she like?'

His eyes soften in the moon light, and a slight but sad smile appears.

'You remember me telling you that?'

'Of course I remember. It's not every day your Commander, the toughest man you know, tells you he was in love. I'm desperate to know what she was like.' I nudge his shoulder.

He takes a deep breath. 'She was... brilliant. Clever. Witty. And my god, what a temper.' He laughs affectionately as he recalls. 'She was in my unit. We grew up together. Much like you and Cassius. She was a better fighter than me. Braver than me.' His smile fades a little. 'She was the other half of me. When she died, I think I died a little too.' He looks back to me and puts on that solemn smile again. 'Which is why I still think that you should have said goodbye to Cassius. If I was in his position and she left the way you did, I would have gone mad. And worse. Been heart broken.'

'How did she die?' I ask, not sure if I'm overstepping and steering the conversation away from Cass. 'If you don't mind me asking.'

'She died because of me,' he says quietly, looking up at the stars.

'Was she bitten?'

'No,' he says absolutely. 'No way. Like you, if she was bitten, I'd have been dead before that could have happened.' He turns to face me and with the help of a deep, courage-inducing breath, he admits, 'She got pregnant. As is the way when two people... well... you know. Get close.'

'You had a baby?!' I gasp.

'She was just starting to show. We had no idea what to do. Our relationship was illegal and we were kids ourselves. They would have taken the baby away from us as soon as it was born, and we would be in serious trouble. Probably sentenced to a lifetime in The Canaries. But then, she started bleeding. Out of nowhere. The bleeding never stopped. I lost them both. Just like that. I was so grief stricken, but I couldn't really mourn. If they ever found out I was the one who got her pregnant I'd have been banished for good. So, I volunteered for a few years with the Canaries to try and work it all out. Back then you could do that. Volunteer a year or two.'

'Bloody hell!' I breathe. 'I'm so sorry. That's awful!' He gives a small, single nod and clears his throat as if clearing the need to cry.

'They see us a number, Kiddo. Not people. You need to remember that. We're expendable. Every single one of us. You... you're not though. You're important. To me. To Noah. And to so many others. The Cadets back home, they look up to you. You're strong. Caring. You fight for the ones who can't fight for themselves.'

'I think you hold a higher opinion of me than you should.'

'I think you are blind if you don't see it. Noah wanted you as a wife not just because of your pretty face. You have the respect of every soldier, both graduate and cadet alike. I wasn't joking when I told you I was inundated with requests from Cadets to be placed with you. I got dozens! And the Grey Coats, they wanted you too. Noah wanted you to be his wife and ensure the loyalty of the soldiers. I think that in the last few years, as The Grey Coats have grown in number and vindictiveness, people have started to have less faith in The Verity. He'll do anything to keep power.' He looks nervously at me. 'If you approve of him. Stand by him. Follow him. The others will too. That's what I think he believes anyway.'

'Guess we'll find out when we get home. Looks like winter is on the way. We may end up snowed in. And all this, coming out here, it may all have been a waste of time. If he threatens my family again, I'll have no choice. I may just have delayed the inevitable. Noah can be very persistent.'

'He's a right little prick, that one. Gods representative, my back-side.'

I can't help but laugh. Elder's complete disregard for the religion has always made me feel a comradery with him. I rest my head on his shoulder and look up at the sky with him as I have so many times before. He's never been this close to any other Cadets. Not that I've noticed anyway.

'I'm really sorry about your lady and your baby,' I tell him.

'Thanks, Kiddo,' he says, patting my arm.

'For the record, I think you would have made an amazing dad. You sure look after me brilliantly. Even when I tell you not to.'

'That means a lot. Thank you.'

'You're welcome.'

The muffled whisperings of Sky and Elder wake me from my brief and uneasy sleep. The sun was starting to rise when I closed my eyes, and as I open them, it's barely up. They don't notice me stirring. I'm still in the graveyard, curled up in a ball with my hood over my face and my head snuggled into the crook of my arm. My right side is stiff and aches from the contorted position I've worked myself into. I'm about to stretch it out when I hear Sky say my name in a hushed angry whisper.

'If there's something we should know,' she says. 'Then you need to tell us. Is Scar in danger?'

Elder groans, 'We're all in danger, Sky. We're not on bloody holiday out here.'

'I know I'm not the sharpest tool in the pond,' she hisses, ignoring Elder's snort of derision. 'But I know that there's something bad waiting for her when we get home and I demand to know what it is so I can protect her from it.'

'If you think that girl needs protection, you don't know her.'

'Let me tell you what I know about her.' I don't open my eyes. Mainly because I don't want to embarrass her. And I'm kinda curious as to what she's gonna say. 'I've seen her face Class Twos alone and not bat an eye. I've seen her sing while surrounded by slobbering, biting monsters. I watched her use her foot to stop me getting bitten.'

'Yeah, she wasn't happy about staining her kicks on that one,' he laughs.

'But she didn't even hesitate or flinch at shoving a part of her body into the mouth of a zombie is what I mean. When we ran out of food she didn't panic. When she dislocated her shoulder, not a word of complaint.'

'What's your point?' he groans tiredly.

'My point is you two don't whisper as quietly as you think ya do. She's not scared of anything out here. But she's terrified of going home. Every time we talk about it she flinches and leaves the conversation. And her mood since we turned around has been really shitty. We're all thrilled to be heading back. Excited. Not her. She wants to stay out here. What could possibly be scarier back home than what we've faced out here?'

'It ain't my place to say,' he replies. I hear him get to his feet. I peek out from my hood and see her grab his arm to stop him. 'I suggest you remove that,' he warns in a low menace I've not heard very often from him.

Not only does she refuse to let him go, but she stands nose to nose with him, looking firmer and more serious than I have ever seen her.

'I didn't grow up with friends, Elder Eight,' she states in a low tone that I would never thought possible for her to produce. 'Everyone thought I was weird. They all said my head was in the clouds. They laughed at my white hair and they called me weak because I let one of *them* scare me so much it changed colour.' Sky briefly told me the story of how her hair turned white. She was cornered by a couple of Class Twos on her first time out. She almost died. Scared her half to death and her hair drained of colour. 'She's the only person who's ever treated me as an equal. As a friend. I will protect her. But I can't if I don't know the threat.'

'There's nothing to concern yourself with,' he snaps, yanking his arm free. 'If she needs your help, she'll ask. But I wouldn't hold your breath.'

'What did she do to Noah Sands?' she asks as he starts to walk away. He slows and stops before slowly turning to look back at her.

'What do you know about it?'

'He's not going to let what she did pass? She's afraid of what he's gonna do to her when she goes home? I heard you two before we left camp. Like I said. You don't whisper as quietly as you think.'

'Neither do you,' I tell her, sitting up straight and lowering my hood. She loses her steely resolve with Elder as I glare at her. Her gaze meets the floor in embarrassment. 'Don't you ever talk to your superiors that way again. Understand?' I order.

'I just want to help,' she complains.

'Then help me get breakfast started.'

'Scar, if Noah's a risk to you, then let me help.'

'You wanna help?'

She lifts her head and nods eagerly, rushing to me. 'Yes! I want to help, Scar. Let me help.'

'Then help me get breakfast going and forget you ever heard us say that man's name. Got it?'

'I just-'

'You got it? Or not?' I jump down from the tombstone and give her a little poke in the chest. I know she's only trying to protect me. *Temper, Scarlett.* But if Noah knows that anyone else has discovered the truth about us, he won't hesitate in silencing them. Permanently. 'Well?'

'I got it. Jeez,' she replies, rolling her eyes and kicking the dirt.

When I head towards the church she follows close by my side.

'You being a bossy cow ain't gonna stop me looking out for you,' she grumbles.

'I know,' I tell her, wrapping my arm around her shoulders. 'Wish it would though. And for the record, you are weird. But I love weird. And I also adore your hair. Screw what others say about you. You just do you, Sky. Because you're brilliant.'

She absolutely beams at me. With a glance to Elder, I see him laughing to himself as he watches us leave.

Inside, Chilli and Loom are talking. From the looks of it, heatedly. They go silent as soon as I walk in.

Great. It's awkward.

'Right!' I call over. 'Breakfast and then we hit the road.'

'We still going to that flower place then?' Chilli asks, pulling his angry and furrowed brow away from a flustered Loom and showing me his over-the-top boyish smirk.

'Yep. It's a couple of hours ride from here. Toss me the saucepan, would ya?' I call over. 'I'll fetch water from the well so we can get breakfast started.'

Although I have my hands held out ready to catch it, Chilli shoves the pan in Loom's hands and nods him in my direction. He gets to his feet looking every bit the uncomfortable prat he is, heads over and hands it to me.

'I'm really sorry,' he says as I take it. 'I was out of line with what I said about your people.'

'You're my people too, Loom.' I remind him. 'And I was out of order as well. No more zombie head football. I promise. Tell you what. I'll just kill them and destroy their brains like any other normal girl. Deal?'

'Deal,' he laughs.

'Good. Then *you* fetch the water and get breakfast started.' I give him back the saucepan. 'I'll do a sweep of the perimeter. I slept funny and need to walk the knots out of my muscles.'

'Anything to get out of cooking, huh?'

'You know my view on things.' I nudge him. 'Men do the cooking. The women kill the undead.'

'Don't I know it,' he chuckles, spinning the saucepan playfully as we separate.

Walking around the edge of the grounds is a welcomed break from the others. Last time we stayed here we camped for a week. There are three villages surrounding us. All with houses and little shops full of supplies. Not to mention the fresh water from a pretty little well.

I follow the fencing which turns into hedges and then a waist high brick wall. The blissful silence and rare moment of serenity is interrupted in a manner I'm becoming all too accustomed to.

Someone yelling.

The panicked hollering has me filled with adrenaline and sprinting in the direction of the well where Loom is currently bellowing for help. I see the well in the middle of an open field as always. But there's no Loom. Nowhere. But I can still hear him. The others pile out of the church doors and stand beside me, all of us ready with our various weapons and all of us completely baffled as to where the hell he is. I'm panting. But not through effort. Through fear. Loom's in trouble and out here? That's deadly.

'Is that Loom?' Sky asks. She does a complete three-sixty and throws her arms in the air. All we see are empty fields. 'Where the hell is he?'

'LOOM?' I call out. 'WHERE THE HELL ARE YA? LOOM!'

'OVER HERE! HELP ME! MY FINGERS ARE SLIPPING.'

His fingers?

'THE WELL!' he shouts. 'HURRY!'

We sprint towards him. The idiot's fallen down the well? I'm out ahead, desperate to help him, my eyes completely on the stone wall of the circular well and stupidly not on where my feet are going.

'I'M COMING,' I tell him. 'Hang on, Loom.'

'Scar! Wait!' he calls.

'I'm coming - Oh shit!' The ground suddenly disappears from beneath my feet and I fall like a sack of bricks into a ditch. I reach out and grab at anything I can get my hands on to stop myself from falling. Especially when I see what's at the bottom of this pit. In a quick move, I slam my sword into the earth and anchor myself from falling any further. Opposite me, Loom is hanging by his fingertips.

'Good move, Boss.' His voice is strained and he's red in the face from the effort it's taking to keep himself from slipping. 'You're quick with that sword. I'll give you that.'

'Err, thanks. What the hell is that?' I look above where there are two small holes in a light canopy above us.

'Someone covered a ditch over with a lid of twigs and leaves!'

We both look down. 'What the hell are they doing down there?'

The five Class Threes below reach up and wrap their disgusting fingers around our ankles and start to pull. With every kick to get them off, we slip a little more.

'GUYS?! GET YOUR ARSES OVER HERE!' I yell, reaffirming my grip on the hilt of my katana. 'AND WATCH OUT FOR THE HOLE!'

'Hole? What-*Woah*!'

Elder grabs Sky by the scruff of her neck and stops her from crashing through the fake floor above us. They use the heels of their boots to smash it away and clear their view. As they all stare at us in a state of disbelief, Loom starts to slip. Chilli grabs his wrist just before he plummets down and hauls him up.

'Where the hell did this come from?' Elder asks.

'A great question,' I reply, still dangling and being yanked by several undead hands. 'Shall we discuss it here? Or maybe you could... I don't know... PULL ME UP?!'

He snaps back to the situation. 'Of course. Sorry, Kiddo.' He leans down and heaves me up quickly and rather violently. I go soaring through the air and he lets me land in an inelegant heap on the floor.

'Ow.'

But no one pays the slightest bit of attention to me. Why should they? They're all peering into the ditch. I join them. The five Class Threes are clawing at the sides, shoving and pushing each other in order to try and get to us.

'Did one of you dig this?' I ask, peering down at the pit.

'Not me,' Elder replies.

Loom glances at Sky. 'Did you?'

'No,' she says with an anxious swallow. 'You?' she asks Chilli, who shakes his head. We all look at Elder. But he just looks into the hole suspiciously, his thoughts racing.

'We're well over two hundred miles from any known scouting locations. Who the hell dug this if not one of us?' I ask. 'Can anyone see a blood rag?'

We all look. But can't see anything.

'Who would put a lid on a zombie trap?' Loom whispers.

I nudge Sky and nod to the contents of the pit. She pulls out her bow. It takes a minute for her to kill them all with very little fuss. Loom and Chilli then jump down, masks up.

'No blood rag,' Loom calls up, kicking the top soil about with his feet. 'It's not one of our traps.'

'Unless one of them ate it. Perhaps another group of Canaries made it out this far and dug it?' Chilli adds.

I feel something plummet in my gut as I look closer. 'What the hell...' I mutter. 'You see what they're wearing?'

The boys flip them over. They're all on their backs, mouths open, bile and pus leaking from their eyes and ears.

'It's army uniform.' Elder kneels down with me to get a closer look. 'All five of them are in the exact same army uniform.'

'We don't wear that,' Chilli states as Sky helps heave him out of the ditch before reaching down to give Loom a hand out. They brush off their clothes and lower their masks. 'That's not Sainted Army garb.'

The dark green mixed with light green in a rough pattern is very odd. I've never seen anything like it. I just thought it was weird that they're all wearing the same rags. But Chilli's right. That's nothing like what we wear.

'Not our army, Chilli,' Elder clarifies. 'It's the old army. Back from before the outbreak. These guys are all soldiers from five decades ago.'

'Weird,' Chilli says very casually with a disinterested shrug. 'You want me to go burn them? Or bury them?'

'Chilli... it's more than weird,' I state.

'How?' he asks. 'The world's full of zombies. They fell into a zombie trap. What's the big deal? It's what's supposed to happen when you make a trap.'

'So, who the hell made *this* trap?' I ask, gesturing to the ditch. 'It wasn't here last time and we didn't make it! And look at where it is. Right by the well. And concealed? Why conceal a zombie trap?

They didn't fall through the roof. We did. The only holes in it are the ones that we made.'

'Probably another group of Canaries made it and couldn't be bothered to fill it in. Or maybe we just didn't notice it before.'

'It wasn't here before, Chilli. Stop being dense.' He goes red as I snap an insult at him. 'Don't you think it's a coincidence that all five of them that just so happened to be in it, all wearing the same thing?'

'They travel in groups sometimes. It's not that strange.' His tone is less certain as he takes another look at the hole, scratching the back of his head. 'I mean... what else could it be?'

'And why are they still even wearing clothes?' Sky asks. She gestures to the almost complete pair of green combat trousers on the one nearest her. 'Most of the one's I've seen are naked or at least wearing a lot less and in much worse condition. But these...' She stands and looks at all five. 'These clothes don't look too bad.'

'Thinking up your next outfit?' Chilli teases her.

'And what if I am?' she argues back. 'Green looks good on me.'

Despite Chilli and Sky bickering off to the side, I get to my feet and glance at Elder and Loom. All three of us share a silent look of deep concern over the mystery of the zombie pit.

'Okay,' Elder puts on his usual easy going yet authoritative demeanour. 'Boys, go and sort breakfast. Sky, finish the sweep and watch out for any more... zombie traps. Kiddo and I will bury the biters.'

Everyone nods and does as instructed. They head back to the church together muttering theories. Once they're clear, he stands close and looks me dead in the eye.

'This is very worrying,' he says quietly.

'You're telling me. Of all the places in the world to find a trap with five relatively clean Class Threes, what's the likelihood of finding it in a site we stayed in a few weeks ago?'

'There are three other Canary groups. I know each of their leaders personally. And none of them would ever come out this far. And none make traps like this.'

'Did you put this location in the pigeon letter you sent back when we last stayed here?' I ask.

He nods slowly and we both look down at the pit once more.

'You know as well as I do. This isn't a zombie trap, Elder. This is a People trap.' I look at him. 'This is a Canary trap!'

'We can't be certain of that,' he says, clearly not believing a word he just said. 'Nonetheless. We should get them buried and get out of here. Quickly.'

'Agreed. Let's get the hell out of here.'

CHAPTER ELEVEN

'What. The hell. Is that?'

'That, Chilli... is a giant greenhouse,' Elder replies, jumping down from his horse and heading towards the balcony ahead of us. We all climb down and follow his lead. 'Would ya look at that...' he mutters, letting out a long appreciative sigh and gently shaking his head side to side. 'Absolutely stunning. Have you ever seen anything so... beautiful?'

At the end of the balcony we all stop and marvel at the scene before us. We're standing along the top of a huge dugout pit. Below is a meandering path leading left to right then right to left, all the way down to the very bottom where at the base are two large dome shapes, covered in moss.

And they are huge!

Probably sixty metres high and two hundred metres wide if I were to hazard a guess. One of them has caved in. The roof is half missing. But the other has lush green foliage spilling out the very top through open slits in the domes.

'I've never seen plants like that!' I say in awe. 'Maybe in the illustrated version of the Jungle book. But not in real life.'

The leaves are thick and must be a minimum of three meters wide.

Loom notices a plaque to our right, wipes it clean of dust and grime, and starts reading aloud.

'Apparently, this place was used to grow plants from all over the world. The dome things *are* greenhouses. Just like Elder said.' He looks over at the large one spouting green. 'That one is from the rainforests, the other is from the Mediterranean. They called it... *The Eden Project.*' He glances at me over his shoulder. 'Well done, Boss. Good call on deciding to come here. Can you imagine all the stuff that's growing in there?'

'Why do you think I wanted to come here? We can harvest seeds and take them home.' I lean over the vista point. Along the paths there are several Class Threes aimlessly wandering about. Arms by their sides, their heads lolling as they continue with their incessant gurgling. Flesh hangs off their thin and decaying corpses. Bile drips from their orifices onto the floor. 'I count twelve. But there will be some more inside the collapsed Mediterranean dome I imagine. And see over there?' I point into the distance to my left. And then to my right. 'There are two smaller buildings. I can't see doors from here, but there may be more in there too. Loom, can you grab my brown satchel?'

'Yes! I love your brown satchel,' Loom says excitedly as he rushes over to Hanzo to fetch it. I open it up and pull out the only other piece of weaponry I love as much as my Katanas. Well, almost as much.

My slingshot.

The handle of which is made from an old Smith and Weston pistol I found a few months ago. No ammo of course. But I don't need bullets. I have something so much better than a shell containing gunpowder.

I climb up onto the ledge of the balcony, the satchel thrown over my shoulder and the slingshot firmly in my hand.

'Let's see what we can lure out.' I dig my hand into the satchel and pull out a balloon which I filled with my own blood. I got the idea from the incident during final assessment. Those suckers really went crazy for my blood. I pop it into the slingshot, take aim and let it fly. As they balloon soars high through the air, the others run to the edge of the balcony to watch. It carries on and lands with a splat in front of the dome.

'Great shot!' Chilli admires. 'Can I have a go?'

'Go bleed yourself if you wanna play with my slingshot. You have any idea how long it takes to make these things?'

The balloon has exploded on the concrete and the smell of my blood attracts every single one of the Class Threes in the vicinity. They turn and smell the air. Their gurgling turns to that chilling screeching as they make their way quickly towards the red puddle on the ground. Most fall flat on their faces to lick it up.

'I really love your blood bombs,' Loom says with a smile. 'You're right too... look at them all come scurrying.' He nods to the building on the left and at the additional Class Threes stumbling towards the blood. They bump into each other and trip over their feet. Some are missing arms. One has the flesh missing from their thigh, showing their bones. I pull out my binoculars.

'Another eight...' I count as they appear.

'We can take them on,' Sky says, retrieving a bow from her quiver.

'Hold it, Sky. Wait for it...'

'Wait for what?'

'Just wait.' They all stand silent. After a minute or so, Loom goes to talk. 'I said wait!'

There it is. A high-pitched shriek followed by a loud smash as a Class Two comes charging out of a building towards the blood. It tosses the others out of its way as if they're nothing more than bowling pins at the end of an alley. When it reaches the blood, it gets on all fours and starts lapping it up.

'Good call,' Elder says quietly.

'Well, it seems to be a trend. Where there's a fair amount of Class Threes, there tends to be a Class Two lurking about. That's twenty Class Threes and a Class Two in total. Here...' I hand Loom the binoculars to hold as I pull out another blood bomb and let it loose towards the building on the right. When it lands on the floor, Loom hands me back the binoculars. We watch in silence as more Class Threes appear from the back of the structure.

'There must be a door to that building around the side, out of sight.' I hear another high-pitched scream. I scan the area but can't see it. 'And there's another Class Two somewhere.' I sigh, looking to the second dome where the roof is half destroyed. 'Sounds like it's in there. Stuck I'd imagine if it can't get to the blood.' I look around us, taking in the details of the area. 'There's no point in attempting to secure the location as a whole. We don't have the time or resources. Not if we want to get home before the snow starts. It's far too large an area for us to build any kind of wall that will be of any real defence against any Class of zom. But...' I gesture to the dome that is lush with life. 'That *must* be kept secured. That's our mission here. Get down there and check if it's been breached. If it has, we clear it and seal it. Agreed?' I look at each and every one of them in turn. Including Elder Eight. They all nod their agreement.

'I can get up on the roof of that building on the left,' Sky says, pointing to the structure. 'I've got thirty arrows. I can put down as many as possible. But once that Class Two sees me it's gonna come straight for me. And it will be able to get up to me. Those things can jump pretty damn high.'

An image of the Class Two leaping on me during evaluation springs to mind. It cleared the first floor easy.

I look to Elder Eight for further instructions. But the team are all watching me. Waiting. Elder simply waits too. He's handing it all over to me. A final test maybe?

'Alright. Sky, you follow this ridge up until you're directly be-hind the building. Then climb down and get on the roof. When you get up there, take out as many Class Threes as you can as quickly as you can. There's no point taking on the Two. Arrows rarely go through the skull anyways. Best not to waste them or piss it off. Me and the others will head down in the standard formation. Three up front. One behind.'

'I'll keep up the rear and get the stragglers,' Elder says. 'You, Loom and Chilli take point.'

I nod. 'Loom to the right. Chilli to the left. Me front and centre. As we go, keep an eye on your arrow recovery.'

'I'll collect them and get them to Sky,' Chilli adds.

'I'll deal with the Class Two,' I tell them. 'Seal the horses up in the foyer building behind us. Give them enough food and water for a few days. Just in case we get stuck. We'll let them have a good rest while we work. They'll be safe in there.'

Everyone goes to sort the horses as Elder joins me at the edge.

'I think we should add this to our list of possibilities,' I tell him. 'What do you think?'

'Hmmm, being on low ground ain't that great. If we do build a secure wall like the one back home and it's breached, everyone would have to climb up the hill to get out. It's not practical.'

'True,' I agree. 'But, if we build the wall from the coast which is two miles south of here...' I point towards the direction of the sea. 'And then go around this place and along for another mile or so before building it back towards the water, we would have plenty of warning from the Green coats on the wall about a breach. And, we could separate this section. Build another wall between this and the land up to the water. Only use this location for growing. No one would sleep here. Just work. That greenhouse dome is filled with life. We can't abandon it.' He nods slowly, thinking it over. 'There are miles of empty farmland surrounding this place. And only three small villages between here and the water. The houses are in good condition. We wouldn't have to do much maintenance.'

'I have to say I agree,' he says. 'I'll add it to the list. We'll need to check for a possible water supply.'

'Judging by those plants, I'd say there's water here somewhere.' We look back out to the giant dome. 'Elder, this would make an excellent settlement. Much better than The Haven.'

'Ready?' Chilli calls over as he pulls up his mask. Sky painted his. It's a set of teeth with a strawberry lodged between them in honour of his crime. Beside him, Loom has his double-bladed axe in his hand. He pulls up his mask in preparation for the fight. His *"Knight in shining armour"* mask. Sky painted it to look like one of those metal helmets on a suit of armour from way back when. Sky stands beside him with her own mask up and every single one of them is watching me. Waiting for my instruction.

For me to lead them.

'I told you they've chosen you,' Elder whispers quietly before taking his place beside them. He draws his sword and pulls up his own mask. Sky drew on a bright red version of his handlebar moustache for him which he thought was hilarious.

'Okay... Sky, get to the roof of the building,' I tell her. 'The rest of us will head down slowly, give you time to get there. And keep an eye out for any other targets we didn't see.'

She nods and sprints off. I turn and head towards the meandering path. The others follow.

It's times like this I always think of my people back home. Of what they're doing right now. I imagine Tee on the wall. I bet she's got close to Owl. They'd make great friends. And then I think of Cass leading his units to locations of recovery and cleansing. The locations of the places we've seen in our long tour of England will be given to the Elders back home, and they'll decide which areas are worth sending a unit to. We provide details of distance to the point of interest and conditions they can expect to find. They'll use that info to decide how many units to send. How long it will take. How many carts they should bring in order to carry stuff home. And so on.

But Elder and I have bigger plans.

We want to create another Haven. Expand our safe zone. Building one down here, in the south of the country, means that we reclaim more land. That the Canaries won't need to spend almost a year out in the wild to gather intel.

Imagine!

Setting up towns all over the country. It's logical! Elder agrees. But convincing everyone back home may prove difficult. They're safe and comfortable in their little cage made of stone.

Especially Noah. Lord of us all.

So, Elder and I have kept our idea to ourselves until we can figure out a way to pitch it to the others back home.

As we reach the end of the path, I see Sky on the roof. Her bow poised and an arrow just waiting to fly. Her face is nothing but focused on her lethal aim. She may have her head in the clouds, but hell, she's one serious archer. I pull up my mask, unsheathe my katanas and give them a playful spin in my palms.

God, I love this.

The targets are all gathered in a circle, clawing at the ground, desperate to try and get even the slightest bit of my blood from the blood bomb. But the Class Two keeps tossing them away so it can lick it all up itself.

I raise my hand and Sky lets the first of her arrows fly. Then another. And another. All strike the heads of the Class Threes she aims for. But the Class Two notices and stands up. It turns and sees us approaching. It throws back its head. Its grey skin is pulled tightly around its ridiculously large muscles. Its fingernails have grown well over two inches and looks like sharpened bone. It digs in its feet, bends its knees, and sprints towards us. The Class Threes following it close behind.

'Death or glory,' I mutter.

'Their death... our glory,' I hear Cass reply in my imagination. *'Kick their arse, Scarlett. Then get yourself home to me.'*

CHAPTER TWELVE

We all charge.

Weapons ready and hearts full of determination. The two armies collide like waves on a cliff. I hear the others shouting and grunting as they swing their swords and axes. I hear them cutting through rotted flesh and brittle bones. I hear the squelch and splat of the blood and limbs they hack free.

I thrust my left blade through the gut of a Class Three, and as another approaches from my right, I swipe straight across its neck, severing its head completely. Heaving my still embedded blade in my left hand upwards, I split the corpse in two from the belly up. Just as the Class Two reaches me. I raise up my weapons in a cross above my head and strike them down. But before I get a chance to introduce its dead flesh to my steel, it body slams me hard and knocks me to the floor. With its full body weight on top of me, my arms are pinned to my chest. But what's worse is the way I've landed has my crossed blades an inch from my neck. As it keeps lunging at me with its teeth, chomping over and over, the blades get closer and closer.

An arrow lands straight in its eye.

Thank you, Sky.

I drop one of my swords and grab the arrow instead. I yank it out and thrust it upwards through its jaw at an angle to clamp its mouth shut. And then I slam my fist, as well as the knuckle-duster, straight into its face again and again and again until I get it far enough off me that I can buck it off. I snatch up my second sword, jump to my feet and attack.

I strike.

It dodges.

I strike again.

It bloody dodges.

I lift up both my blades ready to cut its sodding head off when I feel a set of teeth clamp down on my shoulder. The smell of death and rot comes with it. A Class Three tries desperately to get through the thick wool of my jacket as well as the leather of my coat beneath it.

No way that's gonna happen.

The Class Two claws at its own face, digging its razor-sharp nails into its flesh as it tries to get rid of the arrow keeping its mouth sealed shut.

Suddenly, it grabs its jaws with both hands and wrenches it open, dislodging the arrow and breaking its bones in the process. It wiggles its jaw side to side, lodging the bones back in place before sprinting to me with a snarl. I slam the knuckle-dusters into the face of the Class Three and kick the Class Two hard in the chest before it can reach me. As it staggers back, I take the seconds I've bought myself to turn and slice off the head of the hungry little shit that was trying to nibble my shoulder. I turn back to the oncoming Class Two, duck down low and... *swipe*. Off with its feet. It falls with a furious screech beside me. I jump up and take two more of its weapons away.

Swipe... swipe.

Off with its arms.

I stand over it and try to stifle my smile as I cut the suckers head clean off. But no time to gloat. I stab it through its temple, flick my blades clean - well, *cleaner* - and turn to help the others with the remaining Class Threes.

Chilli has a fist full of arrows and is currently sprinting towards Sky who is crouched low with her arm outstretched, ready to take them. He uses an old, silver table to leap high into the air so he can reach her. The exchange is quick. Seamless. She's back on her feet letting loose arrow after arrow as Chilli runs straight back at the Class Threes, his sword ready and a look of severity on his face that turns him into an entirely different person.

To my right, Loom is dismembering target after target with his double-sided axe. The blade never stops moving. It's like watching Winder. But less ginger.

'Quit daydreaming, Kiddo!' Elder bellows from behind. I turn and watch him effortlessly bring down his sword on a straggler. The head rolls down the hill and lands at my feet. Its jaws are still snapping. They stop after I stick it with my Katana right through its temple. 'Get to bloody work!'

'Err... guys?' Sky calls. I don't even need to look in her direction to know what's got her attention. The dome to the right, the one with its roof caved in, it's spewing zombies! Somehow, they're climbing up the sides from the inside and falling down on the outside. One, then another and another tumble over and land on the floor with a thud. Their legs may be broken. Their torsos twisted and their arms mangled. But they have their eyes on us and they're coming. There's one hell of a crash as the side of the dome breaks apart under the pressure and an army of undead, starving monsters spill out.

'Holy hell... there's hundreds!'

Chilli, Elder and Loom finish their kills and join me, their weapons ready. Even Sky has jumped down to join us.

'There's too many,' I tell them. One thing I've learnt quickly out here, know what fight you can win, and leg it from the ones you can't. 'Abandon mission.'

'We need to get back up the hill!' Loom says. We turn, but more have appeared from behind us and are heading at us from over the ridge. We're completely penned in and there are too many to fight. 'What the hell do we do?'

'We climb!' I point to the dome on the left. 'We climb up the foliage and slip inside through the vents at the top.' I shove Sky in that direction as she stares at the oncoming army of death in horror. 'GO! NOW!'

We all run like hell, slicing and hacking at the ones that manage to reach us, and dodging the rest.

'LOOM, LIFT!' He turns and cups his hands. I leap and he catches me before throwing me high into the air. I toss a blood bomb as far away from us as I can. It lands on the ground and explodes. It drives them crazy, and a few turn their attention to that instead of us. But most prefer the very alive humans to the bag of week old blood. Loom grabs my arm as I land and pulls me towards the dome. I kill one on my right. He kills one on his left. The noise they're making is almost deafening. The smell is more than I can bear!

Ahead, Elder is helping Chilli reach one of the large, thick leaves dangling above him. He grabs it and pulls himself up the side of the giant dome, using that and the vines as rope. The next to reach the side is Sky. She glances back at Loom and me over her shoulder.

'Scar!' she screeches. Elder grabs her before she can turn on her heel to help us, and hurls her upwards. She latches onto the vines and watches us below with dread. Elder looks back at us.

'HURRY UP!' he yells. 'STOP BLOODY DAWDLING!'

'GET UP THERE!' I order him. 'NOW! DON'T WAIT FOR US!' He stows his sword, swears under his breath, takes a few steps back and then sprints at the side of the dome. He leaps and grabs a thick vine.

But the horde around us is getting closer no matter how fast we run.

I slam the butt of my hilt into a dead face. And then stab at one over my shoulder. Loom decapitates one on his left with a forceful swipe and then another as he retracts it. His arms move like a deadly pendulum, as he just keeps cutting down anything that gets in our way. An arrow hisses as it passes my ear and lands through the temple of one an inch from me. I grab the arrow before the corpse gets a chance to fall. A rotting hand wraps around my arm. Another whoosh and an arrow lands in its face. I look up. Sky's on the wall of the dome. Chilli has her by the scruff of her coat as she dangles there with her bow and arrow, letting loose arrow after arrow. She gives us more of a clear path, but there are still too many. I duck as one claws at my face, spinning and driving my blade up through its jaw before continuing my sprinting.

Stab. Kick. Swipe. And then... *screech.*

'CLASS TWO!' Elder bellows, pointing behind us. 'It's charging through the crowd of Class Threes. GET YOUR ARSES UP HERE, THE PAIR OF YOU!'

I've never heard fear in Elder Eight's voice before. But I certainly hear it now.

I grab a plastic tray left on the floor and use it to slam into the face of a Class Three that's got far too close. And then another. And another. Until it shatters in my hands.

The dome is close. Ten metres maybe.

To our right, the screeching's getting louder. I see the Class Threes being tossed out of the way as the Class Two barges through. It's getting real close, real fast.

We reach the dome. Loom turns and cups his hands.

I sheath my swords and run towards him. My foot lands in his palms and he tosses me up. I grab one of the vines and look back down below.

'GET UP HERE!' I yell at him. Sky shoots the last of her arrows, giving him the space and time he needs to do a run and jump up to the vine beside me. He misses a swarm of hands by inches.

He sighs with relief, puffing out his cheeks with wide eyes.

'That was bloody close, huh?'

'Are you okay?' I ask him. 'Are you hurt?'

'I'm fine. You?'

I nod. We look at the mass of dead below. In the not too far distance is the Class Two still steaming towards us. And now we're up high, we can see what exactly had Elder Eight sounding so scared.

'Oh my god!' I whisper. 'What the hell is that?' The Class Two is huge. Seven feet tall and built like a gorilla. Not only that, but it's covered in spikes! Long poles with sharp edges are sticking out from all over its body, but not a single one is near its head. I'd say someone must have tried to take it down and failed miserably. I feel the material beneath us. The walls that make the dome isn't glass. It feels like plastic. It's strong. It can easily hold our weight and a lot more besides I imagine. But the spikes sticking out of that monster look very, very sharp.

'We can't let it touch the sides. Those spikes could tear the wall and the insides will be compromised,' I tell Loom.

'Well you ain't jumping down there to face that thing,' he insists with a horrified scoff.

'Hold me.'

'Hold you?'

'Yeah. Grab my waist and don't drop me. What do you think I meant? A bloody snuggle? I need both my hands. Quick! Before it gets any closer!'

He reaches over and takes hold of me around my waist as instructed, pinning me close to his body and wrapping his leg around mine to keep me close.

'I sure hope this vine stays attached. Or we're both screwed.' he mutters. He ain't wrong.

'Bet you're glad I skip the odd meal now, ain't ya?' I laugh, pulling out my slingshot and loading it with a blood bomb.

'Your pillow talk leaves much to be desired. Snuggle buddy.' He nods to the horde below. 'Focus.'

I aim it at the Class two and fire. It slams into its flesh; the bag explodes as it hits one of the spikes. A couple of the Class Threes turn and look at it with what I imagine confusion for the dead looks like. But it keeps coming. The Class Two makes its way through. The others start sniffing it. I smile and let loose another, feeling more confident in my plan. It hits it square in the face. It slows and starts licking itself so fiercely, it slices its tongue on the spikes protruding from its body. But it's the reaction of the Class Threes around it that I'm interested in. They're turning to face it, their noses in the air.

'You clever thing. It's working...' Loom whispers, as the vine starts to groan. He reaffirms his grip on me, pulling me in tighter. 'Hit it again.'

I pull out another and hit the Class Two in the shoulder. It's almost completely covered in blood now and the others can't resist. One sinks its teeth into its shoulder. The Class Two pulls away and growls at it. I send another which hits its stomach. Another Class Three grabs at it. Then another. It snarls and snaps its jaws at them. It tosses one away, but it's soon replaced by another, hungry and chomping. I reach into my satchel for the last blood bomb. I load it, and send it through the air. It hits it and the air fills with the excited grunting of countless starving, blood-thirsty monsters that can't tell the difference between my blood and the Class Two it's soaked in.

'You bloody genius!' Elder laughs as they all turn on the Class Two, and soon it disappears beneath a pile of zombies. The screeching and the sound of tearing flesh echo off the hillsides surrounding us.

Loom flinches. But I find it the best sound ever.

'Thanks for the hug,' I laugh. 'And such a gentleman. Barely any groping. You really are a knight in shining armour.'

'Anytime,' he chuckles, blushing ever so slightly. 'But if you don't mind, this vine is about to snap.'

I reach over and take a vine of my own and look up at the three others above who stopped to watch. They're all beaming, and Elder Eight looks as proud as I've ever seen.

'Let's go see a jungle.'

CHAPTER THIRTEEN

In the roof are countless open triangular windows, some of which have been torn from their hinges by thick vines. Elder Eight reaches down and hauls Sky up the last stretch. Chilli helps Loom on his final effort to reach the top and when Elder extends his hand to me, I take it gladly. The fight alone was tiring. That climb must have been almost a hundred metres. We're all exhausted! I slump a little when I reach the top and rest my forehead on Elder's shoulder as I catch my breath.

'Holy ja-moly. This is a big greenhouse,' I pant, looking down through one of the windows. 'That is a looong way down.'

Below is the most green I've ever seen. Leaves of all shapes, sizes and colours obscure whatever lies below. There's a chill in the air out here, but there's a warmth emanating from inside and a smell of damp and rotting vegetation that's oddly enticing.

I look at them all. 'Is everyone okay? Anyone hurt?'

They all tell me they're fine, just exhausted and pumped up on adrenaline. Which is a huge relief.

'You?' Elder asks.

'I'm good,' I reply, waving my hand dismissively.

'I'm not,' Chilli wheezes, his head low and his shoulders rising and falling at speed. 'I'm absolutely knackered. Christ... I can hardly breathe.'

'Well,' Elder grumbles. 'I hate to break it to ya, but we've gotta climb down the bloody thing now.'

His words have us all groaning.

'Right...' Elder is attempting to sound filled with energy and enthusiasm. 'Let's get inside and see what we got.'

Chilli slides through the window first, followed closely by Sky. Loom is next and then finally Elder Eight. I watch them all grab hold of various foliage, trunks and vines, before sliding in myself and shimmying down the trunk of a tree of some kind. Every muscle in my body is screaming for rest. But thankfully the adrenaline is still pumping hard, giving me the energy I need not to fall to my death.

'You alright?' Sky asks quietly as I begin to slow. She eyes me nervously, setting her sights on my hands which are white from how hard I'm holding onto the trunk. 'You ain't gonna fall, are ya?'

'I'm fine, Sky. You just concentrate on where your feet are going.'

'You fought hard and you haven't slept much in the last couple of days. You sure you okay to do this climb?'

'That's because you kept me awake again talking about building a rocket and starting a new life on the moon,' I sigh. 'Like I said. I'm fine.'

'You haven't really eaten either,' she mumbles.

'Enough, Sky. Stop. Now is not the time to scold me. Okay?' She's right though. Annoyingly. I'm running on fumes. I haven't slept more than four hours in the last three days. I didn't eat before I left camp because the knot that pit by the well created in my stomach made it impossible. I really hope I don't fall. After everything I've been through, falling to my death would just be embarrassing. I take a deep breath and carry on with the climb.

'We could ya know...' she grumbles to herself as she continues shimmying down. 'It's possible. There must still be rockets-'

'Wait...' I stop climbing and so does she. 'Can you hear that?' We listen. Her eyes narrow as she hears it.

'Is that water?' she asks excitedly.

We look below and see the others have stopped too. We all hear it. The sound of cascading water. We continue down, albeit a little quicker and filled with a little more excitement.

The lower we get, the more we all gasp in awe. And when my feet finally hit the ground, I'm far too excited to give in to my desire to curl up in a ball and sleep.

We stand in a line and marvel at it.

At our beautiful and miraculous find.

The floor is thick with mossy grass and ankle high, vibrant green plants. There are trees reaching up high above us, their leaves stretching out far and wide. Vines connect them all and stretch across the floors like a web. And there are birds and insects making so much noise, it's like a choir made from nature. Like they're all singing to welcome us into their paradise. Their songs echo off the odd plastic material of the dome walls and makes it so much louder than it probably is. But it's not annoying or overwhelming.

It's heavenly.

Compared to the usual grunting and screeching of the dead we have to put up with out in the world, this is bliss. I look at the faces of the others. And they feel it too. Their amazement and joy is as clear to me as any one of the other emotions I know from them all so well. Usually I see determination. A fierceness. A readiness to die. The thrill of the hunt. The excitement of the kill. Even fear. But now they look lost in wonderment. And I'm lost too.

'When we were forced to listen to all those stories of how the world began back at the orphanage... How the Elders described Eden...' Loom walks a few steps ahead of us, his eyes wide and a small, but blissful smile on his face. 'This is exactly what I imagined. They sure got the name of this place spot on.'

Sky's hand wraps around my wrist and she starts to run. I stumble, she pulls me along so quick.

'What the hell?' I have to jump over trunks and stones as she continues guiding me somewhere. She's giggling like a nutter and keeps a tight hold on my hand. 'Sky! What-' She turns around a bend and stops before pointing up above us.

'Bloody hell!' I gasp.

On the other side of the structure is a waterfall cutting a path down from the top of the dome. The water rushes over jagged boulders and lands in a purpose-built stream which runs underneath a wooden bridge, and then travels like veins in all directions, reaching all parts of the dome. This is the source of the water noise, and this is the best thing that I could have hoped for.

'ELDER!' I holler. I needn't have yelled. He followed us right along with the others. He looks up and starts laughing. I can't help it! I laugh too. 'There's water here! Look at it! There's water!' I'm borderline hysterical with joy! I take a sip. 'It's fresh! We can drink it!'

'And fruit!' Loom calls from behind us. We turn but can only see some leaves above us start to shake. He leaps down and lands in front of us with something in his hand.

'Is that...' Sky snatches it out of his hand and peels it. She bites. 'It's a banana!' she gasps. 'I've read about them! Scar, look! Look!' She thrusts it into my hand and I take a bite. All I can manage is a low moan as I taste it for the first time. It's sweet and unlike anything I've ever eaten before. I hand it to Elder and he has a bite too. And then he hands it to Chilli.

'No need to share, guys,' Loom says, as he pulls out two more from his pockets and tosses them at Sky and myself. 'There are hundreds!' He points upwards and sure enough, nestled close to the trunks of the trees are more. Countless more. 'This is unbelievable!'

'It is all very exciting. And better than we could have ever hoped,' I tell him, handing my banana to Elder Eight. 'But first things first. We need to make sure this place is secure. Priority number one. Check the structure. Loom, Chilli, you walk anticlockwise around the wall. Elder and I will go clockwise. We'll meet in the middle. Sky, I want you to get up as high as you can and check the roof. And also try to get a lay of the land. Get up to the top of that waterfall. It seems the highest point.'

'Sure thing, Boss.' She peels her banana and happily skips off, bow over her shoulder and an empty quiver. We'll have to spend some time replenishing her arrows. Luckily, there are plenty of supplies in here to do that. A very happy Loom and Chilli head off towards the wall. Stuffing their faces with banana and laughing triumphantly.

'They're happy.'

'They bloody well should be!' Elder says, heading off and nodding for me to follow. 'This is a big win, Kiddo. A very big win. Look at what you've found!' He opens his arms wide, his handlebar moustache stretched across his face as he grins.

'*We* found.' I correct him. But he shakes his head.

'*You* found it. You wanted to travel south when I said north. You found this place's details in the tourist centre I said was a waste of time to visit. You persuaded us to carry on when every single one of us wanted to stick around North Wessex. And you are the one that found the locations we've added as possible settlements. No other Canaries have ever made it this far and lived to tell the tale.'

'Which is why our pitch to the others back home has to be accepted. If we can set up more settlements in different parts of the country, we wouldn't have to spend so long out here just to get from one end of the country to the other. We have a fortress in the east. We need one in the south, the west and the north at least!' I argue. 'How can we ever hope to reclaim this country if we hide away in that tiny little corner all the time.'

'Hey, I agree,' he says. 'Scarlett, you have found three fantastic locations that would be perfect to build on. That holiday village in Longleat forest. That island a few miles off the coast of what was left of Portsmouth. Now this one! None are a quick fix to this apocalyptic mess. But they're certainly places and outcomes worth fighting for.' He throws his strong arm over my shoulders. I feel ready to buckle under the weight of it. 'Can you imagine, clearing that island! We wouldn't need walls at all. It would take years of hard work. But we could do it! I'm so proud of you, Kiddo.' I look up at him as he smiles at me. 'Cass and the others will be so proud of everything you've achieved.'

'As long as they're still alive, that's more than enough for me.'

He gives me the slightest one-armed hug before steering us left as the others go right.

'See ya in a while,' Chilli calls back with a mouth full of banana before they disappear into the jungle.

'Be safe, boys!' I order back.

Elder and I walk side by side and do our best to follow the walls. It's impossible to see through the thick layer of moss and plant life that has grown all along the inside. It covers the lower half of the wall completely. But we take our time and inspect it as much as we can. I run my fingers along as much of it as possible. Not necessarily feeling for damage, but feeling nature itself. I stumble over a root but quickly straighten myself. I feel Elder watching me. And sure enough, he's got something to say.

'You're not looking after yourself nearly enough. You don't sleep. You barely eat.'

'Not this again. Christ. Are you and Sky on a harassment committee or something? I appreciate your concern. But I'm fine. Honestly.' I stop and look ahead with a sigh. 'The rest is a rock face. It follows the wall around for as far as I can see. Unless we learn to rock climb, there's no way to check it.'

'Yeah well... unless those Class Threes learn to climb the dome or do another body wall like they did in the other dome, I think we're safe. So, let's be careful not to spill our blood or make too much noise, and they should leave this place well enough alone.' He reaches up and grabs a couple of bananas. 'Eat,' he orders, thrusting it in my face. I take it and we continue walking. Eating and laughing as we go.

'This place is unreal!' Chilli chirps as we rendezvous.

'Is it secure?' I ask.

'Oh yeah. The main entrance to this place was sealed up from the outside and the walls are completely intact. No sign of any zoms either. Looks like it was locked up to keep it safe. But never mind that. Look at what we found.' He shakes a bottle he has in his hand. Elder Eight charges past me, pushing me unceremoniously out the way and almost leaps on the poor guy.

'Oh, you amazing, beautiful creature...' he says in a low, seductive tone, taking the bottle in his palms and licking his lips.

'Why thank you, Elder. You're rather beautiful yourself,' Chilli chuckles.

'Not you, ya twit. This!' He holds up the bottle with gentle hands and even more wonderment than he had when we first got in here. 'Rum... oh my dear friend. I've not seen you since I was a young Canary. I do enjoy whiskey. Port too. But rum... that's my real love.' He gives it a kiss and then points at us all with the bottle firmly in hand. 'Right. Let's find that arrow-wielding nutcracker. We're gonna set up camp, gather some grub and drink this bad boy.'

'But... we need to come up with a plan on how to get out of here,' I remind him. 'We're surrounded by the undead. The horses are sealed up in that-' But he's already turned on his heel and started heading towards the waterfall. 'Elder! We have to make a plan! Elder!'

'Not tonight, Kiddo. Tonight... we celebrate!' He lifts the bottle above his head and yells out happily, 'Tonight, we drink. RUM TIME!'

Chilli and Loom stand beside me as we watch him almost skip away.

'Probably best not to tell him we found three cases of that stuff,' Loom adds with a laugh.

'Hell no. He'll never want to leave,' I reply with a soft chuckle. 'Come on. You heard the man. Rum time.'

With an enormous grin on each of our faces, we follow him to find Sky.

As we reach the waterfall, Sky gives a high-pitched whistle. Looking up, we see her right at the top. She waves her arms and squeals gleefully before heading down to meet us.

'You would not believe what is in here,' she says. 'There was some kind of bridge that looks like it went right across this place. It hung from the ceiling.' She points up to a few long pieces of wire cable dangling above us. 'It must have collapsed because there's metal steps laying across the ground over there.' She points to the right. 'It's under a load of undergrowth. And there's a roof of a cabin or hut in that direction.' She points towards the left. 'And over there...'She points to the doors of the dome. 'Over there is a truck-'

Elder slaps her hard on the back. 'Take us to the cabin.'

'But... there's a truck. It might still work considering it's been locked up in here,' she says. 'We could use it to escape.'

'And maybe we can use the wire and metal from the staircase for weapons,' Chilli says.

'Yeah...' Loom agrees. 'We could use that to turn the truck into a battering ram or something.'

'And Sky's out of arrows,' I tell him. 'We need to make some more. There's plenty of-'

'CADET'S! ATTEEEEN-TION!' Elder bellows, making us all jump. His tone is exactly as it was when we were back in training. Its arrival has us all standing in a line, backs straight and palms flat against our thighs. Our reaction is instinctual. Like breathing. He stands in front of us and looks at us each in turn with those analytical and judging eyes we all know so well. He then starts slowly walking up and down.

'Now. I want you all to listen to me *very* closely,' he says. 'And I don't want to hear any of you to say a single goddamned thing till I'm done sayin' what I gotta say. Got it?' We all nod once. 'Good. Now. We have been out in the wild for nine months and three days. We have slept under bridges. In caves. In a camper van that was previously filled with corpses which I swear, I can still smell in my leather coat. We have destroyed the skulls of hundreds of freaking zombies. Washed a ton of coagulated blood from our hair. Wiped our backsides with leaves. Been bitten by fleas. Stung by wasps. Chased by wolves and hunted by the undead. And I'm pretty sure that I slept in a puddle of Chilli's piss three nights ago.' He glares at Chilli who stifles a chuckle. 'We have not had a single moment of real peace, rest or relaxation in the whole nine months and three days we've been out here. The horses are sealed up safely with food and water. Enough to last for four days. So... we are goin' to that cabin Sky has seen. We are gonna gather food that is growing in this dome. We are gonna all sleep at the same time. We are gonna sleep for many, many hours. A whole day in fact. We're gonna take off these goddamned leather coats. Put down our weapons and rest. But first...' He holds up the bottle and gives it a gentle shake. 'We are gonna drink the entire contents of this bottle of rum. I want to hear every single joke you know. I want to hear the best anecdotes you have. Then... and only then... when we have done everything I have just said... will we figure out how to get out of here.' He looks at us all in turn, daring us to argue. 'Have I made myself perfectly clear?' he asks.

I raise my hand slowly. He stares daggers at me.

'Kiddo?' he growls. 'You have a problem?'

'No, Elder. Just thought you might want to know that the boys actually found three cases of the rum. So...' Elder breaks into an enormous, heart-warming smile.

'Perfect,' he says. 'Absolutely perfect.'

The first thing we did when we reached the little bamboo cabin was take off our coats, our weapons and our shoes. Well, it's only polite when entering someone else's house. And it's bloody boiling in here! We're all sweating like crazy in this humidity. We stand in the doorway in our socks, vests and trousers, and have a good look around this odd little structure.

The wide, wooden planks that make up the floor are thick in dust. It puffs up into the air and lingers with every footstep. To the left is a double bed made of crates pushed together. In the far corner is a shoddy shelving unit made of logs tied together with thick string. I press my foot harder on the planks, pressing my body weight onto it. They creak, but hold. Knowing it's safe, I head inside.

The shelves hold pots, pans, plates and bowls. Next to that is a chest. Inside which are cooking tins, magazines and something I know Elder will simply love. I pick up the deck of playing cards and toss it at him. He catches it and chuckles.

'Right!' He grins. 'Chilli, fetch the rest of that rum. Sky, grab some more bananas. Loom, help me sweep these floors, would ya? This dust can't be good for our lungs.'

'Yes, Elder,' they all respond.

'What about me?' I ask.

'Kiddo, sit your backside down and take a breather. Before you fall over.'

'I can help.'

'Please, Boss,' Chilli says as I go to argue. 'Let us look after you for a change, huh? Sit. Drink. Relax.' He winks before heading to the door. 'Because if you're not on top form when we try and get past that horde outside, pretty sure we'll all be torn to shreds. No pressure.'

Loom grabs a couple of brooms from the corner and hands one to Elder as Sky heads out to find some food.

'Fine,' I groan, knowing I'm beat.

I pick up something sitting on a makeshift coffee table called a *"Guide book"* and lay on the bed. Book in hand, back against the wall, and feet well and truly up, I take that breather they're all so keen on me to have. As they sweep, I flick through it.

'What does it say?' Loom asks, cleaning the floor with very little enthusiasm.

'That the hut was built to demonstrate how people live in a real rainforest,' I tell him. 'According to this, this whole dome was designed to be a rainforest ecosystem. Whatever that means.'

'It means they made the atmosphere hotter than normal and more humid so plants that normally couldn't grow in England can thrive,' Elder explains, tossing the broom to the floor and plonking his arse on the bed beside me. 'That'll do. What else does it say?' He puts up his feet and leans his back against the wall just as I have, and gestures for the rum. 'C'mon and sit down, Loom.'

Loom heads over with it in his hand and passes it to Elder before sitting on my other side. We're all chilling with our feet up as Elder opens up the rum. He takes a sip and moans in pleasure before handing it to me.

'It says that the dome's completely self-sufficient. It collects rainwater and has access to an underground stream,' I tell him. 'And, there are over a hundred different types of fruit, vegetables and herbs growing in here. As well as rice plants.' I take a sip and cough as I swallow. 'What the-' cough, splutter, 'That's strong!' I hand it to Loom, as Elder chuckles to himself. I continue to flick through the pages. 'There are recipes in here.'

'Really?' Loom says, leaning over and having a look. 'Recipes?' He takes a sip and gives a little cough as he swallows, but that doesn't stop him having more.

'And all the ingredients are in this dome,' I add, handing it over and pointing out a particularly delicious looking one. 'You think you can make it?'

'Of course. I can make anything.' That's true. He's a fantastic cook. He can make roots taste like... well... not roots. He has another sip and takes the book. 'I'll fetch the ingredients and we can have a real meal tonight.'

'Want some help?' I ask.

'Nah. You stay put.' As he heads to the door, he looks back and points at the bottle. 'Drink. It will help you sleep.'

I doubt that.

I hand the bottle to Elder and sigh deeply. He's watching me closely.

'You're gonna overheat,' he says, gesturing to my leather trousers and corset.

'You're right.' Sitting, I unbuckle my corset and toss it to the floor next to the rest of my leathers.

'You should take off those cuffs too.'

'Nope. Never,' I reply, running my fingers gently over the edge of the leather. 'I never take them off. They've saved my life more times than I can count.'

He takes a sip before getting to his feet.

'They remind you of Cass. Don't pretend otherwise. I'm gonna leave and give you some privacy so you can sleep. I suggest you take off your trousers so you don't overheat.' He picks up his jacket, folds it up and lays it on the bed as a pillow. 'Sleep. That's an order, Kiddo.'

'I appreciate your concern. But honestly, I'm fine. I could do more sweeping if you wanna put your feet up.'

'Scarlett.' His hand lands firmly on my shoulder as I attempt to stand. He holds me in place and glares at me. 'Lay down and sleep willingly. Or I will knock out and you will sleep forcibly.' Part of me kinda believes him. I lay down and rest my head on his coat. 'Good. I'll wake you up when there's food. You want a drink? Water? Rum?'

I shake my head. 'I'm good. And feeling quite looked after. Thank you.'

'You're worried about Noah. I get that. But this distraction is goin' to get you hurt. Or killed.'

'I'm not worried.'

'Lying won't help-'

'I'm terrified,' I admit in a whisper, knotting my hands together in my lap. 'Elder... what if he forces me into marriage when we go home. What if he threatens Winder, Tee and Cass again? If I have no choice, if it's the only way to keep them safe... I won't be able to say no, will I? He hates Cass. He loathes him and I worry that if he hasn't already, he'll kill him. I hate to admit it. Especially to you. But Noah frightens me.'

'I've never heard you say you're frightened before. Does he scare you more than that horde out there?'

I nod. 'A lot more. Those monsters will just kill me. Noah can lock me up for the rest of my life. Force me to be his wife. Force me to give him children. He could sentence my friends to The Canaries.'

'You'll kill him before he ever gets to lay a hand on you. Or them. Of that I'm certain,' he replies.

'And then I'll be executed. No matter what, he'll win. And I'll lose.'

He kneels down and rests his hands over mine. 'We have no idea what's waiting for us when we go home. For all we know, he's moved on and chosen another girl to marry. Cass and Winder are probably loving their time in their unit. Doin' what they do best. And Tee is up on that wall. Safe and sound. And all of them are missing you like crazy. Right now, there's nothing you or I can do about what may or may not happen back home. All we can do is survive the here and now. And you won't survive if you keep yourself up at night worrying about the people you sacrificed everything for in the first place. *They're* safe. They have their coats. They have each other. The protection of the wall. That's why you did this. You can't give any more than you already have. They wouldn't want you to die out here to protect them.'

'But what if Noah's hurt them while I've been away.'

'And what if he hasn't? Hmm? There's no point worrying about something that may not have even happened.'

'What if he forces me into marriage? What if-'

'What if? What if? What if?' he sighs. 'Focus on the facts. We're trapped in a rainforest. A bloody rainforest! There are hundreds of Class Threes between us and our horses. They have four days of food and water until they die. If they die, we're stranded. We need to get to them while keeping this dome's integrity intact.'

'Then I should make arrows-'

'I don't know if you've noticed, but everyone is at their limit. We can't defeat what we need to defeat in our current condition. And you are our main fighter. We need you if we're gonna get out of here. So please, I know you care about your people back home. But these people need you too. We need you to help get us back home.' He looks me straight in the eye. 'Do you hear me? We need you. Alive. And strong.'

I nod and hold his hand as tight as he's holding mine.

'I hear you.'

He slaps a friendly hand on my shoulder and gets to his feet. 'And for the record, if you are forced to be his wife, I'll slit his goddamn throat before he gets a chance to consummate that marriage. I promise you that.' He's being deadly serious. And it makes me feel a lot better. 'Now sleep.'

He turns and heads to the door.

'Thank you, Elder. If I did believe in God, I'd thank him for sending you to me.' He watches me from the door. 'You've had my back since I was five. I'm only alive because of you.'

'That's not true.'

'It is. I was so afraid when I left the orphanage. If you weren't there, if you weren't the one that taught me how to survive, how to fight... well, I just want you to know. Cass, Tee and Winder...' Saying their names makes my insides ache. I have to swallow down a sob. 'They aren't the only ones I consider my family. You're my family too. And if you hadn't volunteered to come with us, I think I would have given up months ago.'

His face falls a little. I think he's angry. But then... there are tears in his eyes. He quickly clears his throat and gives a small, humble nod.

'You have no idea what that means to me,' he says. 'What you just said... I'm very touched. And I want you to know that I feel exactly the same.'

He does?

He clears his throat again and straightens up. 'But if you ever hint to giving up again, I'll kick your arse. Now, get some rest.' He gestures to the makeshift pillow and leaves. Quickly. Wiping his eyes dry as he goes.

As I lay looking up at the ceiling, the sound of the rainforest outside and the water tumbling over the rocks does very little to settle my nerves. Give me a zombie. Give me a weapon to clean. Hell, I'll sweep the floors. Anything to keep me from thinking of the people I left behind. Anything to keep me from the reality of what I'm going to return to. Noah and his wrath. How I betrayed Winder and Tee. How I left Cass so soon after sleeping with him. I don't want to go home. It will put us all in danger. But yet, I long for them more than I long for anything else in this world.

But I love *these* people too. Loom. Chilli. Sky… Elder Eight. They shouldn't have to suffer because I'm a coward. They need to go home. They want to go home. So… I'll get them home.

I close my eyes and much sooner than I expected, I fall fast asleep.

Sky's hysterical giggle wakes me up. I'm still on the bed, sprawled out on my back. And I am sweating hard. My mouth is dry and my head is thumping. I'm overheating, just as Elder warned me I would. This outfit is fantastic for fighting. But not for sleeping in whilst in a rainforest. I undo the buttons of my leather trousers and lift my hips so I can peel them off. I toss them on the floor and sit in my pants and my long black sleeved top.

I slept.

Not sure for how long. But it was deep and I feel better for it. And then I notice a fantastic smell wafting in from outside. Sky gives another giggle. I get to my feet and have a good stretch before heading out to see what's going on.

'SNAP!' Elder hollers as he slams his hand down hard on a crate he's using as a table, making us all jump.

'GODDAMN IT!' Chilli yells back. 'You're too fast!'

Elder chuckles and picks up the pile of cards between them triumphantly before they both continue slamming down card after card. Sky's on her knees watching them play with an enormous grin, her face etched with excitement.

'You're up! Sleep well?' Loom asks quietly. He's sat cross-legged on the floor to my left, stirring a pot that's bubbling away on a small fire. I head down the steps and sit on the very last one and leave the others to play.

'I did. Whatever you're making smells amazing.'

'You must be thirsty.' He hands me his flask. I open it up and drink till my belly's full. He doesn't bat an eye that I'm in my pants. We've lived in each other's pockets for months. Not much shocks us now. Even Sky's taken off her long socks and tucked up her top so her belly is on show. Everyone has a light sheen of sweat but they also look relaxed which is lovely to see.

'How long was I asleep?'

'Only a couple of hours.'

'Oh hey, you're up!' Sky chirps, making everyone look. 'Does that mean we can eat now?'

'Soon,' Loom laughs. 'Eat another banana if you're hungry.'

She jumps to her feet as the others continue playing and heads over to plonk herself on the step next to me.

'I was gonna try and take those trousers off while you were sleeping,' she says, sweeping my sweat-soaked hair from my face. 'But decided I valued my life and left them on,' she teases. 'You must be starving!'

'I am actually. So, what's cooking?'

'It's papaya risotto,' Loom tells me happily. 'Wait till ya taste it. There's beans, papaya, olives, rice... tons of stuff!'

'SNAP!'

With a loud swear word and after sending his cards in the air, Chilli gets to his feet in a huff.

'That's it. I'm not playing anymore.' He charges over to us and sits on the floor with his legs and arms crossed. 'He cheats. That's the only explanation.'

Behind him, Elder's chuckling away as he tidies up the cards. Scooping up his almost empty bottle of rum, he comes and joins us too.

'How's that dinner coming along?' he asks.

Loom has a taste and nods approvingly at his own creation. 'Ready.'

Sky scoops up a pile of plates beside her and hands us one each.

'Right,' Elder says in his usual gruff way, pulling out a new bottle of rum and unscrewing the lid. He points at Chilli. 'A joke or a funny anecdote. Your choice.' He thrusts the bottle in his hand. 'But I fully expect to laugh. Go.'

CHAPTER FOURTEEN

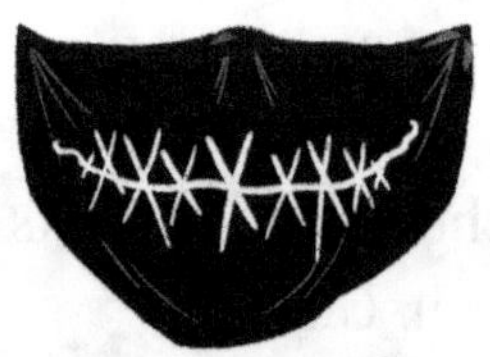

'Hang on. Run that past me again,' Elder groans. His eyes are scrunched closed and his fingers are pinching the ridge of his nose. 'Maybe I'm still drunk. Or maybe I'm just really, really hungover, but I don't understand what your crazy arse is proposing.'

'We take the railings from the fallen stairway,' Chilli explains. 'Attach it to the front of the truck. Add some spikes we can fashion from the branches. And drive through the horde out there. Right up to where the horses are. What's so hard to understand?' His eyes are bloodshot from all the drinking he did last night. And his skin is clammy from the heat. Each swallow he makes look like a desperate attempt not to vomit.

'Great,' Elder grunts. 'Let's charge up the battery with a non-existent power source. Fill up the tank with imaginary diesel. And then get the truck through whatever the hell that wall is made out of, all the while keeping this place intact. I apologise. You're not crazy. You're idiotic!' he barks.

'It's an organic truck!' Chilli argues, waving the guide book in the air. 'According to this-'

'He can read?' Sky groans with her head on her knees and her backside on the floor next to me. 'I didn't know he could read. Do you guys have to be so loud?' She grumbles as I gently pat her on the head. I told her not to drink that much. But would she listen? No. Of course not. She pathetically swats my hand away and moans. 'I think I'm gonna hurl again. Rum is the devil.'

'Yes. I can read. And I can hold my booze too. Unlike you, ya lightweight.' Chilli slaps the booklet over her head making her complain loudly before returning back to Elder Eight. 'According to the guide book, the truck was made with the same sentiment as the rest of this place. To be eco-friendly. It runs on organic material. It's an organic truck! All we have to do is fill it up with stuff off the floor. Leaves and rotten fruit, that kinda stuff, and it should work!'

'That's great,' Elder sighs. 'So we get it to start. How do we get it outside?'

'Well, we can create a pulley system. Use the cables from the fallen bridge to hoist it up... somehow.' He scratches the back of his head as he struggles to create a plan.

'A pulley system?' Elder stares at him like he's insane. 'The roof is over sixty metres high, ya numpty. And how are we gonna get it through the roof even if we do haul it up there? The windows are barely big enough to get *me* through, let alone a sodding truck.'

'We can remove one of the panels,' he says. I'm not sure if it was a question, but it certainly sounded like his resolve was in question.

Elder just stands there with utter disbelief on his face. Even Sky has lifted her head to scowl. Me and Loom have a bowl of leftovers in our hands as we watch the show before us trying hard not to laugh.

'What?' Chilli asks, his face going a little red. 'It could work. We could make the truck into a weapon and drive it down the side of the dome.'

'Or...' I take the guide book from his hands and flick through to a page at the back and show it to him. 'We could use the underground water system they set up.' I tap the page that has a map and details on how it all works. 'Behind the waterfall is a man-made grate. We take that off and climb down into this cavern here. See?' I point to the diagram. 'The water funnels through these tunnels. One goes to the other dome, the other goes to a lake outside.'

'A lake?' Chilli asks, peering at the book. 'I didn't see a lake out there.'

'It's behind that big building to the right where the Class Threes came from before the horde of dome zombies escaped. It's there. And the cavern connects by tunnels big enough to crawl through. I think we should try the tunnels first. If it's flooded or blocked, then we can rethink your truck idea. What do you say?' I look at them all in turn and they all agree. 'Great. I'll finish my breakfast. Sky... sleep off your hangover and then get to work on making arrows. Loom, would you give her a hand?' He nods and carries on shovelling food in his face.

'I'll give you a hand with the grate,' Elder says, still looking at Chilli like he's nothing short of bonkers. 'And Mr pulley system here can gather supplies for the trip home. Seeds and fruit. Bloody truck... down the side of the dome... I mean really.'

'It could have worked,' Chilli mutters to himself as Elder clips him round the ear as he passes.

The grate still hasn't come off after an hour of swearing and shouting. From Elder of course. He's not renowned for his patience. And will he let me help? Course not. I've never heard such language in my whole life actually. And growing up with Winder... I've heard plenty. He must have called those stiff screws every conceivable curse in the English language and then some. If we were at home, he'd have racked up fifty lashes at least. I'm trying so hard not to laugh. Every snigger I'm not able to hold in gets me one hell of a stare as he stands waist-deep in water with his hands and torso reaching behind the waterfall. He's soaked through and keeps getting a face full of tumbling water. But when he slips over and disappears beneath the water completely, I can't stop my hysteria. He jumps up coughing and spluttering as I hold my sides.

'If you think you can do this better,' he snaps, tossing the screw-driver at my head. I protect myself with my arms so I don't get hit. 'Then have at it, you bloody idiot.'

Still roaring with laughter, I double over. His moustache has lost its shape and is sticking up all over the place. He stands there fuming as I fall off the rock I was sitting on and roll about.

'That's it. I'll be back at the hut,' he grunts, wading out the water. 'When you get this sodding thing open, come and get me.'

He storms off, squelching as he goes.

'Need a hand?' Sky asks as they pass each other. He barges into her shoulder muttering profanities to himself leaving her looking to me for an explanation. But I'm still wetting myself. 'What's so funny?'

Finally, I get the last screw loose and can lift the metal grate free.

'Good job,' Sky sings, taking the grate and tossing it to the water's edge before returning to my side. Together, we shove our heads under the cascading water and peer down the dark tunnel. It's brick near the entrance, but further in it becomes a cylindrical metal tunnel which dips downwards into blackness. It's big enough for us to all crawl through. Elder might find it a bit of a squeeze, but as long as it doesn't get any thinner, he should be alright. There's a couple of inches of water trickling steadily down the centre of the funnel, and so far, my plan seems perfect.

'ECHOO-ECHoo-EChoo-echooooo.' Sky watches with wonder as her voice slowly fades away. Then she looks at me with an excited grin. 'Don't you just love this job? Who else can say that they've spent the last twenty-four hours chilling in a jungle, drinking rum and preparing for a journey down a secret tunnel hidden behind a waterfall?!' She whacks my arm and leans in even further. I wrap my fingers around her elbow to stop her from going too far in and taking a tumble. 'It's a bit dark. How will we see where we're going?'

'We'll just have to feel our way. C'mon. Let's go tell the others the tunnel's open.'

It's agreed. One more night and then we head out. We're all worried about the horses, even though they're locked up safe and sound. The sun goes down. The card deck comes out. Loom gets cooking. Elder and Chilli get drinking. Sky's singing made-up songs as she whittles arrows in the corner of the hut, and I'm not in the mood for any of it. As they laugh and joke and sing, I make my excuses and sit alone with my feet in the water, staring at the waterfall that conceals the tunnel out of here. The air is stifling in this place. I feel smothered by the thickness of it. Smothered by the walls. The ceiling. The birds that won't stop tweeting. The crickets that chirp incessantly. This place is amazing. A whole different world than the one out there. But it's still, just another cage. Like the walls back home are. The opening of the grate is right there in front of me. The way out. The pathway back to the real world.

What's wrong with me?

I want to get out of here and out there as soon as possible. I hate just sitting. Waiting. Every second I do nothing, we lose a little more of the world. I could just slide in through that grate. Blow off some steam. Be back before anyone even knew I was gone.

'Sort your head out, Scarlett,' I scold myself. 'Going out there and getting yourself killed won't fix this.' I lower myself into the water completely and cool off.

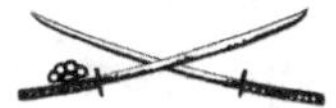

I head back along the path to the others the long way around, wringing out my top as I walk in my underwear. As I approach the hut from the side, I spot Loom and Sky cornering a rather red-faced Elder as Chilli relieves himself behind a tree in the distance. As Elder sits, the other two look very agitated. When they see me, they put on a forced smile and scatter, leaving Elder still sat on the floor looking a bit pissed off.

'What was that about?' I ask, putting my top back on and sitting beside him.

'Nothing,' he grunts, handing me the almost empty bottle of rum.

But a quick glance to Loom and Sky whispering in the distance while glancing at me anxiously tell me that it was something. I take a sip and look at Elder with raised eyebrows.

I just wait.

'Loom heard us talking about Noah,' he says. 'He asked Sky if she knew anything and of course she spilled the beans about what she knows and now they're sticking their beaks in.'

'Did you tell them anything?' I ask, handing back the rum.

'No.' He drains the rest and falls heavily on his back with his eyes closed. 'Now sod off. I'm trying to forget the fact that we have to leave this little slice of paradise tomorrow. Let me relax, will ya?'

Relax? More like drink himself into oblivion. As I watch him, his breathing gets heavier, slower and much deeper. Then... he starts to snore.

Well, a bottle of rum tends to do that.

I reach over and pick up my coat which is tossed over the steps of the hut. I fold it up, gently lift his head to give it to him as a pillow, and lay him back down.

'Thanks, kiddo,' he says sleepily.

'No worries,' I whisper back, patting his shoulder.

As he sleeps, I eat the soup Loom made and watch as he continues talking to Sky. I could go over there. Tell them to cut it out. But to be honest, I can't be bothered to get into it.

'Cards?' Chilli asks, sitting cross-legged in front of me and dealing them out. 'I need to practice if I ever want to beat the old man.'

'Sure. Why not.' I look over at Sky and Loom. 'Hey, you two! Fancy giving the gossiping a rest and having some fun instead?'

I like watching them sleep. Weird. But it's good to see them safe and comfortable. Dreaming their dreams. Not worrying. Not being tense. Sky's mumbling to herself. She always mumbles. I don't make out much. But she keeps giggling and saying - *"Cut it off. Cut it off"*.

She's an odd one.

I get up and have a stretch. We're heading out in a couple of hours. I should really get some sleep myself. As I turn to head inside the hut to do just that, Elder rolls over and mumbles a little himself. Curiosity gets the better of me as I linger.

What the hell does a man like him dream about?

His hand settles on his neck and he starts stroking it. When I look closer, I see a delicate silver chain. It's whatever's at the end of it that he strokes so gently. Then he mumbles my name.

Scarlett.

What the hell?

He falls still and quiet again. His hand falls limp by his side and he continues to snore. I take a look around. Everyone else is still fast asleep. I'm not proud to say, curiosity has definitely got the better of me. I tiptoe over and kneel by his side. My hand lingers just above his chest. The silver of the chain shines in the firelight. Slowly, I reach down and pull it out.

It's a necklace with a silver oval pendant on the end. It's tarnished and very, very old. I can tell that he's worn it for years. There's the faintest engraving on it. I lean in a little closer to get a better look. It's three hearts all entwined with each other.

It's beautiful.

As I look, I see a small catch on the side. I click it and the pendant opens.

Inside is a picture.

A photo.

I've not seen many of those in my time. But it's not the fact that I'm looking at a photo. It's what's in the photo that has me speechless.

'That's not possible.'

'You bloody WHAT?!' Elder bellows in my face and showering me with spit as I finish explaining why he just caught me climbing back through the grate. I'm soaked through and glad to be back in the warmth of the dome after being out there in the bitterly cold, soaking wet. But I needed to get out. I had to. I have no idea what I'm thinking or feeling right now. And for me, that can be dangerous. Explosive. Cass always said I had a temper like a wasp. 'What the hell were you thinking?' he barks. 'You stupid bloody fool!'

'I wanted to make sure the tunnel was clear,' I tell him, wringing water out from my hair and avoiding his stare at all costs.

'What a stupid, irresponsible thing to do,' he snarls. 'You leave without telling anyone. With no weapons and no back up. Through a tunnel that might not even be structurally safe-'

'Well, better it collapses on just me than all of us.'

'Better it bloody doesn't!'

'Let's agree to disagree.' Retying my hair and walking past him without so much as a second glance, I carry on. 'The tunnel's safe and big enough for us all to fit through. It comes out in a clear area. We can get back to the horses without-' As I pass, he grabs my arm roughly. I can't help it. I just react and shove him off me so hard he stumbles back and looks at me completely stunned. 'Don't.' I warn. 'Don't you dare touch me.'

'What the hell is your problem?'

'I have a right not to be touched if I don't want to be,' I snap back. 'Why do you think I volunteered to be out here in the first goddamn place! No man gets to touch me without my permission unless they want the sharp end of my sword up their backside.'

'Don't you liken me to him.'

'Liken him to who?' Loom asks the others quietly.

'None of your damn business,' I snap, before turning back to Elder. 'I'm just doing my job and getting you out of here and back home.'

'Your job ain't to get yourself killed, Kiddo.'

'Scarlett. My name is Scarlett. And your job ain't getting pissed and passing out, Elder Eight,' I argue. His brow furrows as he tries hard not to lose his temper. And so am I. 'We need to get back to the horses.' I look at the others. 'You all wanna get home, right? Chilli, your sentence is almost up. You can get back on the wall. Sky and Loom, you're keen for a break? Some time off before coming back out here? Winter's on its way. With any luck, you can have a few months off if the snow is bad enough. Well, pack up. Your wish is coming true.' I walk away. 'You're all going home. We leave in an hour. Pack your shit.'

'Don't you mean we?' Sky asks as I pass. '*We're* going home?'

'Yeah. Sure. Whatever.'

After shimmying through the tunnel, we emerge in the cold, fresh air by the lake. It's easy enough to get to the horses from here.

'Hello, beautiful boy.' I'm so relieved to see Hanzo and he's clearly happy to see me. I run my fingers through his mane and kiss his face over and over as he nudges me affectionately. 'I missed you too, buddy.'

'So what's the plan?' Loom asks, looking between Elder and me as he runs his hand along the side of his horse. The atmosphere is uncomfortable to say the least.

'Better ask Scarlett,' Elder says, not even turning to respond.

'We could go to the mortuary again?' Sky suggests.

'Oh really?' Chilli groans. 'That place is so creepy. Can't we go back to the church?'

'It's in the wrong direction. We need to start heading east,' I tell him. 'The mortuary's a seven-hour ride from here and it's in the right direction.' And we didn't put that location in a pigeon so it should be safe. 'We'll head there. Good idea, Sky. Everyone ready?'

'Ready,' They all reply.

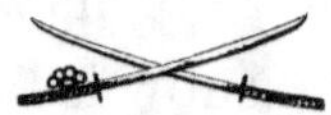

We stick to the main road which cuts through the emptiness of the countryside and leads us clear past the small towns that surround us.

It's a quiet journey.

An awkward journey.

And a bloody cold journey.

The chill in the air has come as quickly as the heat did in the summer. But thankfully we're not too far from our destination now.

'Hello?' Sky says. I look over and see her watching me. 'You alright? You look a million miles away.'

'I'm fine.' I shrug, hating where my thoughts are right now. 'Just cold.'

'I know, right!' she says. 'I'm gonna have to put on some thicker socks.'

'Or some trousers.'

'Nah. I like wearing skirts while I can. Won't be allowed back home. Listen, what's going on with you and the Moustache?'

'Nothing.'

'Is it about Noah?'

'Sky, drop it.'

'Because if it is, you don't need to worry. We got your back-'

'Just drop it!' I almost scream in her face. 'Do you ever shut up? I mean seriously. You just talk and talk and I'm sick of listening to your nonsense. Stop acting like we're friends. We're not, okay! We work together so just stop!' Her whole face falls in a way I've never seen before and her bottom lip even wobbles a little.

Great.

I'm taking out my anger and upset on her. The one person who deserves it the least.

'I'm sorry. I didn't mean-'

'My mistake,' she says quietly. 'I'll err... ride on and make sure the mortuary's secure. *Boss*.' She gives her horse a kick and speeds off as I call after her. The others glare at me as they ride. Elder shakes his head disappointed in my cruelness. I was so out of line.

'Nice one, Kiddo,' he says. 'Real nice.'

'Crap,' I mutter. 'I'll catch up with her and apologise.'

I give Hanzo a kick and he speeds up. He's fast, but he's built more for distance than speed so we can't catch up as easily as I'd like. When she disappears out of sight round the twists and bends of the roads, I start to worry. She's on her own and upset. I'm on my own now too, having left the others behind. But the clatter of hooves behind me makes me turn. Elder Eight catches up.

'If whatever's crawled up your arse and pissed you off gets that girl killed, I'll never forgive you. Ya hear me?' he shouts over the sound of hooves.

'I know. I know! This is my fault and I'm gonna fix it.'

It's another twenty minutes till we reach the large metal gate of the mortuary. It's closed and I worry that she hasn't made it. I climb down from Hanzo and take hold of his reigns so I can lead him through the main gate. It opens with a groan and Elder follows me in.

I'm thrilled to see her standing with her face buried in her horse's neck safe and sound. What doesn't make me happy is the sound of her sobbing.

Elder climbs down before turning to me. 'You *better* fix this,' he says. 'She loves you and you treated her like something you scraped off the bottom of your shoe.'

'Don't lecture me on how I should treat people,' I reply. 'Coming from you, that's a load of hypocritical crap I'm not in the mood for.'

'What the hell is that supposed to mean?' he demands. I turn and head towards Sky. But he has different ideas and abandons his horse to follow me. 'I asked you a question!' he calls after me. Sky lifts her red and tear-streaked face to look at us. I carry on heading towards her, Hanzo's reigns still in my hand and Elder hot on my heels. As I reach her, I secure Hanzo with her horse and rest my hand on her shoulder.

'I'm sorry, Sky. I didn't mean what I said,' I tell her. 'I was just in a bad mood.'

'Hey!' Elder barks, snatching my hand away. 'You owe me a sodding apology too. What the hell is your problem?'

'I don't owe you jack,' I hiss, yanking my hand free. I look back at Sky who's watching us speechlessly. As another little tear slides down her face my guilt goes into overdrive. 'I really didn't mean what I said. I'm just tired and had something else on my mind. You are my friend and I love hearing your nonsense. Honestly. You always put a smile on my face. That reaction was on me and had nothing to do with you. The past few days have been hard for me and I've taken it out on you guys and for that I am really really sorry. You are so much more than just a friend to me. You're family.' I give her a smile which she returns before wiping her tears dry. 'Please forgive me.'

'Of course I forgive you!' she wails, hurling her arms around me and squeezing the life out of me. 'Let's never, ever fight again.'

'Great,' Elder says gruffly, pulling her away and standing in front of me instead. 'What ya got to say to me?'

'Nothing,' I bite back, busying myself with unstrapping my katana harness which has been digging into my side from the speedy ride. 'To you, I have absolutely nothing to say. We're done. I don't like liars. Cos you can't trust them. And trust is all I got.' I lay them gently over Hanzo's back and turn. But he grabs me and hurls me back so I land on my arse before standing between me and the building.

'We ain't done. And you ain't goin' nowhere unarmed. We haven't checked the perimeter yet.'

'I err,' Sky points to the building. 'I'll just head inside and wait for you guys to finish screaming at each other.'

'You don't need to go,' I tell her, getting to my feet and brushing off the dirt. 'Like I said, we're done here.'

'Yeah, I do,' she says. 'It's like watching your parents argue. Ya know,' she shrugs 'If we had parents *to* watch argue.'

'Yeah,' I sigh, glaring at Elder. 'Imagine that. Having parents.' I walk towards him and jab my finger into his chest. Right on top of the locket. 'Just imagine.'

His hand settles over the locket and a wave of realisation washes over his face.

'You saw the locket?'

'Yeah,' I sneer. 'I saw the locket.' I turn and start to walk away, heading towards the mortuary.

'I can explain,' he calls after me.

'No need,' I reply, not even turning to look at him. 'I get it.'

'I don't,' Sky adds.

I turn. 'You wanna know?' I ask her before pointing at Elder. 'He told me that he knocked up a girl back in the day but lost both the baby and the woman before it was even born.'

'Kiddo, you're out of line,' he warns.

'But that was a lie. She had the baby.'

'Stop...'

'And then he took a photo of them all looking *so* happy togeth-er.'

'Scarlett...'

'And then... he donated her. He donated his own child to the army!' I'm trying to keep my calm but I'm shaking with anger.

No.

Hurt.

I'm trembling with a sense of utter betrayal at the picture of the young woman with thick red curls who was the spitting image of me, cradling a baby girl.

Sky doesn't know what to say. It's the first time I've seen her speechless as she looks between Elder and me.

'Does the army mean that much to you?' I snarl at him as he just watches me. 'Did it mean that much, that you gave up your own kid for it?'

'You don't understand,' he says.

'Oh, I understand,' I laugh hatefully, throwing my hands up in the air. 'So, what happened to the woman who gave birth to your bastard daughter? Hmm? Is she still in the army too?'

'Can you let me explain?'

'No need.' I turn and look at Sky. 'Let's get inside.' I walk away from him, scared that if I stay, I'll do something I'll regret.

'Everything I have ever done, every lie I've ever told or choice I have ever made, has been for you. Because I love you!' he calls after me. I slow to a stop, Sky close to my side. 'I reached retirement seven years ago, but I'm still here. Still fighting. Because that's where you are. I'm out here because you are!' I hear him walking towards me.

'Oh my god...' Sky whispers. 'You're her dad?' She's not the quickest. But she's there finally.

Sky's watching him, but I can't bear to turn. He stops behind me.

'You're not a bastard, Scarlett. I married your mum. In secret. She gave birth to you and refused to tell anyone who the father was. I wanted to come forward but she made me promise not to. She knew that I could be executed if I did. When you were born, they took you away and sentenced her to a lifetime in the Canaries, and they put you in the military orphanage to grow up as a soldier. You know the rules we have to follow. It's not like we could be public about our marriage! We had to keep it all secret. When she fell pregnant and got arrested, he made me swear not to tell anyone I was the father. The sentence back then was death, do you understand me?'

'So you had to keep it secret. Fine. But you could have told me! All these years... and not a word.'

'I couldn't risk it. If anyone else found out, if the Grey Coats learned the truth, I would either be killed because of my crime, or I would have been sentenced to a lifetime in the Canaries and then you would have been all alone in the world. And if they knew that you knew, the same fate would have befallen you. I would never risk that. Never!'

'And you just left my mum to die out here alone? After she was sentenced to be a Canary?' I ask, still not able to look at him.

'No,' he says calmly. 'I volunteered. Back then, you did two year stints. I did two stints with your mum before I came back. That's four years.'

'I can count. And then what?'

'She didn't want me to leave her. She had this idea that we could run away and live out here on our own.' He turns me and lifts my chin so I look at him. 'But the orphanage had you. No way I could get you out. They guard it closely, scared that the parents will raid it and take back their children. So I refused to go with her. I had to get back to you. I needed to make sure you were okay. Four years was long enough.'

'You left her?'

'She should never have asked me to choose between her, and our daughter.' Both his hands settle on my cheeks as he smiles at me. 'My dear girl. She was never gonna win that competition.'

'I'll leave you two alone,' Sky says quietly, bowing out and heading towards the door of the mortuary.

'I loved your mum,' he tells me. 'Our love made you. And our circumstances took the chance of raising you as our daughter away from us. I may not have been able to be your father. But I had to have a hand in raising you. Seeing you grow. Watching you laugh. I couldn't get anywhere near you in the Orphanage so I missed your first steps and your first words. I was just a simple soldier and wasn't allowed anywhere near the Orphanage. I had to wait till you were put in The Academy at age five to see ya again. I knew I had five years to get to where I needed to get to. I worked my arse off. Got close to the former Elder Eight. And when he died, I was named his successor. I took his place. I made sure you were in my charge so I could have some say in the way your life turned out. But if anyone ever knew that I was your father, you would have been left completely on your own or even killed. I was about to finally retire. You were gonna get a Red Coat. Or a Black and I could take a step back. Cass had your back. He loves the bloody bones of you, any fool can see that. But then when your stupid backside volunteered for this nonsense, I did too. Cos that's what fathers do for their daughters. They support them. And they keep them safe. Even from the side lines.'

'You did all that for me?' I ask as I try my hardest not to cry. 'You turned your back on your wife and retirement for me?'

'Of course, Scarlett. You're my daughter. I taught you to read. Made sure you didn't get brainwashed by The Verity nonsense. Ensured you grew up strong. Loyal. Tough. That you had good people around you. I always have and always will choose you over everything else. Always.'

'What...' I clear my throat and shuffle my feet, nervous to ask. 'What happened to my mum? Is she still out here somewhere?'

'No,' he says sadly. 'No, Kiddo. She's not still out here.'

'She died on mission?' My voice starts to strain and my throat gets a little tighter. 'Did she-did she turn?'

'No. I told her I couldn't abandon you. That even if we could get you away from the orphanage, this world was no place to raise a child. If we didn't starve we'd be eaten alive or freeze to death when the snow started to fall.' He takes a deep, solemn breath.

'She took her own life, Kiddo. The night before she was due to leave on her third mission. The first one she would have faced without me.'

My lip trembles. I slam my hand over my mouth to stop it. I've never felt like this before. So vulnerable and... and... sad. Not just for the woman who I would have called mum who killed herself. But because of the grief I see so clearly in Elder's eyes.

'I'm sorry,' I whisper. 'If it wasn't for me-'

'None of this is your fault. Never apologise to me. It's me that should apologise to you.'

'You should have told me.'

He nods and lowers his head. 'I won't blame you if you hate me-'

I throw my arms around his neck and hug the hell out of him. His arms wrap around my waist and he hugs me back so tight, my bones crunch a little. But it's the best hug ever.

'Can you forgive me?'

'There's nothing to forgive,' I tell him. 'Even without me having a clue, I always thought you were the best dad I could have ever asked for. I'm sorry I was so cruel. It's me that needs your forgiveness. I acted harshly and said awful things. I'm so sorry.'

'It's alright. It's a shock. I get it. Now, Scarlett. There's something else I need to tell you.'

'What?'

He lets go and looks at me with the kindest expression he's ever worn. 'I wasn't entirely honest with you about what we have been doing out here.'

'What do you mean?'

'I've been working with others. Formulating a plan in which we get to leave Noah and the Grey Coats behind. Where The Verity doesn't rule over us.'

'You mean... treason?'

'The locations we've chosen. The ones that could be new Havens. Well, they will be. For us. We're leaving The Verity behind. It's time to break away and start over without their rule.

Scarlett, they're up to something. Elder One and I... we discovered something terrible. Something-'

A high-pitched, shrill scream has both Elder and I turning to look at the open door of the mortuary.

'SKY?' I call out.

'HELP ME!' she shrieks in a panic. 'PLEASE! HELP ME, SCAR-LETT!' She's absolutely hysterical and the fear in her voice has us both sprinting towards her. When I get in through the door, Elder grabs the waist of my trousers and yanks me back.

'CAREFUL!' he hollers. 'The sodding floor's gone!'

The floorboards have been ripped up making a ditch into the basement. Sky's fallen in and is surrounded by the undead. She's holding one arm to her chest, and wielding a plank in the other as she lashes out at them.

'My arm's broken. I can't move it!' she cries. 'Help me!'

'Hold on!' I tell her as she looks up at me in terror, pleading for help. 'We're gonna get you out!'

She whacks the plank into the head of a Class Three that just stumbles before trying to get to her again.

'There's too many!' She clambers on a pile of bricks and reaches up to a support beam above her head, trying desperately to get out of their reach. But without two hands she can't climb or fight. One grabs her ankle making her scream. She whacks at it with the plank and backs up to the wall.

'I don't wanna die! I don't want them to eat me alive! Help me... please!'

'We're coming,' Elder tells her. As he goes to jump down, I pull him back. 'What are you doin'?'

'I'll fight them. You get rope or something to get us out.'

'You're not goin' down there! You're not even armed!'

'I'm not strong enough to lift you out if you go! Get the rope. I'll be okay.' I take his weapon and give him a shove as he stands, reluctant to obey. Without giving him another chance to argue, I pull up my mask and jump down into the pit.

He disappears from view as I land between her and the Class Threes. I try to swing Elders sword to sever the head of anything that gets too close. But there are too many. I have no swinging space and those I do strike are replaced with more. Their hands grab at me all over. Their jaws are wide as they come for us both. Sky whacks one in the face with her plank, dislocating its jaw and knocking a few of its teeth out.

But that doesn't stop it.

'Scar, we need to get out! There's too many!'

She's right. There are twenty at least.

I slam my foot into the chest of one too close and as it stumbles back, I get enough room to swing the sword and lop its head off. I look up. Still no sign of Elder.

'SCAR, LOOK OUT!' she screams.

I look just in time to see one lunge at me teeth first. I shove my wrist in its face so it gets a mouth full of leather cuff instead. But it's charged at me so hard, I fall back and land on the floor with it on top of me. Then they all start bundling me. The weight of them pushes the air out of my lungs as they all clamber on top of each other, desperate to get to me and Sky. I feel their hands and teeth biting and scratching at the leather protecting my body. I'm not sure if it will hold out against this many. My skin hurts as they chomp down, causing deep bruises. But they don't pierce my skin. Sky snatches the sword from my pinned down hand and starts hacking at them all the while screaming like a banshee. As limbs and guts and black goo go flying everywhere, I see a lone red brick a few feet away. I reach out, wrap my fingers around it tightly and slam it into the skull of the one still gnawing at my wrist cuff. It falls limp on top of me as its head caves in. I hit the one behind that, and the one behind that, until I manage to buck them off and get back to Sky. In a quick move, I pick her up and hurl her up onto the beam. She then stretches out her hand to me.

'CLIMB UP, SCAR!'

I put one hand on the beam and it groans under my additional weight.

'GET UP HERE!' she bellows.

'If I climb up there, it will break and we'll both fall.' I snatch the sword still in her hand. 'Just stay as still as possible and it should hold.'

'What about you?'

I turn and slash at anything that gets too close. They reach up for her, but she's just out of grasp so they turn their attention back to me.

I hack. I hit. I swing and I brawl. I yell and shout as I wield this heavy and cumbersome weapon.

'ELDER!' I call out, slamming the blade through a neck. 'HURRY UP!'

There's a groan. And not the type that comes from a dead thing. The plank holding Sky is giving way and I've ended up on the opposite side of the room. There's a loud creak. I look at Sky and she looks at me. Then with a shriek, the plank snaps and she crashes to the floor.

'SKY?' I scream. 'SKY SAY SOMETHING!'

She doesn't respond and the way they all lift their heads and sniff tell me she's bleeding. They turn away from me and start heading to her.

'SKY!'

Elder lands in front of her, my sword in his hand and a lasso in the other. He swings my blade with skill, killing anything that gets in its way. But it's a wall of monsters. He can't protect her, fight them all and get out.

I see a rusty nail sticking out from the wall and slam my hand onto it hard. And then I pull it down, cutting my flesh in a deep jagged cut. Blood pours from the wound and splatters the floor around me. It works and distracts them. I'm bleeding more than her. That's something.

'HEY!' I yell. 'COME HERE. COME TO ME!'

They all turn and start scrambling to me instead. Behind them, Elder is lifting a barely conscious Sky to her feet and looping the rope under her arms.

'HELLO?'

'LOOM!' Elder shouts back. 'WATCH THE HOLE!'

Loom and Chilli cautiously peer over the edge and survey the carnage below in shock and disbelief. 'What the...'

'PULL HER UP!' I order, bringing the heavy sword down again and again. My grip on the handle is slippery as I continue to bleed. They sprint to the other side and take the rope to heave her up. Once her feet leave the ground, Elder heads to me, cutting through whatever finds itself in his path. Sky is hoisted up and blinks us into focus. As she comes around fully, she starts screaming to be let back down so she can fight. But no one listens. She's no use to us. I swing too hard and the sword flies out of my hands as blood continues to seep from my wound, driving them all crazy. Elder doesn't slow or stop as he forges ahead. He scoops up his sword as he passes it and tosses me my katana which lands in my uninjured hand. Now I can really get to work. This is my weapon. My limb. I drive it through the gut of one and skewer another two behind it like a zombie kebab. Then I yank it up, splitting them both in two. I spin, slicing off the head of another two then reverse my swipe and take another.

This sword is so much lighter. Elder is causing some serious damage with his. Heads, arms and bits of flesh are flying all over the place. When he reaches me, he grabs the back of my head and plants a kiss on my forehead.

'You okay, Kiddo?'

'Fine. You?'

He nods and lifts his sword to bring it down on one behind me as I drive my sword upwards under the chin of one behind him. And when I see Sky's feet disappear over the edge, Chilli reappears with the rope in his hand ready to toss it back down.

'SCAR!' he yells, letting it go. 'GRAB IT!' The floor beneath him starts to groan. The beam that collapsed was holding up a large portion of the floor and without it, they're standing on kindling.

'GET AWAY FOM THE EDGE!' I yell back. 'BEFORE YOU FALL!'

'GRAB THE ROPE!'

A chunk of floor gives way and Loom drags Chilli away just in time. But he drops the rope. I rush forwards to get it back.

'SCARLETT! LOOK OUT!' Elder throws himself between me and a Class Three that leaps at me. He collides with it and lands in a heap.

'ELDER!' I rush over, swinging my katana wildly as I go. When I reach him, he's pinned beneath it. 'ELDER!' I haul it off him and hack its head clean off. 'You okay?' I ask, reaching down and helping him to his feet.

'I'm fine!' he says.

'There's too many. What do we do?'

He wraps his arm around me and pulls me into a hug. 'Elder One,' he says. 'You get back, you tell him our plan. You tell him about the locations we found. You tell him about Noah and his threats. You hear me? No one else. You trust him and you tell no one you're speaking to him. Understand?'

'What-'

'I love you. So much. And I'm so proud of you, Kiddo. You're everything a dad could ever wish for.'

'We're gonna get out of this,' I tell him. 'Why does it sound like you're saying good bye?'

'We don't have long. Fight!'

He lets me go and turns back to the battle. We both do. Side by side. Father and daughter. The floor is so littered with corpses we can barely stand. As we stumble and trip over the pile of bodies beneath us, we never stop fighting. We never stop swinging. And Chilli has Sky's bow, using it to fire arrow after arrow. We add more bodies to the heap and when the last one falls, I clutch my side and gasp for breath before raising my katana high above my head and letting out a victory cry.

'YEAH!' I bellow. 'THAT'S WHAT I'M TALKING ABOUT! WOOO!' I laugh, looking up at the others who are avoiding the edge and watching us with relieved smiles.

'HELL YEAH, GIRL!' Chilli applauds. 'GO, ELDER EIGHT! YEAH!'

'Yeah, great,' Sky breathes. 'Can you both please just get the hell out of there now?'

'Yeah, yeah.' I turn my attention to the floor. 'Do you see the rope?' I look around at the carnage. We're knee deep in bits of zombie. 'Elder, do you see the rope?' I look over at him. He's across the room with his back to me. I can see his shoulders rising and falling as he tries to catch his breath. His sword is still in his hand and he just stands there facing the wall.

'Elder... you alright?' I take a step closer. His breathing gets louder and more laboured. 'Elder?' I ask again.

He drops his sword.

'A-are you okay?' I take another step closer. His body starts to spasm and it sounds like he's choking. His head tilts back and he starts to violently twitch. 'Elder?' I hear the fear in my voice. The dread. The panic and the grief. 'Elder?' But he doesn't say a word.

'Scarlett,' Sky says slowly. 'Scarlett, get away from him.'

But I don't. I take another step closer.

'Elder Eight, can you hear me? Elder... Elder...' I take another step closer and rest my hand on his shoulder. His breathing stops. The twitching. The gurgling. It all ends as soon as he feels me touch him. He stands frozen, looking at the wall.

'Dad?'

CHAPTER FIFTEEN

He turns quickly.

I go to scream. But nothing comes out. My breathing and my voice get stuck in my throat as I stumble back, falling over the bodies of those we just killed together.

His eyes are pure white. His lips are turning black. There's thick, black blood and bile oozing from his mouth and his skin has already started to go grey.

He's been bitten.

It must have happened when he jumped in front of that Class Three meant for me.

He *was* saying goodbye.

He sniffs the air and catches the scent of my blood. All my training's gone out the window. I drop my Katana, fall on my backside and just scramble away as he throws back his head and lets loose the familiar high-pitched howl that comes just before they attack. Everything seems to slow down. I can't get up. I can't get away. I can't say anything.

My Dad's a Class Two zombie.

My dad is dead.

And even as he begins his descent on me, I do nothing but watch. In the background, I hear the muffled yelling of the others. But I can't make out their words. They sound a million miles away. All I can see, all I can hear, is the man that raised me from the age of five. The man that was there for me every day, who taught me how to fight, who gave me advice even when I didn't want it and who protected me from so much.

And now he's gone. He's dead.

But at the same time, he's not!

He's right there.

'SCARLETT!' Chilli yells. 'GET UP! GET YOUR SWORD!' The floor creaks and collapses as they go towards the edge. Elder is on all fours, scrambling over the uneven ground of bodies like a beast as he crawls closer. His teeth bared. Stuff oozing out from his mouth, eyes and ears.

'SCARLETT! FOR GOD'S SAKE! FIGHT!' Loom orders. Elder grabs my ankle. He's snaring like a monster. Barely recognisable. 'SCAR! GET AWAY FROM HIM!'

His other hand grabs my calf. I slam the heel of my shoe into his face and knock him back. But he just tries again. I keep kicking.

'DAD! STOP, PLEASE!'

Kick. Kick. Kick.

I've broken his nose so badly, it's just a hole in his face. His front teeth are gone. And with another kick, his jaw breaks. He screeches as I scream, but he keeps trying to get to me. To kill me.

'STOP, DAD! STOP!'

Kick. Kick. Kick.

'PLEASE!'

He lunges back, and then hurls himself forwards. His limbs scrambling like a spider as I stumble back.

'GET YOUR SWORD!' Sky shouts.

I roll over and claw myself away so I can reach out and grab my katana.

'ON YOUR FEET!' she bellows.

I get to my feet and turn to face him. He still tries to get to me. His face all broken. His body moving in sharp, jarring movements.

'Dad... you're still in there! I know you are.'

'NO. HE'S NOT. KILL HIM, SCARLETT!' Sky orders. 'KILL HIM NOW!'

I have my sword ready. He's getting closer. I back up more and more until I hit the wall. My hands tremble. My whole body does.

'I can't,' I admit in a terrified whisper. 'H-he's my... he...'

They're all screaming my name. Ordering me to kill him. But he's my dad. Even before I knew to call him that, he's always been my dad. His hand wraps around my leg as he pulls himself closer. His other hand grabs me and he drags himself up my body. The others continue screaming at me as Elder pulls himself to his feet. Now in front of me, he opens his wonky jaw and screeches before lunging at my throat. I close my eyes.

This is it.

This is how I die.

And I think... I'm okay with that.

Because I don't think I can live in this hell without him.

I don't think I want to.

My fingers relax their grip on my sword and I feel my body relax all over. We die together.

And that's okay.

That's okay.

'CADET 5-3-6. KILL THE TARGET. THAT'S AN ORDER!' Loom demands, mimicking Elder Eight's voice and tone to perfection. Before I know what's happened, my fingers tighten their grip and my body reacts. Eighteen years of conditioning takes over and I drive the blade of my sword through the side of Elder Eight's skull so far, the hilt becomes slick with his blood. His pale eyes just stare at me. His mouth agape. His whole body goes limp and he falls, bringing me and my sword with him. I pull out my katana and drop it to the floor so I can catch him in my arms.

No... No. No. No. No. NO!

I cradle him and let out a huge, loud, agonising scream that echoes on and on and on. I hold him close.

I rock him.

My Elder.
My friend.
My dad.
Gone.

CHAPTER SIXTEEN

The paper's in my hand. I've written the message. The bird's in the cage right in front of me. But I just sit here, limp and mute on the grass. Staring into the distance. Doing nothing. The air's bitterly cold. I don't feel it. My hand is bleeding. It doesn't hurt. I want to cry. But I can't. I want to scream. But I have no strength.

I'm empty. Completely empty.

'I need to send the bird.'

'Okay. But, Scar, you need to give me your hand,' Sky says gently. She's kneeling beside me with a first aid box in her lap. Her eyes are red and puffy from all the tears she's shed. But as she reaches out for the sixth time to tend the wound on my palm from the nail, I flinch, and she sighs. 'It needs stitches. Please.'

'I need to send the bird.'

'We can do that,' she nods with a little sniffle. 'After I've sewn up your hand-'

'I need to send the bird.'

I'm barely aware of the footsteps behind me. Or Sky looking upwards at someone over my shoulder.

'How's she doing?' Loom asks, his voice strained and over-worked from his grief.

'She just keeps saying she needs to send the bird,' Sky replies. 'She won't let me fix her hand. She won't look at me. She won't let me clean the blood off her.' She stands up. Her legs are in my peripherals. I don't look at them. I just sit and stare out at the world. 'She won't even cry. I think she's broken.'

'Scar doesn't cry,' he adds quietly. Like I won't hear him if he lowers his voice. 'She never has. Not once. She's kinda known for that. And the loop? She's probably in shock. She'll come around. How's your arm?'

'It was just a dislocated shoulder. Chilli popped it back. It'll be fine. I'm more worried about her.'

He walks around and kneels in front of me in my direct line of sight. 'Scarlett?'

'I need to send the bird,' I tell him.

'I know. And we will.'

'I need to send the bird.' I look down at the paper in my hand. 'I need to... I need...' He takes my hands in his. I look him in the eye. 'When did I get out here?' I ask. 'We should get some dinner going or something, right? It's that time of day when we eat. Should we eat?' I nod. 'We should eat.'

'Scarlett, do you understand what happened?' he asks. 'Inside the mortuary, do you remember?'

'I'm not sure,' I admit, looking back over his shoulder at the building. 'You must all be hungry. We should make dinner.'

He lets out a deep breath and gets to his feet to talk to Sky.

'She's in shock. Definitely. She probably won't be able to process exactly what happened for a day or so.' They both look down at me. 'We'll set up camp nearby. Let her have some time...' Their voices fade and everything else seems to shift into focus. The grass beneath me. The sky above me. The chill in the air. The stench of death on my clothes. The pain in my heart.

I killed Elder Eight.

I stabbed him through the head and held him in my arms.

Loom got me out of the pit. I let him manoeuvre my body as if I were a doll. He carried me like a child outside and settled me gently on the grass. Tears streamed down his face. Chilli held Sky as she wailed uncontrollably.

'We really need to stop the bleeding so we don't attract any more... err,'

'Zombies?' I finish. I look up at them both. 'You can say it. He was a zombie when I killed him, right? When I murdered my dad?' As I talk, I feel nothing. The words should make me feel something. Shouldn't it? They both kneel down.

'He was dead before you put him down. You know that,' he tells me. 'You didn't murder him.'

'I stabbed him. I felt his blood on my skin.' I look down. Some of it's still there.

'Scarlett. You listen to me closely.' Loom rests his hands on my shoulders and looks into my eyes. 'Your father was bitten.'

'And I killed him.'

He shakes his head. 'No. You didn't kill your dad. He was bitten. He turned. You put him down before he could bite and turn you. That creature was not your father. You said it yourself, remember? The thing you saw was what killed him. It was wearing him.'

'I'm sorry,' I whisper.

'Sorry?' he asks. 'For what?'

'You were right. They deserve respect. I never thought... I never understood...' I look down at the paper in my hand.

Sky looks behind me and turns a little pale.

I turn to see. And what I see has me to my feet. Everything inside me stops being fuzzy and returns to the sharp, solid and absolute cruelness that has always been my life.

I watch Chilli carry out the body of my father and lie him down on the ground with the utmost kindness and respect. He gives him a small bow and then heads towards us, wiping a tear from his cheek as he does.

He's dead.

That's all there is to it.

But that's not the end of it.

Not by far.

Chilli stands before me. 'Scar, I'm so sorry for your loss. Elder Eight was a great man. And he loved you very much. Even before we all knew who he really was to you, we could all see how much he cared for you.' He reaches out and takes my hands. I feel something in his palm. When I look, it's my dad's locket. 'You should have it. We always called you his favourite, ya know? A Teacher's pet. You totally were his favourite,' Chilli says fondly. 'He called you Kiddo. We all call you The Moustache's Kiddo behind your back. In a nice way.' He then pulls me into a hug and tells me, 'Whatever you need. You got it.'

'I need to understand.'

I manoeuvre around him and head back towards the mortuary, glancing briefly at my father's body as I pass. Only briefly. It hurts to look.

Inside, I stand at the edge of the torn-up floorboards and look down at the carnage below. I have to admit, I'm confused. This floor wasn't damaged before we left. There wasn't so much as a scratch.

The others are all standing by my side looking down with me.

'Sky, when you came into the building, was the door locked?'

'I think you should have a lie down–'

'Sky. Answer my question.'

Loom gives her a small nod. She thinks for a moment, and then shakes her head.

'I locked it when we left,' I tell them. 'I know I did. A hundred percent. I locked that door and gave the key to Elder Eight for safe keeping.' I point to the floorboards. 'They've been torn up. Look.' The splintered remains of the planks litter the edge of the room. 'If it was a collapse, they'd be in the pit. Not up here. The floorboards were stripped and tossed to the side.'

'The hole is too big and purposefully round to be a collapse,' Loom adds. 'And unless a horde of zombies managed to open a locked door, all wander inside, pull up the floor, clamber down, and then close the door after them... this isn't an accident.' He looks at me with shock, his face turning a ghostly white as he realises, 'It's another trap.'

'Like the church. That pit by the well deliberately covered over. Two locations. Two traps. They're not zombie traps.'

'They're Canary traps?' Sky gasps. 'Bloody hell! Someone's trying to off us?'

'Someone seems to be,' I conclude. Elder's final words echo in my head. I know what he wanted. And I think I know that we all want the same thing. I've been with these guys long enough to know they don't respect The Verity. 'Can I ask you all a question?' I turn to face the unit. 'Do you believe in The Verity?'

'In God, you mean?' Chilli asks with a scoff. 'No.'

'No way,' Sky agrees.

'Not a chance,' Loom adds.

'Not God,' I clarify. 'I'm asking if you believe in *The Verity?* Their rules? The way they make us all live? I'm not asking if you believe in God. I couldn't care less if you believe in God or bloody unicorns. I'm asking if you believe in *them?* In Noah? Because I don't. And neither did Elder Eight.'

They all share nervous glances. A conversation like this could end up in some serious punishment back home. But we're not home. We're here.

'No,' Sky says first, glancing at the two others a little worried. 'I don't. You?'

'Me neither,' Loom adds.

Chilli sighs in relief. 'Not even a little bit. The whole system back home is just wrong.'

'Good. Then we're on the same page.' I take a moment to think. And they stand patiently as I do.

'What are you thinking, Boss?' Loom asks.

'Someone murdered Elder Eight,' I tell them. 'He may have been bitten. That I can understand. That I can maybe forgive. But someone human built this trap. Someone human made the trap at the church too. And whoever made them, they're the ones that killed him.'

'The only people that knew we were here are the ones that read the letters he sent back home,' Loom says.

'The church. Maybe. But we didn't put this location in the letters.'

'Then how did anyone know we'd been here?' Sky asks.

'Maybe we're being followed?' Loom suggests.

'Maybe. I don't know. But what I do know is Elder loved my mum. All he wanted was to be her husband. My father. That's not a crime. It hurts no one. And what happened? She got banished and driven to suicide. I got taken away from a family that would have loved me, and I was signed up for a fight before I could even walk. We all were. You,' I point to Chilli. 'You stole a strawberry and got sent out here while the man that grew it, illegally - which in itself is ridiculous - got no punishment whatsoever. Sky, you were so traumatised by an attack when you were little, your hair turned white! And who can blame you. A child up against a Class Two alone? It's a miracle you didn't die. And Loom... well, I have no idea why you volunteered, but-'

'I think this is my fault.' Loom stares at the ground, avoiding all eye contact with any one. 'I think your dad died because they were trying to kill me.'

'Who is trying to kill you?' I ask. He lifts his gaze and it lands on me. 'My Elder... The Elder I had when I was training... well... he used to come into my room, late at night. He wasn't entirely... appropriate.'

'Jesus...' Chilli whispers.

'It was just touching, ya know? But it wasn't right. It went on for about a month. Then, he stopped. Pretended like it never happened. He retired and I never really saw him after that. Then, a week before we left home, I went to the stables to check on the horses, and I walked in on him with a young cadet.' His face screws up in disgust. 'Fucking old pervert. He had his hand down the lad's trousers and I just lost it. I just attacked.'

'I repeat,' Chilli murmurs. 'Jesus!'

'The cadet said he wouldn't tell anyone and we just left him there. The next day, I heard that the old man was in a coma and that the Grey Coats would put whoever did it to death. I panicked and volunteered for the Canaries. What if they found out it was me?'

I close the distance between us and take his hands in mine. There's a deep and dark pain in his eyes. And guilt. How can he feel guilt for this?

'This isn't your fault. Even if this is in retaliation for your actions, it still wouldn't be your fault! What happened to you was awful, Loom. And you putting that old bastard in a coma probably saved a lot of others from the same pain you suffered! But if I'm honest, I think that perhaps, this is because of me. That this is Noah's doing.'

'Noah?'

'He wanted me as his wife,' I confess. 'I said no, so he threatened to kill everyone I care about unless I agreed. I joined the Canaries instead. If anyone gave the orders to have us killed, I would put my bets on him. Either way, this isn't on you and it isn't on me. It's on Noah.' I turn and face them. 'It's on all of them. They all sit under a tent and watch us fight so they can mark us. They take us from our families. They let us die bloody and screaming. They demand we do as they wish. To fight for them. Kill for them. As if taking our freedom and our lives isn't enough, they dare demand our bodies too? That...' I point to pit. 'That was an attempt to kill us by a human. It's wrong. It's us versus the undead. Not us versus other people. Sentenced to this because of stealing, of love, of having a baby, for blasphemy... Joining up because we fear those who are supposed to protect us and keep us safe from harm... it's wrong. I'll die to save my family. You guys. The people I left behind. That's the reason I want to fight. To get this country back.

I don't fight for Noah or Elders or Grey Coats. The only threat anyone should face is from the targets. They should be the only thing we have to fear. But they're not! Back home, being eaten alive is the least of our problems! It's time you know what Elder Eight and I had planned. And what he told me just before he died.' I tell them of our plan to build more settlements. To spread the survivors beyond The Haven. And they're on board completely before I've even finished. 'I propose a world without the sodding Verity. Without the law of donation. Without worshipping a man who is more sinful and cruel than any other man I've known.' I look back down to the pit. 'No one knows about the dome. Or the island off the south coast. We didn't put it in the pigeons.' I turn back to them. 'I propose we leave the Verity behind and make our own life.'

'You want to set up a new base without them?' Loom asks.

'That's precisely what I want to do.'

'I like it,' Chilli nods. 'Where we can love who we want.'

'Where we're not forced to fight,' Loom agrees.

'Where we can have a family.' Sky nods.

'Where we can be free and focus on the real enemy,' I add.

'What do you have in mind?' Loom asks. They're ready to follow any instruction I give them. I see it in their eyes. I keep my promise to Elder and keep the fact Elder One seems to have something to do with this under wraps. After all, it seems that he tried to help poor Loom by sending him out here. 'We're going back. We're not the only ones who want out. We'll go back and tell the others that we plan to leave and if they want to join us, they can. And the person responsible for this...' I gesture to the pit. 'They're gonna pay. Big.' I look at Loom. 'If you don't want to return with us...' I look at them all. 'If any of you want to stay away from home, you can stay at the dome over winter. I can bring others back with me when the snow clears.'

'If we don't do something, more people will suffer,' Loom states. 'We need to return. Together. As a unit. People deserve to choose the kind of life they want to lead.' Loom stands by my side. 'I'm coming back with you.'

'And if Noah or the Grey Coats try to take either of you, they'll get an axe in their face,' Chilli states furiously. His hands tremble as he speaks.

'We have a mission now. It's bigger than us. We know where we can bring others to start over.'

'We're ready to follow you,' Loom states. 'Wherever you decide to take us. Boss.'

'Sure thing,' Sky nods.

'Okay,' I breathe, completely overwhelmed. 'We return home. Gather the people that want to leave. Serve some justice, and then we go.'

'That simple?' Sky asks. 'Who will we ask? What location will we go to?'

According to Elder Eight, Elder One is the man to talk to. But he also said not to mention that to anyone else. So I keep that little nugget of info to myself.

'We can figure the details out on the way back home. I'm going back. I'm gonna find out who did this to Elder Eight. And then, I'm gonna rip their spines out with my bare teeth.'

'I think she's at the anger stage of the grieving process,' Chilli breathes.

'Better believe it. Pass me the pigeon and then let's pack up. We're going home.'

'Yes, Boss,' they all reply.

Canary unit 63.

8/8 bird.

4 alive.

1 deceased.

We're coming home. 1 week out.

CHAPTER SEVENTEEN

Hanzo's getting a little tired. It's been six days of pretty intense travelling, only stopping for nightfall in locations that are unfamiliar and in most cases, unsecure. We can't be too careful. Nowhere we've been before is safe. And I won't risk losing anyone else out here, so everywhere we stop needs to be new. And therefore, cleared from scratch. It's hard work for such little rest. Two sleep. Two on watch. No more than four hours at a time. And as soon as the sun begins to rise, we carry on. Everyone is full of purpose. Worry. Anger. Grief.

And questions.

What's gonna to happen when we turn up with the dead body of an Elder?

Who's been following us?

Was it Noah? Grey Coats?

And for me personally, my question is why Elder One? The man's never spoken to me unless it's been to deliver a punishment or a scalding. What have they been planning? What was Elder Eight talking about?

The others are afraid that I'm returning to my doom. I see their side glances. Hear their secret whisperings. They're twitchy. Uncertain of my choice to go back. They continue to ask if I would be willing to stay out here as *they* return and find out what happened to Elder on my behalf. Sky was more than up for the idea of us camping out in the world together.

But I refused.

I need to find out who the hell's been following us. Why my father died in that pit. I need to see my family. Make sure they're okay. I need to hug the hell out of Tee and hear her sweet little laugh. I need to see Winder's beaming smile. I need to see Cass furrow his brow as I do something he disapproves of, before rolling his eyes and letting the corner of his mouth twitch into a begrudging smile.

And apparently, I need to see Elder One.

But I doubt they'll even want to talk to me. I broke so many promises to them. I swore not to abandon them. That I would always be there. I lied about Noah and the relationship we had in secret. I slept with Cass and then ran off with the Canaries without a word of explanation. My actions led to Elder Eight volunteering. If he hadn't, he'd still be alive and retired. They'll blame me for his death. They loved him too and they should blame me. It's my fault he was out here in the first place. If they didn't hate me, I'd be very surprised. But still, I need to see them. Winder doesn't need to smile at me. I just need to see him smile. Tee doesn't need to laugh with me. I just long to hear that giggle. And Cass, I just need to see those eyes. Even if they're filled with hatred. I just need to see them.

My fingers play with my locket I have around my neck. I've spent hours looking at the picture inside it. My mum had a beautiful smile. It must have been hard for Elder Eight. Looking at me every day. We're so similar in appearance.

'Earth to Scar,' Sky says playfully, trotting right along beside me as we ride east on horseback. She's not left my side since we got out of the pit. None of them have really. They're always watching me. Like they're scared I'm gonna snap. My reaction immediately after they pulled me out of that hole scared them. I was empty and they had no idea what to do.

But I'm better now.

'How's your hand feeling?'

'Fine,' I lie. It's throbbing and stings. Red is starting to seep through the bandage again.

'Will you please let me clean it up?'

'It's fine,' I tell her.

'You haven't been able to fight since Elder died,' she blurts out.

'Cos my hand hurts.' Truth is, every time I look at my sword, the sword I used to kill him, I feel sick.

'I know.' She nods. 'Which is why you need to let me look at it. What if we need your help fighting off a Class Two? What if-'

'My hand hurts. Okay? It will heal when it heals. End of.'

'Alright. Sorry.'

As we ride, she keeps talking. On and on she goes. I have no idea what she's talking about half the time. I just nod and give the occasional, *"yeah"*. I think she feels the need to fill the silence and to distract me. Distract us all from the loudest most painful thing around us.

The bundle that's draped over the back of Elder Eight's horse.

No one can look at it. No one wants to talk about it. I just hold the reigns of the animal carrying the body of my father and stare straight ahead.

Coming into view is the towering wall that protects The Haven.

'We're home.'

As we get closer, my heart starts to race harder. The wall seems taller than I remember.

Weird.

I clutch the reigns of Elder's horse firmly in my hand as we ride. The others have all gotten a little closer, like they're forming a protective barrier around me. And when the main gate with those stupid V's boasting The Verity's authority on the front starts to open, they all stop.

'What are they doing?' Loom asks. 'They never open the gate until they see who we are.' He climbs down and rests his hand on the handle of his axe. 'Scarlett, stay behind us.'

The others all climb down too and stand in a line ahead of me, all with their weapons ready.

'You are not to intervene,' I say firmly. 'No matter who comes through that gate or what they want, you stay out of it and let it happen.' I jump down and stand up front.

The gate has barely opened a crack when a single person squeezes through the gap and starts sprinting towards us, kicking up dust as they run.

'What the hell?' Chilli asks quietly. 'Who is that?'

Sky draws an arrow and points it at the oncoming solider who continues their solitary dash across the wasteland, on foot, straight at us. They're yelling something. But they're too far away for us to hear them. They're moving quick and shouting something in such desperation, I don't know if we should run away from them, or run towards them to help.

'They're yelling your name,' Loom realises, looking at me with a quizzical expression.

'SCARLETT?' they yell. They're so far away, I can barely hear them. 'SCARLETT?'

Sky pulls back her arrow ready to fire. But I lower it and shake my head. Because I think I know who it is.

'SCARLETT? IS SHE THERE WITH YOU?' She screams to us. 'PLEASE. TELL ME SHE'S THERE WITH YOU!'

'Tee...' I whisper. 'Guys, it's Tee!'

'Well, safe to say Tee's happy to see ya at any rate,' Chilli laughs, before looking to me. 'Well? Go on then. What are you waiting for?'

I thrust the reigns of Elder's horse into his hands before breaking into a sprint.

'TEE!' I call out as I run. 'TEE!'

'SCARLETT! IT IS YOU!' She sobs happily, running as fast as her legs will carry her. 'I KNEW IT! I KNEW YOU'D COME HOME!'

I see her tear-streaked face. Her beaming smile. Her relief at seeing me. I feel everything I see on her face and then some. I open my arms. She opens hers.

And we collide.

She grips onto me with everything she has. Her arms are vice-like. Her whole body swamps me. And I know I'm doing exactly the same to her. It would hurt if we both weren't so happy to see each other. She sobs into my neck, talking so fast I have no idea what the hell she's saying. I just hold her. Relieved to feel her hair in my face. To smell her scent. To have the full strength of her hug crushing my ribs.

When she lifts her head, I brush the hair from her face and dry her cheeks with my thumbs. I feel so awful for thinking for even a second that she would ever have it in her to hate me.

'I knew you'd come back in one piece,' she wails, 'You had to. Oh, Scarlett, I've missed you so much. You have no idea.' She pulls me back into a rib-crunching hug which feels so good, I never want it to end.

I bury my face in her neck and just breathe her in. This right here, this is home. 'Is everyone else alright?' I ask. 'The boys, are they okay?'

'They're all fine. But, Scar?' she asks. 'Your letter... who died? Your pigeon.' She looks into my eyes. 'Four alive. One deceased. There was no name. I've been sat up on that wall waiting for you to come back for days. I thought that maybe... it was you.' She glances over my shoulder to where the others are still standing. Her eyes linger on the empty horse carrying a bundle on its back. 'Scar... where's Elder Eight?'

'We-we...' I look over my shoulder at the body draped over the mare. 'We lost him, Tee. I'm so sorry.'

She pulls me back into her arms and once more I bury my face in her neck as she sobs desperately. But these are far from happy tears.

I tell her how sorry I am that I let him die. It's all I seem able to say.

I'm sorry.

I'm so, so sorry.

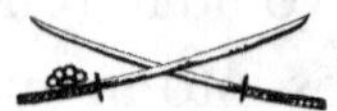

Tee holds Hanzo's reigns as I hold Elder Eight's, and together, we walk them back towards the wall. She's pulled herself together. Just about. But the odd sniffle and whimper doesn't go unnoticed. Our free hands grip onto each other. Her fingers are locked with mine. I'm as reluctant to let her go as she is to release me. Ahead of us, the others walk and lead their own horses. Each one of them looks back at us occasionally. Checking that I'm still there. That I'm okay. They eye her suspiciously. Looking her up and down with clear distrust.

'Wow,' Tee whispers. 'They seem really protective over you.' She looks at me with wide eyes. 'And very hostile. Are they going to attack me?'

'We've been through a lot,' I tell her. 'They won't hurt you. God, I have so much I need to tell you.'

Sky openly sneers at her. As I frown in her direction, she rolls her eyes and returns her attention to the road that leads to the gate.

'Are you sure?' Tee whispers. 'Sky looks like she wants to rip my face off.'

'Err, yeah. I'm sure.' I grip her hand tighter and show her a smile. 'She's harmless. Relatively speaking.' Her eyes shift instead to the increasingly bloody bandage wrapped around the hand I'm using to hold onto Elders horse with.

'You're hurt.'

'I'm fine.'

'You're bleeding.'

'I'm fine, Tee,' I insist a little sharply.

By the time we reach the gate, it's completely open. Sky and the boys head in first and just as I pass the barrier, I hear a joyful cheer before being body slammed with a hug by Owl who's just sprinted down the steps to accost me. Loom draws his sword and gets ready to attack but I shake my head and he holds his position.

'I knew you'd come back, you absolute nutter,' Owl laughs. 'I told Tee that you would, but she refused to budge from my post. Your girl's been up there for days.'

Tee won't release my hand and I can't let go of Elder's horse so it's a bit of an odd embrace. She lets go and holds my shoulders so she can get a good look at me. Her cheery smile soon fades.

'Hang on.' She looks to my side and that look of grief washes over her too. 'Elder Eight? He's the one that... he's not...'

'Yeah. It was him.'

'Oh... oh no...' she whimpers, her hand covering her mouth and her eyes brimming with tears. 'Oh, Scar...'

'I need to go report to Elder One, and...' I nod to the bundle on the back of the horse. I really can't take the look on her face and the sniffles that continue to come from Tee. 'I need to-'

'Of course,' She steps away and gives the saddest little smile while wiping a tear dry. 'Go and do what you need to do.' She throws a nervous glance at Tee. 'Have you told her about... ya know...?'

'I will,' Tee replies, looking between Owl and me with extreme discomfort.

'You need to tell her, Tee.'

'I just want her inside first.'

'So she can't turn tail and leg it?' Owl scorns. 'Like she ever would.'

'We'll see you later, Owl.' Tee gives my hand a light tug and we carry on heading down the path.

'What was that about?' I ask nervously. 'Why would I leg it?'

'Nothing.' She shrugs. That's a massive lie. I wait, watching her expectantly and she knows it. I only need to wait. She'll spill. But Sky doesn't give her a chance to spill on her own. She turns and walks quickly to Tee, stopping so close to her face their noses are almost touching.

'Tell her what you're holding back,' she warns. 'Or I'll make you tell her and you won't enjoy a second of it I promise you.'

Tee looks completely terrified. Without looking away from the girl whose face is in hers, she spills.

'Cass is really angry with her.'

'Is he going to hurt her?' Sky demands.

'N-no one knows what he's going to do,' she stammers. Releasing my hold on the reigns, I rest my bloody palm on Sky's chest and urge her back. She doesn't look away from Tee as she retreats a few steps.

'Don't corner her,' I warn. 'Never. You hear me? I told you. Whatever happens when I return, you're not to get involved. Now, Sky... Back off.'

'Just so you know,' Sky says to Tee. 'Anyone so much as looks at her funny, I'll tear their eyes clear out their skull. Got it?'

'I... err...'

'YOU GOT IT?'

'Sky!' I bark.

'I got it,' Tee whispers, squeezing my hand even tighter as I shove Sky further back and stand between them.

'That's enough!' I hiss. 'Tee's my sister. You'll treat her with some respect. *You* got *that*?' She looks down at my hand and glares at me. 'What?!'

'It's still bleeding. I told you, you need stitches. You need to-'

'I don't need to do anything. You need to take the horses to the stables and get them settled. They're exhausted.'

'But-'

'And then you need to get your arses to the main hall for some food before you get yourselves to bed. We will regroup in the morning. We discussed this. We don't want to draw attention to ourselves!'

'We're not leaving you,' Loom says plainly, his axe out and over his shoulder. 'It's not safe and you know that.'

'GO!' They all watch me. And I glare at them. 'Do not make me repeat myself.'

They obey with a distinct look of annoyance before they turn and carry on ahead of us. I know that if I'm approached by Noah, Grey Coats or even Cass, they'll fight. And my unit will lose. They know their new mission. That's all that matters.

'Wow...' Tee whispers. 'I take it you're the new Canary leader now Elder's gone then?'

I turn to face Tee, who still has her hand in mine. 'I need to know what I'm walking into. Please, Tee. Just tell me.'

With a beaten sigh, she spills. 'Cass says he hates you. He won't let anyone say your name and the other morning, we were sitting in the main hall having breakfast when we heard about the pigeon saying one of you had died. And he-he sort of...'

'What?'

'Said good riddance and stormed off. No one's seen him since.'
Ouch.

She goes on to tell me that after I left, they had no idea what the hell to do or why I did what I did. They went to look for Elder Eight but he'd gone too. Then they all got dragged to the lottery announcement where Elder One called my number as the winner of the lottery. She watches me for a reaction as she talks. My lack of shock comes as no surprise to her.

'You knew you'd be chosen. Didn't you?'

'I can't go into it right now. Please don't ask me to. What happened next?'

'Noah got mad. Like, really mad. He started demanding to know where the winner was. Cass stood up and announced to everybody that you'd left as a Canary that morning. Made a point of the fact that he knew and Noah didn't. There was this really awkward stare between them. Everyone could feel the hatred they had for each other. Then Cass went and said, *"Looks like she'd rather live out there, than be your wife, mate".* Noah ordered Cass be lashed and arrested. He wanted him executed, Scar.'

'What?!'

Nodding, she carries on. 'Cass went quietly. But everyone else kicked off. Even Elder One.' She looks at me with such a serious expression. 'They kicked off big time. Even he was surprised by how many people came to his defence.'

'What charges did he accuse him of?'

'Sex out of wedlock,' she tells me, still watching my face closely. I must have a great poker face because she doesn't pick up on anything. 'He said that Cass must have pressured you into degrading yourself and driven you to flee. That Cass was jealous of him. But Elder One demanded to know what proof Noah had to accuse him of such a thing. And then pointed out how strange it was that Noah knew anything about you or Cass, considering you'd never met. Which of course, now we all know you had met.' Again, she waits for me to add something or deny it all. But I don't, which in itself tells her something I suppose.

'Turns out Noah had no proof about any kind of relationship between you and Cass. And Cass wouldn't deny or confirm his allegations. He just smirked like a prat. And without you here, no one could do anything according to Elder One. But they dragged him off anyway.'

'And then what? Was he okay?'

'The morning after, he was back in the main hall for breakfast. He looked like hell. Beaten black and blue. Wincing as he walked. He wouldn't say what had exactly happened, but he said that he got a punch in.'

'He hit Noah?' I gasp.

'Dunno. That's all he said. Well that, and that you were a selfish coward. That you had got yourself into a mess with Noah and run off leaving him to deal with your crap. And that he never wanted to hear your name again. He said that we're not to talk about you. Or to you. We're to stay away.' She shrugs apologetically. But I'm just glad that Noah didn't have him killed.

'But you're here. Why wait at the gate if he's ordered you to stay away?'

'I'm your sister. I choose you over everyone else. I told him to get stuffed,' she scoffs. 'He may be the Red Coat. But he can't control who I choose to talk to.'

'Has he been awful with you?' I feel terrible.

'He's been so busy with the units, I've not seen him much. He's been okay. Winder and me just try not to talk about you in front of him.'

My whole-body slumps as my insides plummet. She pats my shoulder sympathetically.

Cass hates me. I got him hurt.

'He really said good riddance when he thought I was dead?'

'That's what he said.' She glances over my shoulder to the bundle; a haunted look etches over her features. 'But the look in his eyes when he heard...'

'What? What did he look like?' I hesitate to ask, but I ask anyhow. 'Happy? Sad?'

'Terrified. I think,' she says, her eyes returning back to me as she tries so hard to ignore what lies just behind me. 'I've never seen him look like that before. But Scar, if you had any thoughts of a good reunion between you two, I have to tell you-'

'I don't,' I tell her, swallowing my sadness. 'I know Cass. I know he'll never forgive me.' Her big eyes look into mine with a huge amount of sympathy. 'But I did what I had to do and I can't change it. Even if I wanted to.' My hand slides to her shoulder. 'As long as I've still got you on my side, I'll be fine.'

'Your side *is* my side,' she assures me, her hand resting on mine. 'I'm so glad you're home safe. Well,' she glances at my hand. 'Relatively speaking. Sky is right. Your hand is bleeding. You should get it seen-'

'CANARY 5-3-6?' The formidable tone makes us both jump.

'Ahh crap,' I mutter when I see five Mr Greys blocking our path. 'This can't be good.'

'Scar...?' Tee whispers as she steps a little closer to me. 'What do we do?'

'It's alright, Tee. Just keep quiet. I'll deal with it.' I turn to face them, stepping between her and the weapons they have aimed at us. They're all on foot. Two are pointing arrows at me. Two others have their swords drawn and the fifth is standing front a centre. 'Can I help you, Commander?' I call over, attempting to sound calm. I know it's him that spoke. I know his voice all too well. As ever, all their faces are concealed by their hooded coats. But that won't hinder them killing me where I stand with a more than perfect shot.

'Canary 5-3-6?' he repeats.

'You know who I am, Commander. Is there a problem?'

'You are to come with us. Right now.'

'Why?'

'Surrender your weapons, step away from the Green Coat, and put your hands behind your back.'

'I'll ask again. Why?'

The archers pull back their arrows a fraction as a warning. And when I stay put, they move their aim from me, to Tee.

'I will *not* ask again, Canary,' The commander states. I look at them each in turn. But I can't see a thing beyond their hoods. Noah could very well be among them.

I turn and place the reigns of Elder's horse into Tee's hand. What else is there to do? She trembles as she takes them.

'What do I do?' she whispers in a panic. 'Shall I fetch help? Your unit maybe?'

'Just, just take Elder Eight to Elder HQ. Tell Elder One that the Grey Coats have me. Only him, understand?' I try to pry my hand free. 'I have to go with them, Tee. Let go.'

'I'm not leaving you.' She tightens her grip. Her fingernails dig into my skin.

'Tee, you have to let me go, before they shoot you.' I take hold of her wrist. But she won't release me. 'Tee. Let go!'

'I just got you back. I can't lose you. I really can't!' she exclaims, tears brimming in her eyes. 'You don't understand. You can't leave me again!'

'Canary!'

'Yeah. Hold on, Commander!' I snap. Tee's breaking apart in front of me. Her nails are drawing blood. What the hell is the matter with her? Why does she look so frightened? 'Tee, listen to me. You have to let me go. Everything will be fine.'

'You don't know that!'

'Trust me. It'll be fine.' I manage to pry myself free before they do actually let loose an arrow. With a kiss on her cheek, I step away.

'Your weapons, Canary.'

'Yeah. Yeah.' I undo the buckle on my harness and hand my weapons to Tee. 'Look after those.'

'They can't do this!' she insists.

'Pretty sure they can, cos ya know, they are. Just, take care of Elder Eight for me. And make sure the others stay out of trouble,' I add. 'The last thing I need is for them to come charging after me.'

'Step away, Green Coat,' Commander warns Tee. She steps away, holding my weapons and the reigns firmly in her hand.

'On your knees. Canary. Hands behind your back.'

I lower myself down and put my hands behind my back. She doesn't take her eyes off me as one of the swordsmen makes their way over to cuff my wrists together.

'Everyone knows she doesn't want to marry Noah,' she says in a panic to the Grey Coats. 'He can't force her. Not now.'

Safely restrained, the commander stands before me. I crane my neck upwards and see the slightest smile beneath the hood.

'I think marriage is on the back burner now, Green Coat,' he scoffs. 'He has something else planned.'

'Gonna sentence me to the Canaries?' I laugh.

The next thing I see is his fist as it slams hard into the side of my face. I land on my side in the dirt as Tee screams. The Commander kicks me in the gut. Then again in the ribs, flipping me over so I'm on my back coughing and wheezing as blood fills my mouth. The Grey Coat who cuffed me grabs Tee as she tries to intervene.

'You can't do this!' she cries. 'STOP!'

'You embarrassed him,' The Commander snarls, lifting me by the scruff of my coat and giving me a rough shake. 'Your infidel friend laid hands on the most divine.'

'Yeah. I heard Cass got a punch in,' I mock, although my words slur a little.

'Yeah. Your man got a lucky punch in. *You'll* pay for that insult.' He reaches into his pocket and pulls out a pair of pliers. Big metal things made of solid steel. 'He punched him in the mouth. Knocked out one of his teeth.'

'You just punched me. So, who gets to punch you?' I laugh, but choke on my blood as I do.

'And so, the lord said...' He tosses me on the floor, winded and dizzy. 'If there is harm done, then the one that harms shall pay.' He kneels over me, a leg each side and my arms still cuffed behind my back. His fingers go in my mouth and he prises open my jaw, forcing the pliers in between my teeth. 'An eye for an eye.' He clamps the pliers around my back tooth. Tee is screaming so hard; the Grey coat covers her mouth. 'A tooth for a tooth.' His face scrunches up as he gets a grip. My legs are kicking out as I try to get him off me. I'm yelling a garbled yell past the metal and the blood. 'Welcome home, Canary.' He pulls. The pain as my tooth is yanked from my gum has me furiously yelling. More blood fills my mouth as he admires the molar he's just stolen. He laughs and slides it in his pocket then heaves me to my feet. I try to ignore Tee looking on in a helpless mess as I sway. The Commander spins me. I can tell he has a cruel smile beneath that hood. I spit blood in his face.

'What? Noah not brave enough to torture me himself?'

'Oh. He wants to torture you. He wants to break you. And he will. That was just my own personal welcome home. Come on. Let's go.'

Tee is thrown to the floor but she's soon back on her feet. Tears streaming down her cheeks but a fury like I've never seen in her eyes.

'Where are you taking her?!' she demands.

'Canary 5-3-6 is under arrest.' He throws back over his shoulder, already leading me away.

'For what?'

'For desertion of duty,' he says. 'And you know what that means?' He wraps his fingers in my hair and yanks my head so I'm looking up at him. 'The sentence for which is death.'

'DEATH?!' Tee screeches. 'YOU CAN'T!'

'Your sentence is to be carried out at first light. Until then, Lord Sands will keep you company. And he has much worse things than pliers waiting for you. I assure you.' He looks over his shoulder to Tee. 'Her execution is scheduled for tomorrow morning. Seven am. Attendance is mandatory. We'll see you then, little Green Coat.'

I'm dragged away.

'Go find Elder One, Tee!' I yell back. 'GO! NOW!'

End of part one.

THE VERITY: PART TWO
MJ LAWRIE

CHAPTER ONE

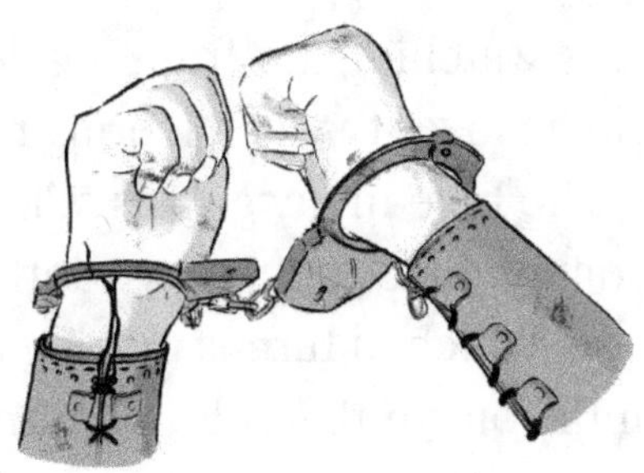

As welcome homes go, this sucks!

Standing in the lobby of the Guardhouse - a building I've only seen from outside and never, not once, had the inclination to enter - has me so anxious and so furious, I could scream. This is where every soldier convicted of a crime severe enough to warrant a death sentence or a Canary Coat is brought. Around the back of this cold, authoritarian building is The Courtyard.

Where they execute people.

Where *I* am to be executed.

This is where every soldier convicted of a crime severe enough to warrant a death sentence or a Canary Coat is brought.

Chilli was brought here when he was sentenced to the Canaries. It's exactly as he described it, too. He even got the smell down. Sad desperation. I never thought that was actually a smell.

But it is.

And it stinks.

The Guardhouse's lobby is a large space with high ceilings and no windows whatsoever. The floors are made of cracked and uneven grey stone-slabs. Cast-iron chairs have been bolted into them and they line every wall. Ahead of me is a bare concrete staircase that twist upwards and out of sight. The Grey Coat Commander disappeared up there several minutes ago and ordered me to stay here.

On the walls, portraits of the Sand's family hang side by side. Noah's face is watching me from a golden frame with that self-righteous grin he loves to wear, leering right at me. I fight the urge to spit at it. The hole in my gum is still bleeding and throbbing. Sodding Commander, taking my tooth. I keep swallowing mouthfuls of blood, which in turn is making me want to hurl.

I've spent months out in the wild. Fighting Class Threes and Class Twos. I've gone days without sleep. Without food. I've defeated foes I had no right in defeating. Survived impossible odds.

And where has it got me?

Stuck in the lobby of the dankest and most depressing building I've ever had the displeasure of seeing, in handcuffs no less, waiting to be executed.

That's where.

I've seen more welcoming sites in the derelict buildings left to rot out beyond the wall.

I'm not allowed to sit and two Grey Coats continue to hold my upper arms so tight, I'm bruising. Two others are positioned by the thick wooden door behind me, marking the only exit. I watch it closely, hoping to see Elder One emerge.

We wait.

I can't believe I had to leave the body of my dead father in the hands of my devastated best friend who just told me that Cass hates me so much, he was glad that I might be dead.

Bastard.

Suppose he's about to get his wish. He can sit upfront when they tie the noose around my neck.

It's been years since they've executed anyone and not once has it ever been mandatory to attend. Usually, they just sentence criminals to the Canaries and let the un-dead do their dirty work for them.

A door creaks as it opens upstairs and the voice of the Commander carries down from above. Shortly after, he appears and gestures for the brutes holding onto me to bring me up.

I glance back longingly at the one and only way out of here.

Still no sign of Elder One.

The Grey Coats push and shove me unnecessarily. If I stumble, they tighten their already impossibly tight grip and watch, keen to hear me complain. But they won't hear me utter a single world.

My lips are sealed.

Up the stairs we go, onto a long landing that looks just as cold, grey, unwelcoming and harsh, as the lobby below. At the end of the hallway is a slightly ajar white door with a silver handle.

We stop this side of the threshold and I smell a burning fire inside. Hypocritical sods. It's not cold enough to light a fire yet. Not for us.

But it would be... for *him*.

Heaven forbid he gets chilly.

The Grey Coat commander raps his knuckles on the door and the heavy footsteps inside get closer. I put on a smile for the man who opens it fully.

'Fancy seeing you here,' I greet.

'Well... hello, Cadet. Long time, no see.'

I look past Noah to the little setup behind him. It's a plain, square room with the same grey walls as the rest of this place. There's a large wooden table to the back, two chairs on opposite sides, a pot of tea in the very middle and two mugs, all set in front of a roaring fire in the fireplace.

'I have been worried sick,' he sighs in apparent relief. His hand reaches out and he tucks my hair behind my ear, just as he always did when he would see me. 'Every day that you have been gone has been torture. Utter torture.' His palm settles on my cheek. His features ease into a disingenuous sadness as he steps closer, pressing his body into mine.

I remain silent as he surveys me. His eyes flick back and forth as he tries to read my raging thoughts. I'm not exactly hiding the hatred I have for him in my sneer but that doesn't stop him staring deep into my eyes and soul.

His other hand holds my hip firmly and he steps even closer. I feel his heart through his chest as it hammers hard, not that you would ever tell by the serenity on his face. My heart races just as hard, hating his closeness and wishing more than anything I had my katanas to hand to force through his neck.

He leans in. His forehead rests on mine as he lets out a long breath, closing his eyes as he does.

'Oh, Cadet. I thought I was never going to see you again. How could you leave like that? Without a word? Without any warning?' His eyes open. The corners of his mouth twitch before he utters his next words. 'It's a miracle that it was only your Elder that perished. Thank the lord that you survived. Praise God that he chose to spare you.'

I snatch my face from his grasp and step back, causing the two Grey Coats still holding onto me to harden their grip.

'God had nothing to do with any of this.'

'God has everything-'

'Fuck God,' I hiss hatefully, leaning towards him slightly. The Grey Coats hands tighten. 'And fuck you. If you're gonna kill me, get on with it. I'd rather the noose around my neck than have to listen to your sanctimonious bullshit, or have to suffer having your hands on me ever again.'

His entire face goes rigid. Pure rage burns behind his eyes as his teeth grind together. But still, he attempts to remain calm.

With a small side-step, he clears the doorway for me to enter. 'You are clearly upset. Come inside. Let's talk.'

'Talk?' I ask. 'About what? Something you want to get off your chest, Noah?'

'Lord Sands to you, Cadet,' he says, his fists balled up by his sides. 'Now, like I said, inside.' He gives a small nod of his head, gesturing me to join him.

'Nah.' I laugh at the mere idea of stepping inside that room alone with him, with no weapons and my hands still cuffed behind my back. 'I don't think so.' I bump into a Grey Coat as I step away.

'I said... inside.' Noah snarls, narrowing his eyes. 'Now!'

'I'm good out here. Thanks.'

'You think there's nothing I won't do to you in here alone that I won't do to you in front of my men?' he laughs angrily. 'Get inside.'

'I'm allowed an Elder representative with me for all hearings. I'll wait.'

He steps forward, not stopping until he's towering over me. His chest is crushed up against mine and I feel him shaking with rage.

'I said get the fuck inside, Cadet. Or I will drag you in here myself.' He's pinned me between his body and the chest of the Grey coat at my back.

'You'll have to drag me in then,' I hiss in reply. 'I am not going in there willingly.'

'As you wish.' He reaches out and wraps his fingers around my throat. He flings me inside and tosses me on the floor, slamming the door shut behind him.

I hit the ground harder than I'd have liked and with my hands still cuffed behind my back, my face takes quite a hit. He remains by the door for a few moments, his back to me as he takes numerous deep breaths in and out. Slowly, his shoulders relax. His fists unclench and when he turns to face me, he seems calmer. He walks slowly and at his leisure around me as I roll myself over onto my back. As I go to sit up, he slams his boot on my chest, keeping me down.

'Despite your hostility towards me, it is good to see you again, Cadet 5-3-6. I have truly missed you.'

'I wish I could say the same. And it's Canary, actually. I graduated. Remember?' I correct him, making his eye twitch. 'So, you want to sentence me to death because I turned you down? Rejected you? Bit pathetic, don't you think? Even for you.'

His fingers flex slightly and he's forcing himself to breathe slow and steady.

'I know that the way we left things wasn't ideal-'

'You threatened to kill my family unless I agreed to be your wife!'

'And I planned to say sorry for that but you left before you gave me the chance.'

'Sorry?' I scoff. 'You're sorry? I glance at his boot which is currently pressing down hard on my chest. 'Yeah... I'm feeling the apology.'

'I'm trying to make this right!' he barks at me, his foot becoming heavier. 'Just... accept my apology and agree to give me another chance.'

'Another chance?'

'Yes. All I have ever done is love you. Train you. Try to protect you! I wanted you to be my wife rather than die bloody in a war that we will never win! Why is that so bad?!'

'Is that all you have done, hmm? Love me? Protect me?' I laugh and shake my head. 'You have destroyed my whole life, Noah. You have done far worse to me than try to make me your wife and you know it.'

'What is that supposed to mean?'

I know there's blood between my teeth and that a steady stream of it is dribbling down my chin, but I still put on a smile for him.

'It means that you're going to pay. And I promise it's going to hurt.'

He lunges down, grabbing my hair. I give an angry yell as he drags me across the room towards the desk before slamming my face down into it so hard, the teacups fall with a crash to the floor. He holds me there with his hand at the base of my neck.

'GET THE HELL OFF ME!'

'No,' he says, taking a fist full of hair and lifting my head before smacking it into the table. The hit knocks me senseless. 'That was for blaspheming.'

'I'll do more than blaspheme if you hit me again.'

'Stop struggling, or I'll give you another hit, Cadet.'

'THAT'S CANARY! YOU HOLIER THAN THOU PIECE OF SHI-'

Bang.

'Language!' he warns as I blink the room back into focus. 'You will not take the Lord's name in vain! You hear me?' He leans down into my face, a nasty smirk on his smug face. 'Now, tell me what you meant by that? What else have I done to you exactly?' He asks, daring me to accuse him of something.

I keep my mouth shut. If I come right out and say that I believe he orchestrated my father's death, he might just cut his losses and kill me here and now. And more than likely my Canaries just in case they suspect him too. The mission my Canaries and I have now is too important to jeopardise this early on. We need proof if I'm to get my revenge without putting the people I care about in danger.

'Well?' he pushes.

'I know you hurt Cass,' I tell him instead. 'You've made him hate me and turned him against me.'

'You did that yourself when you chose him over me and then left us both.'

He leans down and softly runs his nose along my jaw. His free hand runs down my spine before resting on my backside. He moans in pleasure which makes me turn cold from the inside out.

'Get off me, Noah.'

'That's Lord Sands to you. But I will accept husband. Or beloved, if you prefer. But I'll leave that up to you of course. Wife.'

As I laugh in his face, he gives me another hard bang. The pain makes me silent and I struggle to fight the urge to throw up. Knowing I'm far from my normal capabilities after three hard knocks, he loosens his grip and spins me around so I'm on my back across the desk. He rests his forearm across my collar bone and maintains a fair amount of pressure as I blink up at him.

'You're looking a little dazed there, Cadet,' he smirks, brushing my hair from my face. 'Oh, and look...' He wipes my eyebrow with the cuff of his sleeve and shows me the red that stains it. 'I made you bleed.'

'I'll make sure to return the favour one day soon.'

He simply laughs.

'What do you want from me, Noah?'

He presses his arm down a little, making it difficult to get a good breath.

'I'm pretty sure I've made that perfectly clear.' He takes hold of my chin and directs my attention to something in the corner. It's a dress, draped on a hanger. A long, white, lace dress. Complete with a floor-length veil.

'You'll look very pretty in it,' I tell him. 'It'll definitely bring out the psycho in your eyes.'

Whack.

I groan and see spots before I lose the ability to hold my own weight. He has to keep me from sliding off the table. 'Keep hitting me if that makes you feel better,' I slur, shaking the fog away. 'You can do it till my skull breaks and my brain leaks through my ears. But I ain't marrying you. I mean it.'

'As do I,' he replies. 'Every single word I'm about to say. So listen closely. You entered your name into my lottery. You were chosen.'

'And then I left,' I snipe. 'Take a hint. You're coming across as desperate.'

Whack.

'I'm gonna be sick if you do that again,' I warn. 'And I'm a good aim.'

'As I was saying. You were chosen. You still are. So, you're going to take off these trashy clothes you have on, put on that dress, and in ten minutes an Elder will be here to wed us.'

'Not gonna happen.'

His arm slides up and he presses harder on my windpipe.

'Kill me,' I wheeze. 'Better dead... than your ... wife.' He keeps pressing harder, but he won't shut me up.

'You do not have a choice, Cadet.'

'Canary...' I gasp.

'You will marry me. I need you to. Not only because I love you, because I do love you, Cadet. Against my better judgment and common sense, I love you. But also because I need you to help me.'

'Need me to... help... you?'

'I need you to stand by my side. The army's *"darling"*. The one all the others look up to and admire. The one they trust, even above their Elders in some cases.'

'I think you're overestimating... Noah... I can barely breathe!' I wriggle beneath his hold but he refuses to let up.

'I have big plans, Cadet. Huge! Drastic! The survival of humanity is within our grasp and with you by my side, supporting me and loving me, we can start building our new world order.'

'What the hell are you talking about?' I ask breathlessly. 'You sound insane!'

'Just... say yes. Just love me!'

'I came here to be executed. Not to marry you. And certainly not to love you.'

He presses harder. I feel the pressure in my lungs as my body starts to scream for oxygen. My eyes begin to bulge.

'Really?' he asks, eyebrows raised and an expectant look on his amused face.

'Re-a-ll-y.'

'Fine. Then we'll do this with you unconscious. Once the Elder gets here, he'll sign the paper that will legally make you mine. I don't need your permission. Just his signature and his word that you agreed. Which he has guaranteed to give. Even if you prove... resistant. I'll give the announcement in the morning and declare to one and all that you returned from your brave and daring adventures beyond the wall more determined than ever to lead us all to victory, with me by your side as your loving husband. But due to your grief at losing your Elder and the injuries you suffered, you will be resting in private for a while. And then, when you have become more... compliant... you will return. With you by my side and with the Sainted Army looking to us both as their leaders, the real work can begin.'

'You can't – do - this.'

'Yes, I can. I would rather have you willingly wed me, but I know that in time, you will come around to my way of thinking. One way or another. Everyone has a breaking point, Cadet, and I am very excited about finding yours. And when I have stripped all your defiance and disobedience away, you will be mine in totality. So sleep, my love. For when you wake up, you'll be my wife.'

'And I'll slit your throat.'

He holds me down tighter. I'm not getting any air. It's starting to go black. My legs weakly kick out. I try to wriggle free but my hands are still in cuffs and I can't. I'm less than useless. My eyes start to close. This can't be happening! I joined the Canaries to stop exactly this from happening. I lost Elder Eight in the process. And Cass.

'LORD SANDS!' bellows a familiar and most welcomed voice. 'I suggest you release your grip on that Canary and step away, *Sir.*'

'This is of no concern to you, Elder One,' the distant echo of Noah's voice replies. I'm on the very edge of unconsciousness. The very, very edge. 'I suggest you leave. You have no authority over me whatsoever.'

'Perhaps not you, my Lord. But I do have authority over her.'

'Not more than I do, I'm sure.'

'I'm afraid I do,' Elder One insists. 'I have something you need to see.'

There's a moment of agonising silence before thankfully, Noah releases his grip on me and lets me fall to a heap on the floor, gasping and coughing as I greedily take in as much air as possible. Before I get a chance to move, however, he presses his boot down on my neck, applying just enough pressure to keep me down and for barely enough air to get into my lungs I look to the open door where Elder One stands accompanied by Elder Ten - The Elder who still works on the wall and would reward me with apples every time I guessed the correct answers to his riddles - As well as three Black Coats. Elder One has a hand resting on the chest of the man beside him, stopping him from going any further into the room which is clearly all he wants to do. A simple hand gesture and the Black Coat is very begrudgingly obeying him.

It's Titan.

One of the members of my unit before I left home. The gentle giant I grew up with and one of my closest friends.

Boy... am I glad to see him! Even if I am under Noah's boot.

Titan's eyes are on me completely and he looks livid at what's happening. His chest is rising and falling from anger and his fists are clenched as he looks at Noah.

But he stays.

Funny thing is, Titan could easily flatten Noah with a single punch. But no one would ever lay a hand on him. It would mean death. Simple as that. Hundreds of Grey Coats would tear any attacker apart. I couldn't have made any real attempt to fight Noah off even if I wasn't cuffed and bashed about first. One strike, I'd be killed then and there.

'There is no reason for you to be here, Elder One,' Noah says, applying a little more pressure to my neck. 'I have dropped the charges against her. Seems she has returned home to fulfil her duties as my wife, and Elder Two is due any moment to officiate our wedding.'

'I'm afraid you must hand over the girl to me,' Elder One says with a polite smile as Elder Ten openly scoffs at Noah's obvious lies.

'I have the ultimate authority. Over you and over my bride to be. She is my property. Always has been. Always will be. What I do with her is of no concern to you.'

'I intervene with your best interests at heart, my Lord. I personally don't care what goes on between you and the girl.' Elder One shrugs, sounding beyond disinterested. Even bored. 'I am simply following the laws which you and your family put in place.'

Elder One holds out a piece of paper for Noah to take. Everyone stays put. Noah doesn't move an inch and neither do the Elders. This standoff is getting more unbearable with every second. I can barely breathe and his boot isn't getting any lighter.

'Can someone bloody move?' I wheeze. 'A little uncomfortable down here.'

'Language!' Noah warns, before holding out his hand. 'Bring the letter to me, Elder One.'

Elder One bows and heads over. They stand by my head, neither one acknowledging me as Noah takes his sweet time reading. Titan's looking between me and the wedding dress behind me. Elder Ten has his hand wrapped around his wrist, just in case he does decide to charge in and hurl Noah off me. Titan's eyes settle on me.

"You alright?" he mouths silently.

I give the slightest of nods, as much as I can in my current position. Elder Ten gives me a worried wink as he watches us all anxiously.

Noah's eyes dart from the paper to me and there's such hatred in them, I worry he'll just snap my neck and be done with it.

'Did you know about this?' he demands. Instead of giving me the ability to speak, he nudges his foot down a little harder, making my legs kick out. If I could catch a breath, the language I'd be hurling about would probably earn me a thousand lashes.

'She does not,' Elder One replies. 'Which is why I came as soon as I heard she had returned with Elder Eight's body. Now, I must insist you let her up, Lord Sands.' There is slightly more agitation to his voice. But only slight. Noah either doesn't notice or he simply doesn't care. He scrunches up the paper and tosses it into the fire.

'What you have shown me makes no difference. The facts remain the same. This cadet-'

'Canary.'

'Shut up,' he spits at me without even lowering his gaze. 'She put her number into the lottery. She was chosen. And now she has chosen to fulfil her obligations to me.' Someone clears their throat by the door. Everyone turns to see a thin, paled-complexioned man standing in the entrance. 'Ahh. Just in time. Elder Two, come on in. My bride will be ready shortly.'

The newcomer looks down at me pinned beneath Noah's boot and then to Elder Ten and One nervously.

'Now,' Noah sighs with a great amount of agitation. 'Leave us and take your Black Coats with you. It's our special day. One I've waited far too long to enjoy.'

'Don't,' I gasp, looking up at Elder One pleadingly. 'Don't leave me here. I don't consent.' I start to thrash. Is this really going to happen? It can't! I've been through too much to *stop* this from happening. 'I don't consent! I don't con-'

'SHUT UP!' Noah roars.

'NO!' I yell from beneath his hold. The more effort I put into forcing my voice past the force of his boot the more my throat burns, but I will scream until I lose my voice for all eternity before I let this happen to me. 'I DO NOT CONSENT TO THIS AT ALL!'

As I struggle beneath him, he gets angrier. His foot becomes heavier.

And Elder One laughs.

He sodding well laughs at me!

'She's feisty,' he chortles, lowering his gaze to meet mine. 'It's amusing that you think what you do or don't consent to actually matters, Canary.'

'Her feisty nature is nothing a good bit of physical discipline won't resolve,' Noah replies. 'Like I said, if you'll excuse us-'

'I am sorry, my Lord.' Elder One interrupts, resting his hand over his own heart. 'But I simply can't do that. As you read, she is now in my charge. She must come with me. I am sorry, sir, but a wedding between you and this Canary is simply not possible by law. *Your* law, might I add. Even if she has changed her mind and returned home to become your wife.'

'She was eligible when she put her number in!'

'And now she is not eligible. You cannot break your *own* law to fit your desire.'

'Well, I burnt that letter. So-'

'That was merely a copy. The original is back at Elder HQ with six other Elders who have all seen it.'

'And word has gotten out to the rest of the Army of its contents,' Elder Ten adds. 'More will know than not know by now.'

Noah's getting angrier. His foot, heavier. Both Elders simply remain passive.

'She returned less than an hour ago. How has word gotten out?' he snarls.

'Loose lips. I will ensure that whoever owns them will not get the chance to be so careless in the future. I am sorry but the girl cannot legally marry. Not until she reaches the age of retirement at any rate. Not unless you want the whole Sainted Army to revolt. We must follow the law. If *we* do not, why should *they*?' Elder One asks plainly. Noah says nothing. 'And now, I really must insist you remove your boot from her throat and let her up. I have the entire Elder Council waiting for us to return with her and if I don't, the other Elders will simply come in my place. And they will be accompanied by far more than three Black Coats.'

I'm confused as hell and have no idea what was on that paper. Or why I suddenly have the full force of the Elders behind me. But I'll take whatever's going on as a win.

'Are you threatening me?' Noah asks furiously. 'You and your fellow Elders are living on borrowed time, I assure you. So I would be wary of your welfare if you dare threaten me again.'

Borrowed time?

'No, Sir. I am not threatening you. Not at all. I am just stating the facts.' He nods to Noah's foot on my throat. His eyes never leaving Noah's fury-filled face. Begrudgingly, Noah lets go and steps away. 'On your feet!' Elder One orders.

No one helps as I struggle to get myself up. I stumble and sway. I'm definitely a little out of it and I have a trickle of blood making its way down the side of my face.

'Come along, girl.' Elder One steps aside, still not looking at me in the slightest. 'Hurry up. I don't have all day and people are waiting for us.'

As I pass, Noah grabs my arm and stops me. 'She's still under arrest.'

'Any charges brought up against her are to be dealt with by the Elder Council now. But, my Lord, you know that there is no law against joining the Canaries. And there is no law against a betrothed getting cold feet and calling off a wedding.'

He's beat. He knows it. I don't know why exactly, but I'll accept it. With his face in mine, Noah issues me one final threat.

'This isn't over.'

'You're not wrong,' I warn. 'This is far from over. Now, excuse me, *my Lord*.'

I try to leave, but he blocks my path and descends on me, making me back up a few steps. Behind him, Titan shrugs off Elder Ten and attempts to come to my aid, but Elder One holds up his hand and he stops.

I hit the table.

'I will get what I want from you,' Noah says quietly. 'One way or another.'

'Doubtful.' I lean in a little closer and lower my voice. 'And know this, Noah. If I did marry, if I did choose to be with anyone, it would always, always, be *Cass*.' I snarl every word in his horrid little face. 'He's a million times the man you could ever be.'

'If I find out that you have broken the law in any way, you will both be executed. And anyone who protects you, anyone who defends you, anyone who tries to save you... will be executed right alongside you both.' He's filled with such venom and hatred, it's scary.

'Until that day, perhaps you should contain your wrath, my Lord,' Elder One says, picking a stray piece of lint from the elbow of his jacket. 'If anything were to happen to this young woman or her acquaintances after such a careless and public threat...' He gestures to the others he brought with him still by the door. 'Your position and your motives may be called into question. And I would hate for you to lose the loyalty of the army because you could not hold yourself to the laws and standards you demand we live by. And, may I also say, purely out of concern for you, the soldiers adore this girl as well as those she calls family. They respect her and hold her in very high regard. Mistreatment of her or her kin may lead to somewhat of a disturbance. It is not worth losing the respect and loyalty of the Sainted Army over such a petulant and disobedient girl.' Elder One lifts his slightly smug gaze to meet Noah's. 'Don't you agree?'

Noah looks into my eyes. If looks alone could kill...

'I will still end up getting what I want from you, Cadet.'

'Canary.' I correct him.

'Actually,' Elder One says, finally looking at me. 'She's to be addressed as Elder. Elder Eight. And it's time I escorted her to Elder HQ.'

'I-I'm sorry...' I stammer. 'What did you just call me?'

CHAPTER TWO

Elder Ten swiftly removes the cuffs from my wrists. I struggle to stand on my own after the way I've been knocked about, so Titan wraps his arm around my waist and takes all my weight.

'I got ya, Scar,' he whispers in my ear, hugging me close. 'We've got ya.'

With a final bow to the most furious man I have ever seen, they take me out of there, fast.

'Be seeing you *real* soon, my love,' Noah calls after me, the threat in his words as clear as day.

My feet trip over themselves and my head continues to spin as I attempt to navigate the steps. Titan gives up trying to keep me upright and swoops me up in his arms instead. I would usually complain but I know when I'm done.

And I am done.

'We'll get ya outta here, Scarlett,' Elder Ten whispers as Titan carries me through the miserably grey lobby and towards the door, following Elder One closely. Several of Noah's Grey Coats gather by the one and only exit and I ready myself for a fight. But Elder One strides past them with conviction, barely acknowledging their presence. We follow, just the same.

When the cool night air fills my lungs, I breathe a sigh of relief.

But with a glance over Titan's shoulder, I soon lose any relief I had.

'They're following us,' I tell Elder One, watching the six hooded Grey Coats.

'Yep,' Elder says plainly, still striding onwards.

'What's going' on?' I ask as we storm down the path and towards the Soldiers Road. 'Did you mean what you said in there? Am I really-'

'Quiet!' Elder One replies curtly, still maintaining his long and purposeful steps. 'Not here.' He glances back at me over his shoulder, his eyes settling briefly on the pursuing Grey Coats before they rest on me. 'I had you down as smarter than this, you foolish child.'

'What did I do?'

He turns and carries on. 'You came back.'

I hold my tongue, watching Titan glance over his shoulder intermittently as we retreat, and soon enough, far sooner than I was expecting, we reach Elder HQ. The Grey Coats stop several feet away gathered in a huddle, glaring at us all with their fingers resting on the hilts of their various weapons.

'You good?' Titan asks, gently placing me back on my feet. I keep hold of him for a moment and wait for the world to stop hurtling around me. Ahead of us is the mansion dubbed *"Elder HQ"*. I nod to Titan and let go of him. He must remain at the main gates as only Elders are permitted inside the grounds. We all know that.

'I'll wait for you out here,' he promises me with his sweet smile.

'No. I need you to go and do something for me.'

'Nowhere and nothing is more important than being here, Scar.'

'I need you to go and find Tee. I need you to-'

'You!' Elder One interrupts, prodding Titan's chest. 'You need to go to The Academy. They will be serving dinner-'

'With all due respect, sir,' Titan almost yells back. 'I'm hardly hungry and will not abandon one of my dearest friends when she is so hurt and in such danger.'

Elder One stands nose to nose with Titan. His cheeks turn an angry red at Titan's defiance.

'You need to go to the other soldiers and tell as many as will listen that Scarlett is back. That she is alive and well. That she has not been arrested and that her health is not a risk to her life. You need to tell as many as will listen that she is the new Elder Eight and that she has lost all eligibility to be included in Lord Sands' lottery. That she has returned a hero, defied all odds, and come home to lay her beloved Elder to rest. And that she is excited about seeing all her comrades very soon and get back to fighting the fight. You tell them, with a smile and a cheeky laugh, that the Grey Coats weren't too happy with her, but that despite that, she is coming to the Main Hall within the hour. You tell them to wait there for her and that if she does not arrive, they should go in search of her. Do you understand me?'

Despite the fact that Titan stands more than a head taller than his superior and is built twice as broadly, Titan lowers his gaze and nods quickly and obediently.

'Good.' Elder One points to the other Black Coats that came to fetch me. 'The same goes for you two. You all stick together and go straight there. Spread the word.' His eyes flicker briefly to the lingering Grey Coats down the path before he turns to me. 'C'mon. The other Elders are waiting,' he grumbles. 'Let's get this over with.'

'Get what over with? And what did Noah mean... Borrowed time? What's going on?'

But he's already started walking towards HQ.

Titan lets me go, causing me to sway without his support. Elder Ten takes my elbow.

'I've got her. Off you go, son,' he encourages Titan, who glances at the forbidden mansion ahead and then at the enormous gates that are starting to seal closed between us.

I watch them close, wishing more than anything that Titan didn't have to leave. He stretches out his hand between the railings. I hold it tightly in mine.

'It will be okay,' he assures me, rather unconvincingly.

'I know,' I agree, comforting him far better than he is comforting me. 'Go. Do what Elder's instructed. And find Tee. Her heart looked ready to stop when they arrested me. She needs to know I'm not hurt.' His eyes dance over my battered and bloody face, his eyebrows both hitched. 'Relatively speaking that is,' I add.

He plants a kiss on my knuckles before he turns and runs off into the darkness.

'It's alright, Scarlett,' Elder Ten assures me as I watch my friend disappear. 'Everything will be-'

'HURRY UP!' Elder One bellows at us, holding open the mansion doors for us to enter. Behind him, several other faces are watching us intently.

'Elder Ten, what's going on?' I whisper as we walk away from the Grey Coats and towards the huddle of Elders.

'It's complicated.'

'I'm pretty quick at picking things up.'

'Not here, Scarlett,' he says in a hush, glancing over his shoulder. The Grey Coats have gathered by the gates now. 'Come on. Let's get you inside.'

Elder HQ is a much grander building than the one I was just in. The walls are filled with Masterpieces salvaged from museums beyond the wall. Monet. Picasso. Van Gogh. All the greats.

The floors are carpeted. The skirting is polished. There are fresh flowers in vases, fruit in bowls, and not a hint of damp in sight. I follow Elder One up the spiralling staircase made of marble, down a long corridor and into a room at the far end of the hall. He takes my arm and leads me to a purple, floral print sofa. I slump into the cushions and look up at the eight Elders standing around me in silence. One of whom was ready to marry me to Noah a few moments ago.

Elder One joins them, and together, they watch me.

Every bit of movement causes my leathers to squeak. The noise makes some of them twitch so I try to keep still and not bleed too much on the rug.

The Elders all face each other and huddle close, talking in murmurs as I look on. Finally, they break, and Elder One heads towards me.

'Do you understand what I told you at the Guardhouse?' Elder One asks, placing a chair in front of me and taking a seat. 'You look a little dazed.' He hands me a handkerchief so I can catch the blood about to drip from my chin.

'Err...' I look at them all. So many pairs of eyes and each showing me such a variety of emotions at my being here. Anger. Annoyance. Pride. Joy. Amusement. Confusion. This is their inner sanctum. Their haven.

And I'm a woman.

No woman has ever set foot inside these walls.

'I think I need you to tell me again. Cos either I have a con-cussion or you're telling me the impossible.' I look Elder One in the eye and shake my head, rattling my already throbbing brain against the sides of my skull. 'I can't be-'

'It's not the impossible,' Elder One cuts in wearily. 'For goodness sake, girl. Listen. An Elder position is inherited. Elder Eight made it clear in his will that you were to take his position if he were to die. Your return, along with the return of his body, makes you the new Elder Eight. I don't understand what you're struggling to grasp.'

'I err... Are you sure?'

'Positive,' he grunts, watching a stray drop of blood spill from my lips to the cream rug.

I swiftly cover my mouth with the handkerchief to catch any further droplets, but the hole in my gum is still bleeding. I'm forced to swallow a mouthful of it before I speak again.

'There's never been a female Elder before.'

A few of the others mumble in disapproval, looking me up and down with distaste. But not all of them seem displeased. Especially Elder Ten who looks thrilled and is watching their reactions with utter delight.

'That may be,' Elder One says a little loudly, causing the others to stop their whisperings. 'I for one do not care what is or is not between your legs. I care what is in your heart and at the end of your sword. As did your predecessor. I have watched you grow from an easily abashed child, who earned her chosen name from the ease at which the others could make her blush, to a fearless and formidable soldier who is now called Scarlett for the blood you spill.' He looks at the others. 'She is a Canary volunteer and a hell of a lot braver than most. And now, she is a fellow Elder. We will guide her and help her to fill this new role. That is all there is to it.' With that, the others settle. He returns his attention to me and opens his mouth to speak but is cut off by Elder Five.

'Tell us what happened to the former Elder Eight!' he demands.

The others all shift closer, eager to hear the tale. Elder One scowls at his outburst but remains silent and watches me closely, giving me a small nod.

'We were returning home. We decided to stop for rest at a safe location that we cleared and secured several months previously. It was compromised and it had become overrun. The floor had...'

I hesitate about which words I should use next. 'Given way,' I conclude. I look at them all. Each one seems eager for information. As am I. Eager for the truth about who is responsible for my father's death. Did any of them have something to do with the traps? Did they order the floorboards ripped up and dozens of undead monsters to be hurled inside that mortuary? 'Targets had fallen into the basement. One of the unit members fell into the hole. She was injured and unable to fight, so I jumped down to protect her and to get her out.'

'Very brave,' Elder One acknowledges, pulling out another handkerchief from his pocket and swapping it over for the one I've bled through. He glances briefly at the bruises I know must be forming on my face and he flinches. Never before have we sat so close for this long. As his eyes survey the damage Noah and his Grey Coats have inflicted, I see rage within them. As his eyes meet mine, I see that rage turn to concern. Perhaps even compassion. 'What happened next?'

'Well, Elder Eight went to find rope so he could pull her out. We got her out but I got cornered. He jumped down to help me and in the fight, he was bitten.'

Some gasp. Others shake their head.

An Elder sacrificing himself for a mere soldier?

What a waste.

But none of their disdain at the fate of my father will ever outweigh my own.

'After he was bitten...' Elder One continues. 'Who put him down?'

'I did.' I lower my eyes in complete shame. I feel my entire body slump and the heavy burden of guilt within me triple. 'I killed him.'

He slams his hand on my shoulder as he gets to his feet. 'The bite killed him. Not you.'

I look up at him as he stands over me.

'We're soldiers. We fight and we die. That's what we do. But what we don't do is a job half-assed.'

'E-excuse me?'

'For future reference, when you lead your units out beyond the wall again, and when you train others, remember to include all the required details in your pigeons. Writing to say one deceased and no location is hardly informative.'

Any and all compassion I thought I saw inside him has either vanished or was simply a side-effect of my head being slammed into Noah's desk over and over.

I sit up straighter. 'I was a little out of sorts when I wrote the final letter. Next time I am forced to plunge my sword through the temple of someone I care about, I'll be sure to remember protocol.'

'I'll assume that's the concussion causing your cheek,' he grumbles, returning his chair to the side of the room and collecting a bundle of papers from a desk before returning to me and holding them out. 'Paperwork. Sign it. I see your hand is injured. Can you still use it to scrawl a signature?'

'Now hold on!' Elder Five bursts before I can reply. 'That's it? We're not going to ask her anything further?'

'Like what?' Elder One asks back with a shrug.

'Like... this business with Lord Sands' lottery? He wants her as his wife!' He glares at me. 'She belongs with him. Not here.'

'The law clearly states-'

'Laws can be changed. As you well know, Elder One.'

'Yes. Lord Sands has been very busy these past nine months changing his own laws,' he grunts. 'But unfortunately for him, he hasn't changed this one.' Elder One looks at me still sat in the chair, holding his paperwork. 'Not yet anyway. She has been named in a will and as soon as she signs that document, it will be official. Canary 5-3-6 will be an Elder, and thereby exempt from the lottery. The only thing that will excuse her from her duties is retirement or death.' He nods to the paper and pen in my hand and I take the hint. If signing this document will keep me from becoming Noah's wife, then I'll sign it in blood! I write my signature swiftly.

'As you said, Elder One...' Elder Five sneers, folding his arms across his chest. 'Lord Sands hasn't changed this law *yet*. He wants her. He has every right to claim her. He is God's chosen representative on earth, after all.'

I hand back the contract, sealing my fate as the new Elder Eight and watch the hateful stares both Elder Five and Elder Two are throwing me.

What on earth has been going on while we've been away?

'The only way he will be able to claim her is when she turns forty, or when her heart stops beating.' Elder One folds up my contract and slides it into his jacket pocket.

'We'll see,' Elder Five mutters.

'Now,' Elder One turns to me. 'I think the best thing for all involved is a good night's sleep. You-'

'Who receives the pigeons we send back?' I ask.

His eye twitches at my interruption.

'Do they go to the Aviary? The one by the coast? Or do they go somewhere else?' I continue.

'Did that Elder of yours teach you no manners, *girl?*' Elder Two barks at me. 'Do not interrupt your superior.' He steps forwards, displeasure marking every inch of his face. 'And for goodness sake, stop bleeding all over the rug. It's over two-hundred years old and made of the purest silk. Have you no etiquette?'

'I've spent the last nine months sleeping in ditches and shitting in a hole in the ground, Elder Two. So, no. I have no etiquette. And what little I did have was either ripped out of my gum with plyers or smashed out of my skull by Lord Sand's fists. Forgive me for bleeding my blood on your Persian rug while I tell you how the man who basically raised me met his end.' I shunt my chair back so the legs meet the wood instead. 'If the stain upsets you so much, I can tell you the location of another hundred even finer than this one, if you are willing to travel three-hundred miles on horseback, through a zombie-infested country and no real sanctuary or guarantee or lasting the day... let alone the nights... to reach them.'

Several of the other Elders chuckle as he almost convulses with rage. His face has gone the brightest red I have ever witnessed. He takes a step forwards, his hand settling on the hilt of his sword.

'The birds return to the Aviary down by the coastline, where a Green Coat is stationed at all times,' Elder One says, gesturing for his comrade to stay where he is. 'He usually brings all the letters regarding the military to me personally.'

'You?'

'Yes. Me.'

'Hang on. Usually?'

He furrows his brow at me and gives the slightest, barely distin-guishable, shake of his head. He knows something but there are far too many sets of eyes on us for me to push it.

'Go get some rest,' he urges. 'You look like you need it. I will come and see how you are tomorrow.' He glares at me with his eyebrows raised. 'Am I understood?'

'Yes, Elder.'

I force myself to my feet and turn to face the door. Then, I turn back to him.

'Where do I go?' I ask. 'The Academy?'

'I'm afraid your room at the Academy is occupied by two Cadets going through their final year of evaluations.' He heads towards me and hands me a key.

'What's this?'

'A key to your new home. I assume you know where the prop-erty that each Elder Eight inherits is located?'

'Yes,' I whisper sadly, thinking of the forever empty porch that lies in the woods. 'Is that it?' I ask. 'I just go to bed? I thought you wanted me to go to the-'

'What else do you expect?' Elder One cuts in. 'A parade? Just go!'

'I mean... am I still a Canary? Can I stay with my unit even though I'm an Elder?'

'You are still a Canary if that is what you wish. However, if that is the post you choose to keep, you will be responsible for *all* the Canaries and for their training. As Elder Eight was with you and your unit, both before and after you graduated. Like I said. Go get some rest. Stop the bleeding and get that hand of yours seen to.' He gestures to the red bandage wrapped around my palm. 'You need that hand to fight with. Elder Ten, escort her to the gate.'

He's heading out the door without another word, followed by several others. Elder Five barges into my shoulder as he passes and I make sure I give him a good nudge back so he stumbles.

'I'm sorry for your loss, Scarlett,' Elder Ten tells me, taking my arm and gently guiding me out the door. 'That Elder of yours was a good buddy of mine and I know how much you meant to him. If you ever need to talk, you know where to find me.' He places a beautifully green apple in my hand as we reach the staircase.

'No riddle?' I ask, navigating each step carefully. 'Whenever you usually give me an apple, it's because I've answered your riddles correctly.'

He shakes his head and shows me a sombre smile. 'I think there are probably enough riddles rattling around in your head right now, and more than enough questions you want answered.'

'True. Thanks for the apple,' I tell him, holding it between my fingers before sliding it safely into my pocket. 'I'll give it to Tee. My gum is bleeding with a gaping hole in it, and the idea of eating this apple is making my eyes water.'

When we reach the base of the stairs, he guides me towards the back of the house, through a long and thin corridor with rough stone floors, and then out through a small narrow door.

'We need to take the back exit,' he informs me as we head out into the dark. 'Those Grey Coats are still out front.'

'I'm a little confused,' I admit. 'Elder One said to go to the cottage, but earlier, he told Titan to tell everyone I'm heading to the Main Hall. Where am I supposed to be going?'

'The Main Hall. And quickly. The sooner everyone sees you, the better. The Elders will be expecting you to be heading to the cottage, and as you saw, some of them are sympathetic to Noah's desire to have you as his own. They will more than likely inform the Grey Coats where to find you and it's imperative the soldiers see you fit and well before they can catch up with you, in case a mysterious illness or untreated wound suddenly takes you.'

'Oh shit,' I sigh. 'Noah's totally gonna try and kill me, isn't he?'

He shrugs. 'Who knows with that nutter.'

Chuckling away to myself, I carry on following him into the dense woodland.

'So. What's been happening while I've been away? There's definitely dissension in the ranks.'

'Noah's been changing laws left, right and centre. Now, it's mandatory for civilians to marry and start producing children from the age of sixteen.' He scoffs in disgust. 'If they don't choose their own spouse, Noah chooses one for them.'

'No way...'

'And even worse, a year after they have a child, they must conceive another.'

'What?! That's disgusting!'

'Yep,' he grunts. 'He wants to build our numbers. Both within the army and the civilians. The law of donation still applies, unfortunately. He has also removed Elders from punishment detail. Now, all indiscretions are dealt with by Grey Coats only. The number of lashings has tripled and if we try to intervene, the poor sod tied to the post receives ten more strikes. Believe me when I tell you, the Grey Coats aren't shy about dishing out their justice.'

I feel the scars on my back tingle at the memory of my own lashing.

'Noah has started to make moves on removing Elders from having a say in rank allocation, as well as controlling who does what beyond the wall. He also wants to allocate his Grey Coats to the cadets' training. But since he needs a majority vote from the Elders to implement those changes, he hasn't been able to do that yet.'

'What's he trying to achieve?'

'Full control,' he replies plainly. 'The whole idea of the Elders was for them to guide the military while the Sands family guide our spiritual welfare. We protect the Haven and they protect our eternal souls. Or some nonsense like that. Now, Noah wants to control it all and his Grey Coats are more than happy to help him. Luckily, there are certain things he doesn't have a say in yet. You for example. You're protected by the law that Elders are exempt from the lottery.'

Thank you, Dad...

'He'll be wanting to change that I imagine. And as you saw, he has support. Not enough to create a majority but the former Elder Two - his replacement you met while Noah had you pinned beneath his boot - made it clear he would die before he allowed Noah to take full control. Two days later, the poor bastard fell into a pit and was devoured alive. Strange though, how he decided to go out to clear that pit alone. After dark.'

'Noah had him killed?'

'I'd bet my life on it. As would Elder One. His replacement was a Black Coat who hardly ever spoke to Elder Two. It's strange that he ended up being named his successor in his will. But I suspect the fact that he has been trying to convince the Grey Coats to let him join for the last few years may have had something to do with it.' He glances down at me as we walk side by side and waits for me to say something. But what can I say? It's obvious that Noah, who already has the majority of control, wants to take the sliver of power the Elders hold and that he has spies in their ranks. 'What really happened to my friend?' he asks. 'Did he die how you said? Or was there something else going on?' He stops and wraps his hand around my wrist tightly. 'You need to tell me what you know, Scarlett. What happened out there? What did you and your Canaries see?'

In that moment, I suddenly realise I'm in the deep woods with no weapon and with a man I'm not entirely sure I can trust. I spot his sword at his hip and wonder how fast his draw is. My dad's final words echo in my head. *"Trust no one but Elder One".* Although I have known Elder Ten my whole adult life, I wouldn't say I trust him. Not more than I trust my father's dying words at any rate. What if he only remained on the wall to keep an eye on me at Noah's request? What if he was only ever kind to earn my trust? Sure, my dad did mention him a couple of times but not so much as I would assume a deep friendship between them.

I pull my hand free of his grip and step back.

'It was like I said. He fell.'

'That's it? You didn't see anything strange?'

'Like what?' I ask.

He shrugs and continues watching my reactions closely.

'You know what?' I smile. 'I could really use a little time on my own to clear my head. Thank you so much for helping me out today but I think I would rather go on alone.'

He steps forward, shaking his head. 'No. It really isn't safe and you're not even armed. If you get cornered-'

'I'm gonna be honest, Elder. I'm feeling a little cornered right now.'

He takes another step closer. I take one back, my fists clenched.

'If you or your unit saw anything out there, it's vital you tell me.'

'Why? So you can tell Noah?'

'What?! No! How could you even think that?'

There are a series of rustles to our left, causing us both to stop abruptly and stare into the gathering darkness. While he's distracted, I turn and quickly run further into the woods. It's late and there's no light to show me the way. My body is exhausted and my head still thumps from the hits I took, so my retreat is less than graceful. Or efficient, as Elder Ten, a man in his fifties, catches up with me easily. He takes a firm hold of my wrist and yanks. I fall flat on my backside and groan as I collide with the hard ground. As I look up, he stands over me and draws his sword.

'If you're gonna kill me, you better be prepared to face a vengeful and rather unstable Canary unit,' I pant.

He tosses his blade so it spins in the air. With grace, he catches it by the tip of the blade and presents me with the handle. 'You cannot be walking around unarmed, Scarlett. Your life is in danger.' He nods to his weapon. 'Take it and defend yourself if you find yourself in a difficult situation. I will not be the one who allowed my dearest friend's only daughter to die without a sword in her hand.'

'Wait...'

'I know who you are. I've always known. You think I sat up on that wall for the view? Take the sword. Protect yourself. Find people you trust and let yourself trust them. I am sorry I failed in that respect but know that I *am* on your side.' He holds the sword out further. I slide my hands onto the hilt and take it. 'Get up and go,' he orders. 'You run to The Academy and get yourself seen by as many as possible.'

I get myself back on my feet and shake off the dirt and leaves from my clothes.

'I'm just paranoid,' I confess. 'Walk with me. I can barely summon the strength to stand anyways.' I slide my arm into his and together, we start walking through the woods.

'Want me to carry that sword then?'

'I'll keep it for now. Like I said... I'm paranoid.'

He chortles under his breath as we head towards the building I called home for thirteen years.

As Elder Ten and I approach The Academy, I spot Titan lingering in the courtyard in the same spot I punched Cass in the face after evaluation day. After Elder Ten gives a short, sharp whistle, Titan sees us and rushes over. I barely get to say hi before he wraps me in his arms, embracing me tightly, before stepping back to examine my injuries.

'He beat the living daylights out of you!' he says, taking my throbbing face in his hands and flinching at the cut on my brow. 'He needs locking up! You need stitches and your face is swollen.' He feels my waist. 'Damn, Scarlett, you need a decent meal.'

'I need you to let me go,' I laugh softly, prizing his hands off me. 'I'm fine. Just sore and really tired. Where are the others?'

He nods over his shoulder, towards the hole where the revolving doors used to be. 'Inside. Waiting for you.'

'Tee-'

'She's in there too, with your unit. She's shaken up but okay.'

'What about Winder... and Cass?' I ask, feeling them both go tense at my question.

'We're not too sure,' Elder Ten admits.

'Cass and Winder are kinda... missing.' Titan adds.

'Missing?!'

'They haven't been seen since the morning after we heard what was in your letter. No one can find them.'

'Have you been looking for them? They could be hurt or Noah could have taken them. Where have you looked?' I turn on my heel. 'I'm gonna go look for them at Noah's mansion.'

Elder takes hold of my upper arm. 'They're not lost or taken. They're just... away.'

'Away? What does that even mean?' I shake my head. 'I'm gonna go look for them. They might need help. Noah could have them!' I take a single step around him but he steps in front of me.

'That's not a good idea,' Titan tells me. 'Never mind Noah and his Grey Coats, Cass is furious with you and frightened that you're dead. He's like an injured animal and you're the one that injured him. Tee hasn't stopped crying since you left and he blames you for it. Every night, we all hear her crying for you. Her sobs echoed through the halls. He hates you for doing that to her. And then there was the incident with Noah at the lottery announcement. He got arrested and hurt because of you. You betrayed him by leaving and you hurt the sweetest girl alive. Cass will not be happy to see you. Alive or not. He's upset right now, cos he thinks you might be dead. But when he learns that you're not, he'll go back to being angry again.'

'And what about you? Do you hate me?'

'I don't hate you. I know that you had your reasons for doing what you did.'

As his arm reaches out to comfort me and his eyes fill with pity, I find myself getting pretty damn pissed off. I slap his hand away.

'You know what? Fine. Cass hates me. I let you guys down and caused a lot of damage. But I did what I had to do. I did what I had to, to keep all of you safe. And maybe you were in danger because of me in the first sodding place but I wasn't counting on Noah turning into a raging lunatic. I had to leave my home. Leave Tee. Leave my friends and my family to save not only your lives, but mine too. You have no idea what I've been through these last nine months. None. NONE! I've lost so much. Everything! So, if you see Cass, you tell him this. You tell him I'm alive. You tell him if he wants a fight, I'll be waiting. And if he so much as looks at me funny, I'll shove my Katana so far up his arse he'll taste it.' I barge into his shoulder and head inside.

The sound of hundreds of cheering cadets rattles my already pounding head. They clap or rest their hand over their hearts as I pass through the crowd. Hundreds of voices are all talking excitedly as I make my way towards the table ahead where my unit is currently getting to their feet. Unlike the rest, they're not so cheerful. They see the blood and the bruises I gained since seeing them and a fiery rage consumes their faces. Tee is pale and shaking as she charges towards me, her eyes on nothing and no one but me. She collides into my body, her arms pinning me close as she starts to sob. Her cries are drowned out by the saluting and hurrahs that surround us.

'It's okay,' I whisper in her ear, stroking her hair and letting her wail. Her body trembles as she leans on me. I can barely keep myself up, but for her, I find the strength to keep us both on our feet. 'I'm okay, Tee. It's all going to be okay.'

Titan passes us and heads towards my unit where Flash is waiting. Flash gives me a sad wave before talking to Titan. But Loom has grabbed Titan's arm and is furiously talking to him, pointing at me and throwing his arms up in the air. Titan is talking back, his mouth moving at speed.

'He what?!' I see Loom exclaim before shaking his head and making for the door.

Elder Ten intervenes and stops him from, if I were to hazard a guess, trying to go and kill Noah.

They argue.

The soldiers and cadets surrounding us are still celebrating our return.

Sky and Chilli watch Tee and I embracing with tears in their eyes.

In Sky's hand is my father's sword. She holds it as if it's made of glass.

It's all too much.

The hall falls silent as I stand by the door and raise a glass of water in the air. Everyone grabs whatever drink is close and follows suit.

'To Elder Eight,' I call out proudly. 'Truly, the best teacher, mentor and Elder we could have ever wished for. He will be greatly...' My words get stuck in my throat. 'He will be greatly missed.'

'TO ELDER EIGHT!' They bellow back in unison, placing their free hands over their hearts and bowing their heads, as is customary when we mourn the loss of one of our own.

One minute.

That's all we allow ourselves. One minute of silence in which we're to reflect on the life and loss of whoever we have just raised our glasses to and then we're supposed to just move on. Leave them in the past and carry on with our lives, until the day they raise their glasses to us for a full sixty seconds.

All I can think about in this unbearable stillness is how many times I've raised a glass like this in my life.

How many moments have I spent contemplating the loss of a friend?

I should know, right? I should know how many people have died in this fight. This never-ending war.

But I don't.

I stopped counting years ago.

The minute is up, and yet my glass is still raised high. In my heart, this hand will never be lowered and I know it. I will never stop thinking of my father and the manner of his death. Noah's smug face flashes into my mind and my rage goes into overdrive. My hand clenches and the glass breaks around my grip. The sound of it shattering to the floor echoes all around us and creates even more silence.

'I... err...' I struggle to lift my gaze from the shard of glass embedded in the bandage still wrapped around my palm. I see the memory of my hand impaled onto the nail down in the pit at the mortuary. I hear the tearing of my flesh and the sniffing of the targets as they caught my blood's scent. 'I wanted to tell you...' I pick out the glass and let it fall to the floor. When it lands, I don't hear glass hitting stone. I hear the twang of my father's sword as it fell while he juddered and convulsed. 'As your new... as Elder's... replacement...' More red spreads throughout my bandage and as everything falls into nothing, my ears suddenly fill with the inhuman roar of my undead father.

'As you can probably tell,' Elder One calls across the hall, making me jump and return to reality. He's standing by my side and standing tall. I didn't even notice him arrive. 'The last few months have taken its toll. The Canaries are tired from their travels and mourning the loss of a most beloved Elder. Allow me to speak on their behalf. Yes. I can confirm that the rumours are true. Canary 5-3-6, or as you call her, Scarlett, is the new Elder Eight. Not that anyone can replace her predecessor but she will be taking up his position from this moment on.' He keeps his focus on the sea of faces before us, his hands cupped behind his back. 'As you may also see, she has suffered some injuries while out beyond the wall. All in the line of duty.'

Loom scoffs loudly making Elder growl quietly beneath his breath.

'Now... I think everyone should be heading either to bed or to their night-time postings-'

'Before you all leave,' I call out, stepping forwards and filled with a venomous anger towards Noah and all he has done. 'I want to make it clear to you all that I fully intend on continuing my work with the Canaries.' The crowd starts to mumble. 'And I want to remind you that you all have the option to join me.'

'Join *us*!' Loom adds proudly.

'Out there, the world is healing.' My words have everyone quiet once more. 'The land that surrounds the Haven is dry and brittle. It's lifeless and swarming with targets. Death surrounds us. It walks freely through deserted streets and lost homes. But further south, the grass is growing freely. Up to our shoulders in some places. There are fish swimming in streams. Fruit growing from trees. Vegetables pushing their way up through fertile soil.'

'That can't be true!' Someone calls out from the crowd, fuelling the already fierce fire in my soul.

'No one dares venture further than twenty miles from here. You never see more than a dead and decaying world,' I call back. 'But what I say is the truth.' Elder One glances sideways at me. I expect to be silenced. Instead, I see the slightest smile pulling at his mouth. 'All I will say to you tonight is this. If you wish to see it for yourself, if you want to witness life in a manner far more than this…' I hold open my arms and drop them down by my sides. 'If you want to stop hiding behind walls and live your days without the threat of a whip at your back and a boot on your throat,' I hiss hatefully, not caring if any Grey Coats hear my words. 'If you want to live in the world instead of hiding from it, then come see me with a transfer request. I will take you into my unit and I will show you what we are really fighting for. And I swear to you, it's not a single man or a higher power.' They all gasp at my words. 'It's us.' I gesture to the crowd. 'It's you.'

'What are you saying?' Someone calls.

'I'm saying… The Canaries are recruiting. We're taking England back. Bit by bit. Kill by kill. And we want you to help. If you have questions, come see us. My unit and I will be at Elder Eight's cottage. Good night, Cadets. Good night, Soldiers.' As they all explode into conversation, discussing all that I have said, I turn to Elder One.

'Recruiting?' he smirks.

'I need to speak to you in private as a matter of urgency.'

'And I you. How about you and I head to-'

'Elder One!' calls a familiar voice.

The entire hall turns to see Noah standing by the door, flanked by a dozen Grey Coats. His eyes settle on me.

'Elder Eight,' he adds bitterly to me. 'Already hard at work? Trying to lure these good people to their deaths?'

'Far from it. I'm inviting them to live.'

'Is that so,' he chortles.

'No law against recruiting, is there?' I take a step forward. 'Not yet anyway.'

'My lord,' Elder One greets pleasantly, stepping ever so slightly between us and encouraging me back. 'What brings you out here at this late hour.'

'I just wanted to offer my condolences to you all for the loss of poor Elder Eight. The former, of course.' He smirks, the bastard. 'And to wish his successor all the best in her ventures.' He walks towards me. Elder One stands taller, but I have never been one to shy away from a fight. I step around him and meet Noah. 'I wish you luck, Elder Eight.' He stretches out his hand. The hand he offers means that the hand I must give is the one currently bleeding through several layers of thick bandage. 'Will you not take the hand of you lord, Cadet?' he asks, flexing out his fingers. 'I may take offence.'

'We wouldn't want that,' I reply, offering my hand. His grip is painful. My bones grind together and the wound opens a little more. I simply smile. 'And it's Elder. Not Cadet.'

'Oh...' he whispers, smirking from ear to ear. 'You will always be my Cadet, *Cadet*.' He chews down on his lower lip as he watches me with amusement. 'Elder One,' he suddenly says cheerfully, his charming smile on full display for the crowd. 'My dear friend. I have a matter of urgency I must discuss with you.' He releases my hand, massaging the pooled blood he's accumulated from my wound into his palm. 'Please. Come with me. I am in desperate need of your assistance.'

'As you wish, my lord,' Elder replies.

'The rest of you...' Noah glances at the crowd around us. 'I am certain there are places you are supposed to be.'

Everyone gathers their belongings and starts to file out, muttering and chatting away to each other.

As Elder One passes me, I take hold of his wrist.

'Don't,' I whisper.

'I will be fine, Scarlett. You and your friends should retire for the night. Together. You hear me?'

'But-'

'I look forward to seeing you all for morning service,' he says loudly to the rest of them as they all pass us.

'I will come with you,' I insist, watching Noah stand with his Grey Coats by the door.

'No. You will not,' Elder One tells me, stepping close and lowering his voice. 'You and your unit, as well as your friends, are to retire. You need to clean yourself up and get some rest. You will need every ounce of strength you can muster in the coming days.'

'But if you go with him, you may not come back.'

'Noah has a lot of power but not enough to make me disappear quite so easy. He may have his Grey Coats, but I've got my own guards.' Six Black Coats stand close by the door, ready to escort him wherever he's about to go. 'I will come to see you as soon as I am able but in the meantime, no matter what, you must stay as far away from Noah as possible.' He leans in and whispers into my ear. 'When I return, we will talk about your father's plans. And if I fail to return, trust Elder Ten.'

He turns and heads out of the hall without another word, leaving me mouth open and speechless.

Noah throws me his best smug grin before he turns and leaves with him.

I hate that I have no choice but to watch them go.

My unit gathers around me. Sky, Loom and Chilli along with Tee, Flash and Titan.

'You alright?' Sky asks me.

'I'm fine,' I reply curtly, retaking Tee's hand in mine. 'C'mon. Let's go home.' I look at them all. 'Let's all go home.'

CHAPTER THREE

We all head back to the main path. Our boots echo off the concrete and the wind blows in my ears. No Grey Coats follow us. No one speaks as we walk. Those few that we pass merely nod a hello and carry on.

I don't even need to think about where I'm walking. My feet take me to the cottage instinctively. When I reach the small, meandering path that takes me to the porch, I stop. My heart is in my throat and the beginnings of tears sting my eyes.

It's completely as I remember it. Nothing's changed one bit. Even his rocking chair is exactly where he left it. As a breeze blows my hair across my face, it moves the chair a little. The creak of the wood on wood makes me ache. I would sit on those steps and read his books to him. He taught me how to read right here. I couldn't grasp it at The Academy. They just didn't explain it in a way I could understand. So, he would teach me himself late at night by candlelight, out here, on this porch. Or inside at his kitchen table. God, I moaned. I complained. He would have me reading the same thing over and over for hours and hours.

But the stories were good.

Filled with magic and adventures. Tales of great heroes overcoming terrible odds and malevolent enemies. Come to think of it, those stories made me excited to be part of the fight. To defeat the monsters in my own story. I guess he was just preparing me. In his own way. Shame he couldn't prepare me for it all.

For losing him.

I look to my left and see Tee looking up at the cottage with tears spilling down her cheeks. To my right, Titan holds Flash's hand tightly, grief swimming in his eyes. It seems too much for Flash because he pulls his hand free of Titan's and wraps his arms around himself instead. My unit lingers behind us.

'This isn't gonna get any easier by freezing our arses off out here,' I tell them, taking a courage inducing breath and fiddling with the keys in my hand. 'Let's get inside.'

I walk up the porch steps, stroking the arm of the painfully empty chair as I pass and dry my eyes before a single tear escapes.

I unlock the door and head inside. It's been nine months since he was here and I can still smell him. I take the matches left on the table by the door and light the first candle. Loom takes them from me and heads inside to light the rest.

'Come in,' I tell the others, who are all waiting anxiously on the porch. 'Head down the hall to the kitchen. See if there's anything to eat or drink. Get yourselves comfortable.'

They file past me as I watch the flame of the candle flicker against the bitter wind that has followed us in. When Tee closes the door, the flame falls still. I can't tear my eyes away from it because I know that when I look up, I'll see his home. His life. His death.

'You okay, Scar?' Tee asks sweetly, resting her palm on my back.

'Hmm,' I reply. 'Could you put some water on the boil for me, please? Saucepans are under the sink. Let the tap run for a minute. It always comes out murky at first.'

'Okay.' She gives my cheek a kiss and joins the others in the kitchen. After a few moments, I finally lift my gaze.

This place was always cluttered and it still is. Books. Trinkets. Broken furniture that he insisted he could fix. He always said… *'I'll get around to it.'* But he never did. He said he was always too busy making sure his Cadets didn't get killed. On my right is what he called his *"study"*. It's where he stored his countless books. There's barely any room to move in there and it's so full of dust, the slightest bit of disturbance and you'll be coughing for a week. To my left, there's a doorway that leads into a lounge with a musty old sofa, a fireplace and the furniture he did get around to mending. He never sat in there though. He sat where everyone else is gathered right now. In the kitchen at the end of the hallway. So that's where I go.

As I walk in, I see Sky and Chilli sitting at the beat-up old table in the very centre of the room. Loom, Flash and Titan are leaning against the kitchen worktop, deep in conversation. And Tee is looking out the window with her hands wrapped around the edge of the sink so tight, her knuckles are white. The tap is running clear, but I don't think she's noticed.

I head straight towards her and place the saucepan beneath the cascading water, shutting the tap off when the pan's half-full and placing it on the small gas stove my dad kept.

'Chilli?'

'Yep?'

'Cupboard by your leg. Behind the line of books.'

He heads over and opens up the doors, pulling out a couple of books from the line of Charles Dickens' complete works.

'Oh,' Chilli sighs. 'Good old Elder Eight.' He holds up the bottle of Wild Turkey bourbon. 'He always did have good taste.'

'Glasses are in the next cupboard,' I tell him. As he rummages and clinks away, I glance at Tee. If she was any paler, she'd pass out. Her whole body shakes and she looks like she's in shock. I take her face in my hands. 'Now, Tee, you sit next to Sky at the table. Have a drink with us and take a deep breath, okay? Everything is fine. As you can see, I wasn't executed.'

'Look at your face...' she whimpers. 'And now he's taken Elder One.'

'He just knocked me about a bit. It probably looks worse than it is.' Her hand settles on mine and she squeezes, reluctant to let me go. The pain her touch creates in my cut is agony but I remain calm and comforting for her. 'I'm right here. I'm fine and so are you. But, I have a very sore hand which needs sorting out right now. So take a seat, have a drink, and let's take a moment to just gather ourselves. Okay?'

But still, she doesn't budge.

'C'mon, Q-Tee,' Sky says, her voice full of warmth as she heads towards her. 'Come sit with me. You're an archer too, right?' she asks, guiding her gently away from me and towards the table. 'What wood do you like to make your arrows with? I like pine. But some prefer cedar.' She pulls out a chair and sits her down, all the while chattering on about the pros and cons of the different materials they can use for their weapons. If Sky is good at any-thing, it's talking, and right now that's exactly what we all need. Distracting.

"Thank you" I mouth. She gives me a wink and leans in close, full of interest as Tee starts to talk back.

Loom helps Chilli put the glasses on the table and Titan and Flash linger by the counter.

'Hiya, Flash,' I say kindly. 'You're looking good. The Green coat clearly agrees with you. I'm glad.'

'Really good to see you again, Scarlett. You had us worried for a while there.'

'Never need to worry about me. You know that.' I gesture for them both to sit. They do, and Loom pours everyone a drink. 'This stuff is banned here, so if you would rather not drink it-'

Everyone has already taken their drinks and started sipping.

I turn back to the slowly simmering water and shut off the gas before I start to unravel the bandage from my palm. It's stuck fast to my skin and stings as I slowly peel it off. The wound is angry. The cut is deep and the edges are red and swollen. I rest my fingers over it. It's hot. Damn. It's showing signs of an infection. I run it under some cold water from the tap and clench my teeth together to stop myself from crying out.

'Here.' Loom holds out the bottle and watches the way I grit my teeth. 'It will help with the pain.' I almost snatch it from him before I take some big gulps. 'I'll fetch you some Aloe Vera and coconut oil from the doctor when the sun comes up. It should help. What happened? Titan said Noah arrested you? That he attacked you?' He keeps his voice low so the others don't hear over their own conversations.

'Yeah,' I sigh. 'Noah attacked me and that arse of a Grey Coat Commander pulled out one of my teeth with plyers in retaliation for Cass punching Noah.' I open my mouth and he peers inside. His face scrunches and he inhales sharply through his teeth.

'Ouch.'

'I'll be fine. It's stopped bleeding. I'm more concerned about this cut on my hand. The nail I used wasn't exactly clean. Pass me that cloth, would ya?' He passes it over and I use it to soak up the hot water so I can clean my hand a little.

'Does it hurt bad?'

'Doesn't tickle. So, what happened while I was gone?'

'We did as you told us to do. We stabled the horses and went to the Main Hall. Then your girl came charging into the Main Hall in hysterics, telling us that you'd been arrested. She was so worried and in such a rush, she dragged the horse inside the hall too. Complete with Elder Eight still attached to the back of it. Chilli took the horse and Elder to HQ. Sky and I went to the Gatehouse to try and help you. Got there the same time as Elder One and your gigantic friend over there. Elder told us to go back to the Main Hall and wait. That's about it.'

'So, where's his body now?' I ask painfully.

'Still at HQ, I guess.'

'I don't suppose… by any chance… you've seen Winder or Cass?'

'No. I'm sorry. No one knows where they are. I asked, but…' He nods to my hand. 'You need stitches.'

'What I need is a good night's sleep.'

'What are we going to do? What if Noah comes after you again?'

'Not if. When. He is far from done. Doesn't matter anyway. It's not like we're staying long, is it?'

'We got the third degree from some other soldiers, asking where we'd been and what we'd been up to. Everyone's keen to know what the world is like, which is good I guess. Considering we're gonna offer them to come and live in it with us. I thought we were gonna do it a little more on the quiet than declaring it to the whole Academy, mind.'

'I only invited them to consider joining up as a Canary. That's all.' I shrug.

'Recruiting…'

'Recruiting.' I agree. Whereas he looks worried, I have a slight grin.

'Noah won't like what you said.'

'I don't really give a shit. You know our mission, Loom. We gather others who want to leave and we leave. We leave The Verity behind us all for good after I kill the people responsible for my father's death.'

'Killing Noah won't be easy,' he whispers. 'Can't we just go?'

'No!' I bark, tossing the pan into the sink and spilling water all over the place. He steps back as I glare at him. The others have all fallen silent and turned their attention to us. I'm shaking with anger and unfortunately for Loom, he's just the closest, so he gets the brunt of it. 'We came back here for a god damn reason. Or did you forget that? HUH?'

'No. I didn't-'

'We will not just run away, Loom. The man responsible for killing our Elder will pay. Do you hear me?' I turn to the others. 'Do you all hear me? If this has scared you...' I gesture to my face. 'If a few cuts and bruises have made you rethink what we agreed and you no longer want to be a part of our plan, THEN GET THE FUCK OUT OF MY HOUSE!'

As I scream, Tee jumps a mile and drops her glass.

'P-plan?' Titan asks. 'You guys have a plan?'

As I open my mouth, there's a knock on the front door. We all fall silent and look to the empty hallway. Waiting.

They knock again.

Chilli gets to his feet. 'I got it. If it's Grey Coats, I'll holler.'

We all sit, straining our ears for any indication of what's going on out in the hall. There's no yelling. No swords meeting in battle. Just calm and mumbled conversation.

'I haven't changed my mind,' Loom tells me as we wait. 'I guess I'm just worried.' He picks up a dry towel and rests it on my bleeding hand. 'I don't like the idea of you getting hurt, okay? And I have a very strong feeling that Noah isn't going to let you walk around breathing much longer. Not with you declaring ideas like you did in the hall today.'

'Did you know that they're forcing the civilians to marry at sixteen now? That a year after they give birth, they must conceive again? How many children will be taken from wailing mothers and fathers in the coming years? How many must lose their children to die in this fight? To grow up alone? To learn how to whittle arrows before they even learn how to write? This can't carry on. I. Won't. Let. It.'

'Guys... what are you talking about?' Tee asks nervously. 'What's your plan?'

The door closes and Chilli returns holding a few sheets of paper in his hand and a smile on his face.

'Three transfer requests from three very excited Black Coats,' he announces, handing them over to me. 'Two girls and one guy, all keen to see what life outside these walls is like. Looks like your speech piqued some interest.'

I hold the papers in my hand and can't believe that I just got three volunteers. Other than Sky, Loom and me, there haven't been any volunteers for the last two years. Just convictions.

'What about the civilians?' Loom asks. 'We can't offer for them to join and if what you say is true-'

'It's true,' Tee adds. 'Noah implemented the new marriage law three months ago. When the people complained, he cut their food rations in half.'

'He did what?'

'They're still on half-rations and will be until they agree,' she concludes, but then the corner of her mouth twitches.

'What?' I ask.

'Well, Cass, Winder and I have been sneaking in the rest of their rations after dark,' she giggles. Her confession has not just my eyebrows raised in surprise, but everyone else's too. 'What?' she huffs. 'Didn't think I had the balls?'

'No,' Chilli laughs. 'But impressed that you do!'

'Hey. Don't let all this weeping fool you. I'm actually a tough cookie when I need to be. I just have a serious weak spot where Scarlett's concerned.' She looks over at me. 'Turns out I can't live without her.'

'Join the club,' Sky laughs, nudging her shoulder and beaming ear to ear. 'Way to go, Tee! Sticking it to the man. So, what's the general feeling like in civi life? You think that if they had a choice, they might wanna relocate to a Verity free zone?'

'Erm... maybe.' Tee furrows her brow. 'Why? Is that what you're planning?'

'Like I said,' I interrupt. 'We're recruiting. What do you say?' I ask her. 'You fancy-'

The sound of metal soaring through the air, followed by a thud, silences me. Embedded in the frame of the window by my head and still slowly wobbling from impact, is a haladie.

Standing in the doorway, looking at me with a scowl and his arm still in the same position it was when he hurled his weapon at me, is Cass. Behind him, Winder is looking stuck between a rock and a hard place. The scraping of chairs is deafening as Chilli and Sky spring to their feet, each drawing a weapon. I'm amazed at how quickly Sky retrieves her bow from the back of her chair. She pulls back an arrow, the tip pointed right at Cass's heart.

'Don't!' I order quickly, stretching out my arms and stepping forwards, terrified that Cass will get an arrow in the heart before he can blink. 'No one attack. You hear me?' They stay perfectly still as they obey me without question or hesitation. Cass continues to stare at me with a steely resolve as he lowers his arm. His chest is rising and falling slowly.

'He just tried to kill you,' Sky says darkly.

I wrap my fingers around his haladie and pull it from the frame. 'If he wanted me dead, he wouldn't have missed.'

'It's a mistake I won't make again,' Cass growls. I hate the anger I hear in his voice. It hurts to see the hatred not only in his eyes but throughout the whole of his body. Those arms that once held me now look like they want to break me into tiny pieces. His hands which tended to me gently for so many years, twitch as they fight the urge to wring my neck.

I turn and walk towards him. Those steely grey eyes watch me closely and glance at his weapon which I hold in my hand. When I reach him, I smell his scent. It feels like home and makes me ache inside knowing that it's a place I'm no longer wanted.

'Doing what you just did to an Elder is punishable by death,' I tell him, stopping a few feet away.

'You gonna have me killed?' he asks with calm contempt. *Elder?*'

'Can we talk?' I ask, handing him back his weapon. 'In private?'

He laughs at me, shaking his head. 'All I want to say to you is go. Leave. You're not wanted here. And you sure as hell ain't taking Tee out there with you. Do you hear me?'

We stare unblinking into each other's eyes. The room is silent.

'Get your stuff, Tee,' he barks. 'We're leaving.'

Tee gets to her feet, the legs of the chair scrape against the tiles. That's all I hear.

'I'm not leaving her,' she says. 'Cass, she just got back.'

'I said get your stuff,' he warns.

'She doesn't want to leave,' Sky snarls at him, 'But you could always try and make her leave with you. That would be fun.' She pulls back her arrow a little. 'For me at least.'

'Alright, guys,' Winder says from behind Cass. 'Let's not get nasty.' He looks at me over Cass's shoulder. 'I'm really happy to see you again, Scar. Seriously. So happy you're okay.'

'You too, Winder. If you like, you're welcome to stay for a drink? For Elder Eight?' I look at him and Cass. 'You both can. He loved you guys.'

'That would be great.'

'Whose side are you on?' Cass snipes at Winder.

Winder shrugs apologetically. 'Everyone's?'

'Hey, Winder, right?' Sky calls over. She smiles a cheeky smile at Winder. 'Scarlett's told me a lot about you. Stay. You... can't,' she adds to Cass. 'I don't like you.'

Winder shuffles around Cass keeping his gaze lowered, and heads towards the table to stand side by side with the others.

'Traitor,' Cass scoffs.

'Mate, she's family. I'm just happy she's home and alive. Look at her. She looks like she's been through hell. Come sit and have a drink to the old man's memory. Let's meet her new unit.' He blushes as he looks at Sky who beams at him. Her bow and arrow still poised and directed at Cass of course.

'I'll fetch some more glasses,' Loom adds. 'Stay, Cassius. We've heard loads about you.'

'I couldn't give a shit what you've heard about me. Winder? Tee? Titan? Flash? How can you not care about what she's done? About how she left Tee to cry herself to sleep every night?'

'I didn't cry *every* night,' Tee protests, turning a little pink.

'She left our unit one man down! She roped Elder Eight into leaving with her!'

'If you could just give me a second to explain-'

'I thought nothing else you could do would ever shock me. You left. Abandoned us. Abandoned me to your boyfriend's wrath-'

'He's not-'

'I thought you couldn't stoop any lower than that cowardice. Than that selfishness.'

'Just listen-'

'But then you return to try and lure others out there to die with you? You return with the body of the man who basically raised us because he died saving your pathetic and unworthy arse.' He jabs his finger into my collar bone, jarring the bruises that are forming from Noah's boot. 'You...' *Jab* 'Are the reason...' *Jab* 'That Elder Eight...' *Jab.*

'Don't you dare,' I warn.

'Is dead.'

I react to his words with a right hook straight to his ribs followed by a swift uppercut to his chin. As he stumbles back, I finish him off with a straight cross, right on his nose which sends him to his arse, grabbing his bloody and broken nose.

I lean down in Cass's face. I've never been so angry. I've never hated him so much in my life. Even he's taken aback by the loathsome expression I wear clearly on my face. I wanted to tell him why I did what I did. I wanted to make it right.

Not anymore.

'Get the hell out of my house before I cut your tongue out of your head,' I threaten. 'You are never welcome here again. You so much as look at me, talk about me... think about me, and I will kill you. Do you hear me?'

'I hear you,' he replies, spitting a mouthful of blood on the floor.

I can't stay in here. I need to leave. Now. As I head upstairs and reach the landing, I hear yelling. They're telling him to leave.

He's calling everyone traitors and fools. As I linger with a heart thumping hard against my chest and a fierce anger that burns the back of my throat, I struggle to fight the urge to go back down there and tear his head off. There's one hell of a commotion. By the sounds of it, he's trying to get Tee and the others to leave with him but they refuse. So, Loom and Chilli are in the process of hurling him out the door. He's not going quietly. The things he's shouting at me, calling me a liar, a manipulator... a murderer.

Boy, they weren't joking about how much he hates me.

Finally, the door slams shut and the house falls quiet. That is until they start murmuring about whether or not someone should come up to see me. I head inside the bedroom facing the back of the house and slam the door shut.

No one comes.

Good.

I light some candles.

This is the biggest bedroom but Elder never used it. He slept in the small room at the front of the house. He always said that this room felt like it was meant for a couple. Not a lonely, old git like him. There's a cast-iron fireplace. Next to that, a beat-up old rocking chair. An old floral rug covers the wooden floor and a wonky double bed lies beside the open window. There's been a leak in the roof at some point. It's watermarked and bulging a little. In the far left corner is another door. As I walk towards it, I slide off my coat and drape it over the end of the bed. I unbuckle my corset and let it fall to the floor before stretching my arms out and working loose the aches in my muscles. I push open the bathroom door, taking a single candle with me. What was once green paint is now heavily marked and peeling from the walls. A single sink sits beneath the window, covered in grime. Barely clinging to the wall is an old and rotten cabinet and against the wall is a free-standing, cast-iron bathtub. I sit on the edge of the tub with the candle balancing beside me and sluggishly I pull off my kicks. I reach over and turn on the tap. The water's cold and the pipes groan and creak as the water forces its way through. So much so, the floorboards shake. I unwind my leather wrappings and slide off my trousers before tossing them all in the sink. The leather wrappings need replacing. They're beyond damaged. They were once cream and now... I pick them up and look closer. They're heavily stained with blood.

Zombie blood.

My father's blood.

I drop them into the sink and stagger back feeling as though ice has been thrown over my entire body. My chest grows tight and my breathing becomes strained. I clasp my chest and feel the way my heart pounds wildly beneath my palm. As the blood starts to pump furiously through my ears, the room starts to spin. In my head, all I can hear is the screeching of my father and the snapping of his jaws. I smell the death on his breath and feel his clawing fingers on my legs. I hear his bones shatter as I pound my foot into his face over... and over... and over again.

I can't breathe!

My vision is going black.

Am I dying? Or worse... am I turning?

Have I accidentally contaminated myself? Has the dried blood from my wrappings got into the cut on my hand?

I grip the edge of the sink tightly, desperate to stay upright. To stay alive. When I cry out for Tee, nothing but a strained wheezing escapes my lips. Water fills my eyes as I continue struggling for air.

I step forward, my eyes on the door. I have to get help! I let go of the sink and stumble, falling into the cabinet. The rotten wood crumbles under my weight and the whole thing crashes to the floor.

The bathroom door hurtles open.

Standing in the doorway is Cass.

His haladie is in his hand, ready to be wielded. Fury and anger covers every inch of his face as he checks I'm alone. Unable to stand for a second longer I start to fall. He lunges forward, the dagger in his hand.

Everything goes black.

CHAPTER FOUR

The sound of distant mumbling pierces through the thick, heavy fog that has consumed my mind.

I can't make it out. Not the words. Not the emotion. Not the voice.

My body is aching. My head is pounding.

But that doesn't stop me.

Because when I open my eyes, I see Cass, and he's coming at me with a knife.

I'm up and charging him, screaming threats and obscenities as I do. In the confusion of my sudden attack, he drops the knife and backs away. I get two punches in before he overpowers me and takes an unbearably tight grip of my wrists. He pushes me backwards, not easing up on his hold one bit.

'Don't fight me!' he orders.

Like hell!

I raise my foot and slam it into his stomach. He doubles over and I twist my wrists around, forcing him to let me go.

All this activity makes me dizzy. I grip the table I was just lying on and shake my head clear.

'Stop it!' he warns, pointing his finger at me and standing up straight. 'You stubborn bloody woman!'

As the room stops spinning, I realise I have no idea where the hell I am. It's not the cottage and my unit aren't here. By my foot is the knife Cass just dropped. It's not a knife. It's a scalpel. I snatch it up.

'You wanna kill me?' I ask, twirling the small blade in my fingers. 'Get in line. But just so ya know, I won't make it easy for you!' I scream as I rush him, pushing myself from the table to put some momentum into my otherwise weak and cumbersome movements. I slice and slash at him. He ducks and weaves. As I attack, I knock over small tables. Vases. Books. Cups. I notice that lining the walls are dozens upon dozens of shelves, showcasing the most hideous mugs with grotesque faces I have ever seen.

Where the hell am I?

Cass blocks me with perfection at every turn, which only fuels my rage. The room spins and I stagger, grasping the side of my head which pounds relentlessly. Cass steps closer, his hand outstretched. I charge. He sprints towards me, shoving me backwards. My feet trip over themselves and he doesn't stop till my back slams flat on the same table I was just unconscious on. My legs kick out as he concentrates on pinning down my hands.

'Drop the knife!' he demands.

'SCREW YOU!'

'Keep your sodding voice down-'

I let out a high-pitched scream filled with hatred. Cass slams his hand over my mouth and starts hitting my scalpel-wielding hand against the wooden tabletop.

'Drop,' *Thud.* 'The sodding,' *Thud.* 'Scalpel!' *THUD!*

My fingers relinquish their grip and the blade falls to the floor. He's between my legs and manages to take both my wrists in one hand while his other steals my screams.

'Stop it!' he says, as I thrash beneath him. 'Scarlett, will you please- argh!' I bite down hard on his hand until I taste the metallic liquid of his blood. But he doesn't let up. 'For God's sake. Listen to me... Stop... Will you just...' I never let up. I thrash and I bite and I scream. 'I LOVE YOU, SCARLETT! I'M TRYING TO HELP YOU! JUST STOP FUCKING FIGHTING ME!'

I fall still. I lay there, held fast, his blood dripping into my mouth and his entire body weight holding me down while I pant.

'*Hummphh diiiu shhaaayy faw meh?*' I ask, his hand muffling my voice.

'What?' he asks, with a quizzical furrow on his brow. I remove my teeth from his palm. 'Oh. Right. Sorry.' He moves it away so I can talk.

'What did you just say to me?' I whisper breathlessly.

'You heard. I love you, you crazy bint. Now listen...' He carries on like what he just said was beyond obvious. 'I'm not trying to hurt you or kill you.'

'You had a knife.'

'A scalpel. If you look over there, you'll also see hot water, a suture kit, and clean bandages.' He eases his grip on my hands and shows me the freshly sewn-up wound on my palm. 'I was just cutting the silk from your stitches. That's all. Now, if I let you go, will you stop trying to kill me?'

'I... I err... *You* want to kill *me*... Don't you?'

'No. Of course not! Look, I know you left cos of Noah. I know he threatened us all unless you did what he wanted and agree to be his wife. I know that's why you had no choice but to leave. And you did the right thing by leaving, even if you went about it like a prat. I would have done the same thing if I was in your position.'

'What? How-'

'Winder told me about Noah, okay? Just before we got herded into the lottery. He told me Noah was trying to force you into being his wife. I gathered that your leaving was the only way to stop that happening.' He lets me go and helps me to sit, remaining close with my legs either side of his hips. He holds my shoulders as I sway. 'Scarlett, when did you last eat?' His hand rests on my cheek as he looks into my eyes with deep concern. 'I've never seen you so weak and thin. You're as pale as the dead!'

I lower his hand and shake my head.

'You charged into my bathroom with your haladie. You were going to kill me.'

'I snuck in through your window hoping to talk to you in private. I heard you in the bathroom gasping and then there was a mighty crash. I thought Noah was in there with you or something! I charged in ready to kill whoever was attacking you! You saw me, then your eyes rolled into the back of your head and you passed out. I caught you before you cracked your skull open on the edge of the bathtub. When I saw how bad you were, I brought you here. I was so scared. I thought you were dying!'

I look around the room I'm in. It's nice. Too nice to be any-thing to do with the army. There are large ornate candlesticks on various antique units, all casting a warm glow in this cosy room. Behind Cass, there's a royal-blue sofa made of velvet with tasselled throw cushions and even a matching footstool. There's no damp. No weapons. No holes in the wall. And dozens of pottery mugs of old man heads watching us.

'Where exactly is *here?* Where have you brought me? And what the hell are those creepy mug things?"

'You are in my house and they are my Royal Doulton Toby mugs.'

I spin, throwing my gaze over my shoulder to the door where Elder One stands.

'He brought you here a couple of hours ago, unconscious and...' Elder One glances at my legs. 'Half-naked. Was a bit of a shock, I tell ya.' He walks in and places a bowl of leek and potato soup on the table. 'Let him finish fixing you up, Scarlett. He is of absolutely no threat to you and that hand's getting infected. And the eat this. All of it. You're skin and bones.' He turns, heading towards the door. 'And if you've broken any of my mugs, I won't be bloody happy. That collection took twenty years to put together!' He slams the door shut behind him.

Slowly, I turn back to Cass. He takes the bowl of soup, lifts the spoon and holds it to my lips. But they remain sealed shut. His eyes meet mine.

'You must eat.'

I don't need to say anything. He always could read me. It's like he can read my thoughts, as if they were printed on the whites of my eyes.

He lowers the spoon and places the bowl back on the table. 'I didn't mean what I said back at the kitchen in the slightest,' he tells me. 'What I said to you was unforgivable. Even though it was a lie.'

'No, it wasn't.'

'I didn't mean it. I only said it to make it look like I hated you.'

'It wasn't a lie, Cass.' My head falls forward. 'He *would* still be here if it wasn't for me.' I let out a long and painful breath. 'His death is all my fault. Elder Eight died... because of me.'

His finger settles under my chin so he can lift it. 'Elder Eight lived for you! You were his entire world, Scarlett. You have to know that.'

I shake my head and start pushing him away.

'Don't do that,' he says softly, taking my face in his hands and resting his nose against mine. 'You are not to blame for your father's death.'

'Then why say it? Hold on. My father? You know?'

He just keeps looking at me with a kind of dazed expression. His fingers run through my hair and glide softly along my jaw.

'Cass... what are you doing?'

'I'm sorry. I just... I can't believe you're really here. I thought... I was so afraid that I would never see you again.' He snaps back to reality and pulls out a piece of paper from his inside pocket. 'I know, because your dad told me.' He puts the paper in my hand. It's well worn. He's clearly handled it a lot. 'He wrote me a letter before you left that explained everything.' As I open it up and read, he strokes my arms. He caresses my hair. It's like he has to touch me as much as possible. The letter does tell him everything. My dad laid it all out in very simple terms. Me. Noah. Him and my mum. Even about our apple tree. He asked Cass to water it while we were gone. I look away from the paper and into his eyes. His silver-grey eyes that I've missed so much. He leans in and kisses me. But I pull away.

'I don't understand,' I tell him, looking at the paper clutched in my hand. 'Why behave like you did? Why-'

'Pretend that I hated you? Because if Noah thinks for even a second that you and I are anything less than enemies, he'll have us both arrested for unlawful relations and have us put to death. But not before destroying the people we both care about. Winder, Flash, Titan-'

'Tee. My unit. But you didn't need to say the things you did back at the cottage. Noah couldn't see us or hear us there.'

'Yes. He could, Scarlett.'

'What are you talking about?'

'Noah knew about us staying the night at the arcades before you left.'

'Impossible.'

'He knew. Someone told him. Believe me.' He lifts his shirt. All across his abdomen are light pink scars and scorch marks. Horrified, I gasp as I touch them all in turn. Some are really deep and there are too many to count. 'He had me tortured after I was arrested, to make me admit I took your virtue that night. He didn't just know we stayed inside the building. He knew we ate peanut butter. He knew we used that old generator to play the games on. He demolished the pier, saying that we will never have a place to call our own again.'

'That doesn't prove one of our own is his spy.'

'Maybe not. Maybe he was just guessing. Maybe he was just guessing Tee would always sleep in your bed. That you tried to kiss me all those years ago out in the snow.' He shrugs. 'I personally believe that someone who knows us fed him that intel. My money is on Flash. That little shit always hated me.'

'You hated him first,' I remind him. 'But even still, Flash? Really? Why?'

'For a Grey Coat, maybe?' He lowers his shirt to stop me antagonising over the marks he has because of me.

'This is all my fault. Your scars. Elders death.'

'It's Noah's fault. Not yours. Look. Maybe someone is feeding him information. Maybe they're not. Either way, I'm not risking it. So, as far as anyone else is concerned, you and I hate each other. I won't risk your safety. Noah is obsessed with you. Completely and utterly obsessed. He would have killed me if Elder One and a load of Black Coats hadn't charged in to get me out after I was arrested. Noah loves you and he's a psychopath. And a psychopath who thinks he's in love is pretty damn terrifying. Especially when it's the woman *I* love that he wants as his own. I won't let him hurt you any more than he already has.' My heart hammers as he makes that statement so absolutely. 'I am sorry, but if I don't do this right now, I'm going to explode.'

'Do what?'

His lips crash onto mine. His arms wrap around my body and he pins me close. His kiss is desperate and I meet his desperation with a fiery need of my own. My legs wrap around his waist and we continue our passionate embrace.

Until Elder One clears his throat from the doorway.

I shove Cass away hard, leaping to my feet and turning crimson.

'Yes. Yes. It's all very dramatic and touching. You love each other and by some miracle, you're both still alive. How about we work on keeping it that way, hmm? When you have quite finished reuniting, we need to talk.' He tosses me a pair of leggings. 'Because I need your help.'

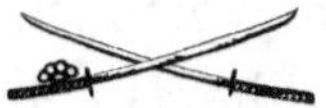

Elder One pours us a glass of whiskey before sitting himself on the velvet sofa. He averts his eyes while I pull on some clothes and Cass gives me his hooded jumper to wear. I let it swamp me, my nostrils filling with his scent.

'Sit,' Elder One tells us, 'Drink.' He gestures to the glasses on the table which I watch suspiciously. Drinking is forbidden. 'Don't tell me that dad of yours never shared his whiskey with you? I know for a fact that he kept a healthy stash of it hidden in that kitchen unit behind those books.'

'How did you know he is... I mean, was... Did everybody know he was my dad but me?'

'Who do you think married him and your mum? Hmm?' he says, taking a sip. 'I was a young Elder back then. He was my best friend. But never mind all that. What I need to know is... are you onboard?'

'Onboard?' I ask, still standing. 'Onboard for what?'

'Surely your dad told you.'

'Told me what?'

'For goodness sake,' he snaps. 'Let's just cut to the chase, shall we?' He gestures again for me to sit. It takes Cass nudging me in the back to actually plonk my backside down on the sofa. Cass sits beside me, his hand resting in mine. I'm worried about our intimacy, but Elder isn't remotely interested.

'Your dad and I had been discussing the possibility of breaking away from The Verity for a few years now. And then he had to go and die saving his daughter so we never got any further than just talking about it.' He looks at me a little sadly. 'He really loved you. You know that, right? He thought the absolute world of you.' He looks at Cass. 'And he approved of you. He said you were the only one that could make her happy. I was worried he'd given you more credit than you're worth when you started spouting off about how much you hated her. Even I believed you for a while there, until you disappeared when you thought she might have died. But as long as Noah believes you two aren't speaking, that's all that matters.' He raises his glass and takes a sip. 'How did you know you could trust me? Bringing her here was a big risk.'

'No it wasn't,' Cass replies. 'Her dad told me I could trust you in a letter he left me.'

'Well, that saves us some time I suppose. We can all trust each other. Isn't that peachy? So, me, your dad and Elder Ten. We've all been planning a coup, of sorts.'

'A coup?' Cass asks.

'You know what one of those is, don't ya?' Elder laughs. 'We don't like the government. We don't like their rule and we think we can do it better. Problem is, everyone's scared of Noah and his Grey Coats. Anytime someone stands up to him or tries to change how things are done around here, they either fall into a target-pit or get sentenced to The Canaries. And those who do defy him and leave these walls, never return. Noah and his Grey Coat's treatment of all of us is ruthless and they're only getting worse. We couldn't get enough people to stand with us in a coup, so we planned to take those who wanted to leave and go somewhere else instead. If Noah gets even a hint of dissension in the ranks, he stubs it out quicker than you can say zombie bite. No one dares defy him.' He points at me. 'Not until you.'

'Me?'

'Everyone knows how much you love the military and what they stand for. The cause. Defeating the targets and winning back our country! And now everyone knows he fixed that lottery because not a single person believes that you would put your name *in* that lottery to begin with. Then he threw his tantrum, demanding to know where *"Scarlett"* was. When he used your name, everyone knew that he knew who you were. That the lottery wasn't random at all. After all, he was only given your Cadet number. He showed everyone a glimpse of the kind of man he truly is after taking Cass and losing his temper so violently. No one liked what they saw. The other girls who put their number in? They wanted to withdraw it. Just in case he decided to redo the lottery later on and he picked them. You defied him, then left. But unlike the others in the past, you returned. And you returned as an Elder. You were arrested but you're still free. The soldiers are looking to you now.'

'To me? For what?'

'For what they can get away with. But that's not the point.' He leans forward in his chair. 'You see the point, don't you?'

'They *want* to disobey,' Cass says. 'They don't want to follow his rules and now they know that they don't have to.'

'Precisely. They're on the fence,' Elder says. 'You said you were recruiting. I'm assuming you have found some locations which we can relocate to? That's what you were getting at, right? When you gave your speech in the hall? Your dad and I kept talking about setting up a new base but we couldn't get far enough into the world to find anything decent. Did you find anything?'

'Erm...' My eyes dance left to right. 'I...'

'She ate anything yet?' Elder One asks Cass quietly, like I won't hear him if he mumbles. 'She still looks out of it.'

'I haven't eaten anything yet, no.' I give Cass my whiskey and rest my head in my hands. 'I just need a minute. Okay?'

'We don't have a minute, Scarlett,' Elder urges. 'We're pushing it, you being here at my house, as it is. Have you found any locations suitable for us to move to?!'

I nod and lift my head. 'Yes. Yes, I have. Elder Eight and I kept them to ourselves. We didn't want The Verity to know about them so they couldn't find us after we left. We didn't put them in any of the pigeon letters back home.'

'Tell me about the locations.'

'No.'

'No?' he snarls.

'No. I'm sorry, but I'm not really with it after Noah smacking my head into his desk and not eating or sleeping properly for days. I know when I can trust my judgment and I can't trust it right now.'

'Before you slot me into your *"do not trust"* pile, just think about who got both of you away from Noah. He was about to carve you open, Cassius. And Scarlett, you were barely conscious, under his boot and about to be forcibly married to him before I saved your backside. And that old man of yours? The one who died in order to save you? He was my closest and dearest friend. He was my goddamn brother and he died to save your sorry arse. You think I would ever betray the person he loved most? That I would side with the man who is more than likely the one who caused his death?!' His anger contaminates the air. He looks at me with enraged eyes and white knuckles. 'Never mind the fact that you are in my house, talking treason, drinking whiskey, and only a moment ago, you were half-naked with your tongue down your boyfriend's throat! If I was on Noah's side, don't you think I would have called him here? Huh? Handed you and Cass over to him?'

'I-I'm sorry,' I offer.

'You better bloody be!' he huffs, downing the remainder of his drink and getting to his feet. His eyes watch me with every step he takes, right up until he has left the room entirely.

'Can you not piss him off?' Cass mutters, squeezing my hand. 'We're not exactly drowning in allies here.'

'I didn't mean too,' I reply is a hush. 'But I have no idea who to trust, Cass. After everything you've said... Everything that's happened... Everything I've lost! How can I trust him? How can I trust anyone? All it would take is the wrong word said in the wrong ear and more people will die. I can't be responsible for anyone else dying. If I hadn't have yelled at Sky and upset her, she would never have run off the way she did. She wouldn't have rushed into the mortuary. She wouldn't have fallen in! If Elder Eight hadn't have jumped down to save me... If-'

He turns. His hands cup my face and his eyes search mine.

'You are not responsible for anyone's death.'

As I scoff, he firms his grip and raises his brows. He refuses to let my face go and leans in a little closer.

'You. Are not. Responsible. His death was *not* your fault!'

With a stoic stare, he waits for me to accept his words. But I know that no matter what he says or how often he says it, I will never rid myself of this soul-crushing, mind-numbing, heart-breaking guilt.

The nod I offer is half-hearted at best, and I think he knows that. I think he knows that this is the best I can offer. But he accepts it. He also accepts my inability to shed a tear for my fallen father just as he has accepted my inability to say the words I know he longs to hear. Those three words have never passed my lips. I never said them to my father and the pain I am suffering is unbearable. I dread to think how much worse it would be for me if I had said them. If I had allowed myself to really love him. Cass would never question that my lack of tears would ever reflect on just how much I miss Elder Eight. He wasn't only the man I know now as my biological father, but also the man who taught me how to survive this world and find joy and safety in amongst all this death, destruction and pain. Elder wanted me to love. He tried endlessly to get me to admit that I not only cared for my family, but that I needed them as much as they needed me. It confused him for years, that the only emotion I was capable of showing to anyone for the first decade of my life was embarrassment. My body gave it away. My cheeks would turn crimson. But I wouldn't laugh. I wouldn't cry. I wouldn't get jealous or even angry. Elder never gave up trying to get me to open myself up to others. Neither did my family. Winder, Tee and Cass stood by my side through everything, with Elder Eight always lingering somewhere close by, and they taught me together how to feel. And now I can't face feeling anything.

'Do you trust me?' Cass asks, pulling my wandering thoughts back to the here and now.

'Yes,' I reply, resting my hand over his as his thumb traces back and forth over my cheek. 'I do. More than I trust myself right now.'

'Then let me judge who we can trust until you feel ready to. Trust *me*, Scarlett. Let me help you.'

We lean in, our lips meet for no longer than a second when Elder One returns with a binder. He drops it on my lap and re-takes his seat.

'What's this?'

'Open your eyes and see for yourself.'

I flick through its pages and see it's a ledger.

A death ledger.

'Funny thing,' Elder says, jabbing his finger at one letter stating the death of six Canaries. 'Two years ago, the average survival rate of a Canary unit plummeted. And I mean... *plummeted*. Before, twenty percent of those that left didn't come back. Not a great statistic, to be fair. But much better than what we have today. Now, an average of ninety percent are killed in action.'

'That many?' I whisper, horrified. 'I didn't know that.'

'That's because no one knows who has been sentenced or who has volunteered anymore. Or when they leave. Or how long they are supposed to be gone for. Two years ago, it all changed. Noah took control of the Canaries and now, he carries out the sentencing. He's the only one who knows who has left and how long they are leaving for.'

'He didn't know about me leaving,' I reply.

'Yes. Well, that's because you and your father technically were never Canaries. Your dad broke into the Guardhouse and took the names of the next Canary unit due to leave and lied to them, saying that he was leading the mission and that their departure date had been moved up. There was no paperwork at all. He didn't even tell me what he was planning. He just did what he needed to do to get you away from Noah before the lottery announcement.'

'But... he had Canary coats for us both.'

'He had his old Canary coat. And he had your mums old Canary coat, which, he gave to you.'

My hand grips Cass's tightly as I realise I've been wearing my dead mother's coat all this time.

'What does that tell you? About the sudden death rate increase? Are the targets getting smarter out there? Are our training techniques worse now than they were ten years ago? No,' he says, not giving us a chance to answer. 'Our soldiers are the best they have ever been and those monsters out there aren't getting any the wiser on catching us. There's more.'

'More?' I ask with dread.

'I discovered only a few weeks ago that Noah has been rewarding those who do return from Canary missions with honorary Grey Coat positions.'

'Really? He has? I didn't know that.'

'No one did. I only discovered it through chance. I overheard a group of Grey Coats talking about it when they thought no one was around. So. We have a group of people leaving The Haven as Canaries and then only one, sometimes two, return. On occasion, none return at all. But those who do return, they report straight to Noah as soon as they set foot inside The Haven. No one knows who it is that comes back because they go straight to Noah's mansion by the sea and walk out wearing those stupid Grey hoods. Want to know my theory?'

I know exactly what he suspects. 'Someone is sabotaging the Canaries. And you think it's the ones who return.'

'I do,' he sighs sadly. 'It's too much of a coincidence otherwise. The Canaries leave, and most of the time, they never return. That's all we know. That's all we're told.'

'That's all we see,' I agree, thinking of all the soldiers who I've known that left as a Canary for some unknown crime, never to return.

'Precisely. At least, that's how it's been the last couple of years. These sole survivors return and report to Noah. I can't tell you how many of the Grey Coats were once Canaries. I simply don't know.'

'So, you believe that perhaps these Canaries, the survivors, they are working for Noah from the word go? That they leave with the units under his instruction?'

Elder One nods. 'I'm betting that Noah already knows all of your safe locations. I'm betting that Noah knows everywhere you went. What you saw. What you faced and how often you took a piss. Because if the past few years are anything to go by, I'm pretty damn sure that one of your lot was working for him all along. But that still doesn't change the fact that we need to leave and you are the only people who know of any hospitable areas in which we could survive.'

'None of my unit would betray us.' I shake my head adamantly, my hair flicking my face as I do. 'Not a one. Nope. No way!'

'Hmmm.' Elder sits back, surveying me with scrutiny. 'How about you tell me how your dad *really* died? Tell me what you couldn't tell me back at Elder HQ.'

I glance to Cass, who nods me on in encouragement.

'The pit that Sky fell into was *made*. The floor didn't give way. It was torn up and the targets were put down in that hole. There was another pit at a separate location too. The targets looked neat. They had clothes on. They might not have even been that old.'

'So, who fell into these pits?' he asks.

'Loom and me at the first one by the church. Sky at the mortuary. I jumped in to save her. And Elder... I mean... my dad, he jumped in to save me.'

'So, Chilli didn't fall in?' Cass says suspiciously.

'No.'

'Then he must be the spy.'

'But there's no way he could have disappeared long enough to make the traps without us noticing he was gone. No way. We slept in shifts. Three hours max. It's not physically possible!'

'Not for him, maybe,' Cass says. 'But there are ways to get messages to people. He could have let others know where you would be. Other Grey Coats, maybe? And you know that I'm pretty sure someone was reporting to Noah before you left too. How else would he know all that stuff, huh? About the arcades? About Tee?'

'I... I don't think Chilli would. I don't think any of them would.' I look between them. Surely, they can't be serious. 'I think you're wrong. As you said, my unit was different. We left sooner than we were supposed to. Noah probably didn't have a chance to insert his spy yet.'

'I know it's hard to suspect someone you've fought with in such close quarters,' Elder says. 'But Scarlett, that floor didn't rip *itself* up and the trail of dead Canaries can't just be a coincidence!'

'But... Noah wanted me *back*. Not dead,' I argue. 'He loves me, right? He wants me to marry him. Would he risk killing me? And only one of us died. Not like the others where whole units have been wiped out. And as far as I'm aware, none of us is being handed a Grey Coat.'

'You hit the nail on the head. Noah wanted you back. Not dead. And what brought you back?' Cass asks with a knowing look. 'What happened that the law states you must return home for? When a soldier dies after being sentenced to the Canaries, the unit is entitled to bring their body home for burial. Then, they head out again. Someone died, you came home. And if it is an Elder, it is the law! You must return!'

He and Elder One glance at each other as the pieces of their puzzle slot so perfectly together. But the pieces still fail to fit for me.

'You truly think that someone killed my dad all so I would return home and marry Noah? And they did it for, what? A Grey Coat?' I laugh and shake my head. 'No way.'

'Either way, I think it best we play it safe. We should assume Noah knows all the locations you discovered.' Elder leans over and turns the pages of the ledger still in my lap. 'You should also look at this.'

I look at the list of names, beside them are dates and ages. 'What's this?'

'The missing,' he tells me. 'Civilians and soldiers alike. I started getting reports from the village a few months ago. Apparently, they were telling the Grey Coats that people were going missing. But they didn't do anything about it. They just said that sometimes people run away. So, one of the village leaders snuck into the military village and sought me out personally to ask for my help. I looked into it. Over the last two years, over a hundred civilians have gone missing and nothing has been done to look for them.'

We look at each other for a fair amount of time as it sinks in. All the information he is sharing is far more than troubling. It's downright terrifying. Cass's grip on me tightens.

'Noah has declared no one is to go beyond the wall until winter is over,' Elder tells us. 'Not Black Coats, Cadets or Canaries. Despite the fact that snow hasn't even started to fall. That's why he wanted to talk to me earlier. To implement his... *"lockdown"*. He's put Grey Coats up on the wall, along with the Green Coats, to make sure no one leaves.'

'We're trapped?'

'Yes. At least until the snow has finished falling.' He rests his hand on mine. 'He doesn't want you to leave, Scarlett. He wanted me to revoke your Elder status so you were eligible for marriage once again. I refused, of course. But I fear it is only a matter of time until he finds a way around it.'

'Around you, you mean.'

He nods slowly.

'Yes. He's made it pretty damn clear that unless I release you as Elder, he'll remove any and all obstacles that stand between his plans to wed you.'

'He means to kill you, Elder.'

'He means to kill anyone who stands between him and you,' he states plainly, his eyes flicking briefly to Cass.

'I will not allow anyone else to die for me!' I snap, shoving off their comforting hands and getting to my feet. 'I won't!'

My toes sink beneath the deep-pile carpet as I walk up and down, up and down. My mind is raging. My thoughts are screaming over themselves as each one tries to get my attention. Images of my unit, of all we faced, all the laughs we shared and the times we saved each other. Are they lies? Manipulations? What if Elder Eight and I were the only genuine members? What if the reason no one else died out beyond the wall is that no one else was supposed to? How can I know who to trust? Who do I try to save when I can't see who my enemies are?

Where are the missing civilians? Why is this happening? We have monsters desperate to eat us alive and a planet screaming to be rescued. How... *how* can it possibly be that the biggest threat to humanity is other bloody humans?

The other two leave me to stalk the room as they discuss their plans. They want to leave. They want to flee The Haven and set up somewhere new. They discuss methods of sneaking past the guarded wall. They debate what supplies are most important. Who to trust. Who must be taken with us and how we will fight when Noah tries to stop us.

I stop pacing. At that moment, it's as if I've been struck by lightning. All my thoughts and conflictions, my anger and hatred, it all falls silent and now my mind is as calm and still as a millpond.

'None of that matters,' I say over them, cutting off their conversation and turning to face them. 'How we escape... It doesn't matter.'

'How can you say that?' Cass complains. 'Of course it matters. We need to be careful. We need to plan, Scarlett. One miss-step and Noah will end us all. One wrong move and he will kill us and take you as he pleases! And with all the dead Canaries and missing people-'

'It doesn't matter, because we're not leaving. We're not abandoning this place. These people. The civilians, who, as you said, are disappearing. Who are now forced to breed more than our livestock? Who can't even choose who they want to love? Who have their children stolen and forced into this life.' I look at Cass. 'I won't leave them. I won't leave my friends, my comrades, the children in the orphanage, the Brown Coat Cadets… I will not leave a single one behind.' I look at Elder. 'If we leave, we abandon them to a life of misery. And life is so rare to come by, it shouldn't have to be miserable as well. You said you were planning a coup? Then let's do it! Let's overthrow the government. Let's kick Noah and the Grey Coats out of the home *we* built. Let's banish *them* to a life beyond the wall.'

'Atta girl,' Elder smirks. 'There's my best friend's daughter.'

'Okay then…' Cass lets out a long breath and drags his fingers through his hair. 'So what's the plan?'

'I have three Elders that I know will fight against Noah,' Elder One informs us. 'Five including you and me. Elder Six, Nine and Ten will stand against Noah. But there are two I know who will not. Elder Two and Elder Five have been reporting back to Noah on everything the other Elders and I have been doing for a while now. I wish I could tell you how long for. It could be years. It could be months. The other Elders, Elders Three, Four and Seven are simply terrified of Noah and they could go either way.'

'Can we make a move without them?'

'We can try but if we go to them and they decide that telling Noah our plans would be safer for them, then we'll be done before we even start. By done, I mean dead. Their Cadets are loyal to them. If they side with Noah, they might too.'

There's a knock on his front door.

We all fall silent and look to the hallway.

'Are you expecting company?' Cass whispers, looking to the clock on the wall telling us it's three am.

Elder shakes his head.

They knock again. Harder this time.

'Elder One!' Calls a familiar voice.

'It's the Grey Coat Commander,' I whisper. 'The bastard that pulled my tooth out when I got back.'

'He did what?' Cass hisses, leaping to his feet and wrapping his arm around my waist. He tries to look inside my mouth.

The Commander knocks again. 'We know you're in there. Open up!'

'Take her out the back,' Elder orders, nudging us into the hallway. As we turn to the back of the house, the knocking continues from the same direction Elder was leading us. 'Damn. We're surrounded.' Without a moment's hesitation, Elder grabs my elbow and drags me back inside the lounge. Cass and I watch as he takes hold of one of the shelving units and pulls, revealing behind it a hidden cupboard. It's a small square lined with more shelves. And on those shelves are countless bottles of alcohol, cigars, books, tinned food, chocolates and sweets.

'In. Quick!'

Elder pushes me and Cass inside. It's a small cupboard and we're crushed together, both our backs are pressed against the shelving and our chests are wedged together.

'Don't make a sound,' Elder warns, stashing away the glasses of spirit we were drinking on one of the shelves behind me. 'No matter what, you don't come out. Do you hear me? That's an order. And don't break or eat anything. This is my life's savings.' He seals us in. Only the slightest sliver of light sneaks in through the very top of the concealed door. I look up at Cass who peers down at me with narrowed eyes.

'We can't just hide in here,' I whisper. 'If they hurt him-'

'He can handle it.'

'But-'

'Shh!' Elder warns through the door.

Cass is on high alert. Every muscle in his body is ready and raring to fight. I take his hand in mine and we wait.

We hear more knocking.

'Yeah... alright. Keep your hair on.' Elder opens the front door and several pairs of feet thump inside his home. Their voices mumble and I can't make out what they're saying from out in the hall. Not until Elder One and the Commander enter the room in which we're hiding.

'I've already told you,' Elder sighs. 'I can't revoke the girl's Eldership, even if I wanted to. Lord Sands will need to find another pretty, young thing to keep him warm at night.'

'Well,' the Commander replies leisurely, 'That is a shame. Lord Sands will be most disappointed.' I hear his feet shuffle, and then with a hint of callous joy, he adds, 'Until he gets what he wants anyway. As he always does.'

Elder grunts in reply.

'Nonetheless, the girl is not the reason for my visit.'

'So, what is the reason for your visit to my home at three am precisely?'

'We are looking for a Red Coat. I believe you know him.'

'I should hope so. I'm the Elder in charge. If I didn't know my Red Coats I'd be a pretty poor excuse of an Elder. Which one are you looking for?'

'I think you know,' the Commander sneers.

'I have more than thirty. Perhaps a name-'

'You lot don't have names. You are merely worker ants, insignificant and forgettable.'

'And yet there is an insignificant and forgettable ant that has you and six of your men out in the early hours, searching my house.' I hear the mocking tone in Elder's voice.

There are some slow and steady footsteps. I feel my body prepare for battle, just as Cass's has. He takes both my wrists firmly in hand, holding me in place.

'He's vain. Egotistical. Self-righteous and blasphemous. Just as his given name would suggest.'

'Gonna need a little more than that.'

'Cassius. Where. Is. Cassius?'

'Ahhh,' Elder breathes. '*That* Red Coat. Nope. Haven't seen him. Not since he left the Main Hall after we received word that one of the Canaries had passed away.'

'Is that so? Well, I have received a report that the cretin attempted to kill that new Elder of yours.'

'He did, hmm? How so?'

'He threw a knife at her head.'

'Ahh, well, I would probably guess that he didn't intend to kill her. If he had wanted to bury the blade of his haladie in her skull, he wouldn't have missed.'

'You seem pretty sure of that.'

'I've seen the kid use that thing. No one better. And he doesn't miss. Ever. So I would probably say it was more of an argument than attempted murder.'

'Well, his poor aim doesn't defer from the fact that he threw a bladed weapon at his superior. At the woman our Lord and Commander cares so deeply for.' His words are far from genuine, I can almost taste the sarcasm. 'Then there is the matter of his behaviour with the Black Coat girl in his unit.'

'What behaviour?'

Cass tenses even further. As I glance up at him, he avoids looking me in the eye.

'We have received reports that he was seen in a rather compromising position with a young lady.'

'Compromising position?' Elder repeats.

'And the young girl has confirmed this. She has also stated that the attention she received from him was one-sided and... not consensual.'

Cass's eyebrows narrow together as anger stirs from within.

'If you are talking about the young blonde the others call *"Melody"*,' Elder One says. 'Then I have heard similar rumours. However, I assure you that their brief dalliance was far from non-consensual. It was the girl, Melody, I heard boasting about her actions with her Red Coat. In fact-'

'The poor girl gave public testimony.'

'Public testimony?'

'Oh yes. She stood before the soldiers a few hours ago and she informed them all of his barbaric behaviours. There is a warrant out for the arrest of the Red Coat named Cassius for the charge of attempted murder... and rape,' The Commander states. 'If you see him, you are to hand him over immediately. Anyone found harbouring him or protecting him will meet the same fate as he is now intended for.'

'And what fate is that? You gonna sentence the lad to the Canaries?'

'Oh no,' the Commander laughs darkly. 'Cassius is to be arrested... and executed. On-sight. As soon as one of my men lays eyes on him, he will be terminated then and there.'

'You can't do that,' Elder replies sternly, rising to his feet. 'Every man and every woman has the right to a trial. You cannot kill him on-sight!'

'You didn't hear?' The Commander mocks. 'Lord Sands has changed the laws regarding how and when a guilty bastard like him meets his end.'

'Since when? How long has this warrant for his death been out?'

'From the moment you took Lord Sand's bride away from him.'

The sound of more men joining them in the room has me tense even further. Elder is so outnumbered and neither Cass or I have our weapons. And now Cass is to be killed immediately if seen? What the hell do we do?

'Well?' the Commander demands.

'Nothing, Sir,' replies an unknown and unfamiliar voice. 'We searched everywhere. No one else is here.'

'Well, I told you that when you barged your way inside,' Elder grunts, slumping down in his settee with a weary groan. 'Anything else I can help you with? A cup of water, perhaps? I think I have some stale bread in a coat pocket somewhere.'

The men pile out. Footsteps fade away until all I can hear are a few mumbling voices and then a closing door.

Moments pass. It feels like hours with Cass's stare burning into the side of my head. Finally, Elder One opens the door and I launch myself out.

'He's talking shit!' Cass insists, reaching out to take my hand. 'I would never force myself on anyone. That's a load of crap!'

I snatch my hand away and shake my head.

'What brief dalliance?' I ask, looking between Elder and Cass. 'Who the hell is Melody and why is she standing in front of the entire army saying you raped her?!'

'Melody is in my unit,' Cass replies softly, still reaching out for me. I pull my hand away and step back, disgust and betrayal coursing through my veins. 'Noah's obviously forced her to say those things. I barely touched her! For God's sake, Scarlett. You can't actually believe-'

'Did you kiss her?' I ask. 'When I was gone? Did you kiss her?'

He looks stuck. Like he wants to talk but the words are failing to form.

'Did you have sex with her?'

'No!' he insists, shaking his head violently from side to side. 'Never. I would never betray you like that.'

'But you kissed her?'

'She caught me at a bad time. It was one, single kiss! I swear to you. One kiss which I ended after a few moments. She wanted more. I had to stop her from pulling off my trousers-'

'I can't deal with this right now.' I turn away, shaking my head and covering my face with my hands. I take no more than two deep breaths before Elder One speaks.

'Cass didn't force himself on anyone. You know that's all a load of rubbish. I heard Melody bragging to another girl that she kissed Cass. Noah is just coming up with excuses for this vile execution order he's issued. A rapist that tried to kill an Elder is a far easier sell for an immediate execution than a devoted soldier who holds the heart of the one he loves. He's jealous, Scarlett. And he's lying.'

'I know that!' I snap back. 'Of course I know he's lying. I know Cass would never do anything like that.' I look at Cass who still seems both enraged and agonised over this disgusting accusation. 'He's going to kill you!' I slump down on the sofa, my face buried in my hands. 'And it's all my fault. Again.'

Cass sits beside me, his arm draped over my shoulders.

'It's not your fault! Scarlett... look at me.' He lifts my chin with his finger. Our eyes meet and I hate the guilt I see in his gaze. 'I'm sorry I kissed Melody. It truly meant nothing.'

'You kissed Melody. I kissed Noah.' I shrug. 'Both those kisses have really fucked us over. Now I have a psychopath in love with me and you have a girl calling you a rapist.'

There is no doubt whatsoever in my mind that this is all a lie. Cass is not capable of anything like that. He has the scars on his back from beating a man who touched Tee without her consent several years ago. 'How can you hope to last the day with every Grey Coat looking for you with the orders to kill you on-sight?'

I reach out and take his face in my hands. I can't bear the thought of losing him. Of seeing him slaughtered. Of living in the world without him.

His hands cup my face and he puts on his most charming smile.

'You don't need to worry about me. I mean... I am the Red Coat after all. They didn't give me this coat because it brings out the colour of my eyes.' He gives me a cheeky little wink as I roll my eyes. 'Besides. We're starting a revolution. All our heads will roll if we fail.'

'Worst pep talk ever.'

'Well,' Elder One huffs. 'Now that's all sorted, we'll wait for the sun to rise and you can be on your way, Scarlett. In the meantime, we need to figure out who it was that told them about your little dagger throwing display.'

'Had to be someone in the kitchen. Everyone was there. All the Canaries and all of our old unit. It could have been any of them.'

'When the Commander finishes his search of the cottage, Scarlett, you better get over there and start asking some questions. See if you can shake something loose-'

'Wait. What?' I leap to my feet. 'The cottage? He's gone to the cottage? Now?'

'Yes. That's where they're heading now. To look for Cass,' he replies with a shrug. 'Good job you're here or they might have ended up arresting you on some trumped-up charge.'

'Shit,' I hiss, running to the door. Cass grabs my arm and pulls me back.

'You're not going out there alone in the dark. You're not even at full strength and you're unarmed as well as injured! Just let him look for me there. He won't find me and he'll move on. I don't want you anywhere near the Grey Coats or whoever it was that told him about our fight in the kitchen!'

'They have my dad's whiskey out!' I tell him, pulling my arm free.

'Ah,' Elder says. 'Well... yes. That is a problem.'

'Noah will take any excuse to dish out punishment to those I care about. I can't just hide here while they're in danger.'

'I'll come with you then,' Cass insists.

'No, you won't. There are orders to kill you if seen.' I turn, but he pulls me back. I land in his arms and there's a deep terror on his face as he looks down at me.

'I just got you back. I can't lose you again.'

'Likewise.' I lean up and kiss him. I kiss him with everything I have. When we part, I look at Elder One and nod. He attaches the handcuffs I saw him pull from his pocket to Cass's wrist and tethers him to the doorknob. I step back, out of Cass's reach. 'Stay put. I'll come back as soon as I can.'

I charge out of the room, through the back door, and sprint as fast as I can through the woods.

CHAPTER FIVE

By the time I reach the cottage I'm out of breath, light-headed and covered in dirt and twigs. I notice that the Commander and his hooligans are already there. I watch them from outside the kitchen window. Loom and Chilli are following every single Grey Coat around as they search the house. Winder and Tee are sat at the kitchen table being questioned. They look like they've just woken up. Their hair's a mess and their eyes are puffy. But they seem perfectly calm and composed as they answer whatever questions they are being asked. A hand lands on my shoulder. I spin around, my fist clenched and ready to fly.

'Easy, Scar,' Sky whispers, holding up her hands and stepping back. 'It's only me.'

'Sky? What are you doing out here?'

'Looking for you of course.' She steps closer, pulling out the twigs from my hair. 'Where have you been? Are you alright?'

'I'm fine. I needed a walk is all,' I lie, trying hard to slow down my breathing. 'What are you doing out here?' I look back to the window. 'And what are they doing in there?'

'They're looking for Cass,' she tells me. 'When the Grey Coats started hammering on the door a few moments ago, I ran upstairs to wake you up but you weren't there. The window was open so I assumed you snuck out. I snuck out too, to avoid the Grey Coats and to try and find you. As I was leaving, I heard that they were looking for Cass.'

'C'mon. We should go in there.'

'Maybe you shouldn't,' she suggests. 'The last time you faced them, they stole one of your teeth!'

'It's okay. I have a couple dozen more.' I attempt a smile but she doesn't return it. Instead, she folds her arms across her chest and glares at me. 'You've already been spending too much time with Tee. You've got her scowl down perfectly. C'mon.'

Together, we head around the side of the house and go inside.

As soon as I enter the kitchen, Tee and Winder get to their feet and the Grey Coat questioning them turns to face me.

'Where have you been?' he demands.

'Good evening, Commander,' I greet, recognising his voice instantly. 'Or should I say morning? What are you doing here?'

'I asked you a question. Where have you been?'

'For a walk,' Sky replies, linking her arm with mine. 'With me.'

'A walk where?'

'The woods,' she replies, with her usual sweet smile.

'At this hour?'

'Well, if it's a good enough time for you to wake everyone up and search her house for no reason whatsoever, why is it out of the question to go for a walk?'

'I'm not talking to you, Canary. If you open your mouth again, I'll have it wired shut. You hear me?'

I see her about to throw back a snide remark and cut her off before she gets a chance.

'I couldn't sleep so I went for a walk. Sky kept me company. What do you want?'

He takes a few steps towards me and asks, 'Where is the Red Coat you call Cassius?'

I shrug. 'No idea.'

'So, you haven't seen him since returning?'

'I have seen him,' I reply. 'He was here earlier. We argued and he left.' Tee looks shocked that I've admitted to that. But I know the Commander already knows what happened, so lying would be pointless.

'Cass isn't here so if you don't mind-'

'You think you're clever.'

'Not really. Like I said. Cass isn't here. So get out of my house.'

'Nice top,' he says, gesturing to Cass's hoody which I'm currently wearing. 'A little large for you.'

'Because it's mine,' Winder tells him. 'I lent it to her until she gets a chance to wash her clothes. No law against that, is there?'

'Not yet there isn't, Winder. But give it time.' I raise my eyebrows and continue to watch the Commander. 'Anything else?'

'What's the Black Coat doing here?' The Commander asks, nodding to Winder. 'And why are the Canaries and the little Green Coat not in the Warren where they belong?'

'The Canaries are my unit. They stay where I tell them to stay. And I've told them to stay here. The Black Coat and the Green Coat are my friends and I've told them they can stay as often as they want.'

We stand in silence, not looking away as we listen to my house being turned upside down. After ten minutes of banging and smashing, the Grey Coats all return to their Commander, followed closely by Chilli and Loom.

'Nothing, Commander.' One of the faceless prats report.

'Are you sure? You looked... everywhere?'

'Did you check under the beds?' I ask with a smirk. 'Or perhaps Cass is in the wardrobe.'

'Oh, they looked there,' Loom says darkly. 'Even in the kitchen cupboard, behind the books.'

'Huh,' I nod, knowing full well that that is where Elder hid his booze. 'Find anything?'

'Nope,' Chilli grins. 'Not a thing, huh lads?'

'Shame. Maybe next time. You can show yourself out.' I gesture to the door and watch the Grey Coats pile thorough it.

All except the Commander who remains by the door.

He turns to the room as a whole. 'There is a warrant out for the arrest of the Red Coat you call Cassius,' he declares. 'If you see him or know of his location, you are to report it to us immediately. If you are discovered to be protecting him, hiding him or helping him, you will meet the same fate as he will.'

'Gonna sentence us all to the Canaries?' Chilli scoffs.

'No,' The Commander replies, turning on his heel and walking out the door. 'We'll kill you right alongside the traitorous little heathen. Good night, Elder Eight. I'll pass your regards on to Lord Sands.'

When the door slams closed, all eyes turn on me.

'What the hell was that about?'

'Cass has an execution order?'

'Where were you?'

'What's going on?'

I lower my tired head and hold my hand up, silencing them all.

'Did they find anything?' I ask sharply, lifting my gaze to them each in turn.

'No,' Tee replies, stepping closer to Winder. His arm wraps around her waist as she pulls at the hem of her oversized t-shirt. 'They looked in all the places Elder hid all his secret stash. I thought for sure we were done for.'

'They didn't find anything?' I ask, completely confused. 'He had at least a dozen bottles of booze hidden in that cupboard.'

'After you guys went to bed, I tidied up,' Loom says. His eyes dart around the room, landing on each and every one of them in turn. 'I moved them.'

'Where to?' Chilli asks.

I meet Looms gaze and shake my head. We share a knowing look. The same look we had over the pit we fell into. The same look we shared as we stood over the torn-up floorboards at the mortuary.

Someone passed on information about the location of that alcohol to the Grey Coats. Someone told them about Cass coming to the house earlier.

I slump down into the nearest chair, utterly exhausted and with so much information swirling around in my head, I can barely think straight.

'You should all go to bed. Try and get some sleep.' I pinch the bridge of my nose and close my eyes. 'We'll face this all after some rest.'

'Sure thing, Boss.' Loom holds open the kitchen door and they leave.

It takes a moment for me to realise that Tee and Winder have stayed. I lower my hand and look up at them.

Tee sits beside me.

'Are you okay?' she asks.

I shake my head.

'Noah's declared that Cass is to be killed as soon as he's found.' I sigh and lean forwards, resting my elbows on the table. 'He's trying to accuse him of raping some girl called Melody and trying to kill me. I know it's all a load of rubbish but Noah wants him gone.'

'*Bastard!*' Winder hisses, slamming his hand down on the table. 'Is Cass okay? Where is he?' He gestures to my clothes. 'I know that's Cass's hoody. You've seen him, haven't you?'

'I can't tell you that right now.'

He sits at the table and lowers his voice.

'Is he safe?' he asks painfully. 'Can you at least tell me that? He's my brother, Scar. Please. Just tell me that he's safe?'

I nod. 'He's safe. For now.' I groan loudly and let my forehead lay on the table. My head thumps into the wood repeatedly, like perhaps I can knock a brilliant idea into my brain somehow. 'This is such a mess.'

Tee rests her hand out and catches my forehead.

'Let's go to bed and get some sleep.'

'I'll sleep here. You two go and have my bed upstairs.'

'Nonsense. We're family. We stick together. Come on.'

'I can't be arsed to move,' I yawn.

'Lazy cow,' he laughs, scooping me up tossing me over his shoulder.

I'm laid on the bed and just as we used to do when we very first left the orphanage, when we were scared little children no older than five, we all snuggle down together, gripping each other's hands tightly.

The only one missing is Cass.

The open window brings with it a chill in the air. The breeze blows the curtain, dazzling me every so often as the sunlight sneaks past the billowing drape.

I sit and find the bed empty.

My head's still spinning from everything I've faced since walking through Haven's gates.

I'm an Elder.

Cass still loves me.

There's a spy amongst us.

We're plotting treason and revolution.

My father is dead…

I push that last thought from my head and get myself up. Still wearing Cass's hoody and a pair of black joggers, I head onto the landing.

There's a note pinned to the bedroom door.

"Scar, we had to go to work. Didn't want to wake you. I'm on the wall at the fifth mile. Come see me.

Tee xx"

Propped up against the wall are my Katanas. I reach out but I can only bring the very tips of my fingers to touch them. My throat feels tight at the mere idea of picking them up. My hand begins to tremble.

What the hell?

I retract my hand and feel better instantly. When I attempt to pick them up again, I react even worse and struggle to breathe. Flashes of my father, juddering and convulsing, snarling and biting, fill my head. My throat starts to close, just like it did last night in the bathroom before I passed out.

I step away. I distance myself from my swords. I won't take them. I don't need to. Not if I go straight to the wall and see Tee.

I pull up my hood and leave. Downstairs, Loom and Chilli are curled up on the old musty sofa in the lounge still snoring heavily. Sky is laying on the floor under a large blanket, mumbling to herself in her sleep. I leave them to catch up on their rest and head outside.

On the porch, Titan is sitting on the steps. He jumps to his feet when he spots me.

'You're up!' he says. 'How are you feeling?'

'Fine,' I tell him, suddenly feeling very cautious. If someone is reporting back to Noah about me, it could be Titan. 'What are you doing out here?'

'I've been keeping watch. Ya know… in case anyone came looking for trouble. Again. I heard the Grey Coats came by.'

'How did you hear about that?'

'Flash told me.'

'How did Flash know? He wasn't here last night.'

'I think Chilli told him when he came by this morning.'

'Flash came by? Why?'

'He was worried about you,' he says with a light shrug. 'He left about an hour ago to report for work up on the wall. Oh, and here.' He holds out a handful of envelopes for me to take.

'What are these?' I ask, taking them.

'Thirteen transfer requests,' he says. 'Folks have been coming over all morning.'

'Thanks.'

Titan's feet shuffle in the dirt. 'I err... well, I want you to know that I want to put in a request too,' he tells me.

'You do?'

'I do. But, well, Flash isn't too sure. You know how he is beyond the wall. But I'm working on getting him to change his mind. I can't leave him behind. You understand, right?'

'Of course.'

'Have you heard? About the warrant for Cass's arrest?'

I start walking down the steps. 'Yeah. I heard.'

'What are we gonna do?' he asks. 'We can't let him be executed!'

'Right now, I honestly have no idea.'

'Do you know where he is? Is he okay?'

'I don't know if I said thank you for helping me yesterday. In case I didn't... Thanks. I'll be back later.'

'Scar, please! Let me help? Don't go off on your own! We've already lost Elder Eight. Cass is missing and you're on the rather scary side of a tyrant who wants to hurt you. Please.' He looks at me with those sad and pleading eyes. It's so strange that such a brute of a man has such a tender and loving soul. 'I don't want to lose any more of my family. Stay here at the cottage.'

'Elder Eight!'

I look over my shoulder and see Elder One summoning me with his finger. I turn back to Titan and reach up, wrapping my arms around his neck.

'I'll be fine, Titan,' I promise as we share a hug. 'I'll be back later.'

I turn and leave to follow Elder One who has already started walking away.

'Everyone still in one piece?' he asks once we're out of earshot. 'The Commander cause too much trouble?'

'Not too much,' I reply. 'He said he was looking for Cass but spent a large portion of time searching the cupboards where Elder Eight used to hide his liquor.'

'Cupboard in the kitchen? They knew about that?'

'Yep. But Loom had moved them all when the others had gone to bed, so they didn't find anything.'

We share a look.

'So. Loom fell into the pit *and* he moved the booze. Doesn't change the fact that he did volunteer. That's suspicious.'

'He volunteered because he was scared.'

'Of what?'

'Well, apparently he got into a fight. One he won. By a lot. Not sure the other guy woke up if I'm honest. He was scared that he was going to be executed so he volunteered to get away.'

Elder's feet slow to a stop as a look of realisation washes over his face. He looks at me.

'The chap he got into a fight with. I don't suppose he was a disgusting paedophile who also happened to be an Elder back when Loom was a young Cadet by any chance?'

'Well. I wouldn't like to say-'

'Loom's safe,' he says firmly, carrying on with his quick and steady pace. 'Truth be told, I went to visit the old bastard after he was attacked. He was so out of it and in such a delirious state, he told me all about what he had been up to with his *"Little Lads"* with a vile little grin on his face. Like he was reminiscing over summer romances gone by.'

Elder scrunches up his face, like the taste of shit lingers in his mouth.

'Did he tell them who attacked him?' I ask nervously.

'Nope. Didn't get a chance. I put a pillow over his face and watched the sick freak die,' he confesses bluntly. 'You can tell Loom to rest easy. No one knows. What about the rest? Anything suspicious?'

Elder One is surprising me more and more. I can see why he and my dad got on so well.

'Sky was outside when I got there. She said she came upstairs to warn me that the Commander was at the front door, saw the open window and that I was gone, and climbed out to find me. When we went inside, she covered for me. She told them that we went for a walk together.'

'Plus, she almost died in that pit, so it's unlikely that she had anything to do with making it. Anyone else?'

'Commander knew I was wearing a man's jumper. Winder told him it was his. But I tell you what is a little off. Chilli told Flash that the Commander came to the house. Flash told Titan.'

'Cass is adamant that it's Flash that's been telling Noah about you. They never really did get on those two.' He looks at me as we continue walking. 'What do you think?'

'I think…' I sigh heavily and give in to the obvious. 'It's probably Flash. And perhaps Chilli. As much as I hate to even think it, I just can't think of anyone else. I mean… a strawberry? Who gets sentenced to the Canaries for stealing a strawberry?'

'Is that what he did?' Elder chuckles. 'Truth be told, Elder Ten got sentenced to three months beyond the wall for pinching an apple when he was younger. That's where he met your mum and dad so he may be telling the truth. But he didn't fall into the pits and he's talking to Flash so perhaps it is him.' We turn onto the Soldiers road and start heading towards the Military village. We have to pass through it to reach the wall. 'Let's play it safe and keep everything close to our chests.'

'I'm telling Tee everything,' I inform him. 'I trust her completely and Noah knows she means the world to me. She needs to know the truth so she can protect herself.' I expect him to argue, but he simply nods and we carry on. The further we walk, The more soldiers we see. As they pass us, some whisper or avoid meeting our gaze. Others nod with a polite *"Good morning, Elders".*

'That's fine. He had me fetch Winder this morning. He's back at the house with him now, filling him in on everything. I sure hope neither of you has poor character judgments is all I'm saying.'

'Is he okay?' I ask quietly, smiling to a couple of Black Coat girls who give me a wave. 'Cass, I mean?'

'He's fine. Worried about you and pissed off with me. He spent the night handcuffed to my door, threatening that if you get hurt because he wasn't there to protect you, he'd kill me. He's currently in my lounge with Winder and they're both ready to hurl themselves into my hidey-hole again if anyone comes knocking. Listen. I'm on my way to speak with some Elders... oh dear lord...'

We both stop dead as we enter the military village.

'What the...' I look around in utter horror. Pinned to every wall, every tree, every post and being handed out by several Grey Coats are flyers with a drawing of Cass's face on them, along with the words:

Wanted. Dead or alive for attempted murder and sexual assault.

I reach out and snatch one from the hands of a young Brown Coat Cadet.

Never mind the words, which are not only lies but disgusting too, the way Cass has been drawn makes him look demonic. They've narrowed his eyes and given him a malicious grin. What's worse are all the soldiers looking at them, nodding and agreeing that there was *"always something not quite right about that guy".*

Without a second to spare, I start tearing them down. Within minutes, my hands are full of crumpled sheets of paper and yet they are still all I can see when I look around.

'Scarlett!'

I spin on my heel, raging and ready to fight. I see Owl, my friend who is a Green Coat from the wall, walking towards me. She's followed by two others I recognise as Bowzer and Tan, another two Green Coats. As they make their way closer, they snatch the flyers from people's hands and tear them from the trees just as I am doing.

'Can you believe this bull?' she barks angrily, looking around at the others. 'It's all lies!' she bellows. 'This is all utter crap! And you are a fool if you believe it.'

Across the courtyard, the Grey Coats have all turned to watch us. I take a step forwards, furious and desperately wanting to attack.

'Don't you dare,' Elder warns, taking my elbow and keeping me at his side.

'They can't do this!'

'Apparently, they can,' Elder mumbles. 'Let it go. Choose your battles. This one isn't worth fighting.' He turns me and raises his brow expectantly. 'Am I clear?'

I grind my teeth together and nod. 'Yes, Elder.'

'Good. Come on. We have places to be. You lot...' He looks at Owl and her friends. 'I want you to tell as many as will listen that this is all nonsense and not to believe it. That's coming from me. So, if you get any trouble, you point them in my direction. Got it?'

'Yes, Elder One,' Owl replies. 'And Elder Eight?' She turns to face me. 'What you said last night? About recruiting? About the world beyond not being the same dead lands we see around The Haven? Was that the truth?'

Tan and Bowzer step closer, eager to hear.

'Absolutely,' I reply. 'The world's healing. The further south you go, the healthier it all is. I've seen entire villages covered in moss and cars lost beneath long grass. It's beautiful. And if you want to join us in reclaiming it then you are always welcome.'

She nods and pulls out an envelope from her pocket. 'Then this is for you.'

Behind her, Bowzer and Tan also hold out an envelope.

'What's this?' I ask, taking them in hand.

'Transfer requests.' Owl looks over my shoulder to the Grey Coats still watching us. 'We want to join up. The sooner, the better. The Grey Coats are going too far and we've had enough. They've taken over our postings at the wall now as well. What else is there to do but go out there and fight?'

Elder One gives her a firm slap on the back.

'Good on ya!' he beams, turning to look at me with an excited smile. 'The more the merrier. Consider yourselves a Canary.'

'Really? That easy?'

'Yep. Now c'mon, Elder Eight.' He nudges me towards the path leading to the wall. His eyes linger on the gathering Grey Coats as they all start to face us. 'We have places to be.'

As we leave the military village. Elder glances over his shoulder.

'Listen. I want you to go straight to the wall and find Tee. She should never have gone up there alone. Not with all the Grey Coats swarming over it.' When we lose sight of the main courtyard, he stops me. 'I need to meet some Elders and a couple of Red Coats. I'm already late. You go talk to Tee and go to my house to see Cass as soon as you can. Will you be alright going the rest of the way on your own?'

'I'll be fine. Good luck.'

'You too.'

'Oh, Elder?' I ask as he turns to walk away. He stops and looks back at me over his shoulder expectantly. 'W-where is he?'

'Who?' he asks.

'Elder Eight... I mean... my dad?' I clear my throat to ease how it has started to constrict. 'Where is his body? I-is he safe? Is he-'

'He's safe,' he says kindly, turning to face me completely. 'He's waiting.'

'Waiting?' I swallow hard, fighting the urge to cry.

'For us to say goodbye. Properly. We'll give him a burial, Scarlett. I promise. But first, we must do our job. Time, I'm afraid, is not on our side.'

He shows me a compassionate smile and waits for me to nod my understanding.

'Be safe. You hear me?' he states.

'Yes, Sir. You too.'

We separate. He goes left and I head right.

When I see the wall, I breathe a sigh of relief. I'm at the fourth mile and a need to get to Tee as fast as possible has me running towards the fifth. All along the top, I notice several grey hooded heads peer over the edge. I have my own hood up and my head down so I don't think they know who I am. I reach the marker for the fifth mile, look up at the towering wall and whistle.

'TEE?' I call. 'TEE, YOU UP THERE?'

Nothing.

'TEE?'

A tumbling length of rope falls. I take it in hand and grip it tight, readying myself for the climb. I lift myself up. My feet leave the ground and I start my ascent. My sewn-up hand hinders me but it won't stop me. I climb that rope right to the top. To my Tee. And when a hand reaches over the edge, I grip it tightly and she pulls me up. I stumble as my feet land on the wall and I'm steadied by a strong pair of arms.

I don't see Tee. Instead, I come face to face with a Grey Coat whose features are hidden by that stupid hood. He has a giant, double-bladed axe strapped to his back.

'Well hello there,' he drawls, pinning me close to his body and laughing a deep and throaty laugh. 'And what are you doing up here?' His hand slides down and lands on my backside. 'Come to join the part-'

He doesn't get a chance to finish speaking before I slam my knee between his legs and my forehead into where I know his nose should be. He staggers back, holding his private area as I grasp my knee. He's so solid, it felt like hitting a brick wall! I look around and see Tee between two other Grey Coats. She looks like a startled rabbit as they both tower over her. I hold out my hand and she sprints to my side. Placing myself between her and the three arseholes, I face them all with my head held high.

'How dare you strike me!'

'How dare you grab an Elder so inappropriately!' I lower my hood. 'Shall I tell Lord Sands that you just groped the woman he loves? Or should you?'

The Grey Coat takes a few steps back and remains silent.

That's lucky. I have no idea if Noah would give a rat's arse if anyone touched me. Not anymore.

'Yeah. I didn't think so. Tee, grab the rope and start climbing down.'

'The little Green Coat's still got six hours of duty,' the Grey Coat snipes, straightening himself up and grunting against the pain I've inflicted between his legs. 'And we were so enjoying her company.'

'She's not a Green Coat any longer,' I retort. 'She's a Canary. My Canary. Tee, did they hurt you?'

'No,' she tells me. 'They just kept asking if I knew where Cass was. Which I don't!' She adds firmly to the Grey Coats. 'So why don't you find something better to do with your time, say, kill some targets? Rather than chase innocent people down on trumped-up charges?!'

The Grey Coat I hit chortles. 'Aren't you a feisty little thing? I like that. The Green Coat is very much wasted on you... *Q-Tee.*' The way he says her name makes both Tee and I shudder.

'Did they touch you?' I ask Tee through gritted teeth, stepping closer to the Grey Coats. 'If they touched you, I swear to-'

'No, Scar,' she insists, reaching out and holding me back as I take another step forward. 'They didn't. Please, let's just go.' She pulls me towards the wall's edge but I'm reluctant to go. I refuse to turn my back to the three ahead of us as she guides me towards the rope. 'Scar,' she whispers in my ear. 'Please? We're not a match for them. You're not even armed.'

'You heard her,' the Grey Coat jeers. 'You're no match for us. Off you go.'

As Tee takes hold of the rope and topples herself over the edge, I point my finger at the Grey Coat. 'If I find out you so much as breathed on her, you'll be sorry.'

'Don't you dare threaten me,' he snarls back in response. 'You are in no position to talk to your superiors so disrespectfully. Not until our Lord gets that ring on your finger and even then-'

I stalk up to him. 'I'm not threatening you, Grey Coat. I'm promising you.' I'm furious. Filled with a wrathful hatred and anger that they couldn't hope to douse. I step closer, my fists by my side itching to hurl them into his face. 'Noah may have spent the last few months changing his own laws to better suit him but you can't do jack to an Elder, so until the day comes when he gets around to changing that rule too, you stay away from my Canaries. Do you hear me?'

I shove him away from me as I turn to the rope. Tee kicks off and starts abseiling down. As I stand on the edge with nothing but fifty feet of air between me and the ground, the Grey Coat positions himself just in front of me.

'I can't wait for Lord Sands to get you under his heel. Because he will. Mark my words. And then we'll see how tough you really are.'

'He will never get me under his heel. Or anything else. And if you so much as look at Tee again, I'll take that big axe strapped to your back and shove it up your arse.' I lean back, my hands gripping the rope. 'And then we'll see how tough *you* really are!'

And with that, I swiftly abseil down, half expecting him to cut the rope so we both plummet to our deaths.

But we both make it safely to the ground. As soon as my feet touch the grass, I take Tee's face in my hands. She's pale and shaking. Her eyes are wide and her breathing is jagged.

'Are you okay? Did they hurt you?'

'No.' She shakes her head. 'I got up there for my shift about an hour ago and they all turned up shortly after. They wouldn't leave me alone and they wouldn't let me go. God!' She shudders and lets out an angry growl, looking up at the wall hatefully. 'Bloody bastards. They were so creepy. And the one with the axe?' She looks at me with a confused little frown. 'He kept sniffing my hair. How weird is that?'

I nod in agreement and rub my knee again. 'Pretty damn weird. When I hit him, he was solid! I've never hit anyone that felt so hard. My knee is killing me! What the hell are they feeding those Grey Coats?' We both look up at the wall. Above our heads, three grey hoods peer over the edge. 'Why on earth did you come up here on your own this morning?'

'I had to. It's my job. If we don't report for duties, we get ten lashes.'

'Since when?'

'A couple of months now. So... I'm a Canary now?' She turns to me and I'm thrilled to see her smiling from ear to ear. 'I didn't even get a chance to give you my transfer request.' She then promptly pulls out an envelope from her pocket and hands it to me. 'How did you know I was joining up?'

I can't help but chuckle. I open it up and read her transfer request. 'I didn't. But I'm so happy that you want to.' I take Tee's hand in mine and give a final look at the three hoods still watching us. 'C'mon. We need to get outta here. And we need to talk. There are a few things you really need to know.'

As we walk, we talk.

Oh boy, do we talk.

It's not long until I've filled her in on everything. All of it. Noah and his threats. Cass and our relationship. The truth about my father. The painful revelations that surround his death. The likelihood of a traitor in our small group and what Elder One, Cass and I are planning. It all tumbles out of my mouth as we walk through the secluded woodland and she listens quietly as I spill.

'Okay...' she breathes, slowly nodding her head. 'So. Overpowering Noah and the Grey Coats. That's gonna be...'

'Hard. Dangerous-'

'Fun!' she corrects me. 'And well deserved. Elder's gone because of him and he'll pay for that. Big time!' She takes my hand and looks at me with sad eyes and I know that her next words will be about my dad. Right now, they're words I'm just not ready to hear.

'Tell me about you,' I interrupt as she opens her mouth. 'I want to hear all about what's been going on since I left.'

I think she spots the pleading in my eyes to move on. She obliges.

She tells me about her life since I've been gone. About her new home in the Warren which she hates. The building that house the graduated cadets was a prison back when the world hadn't ended. Her bedroom is a cell. She tells me that she's been spending most of her time on the wall during the day, but once a week she goes out with Winder, Titan and Cass in their unit to help salvage or clear out traps. There are three other members of their usual unit. Two girls and a guy.

'There's... wait for it... Bone-ache.'

'Bone-ache?' I ask.

'Yeah. He's always complaining that he's tired and that his bones literally ache. I mean... I can't even...' She shakes her head and takes a sip of water from her flask as we continue strolling through the trees. 'He complains about everything, Scar. Everything! His shoes are too tight. His coat is too heavy. I breathe too loud when

I stand next to him. Cass mutters too much. His horse keeps looking at him funny. I swear, he's insane. He kinda goes from unit to unit. He drives everyone mad so they shunt him around a bit.'

'What about the other two?'

'Well, there's Liddy. She's pretty plain. Doesn't have much personality if you ask me. She just does as she's told without question. A typical worker-bee. I tried talking to her about the weather on our first time out and she just looked at me with this blank expression.' She mimics the girl, gawping at me like a stunned fish. 'Seriously. I had to ask her if she was okay or having a stroke. And then there's...' She looks at me with a hateful sneer. '*Melody.*' Her nose scrunches up and she shakes her head in distaste. 'Silly, lying cow.'

'*Melody.*' I repeat, my own nose bunching up. 'Yeah. Melody and I are gonna have to have a little chat very soon. What's she like? Other than a lying, life-ruining bitch?'

'Melody is pretty and she knows it. She and Liddy were part of a unit which was not classed as successful. One of their people died in training. One declared she was a lesbian and ran off in the middle of the night two years ago before they could arrest her. She was never seen again. One was ordered to repeat their final test and died when they did. Liddy and Melody were the only ones left so they put them with Winder and Cass. Melody, she does this thing with her hair...' She does this exaggerated swish with her ponytail and then twirls it in her finger while looking at me like a starving harlot. 'And she has this horrible giggle.' She lets out this forced and flirty laugh. 'And she's spent the past few months throwing it all at Winder and Cass. Like this.' She strokes my arm and holds my hand while twirling her hair and laughing that laugh.

'Well, it must have worked, because Cass kissed her.'

'Melody likes him a lot. Much more than Winder. I think it's something to do with him in that Red Coat. Makes the girls weak at the knees,' she teases, jabbing her elbow into my side as she smirks. But I find it all far from funny. 'I think she just wore him down, to be honest. She's pretty intense with the touching and flirting. Which is why this accusation of hers is ridiculous. Honestly. I've never seen anyone so desperate for male attention in all my life.'

'Did Winder kiss her? Did she wear him down too?'

'Well... no. He told her that... well...' Her cheeks go pink. 'He said he had feelings for someone else and wasn't interested.'

'Feelings for who?' I wait, but she just shrugs and looks out into the distance. 'You two need your heads knocking together.'

'I don't know what you mean.'

'Yes, you do. For goodness sake. We're about to pick one hell of a fight. If I were you, I'd tell Winder how you feel. It's clear as day that he feels the same.'

'Coming from the girl that left home knowing she was probably going to die and still

refused to tell the man she loves how she feels.'

Her head turns and she waits for me to argue with a playful grin and raised eyebrows.

'Point taken,' I reply begrudgingly. 'Still can't believe they kissed,' I grumble.

'Pot. Kettle. Black... Little Miss *"smooching the resident tyrant-slash-psychopath"*.'

'Hey. You're supposed to be on my side!'

'Always, Scar. I am being on your side. If I let you, you'll talk yourself out of forgiving Cass for that one stupid mistake and end up miserable and alone. I'm just reminding you in a loving and sisterly way, that you messed up too. Besides. After that *one* kiss, Cass has been all business and barely talks to her unless it's to issue orders.' She pats my shoulder. 'It's not been easy since you left. Plus, being a Red Coat and in charge of all those new Black Coats hasn't been easy. He's not been himself at all. So, cut him some slack.'

I'll cut him something alright.

'I am sorry I left you. If I had any other choice, I wouldn't have. You know that, right?'

She nods. 'Of course I know that,' she says, ducking below a branch as we continue on. 'Oh. Before I forget.'

Whack!

'OW! What was that for?' I complain, rubbing my arm.

'First, not telling me you and Noah had a thing going. We're sisters. You should have told me.'

'I couldn't. Do you know how much trouble-'

Whack.

'Ow! Will you stop hitting me?! I have enough bruises.'

'Second, how dare you think I would have told anyone. You think so little of me? Third...' *Whack.* 'Why would you let me put my number in to marry a psychotic guy you were sleeping with?!'

'First...' I poke her in the arm. 'I wasn't sleeping with him! We kissed twice. That's all. And second...' *Poke.* 'Elder Eight and I took your number out of the lottery and he didn't report you entered it at all. Sorry.'

'Fourth...'

'Christ, how many punches am I getting?' I ask, stopping and facing her. But she throws her arms around me and wraps me in her best Tee-hug.

'I am so so sorry about Elder Eight. I mean, your dad. I can't believe... I had no idea... I should have been there for you. You should never have gone through that alone.'

I sink into her hug, feeling her love through her embrace.

As we stand in the solitude of the woodland, a sound suddenly pierces through the air. One that has us both turning West.

'Did you hear that?' she asks.

'I did. It sounded like...'

The high-pitched scream of a woman travels once more through the air and we both sprint in the direction it's coming from. It's not until the woods start to clear that I realise we have walked so far together, we have found our way into the civilian's village. The closer we get, the louder the short, sharp, shrill screams become. Tee and I are going as fast as we can. We emerge through the trees and come to a path. There are small, rickety cabins lining the dirt path and not a soul to be seen.

'This way,' Tee tells me, urging me on as she runs further down the path. I follow as she weaves between huts and old brick buildings. She cuts through alleyways and darts over muddy gardens. She knows exactly where she's heading, which is strange because I haven't set foot in the civilian part of the Haven for more than a decade.

'How do you know where we're going?'

'The boys and I have been sneaking food to these people for months now. I know where I'm going. Trust me.'

The wailing is unbearably loud now. The unknown girl's voice travels through the bitterly cold air, turning my insides just as icy. Her cries are full of pain. Her whimpering sends a shiver down my spine. As we continue making our way to her, we catch another sound. A sharp whistle, followed by a snap. Then another of her agonised cries.

We emerge between two makeshift houses onto a vast concrete square. It's absolutely full of people, but no one says a word. Tears slide down many of their faces. They hold onto each other for comfort as they watch whatever is unfolding in the centre of the square. Above their heads, I see the tall plinth of a whipping post.

Another whistle followed by a snap and I know, without doubt, that some poor girl is strapped to that post and being punished.

Tee and I barge through the people and stop when we come face to face with a circle of Grey Coats surrounding the lashing post, all with their weapons drawn and pointed at the group of civilians around them, ready to attack if they try to intervene.

I peer past the one with an arrow primed for release in his bow and see that there are in fact three posts in the square. Either side of the tall one, are two shorter ones. There are people strapped to each. Two men, and in the middle, a girl.

She can't be any older than sixteen. She's a frail little thing. Her long blonde hair is plastered to her bloody back as she sobs. All her clothes, except her knickers, have been torn away. She kneels in the mud, shivering uncontrollably in the cold. Her eyes remain on the teenage boy to her left. She's calling his name desperately, over and over, despite being in unbearable pain she cares only that the boy she calls Logan answers her.

He's slumped in the mud. His body is still and his back is so badly lashed, blood pools all around him and I can see bone.

The Grey Coat lifts his whip and brings it crashing down onto the unconscious boy. She screams once more as chunks of flesh are pulled from his form.

I'm pretty sure he's dead.

'YOU WILL DO AS YOUR LORD BIDS!' The Grey Coat roars at her, bringing it down on him again. Another strike. His body moves but no warm breath leaves his lips.

'I SAID I WILL!' she cries. 'PLEASE! PLEASE STOP!'

I go to intervene. No way I let this carry on!

I'm grabbed by a man I've never seen before. He wraps his arms around my waist and pins me to his side. His long grey hair is tied in a ponytail and his skin is weather-beaten and dry.

'Don't, girl. You will only make it worse. You intervene, she gets ten more lashes and you get twice as many.'

'I don't give a damn,' I hiss in reply.

'Her brother is dead!' he snaps in my ear, holding me tighter as I try to get free. 'And her lashes are done. No good will come of your interference! It's done!'

'Samuel's right,' Tee agrees quietly, taking my arm. 'They can't know you're here, Scar. Please.'

The Grey Coat is stepping back. The crowd lets out the breaths they've been holding and I nod, begrudgingly. Samuel, whoever he is, releases me. He swiftly removes his thick woollen coat and throws it over Tee's shoulders, pulling up the hood to cover her face from view.

'Keep your Green Coat hidden, Tee,' he whispers. 'They see you here, they'll be hell to pay.'

The Grey Coat turns to the crowd and with the blood still dripping from the whip, he points at us all.

'You have a duty to your Lord. You farm the land. You marry. You reproduce and you do as you are told! If you do not fulfil your duties, we have no need for you!' He looks to the weeping girl who is still sobbing her dead brother's name, and then points to another boy positioned on his knees, trembling and staring at the ground beside the third post. 'This is the partner Lord Sands has designated to you. This man is to be your husband! You will marry and you will reproduce or the next member of your family I pull up here will be your little sister! Am I clear?'

'But I don't love him!' The girl wails.

'AM I CLEAR? OR SHALL I FETCH YOUR SISTER?'

'YES!' she screams. 'YES! YOU'RE CLEAR! YES! I'LL DO IT!'

'Good,' he scoffs, sliding his fingers down the length of his whip and flicking off the blood that remains there. 'We will return in a week to confirm you are no longer virtuous. Along with the rest of those due to marry. We have already cut your food rations in half. This is what awaits you if you still refuse to follow the law! Your Lord is good and kind. He will save you all. Remember that. We all have our part to play in the survival of our race. This is yours. Now return to your homes. If we see anyone in the street, they will join Logan here.' He looks at the still lingering crowd. 'GO!'

Everyone turns and leaves.

'Tee, go to my cabin and wait for me there. I must help Taylor.'

Tee nods as he heads towards the girl and starts unbinding her. She crawls to her brother and cradles him in her lap, wailing like a dying animal.

As Tee leads me through the throng of people, I notice how thin they all are. How their skin looks grey with malnutrition and sickness. That they have bruises on their faces and their clothes are tattered and torn. Rags barely cling to their frail frames.

'What's going on here?' I whisper to Tee horrified. I suddenly notice the stench that floats through the air. 'And what's that smell?'

'That's the smell of human waste and vomit from drinking dirty water. C'mon, Scar. We need to get you inside before the Grey Coats spot you. Noah won't want you seeing this.'

She leads me by the hand through the streets. People return to their homes, sealing themselves inside their rickety places of refuge. Tee takes me into a what I can barely call a shack, made of wood and metal sheeting. It looks like one good gust of wind would have it blowing through the streets in pieces. She closes the door behind us and lets out a long breath.

'So yeah. Like I said. Noah's changed some rules since you've been away.'

'Changed some... what the hell is going on here?'

The door opens and the man named Samuel joins us. He looks between Tee and me.

'So, this must be the famous Scarlett?' he says, 'Tee's told me a lot-'

'Where's the girl?' I demand. 'Is she okay? That boy... her brother... is he-'

'Dead. Yes. The girl will recover well enough from her physical injuries but it may take some time for her heart to heal.'

'They can't get away with this!' I'm up and pacing. 'They can't-'

'Right now, if you step foot outside that door, you will either be arrested or get an arrow through your skull.' Samuel gestures to an old chair. 'Sit down. You and me? We need to talk.'

'Who the hell are you? And how do you know Tee? And more importantly, why should I trust you?'

'Because I'm the Village Overseer. And I've been working with your friends, Tee, Winder and Cass, to keep my people alive. I have also been meeting with your Elder One while he has been investigating my missing people. If you trust them, then please rest assured that you can trust me.'

I simply look to Tee. She nods.

Samuel starts boiling water in a pan over a small fire and preparing tea. 'The new law in which arranged marriages and children birthed to quota hasn't gone down too well. So far everyone has refused. They cut our food and now they're lashing people. These kids are being forced together and they're not ready nor are they willing to become breeding stock. What you saw is the result of us refusing to bow down to Noah's insane demands.' He hands me a small cup of tea and sits, offering once more for me to join him. 'I apologise for the awful tea. I only have enough for that one cup and the tea leaves have been used so much, it probably has no taste whatsoever.' I lower myself down, perching myself on the very edge of the chair so Tee can sit beside me.

'When did all this start?'

'Things started getting harder about two years ago. Shortly before Noah's father died.'

'I thought so. Everything seems to have changed in the last two years.'

'The Grey Coat presence tripled. Our food rations are cut for the most minor offences. And now, on top of the forced marriages, people are going missing.' He leans forwards, his voice lowers. 'I saw them. Last night I was out, sneaking back from checking on the crops. Three Grey Coats barged into the farm down the road. They took the whole family. Four of them. Sacks over their heads and hands tied behind their backs. They tossed them over the backs of their horses and rode off.'

I swallow hard, his words causing both anger and fear to course through me.

'Where did they take them?' My words come out dry as I force myself to remain calm.

He sits back and shrugs. 'All I heard was one word. Arrested.'

'Arrested?'

'That's what they said. I have to guess that's where the missing members of my village have gone. I planned to visit your Elder One today. See if he knew what was going on.'

'Arrest? Are you sure you heard that word?' I ask again, handing Tee my cup. He nods. 'But we don't arrest civilians.' I look between them. They both look as bemused as I do. 'We don't even have a prison. Except for the Warren but that's full of hundreds of soldiers. They'd notice if a bunch of terrified civilians suddenly turned up. We get punished and sent on our way. Unless we do something tremendously wrong, then we get sentenced to the Canaries. But that's just soldiers that get that particular treat. You lot don't get sent out beyond the wall.'

'Precisely.'

'So where are they taking them?'

'The Grey Coats have taken fifty-two of my people in the last six weeks.'

'Did the missing people do anything wrong?' I ask.

'I have no idea,' he sighs. He gets to his feet and heads to the slight gap in the wall made of metal sheeting, and peers out into the muddy pathway. 'I plan on finding out why they were taken. Believe me. And I won't rest until I get them back.'

'Samuel snuck into the military village to steal food for his people,' Tee tells me. 'Winder and I caught him in the stables stealing the horse feed. When he told us what was going on, we insisted we helped him. We got Cass to help and we've been sneaking food from the kitchens to give to them ever since.'

'And thank goodness you have,' Samuel says, turning to look at Tee affectionately.

There's some yelling from outside. I get to my feet and look out through the small gap. A group of Grey Coats are hurling threats to no one in particular as they stalk through the streets. They kick doors and knock over water barrels as they pass by.

'It's like they don't care anymore.'

'Care?' I ask Samuel.

He glances down at me. 'If we live or die. They don't even care enough to keep us strong so we can continue farming the land. We haven't even been permitted to tend to the fields in over a week. The crops need constant attention or they die. They simply don't care. All they want from us now...' He looks back out the window and lets out a long and tired breath. 'Is to breed or to die.'

We have to wait till nightfall until we can leave. While we wait, we share with Samuel the beginnings of our plan. I also ask him to tell the others that they do *not* have to marry! I fully plan on causing some trouble long before they return to check the girls and I'll be damned if anyone is forced to marry someone they don't want to be with.

Samuel also hears about the warrant out on Cass. He tells us that his home will always welcome him and protect him. He shows us the small dug-out pit in the corner of his house beneath a wooden trap door. If needs be, he can hide here with him.

The sun sets. I pull my hood up over my hair and Tee takes a spare jumper from Samuel to cover her Green Coat.

'You take care of yourself. You hear me?' he tells her, taking her face in his hands and kissing the very top of her head. 'And you send those boys my best.' He turns to face me. 'And you. Be careful. That Noah is as far from a good man as could be, and he has his eyes on you. These are dark times, and you and your Elder One are the light that we have all been waiting for. I want you to know that myself and my people, we are at your service. If you need us to stand with you against Noah and his band of brutal hooligans, you just say the word. We may not be able to brandish a sword or fire an arrow. Hell, we can't even really ride a horse. But we're strong. Determined. And loyal to humanity's survival in a world otherwise inhabited by death and cruelty. We will fight with you, Scarlett. I give you my word.'

I reach out and shake his calloused hand. He grips it firmly, demonstrating just a hint of the strength that a lifetime of manual labour has given him.

'We will try and get you some more food,' Tee promises.

After that, Tee and I duck out into the streets and disappear into the woodland, making our way back home.

CHAPTER SIX

Back at the cottage, the smell of Loom's cooking greets us, as well as the cheerful banter of a fair few voices. But what has me speechless is the house itself. It's been completely cleaned. The floors, the walls, the ceiling, all spotless. Paintings are hanging on the wall and books are on display on brand new shelves. The study's been cleared and has been cleaned top to bottom. There's a single bed in there now with a bedside table and a candle lamp. A pair of curtains have been washed and hung and there's not a speck of dust to be seen. The lounge has been turned-out too. The sofa's been fashioned into a bed and pushed against the wall. The desk that was once in the study is now in there and has a few books, weapons and clothes placed neatly upon it. The old furniture that was once broken and left to gather dust, has all been cleaned and mended.

'They must have worked all day,' Tee whispers. 'This place looks amazing. Oh, Scar... look!' She points to the wall that leads up the stairs. Someone, I'm guessing Sky judging by the way the letters curve around delicate flowers, has painted a simple message on the wall.

"Welcome home, Kiddo."

'That's so sweet,' she says, her voice straining as she tries not to cry.

'All his furniture. All that art he brought home from beyond the wall. They've fixed it all for him.' I feel so humbled by them. And when I walk into the kitchen, everyone stops what they're doing and smiles.

'What do you think?' Sky asks a little nervously. 'We've been working on it all day.'

I rush towards her. She staggers back a few steps.

'I'm sorry! I thought it would make you hap-'

I give her a hug. A great big hug.

'Oh my...' she whispers. 'She's hugging me! Guys look! Scar's hugging me!'

'We can see,' Loom chuckles, still stirring his bubbling pot.

'It's amazing,' I tell her. 'Thank you.'

'We all helped ya know,' Chilli calls over. 'Where's our hug?'

I let her go and look at them all in turn. Loom, standing by his boiling pot at the stove. Chilli and Winder, on the floor with their sleeves rolled up and some contraption between them. And Titan, washing dishes in the sink.

I can't see a single one of these people ever betraying me. Not a one. But then again, someone is missing.

'Flash here?' I ask Titan.

'Working,' he replies. 'He said he'll be here later.'

Hmm. I bet.

'Any trouble while I was gone?'

'Nope. Oh, you got another fifteen transfer requests today.' Loom nods to the pile of letters on the worktop. 'How about you? Any trouble?'

'Not really,' I shrug, taking the papers in my hand.

'Where did you go?' Chilli asks. 'We woke up and you were gone.'

'I'm sure if we need to know, Scarlett will tell us,' Loom cuts in. 'Isn't that right?' He throws a look my way, a silent warning that we don't know who's ears to trust.

'Just spending time with Tee,' I reply. 'What is that?' I ask, nodding to the odd contraption between Chilli and Winder. An excited Sky claps her hands together and jumps up and down with glee.

'We found it in the lounge amongst the old furniture. I have no idea where Elder found it, it's a gramophone!'

'A what?'

'It plays old music,' Chilli tells me. 'Like, ancient music, but you wind it up to make it work. It doesn't need power so if we can fix it, we might be able to use it. There are some old records for it over there.'

'How do you even know what it is?' Tee asks, heading over and kneeling down to get a better look.

Winder hands her an open book. 'Elder had books on a lot of things he found out there. This is a manual for it. Looks like he tried to fix this thing up a few times but couldn't get it right.'

'You guys will do it.' I grin. 'Definitely. You did great here. You shouldn't have worked so hard though.'

'It's the least we could do. For you and for him. We were happy to do it. Now,' Sky gestures to the table. 'Sit. Loom has made another masterpiece for us to eat. Turns out Elder was an extreme hoarder. We found tins of food in the cupboard under the stairs and most of it was edible so we're making a send-off meal for him.'

'He always liked my cooking,' Loom says sadly, staring into the pot.

We eat.

We drink.

It's the most civilised two hours of my life!

I half expect Elder One to come and see me. I wait and wait, but he never shows. My eyes grow heavier. I want to wait and see if

Flash turns up. I have some serious questions for him. But I give in to my body's overwhelming desire to sleep.

'I'm off to bed,' I announce, getting to my feet. Tee is hot on my heels as I walk to the door. And apparently, so is Sky.

'Err... Scar?'

I stop by the door and wait as she skips over.

'What's the plan?' she whispers. 'Ya know... about...' She glances at Tee briefly. 'Ya know. The plan...'

'I'm working on it,' I reply, patting the top of her arm. 'Just rest and relax tonight and we'll get working on it tomorrow.'

She nods and returns to the others.

'C'mon, fellas. Let's do the dishes and get some shuteye.' She claps her hands together, jumping from foot to foot. 'First night on a bed with a real duvet in months. I'm so excited!'

Tee and I leave them all to it and head to my room.

I fall forwards, landing with a heavy groan on the mattress. The springs creak and a musty smell surrounds me.

Tee pulls off my kicks and places them at the end of the bed.

'I can't believe these things are still in one piece,' she chuckles softly, dragging out the duvet from beneath me and tossing it over my body.

'My kicks will outlive me,' I mumble, feeling the almighty pull of sleep tugging at my consciousness.

'They better not,' she scoffs, pulling off her boots and sliding under the covers with me. I know she's watching me. I can feel her eyes on me and the warmth of her breath tickling my skin, but I lack the energy to open my eyes. 'What *is* the plan?' she whispers. 'What are we going to do?'

'We'll talk to Elder One when the sun rises. See how he got on with the other Elders. Then... then we'll...' I yawn deeply. 'I've never known exhaustion like this, Tee. I'm just so... tired.'

Her fingers run through my hair slowly, calming my very soul. 'Sleep, Scar. Rest now. I love you.'

After a few moments, I mumble, 'I love you, too.'

The last thing I hear before I fall asleep is her, quietly weeping, "About bloody time".

'SCARLETT! FIGHT!'
  'DAD! STOP, PLEASE!'
Kick. Kick. Kick.
His nose is just a hole in his face. His front teeth are gone.
He screeches and keeps trying to kill me.
'STOP, DAD! STOP!'
'GET YOUR SWORD!' Sky shouts.
His face is all broken. His body moving in sharp, jarring movements.
  'Dad... you're still in there! I know you are.'
'NO. HE'S NOT. KILL HIM, SCARLETT!'
'I can't!'
He opens his broken jaw and lunges at my throat. His teeth sink into my flesh as I scream.
  'Dad, please don't kill me. Please... Please don't leave me!'
'Wake up! Wake up, Scarlett! Can you hear me? Hey!'

I open my eyes and see Cass leaning over me with worried eyes. I'm on the bed, panting and dripping with sweat from my nightmare. I sit up with a violent jerk and stare at him before reaching out and grabbing at his collar.

Something's wrong.

I... I can't breathe!

Just as before, when I was in the bathroom. No air reaches my lungs and my heart hammers harder than I ever thought possible. I try to speak but I can't. I really can't.

I tighten my grip, pleading with nothing but my eyes for him to help me.

As the sound of pumping blood floods my ears, my vision begins to blur and I see Cass start to panic.

He speaks but all I can hear is the rattling of my dad's breath.

Cass takes my face in his hands but all I feel are my father's hands clawing at me.

'Scarlett, breathe. You need to take a breath!' Cass says, watching me clutch my chest and giving me a shake. Am I choking? Or worse... Am I turning? That thought has me shove him away from me and scrambling across the bed. I fall off the edge and hit the floor, desperate to distance myself in case I am turning.

'Scar, take a breath!' he repeats, leaping over the bed and kneeling before me.

I kick at him. If I'm turning, he can't be here! I'll kill him!

I feel for a pulse. I check that the skin on my hands aren't turning grey.

He takes them in his.

'You're not turning, baby. It's a panic attack. That's all. Hey, look at me!'

'Move!'

Tee suddenly appears and delivers a sharp slap to my face.

That does the trick.

Although my throat is unbearably tight and my heart is hammering so hard it hurts, I finally manage to take a breath. But I still can't talk. All I can do is shake and gasp. He takes hold of my shoulders and forces me to look at him.

'It's okay. It's okay. You're okay. Look at me, Scarlett. Eyes on me.'

He keeps my face held fast in his hands and his eyes never stray from mine. Slowly, he takes a deep breath in. I copy.

'That's it. Good job. Keep breathing. Nice and slow. You alright?' he asks after I get in a few good gasps of air.

I try to lower his hands and push him away as every touch feels like my father's cold, lifeless hands.

'Stop that. Tee told me she knows about us and no one else can see us up here. Are you alright? Scar... hey... look at me. Talk to me.'

I have no words. Just pain.

They both surround me, both hugging and offering me words of comfort and love.

It's too much.

'I have to go,' I gasp, forcing myself to my feet and staggering a little as I walk towards the door. 'I have stuff... stuff to do. I need to talk to Elder One. Get off me. I don't want you pawing at me.' But he keeps hold of my wrist. I just react and my fist goes for his face. 'I SAID GET OFF!'

'Woah! Hey! What the hell was that for?' he says, lunging back and missing my cumbersome attack easily.

'Stop treating me like glass! I'm fine! People keep trying to tell me what to do a-and what to think!' I turn and head to the door. Feeling light-headed, I trip and fall, but he catches me. 'You shouldn't even be here! It's too dangerous.'

'I needed to check on you.'

'I'm fine! Let me go. I have a job to do.'

'You are not fine! And you are not going anywhere! It's the middle of the night. Your Canaries are downstairs and we have no idea who we can trust yet. Never mind the fact that you can barely walk!'

'I have to go,' I tell him, snatching my hand away. 'I need to talk to my dad.'

My hand rests on the door handle.

'Your dad is dead!' Cass says bluntly.

My still trembling hand stays firm on the door handle. I hear him take a step closer.

'You think no one's noticed?' he says sharply. 'You think your Canaries haven't said anything to Tee? Everyone knows that you've not been sleeping and that when you do, you've been having nightmares. Everyone knows that you're not eating and that you haven't touched your Katanas. All of this started when your dad died. You're not functioning, Scarlett, and it's going to get you killed.'

'You've been talking about me behind my back?' I snarl, venom filling my mouth. 'You've been talking to my unit, Tee?'

'I have,' she admits. 'I'm worried about you.' She gestures to Cass. 'We all are. This isn't like you.'

I can't help the bout of laughter that erupts from me. It's fuelled by a righteous anger, deep within my belly.

'You... worried about me?' I mock, turning on my heel to face them. I may be wearing a smile but it's far from a kind one. 'You? No. No, you don't get to be worried about me. I don't need your worry. I am more than capable of looking after myself. Unlike you.'

'Hey,' she whispers. 'That's uncalled for.'

'You were so desperate to avoid the fight, you willingly threw your name into that lottery. You would rather spend the rest of your life popping out a stranger's kids than risk your life fighting for the survival of your friends. Your family!'

'Scarlett!' Cass warns.

'And you!' I charge over and shove him in the chest. 'I left to save you. I lived out there for months. All so you would be safe. So Noah didn't send you out there. And while I was fighting tooth-and-nail for survival, witnessing things you couldn't possibly imagine, you were here. Snogging a girl who is now accusing you of raping her! And you know what gets me? You knew! You knew why I left. Elder Eight, he wrote you a letter. You knew I left for you! For all of you!'

'You hypocritical bitch,' he hisses, charging forwards and pointing his finger in my face. 'Noah told me.'

'Told you what?' I snap, slapping his hand out of the way.

'He came to see me just as I was leaving on a two-day salvage and took *great* joy in telling me some tales of your time together. Probably to put me off my game so I wouldn't come back.'

'What *tales?*'

'Of your first kiss. Remember when I broke my rib a few years back? The day you were supposed to check out the second floor of that old apartment building but you said you had a stitch? I had to do it instead and the floor collapsed beneath me. I fell and broke my rib because you couldn't be bothered. I was laid up and you were with him. I was suffering because of you and you were kissing him! So I was a little upset. We were out beyond the wall and she was just there. It was a single, short kiss that I regretted as soon as it happened. That guy of yours is a psycho. An egotistical nut-job. And I'm shocked that someone like you would ever let him touch you.' He throws his hands up and turns away, shaking his head and muttering to himself.

'When you got hurt instead of me, I went to the beach to clear my head. And he was there.'

'Yeah. I bet.' He snatches up his coat. 'Glad to learn that while I was in pain, you were snogging a psycho.'

I grab his arm to spin him back to face me. 'I don't know if you recall,' I snarl, still trying to keep my voice low so our fight doesn't wake up the rest of the house. 'But I was the one that got you back home in one piece after you fell. I stayed with you for hours after you got hurt and the whole time you berated me. You said I was a lazy, responsibility-phobic idiot. You told me to piss off and come back when I'd earned the right to work with you. So I went, and he was there, and he was nice.' I give him a shove as Tee looks on awkwardly. 'And for your information, I didn't have a stitch. That morning, you were in charge of saddling the horses and you didn't buckle Hanzo up properly. When I went to get on, the bloody saddle slipped and I twisted my ankle when I landed. I could barely walk. I didn't tell you because I didn't want to make you feel bad. I was in too much pain to go up those stairs. But despite the fact that it was swollen, bruised and utter agony, when you fell, I carried you back to your horse and got you home safely. My ankle was fucked for three weeks after that. Elder Eight had to strap it up and help me get it moving again. It still aches when it gets cold. Even after all this time.' I turn and head to the door, snatching up my hoodie and my shoes as I pass. 'Now, if you don't mind, I have somewhere I need to be.'

My katanas are still leaning against the wall. I reach out to take them. It's dark out. Sunrise a good couple of hours away. I should take a weapon in case I get cornered by some Grey Coats. But when the tips of my fingers touch the hilt, they begin to shake. My chest gets tight and I start to gasp.

'Damn!' I growl under my breath, hating that I feel this way towards them. I open the door.

'Scarlett, wait...'

'Get lost.'

'Scar- Goddamnit!'

I shut the door and leave the git where he is.

Downstairs is quiet. The kitchen's been cleaned after our meal and the sound of snoring tells me everyone's gone to bed. I poke my head around the door to the lounge. Loom and Chilli are fast asleep and in the study, Sky's is too. I leave them to it, open the front door and head out into the dark, pulling my hood up as I go. I divert from the path and duck into the woodland.

Cass is right behind me.

'Go back to Elder One's house, Cass. If you're seen, you'll be killed.'

'I'm a dick and I'm sorry.'

'I said go.' I pull my hand away when he tries to take it.

'Scarlett, don't push me away-'

'Go!' I snap, shoving him. 'Do as your Elder tells you and piss off.' I walk away, feeling his eyes watching me as I leave.

'But... you are my home,' he calls sadly. 'Please don't leave me.'

My feet slow to a stop.

'I lost you once. When you rode away from me the morning of the lottery, I literally felt my heart break. You broke me, Scarlett. You not being in my life every day. Not knowing if you were alive or dead, if you were out there alone, stranded or starving. It tore me apart. Every night I had nightmares. I didn't sleep for months. I couldn't eat and I was angry at everyone. I'm amazed Winder didn't take his axe to me.'

'Your point?'

'I told Winder everything and I sobbed like a god damn baby. It helped, Scarlett. Whatever you're going through? Whatever is causing your insomnia and nightmares? The panic attacks and this inability to touch your own swords? Maybe talking will help?'

'So, what? You want me to have a little cry and you think I'll feel better? You think that talking will snap me out of whatever this is?' I gesture back towards the cottage. 'I can't even hold my swords without freaking out!'

'You need to grieve. You've spent so much of your life refusing to feel. Refusing to live a real life where you laugh and love. You've buried yourself in your work. You've desensitised yourself to death.'

He stretches out his hand. I swiftly slap it away.

'I've seen more death in the past nine months than you have in your entire life.'

'I can't imagine how many targets-'

'Not targets.' I shake my head and feel a cold wave crash over me as I remember all that I saw. 'The world out there, it just stopped one day. And for everyone it was different. Some were torn limb from limb, Cass. There were streets that we walked down and you could have collected the bones up like jigsaw pieces. They were all scattered and mixed up. There was so much blood, it's still staining the pavements fifty years later. You can still see drag marks from where they were ripped apart.' I hear how hollow my voice has become. I feel my lip tremble. 'I've seen mummified corpses hanging from lamp posts. Bloodstained bathtubs with rusted blades perched on the side. Skulls covered with teeth marks. Dozens of final embraces. Hundreds of suicide notes.'

'Oh, Scar-'

'There was an old farm. Out in the middle of nowhere. We needed a place to sleep so we broke in. We had to kill a target. Just one. It was trapped inside and just... wandering. But when I went upstairs to check it was clear, there was... there was...' I swallow hard and shake away my inability to talk. 'The bones of a woman laid in the hallway. Blood was all over the walls. The floors. And... and over one door in particular. She'd locked her...her baby in there, and died protecting it. When I opened the door... the bones were so little.' My voice has turned into a quivering mess. 'I can hear that baby crying in my dreams. I can hear him, Cass. Hungry and afraid and all alone, wondering where his mummy and daddy are. Why no one comes when he screams.'

'Scar-'

'You think by telling you how I stabbed my own dad in the head, I'll stop hearing his lungs liquefying and bubbling up through his mouth as he turned?' My throat begins to tighten and I feel a hot burning sensation in my eyes. 'You think that by... by talking about the fact that my leather wrappings are stained with his blood... because I had to kick him in the face over and over and over again to stop him from biting me, it will make me sleep easier? That I'll stop seeing his messed-up face? How his jaw snapped and his nose turned into nothing more than a hole with splinters of bone sticking out in all directions?' I'm starting to gasp and my chest feels full of lead. He walks towards me calmly as if trying not to startle me. I see the reddening of his eyes and how they shimmer with tears. 'You think that... that... oh God... I killed him! I took my katana and I pushed it through his head!' I slam my hand over my mouth, catching the sobs trying to claw up my throat. I daren't look away from him. I fear that if I do, I'll just dissolve. That all I'm trying not to feel, not to face, will explode and tear me limb from limb.

His hand settles on my cheek and I watch as his tears slide freely down his face. My hand glides onto his and as soon as my lips are free, they mutter words that undo me completely.

'I want my dad back,' I whisper. My lip trembles more and the tears in my eyes brim thick and fast. 'I want my dad back!' They spill over, tumbling down my cheeks and trickling over our hands. 'I want my dad!' I let out a desperate sob. 'I WANT MY DAD!'

I come undone.

My legs buckle and I fall into Cass's chest. He lowers us down and engulfs me in his arms as I cry, for the first time in my living memory, I cry. I cling onto him harder than I ever have. I climb into his lap, desperate for him to surround me as much as one person can surround another. His fingertips dig into my skin he's holding me so tight. My body judders and clenches as I wail in his loving arms.

And he cries too.

'He's with you, Scarlett. Every day. He'll never leave you. The man you remember? The one who taught you to read? To fight? To stand up for what's right? He'll always be a part of you. The way he died, it was terrible. But he died saving you and I know that he would never, ever blame you or hold any resentment towards you for that. In fact, I think that if he was here, he'd give you a telling off and tell you to get your shit together.'

He's right. I know that. He would be furious with me.

'And all those things you saw out there? We won't let that happen again. We won't.' He kisses the top of my head and lets me cry. It's such a release, I never thought that actually letting myself feel so sad would feel so freeing.

Together, alone in the darkness, deep in the woods, hiding and risking everything, we grieve.

The heartless Canary and the hard as nails Red Coat.

One perfect imperfect pair.

When my cries start to slow, he leans in close. 'I love you, Scarlett,' he whispers in my ear. 'I know you won't say it back. I know that you still believe in the curse, that saying I love you to anyone will mean that they will die. That's okay. You don't need to say it back. Just know that I do-'

'I love you too, Cass.'

He sits up and looks at my tear-streaked face with a little wonderment in his eyes.

'You do?'

'Of course I do.' With my thumb, I dry his tears. 'It's always been you. It always will be.'

'You have no idea how long I've waited to hear those words come out of that mouth of yours.'

'Well, do you have any idea how long I've waited to do this?'

We lock in a fiery embrace. Sinking into the undergrowth we reunite, the way two lovers should.

Because we want to.

Because we love each other.

Because it's right.

CHAPTER SEVEN

I wake when a hand slams over my mouth before being yanked violently to my feet. I blink open my eyes and grab hold of my attacker as they hurl me against a tree.

When I gain my focus as well as my senses, I see it's Cass. It's still dark. He presses his body against mine, his hand still firmly on my mouth and his eyes wide and wary as they stare intently over my shoulder. I'm about to hurl abuse at him when I catch the sound of hooves.

'Shh,' he whispers, still watching the distance. He nods in the direction he's looking and slowly prises his hand from my mouth.

I carefully look past the large tree he's hidden us behind. Through the darkness I see half a dozen Grey Coats on horseback, riding along the path.

'Shit...' I breathe, watching them all pass and clinging onto Cass a little tighter, hoping that the extra millimetre I pull him in will spare him from being seen. 'I think they're heading in the direction of the cottage.'

'Or out looking for you.'

'Or you,' I counter.

We let them pass, manoeuvring ourselves around the tree to keep out of sight. I've missed how we work so well together. Even just this small action, carefully moving as one, knowing exactly where to go and what the other will do, I've truly missed it. Our eyes never leave the group, not until they're out of sight.

'I need to go. If they're heading towards the cottage I need to be there. I can't leave the others to face them alone.'

He nods, albeit reluctantly, before taking another kiss. 'I'll get back to Elder One's house and tell him that he should get over to you.' He groans and closes his eyes. 'He's gonna tear me a new one for sneaking out.'

'I'm really glad that you did,' I grin. 'Thank you so much.'

'You're thanking me?' he smirks. 'For sex?'

'No,' I chuckle. 'For talking to me. For listening. I needed it.' I pat his chest. 'Now move. I really need to get back before the Grey Coats reach the cottage. If I cut through the woods and run, I should make it.'

He takes my face firmly in his hands, kissing me fiercely one more time before letting me go. He looks to the floor, scooping up our discarded clothing.

'Where the hell are my trousers?' he mutters.

I can't help but laugh when I see them hanging from a branch above us, swaying in the breeze.

I make it back to the cottage just as I see the group of Grey Coats dismounting outside.

I can't go in through the front door. Not without being bombarded with questions as to why I'm wandering around outside in the early hours. I try the kitchen window but it's sealed shut and no one's in there to help me sneak inside.

Muttering my annoyance, I look upwards.

I guess I'm climbing.

I use the drain pipes, the foliage, the window ledges and any cracks I can find. I make my way up easily enough and take hold of the ledge to my bedroom window. I give the rickety glass a firm push and haul myself inside. I'm half in, half dangling out when I stop dead in my tracks. I just hang there staring, like a stunned fish, watching the scene before me in shock.

Dressed in an oversized t-shirt and pushed up against the wall is Tee. The man pressing her against that wall, with his hands caressing her and his lips kissing her mouth and neck, is Winder.

I can't climb back down. I need to get inside!

'So... this is awkward...' I announce.

Tee shoves Winder off her so hard, he staggers back and lands flat on his arse. They both watch me, horrified and embarrassed as I smirk ear to ear at them.

'Hello,' I greet. 'Am I interrupting?'

'It's not what it looks like!' Tee insists, smoothing down her hair and pulling down her t-shirt so it covers more of her thighs.

'I kinda hope it is, Tee,' I reply, trying to contain my laughter. 'Cos that's not how you're supposed to perform the Heimlich manoeuvre.'

Winder chuckles as he pushes himself to his feet, ruffling his hair in an attempt to smooth it down. 'What the hell are you doing?' he asks me. 'This is your house, you know? No need to sneak in.'

There's a series of loud bangs on the front door below.

'Got another Grey Coat visit,' I tell them, dragging myself inside. 'Get yourselves decent.'

Winder hurriedly pulls on his coat and shoes as I throw Tee a playful wink. She looks fit to burst with happiness as they share a kiss and a few whispers meant for only them.

I stride through the room, scooping up my Canary coat which still hangs over the end of the bed, and then I head out the bedroom door. As I pass, I see my two Katanas still propped against the wall. I look at them as I slide on my mother's coat.

Downstairs, I hear that the Grey Coats have come inside. Winder scoots past me quickly, getting himself out in the hallway before anyone sees him in a bedroom with two girls. Tee hastily gets her clothes on and stands beside me.

'Everything okay?' she asks.

I flatten down her hair so it falls neatly over her shoulder. 'Not yet. But it will be. Come on.'

I reach out and take my swords before heading out onto the hall. And for the first time since my father died, they don't frighten me.

As I head down the stairs with Tee by my side and Winder following close behind, I tighten my back harness, loving the weight of my swords being back where they belong. I see my entrance hall filled with Grey Coats. Loom and Sky stand against the wall with their arms folded. They may have just been woken up but they're wide awake and as alert as I've ever seen.

We're used to this. Sudden rousing from sleep with life and death situations snapping at our heels.

Sometimes literally.

Loom sees my swords and a relieved look sweeps across his features.

'Chilli?' I mouth as I descend.

He gives the slightest shrug and a tiny shake of the head.

As my feet hit the ground floor I face the darkened shadows beneath the hoods.

'What do you want this time?'

The faceless figure simply points towards the kitchen.

'Alright then,' I sigh, making my way over.

As the others go to follow, the Grey Coats stop them.

Every attempt they make to pass them, the Grey Coats block their path. From the kitchen, I hear the clinking of china and the pouring of water. Then, the smell of coffee wafts through the air.

Coffee is such a luxury, only one man would ever have access to it.

Legally, anyway.

'Guys, wait outside.'

'No chance,' Sky insists.

'That's an order!' I snap back.

'Scar...' Winder pleads. 'Don't go in there alone.'

I look back at him over my shoulder and let him see my eyes dance briefly to Tee. Noah knows how much I care for her. If he gets a chance, he'll use her against me. And now I've seen that Winder has admitted his true feelings towards her, no way he puts her in harm's way.

'Wait. Outside.' My words are final. Sky and Loom nod. Reluctantly, but obediently nonetheless. Winder takes Tee's elbow and guides her away. Her eyes don't leave me until the front door closes.

I turn to the kitchen and head inside.

The door is closed behind me and I'm left alone with the man whose throat I long to slice from ear to ear.

He stands at the worktop with his back facing me. He doesn't turn. He just continues making his coffee.

'You've been a busy little bee, I hear,' Noah says as he stirs his drink. 'Not even been back two days and you've stolen a rather large chunk of my soldiers.'

'I've not stolen anyone. That would imply you own them. That's something you could never understand, Noah. People don't belong to you.'

'Is that so?' he replies quietly, purposefully placing down his teaspoon and picking up the two mugs of steaming coffee. He turns to face me and extends one. 'Take it,' he orders, nodding to the cup. 'Or else I may be offended.'

He waits, hand still outstretched.

'Don't make me repeat myself, Cadet. I'm not in the mood.'

I close the gap between us and take the mug. As he sips his, I swiftly toss mine down the sink and place the cup on the table.

'Delicious. Now. Why are you here in the early hours of the morning? Don't you sleep?'

He strides past me and takes a seat at the table. He then kicks out the chair opposite and gestures for me to sit.

His eyebrows raise and a low growl rumbles from the back of his throat.

I sit.

'Where is he?'

'Who?' I ask innocently.

'Don't play dumb. It doesn't suit you.' He rests his coffee on the table and leans forward, his elbows settle on his knees and his eyes bore into mine. 'Where is he, Cadet? Where's Cassius?'

I rest my elbows on my own knees and lean forwards.

I don't hide the smug grin hitching the corner of my mouth as I reply, 'That's Elder Eight to you, my Lord. And I have no idea where he is. Why? Can't you find him?'

He leans forwards so his face is in mine. I feel his breath on my skin and the heat of his anger radiating off him.

That makes me happy.

'If you're hiding him-'

'You've searched my house. Well, your Grey Coat lackeys did at any rate. They didn't find him or anything else. So, I'll ask you again, *My Lord*. Why are you here?'

He glances at my mouth and bites his lip before returning his attention back to my eyes.

'You still have your fire. I thought, after everything you went through, that perhaps it might have dampened down a little.'

'Nope.'

'I guess I'll just have to try harder then.'

'Meaning?'

He laughs as he sits back in his chair and starts tapping his fingers on the table as he thinks.

'I'm going to need the numbers of every soldier who has requested a transfer into your unit,' he states. 'And you are to stop your *"recruiting"* immediately.'

'Why do you want their numbers?'

'That's absolutely none of your concern. All you are to be concerned with is doing as you are ordered and I am ordering you to give me the numbers.' He holds out his hand. 'Give me the transfer requests right now, Cadet, as well as your word that you will stop trying to convince my soldiers to go out there to die.'

'What's in it for me?'

'You get to keep breathing.'

'Ya know?' I lean back with a sigh. 'I can't recall their numbers. And I foolishly burnt all the transfer requests.'

'Is that so...'

'Yep.'

He scoffs, glaring at me as his mind ticks over. Again, his fingers tap on the wood.

'Do you remember the night before you left?' he asks. 'When we sat together outside, under the tree? I asked you a question.'

'I remember you sexually assaulting me and then lashing me because I fought you off,' I retort.

'I asked you what you wanted,' he reminds me with a clenched jaw. 'Do you remember that?'

I offer nothing more than a shrug.

'I gave you a chance that night to have everything you wanted. Back then, it was a Red Coat.'

'In exchange for sending everyone I care about out beyond the wall. Yeah. I remember.'

'Well, I'm going to ask you the same question now. And I want an honest answer.'

'Anything I say to you will have me swinging at the end of a rope before sunrise, so no, *My Lord.* I will not answer.'

'Oh, come now,' he grins. 'We've been friends for years. Spent countless hours together. We've shared our hopes and dreams with each other. And I don't care what you say, the kisses we shared? They meant something.'

'Yeah. Regret.'

'It's just us. I want to figure out exactly why you came back here. I want to know what you want, Cadet-'

'Elder.'

His eye twitches.

'Just tell me what you want. Maybe I can give it to you.'

'And what do you want in exchange?'

'I need to know if I can give you what you want first.'

'I want you to leave me alone.'

'Oh,' he laughs, shaking his head. 'That will never happen.'

'Why? Because you love me?' I scoff.

'Precisely,' he snarls in response. 'You may not believe me, but I do love you.'

'Don't make me laugh,' I mock.

'I do love you.'

I let out a snort of derision and roll my eyes.

He lunges forwards, leaping to his feet and wrapping his fingers in my hair as he towers over me. He yanks, tilting my head back as he puts his face in mine.

'I hate how much I love you. I fucking loathe how much I want you. I can't stand that you're all I think about.'

'I'm flattered,' I tell him, careful to keep my composure and remain still as he tightens his fingers, pulling a few strands of hair from the root. 'But I'm not interested.'

'Do you think I want to feel like this?' he spits furiously, a vein throbbing in his neck and his eyes wide in an intense, fevered stare. 'You think I enjoy needing you? Craving you?' His free hand settles on my side. 'You're intoxicating. Addictive. You're-'

'Unattainable and not... interested,' I reply coldly with a heaving chest as I draw in furry-filled breath after fury-filled breath.

'Tell me the numbers of your transfers.'

'Can't. Don't remember.'

He yanks my hair causing me to let out a low, guttural growl. I clench my fists knowing that if I lash out, my friends outside will be hurt in retaliation.

'Where's Cassius?'

'No idea.'

With a roar, he pulls me to my feet and shoves me backwards. My back hits the counter and his hand moves from my hair to my throat. He gives me a shake and leans over me.

I make damn sure I show nothing but the hatred I feel. That his actions fail to frighten me or weaken my resolve.

'Tell me what you want. Tell me, and I will give it to you. I will give it to you if you agree to submit!'

'You want to know what I want?' I hold my chin up and speak calmly, but the malice in my words echo all around us. 'I want to stand over you one day with my sword and drive it slowly through your skull.'

'Just like you did to daddy?'

The hateful laugh that comes out of me does no justice to the utter disgust and feral loathing I feel for this man. But I hold my tongue. One thing's for certain. Someone told him about my father and only a handful of people know that truth.

The kitchen door opens wide. It slams into the wall hard, putting a hole in the plaster. In strides Elder One. Close behind is Elder Ten, Elder Six, Elder Nine, Sky, Chilli, Winder, Tee, Titan, along with several others all wearing large black hooded jumpers. Like the Grey Coats, their faces are covered. They stand silently and as I peer past Noah's frame, I see them filling the hallway and even stretching outside the front of the cottage. Dozens upon dozens of hooded figures. Only the Elders and my friends have their faces showing.

'Lord Sands. Remove your hands from her,' Elder One orders. 'Immediately.'

'What's the meaning of this?' Noah seethes, slowly standing up and releasing his hold on my throat. He sees quickly that he's outnumbered, despite his Grey Coat guards standing between him and the others. 'What are your intentions here, Elder One?'

'To protect. That's my intention. What are your intentions?' He looks at me briefly before returning his focus back to Noah. 'This is the second time I have walked in on you with your hands on this girl. She has made it abundantly clear she has no interest in being your wife. Considering the death order you have placed on one of my Red Coats, I would have thought that perhaps you were against the mistreatment of women?'

'I strongly advise you to turn around and leave.'

'That's funny. I was just about to say the same thing to you,' Elder retorts. 'I would hate for things to become unpleasant here. You lot. Tend to your Commander.' He nods his head in my direction.

Sky, Tee, Winder, Loom and Titan all walk past Elder One and place themselves by my side. They stand tall. Fearless. Formidable. True warriors. True friends.

Noah goes to grab my wrist.

Sky leaps in front of me and just stands there.

'Move, girl.'

She doesn't. He shoves her out of the way.

Tee takes her place.

He makes another move to reach me.

Titan stands between us. He towers over Noah.

Noah's eyes meet mine and within them, I see a promise. A promise of revenge. A promise of pain. A promise of misery.

A promise that this is far from over.

He steps back.

'As of now, the Canary units are disbanded. If you attempt to continue recruiting, you, along with anyone who joins you, will be treated as deserters. Traitors. And you will be sentenced to death. It's time to stop running, Cadet.'

'Elder.'

'Your place is here. Your job is to secure humanity's future. That's all. For us to survive. To win. I can't have you taking my army. I can't have you leading them to their deaths. Not when the fate of our entire existence is at stake. The Canaries are no more.' He turns to the others and puts on that fake, all-knowing and wise tone that I heard him don at every one of his public speeches. 'You are all so important to our work here. If you leave, you will die. We will all die. She tells you of greener pastures. Of a life beyond the wall. A world without rules or consequences. Do you so easily forget how this world of ours perished in the first place? Of how humans boiled this planet with toxins and pollution? How they hollowed it out, causing the ground to crack and the oceans to rise? All that destruction and chaos. All the cruelty and suffering. And for what? For greener pastures. For a promise of an easier tomorrow. If you abandon us, you abandon God. And you hand over this world once more to the Devil.'

'We have the right to choose how we live,' I tell him. 'We have the right to live how we desire. Not to be ordered to die this death every day. The Devil has nothing to do with it.'

'That's the thing about the Devil. He disguises himself as all that you desire. We are all that is left of humanity. We must survive. It's not pretty, this way of life. It's not easy. I've made hard calls and implemented tough laws. But everything I have done has not only kept you safe and alive, but it's also guaranteed us a future. My path is the right path. If you lead these people astray, the world and everyone in it will perish. And if it does, on your head be it, Cadet. On your head be it.' He once more turns to the sea of black hoods. 'Leave now. Return to your postings or to your beds and all will be forgiven. You have my word. But if you stay here, I will be forced to react to this threat of treason. And that is the last thing I wish to happen to you all.'

He turns on his heel and strides out of the room, followed closely by his Grey Coats.

Before he leaves, he adds, 'Whoever brings me the Red Coat know as Cassius will be rewarded beyond their wildest dreams. If I discover anyone hiding him, however, they will be executed right alongside him.'

He storms out of the house and the sound of hooves thundering away is followed by a long exhale of breath from everyone in the room.

'Are you okay?' Sky asks, resting her hand on my arm. 'Did he hurt you?'

'I'm fine,' I tell her. I head to Elder One and look at the sea of black-hooded figures filling the cottage almost to capacity. 'He's gonna come back here with more Grey Coats. No way he lets this pass.'

'No way *we* let this pass!' calls out a voice from the hooded masses.

'I guess it's official? We're making a stand?' Sky asks.

'Damn right we are,' says Owl, pulling down her hood. Her eyes are red and puffy and the left side of her face is swollen with deep purple bruises.

'What happened to you?' I gasp, rushing to her and checking her injury. 'It looks like you've fractured your eye socket!'

'They took them, Scar.' I see how hard she's trying to hold back her tears. But there's also a rage within her as she speaks. 'They took Bowzer and Tan.'

'Who took them?' asks Sky.

'Grey Coats,' Owl tells her. 'A couple of hours ago. A group of them charged into The Warren declaring they were performing a search for Cass. They sent us all outside to wait. I told them they were wrong about him and one of them punched me in the face.' She gestures to the swollen and bloody mess that's been inflicted on her. 'I've never been hit so hard in my life. I thought he hit me with a bloody brick! He tried to grab me. A couple other guys kicked off in my defence. It all got a little messy and we scattered.

Then we all regrouped shortly after. That's when we realised... people were missing!'

'Missing?' I repeat.

'Bowzer. Tan. Thirteen other Green Coats and ten Black Coats. That's as far as we know. That's all we managed to count.' She weakly throws up her hands. 'There could be more.'

'There are more,' I whisper, thinking of all the civilians that have been taken from the village. 'Names. I need the names of those taken,' I insist.

'Erm. Well, there was Bowzer and Tan,' Owl recalls. 'Lizzy. Red-'

'Numbers. Give me numbers.'

'238,' calls a voice from the crowd.

'699 and 558,' calls another.

Numbers are called out from all directions and I recognise them all.

'They're transfers,' I tell them all. 'Every single number that was just called out is a transfer request. I memorised them.'

'You certain?' Elder One asks. 'You've received a lot. How could you possibly remember them all?'

'I remember every single one.' I look to the Black Hoods. 'All of you. I need you to disperse. Noah will return and if he sees you all, he will take you, I'm positive. Please, leave, lower your hoods and return to your duties.' They mutter angrily amongst themselves, calling me a coward. 'This is not me giving in!' I promise. 'This is me saving as many of you as I can. We will stand and we will fight. We will get our stolen friends back. I swear it. But we are not ready and we are outnumbered. We need to organise. Give me time.'

'When will you be ready?' calls out a voice.

'I'll let you know. Soon. Be on your guard and be careful who to trust. Stay together. Don't walk anywhere alone.' I nod to the door. 'Go. Prepare. The time of The Verity is over. It's up to us to ensure it.'

They turn and file out of the cottage. I watch them all run into the dark woodland in every direction.

I turn to the others who have remained inside. Tee. Winder. Loom. Sky. Titan and Elder One.

'No idea where Chilli is?' I ask them.

Loom shakes his head. 'Woke up and he was gone. You think they took him?'

'Why just him?' I ask. 'Why not take us all and how did no one notice him being taken? He wouldn't have gone quietly.' I shake my head, hiding my hateful grimace at the conclusion I've arrived at. I look to Titan. 'Where's Flash?'

'On duty at the wall,' he says. 'He left an hour ago. Same as always. Why?'

'Because not only do I remember the numbers of every transfer. I also remember when and where I received their transfer requests. Someone volunteering to join us is not something I would easily forget.' I feel every muscle in my body become rigid and the hatred I have inside is almost deafening as it causes my blood to pump hard and fast throughout my body. 'Yesterday morning, you handed me a pile of transfer requests. Remember?'

'Yeah,' Titan replies uneasily.

'You said that Flash took them from the soldiers and asked you to hand them to me. Is that true?'

'Well... yeah,' he shrugs. 'So-'

'Ten of the missing were in that pile, Titan. Did you look at the requests?'

'He wouldn't...' he whispers.

'Did you look at the requests?' I repeat.

He lifts his gaze and solemnly shakes his head.

'He wouldn't. Flash wouldn't.'

'Oh please!' Winder snaps. 'That guy cares only about himself, Titan. For as long as I can remember he's done everything and anything he could to keep himself safely out of harm's way. On evaluation day, he didn't give one shit about leaving you alone to hold that warehouse door closed. He kicked Scar in the face, made her bleed, and hid up on the roof of that lorry. The only person he cares about is himself. Do you seriously think that he wouldn't betray any one of us in order to keep his cowardly arse safe?'

Titan looks lost in despair filled thoughts and can only manage a slow shake of his head and the uttered words, 'He wouldn't.'

'Well. Someone's been reporting to Noah about us all. Both before we left as Canaries, and after,' I tell him. 'Noah knows things. Things that no one but us should know. Someone's been telling him our secrets. Winder's right. Flash is the traitor. He's terrified of this life and will do anything to survive it. We all know how much he wanted to be a Grey Coat growing up. He tried out and failed. What if he didn't? What if he's been working with them all along? Passing on intel? Every time there was a raid for contraband items, the Grey Coats always knew where to look. Every time two soldiers were getting close to each other, they would always be discovered.'

'He may be afraid, Scar, but he's not a traitor!' Titan insists. 'He would never betray us.' He rests his hand over his heart. 'He would never betray me.'

'Yeah well, I wouldn't be too sure about that,' Sky mutters.

'What would you know about it?' Titan barks at her.

'More than you. Clearly,' she snipes, folding her arms across her chest as her hip pops out to the side. 'Considering I saw him with his tongue down someone else's throat yesterday at the stables.'

'That's a lie!' Titan bites back, his voice raised and shaking. 'He would never betray me. No way!'

'I wasn't gonna say nothing. It ain't my place, but you better believe me when I tell you it is my place if his actions have put any of my friends lives in danger. There's not much I won't forgive. But traitors are amongst the most vile, disgusting and despicable people in this crappy world.'

'Well, maybe you should look closer to home if you're looking for a traitor!' Titan argues back, stepping towards her with his fists balled up at his sides. I charge between them and stand in his path. He towers over me by almost two head heights, but my palm resting flat on his chest stops his descent on her. 'I don't see your precious Chilli here. That's a bit of a coincidence, don't you think?'

'Chilli?' Sky laughs loudly, the mocking in her giggle infuriates Titan further. 'Sorry, Black Coat. But no one in our unit would ever betray us. Loom, Scar, Chilli and I are a family. We'd die for each other. Hell, we almost did every day for the past nine months.'

'Then where is he?'

'Maybe with your boyfriend, snogging his traitorous little face off.'

'Fuck you!' Titan roars.

'In your dreams, Gigantor!' She sticks out her tongue and blows a raspberry in his face.

As Titan goes for her, I shove him hard. But it takes both Winder and Loom helping me to actually create any distance between the pair.

'That's enough!' I order. 'Both of you! We have enough enemies to contend with, without turning on each other.'

We all take a breath and give Titan a second to calm himself. I turn to Sky.

'I'm sorry. But I believe that Titan's right. It's painful to even contemplate it, but the facts are right there.'

'What facts?' Sky scoffs, sneering at Titan over my shoulder.

'The facts that Chilli can't be trusted.'

'You can't be serious,' Loom replies.

'I know it's painful to even consider it but three of the lost soldiers are the three requests he handed me the first night home. There's also the fact that out of all of us, he didn't fall victim to the traps we all fell into. The traps that were made in locations only we knew about. Me, you and Sky nearly died in those traps. Elder did. Nothing happened to him at all. This morning, they looked for the booze in the places he thought we hid them. He didn't know Loom had moved it. So please, tell me who else would it be?'

'Who says it's anyone? Why would he?'

'To be a Grey Coat,' I reply. 'Did you know, that in the past, surviving Canaries, the solitary soldier who returns when their entire unit was wiped out, has been rewarded with a Grey Coat? Look at the facts. Everyone thinks the country's dead. We know it's not. Other Canaries will have seen it too. But the death rate is high, they hardly ever come back. In the last two years, the survival rate has plummeted from eighty percent, to ten. Volunteer numbers are lower than ever. No one wants to go out there. So we all just stay put. Which lets Noah and the Grey Coats keep their power. He tells us all that the world is a wasteland, full of targets. Those who leave here hardly ever return. But we've seen it! We've seen the world and just how alive it is.'

'You think Noah's really going after the Canaries?' he asks, obviously not as sure about his conviction as before.

'I'm willing to bet my life on it.'

'Okay. I believe you. About Noah, and him sabotaging Canaries. I do. The evidence is pretty clear. But Chilli? Really?'

'It's Chilli!' Sky says pathetically, devastated at the mere idea.

'Until we know for sure, both Chilli and Flash are out. They know nothing about what we're doing, where we go or who we talk to. Understand? Now go. Get dressed. Collect your weapons. We're heading out.'

'Where are we going?'

'To get our soldiers back.'

CHAPTER EIGHT

I drag Tee up the stairs and pull her into my bedroom.

'Arm yourself,' I tell her, pulling out various weapons from the chest of drawers and tossing them on the bed. I snatch out a small rucksack and start shoving in supplies. She begins preparing herself, pulling out her bow and quiver as well as securing daggers to the harnesses she attaches to her thigh.

When I open the bathroom door, I stop dead in my tracks.

Before me is a girl. Her face is bruised and covered in scratches. Her eyes are wide and her lips quiver. There's dried blood in her blonde hair and she smells of sweat and urine.

'Who the hell are you?' I ask. 'Why are you in my bathroom?'

'You...' Tee growls. I hear Tee storming up behind me before she grabs the girl by the throat. 'What are you doing here?'

'Who is it?' I ask her.

Tee's whole face is tight with anger as she slams the girl into the door. 'Scar... meet Melody. Melody... this Scarlett. The Canary Leader. The new Elder Eight. Oh yeah... and Cass's girlfriend.'

Before I've even had a chance to think, I've taken Melody from Tee and tossed her across my bedroom. She lands on the bed with a whimper as I retrieve my sword from my harness and press the blade threateningly against her throat.

Every inch of me wants nothing more than to severe her lying head from her despicable body. But the girl just lays beneath me with her hands by her head, sobbing uncontrollably.

'Why are you here?!'

'I-I n-need your h-help!' she wails, tears streaming down her cheeks, wetting the dried blood that cakes them. Red droplets tumble onto the bedcovers and snot bubbles from her nose.

'Help?' I scoff. 'You accuse the man I love of raping you and you dare come to me asking for help? You stood in front of the soldiers. You stood in front of the Elders and told them that he-'

'T-they made me, Scar. They forced me to-'

'Only my friends get to call me Scar. You are not my friend.' I press the blade in a little harder. If I apply any more pressure, I'll slit her throat. Part of me doesn't care. 'Who forced you? Noah?'

'Yes...' she whispers. 'Noah forced me to stand up there and lie. Cass was only ever good to me. I swear it. P-please! You have to h-h-help me!'

I lean down and put my face in hers. 'Why should I?'

'They took us. They tried to kill me. They still have Liddy! Please!' She grabs my wrists, but not as a way of pushing me off. She clings to me, her eyes magnified by tears and swimming with terror.

'What are you talking about? Take you where?'

She gasps, struggling to catch her breath as she continues to cry and tremble.

'SPEAK!'

Elder One, Tee and I stand opposite Melody as she sits on the edge of the bed rocking backwards and forwards.

'Tell him what you just told me,' I order her. She nods, and tells her tale. I need to know if Elder One believes her. 'Quickly. We don't have much time!'

'Someone heard me talking to Liddy, my friend, about me kissing Cass.' She glances nervously to me. 'They must have told Noah because the morning you returned Noah came to see me. Liddy was with me. He ordered his Grey Coats to hurt her. They kept hitting her.' Her lip trembles as she says the words and her eyes close causing more tears to spill down her cheeks. 'He said he was going to kill her unless I did as he wanted.'

'He wanted you to lie about Cass?' Elder One asks.

She nods.

'His Grey Coats took Liddy away. He said she would come back to me after I told them all what he wanted me to tell them.'

'I'm guessing he didn't hold up his end of the bargain?'

'No. After I made the statement, I was led away and one of his Grey Coats knocked me out. I woke up with a sack over my head. I could hear hooves and I was being tossed about. I realised quickly I was in a large crate attached to a horse-drawn carriage. And I wasn't alone. There was a gag in my mouth. The place reeked of wee and there was muffled yelling and crying all around. Bodies were pressed against me from all sides. No one could move. No one could talk. No one could see.' She becomes distant as she recalls it all in her mind. I clear my throat. 'Sorry. There was one hell of a bang followed by some pretty nasty snarling. Then the sound of smashing wood and screams.' More tears slide down her face. 'I listened to the sound of the Class Twos tearing into them. I heard them, screaming for help. For someone to untie their hands. No one came.'

'How did you escape?' Elder asks.

'I felt the breeze on my face and got to my feet. I clambered over... Christ... I have no idea how many people. We were all trying to get up and get away. All just blindly staggering and rolling about. I fell. I think I must have fallen off the cart cos I felt dirt when I landed. I got up and just ran as hard and as fast as I could. I had no idea where I was going or if anyone was chasing me. I just listened to the sound of tearing flesh, agonised screams and the targets screaming that hollow shriek, and I ran as far away from it all as I could.'

She breaks down again, burying her face in her hands and shaking with the force of her tears.

'You buying this?' Elder asks me quietly as she continues howling. 'How did she get here? How did she escape the bindings on her wrists?'

I nod to the welts visible beneath the cuffs of her hoody. 'She found an old building. Stumbled inside and hacked at the rope on a shard of glass from a broken window. She said that when the sun started to rise she figured out she was North of the wall. She just kept running back towards the direction of The Haven and luckily came across one of the horses that was pulling the crate. It had escaped the attack. She says she jumped on and rode for hours.'

'I rode it till it died,' she cries. 'I think it h-had a heart at-t-tack.'

That causes yet more sobbing.

'I ran the last few miles,' she snivels, wiping her nose along her sleeve. 'I ran for hours.'

'So she says,' Tee adds, her arms folded across her chest as she glares murderously at Melody. 'She's probably lying. It's what she does best after all.'

Melody swiftly starts pulling off her boots and thrusts her feet upwards.

'Bloody hell!' Elder gasps, looking at her swollen, bruised and blistered feet. They're rubbed raw. She quickly shows us her wrists too, proving to us that she's far from lying about her ordeal.

'I'm not lying. I swear to you. They took Liddy! I love her like you love Tee!'

'Is that what they've been doing?' I whisper horrified. 'They're dumping the people they've taken for Class Twos to devour?'

'The ones that are causing trouble. The ones that want to leave with you,' Elder One murmurs. 'They're killing them!'

The bedroom door hurtles open and in rushes Cass, sweating and panting.

'They're coming,' he breathes, gesturing out the window. 'Grey Coats. They're coming for you. Armed and...'

His eyes flick momentarily to Melody. It takes him a moment to realise who she is.

'YOU!' he roars, pouncing across the room and withdrawing his haladie. In an instant, his blade is at her throat.

'STOP!' I yell.

He halts. The tip of his blade piercing her flesh just enough that a small bead of blood slides down to the hilt.

Behind him, Loom and Winder run in.

'Grey Coats,' Winder says. 'An army of them are heading this way... Cass? What are you doing here? Melody?!'

'No time!' I throw open the window. 'Everyone out, right now.' They linger, looking at each other not sure who is supposed to be here or who is to be trusted. 'DID I STUTTER? GET THE HELL OUT! RUN!'

Cass drags Melody to her feet as the others run past us to the window.

'Where's Titan?' I ask Loom as he passes. 'And Sky?'

'Titan stormed off to find Flash. We tried to stop him but he pushed past us. Sky felt bad for upsetting him and followed him.'

'We'll find them. C'mon. We need to go.'

They all leap out and shimmy down with no trouble.

Melody is haphazardly forcing her boots back onto her feet, wincing and whimpering as she does. Cass never lets go of her.

'There better be a damn good reason why you just saved her life,' he warns me.

'There's a reason,' I tell him, making sure Tee gets out the window. 'It's not good, Cass. In fact, it's downright bad.'

On the ground, we all sprint into the trees. Behind us, I hear the front door of my father's cottage being obliterated and the sound of angry Grey Coats storming the house. Winder grabs hold of Tee's hand as we run. Cass has a firm hold on the back of Melody's neck, determined not to let her get away. Not that she wants to. The Grey Coats won't want her telling anyone about what she saw. That's for sure.

Ahead, Loom runs with Elder One. They yell when two others jump out from behind a tree and lower their hoods. It's Owl and Elder Ten.

'Holy shit!' Loom gasps, clutching his chest. 'What the hell are ya doing? Trying to give us a heart attack?'

'We stayed to make sure you guys were okay.' Owl gives a whistle. From behind more trees, another dozen hooded figures appear. They lower their hoods and expose their faces. I recognise them all. Not only as transfers but as friends. Cadets who trained under the guidance of my dad. Cadets I grew up with. Owl looks past us and pulls her bow from over her shoulder. 'They're coming.'

'And we're leaving!' Elder One states, taking her by the elbow and pulling her away from the incoming Grey Coats and deeper into the woods. 'We need to gather our allies. If they catch us now, we're done!'

Everyone turns and obeys his orders.

We flee.

'Where the hell do we go?' Loom asks as we continue running.

'I have an idea,' Elder One tells us, glancing back over his shoulder. 'If we can get to-'

An axe comes hurtling from our right and embeds itself in the trunk of an oak just in front of Elder One. He skids to a stop and lands on his backside, narrowly missing it.

Tee has already reacted and has her bow poised with an arrow ready to fly.

The moon above offers little light. Only enough to show us the eerie shadows of branches swaying in the wind. There's no other movement in the gloom of the night. I have my katana drawn as I strain my eyes for any sight of the person who hurled the axe.

All around me, the soldiers stand on high alert. I can barely hear them breathing.

We may not be able to see them or hear them but we know they're here.

As I look, I start to see their silhouettes begin to move as they remain close to the trees.

I risk a quick look to Cass who has planted his feet by my side.

'You see them?' I whisper.

He nods. 'Ready?'

'You know me.'

'Wahoo?'

I spin my katana in my palm. 'Wahoo.' I smirk.

It all kicks-off in the blink of an eye. Grey Coats emerge from the trees and start their silent attack. They move quickly. Noah's best of the best. Their skills unrivalled.

The sound of steel meeting steel and the heavy grunts that accompany each swing, echo all around us as we fight deep in the woods, hidden from sight. I can't see anything more than the hooded shape coming at me with a sword. I fend off each of his attacks but his blows are more powerful than anything I've ever experienced. Luckily, my skills outmatch his and despite his brute strength, I manage to disarm him. His sword falls to the floor but his arm sweeps through the air and I slam into a tree. I regain my senses and my sword, and return to my feet.

'Bastard,' I snarl, charging at him.

With each blow I deliver, he manages to counter. All around me my friends fight, but when more Grey Coats emerge from the treeline, we know we have no choice but to run. We're outnumbered three to one at least.

I'm still swinging my weapon at two Grey Coats when Cass grabs me.

'Time to run!' he tells me, wrapping his arm around my waist and yanking me away just as I was about to deliver a blow to a Grey Coat's neck.

I miss my mark and prepare to fend Cass off so I can win my match.

But when I see all the other Grey Coats charging, I know we have no other choice.

'RUN!' I bellow into the darkness.

We scatter. I see Winder has Tee's hand in his as they disappear ahead.

Cass has grabbed Melody.

'C'MON!' he barks at me as I hesitate.

I need to make sure no one has fallen. That we leave no one behind. I scour the floor.

'Everyone's running and we should be too!' He gives me a firm nudge. 'GO!'

With a furious and reluctant grunt, I turn on my heel and run.

Through the trees, we hear the voices of those who have chosen to fight on our side. They call each other's names. They tell others to follow them. They share words of encouragement.

And then they start screaming.

One by one.

They yell out and threaten to kill whoever has grabbed them. I see their shadows as we run. Three Grey Coats have surrounded one of ours. Six have corned another two. I veer off-course to go to their aid. Cass has other ideas. He wraps his fingers around my wrist and refuses to let me help.

'We're outnumbered!'

'I don't care!'

'I won't let Noah get his hands on you, Scarlett!'

I manage to pry myself free and turn away.

Then I hear Tee scream from the other direction.

I spin around and look into the night. When I hear her again, no one on earth will stop me going to her.

'GET OFF ME!' she screams. 'I SAID GET OFF!'

I'm running faster than ever before. Not even when I was being chased by the horde of undead at the rainforest domes did I run this hard. My muscles scream at me to slow down. My lungs struggle to catch enough air through my terror.

Ahead, I see a small clearing. Tee and Winder are slap bang in the middle of it, surrounded by Grey Coats.

They already have Tee. Her hands are tied behind her back and they're trying to gag her whilst she thrashes violently in their arms. Winder is swinging his axe at anyone standing between him and her. He's so desperate to reach her, he doesn't see the attackers coming from behind until it's too late. They smack him over the head and he crumples to the floor.

'WINDE-'

Cass slams his hand over my mouth and shoves me to the floor, landing on top of me with his whole-bodyweight. The more I struggle, the firmer his grip becomes. Cowering behind a tree is Melody. Her head is buried in her knees and she shakes wildly. Cass twists my head and shows me what I failed to see, whispering for me to hush.

Noah is standing to the side of the clearing, watching my friends being captured. Behind him is a small army of Grey Coats.

Tee and Winder are dragged away, gagged and restrained. Along with many of my transfers, they're shoved into a large wooden crate attached to horses.

'Where is my bride?' Noah asks.

'Here somewhere, my Lord. As well as the Red Coat traitor,' replies the Commander.

'Who *do* we have?'

'These two. The one they call Loom. Elder Ten as well. Along with a dozen of the fools wearing the black hoodies. There are still other's out there. Our men will find them. Your future bride included.'

Noah snorts as he searches the darkness. 'She'll pay dearly for this. Rest assured. I'll have her begging for my forgiveness soon enough.'

'This wasn't part of the plan, My Lord. Taking all these soldiers? We need them.'

'True. This wasn't part of the plan. It's a good job I'm fantastic at adapting.' He faces the Commander. 'I want her found. I want her brought to me and I want her lover hung, drawn and quartered. I'll serve his head to her on a silver platter as a wedding gift.'

'My Lord, with all due respect, why are you so determined to claim her? There are so many others far more deserving of your divine devotions.'

Noah gives a light chuckle. 'You've clearly never been in love, have you, Commander? No... she's the one. She's the *only* one that can do what I need *my* wife to do. And despite her wilful disobedience, I do love her. And she'll love me back. In time. Find her. I want her in my custody before the sun rises.'

Cass pins me down even harder and even seals my nose so I can't make a sound or even take a breath. I thrash beneath him, failing to free myself.

Noah mounts his horse. 'Load the captured traitors up with the others and get them out of The Haven. We can't risk anyone else finding them and setting them free. They know too much. Send them where the other useless and disobedient stock have been taken.'

'Understood, My Lord.'

Noah, along with the crate, rides away, followed by several of his guards. They disappear from sight.

The Commander starts ordering his men to search the area for me, as well as Cass and anyone else they can find. They're about to head in our direction before Elder One's voice travels from the west.

'THIS WAY, SCARLETT!' he bellows. 'THAT'S RIGHT! FOLLOW ME!'

The Grey Coats turn and run in the opposite direction.

Cass watches them closely as they charge away from us. I, on the other hand, don't look away from the direction Tee has been taken.

'Elder's leading them away from us,' Cass whispers in my ear, still watching the Grey Coats leaving. 'C'mon-'

As soon as he eases his grip I buck him off and roll over, swiftly getting to my feet and making my way to Tee. His hand wraps around my ankle and I fall flat on my face. As I kick and squirm against his hold, he manages to crawl up my body and once more uses his weight to hold me down.

'Get off me!' I warn. 'You coward. If you're too scared to face them then I will.'

'I'm not a coward. I'm being smart.' He glances towards the direction the crate has left. 'It's the same kind of crate Melody said she was in. They're taking them out of the Haven.'

'Like hell!' I hiss furiously, pushing against his chest. Pointlessly.

'We're outnumbered, Scarlett! If you go over there it will achieve nothing but death! I'll be killed. You'll be handed to Noah. Tee, Winder as well as everyone else will be left for zombie chow out beyond the wall.'

I know he's talking sense, but I can't help it. My instincts are to protect my family at any cost.

'Be smart, Scarlett. You must be a soldier now. A Canary. An Elder. Your people are in trouble. If we get captured there will be no one to save them.'

It takes everything I have not to slam my face into his and toss him off me. I seal my lips shut, grip his arms tightly and force myself to stay put.

The sound of the horses leaving and the muffled cries of my family start to fade.

He looks at Melody who has lifted her head. 'Do you remember how to get back to where you were when you escaped?'

'I-I think so,' she whispers, nodding maniacally. 'From where the sun was rising and how close we were to the sea...' She wipes her tears dry and looks a little more focused. 'Yes. Yes, I swear it. I'll get you there.'

There's a series of rustling leaves and snapping twigs. We all spin around and see a rather out of breath Elder One.

'Bloody close that, huh? Who'd they get?' he huffs.

I look and see Owl close behind him, glancing over her shoulder anxiously.

'Are you all that's left?' I ask. 'Elder Ten? Loom? Anyone?'

'It's just us.' Owl replies.

'Then they got everyone,' I tell them, looking painfully at the empty clearing. 'They got everyone.'

'Not for long. C'mon,' Cass says. 'Let's go get them.'

Elder One leads us with purpose through the dark woodland.

'You'll take the tunnel hidden in Elder HQ,' he says. 'It will take you out beyond the wall.'

'There's a tunnel in Elder HQ?' Owl asks, ducking beneath a low hanging branch as we follow.

'Yep. In the garden at the very back, there's a small stable where we keep our horses. Inside is a hidden hatch in the ground. It was made decades ago using old sewer lines, just in case there was ever a breach and we needed to evacuate. We keep the horses there for a swift getaway. We need to be quick. Elder Two and Elder Five have made it perfectly clear that they are standing with Noah. When word gets out that we're not safely detained by the Grey Coats, they'll seal off any and all exits. This one included.'

Although he's speaking, I can barely focus on his actual words.

I'm struggling to act as a soldier should. All my training, everything I know I should be doing right now, has just abandoned me.

None of my thoughts can get themselves in order. I should be planning. Preparing for a fight. Thinking of routes to take. How to fend-off targets in the dark. How to attack the Grey Coats, or coming up with methods of breaking open the crate holding Tee and the others hostage. But all I can think about is the worst-case scenario. What if she's been bitten? Will I be able to put her down like I did my father? What if I find nothing but torn limbs and blood? There's a never-ending pit of despair in my gut. It makes it hard to swallow. Hard to breathe.

Cass has hold of my hand as he guides me through the trees.

We hop over the wall surrounding Elder HQ and skulk through the grounds to the rear of the garden. Elder One leads us to a small wooden stable and pulls open the door. Quickly, he lights a gas lamp and hands it to Melody as Cass and Owl help him saddle the horses. One of them leans over its stable door and nudges me affectionately.

I recognise it as my dad's horse.

'You will come out two miles from the wall, on the coast,' Elder explains, fitting the saddle in place. 'Sunrise is less than two hours away. The tunnel is wide enough for you to go one by one but take it easy. They're old tunnels.' He thrusts the reins into my hand. 'You go and fetch the others back. I will remain here and gather those who want to fight. We will prepare to make our final stand against Noah. If you have not returned by sunrise tomorrow, we will make our move without you. Twenty-four hours. That's the longest we can wait. Any longer and we risk capture.' He settles his hands on my shoulders. I blink up at him. 'I know you're scared, Scarlett. Tee's been taken and after losing your dad the way you did I wouldn't blame you for freaking out right now. But you must pull yourself together. This fear of yours, use it. Get it under control and use it to your advantage.'

'I've never been this afraid before,' I admit in a shameful whisper. 'I don't know how to use it. I can't get past it. What if we're too late?'

Cass taps Elder on the shoulder. He moves aside and lets Cass stand before me instead.

'Scarlett. Stop thinking about the what if's. Focus on the facts. The facts shouldn't frighten you. They should piss you off. There is a man who wants to force you to marry him. There is a man who wants to butcher everyone you love. There is a man who will see the very people he swore to protect, starve, be bred like cattle, hand over child after child to a life of being nothing more than a sacrificial-soldier.' He takes my face in his hands. 'Noah Sands is the man responsible for your father's death and don't you dare forget it!'

As he speaks, my once fierce rage begins to stir. The barely burning embers spark and grow brighter.

'He has just taken our family from us. My brother. Your sister. Your unit. Our allies. Will you let that pass? Will you take all of this lying down? Will you give in? Really? You?'

I shake my head.

'I didn't catch that, Canary. Elder. Friend. Lover. Sister. Warrior. I said... Will you let this pass?'

'No...'

'Sorry?' he urges. 'What did you say?'

'I said no! I won't let anything that man has done, pass.' I stand straighter and feel the full force of my inner flame burn with vengeance and hatred. 'We're gonna get them back and we're gonna come back here and I'm gonna tear Noah's head from his god damn body!'

'That's my girl.'

We ride through the dark tunnel with nothing but the gas lamp Elder gave us to light our way. The walls are made of old brick and patches of steel and concrete. Wooden posts that look rotten and fragile hold up the areas that are crumbling and the air is full of damp, stagnant water and mould. Enough to make my throat burn.

None of that matters.

Even if this tunnel falls on my head, I will dig my way from the earth and rise from beneath my enemy's feet to stop their victory and save my family.

After almost an hour of navigating the tunnel, we reach the exit. It's an old metal-grate looking out on the beach. I pull out the key Elder gave me just before we left and unlock the chunky padlock which is almost rusted shut. The rising sun greets us as we lead out the horses, re-seal the grate, mount up and turn to Melody.

'Well?' I ask impatiently. 'Which way?'

She looks at the rising sun and takes in our position on the beach.

As do I.

I know this place. I've ridden past it many times. About half an hours ride north is the pier we used to sneak off to.

'That way,' Melody tells us, gesturing north. 'There's a pile of rubble disappearing into the sea. I'd been running for about an hour when I came across that.'

'Let's get on the road. Running on the concrete rather than sand will save the horse's energy,' I tell them, heading away from the ocean and towards the street lined with rotted beach huts and old candy stands.

After some pretty hard riding, we arrive at the remains of our beloved amusements. We pass by it wordlessly, but Cass and I share a melancholy glance to the only place we ever called ours.

Ahead of us are several targets huddled in a pile. We hear the sound of tearing flesh and their vile gurgling and chewing.

My heart thumps in my chest as we approach.

It thumps even harder when I spot something I recognise hanging from a branch, gently blowing in the wind. I reach out and take it.

It's Winder's face mask. The one with the giant grin Tee drew on years ago. I look ahead at the gathering of eating targets.

'Please...' I whisper. 'No!'

With Owl's shooting, there's no need to engage with any of them. They all fall dead as her arrows find their mark and I jump down to run to the pile, praying to a god I don't believe in for the body they're feasting on not to be one of my friends.

I let out an enormous sigh of relief when I see that they were feeding on the carcass of a horse instead.

It's saddled and not long dead.

I look to Melody. Cass remains close to her, concerned that she'll bolt at the first sign of trouble. He's tethered their horses together.

'What colour was your horse?' I ask her. 'The one you rode until it died?'

'White,' she answers painfully.

Owl pours a little of the water from her flask over some of the blood-soaked hair and reveals that yes, this is the white horse she rode until it gave out. I recognise the saddle as a Verity issue too.

'We're on the right track at any rate,' I tell Owl, looking at the sad creature by our feet and handing her the face mask. 'It's Winder's. He was here.'

She examines the mask. 'No blood. That's good.' She hands it back and nods to Melody. 'And she wasn't lying about her escape either.'

Owl has a sip of water and hands her flask to me. I take a sip and return it to her.

'You holding up okay?' she asks.

'Just trying not to think about it. You?'

She shakes her head and runs her fingers through her hair. 'Bowzer's tough. He's almost as tough as you but I'm still freaking out. I love that guy. If anything happens to him I swear... I'll burn those responsible alive.' She looks at me and I see the fear in her eyes.

'Isn't he a pyromaniac?' I ask. 'I remember Elder Eight telling me that some time ago.'

She chuckles and nods. 'Yeah. He was a Black Coat for a couple of years but Elder Eight made him a Green Coat because he kept collecting explosives from beyond the wall and using chemicals to make bombs. He'd sneak out after dark to blow stuff up.' She carries on laughing fondly at her memories. 'The Grey Coats caught on and knew someone was setting fire to the old buildings out here or strapping bombs to targets. Elder Eight hid him up on the wall.'

'He sounds interesting, your Bowzer.' I smirk.

'He's the best,' she agrees, blushing a little. Then her face falls as she remembers that he's not safely by her side.

'They'll be okay, Owl.' We turn and start making our way to the horses. 'They'll all be...' My feet stop as my words peter-out. I don't know what it is but something's not right. I look to Cass and watch him observing me. I feel my brow knit together as I chew my lip.

'Scar?' Owl says softly. 'You okay?'

It takes a moment for all the noise created by my fear and anger to simmer down.

I start walking backwards, back towards the targets that lay limp around the remains of the horse. I kick off one of the targets, exposing the one beneath. Rolling it over I see what it was that caused my brain to hiccup.

'Cass?' I call over. He heads on over, pulling Melody alongside. We stand around the huddle. 'You see this?'

He leans down and using the bladed tip of his haladie dagger, he scrapes off some of the horse's torn flesh stuck to the fibres of its coat.

'Well I'll be...' he mutters. He checks the others and after a few moments, he gets to his feet. 'One wearing a German policeman's coat and another wearing combat gear with the French flag stitched into the sleeve.' He lifts his gaze to meet mine. 'Another German policeman, like the one you found in the trap before you left.'

'That's weird, right?' Owl interjects, rather enthusiastically which causes us all to look at her quizzically. 'It's just, in the last few months, I've killed some odd targets while up on the wall. Some were wearing clothes, just like this one. A lot of French and some Irish. I could tell by their uniforms. I don't see many still wearing clothes so it was really weird.'

We all look down at the targets.

'It is extremely weird,' I agree.

'We need to carry on.' I swallow my dread, and with it, the thought that my Tee might be out here alone, wandering around injured, or worse, searching for flesh and blood to devour. 'We can't wait around here any longer.' I give Cass Winder's mask. 'They're close' I take hold of my father's horse and climb on up. 'We need to find them. Now.'

We ride on. We're not hanging about. This isn't a sightseeing mission and it's not about elimination either. We pass targets and avoid engaging them if at all possible, but every single one we pass we look at them closely. None of them are our friends.

We continue following the road which turns away from the water and leads inland. We divert to the coastal path instead in order to keep the ocean in our sights.

'You know where we're heading, don't you?' Cass asks knowingly as we ride. 'If we carry on in this direction, we're going to end up in-'

'A level one zone,' I reply. 'Yeah. I know. Makes sense, if they're dumping people to be eaten they'd want to do it where they'd definitely have enough targets.'

'Level one?' Melody asks. 'What's a level one?' Her eyes dart between Cass and me, dreading to hear our answer.

'No wonder you failed your final assessment,' I snipe. 'How can you not know what a level one is?'

'I... I don't-'

'It's an area with the highest risk possible and not recommended to be approached at any cost.' I explain. 'There are four levels. Level four is little to no risk. Level three is a location that has been secured but may have been breached since last visiting. Level two is very dangerous. Level One is a lost cause. Like London or Plymouth. We passed those a few months back and they were swarming with the dead and the buildings were unsafe from bomb or fire damage.'

'Translation. Certain death,' Owl clarifies.

'There are three level ones near The Haven. We're forbidden to go anywhere near them. Norwich, Ipswich, and another town which just so happens to be right where we're heading. There's supposed to be some kind of old power station there. The targets are attracted to it. Don't suppose you recall seeing something like a level one zone when you fled to save your own ass and left everyone else to be eaten alive?'

'Scar!' Cass snaps. 'That's out of line.'

'Oh, you can shut up as well. The bloody pair of you can both piss off. If you hadn't kissed her and if you hadn't had lied about him assaulting you and if you'd have let me help Tee instead of making me hide-'

'We'd all be either dead or captured! And if someone kissing someone else is the real reason this is happening, I think you need to look in the mirror!'

'Bite me, Cass.'

'Poor choice of words out here, Scar,' Owl chuckles, desperately trying to lighten the mood.

Her attempt at humour falls like a lead balloon.

'We need to find them.'

'We will, Scarlett,' he promises. 'We will!'

'I'm gonna go to that hill over there and see what lies ahead,' I tell them all, pointing into the distance. 'You carry on following the coast path. We don't want to miss anything.'

'Not on your own you're not.' Cass laughs angrily. 'Besides, that hill is inland. Melody said she was near the coast when she escaped.'

'She was blindfolded. She ran in an unknown direction for an unknown amount of time. I'm not risking losing them.'

I give my horse a nudge and divert inland. The sound of hooves follows close behind me.

'What do you want?'

'To help,' Melody replies quietly.

'You can help by shutting up and concentrating on trying to recognise where we are.'

She follows me closely and I feel her eyes on me every step of the way.

'I'm sorry,' she says weakly.

'You didn't have a choice,' I sigh, knowing that in reality, she had as little choice as I did once Noah issued his threats. 'Making your statement-'

'I made the choice to go after Cass,' she tells me. 'I knew... we all knew... that you and he loved each other. Even though you two didn't even seem to notice how you each felt. But we all knew. And I still went after him.'

'Why did you?'

'Cos, he was unattainable. The best soldier. The most attractive.'

I look back at her. Is that all it takes to want someone?

'I guess,' she takes a second to compose her next words. 'I'm a crap soldier. I'm not a particularly popular person either. If he liked me the way he liked you, it would have made me worthy.'

'Of what?'

'Not sure. But you're the best soldier too. The most popular. Everyone looks up to you and the Elders adore you. Most of them anyway. I guess I thought that if he liked me the way he liked you, I'd be worth something too. Like you are.'

'That's really stupid.'

'Yeah. Guess so.'

We carry on in silence.

'Look,' I say after a moment of unbearable awkwardness. 'We all do crazy things for random reasons that seem to make sense at the time. We make mistakes. We hurt people. We do things that cause nothing but trouble, but we learn and we move on. You're not as shit a soldier as you think you are. You survived this. You were brave enough to come to me for help, knowing that I would more than likely defend Cass instead of you. And you have Liddy. So who cares if you're not popular. As long as you have someone who you love as much as they love you, that's more than enough.' I think of Tee again and images of her bound and gagged in that crate sends my heart into overdrive.

'What if Liddy was in that crate too?' she says painfully, uttering the words that she's been too afraid to face.

'You can't think like that.'

'What if when I was running, I was leaving her behind to die?'

'As I said, you can't think like that. You were in no position to save anyone but yourself. You-'

'Would you have run?' she asks. 'If you suspected, even for a second, that Tee was in that crate with you? Would you have run?'

I look back at her over my shoulder. 'No,' I reply in truth. 'I would never have run. Something you don't know about me, Melody. Something that only really Cass and Tee knows. Perhaps even Elder Eight did. I don't particularly care for living. I only really do it for them. They'd be far too hurt if I did die. I live for them. Totally. I only really realised that when Elder Eight passed. I'd die before I'd ever let a single one of my friends perish. Because if they die, I'm nothing. I will die for them. Of that I'm pretty damn certain. And I'm okay with that. So you see? Being me ain't all that great. I may look like I have my shit together, Melody.

But I'm damaged and the worst part is they know it.' I nod to Cass who keeps glancing in our direction from the edge of the cliffs. 'They all watch me like a hawk, scared that one day I'm gonna decide that they're not enough for me to keep going or one of my crazy stunts will get me eaten alive. I jump headfirst into things I probably shouldn't without thinking of the consequences because, in reality, any consequence I suffer is mine to bear. As long as they don't have to bear it, as long as they don't die, that's all that matters.' I give a shrug and a slight laugh. 'Because I sure as hell ain't enough to keep myself going.' I look ahead. 'We're almost at the top of the hill. Do you recognise where we are?'

'No.'

We reach the summit and below us is a valley with a path of churned up the dirt.

'They look like wheel marks if you ask me,' I tell Melody, turning to Cass and whistling him over.

'For the record, I think you're pretty awesome,' she tells me. 'If I had friends like yours and a man like Cass, I think I'd die a happy girl.'

'Let's just try and avoid dying for now, huh?' I give her a playful nudge. 'We're good. No hard feelings, Melody.'

Cass and Owl promptly make their way over and agree that the marks indented in the ground look like what we have been searching for. As we descend and dismount, we quickly see that not only are they wheel tracks, but there are multiple tracks.

'More than one carriage? Or one carriage more than once?' Cass asks.

'Let's follow the tracks and see,' I reply, mounting my horse and swiftly galloping on ahead. They all follow, desperate and terrified to see where these tracks lead us.

The answer presents itself when we follow the path around the base of another hill and come across the carriage.

Upon seeing the carnage, Melody starts to heave and violently vomit.

Even my stomach does a flip.

It looks like it lost a wheel when it hit a rock embedded in the ground. I can see that it dragged for a few feet before becoming stuck. I dismount and head over, withdrawing my katana as I do.

'Owl... watch our backs,' I tell her. I hear her withdraw an arrow from her quiver as Melody continues being sick.

Cass stays close, his eyes darting in every direction with his haladies in his hand.

The side of the carriage has been torn and a hole's been created by what I guess was a group of very hungry Class Twos. The splinters of the wood litter the floor around us from where it hurled it away in its frantic effort to smash its way inside. With each step, more blood soaks the earth. Limbs lie half-eaten and torn apart all around us. The stench of death lingers in the air and the sound of buzzing flies become louder and louder.

Slowly, cautiously, we approach the crate and peer inside.

It's Cass's turn to sprint away and vomits.

It's beyond a massacre. I've never seen so much death, so fresh, in all my life. Their white faces, all drained of blood from missing limbs and vicious bites, stare into nothing. The last look of real terror and agony remains. As the wind howls through the gaps of their final cage, I swear, I hear their screams.

I step back, fighting to keep the little food I have in my belly from forcing its way up my throat.

I glance at Cass who's shaking his head in disbelief.

We've seen death, every day for as long as we can remember.

But never like this.

'I-is she in there?' Melody calls over, gasping and desperate to be told that, no, her beloved friend is not amongst this slaughter.

But truth be told, even if I knew what Liddy looked like, I couldn't tell for certain who any of these people were. They're too gnawed up, bloody and covered in too much flesh from others to even hazard a guess.

After Cass recomposes himself he joins me by my side and forces himself to look within. After muttering a swear word under his breath, he looks at me.

'She's in there. See that hand? The one in the corner?' He gestures to the severed limb. There's a large scar running straight across it. 'Liddy got that scar in her evaluation.'

'You better go and tell her. It will be better coming from you.'

He nods but remains by my side.

'How could they do this?' he asks painfully. 'We've given them everything and they do this to us?'

I rest my hand on his cheek. He leans into my touch and finds some comfort there.

'We didn't give anything. They took. And now we're going to take it back.' I nod to Melody. 'Go. I'll take a look around.'

He walks to her and rests his hands on her shoulders. Soon enough, she howls like a wounded animal and falls to the floor on her knees. Cass kneels beside her, holding her as she cries.

Owl joins me.

'Do I want to look in the crate?'

'Not if you ever want to sleep again, no,' I reply, kicking the dirt. 'There are no targets here.'

'That's good, right?'

'It doesn't make sense. This crate... these bodies... No way a target would leave this much behind. No way!'

I follow the tracks around the base of the hill. They disappear out of sight, but something catches my eye. A small piece of cloth in the dirt. I run towards it and snatch it up.

It's Tee's face mask. The same one that I drew her zigzag smile on. Ahead are several Class Twos, beheaded.

It all makes sense.

Owl and I return to the others. Cass helps a tearful Melody to her feet and steadies her. I feel for her, I do, but Tee and the others are still out here somewhere. That's what matters now.

'They didn't dump the crate here,' I tell them all. 'The wheel fell off and it was attacked by targets. This wasn't supposed to happen. The targets are around the bend. Dead! The tracks carry on. It's clear that this route has been taken many times. The dirt is all torn up. I'm betting that the crate Tee and the others are in carried on in that direction and look!' I give Cass the mask.

'It's Tee's!'

'It's Tee's.' I beam. 'She left it for us. I have no idea where they're taking them but wherever it is, they're leaving us a trail to follow!'

Cass lands a kiss on my lips. 'Then let's follow it and get our family back!'

We ride hard as we follow the tracks. I've wrapped Tee's mask around my palm and I hold it tightly, vowing that I'll return it to her. The sun has started to go down. We've been out here all day. The wind is unbearably cold. The air hurts as I breathe it in and my fingers struggle to hold onto the reins of the horse. When we find another mask in the dirt, I recognise it straight away as Loom's. I remember Sky drawing his, the helmet of a suit of armour. I hope that Sky's okay. Finger's crossed she found Elder One and they're together, gathering the others. I stow it safely in my pocket and we carry on.

When we round the base of yet another hill we see that the tracks lead down a slope. Cass and I dismount, telling Owl and Melody that we're going to follow the incline and see if we can get any sights on the Grey Coat carriage from above.

As we reach the top, I grab Cass by the collar and drag him to the floor.

'What the fu–'

'Hush!' I hiss, slamming my hand over his mouth. I point ahead. 'They're over there!'

I take my hand from his lips and let him up. Together, we see that there are two Grey Coats riding horses, escorting a crate in similar size and shape as the one we found further down the road. Four horses pull the crate and two further Grey Coats sit atop the crate holding the reins. They're moving at a steady pace. I imagine that much like our horses, theirs are tired so they've had to slow down. I hear them laughing and talking amongst themselves.

'We need to get ahead of them,' I whisper. 'If we attack from behind, they could bolt.'

'What do you want to do?'

'We ride ahead and attack. Melody and Owl can take the rear.'

He nods and we return to the others below to tell them that finally, we've found them.

We ride as fast as our exhausted horses will carry us.

Above, thick, grey clouds are starting to form in the dwindling daylight. The air has an extra bite to it, threatening the snow we all know is on its way.

I raise my hand, giving the signal for Owl and Melody to fall back and ascend the hilltop. I watch them break away, knowing that the pace we held has put us ahead of the carriage still travelling below in the valley. Cass and I carry on, turning a corner, passing some trees and protruding boulders. We dismount the horses and hide them out of sight before positioning ourselves atop a jagged ledge which juts out of the hillside.

I peer behind us, further down the valley, and see Owl wave her hand high in the air.

'They're in position,' I tell Cass. 'And I hear the carriage coming.'

I turn to face him. He has his steely resolve and his determination to win etched across his face. His eyes are narrowed, taking in every bit of his surroundings. Every muscle in his body is rigid, ready and raring to go. To fight. To kill. To win.

Our eyes meet.

'I love you,' I tell him.

'You better not be saying goodbye,' he smirks, heading over to readjust my collar. Gently and calmly, he sweeps my hair from beneath my mother's coat and places it neatly over my shoulders. 'Because if you die, I will bloody kill you.'

'You better.' I grin. 'I'm not saying goodbye,' I tell him, brushing his hair from his eyes. 'Just telling you something that I really like saying. I.' I take a step closer. 'Love.' His hand settles on my hip. My head tilts up as he looks down. Our noses touch and we each smile a content little smile. 'You,' I conclude.

'I love you too.' He takes my face in his hands. 'Don't do anything stupid out there.'

'You know me.'

'Yes,' he sighs, a smile still pulling at his lips. 'I do. So I'll say it again. Don't do anything stupid, Scarlett. Together,' he says. 'We do this together and we come out of this together.'

'Always, Cass. Always.'

We collide together in a consuming embrace. His lips meet mine and we hold each other impossibly close.

All this time. All those years. I pushed the very idea of allowing myself to love someone far from my mind as well as my heart. I thought it a curse. A weakness. A destructive force that does nothing but devour and destroy.

But I've loved for a long time. Cass. Tee. Winder. My dad. Even Flash, Titan and my Canaries. Despite betrayers among them, I love them still. How could I not? They gave me years of smiles. Of laughter. Of hope. Of friendship.

A reason to live.

I grip Cass tightly, the sound of hooves and the rattling of the cart's wheels grow louder.

Our kiss slows and with an exhale, we rest our foreheads together and look deep into each other's eyes.

'Ready?' he asks.

'Ready.'

'Death or glory.'

I take Tee's mask and place it on my face. 'Their death.'

He puts on Winder's mask. 'Our glory.'

He holds out his hand and as we've always done before any battle, I rest my hand on his.

'Let's do this.'

CHAPTER TEN

Crouching low, we wait for the Grey Coats to pass below. When the two leading the troop are in the right position, we leap down, taking them by surprise from above. I land with both swords in hand, Tee's mask covering my mouth, my hood up and my coat buttoned.

Cass is by my side, his haladies in his grip, Winder's mask on his face, his hood up and a low growl resonating from his throat.

The Grey Coats leap back, startled by our sudden appearance.

'Afternoon, fellas,' I greet, spinning my sword in my palm. 'How's it going?'

'What are you–'

'I'll answer her question for you,' Cass announces, pointing the bladed tip of one of his haladies at the Grey Coat's face. 'Badly. For you, it's about to go really, *really* badly.'

'One chance. That's all you get.' I point at the crate behind them with my weapon. 'Give us back the people you've stolen and we'll let you go.'

The two Grey Coats glance at each other and share a laugh.

'You think you two can overpower us?' The one in front of Cass scoffs as he withdraws his sword. 'You're foolish to-'

A whooshing sound grows louder, then *thump.*

The Grey Coat gets an arrow through his gloved hand, causing him to drop his sword and loudly yell.

They look behind and see Owl. She's got high ground and a quiver full of arrows. Her next one is already poised and ready to fly.

'Hi there,' she calls down. 'I feel I gotta warn ya, I'm an extremely good shot and in a really shitty mood.' She pulls back the arrow a little further in warning. 'This one's aimed at your neck.'

The Grey Coat holds his hand and lets out a furious roar before lifting his head to look at Cass and me.

'TODD!' he yells. 'KILL THE ARCHER!'

The Grey Coat at the rear leaps off his horse and sprints towards Owl. She shifts her aim to Todd instead. She fires but he cuts the arrow out the air with his sword.

'I don't think he's gonna give them back,' I huff, looking at the Grey Coat before me as the one ahead of Cass yanks free the arrow from his hand.

'I think you're right,' Cass agrees. 'Wahoo?'

'Oh yeah,' I grin back, firming the hold on my sword. 'Wahoo.'

I raise my katana and strike my first blow. The Grey Coat unsheathes his sword in a swift and impressive move, blocking my steel from meeting his neck. With a hard shove, he sends me backwards. I'm taken aback by the force of his shove.

Meanwhile, the Grey Coat facing Cass has scooped up his sword and lunged. The anger from being shot comes out in a menacing grunt as he attacks.

My Grey Coat has raised his sword above his head and intends to bring it down on my skull. I lunge to the left and feel the wind brush my cheek as I miss it by a hair. He's already pulling his sword back. As it descends on me, I pull my katana and block him. The sheer brute strength of his steel meeting mine creates a glorious twang but also sends my feet skidding backwards over the dirt. Our blades are still crossed and less than an inch from my face.

He's strong.

Phenomenally so.

That's okay.

I'm quick.

I fall to my knees. While one sword keeps his at bay, my other swipes at his feet. He leaps backwards, relinquishing his attack and freeing up my hands.

I swing both weapons fiercely and skilfully, striking again and again. He has one sword while I have two and he struggles to keep his eyes on both of mine as I wield them. He steps back after each of my attacks, hoping to get enough room between us to slow me down or at least so he can see my strikes coming or anticipate them. He can't counter both my weapons so has no choice but to continue retreating, dodging my left blade with his body while blocking my right with his own sword.

I take my chance when I see it and bring down both swords on his neck.

He lunges low and annoyingly, they soar over his head.

He launches his attack, hammering down blow after blow with almighty force. With each strike he delivers, the strength of it hammers into me unlike anything I have ever experienced before.

Cass is taking on the raging lunatic off to the side of me, his haladies are almost a blur as he fights. He ducks and weaves and the Grey Coat fails to land a single blow.

The Grey Coats atop the crate have climbed down. One has an axe in hand, and the other, a giant of a man, has a sword. Every attempt they take to reach us is met with an arrow. They leap out of the way of each one as Owl continues trying to lure them away from us and the crate. When Owl lands one into the shoulder of the axe-man, he turns on his heel and makes his way towards her.

Owl's high and anyone who wants to reach her will have to climb. She holds her position and will continue to hold her position until everyone is far enough away from the crate to let Melody do what she needs to do. I see her, Melody, crouching behind a boulder on the other side of the crate. She's watching, waiting for the perfect opportunity to reach the crate and break it open.

Cass and I keep two of the Grey Coats busy and Owl has successfully lured the other two away. But the giant remains by the crate, his sword ready as he surveys the surrounding area. He's using the crate to protect himself from our archer and it doesn't look like he's going to shift.

Crap.

I hear a thud and see Cass slam hard into the floor, clasping his side. His Grey Coat raises his sword and runs at him, hollering like a beast. Cass waits, and just as he gets close enough, he slams the heel of his boot into his crotch. When the Grey Coat doubles over, Cass kicks him in the face sending him flat on his backside. He sees his chance. A clear path between him and the crate holding our friends hostage.

He flips himself to his feet and sprints forwards.

The giant Grey Coat steps out from behind the crate and throws a punch. Cass falls to the floor, skidding on his leg as he passes beneath the mighty blow, then he returns to his feet.

I keep my own Grey Coat busy, swinging my katanas down on him over and over, despite his incessant blocking.

When Cass's Grey Coat turns to run after him, I place myself between them both. I face the two Grey Coats with both my katanas in hand and my feet dug into the ground.

They attack. I duck and dodge and block and strike with every bit of skill I have. We're all so well trained, but these Grey Coats have some serious strength. I know I can't keep it up. Not at all! I have no choice but to step back with each of their attacks. When one of them knocks a katana from my hand, I turn and run towards the crate.

Melody has emerged from her hiding spot and is running to our aid. The giant Grey Coat has planted himself between the door to the crate, and Cass and Melody. Cass sees me running towards them and launches an attack on the giant. He lets the giant have dominance, making him believe that with each of his strikes, Cass and Melody must retreat. This draws the giant away from the crate.

Behind me, the two Grey Coats are giving chase.

From up on the hill, Owl starts firing arrows. It slows them down as they dodge them or cut them from the air. The other two who went after her have made it halfway up the ridge. She's stopped protecting herself in order to give me time. I hop on the crate and thrust my sword between the lock and the wood and with every bit of strength I have, I prise them apart. The wood splinters and the metal groans. I yell as I give even more. My feet slam into the door and I haul with my whole body.

'C'MON!' I shout angrily at the stubborn lock. I lift my gaze and see the two Grey Coats heading my way. 'Bugger!'

I pull and I pull. Little by little, the metal pulls further and further away from the wood. Melody appears behind me, wrapping her arms around me and slamming her feet beside mine. Together we heave, yelling and grunting as we give our all. The two Grey Coats are inches from us. Behind me, Cass has taken a heavy hit from the giant and been tossed backwards. The two Grey Coats ascending the ridge see us at the door and start descending.

'IF ANYONE'S IN THERE,' I yell, slamming my foot on the wood. 'PUSH!'

The door starts to bulge outwards as we continue pulling and pulling. The Giant grabs Melody and tosses her away. He turns back, ready to grab me.

With a final and begrudging groan, the metal lock relinquishes its hold and comes apart. I land in the dirt, narrowly missing the giant's hand. Melody dives past us both, straight into the darkened crate, just as the giant reaches me. The point of his sword rests at my throat as he looks down at me, and I peer up into the darkness beneath the hood. His hand tightens on the handle of his sword. His shoulders rise and fall as he takes in deep breath after deep breath.

I lie there, the sharp tip of his deadly weapon resting menacingly into my flesh.

But he just stands there, watching me.

'KILL HER!' One of the Grey Coats bellows. 'THAT'S AN OR-DER!'

Cass has shot around the other side of the crate and is making his way behind the two descending Grey Coats.

I see my katana lying a few feet away. My fingers twitch with the need to reach for it but I know that this Grey Coat can kill me easily if I so much as breathe too much.

'I SAID, KILL HE-'

Cass buries his haladie into the Grey Coat's temple from be-hind. When he pulls free his weapon, the Grey Coat slides to the floor in a lifeless heap.

'Get away from her,' Cass warns, pointing his weapon in the giant's direction. 'Or you're next.'

The second Grey Coat turns away from the crate and goes after Cass.

Owl has run out of arrows and is now following the two other Grey Coats who are descending the ridge.

The Giant looks back down to me.

He's hesitating.

I see the slight tremble in his hand. His hard and jagged breath-ing. But that's not all I notice.

I see the hilt of his weapon where embroidered into the bind-ings are two initials.

I recognise them.

Hell, I helped put them there.

I lift my eyes and stare heartbroken under the hood. I had it wrong. I had it all wrong! The traitor isn't Flash.

'No…' I whisper. 'No… not you!'

His feet shuffle and his fingers flex on his weapon.

'Why?' I ask.

'For him,' he replies. 'For love. I had to keep him safe, Scar. I won't kill you. Noah wants you alive but I can't let you leave here. We can't let any of you leave here.'

There's a furious yell from inside the crate as Flash leaps out, crashing into the giant. They both fall to the floor before a dozen others fly out from inside their prison, yelling and hollering in anger.

The transfers are first. The various soldiers who came to the cottage in my defence. Then Bowzer, Tan and Elder Ten emerge. They snatch up rocks from the ground and clamber on top of the crate to retrieve a large, locked chest strapped to the roof. They start smashing the rocks into the lock which is sealing it shut. When it opens, they start tossing out the confiscated weapons that were hidden inside. The grateful transfers open their arms and catch swords, axes, bows, daggers and hammers. They all swiftly turn and start attacking the remaining Grey Coats.

A hand reaches out to me.

It's Chilli.

He hauls me to my feet.

'Boy am I glad to see you!' He pulls me in for a hug. 'Cheers for the rescue, Boss,' he says. 'You're timing always was perfect.'

'Chilli?' I whisper, stunned to see him as one of the prisoners. I pull back and rest my hand on his cheek as I take in his black eye and swollen jaw with a cut protruding from his lip. 'What are you doing in there? You weren't with us at the cottage. How-'

'It's a long story. I know you thought I was the traitor. Tee told me. But I'm not, I swear it.' He glances over my shoulder and pats me on the arm. A murderous expression contorts his face. 'Excuse me. Mind if I borrow this?' He scoops up one of my katanas. 'I need to help my boyfriend.' And with that, he sprints towards Flash.

'Boyfriend?'

'SCAR!' Tee hollers. I look over and see her step out from inside the crate hand in hand with Winder. Relief overcomes me but the look on her face as she points behind me is far from happy. 'LOOK OUT!'

I turn and manage to dodge the axe coming down on me. The Grey Coat raises it again, yelling as he does.

Swipe. Swipe. Swipe.

It's a frenzied onslaught as he hacks and hacks at me. I leap back, sidestepping and twisting my body to avoid his deadly blows.

I trip over a large rock half-buried in the ground and fall backwards, but I manage to gain control over my tumble and backwards-roll away from him before planting my feet in the ground and pushing myself off so I can charge him. As he goes to grab me, I curve myself around his body and leap on his shoulders. I reach my hands beneath his hood and find his eye sockets before plunging my thumbs deep inside them. Warm liquid seeps through my fingers as he screams out in both fury and agony. He drops his axe and grabs me instead, tossing me off his body. I land in the dirt, rolling several meters before coming to a stop and pushing myself swiftly back on my feet. I sprint at him, snatching up his discarded weapon as I pass it. He's holding his face in his hands, bellowing furiously at the loss of his sight. I run at him, his axe above my head. I leap and soar through the air silently. And he falls silent too when I bury the blade of his own weapon into his skull.

I land gracefully before him and watch as his arms fall limp by his side. He sways, and after a push from me, he falls dead on the floor. I step over his body and walk towards Cass who has my second katana in his hand. He passes it to me.

I look around and see that the Grey Coats and the freed prisoners are fighting. There's only two of them left and there are over a dozen of us. One is cornered and being stabbed over and over.

The final Grey Coat disappears around the bend followed swiftly by furious soldiers. Seconds pass before we hear a cheer. They return to us victorious with their weapons high above their heads and arms around each other's shoulders.

We've won!

'Alright?' Cass asks, resting his hand on my lower back.

I shake my head and look over my shoulder. Towards Flash and Chilli who have cornered the one and only remaining giant of a Grey Coat. They have swords pointed at him but he just stands there silent, hood still up and sword in hand by his side. More and more surround him.

Tee is dashing through the crowd, her eyes solely on me. I throw open my arms and we crash into each other.

'I knew you'd get us out of there.'

'Better believe it,' I tell her, hugging her close. 'Very clever of you, leaving your masks as a trail for us to follow. We may not have found you if you hadn't.'

'I managed to get my gag off and we all worked together to get a few of us free. We poked the masks through a small hole in the floor hoping that you managed to get out of The Haven after the attack. We were about to poke Chilli's out when you caught up with us.'

I still watch the gathering crowd and how Flash cries and shakes as he points his sword at the Grey Coat. Whatever Flash is saying, it's coming out in a long tirade of intense rage. Chilli holds him back when he tries to attack. The whole group that surrounds the Grey Coat leave plenty of space between them and the giant.

I feel tears sting my eyes.

'Scar,' Tee whispers in my ear, sadness cracking her voice as her arms tense around me. 'There's something you need to know. Flash and Chilli are-'

'I know.'

'The traitor... it's-'

'I know, Tee. I know.'

Winder appears beside Cass and they share an embrace.

'What's going on over there?' Cass asks when Winder lets him go. 'Why aren't they killing the Grey Coat? And Chilli and Flash were in the crate with you?' He looks to me with a wrinkled brow. 'They're the traitors though. Aren't they?'

Winder, Tee and I all share a knowing look. They must have figured it out when they saw Chilli and Flash in the crate with them. Just as I figured it out when I saw the initials T&F embroidered on the Grey Coats sword.

'No,' I tell him, letting out a painful sigh and looking back to the cornered Grey Coat. 'It's not Flash or Chilli.'

I head towards them. Tee, Winder and Cass follow. I pass Loom in the crowd. He pats me gently on the back as I pass and joins the others as we make our way closer to the Grey Coat. They all part as we approach. The sympathy they show in their eyes tell me that they all know who it is beneath that hood.

I stop beside Flash and Chilli. Tears stream down Flash's face. A mixture of devastation, betrayal and hatred confuses every one of his features.

I look at the Grey Coat and shrug.

'You might as well lower that hood,' I tell him. 'We all know who you are under there.'

'A traitorous, evil, conniving–'

'Easy, Flash,' Chilli soothes, resting his hand flat on his chest as he takes a step closer.

'Lower the hood. Face us.' I gesture to the crowd surrounding him. 'Face those who love you. Who protected you. Who fought by your side every day since we were five. Lower your hood, Titan, and tell us why you have betrayed us.'

Cass lets out a short burst of laughter in disbelief.

'Are you mad?' he asks me. 'Titan would never...'

The Grey Coat lowers his hood.

Titan... lowers his hood.

The once gentle giant who avoided confrontation at any cost, who defended everyone no matter what, stands before us now an enemy.

'How?' I ask. 'How could you do this? Why?'

'This is all your fault,' he snarls at me. His eyes, which I always saw as soft and loving, are now cold and hard. He points a finger at me. 'This all happened because of you!'

'Don't you dare put this on me. Nothing I have done would ever warrant this,' I argue.

'If you had steered clear of Noah, if you hadn't led him on and made him fall in love with you-'

'I did nothing of the sort-'

'He came to me!' he barks. 'He knew about my relationship with Flash. He said if I didn't pass on intel about you, he'd banish Flash to the Canaries.'

'You should have told me! We would have figured it out-'

'You told him!' he shouts. 'You told Noah about us!'

'I bloody didn't!' I bite back. 'I would never tell anyone about your relationship. I'd have died protecting the pair of you and you know that!' Anger has me stepping forwards. 'In the evaluation as well as after it, I protected Flash. I nearly died doing so. Because I love him and I love you! I would never have told anyone about you two. Never!'

'He told me. He told me that you told him.' His anger shakes his voice.

'If you believed him, that's your mistake, Titan. Not mine,' I reply bluntly. 'You will not blame me for turning on your own family. We're as close to blood as we will ever have and you turned on us all. So it was you that told him all our secrets? You told him about the amusements? About Cass and me? About Tee?'

'I told him anything he asked because if I didn't, he would have taken Flash from me.' Titan looks at Flash. 'I sacrificed everything for you and you leave me for that?!' He turns his finger to Chilli. 'You swore to me that he meant nothing to you! That your affair was a mistake! Then you tell me you're in love with him? That you're leaving me for him?'

'Was it you?' Flash asks in a menacing growl. 'Did you report Chilli to the Grey Coats? Did you tell them he was gay? Did you have Chilli sentenced to the Canaries?'

Titan leans forwards and with a hateful-sneer replies, 'Yes. I reported him directly to Noah myself.'

Flash attempts yet again to go for Titan. Chilli and Loom both hold him back. More tears slide down his face as he confronts his former lover.

'You sent the man I love to his death!'

'I tried.'

'You betrayed Scarlett. You would have her marry Noah against her will? How could you do this? She's family!'

'They're not our family,' Titan scoffs, looking me up and down with distaste. 'They excluded us from everything. They never invited us or included us–'

'Because I asked them not to!' he snaps back. 'Years ago. I asked them not to. It was you that insisted you remain by my side instead of going with them when they went out beyond the wall or snuck out together after nightfall. I'm not like them!' Flash admits, shame cutting into his words. 'They go beyond the wall. They break the rules. They enjoy fighting and they're better at it than I am. If I went out there with them, I'd get them killed. I'm scared, Titan. This whole world terrifies me. I don't want to be lashed. I don't want to be sent out beyond the wall. I just wanted to survive! The only thing I was ever brave about was loving you and I did love you. But you changed. You became possessive and jealous. You wanted to control everything I was and everything I did. You disappeared for days and refused to tell me where you were and got angry every time I asked. So I stopped asking.' He looks at Chilli. 'I fell in love with someone else. I told you we were over. I said I was sorry and you said you accepted that. But you had him sent away anyway and your meddling forced Scarlett to leave too. You destroyed so many lives, Titan. Mine. Chilli's. Scarlett's. Cass's. Tee's. Winder's. And Elder Eight, the man who protected us and kept our secret, he died out there. Now look at us?' Flash throws up his arms.

'Yeah. Look at you.' Titan looks at Cass and I as well as Chilli and Flash. 'You all have each other.' He glares at Chilli. 'He should never have come back. That wasn't part of the agreement!'

Everyone looks at Titan.

'What agreement?' Chilli asks.

Titan remains silent.

'If we understand, perhaps we'll show you mercy,' I offer.

'Chilli gets sent away.' Titan stands a little taller as he speaks. 'I get Flash back with him gone and Noah makes us Grey Coats. We'd be safe when Noah's new world order started.'

'What does that mean?' I ask. 'New world order?'

'You'll see.'

'And what did Noah get in return?' Cass asks. 'For you getting Flash and the pair of you becoming Grey Coats?'

Titan's eyes land on me. 'You.'

'Me?'

'He wanted me to get closer to you. Learn all your secrets. Your hopes. Your fears. I was to pass it all onto him so he could make you his. Like I said. This is all your fault. He never would have turned his attention on me and Flash if it wasn't for you. I was a good boyfriend before he had me doing his dirty work. It was disgusting, snooping on you all. Passing on everything I saw to him.'

'Did you tell him other people's secrets too?' Winder asks him. I see how he's struggling to hold his temper. 'All the couples that have been exposed in the last few months. All the raids and searches. Was that you?'

'He made me-'

'No,' I shake my head and walk to him. Cass reaches out to me but I snatch my hand from his grasp and stop right in front of Titan.

'You had a choice. We would have protected you. We're a family. We've been together since we were five years old. We love you.'

'Loved,' Winder corrects.

'You made a choice,' I tell him. 'You turned on us all. You took the people that love you, tied them up and shoved them in a crate today. You were happily taking them to their deaths. The man you claim to love and who you say you did all this for, included. You're a coward, Titan. You have no honour. No loyalty. And now you have no family.'

'Are you going to kill me?' he asks. '*Elder.*'

'That's not up to me.' I look at Flash. 'I'll leave his fate in your hands.'

Flash thinks for a moment. He chews his lip and taps his foot. Chilli and he share a look. No words are uttered but the smile on Chilli's lips are of forgiveness. Of compassion.

Flash turns to me.

'We take him back to The Haven and he can confess everything to the others. Hopefully, it will help sway those who are unsure if they want to stand against Noah. It's time everyone knew what kind of a leader we have.'

I'm impressed. If I was in his position, I'd already have killed Titan.

'Drop your sword, Grey Coat,' Flash orders. 'And put your hands behind your back. You're under arrest.'

'Great,' I sigh, turning on my heel and walking away from Titan. 'Now, let's get back home and kill the rest of these bastards. My katanas have a long-overdue date with Noah's neck. Let's end this. Once and for all.'

We check over the four horses that were pulling the carriage. They're not harmed and they're strong creatures with plenty of remaining energy. With them pulling the crate as well as the majority of the freed prisoners, along with the three horses previously ridden by the now-dead Grey Coats, *and* the four horses we rode here, we have enough horses to get everyone back to the Haven well before sunrise. It will mean riding through the night. A dangerous and hard challenge. Targets don't sleep when the sun goes down. They'll be out here, hidden in the obscurity of nightfall. But if we intend to get back to help Elder One in his stand against Noah and the Grey Coats, we must make the journey.

At the base of the jagged hillside, Titan sits bound and gagged watching us. Watching me.

'What he did,' Chilli announces, walking up to help me adjust the saddle of my father's horse. 'It's not your fault. He says it is but it isn't.'

'I know that,' I reply sadly, looking away from Titan and instead to Chilli. 'So... Flash. So much for stealing a strawberry, huh?' I smirk. 'Can I ask you something?'

'Why him?' he asks. 'Of all people, why Flash?' He runs his palm down my horse's nose. 'He's funny. Cute. He's got this vulnerability and goodness that you don't see in most people like us. Soldiers in the Sainted Army tend to be...' He glances at me with a smirk. 'A bit emotionally stunted.'

'Cheers,' I chuckle.

'He wears his heart on his sleeve.' He looks to Flash who is helping the injured soldiers into the crate. 'He may not be the bravest but he is the kindest man I have ever known. How could I not fall in love with him?'

'I wasn't going to ask that,' I reply. 'I know why you love a man like Flash. I love him too.'

'Did you just say love?' Chilli says stunned. 'You? What about the curse? I thought that you believed that telling someone you love them will bring death, or some crazy nonsense like that.'

'Yeah.' I shrug. 'I've made a bit of a breakthrough. Not quite as superstitious or emotionally stunted as I once was,' I tease, making him laugh softly. 'I was going to ask why you lied to me? Why did you say you were sentenced to the Canaries for stealing a strawberry?'

'Guess I didn't know if I could trust you,' he admits. 'Being gay, most people aren't too accepting of that. Especially because it's forbidden back home.'

'You can trust me, Chilli.' I rest my hand on his shoulder. 'Always. And I am so sorry for doubting you. I thought you were the traitor and I am so so sorry.'

'I was sneaking about behind your back, meeting Flash and stuff. I don't blame you.' His eyes glance past my shoulder. 'Sky not with you?'

'No. I thought maybe she was in the crate with you.'

He shakes his head.

'Hope the little nutcracker's alright.'

'Me too.'

I turn and see Cass heading over. When he reaches me, he wraps his arm around my waist and plants a chaste kiss on my lips.

'Talking about sneaking,' Chilli states with a smug grin as he looks between us. 'I thought you were furious with her and not speaking to her?'

'Only sometimes,' Cass replies. 'Mainly when she refuses to look after herself or does something stupid.'

'So all the time?' Chilli laughs.

'Basically, yeah,' Cass agrees with a chuckle.

'You love her?'

'With everything I have.' He looks down at me. 'You ready to go and overthrow a tyrannical leader?'

'Hell yeah. Let's go kick some Grey Coat arse!' But something is niggling me. Something I can't let go.

'I know that look,' Cass says tiredly. 'What's on your mind?'

'It's just...' I chew my lip and take a look at the ground. 'These tracks. They don't end here. The last crate, the one with the other's inside that didn't make it, it wasn't dumped. It broke down.' I take a few steps and plant my feet in the very middle of the tracks, looking at how they follow the bend of the hills. 'Where were they taking them?'

'I know someone we could ask,' Chilli says, nodding towards Titan.

'Hmm. Let's do that. In the meantime, Chilli? Take Loom and Owl further down the track. See if you can spot anything from high ground. Owl's got phenomenal eyesight. If there's something there, she'll see it. We'll hold on for you but make it quick.'

'You got it, Boss.'

He ducks out, running towards Loom and Owl.

As I watch them leave, my mind rages with horrid thoughts about what fate Noah and his Grey Coats all had in mind for them. As I take a step towards Titan, Cass takes my hand and spins me into his body.

'What are you-'

His lips meet mine as he holds me close. The outside world melts away. The chattering of the Canaries, both old and new, fade into nothing as we sink into our own world. Cass and Scarlett. Just us. This kiss. Our love.

My hands run through his hair as his slides behind my ear.

When his embrace eases and our lips part, I'm breathless and flushed.

As is he.

'What was that for?' I ask.

'Because I can,' he shrugs. 'We're both still alive and we're together. If that's not worth a kiss I don't know what the hell is.'

I suddenly realise that our passionate and sudden embrace hasn't gone unnoticed. We glance around and see that everyone has fallen still and silent. Every pair of eyes are on us and their mouths are open in a hollow O.

'Nothing to see here!' Tee laughs aloud. 'Just and Elder and a Red Coat snogging each other. Not seen two people in love kiss before?'

'No.'

'Nope.'

'Nuh-uh.'

'Looks fun!'

The group all chuckle and return to their business, nodding their approval.

'Marry me,' Cass whispers in my ear.

I spin my head so fast he has to flinch to avoid our noses smashing into each other.

'What did you say?'

'I asked you to marry me,' he replies as if stating the obvious. 'You know, husband... wife... together forever kinda thing.'

'You're just saying that because you think we're gonna die.'

'I've told you a hundred times. If you die, I will bloody kill you. So no, not because I think we're gonna die.' He stands before me, takes my face in his hands and kisses my forehead. 'Because we're gonna live. We're gonna win. And you're gonna show me the world. Starting with that rainforest. So...'

He puts his hand into his pocket and pulls out a thick, white gold ring. It's rough, unpolished and been hammered into shape.

He lowers himself onto one knee.

'Bloody hell...' I whisper.

Behind him, I see Tee smack Winder on the arm and point to us. Once again, the soldiers have fallen deadly silent and I feel them all looking.

I couldn't care less.

'Scarlett. Spend the rest of your life with me? Let me love you till the day I die because I swear to you, I will love you long after I'm gone from this world. Will you-'

'Yes.' I nod, giving him my hand and grinning from ear to ear. 'You better believe I will!'

He slides the ring on and leaps to his feet.

As we share a kiss through grinning lips, the crowd around us cheers.

The cart, minus the door, is loaded with soldiers. Most sit on the roof, refusing to get back inside.

Cass, Winder, Tee, Chilli, Flash and I will ride the remaining horses home.

As we wait for Owl, Loom and Chilli to return from their scouting exhibition, I've attempted to try and get some information from Titan.

He's not saying a word.

Where were you taking the kidnapped soldiers?

Silence.

Are the missing soldiers and civilians still alive and if so, where are they?

Not a word.

What did you mean by "Noah's new world order?"

Nothing.

'We could torture him?' Suggests Winder. I'm uncertain if he's joking.

'Not sure that's the best way to start our new way of life, Winder,' Elder Ten says. 'Think we want to be a bit more civilised and compassionate than the ruler we have at the moment.'

Winder shrugs. 'It was just a suggestion.' He attempts humour, but I see the loathing he has for Titan and his deeds and knows that he wants to hurt him. Winder refuses to let go of Tee's hand.

Not that she's complaining. She looks as happy as I have ever seen her, despite the ordeal she's been through.

Knowing Titan will never talk, we get him on one of the horses. He's tied to the saddle and the horse is tethered to the cart.

As I make the final preparations for the journey home, I hear a sharp whistle. I look up and see Loom atop a hill, waving me over.

I'm on my horse and galloping his way immediately. Cass, Tee and Winder are hot on my heels as the rest wait below in the valley.

'What is it?' I ask when I reach him.

'Just follow me.'

He turns and starts riding. We all follow. He leads us through the valley and onto another hill, to Owl and Chilli who are standing with their backs to us. Owl has a pair of binoculars to her eyes and only looks away from whatever has her attention when Loom gives her a whack. 'Is it still there?' he asks her.

'Yeah. Still there. You can only see it standing here though. Move an inch either way, it's blocked by the landscape.'

'What is it? Class Two?' I ask, gesturing for the binoculars. 'More Grey Coats?' I peer through them. It ain't a Class Two. 'Is that...?'

'It's a boat,' Winder says. I hand Cass the binoculars, and he hands it to Tee who then hands it to Winder. Everyone has a look and sees it for themselves.

'Gotta be a big boat if we can see it all the way from here,' Loom adds.

'It could be people from another country?' Winder says, lowering the binoculars and looking at us each in turn with an excited grin. 'Maybe they're survivors that need help. Or they're coming to help *us*!'

But Owl shakes her head. 'I don't think so. Take another look. It's leaving.'

'Leaving?' I grab the binoculars and look again. 'How can you know it's leaving?'

'Cos, it was closer before. *Obviously*,' she replies sarcastically.

'Okay. Smart arse. We need to see if we can see any other signs of boats. Or any signs that someone has moored close by.' I take another look at the boat and watch as it disappears into the horizon.

'But we need to get back to the Haven,' Tee reminds me. 'Elder One and the others, they need us there for when they make their stand.'

I struggle to tear my eyes away from the boat heading off into the setting sun.

'Where are they going?' I ponder.

'Where have they been?' Cass adds, taking the binoculars and having another look for himself. 'Let's head down to the beach. See if we can spot anything odd. Perhaps we'll see where, or if, they docked.'

We head towards the water and stop on the cliff-edge. The tide is on its way in, so there's a good bit of beach and it stretches on for miles and miles. There's no sign of any boats. Just the water and the dunes.

'Look at the sand,' Tee says, pointing below. 'Scarlett, look at the sand!'

I do.

'What the hell?' Cass whispers.

'I second that,' Winder says.

'Are they...' Owl mumbles.

'Footprints,' I conclude.

For miles, the beach is perfectly smooth. But somehow, between the water's edge, leading through the gap in the cliffs and disappearing inland, are hundreds of footprints. And I mean hundreds.

'It looks like a small army walked through here,' Winder says, pointing to the line of marks. 'And the direction of the prints are all inland.' He looks at me with a very warranted amount of concern. 'It looks like that boat dropped a hell of a lot of people off.'

'That makes no sense. Why would anyone drop off people and then leave?'

'Maybe it's another country's military?' Tee suggests. But I don't buy that.

'If we went to another country, in the condition the world is in right now, would you let the only way off that island leave you behind?' I ask. 'We need to see where the tracks lead. Maybe we can find who made them.'

We take off at a gallop, following the tracks.

It doesn't take long to find the answer to our mystery.

Soon enough, we're standing along a high hilltop looking down at a small town below.

'Oh-my-god,' Cass whispers.

'What the hell is going on?' Owl gasps, looking below in horror.

'What – why - how...?' Loom mutters.

We all keep our voices low. Our movements to a minimum. And our terror and shock under as much control as possible.

'There were targets on that boat,' Cass whispers in disbelief. 'Someone dumped zombies on our shore and sailed away.'

Below, the small town is swamped. Hundreds, no, thousands of undead are aimlessly wandering about. *They* created the tracks. The tracks from the shore, straight to the town they've infested.

'But, who would do this?' Tee asks. 'Why?'

Everyone is horror-stricken. Completely and utterly lost for words.

'What the hell do we do now?' Tee asks.

And they all look at me.

What the hell *do* we do?

All I can do is look around me and shake my head.

This is far worse than I ever thought possible.

'I think we've seen enough. We need to get home and tell them what's going on,' I insist. 'They're taking people against their will to do god knows what with. They're lying about the land, telling everyone the world is dead and uninhabitable when it's not. They're sabotaging Canaries, killing them so they can't tell anyone else the truth of what they see. And now, there are boats bringing targets to our shores.' I shake my head.

'Is that even possible?' Tee asks. 'Bringing more targets? From where?'

'I'm gonna guess Germany, France and Ireland.' I say simply. 'We've all seen it. The odd uniforms on the targets we've killed. The German policeman from that wire trap shortly after evaluation day and the French soldier earlier? I don't know how he's doing it, but this is Noah. I know it. He's bringing infected over from other countries.'

'Why would he?' Owl asks horrified.

'I'm not sure but this has to stop. Now.'

'Agreed,' Cass says. 'We need to head back and tell them what we've seen.'

I jump down from my horse and take a few steps closer to the horde below. 'All the work we do. All the lives that have been lost fighting them and he's been bringing more in? It's been for nothing. All the death... donation... my dad... For nothing! We dedicate our whole lives, no, we're *forced* to dedicate our whole lives to fighting the dead. And the people forcing us to fight are the ones ensuring we don't have a hope in hell of winning by restocking the enemy?!'

'It's not for nothing,' Cass tells me. We've trained our whole life to fight our enemies and today, our enemy is Noah Sands. We're the best of the best and now... it ends. Let's go home and win our freedom. The time of The Verity is over.' He lifts my face by placing his finger under my chin. 'Let's go and kill Noah Sands. What do you say?'

We all ride hard. I wanted to get the crate out of the valley and travel a road that the Grey Coats may not think to take, but the hills are too steep, there aren't enough horses to carry us all individually and the distance is too great to double-up on them. The cart is tossed about over the uneven ground and the soldiers on top grip it tightly as they scan the area around us with keen eyes. The sunsets beyond the sea and takes the little warmth we had. The air is so icy, it's a little painful to breathe. From beneath each hood comes our hot, thick breath. The ground is getting harder and harder from the increasing cold and everyone starts to shiver.

Luckily, the moon is full and the sky is clear. We can see. Just.

Cass and I ride upfront.

Winder and Tee are positioned to the left of the crate.

Owl and Loom to the right, and on the final horse, still restrained and following the crate directly behind and under the watchful eye of two soldiers with arrows aimed at his heart, is Titan.

Despite everything, we're all filled with purpose and determination. The theories about the boat vary from England being a dumping ground for targets from other countries, to targets evolving enough sense to learn how to sail a boat to find a country with no humans.

Sadly, the targets we saw were very run of the mill, ambling about, half-decayed, snarling and mindless beasts. So that put the clever-zombies theory out the running.

I know that this is Noah. I know it.

No matter what the reason, it's bad.

Very, very bad.

As we turn the corner in the gloom, we see another crate. It takes a second to realise that two hooded figures are standing on top of it.

Grey Coats.

We pull on our reins and the horses rear-up, neighing in anger. The rest of the convoy all halt and together we face them.

'Give us Scarlett!' one of them calls, a male. His voice is one I don't recognise. 'Give her to us and then surrender yourselves to your lord's will!'

'And what is our Lord's will exactly?' Winder scoffs.

'To die, of course.' The one who spoke looks to me and points.

'There you are,' he says smugly. 'The swords you wear are a dead giveaway. Even with all your hoods up I see you and it is time you returned to your master.'

I withdraw my weapons.

'I have no master. And you will not kill anyone.'

He puts his fingers in his mouth and lets out a whistle.

From behind the crate emerge half a dozen more Grey Coats.

'Secure Scarlett,' he orders. 'Kill the rest.'

With that, the two Grey Coats standing on the crate heave two large lengths of rope upwards and the side of the crate facing us falls outwards, landing in the dirt and creating a ramp.

The sound of snarling and snapping jaws is swiftly followed by the appearance of four Class Two targets and several Class Threes, all coming straight for us.

'TARGETS!' I yell. 'INCOMING!'

I look to Cass and we share a nod.

'ATTACK!' we both roar.

Everyone springs into action.

Including the Grey Coats.

They withdraw their weapons and charge at us, right behind the targets.

Our soldiers from the crate leap down ready to fight.

Cass and I jump down from our horses and charge, meeting the Class Twos first. But the soldiers behind have also charged and soon the sound of yelling, screaming and snarling travel through the air as we all merge on the battlefield. Metal meets metal as the Grey Coats battle the soldiers. Weapons slice dead flesh and teeth pierce the living.

Tee, Owl and two other archers stand on the crate firing arrow after arrow, shooting as many as they can. Our training takes over. Two soldiers take arrow recovery. Two others grab all the horses, including the ones they untie from the crate, and ride them up the hill, far from the fight.

I go for the Class Two nearest me, ducking and weaving between its snapping jaws and clawing hands. The air moves as it tries to grab me and misses. My Katana slices through its gut, making it double over. It lifts its head and roars in my face.

I roar right back and raise my sword high. As it goes for me, I swipe and sever its head from its body. As it lands at my feet, I then kick it as hard as I can, sending it far overhead and out of sight.

'ZOMBIE HEAD FOOTBALL!' Chilli bellows with a laugh from somewhere in the mass of people.

I turn back to the fight, hacking and slicing and stabbing as I jump around.

Winder uses his hammer to smash the skull of one of the Class Threes. A whoosh passes my ear as one of Tee's arrow's goes straight between the eyes of a Grey Coat behind me as I plunge my blade through the gut of a Class Three approaching my side. I pull up, slicing it in two.

I see Flash and Chilli, side by side, battling the targets.

Cass appears from the crowd and takes my hand, dragging me behind the crate and pulling me down to our knees. He starts pulling off my back harness.

'What are you doing?!'

'The Grey Coats are looking for you! They're going to take you while we're fighting. You're harness and your coat-'

'Of course!' I slide off my harness and take off my coat, leaving me in nothing but Cass's borrowed hooded jumper.

He tucks my hair in my hood and pulls up Tee's mask to cover my face.

He then takes my face in his hands and looks into my eyes.

'Together. We get out of this together.'

'Always,' I reply, as I always have.

We get back to our feet and re-join the fight.

More swiping. Kicking. Stabbing. Ducking. Dodging.

All around me, everyone fights for their life. Blades flying. Decapitating, slicing and destroying target after target as a shower of arrows fall from the archers, landing exactly where they need to land.

I see The Grey Coats are holding back when they engage us, unless they're certain that the hooded soldier they're facing isn't me.

Then they're swift and deadly.

The targets are too quick. The night is too dark. We're tired and the Grey Coats are relentless.

We're losing.

With a quick glance to the hilltop, I spot the horses.

'RETREAT!' I order.

No one pays attention.

'I SAID RETREAT!' I grab the neck of the nearest figure not wearing a Grey Coat and shove them in the direction of the horses. I grab another and another, ordering them to get to the horses and ride!

'Retreat?' Cass pants, appearing beside me with blood trickling down the side of his face. 'We can win!'

'We can't! We need to get back and warn the others about the boats. If we all stay here, we'll die and no one will know!' I look around the crowd. Many have heard my order and turned to flee. The targets give chase. Tee and the other archers jump down and start making their way through the mess.

The Grey Coats start fighting with more carelessness than before, desperate not to let a single one of us get away. Those who get past grab a horse and ride back to us, reaching out an arm and hauling up one of their comrades before turning and riding away.

Just as we were taught to do.

We're attacked by two targets. A Class Three as well as a Class Two. We take them out together, working as a team and striking a blow to save each other and ending the un-life of the walking corpses.

Owl appears at my side.

'Give me one of your haladies!' Owl orders Cass as we watch her slide on my coat and empty harness.

'What the hell are you doing?' I hiss angrily.

'We're gonna draw the Grey Coats away so the others can escape. Cass... Haladie!'

He swiftly hands one of his beloved weapons to Owl.

'We? Who's we?' I demand.

Owl steps back and pulls up her hood, reaching out her hand.

'Bowzer and I will ride away. They'll think it's you two. The Grey Coats will chase us and you lot will have a better chance of getting back home to help the others.'

'This is not a good idea!' I insist. 'What if they catch you?'

'They won't.'

'They might!'

'Well,' she smiles, backing up, her hand still outstretched. 'We all gotta die some time. Might as well make it worthwhile. Get your arses back to Elder One and get this revolution going. We're counting on you, Elder Eight.' She nods to Cass. 'Look after my friend, Red Coat.'

'Bet your arse I will.'

Bowzer rides past and reaches out for Owl, heaving her onto the back of the horse as he passes, in a seamless and beautiful move. She hands Bowzer the haladie which he uses to stab the targets as he rides. To anyone else, it looks like Cass and me riding away.

Cass pins me to the side of the crate as several of the Grey Coats run after them.

Other Grey Coats make for the escaping soldiers.

It grows quieter.

Only the gurgling and snarling of the targets remain. I hear them eating. I close my eyes and try to ignore their chewing and moaning as they feast on the flesh of my fallen friends.

We peer out from the side and find everyone has left.

'We need a horse,' Cass whispers, looking around the hillside trying to detect anyone in the darkness with a horse.

We step out, hand in hand.

'Go and see if you can find one. I'll deal with these,' I tell him, gesturing to the remaining targets who are so engrossed in their meal, they pay no attention to us.

'We should stick together.'

'Probably. But we have to get back as soon as possible and I'm not leaving these people here.' I look down and see one of our own with black lips and bile oozing from her mouth, reaching out to me as she crawls across the frozen ground. 'Let me put them out of their misery as you secure our ride home. I'll be fine. Go.'

After a kiss, he runs towards the hill. I turn my attention to the poor creatures writhing in blood and guts on the ground.

'I'm sorry,' I tell the girl I knew as Tan by my feet as she reaches out for my foot with her mouth wide open. Her legs trail behind her, half gone from the blow of another's axe. 'I'll tell Owl you died bravely and I swear, I'll avenge you.'

The tip of my katana pierces her temple and she falls still.

At rest.

There are two others of our own, dead and being devoured. I deal with the Class Threes that surround them.

Then, I hear a scream.

Tee's scream.

I lift my head and look in the direction that it came from. I hear her again and I rush towards her.

'STOP!' she pleads over the sound of a heavy punch slamming into someone. 'TITAN, YOU'RE KILLING HIM!'

'GET OUTTA HERE, TEE!' Titan hollers. 'I DON'T WANNA KILL YA, BUT I WILL IF YA DON'T LEAVE!'

The next thump is followed by a heavy groan.

Flash's groan.

I run around the corner and skid to a halt when I meet a steep drop of at least fifteen feet. Rocks and pebbles roll over the edge as I barely manage to stop myself from falling into the wide trench. Below, Titan has Flash by the scuff of his neck and is beating the hell out of him. His face is a swollen mess of blood and bruises. He barely manages to stay on his feet as Titan delivers another blow.

He must be holding back or Flash would already be dead. I see tears streaming down Titan's face, hating that he's hurting the man he claims to love but unable to stop nonetheless.

'TELL ME YOU STILL LOVE ME!' Titan cries, holding up his fist in warning. 'TELL ME!'

'N-never...' Flash mumbles through his broken jaw. 'Y-you're a m-monster.'

Tee pulls at his arm, trying with all her might to stop another hit meeting Flash.

'Stop!' she pleads. 'If you love him, stop!'

'I'm doing this *because* I love him!' he insists, trying to shake her off. 'If I can't have him...' He shakes his head and adds menacingly, 'No one can.'

'That's not love!' Tee argues desperately. 'If you love him, you would let him go!'

'I can't. Noah will never let you both live knowing what you know and I will not let him die with another man. I won't! Now, get off me!'

She refuses to relinquish her grip despite his attempts to shake her off.

Cass appears by my side with a horse in tow.

'Winder and Loom have a horse each. They're coming back for Chilli and Tee.' He looks below. 'Shit,' he whispers, knowing as well as I do that one more strike and Flash will be dead before he hits the ground. Cass looks around and sees a stony slope that leads down into the trench. We're too high to jump down. The rough path is the only other way. 'Stay here!' he orders me, thrusting the reins in my hand before running towards it.

'I SAID GET OFF ME!' Titan bellows, letting go of Flash and taking hold of her wrist. Flash falls in a heap on the floor as Titan twists Tee's arm, bending it till she has no choice but to let go of his arm. He pulls her in close, leering into her face and snarls, 'If you wanna live, run. If you wanna die, get in my way again.' And with that, he shoves her hard to the floor.

He turns his attention back to Flash who's crawling away, telling Tee to leave. To run. To save herself. He drags his body across the ground, his legs barely able to move, looking up as the man he once loved completely slowly descends on him. On the floor is Flash's sword. Titan leans down and picks it up as he passes it.

'This is your last chance,' Titan tells Flash. 'Join me. It's not too late. Join Noah and take your place in his new world order. Take the place you have, only because I did all this for you. Make all this pain worthwhile, Flash. Choose the winning side.'

'I have,' Flash replies, still dragging himself away. 'It's you who have chosen wrong.'

I look below. In the darkness, I see my family and I see them about to die. Tee pushes herself back on her feet and runs between them. She plants her feet in the stony ground and uses herself to protect Flash. In her hand, I see a single arrow. That's all she has against a giant and a sword.

Cass is only halfway down the hill.

He's not gonna get there in time.

'Move, Tee,' Titan warns.

'No,' she states, shaking her head. 'I won't.'

'Fine.' Titan firms his hold on Flash's sword and draws his back his arm. 'Then you'll die with him.'

Move... move... MOVE!

She stands taller.

'So be it,' she says, gripping her arrow tightly and readying herself for his attack.

Cass is going as fast as he can and starts yelling.

He's not going to make it and Titan isn't going to stop.

His arm is all the way back. The tip of the sword is aimed straight at Tee's chest.

No...

I back up and take off at the fastest sprint I'm capable of creating. When I reach the edge, I push off with all my might and I soar through the air. My arms swing, urging my body further and further. I make it over Titans head and land directly between them, my back to him and my face in front of Tee.

As I land, I hear my ankle snap. I feel the bone break and rupture my skin. I stagger but force myself to stay on my feet, my body tall. My face calm. Tee's horrified expression at my sudden appearance has her eyes wide. Everything slows down as the sound of tearing cloth and flesh are followed by a hot, searing pain ripping through my body. The force of it makes all my nerves scream in agony, leaving me speechless. My mouth's open and eyes wide as it claims me completely. The pain. The agony. It's all-consuming. Tee looks down. I follow her gaze and see ten inches of steel protruding from my belly. Thick red blood hugs the blade and drips slowly to the floor. The tip is an inch from Tee's heart.

'No...' she whispers, lifting her horror-stricken face to mine. 'No.... No... No!'

I see the arrow still in her hand as she shakes her head in disbelief.

Slowly, so, so slowly, Titan retrieves his sword. I watch it slide back through me like I'm soft butter.

I snatch the arrow from her hand and when the sword leaves my body, I turn and drive it with my last remaining strength through Titan's temple.

I look into his eyes which bulge and glaze over as his face slackens and mouth falls agape. He sways.

I know that I've killed him.

I know too, that he has killed me.

If I let go of his body, which still sways, I'll fall. When I fall, I will never again get back up.

The sounds around me muffle. Tee's gasp could be a million miles away. Cass is screaming my name as he runs down the hill. It echoes as if he's at the other end of a long tunnel. My own breathing, which has become laboured and choked with blood as it forces its way up my throat, is unbearably loud.

Titan starts to fall.

His eyes roll into the back of his head and I let him go.

My knees buckle and I collapse, only to be caught in the arms of the man I love.

Gently, Cass falls to his knees and lowers me into his lap.

'Scarlett?! No... no... no...' He slams his hand over the wound and pushes down as hard as possible, making a fresh jolt of pain shoot through my body. Looking down at me, he tells me I'm going to be okay. It's all he seems to be able to say. Over and over and over, tears brimming in his eyes.

'You'll be okay. You'll be okay.'

All I can manage are short shallow breaths as I lay in an ever-growing pool of my own blood.

'No. No. No. No. NO!' The look on his face says more to me than any words ever could. As he examines my wound, I see it in in his eyes.

The fear. The pain. The grief.

'GET A MEDIC-KIT!' he yells. To who? I have no idea. He looks down at me, 'You're gonna be fine, baby. Absolutely fine.'

Tee falls to her knees and slams her hand over my wound too. Blood seeps between both their fingers.

'Oh god, there's so much blood,' Tee sobs. 'Cass-'

'She's gonna be okay,' Cass tells her. 'She's... she's gonna be okay.'

'What's happened?' Winders voice calls from up on the ridge. They both look up.

'FIND A MEDIC-KIT, WINDER!' I see Cass's tears glisten in the moonlight. 'HURRY!'

Both Tee and Cass look back down at me in complete devastation. Running down the ridge is Loom and Chilli, both rushing to help and skidding down the loose and uneven slope.

Chilli goes to Flash who is trying to get himself up and over to me. Loom stops by my head and looks down at me in silent shock before falling to his knees.

'Scar...' he says sadly. He looks to Cass. 'She's been stabbed?'

'She's gonna be ok!' Cass insists as more tears fall. 'WHERE'S THE MEDIC-KIT?!'

I try to talk, but it's the hardest thing I've ever had to do.

'I-I can't... I can't...'

'What?' he asks me. 'What can't you?' He taps my cheek as shock starts to set in. 'Stay with me, baby. What *can't* you? What can't you do?'

Blinking up at him, I tell him, 'I can't move m-my legs.'

He nods as several tears tumble down his cheeks. 'That's... it... it's because...'

'Cass...'

'You've been ...' He takes another deep breath. 'You've been stabbed through the spine, Scarlett.'

Winder skids to a stop as he reaches us and seeing me, falls to his knees. His eyes evaluate my injury and he looks at Cass with an agonised realisation of what's happened.

'We need to stop this bleeding or she's not gonna last much longer.' Cass holds out his hand. 'Where's that medic-kit!'

Cass snatches the white box from the stunned Winder and starts pulling out bandages one-handed.

'Cass,' Winder says gently. 'This bleeding ain't gonna stop with bandages.'

'You're right. We need the powder. Get the powder.' He drops the bandages and shoves the box into Winders hands. 'GET THE FUCKING POWDER OUT!'

Winder nods and quickly pulls out a tin. Tee lifts my top as Cass keeps pressure on the wound.

'Okay,' Cass sighs fearfully. I hear his voice shaking as he meets my frightened stare. I haven't taken my eyes off him. I daren't. 'We're gonna cauterise the wound and get you back to the Haven. To a doctor. You'll be okay.'

'Cass,' Loom says slowly, looking from the hole in my belly to him. 'Cass, the wound's too bad. The powder won't help-'

'JUST SHUT THE HELL UP!' Tee roars at him. He flinches at her aggression. 'Or I swear, Loom... I will shut you up. If you ain't gonna help, PISS OFF!' She gestures for Cass to carry on.

He tips the powder from the tin onto my belly. Winder lights a match as Cass grips my fingers tightly with his free hand.

'Ready?' Cass asks me, a hopeful look on his face.

'Mate,' Winder says gently, kneeling beside me and looking me dead in the eye. He knows the same as I do that this is it. 'Loom's right. The wound's-'

'Just light it, Winder,' he warns.

'Cass...' I shake my head. 'I'm dying. The powder ain't gonna-'

Cass snatches the lit match from a reluctant Winder and drops it on the powder. A small but fierce fire erupts on my flesh. I scream so hard and so loud and so desperately, I think the whole world just heard me. Tee holds my hand firmly, kissing my knuckles as I writhe in agony.

'We need to roll you over,' Cass says through desperate sobs as soon as it ends. 'We need to do your back.'

'No...' I wail. 'Please, it's too much p-pain.'

But I'm rolled over despite my words and with my face in the dirt, I let loose another agony filled shriek as they set off a second small explosion to seal my wound.

Everything starts to blur.

Cass rolls me back over and settles me in his lap. 'Scarlett… hey, hey, baby? Don't you close your eyes.' He taps my cheek and my eyes re-open before I give in to the pull of unconsciousness. 'We have a horse. I'm gonna get you back-'

'No.'

'We can fix this-'

'No!'

'C'mon.' He puts his arms beneath my body. When he goes to lift, the pain is unbearable and I scream out. It's like being slowly torn in half.

'STOP!' I screech. 'PLEASE! STOP!'

He lowers me back down.

'We have to go. You need-'

'LISTEN!' I sob, desperately trying not to pass out from the pain and to get him to listen to me. He hears the anguish in my voice. The desperation. I reach up and rest my hand on his cheek and feel the warmth of his tears. 'Cass. My love. I can't move. I can't walk.' He opens his mouth to argue. I cut him off. 'It's over.'

'I know the odds, okay?!' Cass tells me, his voice breaking as we both look at my swollen, purple stomach. 'But I can't just give up. We have to try. We're gonna get you fixed up. You're gonna be fine.'

I swallow a mouthful of blood as he turns to Winder.

'Bring the horses down here. We'll get her on and ride her home.'

Winder looks at me. He knows this is futile. The look on Loom, Chilli and Flash's faces are the same, but Tee and Cass are lost in a fog of denial.

I have hours. If that. No way I survive the ride home and even if by some miracle I did, I'd never walk again.

I'm done.

But still, he tries.

Cass lifts me in his arms.

I scream and blood pools in my mouth thick and fast as my ripped-up insides split further. I start choking. He lowers me again and helps me as I cough it up. It's still there. Spilling out through my organs and pooling inside no matter how much I spit out.

'Please... stop moving me,' I whimper. 'Please.' I slump. My body going limp as I lay in his arms, blood dripping down my chin and tears blurring my vision. 'Cass, I'm begging you.' I reach up and stroke his face. My fingers trace his jaw and settle on his lips. 'Let me go. Put me out of my misery and go.'

He shakes his head. 'No...' He tries not to let the desperate sadness I see in his eyes show in his voice. But I nod and show him a comforting smile.

'Cass, I'm dying.'

'Don't say that.'

'You know what needs to be done. Get on the horse, ride back and do it.'

'I... I can't let you go.' His tears spill over his face, slide down his cheeks and land on me. Leaning down, he rests his nose against mine and lets out a heartbroken sigh. 'We can't end like this.'

'I love you.'

His eyes scrunch up tight and a small sob escapes his lips.

'I know,' he whispers. 'And I love you too. More than anything. I love you, Scarlett. This can't be happening. This isn't real.'

I lean up and I kiss him. His lips meet mine with such tenderness and devotion, I wish that it would never end.

Everyone else has gathered around us. Tee sobs as she buries her face in our hands as we grip onto each other. Her cries are of pure grief. I've never heard anything like it. It's a real goodbye. A forever goodbye.

And everyone knows it.

We've been soldiers for far too long. We all know a mortal wound when we see one. This is as mortal as it gets. Winder engulfs Tee in his arms as he looks down at me. Tears slide down his face fast and plenty.

'It's over for me.' I look at them all. My family. The people I love completely. If these faces are the last thing I see before I die, I'll die content. 'You promise me, you'll bring the bastard to his knees.'

'I'm not leaving you here,' Cass cries, sitting on the ground and pulling me into his chest.

'You must.'

'I won't.'

'Finish me off and go!'

His arms fold around me as he shakes his head.

'No. You stay, I stay. I won't leave you here and I will not kill you.'

'Neither will I!' Tee sniffs, moving from her knees to her back-side and crossing her legs. She takes my hand with both of hers. 'This is my fault. That blade was meant for me. I'm not leaving you.'

'This is n-not... not your fault.' It's getting harder to talk.

Above us on the ridge, we all hear the familiar screech of a Class Two. Everyone looks up.

'We're staying,' Tee says plainly, her eyes still on the hillside and her cheeks soaked with tears. 'Right, Winder? We're staying with her till the end.'

Winder looks from the ridge to me. And then to Tee.

He chews his lip and we share a look.

I nod.

'Of course,' he agrees, the lie clear in his eyes but not in his voice.

More screeching and moaning come from above us.

Targets are coming and lots of them.

All the blood, both from me and the others injured or killed in the fight, is beckoning them closer.

'Chilli, get the horses down here.' I order. 'You, Flash and Loom must get b-back. Warn the others... about t-the boats. Stop Noah, you hear me?'

He eases Flash to the ground and runs off up the stone path.

Cass strokes the hair from my face as Tee wipes the blood from my lips.

Flash hauls himself towards us. I look up and try so hard not to show my pain and fear.

'This is my fault,' he sobs, leaning down and kissing my forehead. He stays there, his eyes closed as he weeps.

'Hey...' I soothe, 'Don't you dare. Don't you dare, any of you.'

He opens his eyes.

I don't have long. I can sense it.

And I'm terrified.

It takes everything I have not to let it show.

Winder kneels beside Tee. Loom beside Cass. Chilli has bought three horses down the path and rushed back to us, taking Flash in his arms.

They surround me.

My family.

'Now, you all listen to me.' I look at them all in turn. 'You have a mission now. That's what m-matters. You carry on and you keep fighting. You don't stop until we win.'

The screeching and groaning get louder. I look up and see some loose stones tumble from above.

'Go. Now. Before they reach us.'

Flash leans down and kisses my forehead.

'I love you,' he says solemnly.

'I love you too. Be happy, Flash.'

He nods and Chilli leans down to kiss me too.

'Take care of him,'

'I will, Boss.' Chilli says sadly, getting to his feet and taking Flash with him to the horses.

'Cass, Tee, you have to go.'

'No,' Cass tells me, cradling me in his arms and smiling lovingly down at me. 'I'm not going anywhere.'

'Me neither,' Tee says, cutting me off before I can say another word.

Winder leans over and kisses me on the cheek.

'I love you,' he whispers in my ear. 'I love you so much and I will never, ever forget you.'

'I love you too. Keep her safe, Winder. You make her happy. You hear me?' I whisper in his ear.

'You have my word.'

He leans down and plants one final kiss on my cheek before swiftly getting to his feet and wrapping his arms around Tee's waist. He yanks her away from me as I let go of her hand.

'NO!' she screams, desperately clawing at him and thrashing in his arms. Her arms reach out for me. 'NO! GET OFF! GET OFF ME! SCAR!'

He drags her away, holding her firmly around the waist as she screams and sobs my name hysterically.

I look up at Cass. He's still watching me, resigned to the fact that he will die here with me. I reach up slide my hand behind his head, pulling him down and kissing his lips.

'I love you,' I whisper, opening my eyes to see his devotion-filled eyes looking back at me. 'I wish I could have married you. I wish I could have shown you the world. I wish we could have grown old together.'

He gently tucks my hair behind my ear and looks content. Behind him, Winder has got the still screaming and writhing Tee on his horse. They're mounted and ready to go. Flash and Chilli too. They watch as Loom silently heads towards us.

'I always said that some people are worth dying for,' I tell Cass, catching a tear before it meets his lips. 'I'm happy to die for you. For all of you.'

'As am I,' he nods, kissing my lips once more. 'Since we were five, we've done everything together. Trained together. Played together. Laughed together and screamed together.' He takes my hand in his and looks at the ring he placed on my finger not even two hours ago. 'I always knew we would die together too. I'm ready. Me and you, Scarlett. Together. Always.'

I take a courage inducing breathe, and shake my head.

'Not this time, my love. Not this time.' I look past his shoulder. 'Loom.'

In a sudden move, Loom grabs Cass under the arms and drags him away from me.

'NO!' Cass yells. 'WHAT THE HELL ARE YOU DOING?!'

I hold in the agony of being dropped as I watch Cass kick and holler violently against Loom's grasp.

'LET ME GO, YOU BASTARD! LET ME GO!'

There's a feral desperation in his face and voice as he's hauled further and further away from me.

'Thank you,' I weakly whimper, watching him be pulled further and further away.

'WE CAN'T JUST LEAVE HER! WE CAN'T! THEY'LL TEAR HER TO PIECES! THEY'LL-'

'I'll end her suffering, Cass,' Loom promises. 'I swear it. I'll-'

Everyone falls still and silent when a Class Two lands directly between us. It's over six feet tall, its skin pulled taught over its muscles and its nails long and sharp.

More stones fall from above before three more Class Twos leap down from the ridge, planting their feet beside the other one. They snarl and flex their fingers. Their feet shift in the ground.

Tears fill my eyes as they all turn to face me, their noses in the air as they sniff the blood all around me. Drool and bile drip from their mouths. Their lips pull back showing jagged teeth.

'Go...' I whisper, my voice weak from fear and pain. I tear my eyes away from the monsters and look past them to my family. I swallow the blood in my mouth and force myself to be brave. They can't face them all. Not with half of their weapons missing and one of them barely able to stand. 'GO!' I yell. 'BEFORE THEY KILL YOU!'

'No...' Cass shakes his head as they turn their bodies towards me. 'Loom... Loom let me go!' He warns in a menacing tone before carrying on trying to get free. Pulling and hitting against Looms grip. 'LET ME GO! GOD DAMN IT, LET ME GO!'

'GO!' I scream, choking on blood and tears.

Cass and Tee are screeching and wailing. Their arms reach out for me.

One of the monsters spin to face them.

'GO!!' I plead. 'GO!! NOW!'

'I WON'T LEAVE YOU HERE TO BE TORN TO PIECES!'

'GET THEM OUT OF HERE!' I scream as the Class Twos start stalking slowly towards me. 'DON'T LET THEM SEE ME DIE LIKE THIS!'

With a mighty thump, Loom knocks Cass out cold and tosses him on the horse before leaping on it himself.

One of the Class Twos sprints at them. Loom, Chilli and Winder kick their horses.

I slam my hand over my mouth, stifling my overwhelming urge to beg them to help me. To kill me. Not to let me be torn limb from limb.

I close my eyes. Tears pour down my face as I shake with every sob.

I listen to Tee's screams fade into the distance until all I can hear is the laboured breathing of the three remaining targets.

I take two, deep breathes and shake away my fear and pain.

I lower my hand and open my eyes. They're right over me, sniffing, moaning, gurgling. I look past them, up into the night's sky.

It's gonna snow soon. I know it. I can smell it in the air. A day or two maybe, and then the ground will become a blanket of white. I smile as I remember last time it snowed, when Cass and I snuck into the woods. I kicked his arse in a snowball fight and then he taught me to make snow angels. We laid side by side on the ground and watched the snowfall. I said it looked like ash. That maybe the sky was on fire and that's all snow really was. He told me I should be more romantic in the way I looked at life. That snow is beautiful.

I said he was beautiful. Inside and out.

He held my hand and said I was too.

I wanted to show him the jungle dome. To catch fish with him in the streams cutting through the moors. To lay in his arms and watch the stars in the crystal-clear sky above us. To kiss him openly. To walk and hold his hand through crowds of people. To tell him I love him every single day for the rest of my life.

I won't get that.

But knowing that Noah will fail. Knowing that he will die and lose everything because of my family, that makes me smile. That makes me laugh. It overrides the fear of my impending and brutal death.

I look up into the sky, laughing like a lunatic. I pull up Tee's mask, feeling a little less alone with that small part of her so close to me. As one of the Class Twos lunges at me with its teeth, I close my eyes.

'I'm coming, Dad,' I say. 'I'm coming.'

The first set of teeth tear into me.

CHAPTER ELEVEN

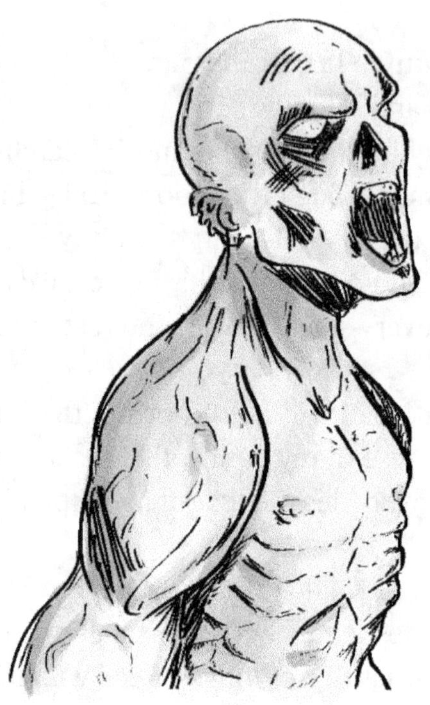

I scream as another joins its attack. Two rip and tear away chunks of my body. Blood squirts all around me, splattering my face. The familiar gurgling of the undead creatures echoes in my ear as it chews my flesh before reaching down to take another bite.

Suddenly, it falls silent.

Just like that.

It stops.

I open my eyes and see its face right in front of mine. It's jaw slack and oozing with my blood and shredded flesh. Its eyes are drooped. Its arms limp at its side and the tip of a sword is sticking through its forehead.

The blade is retracted and it slumps sideways in a heap.

Behind it is a solitary figure, one of my katanas in their hand. Their fingers slotted through the knuckle dusters.

It's a Grey Coat.

They spin, the blade soaring through the air as the other Class Two's attack. I've never seen anyone move so fast in my entire life. The force behind each blow cuts the targets deep and each strike is precise and deadly.

Three moves. That's it. Three remarkably skilled strikes and each of the target's heads are severed from their bodies.

The Grey coat has their back to me when the last of their victim's lands in the dirt. Their head turns and they peer over their shoulder at me, their face concealed not only by the darkness of the night, but also by their hood.

They lower my sword and turn to face me.

I cough on the blood clogging up my throat and groan against the pain throughout my body as I feel the warm, tingling sensation of the venom from the bites spreading deeper into my body. Shakily, my hand goes to my neck. There's a great big chunk missing and so much blood, there's really very little point in attempting to stop it.

I've been bitten anyhow. I have minutes till I turn.

The Grey Coat walks slowly towards me. My sword swinging by their side. They lift it, swaying it gracefully left to right, tormenting me as the tip of my own beloved weapon gets closer and closer.

'You may think I stopped them eating you as an act of mercy,' she says. 'But I must admit, I did it for myself. I want to see you as a mindless monster. Watch you scurry about in the dirt like the savage you are. Watch as you slowly rot and decay. Watch as your insides decompose and spill out through your mouth. Ever since I met Scarlett and she told me of you, when I saw the love she held for you, I knew without a doubt, that I had to get rid of you, Tee.'

She stops with the tip of my sword at my throat and crouches.

'She's mine, you see. Mine and my Lords. Once we have taken everyone she loves, we will have her. She will be his bride and my sister. I have never had a family, you see, Tee. Scarlett was the first person to ever care for me. I will replace you as her most beloved sister.' She laughs. 'I may even take Winder for my own too. He's kinda cute.'

I know the voice. It's unmistakable. It doesn't make any sense though.

'Don't worry, Tee. I'll take good care of them.' She stands, the tip of my sword resting under my chin. 'I'm going to watch you turn. The person you are will die and a monster will walk this world wearing your skin for all eternity.'

I could speak out. I could let her know that it is me beneath this hood and mask. She wants me alive. Noah wants me alive.

But I'm already dead.

If it keeps Tee safe, I'll walk the world a monster.

Gladly.

'Oh… one more thing before you go.'

She lifts her foot and kicks me hard in the side. The force of it rolls me twice before I land face down in the dirt, coughing and gasping in utter torture.

'S-Scar?' She shuffles her feet. 'It can't be… is that… Scar, is that you?'

She runs to me and rolls me onto my back before yanking down my mask.

'Scar!' she gasps, slamming her hand over her mouth and landing on her knees beside me. 'No! No! This wasn't supposed to happen!' She slams her hand over my neck before her attention shifts to my belly. 'You're dying. You're infected!'

I raise my hand and weakly lower her hood.

Sky's ashen streaked hair tumbles out as she looks down at me with wide eyes.

'Why?' I ask in barely a whisper, my voice waning as I lose my strength.

Her eyes dance left to right as her thoughts rage. Her teeth clamp down on her lower lip and she lets out a long, child-like whine of uncertainty. Then, her eyes meet mine and her indecisiveness abandons her, replaced instead with a clarity of some kind.

'I can fix this,' she says in an urgent whisper, nodding her head. 'Yes. Yes. I can fix this!' She starts searching her pockets, digging her hands in deep to the first, second, and then diving into her inside pocket. 'He wants her. He loves her. This will work. This *has* to work!'

'Wh-what are you d-doing?'

'You're dying. But I can fix it. I can-'

'Fix?' I feel the warmth of the bite spreading further and further. It grows hotter and hotter, coursing through my muscles.

'The Elders will not get away with this. Not with any of it,' she tells me, still rummaging. 'Rising up against us. This is all their fault. You were never supposed to be hurt like this. But it will be okay. He wants you like this anyway. I know... I know he wanted to be the one to do it.' She nods her head as if convincing herself that this is the right course of action. 'AH-HA!' She pulls out a small black box from one of her pockets and sits on her knees, holding it like it's made of glass. 'I thought for a minute there I'd lost it!' she grins.

'What...' I'm slipping. I know I am. Everything inside is shutting down. My body yearning for me to just close my eyes and go peacefully while the heat of the infection grows. 'Sky? What are you doing?'

'It will be over soon and then the real work can begin. Our new world order begins right now. Right here. We're going to save this world. You'll see.' She rests her hand on my arm. 'God is great and he will resurrect you. You'll see.'

I look at her like she's insane. She opens the box and pulls out a large needle and a vial full of bright blue liquid.

'W-what is that?'

'Can I tell you a story?' she asks, gently piercing the seal of the vial with the needle and drawing out the liquid.

'Sky...'

'Once, there was a girl,' she says, watching the slow and steady transfer of liquid. 'And she was the best soldier to ever exist. So good in fact, that she was selected to try out for a Grey Coat position at the mere age of twelve.'

My every nerve starts to burn as if on fire.

'But sadly, upon venturing out into the world for her evaluation, she was attacked,' she says, still watching the liquid fill up the syringe. 'Not by the targets. Oh no. But by her competition. Four went out that day. Three boys and one girl. The boys weren't as good as the girl and they knew it. So, they cornered her, beat her, did terrible things to her, and left her out there to die.'

My blood feels like acid and my heart hammers so hard I think it's gonna explode any second.

'Three weeks she was out there. Three! All alone. No weapons. A broken ankle. Trapped in the cellar where they left her. If it hadn't have been for the rats and the leak in the roof, she would have died of starvation and dehydration. That's when *he* came.' She looks to the sky as if seeing the most beautiful sunrise. 'My great and wonderful Lord. He found me and carried me back home on his horse. He made me an honorary Grey Coat. He blessed me, Scar. He made my body strong. He made me impervious to harm.' She finishes drawing out the liquid and drops the empty vial to the ground, lifting the syringe and gazing at it in wonder. 'With this.'

My head's ablaze, my brain is swelling and pushing itself against my skull.

She strokes the hair from my face and brushes it away from the hole in my neck. 'He told me his plans for this world and the people within it. It's a thing of beauty, Scar. Real beauty. You'll see.'

I can't hold in the pain as my body arches and starts convulsing. I scream and fit as she simply shushes me as if to comfort my misery.

'Together, we will punish the wicked and exalt the good. You and me? We're good, Scar. We're the best!' She nods excitedly and places the needle between her fingers, her thumb rests on the plunger. 'The Elders and all those civilians living in filth? The disobedient soldiers and lustful sinners? They're wicked. Your friends? They're the epitome of evil. They want to abolish the divine. Kill Noah. But if they do, we will all die. Noah has *such* a plan and we need you to help spread the good word to all the others.'

The blood vessels in my eyes pop. I hear them. My vision goes red. My insides are rupturing. Blood fills my lungs. I can't scream. I just writhe and judder. Just as my father did.

'You must help us convince them. Only you can. They love you. They trust you. They will follow you. We can start his new world together! You, me and Noah. Our own family.' She rises up as I start to snarl and thrash. Her palm holds down my head and I feel myself disappearing, being replaced instead with a fierce and uncontrollable rage and hunger. My torso jerks. I start to gurgle and gasp. My voice changes from a human scream to a monstrous roar.

'I really hope this works,' she giggles excitedly.

Those are the last words I hear before she stabs the needle into my neck and pushes down the plunger.

CHAPTER TWELVE

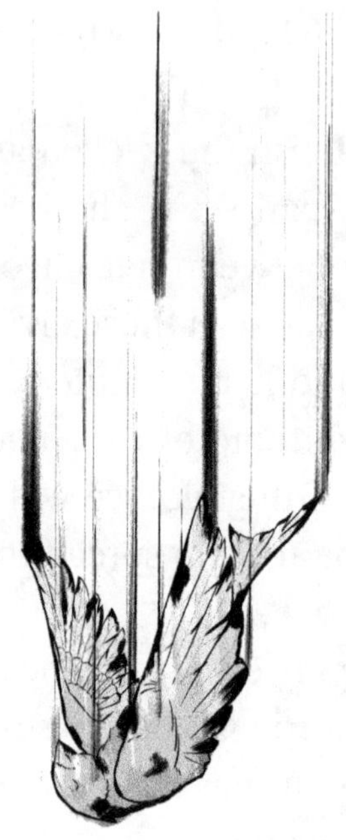

'When will she wake?' Sky asks.

'Her body was severely damaged,' a man replies. 'Plus, she was bitten, Mistress. We have never used the serum on an infected subject before. She may not wake at all. Or... I hate to even suggest it... It may not have worked. She may be just another mindless target.'

'It has worked. Look at her! Look at her hair and eyes. Her skin. That always changes first, right? Then the rest of the body changes? The blessing has worked, I know it. So, answer my question, you grunt. When will she wake up?'

He sighs. 'Usually, it takes a day or two,' he replies, less than convinced. 'Once injected, the serum spreads and changes the host bit by bit.'

'In that case, I will return to our Lord,' Sky chirps happily, giggling as she runs her fingers through my hair. 'I will tell him the fantastic news. He will wish to be here when she wakes. He does love her ever so.'

She presses her lips to my cheek, kissing me lovingly.

'She may be cross when she does wake,' Sky adds. 'She isn't best known for her placid nature. I advise you to keep your distance. In fact, I would probably pop her in a holding room before she does wake up. Just in case.'

I hear her walk away.

'Erm, Mistress?' the man calls after her.

'Yep?'

'When will the men and I be blessed?' he asks nervously, his voice holding a slight tremor as he speaks. 'We run this facility efficiently and beyond reproach. Our loyalty is unmatched, I assure you. Yet, Lord Sands has not blessed us.'

'He will,' she sings, smacking her lips together. 'When he has deemed you worthy. When we have secured enough *true* servants who will serve our great master whole-heartedly, then he will bless all you brave and selfless little worker-bees.'

I hear the mocking in her tone and the derisive chuckle as she turns and leaves.

I lay still.

As still and silent as the dead.

In the hall, I hear Sky's footsteps fade and a door close shut in the distance.

The man walks around the room, muttering to himself, repeating the words she said with an angry and mocking jeer. Metal trays clang as he slams them angrily on the sides, huffing and puffing in frustration.

He stops, letting out a long, drawn-out breath, before slowly heading towards me.

'I don't know whether to be jealous of you or feel sorry for you,' he tells me, tapping his fingers beside me. 'So... you're to be our Lord's wife? I personally don't know what all the fuss is about. You're not the most beautiful girl *I've* ever seen and stories of your disobedience and hard-headedness are legendary. What is it about you, hmm?'

Again, he taps his fingertips beside me.

'I wonder...' he mutters under his breath. 'Perhaps it's something else?'

I feel him lower his face close to mine. His breath stinks of old coffee and onions. It's enough to make me gag, but I remain still.

His fingertips land gently on my leg and I feel his hand slide upwards, running his grubby palm past my knee and up my thigh.

I only now realise I must be naked.

'Perhaps it's what's between those lovely, athletic legs of yours?' he murmurs with a low chuckle. His palm flattens out on my inner thigh and continues upwards. 'I'm sure our great Lord won't mind me having a little taste.' His lips land on mine and his tongue slides into my mouth with a lustful moan.

When my hand reaches out and grabs his throat, it brings with it a torn and broken restraint. I barely felt any resistance as I yanked metal from metal. His neck feels like a matchstick in my hand.

His wide, petrified eyes are odd colours, one is a dark blue and the other is a dull green. They stare at me in terror as I tug free my other hand.

'T-that's not possible!' he gasps. 'How are you awake?'

'Were you about to molest me?' I growl as I sit up on the metal slab I was laying on with his throat still firmly in my grasp. 'Because that would have been a very, very bad idea on your part if that's what you were about to do to me.'

He tries to shake his head as best as he can while in my stone-like clutches.

The room I'm in is bright. White. Alien. I see a machine. A *working* machine! I recognise it as something from a hospital. I must be hallucinating. Especially as I realise, this room is lit by electricity.

'Where the hell am I?'

The door opens and a second man walks in with a hot cup of coffee in his hand. I smell it as if it were placed directly under my nose. I can almost taste it!

'Hey, Kenny? Did she make it?' he asks, his nose buried in a load of paperwork. 'We better get her moved before she wakes up either way. Mistress says she's a bit of a hand*fuuuulll*...' He stops mid-step and looks at us both like a terrified rabbit. 'This can't be good.'

'You could say that,' I tell him, snatching a scalpel from the tray beside me and tossing it into his eyeball with ease. He falls forwards. The scalpel disappears inside his skull when he falls face-first into the stone floor. Behind him, the door closes softly with a small little thud.

'He's right. I am a bit of a handful.' I return my attention to the pervert and look him dead in the eye as I tear away the bindings around my feet like paper and swing my legs over the edge of the table. I hear his heart racing in his chest. I see the beads of sweat fall with crystal clear clarity. I can smell him as if my face were buried in his neck. And then, I catch sight of myself in the mirrored-glass behind him.

My hair is ashen. My eyes have turned a piercing blue and the skin surrounding them is dark. The rest of my complexion is pale. Deathly white in fact. The edges of my lips are almost black.

I lift him clear from the floor and stand up. I have to make an effort not to kill him. I'm twenty-times stronger than I was. I look into his eyes as I pin him against the wall. He gasps and grabs at my hand. It's like holding feathers! There's no weight to feel at all and he has a good four stone on me.

'Kenny, right?'

He nods.

'What's happening to me, Kenny?' I slam him into the wall, breaking the plaster around him with the force I now yield.

'We-we blessed you,' he wheezes.

'Blessed?!' I squeeze a little tighter. I want to tear his head off. I want to rip his arms from their sockets and shove them into his mouth.

Wow, my emotions are way out of control.

He starts weakly slapping my hand as his face goes blue. His heart starts to slow.

I let him go, dropping him to the floor like a sack of bricks. He scrambles away from me but he's got nowhere to go with his back to the wall and me between him and the door.

'Explain. Now!' I snarl.

'You were going to die,' he says fearfully. 'To turn! It was the only way to save you.'

I look down at my naked body and see no trace of the wounds that should have killed me. I glide my hand over my abdomen and feel nothing but perfectly smooth, cold to the touch, skin. I touch my neck. The bite has healed. It's like nothing ever happened.

'What did Sky do to me?'

'She injected you...'

'With?'

He takes a pain-filled swallow as he builds the courage he needs to say the next part of his sentence.

'With a virus,' he whispers, his hands raised over his face, like that will protect him. 'The same virus that created the Class Two's and Three's but the one we injected you with has additional enzymes and anti-bodies-'

'Cut to the chase. What am I?'

'You're... you're...'

I rest my fingers to my throat and feel no pulse. I only now notice that I have no need for breath.

'I'm dead? You turned me into a target?! A zombie?! A BLOODY ZOMBIE? WHY?!' I demand.

'He loves you. Lord Sands would never let you - He needs you – He-'

'What's he planning? Tell me, or I swear, I will tear your arms off and SHOVE THEM UP YOUR ARSE.'

When he remains quiet, I lunge forwards and grab his wrist.

'Got any oil? Or should we do this dry?' I ask., Pulling at his arm.

'WAIT!' he cries. 'WAIT! WAIT!'

'Waiting.'

'Lord Sands, he will make us all like you. Strong. Fierce. Immortal. You... you're the future and this is where it will begin.'

'Where what will begin?'

'His new world order.' He lifts his frightened gaze and peers up at me. 'We will be the new, superior creatures on earth. Don't you see? We will survive this apocalypse because of what he has done. He has birthed a new species. Lord Sands is a God.'

'He is no God. He's a murderer and a psychopath. God should bring life, not death.' The more fear he feels, the more I realise that my stomach is aching. 'Why do I feel hungry?'

He swallows loudly, his mouth moving but no words mange to form.

'If I have to ask again, that arm is going up your backside.'

'B-because you are,' he stammers. 'N-not necessarily h-hungry... b-b-but craving.'

'Craving?'

'Fear. A-anger. L-lust. When the living around you feel strong emotions, you c-c-crave it. Just like they do. The targets. You, like them, crave life.'

'They eat us... because they crave our humanity?'

He nods. 'B-but you don't *need* to feed. Your body doesn't need it to survive and unlike the class twos and threes, you have control over your urges. They're just beasts but you? You're sentient! You're-'

'I'm pissed off. I'm dead. And I'm hungry. So I suggest you shut the hell up before I sink my teeth into your neck.'

He silences instantly.

'What is this place? This technology doesn't exist anymore. We don't have power. We don't have light bulbs but here it is. Tell me or I will tear your intestines out and eat them while you watch!'

'W-w-we're in the old power station,' he stammers, shaking and cowering.

'What's Noah planning?' I ask. 'Where has he taken the people he stole from The Haven? Are they alive? Are they here?'

When he doesn't answer, I slam my foot into his throat and push him against the wall.

'WHAT'S HE PLANNING?!' I roar. Literally. My voice sounds otherworldly and I feel a surge of adrenaline course through me making my already raging body want to start tearing this place down brick by brick. As anger rises from inside my chest, black lines, like veins, spread up my neck and face. When he sees them, despite being choked, his terror increases. I smell it. I taste it.

He gurgles and chokes as I stand patiently and wait. Finally, when he's about to pass out, he taps my foot and I ease up.

'A new world order,' he gasps. 'Oh God, save me,' he prays, closing his eyes and tucking himself in. 'If I tell you, he will kill me.'

'If you don't, I will eat you,' I reply.

'They're here,' he says in a hush. 'The unworthy, he removed them from the others and placed them here for reproduction.'

I look down at the man and crouch low so my face is in his. I force the rage inside me to remain inside, or else this man will be torn apart by it before I can get the information I need from him. I know that the veins are there, spreading as my adrenaline surges. And he knows that if he doesn't tell me what I want to know plainly, he will die bloody. I see the realisation of his situation in his eyes.

'Tell me now what Noah's plan is in very simple words.'

'He wants to make more like you.'

'How many?'

'The worthy. The strong. The ones trained to fight.'

'He wants to turn the army into the same creature I am?'

He nods.

'And what of the missing? The *"unworthy"*?'

'They are stored here. F-f-for reproduction.'

I grab him by the scruff of the neck and haul him to his feet.

'Show me. But first... give me my clothes. *And* the sword Sky stole from me.'

Dressed in my bloodied and torn clothes and my Nike kicks, I stand on a metal balcony with Kenny held fast by the scruff of his neck, and look down below. In my free hand is my one remaining katana, my fingers slotted through the knuckle duster.

What I see would have me vomiting, but I don't think I do that anymore.

Below, there are cages made of iron bars. Inside are groups of people in dirty grey clothes either sat on the floor or wandering aimlessly. The sound of sobbing, retching, groaning, shouting, threatening and pleading is almost deafening.

My sense of smell, which is now keener than ever, has me gagging and covering my nose. The stench of their filth and desperation outweighs any hunger I could feel right now.

In one cage, there are pregnant woman cradling bellies. The fear in their eyes as they cling to their bumps is a hard thing to witness.

In others, men demand their freedom, kicking and slamming themselves against the bars.

In others, children. They huddle together in groups, peering up in terror, scared to make the slightest move or sound. The youngest looks around five. The oldest, maybe ten.

'Reproduction...' I whisper, looking at the sight before me. 'Explain. Now!'

'The unworthy, they will breed,' he says with a quaking voice, trembling uncontrollably in my grasp. 'We will take the children. Those that are worthy will be trained, just as you were, and then blessed on their eighteenth birthday.'

'What makes them worthy?'

'Their physical attributes. Eye colour. Hair colour. Intelligence-'

'And what of the unworthy babies?' I ask through gritted teeth.

'They will be kept here. To... to...'

'To?'

He nods to the pregnant women below. 'Breed.'

'So Noah can continue building his perfect army of dead soldiers?'

He nods.

Makes a twisted kind of sense. If he turns everyone, that will be it. I'm assuming that we can't have kids, being dead and all. So he plans on keeping a human reserve so he can continue building his numbers.

Over my dead body.

Literally... apparently.

'Are any eaten?' I ask. 'By the blessed?'

'There have been... mishaps.'

'Mishaps?'

'Self-control can sometimes fail even the strongest of people.'

A low, animalistic growl rumbles out from my throat.

'How many children have been born here?'

'We're expecting our first crop within the month,' he says, his finger extended and pointed at the heavily pregnant women below. 'We only started production nine months ago.'

All this, it all started shortly after I left?

Did my leaving act as a catalyst for Noah's insanity?

I spin him and wrap my fingers instead around his throat. His knees buckle under my hold as I keep him suspended before me.

'These people are not *"crop"*. They are human beings and do not deserve this.'

'How else will we increase our numbe-'

I squeeze harder, stealing his vile voice. 'I saw a boat sailing away a few miles from where I was stabbed. It can't be too far from here.' I loosen my grip ever so slightly, giving him just enough room to speak. 'Explain.'

'Boats?' he wheezes, shaking his head. 'I don't know what-'

'When people lie, their eyes go dry and they flicker to the left.' I pull him closer, his toes dragging over the floor. 'Their hearts beat faster too. I can hear yours like a manic little drum in my ears. *Thumpthumpthump.*' I lean into his ear and whisper, 'Lie to me again and it will be the very last thing you do. You hear me?'

'He's bringing them over from across the sea.'

'Infected?'

His head nods quickly.

'Why?'

'To keep you scared,' he croaks. 'To keep you in The Haven. To make you... make you... see.' His fingernails claw at my skin as he tries to lessen my grip.

'See?'

'That the only way... to survive... to win... is to change. He needs them all... to believe!'

A man yelling from below catches my attention. He charges through the group of men in his cage and reaches through the bars, anger and retribution coursing through him as he yells for release.

It's Samuel, the leader at the civilian's village. As I look, I see many soldiers too. Those who graduated long before I did. They're hard-core warriors. Dedicated to defeating the undead. I expect they're here because Noah knows that they would never agree to be what I am.

'He wouldn't want a load of super-strong, un-dead soldiers to turn against him,' I mutter to myself before turning back to him. 'The serum that you injected me with. Is there more here?' I ask, diverting my gaze from the human-farming operation below to the pervy shit-bag I have in my hand.

'No,' he wheezes, his blinks are growing longer each time.

'Where is the rest of it?'

'U-under Noah's house, s-sealed in a vault.'

'Great. Thanks for all your help.' I drop him and he falls to his knees, clutching his bruised and swollen throat as he coughs and gasps.

He peers up at me, a confused furrow on his brow. 'What are you?'

'What do you mean?'

'Those veins. The way your eyes went black. You should have been out for hours. Days even! But you healed so fast! And your strength!' He rests his hand on his throat. 'You tore those cuffs like they were nothing! The others, they're strong, but you? You-'

He stops suddenly, gagging as if something is lodged in his throat. He wretches, clasping at his chest and struggling for breath.

The roots of his hair start to turn from dark brown to white. Slowly, it spreads further and further, reaching down to the tips. His eyes change. Both turn to the same vivid blue as mine. He looks at hands as they turn the same ghostly white and I hear his heart suddenly stop beating.

Then, he laughs.

'You turned me!' he exclaims. 'I am blessed!' His fingers rest on his lips as his eyes flick left to right in thought. 'I kissed you. I kissed you and you infected me! Finally, I am blessed.' Gleefully, he looks up at me. 'You're contagious! You... you have the power to spread the virus without the need of injection!' 'The others, they're not contagious?' I ask with confusion.

He shakes his head, lost in the joy of his sudden loss of life. 'No. Only the serum can turn us and Noah holds it all at his home. 'He looks up at me with dim-witted euphoria. 'Perhaps because you were infected before Sky injected you? You. You are something new! Thank yo-'

I take his head in my hands and grip it tight. 'What I am is a Canary. And everyone knows... you don't fuck with the Canaries!' I twist so all the bones in his neck splinter. I clearly have no idea of my strength as I find myself still holding his head as his body slumps at my feet. I lift Kenny's severed head. His eyes are glazed and any humanity or consciousness that was there has gone. He looks like any other target as his mouth still moves. *Chomp. Chomp. Chomp.* 'Thanks for being so helpful, Kenny. Laters.'

I drop his head and make my way to the very edge of the platform to watch as two men in white coats emerge from a steel door along the corridor below. One of them has a long silver stick. He lifts it and I hear a crackle and see sparks shoot out of the end of it. He thrusts it through the bars and imbeds it into Samuel's stomach, causing him to double over and yell in pain.

I leap over and jump down to the platform below. I land not only with grace, but silently.

'Keep it down, old-timer!' the white coat spits, jabbing Samuel relentlessly. 'Or I'll-'

My hands grab his head and I twist, a little gentler this time, snapping his neck but not decapitating it. He falls in a lifeless heap. The other white coat staggers back.

'Oh shi-'

I punch him. I feel his skull break around my fist and feel the warmth of his blood slide along my skin.

He joins his colleague dead on the floor.

When I turn to face the cage of soldiers and farmers they stagger back, pressing themselves against the wall. Samuel is still on the floor but is regaining his senses.

'You okay?' I ask him.

'Scarlett? Is that-' He lifts his head and sees me. His face drains of colour. 'What the hell happened to you?'

'It's a long story. Are you okay?' As I step closer to the door, he scrambles back. 'I'm not going to hurt you.'

His eyes scan the bodies at my feet and then land back on me with a raised brow and a cynical cocking of the head.

'I know it looks bad but I'm not going to hurt you, Samuel. Please. We don't have much time. Things are happening right now that we need to stop. The others, back at the Haven, they're making their stand against Noah when the sun rises. They have no idea that Noah has turned people into...' I gesture to myself. 'Whatever the hell he's turned me into.' I look at them all. Their fists are clenched and they watch my every movement, just as I do when facing a target. Reaching down, I rummage in the pockets of the white coat hoping to find a key.

Nothing.

I return to my feet and grab the bars.

'I'm going to get you out of there. Just, don't try to kill me when I do. I promise, I mean you no harm but I'm not sure about my own strength or restraint and I really, really don't want to accidentally hurt you.'

I pull on the door. The metal hinges groan and creek. I watch them bend and eventually, it breaks and I toss it behind me.

They're free but they remain inside, huddled to the bars.

'You gonna eat us?' Samuel asks.

'Not if I can help it. Now, when you've all finished pissing your pants, perhaps you can give me a hand rescuing the others?' I jibe, walking off to the other cells.

I find three cells full of able-bodied men and women. I free them first and they swiftly tend to the cages holding the more vulnerable prisoners.

'What did they do to you?' Samuel asks me as I step to the side allowing the pregnant women to pass.

'They killed me,' I tell him, tossing the mangled door to the side. 'Well, technically Titan killed me. Listen. I have to get back to The Haven. The sun is rising soon and when it does, Elder One will start the revolution. But Noah has a serum which turns people into whatever it is I am. I'm strong.'

'I can see that,' he mutters, looking at the pile of discarded doors.

'But I'm also dangerous, Samuel. I'm able to control it but the others may not be able to.'

'Control what?'

'The hunger. You all smell really good and I feel like I'm starving.'

'Oh bugger.'

'Yeah. Bugger. I have no idea how many creatures there are like me. If Elder One leads the soldiers to Noah unprepared, they'll be killed. I have to get back to them. I have to help them.' I think of my family, mourning my brutal death and setting their sights and their revenge on Noah. If any of the Grey Coats are like me, they'll be ripped to pieces. 'Will you be okay?' I look beyond him, to the ever-filling hall as more and more prisoners are freed. 'If you follow the coast south, you will reach The Haven.'

'We're not going anywhere until we've torn this place apart.' I turn and see a young brunette girl watching us. She has a purple birthmark covering the left side of her face and a slight bump of a belly. 'They took me in the middle of the night from my bed and brought me here to be raped by a farmer's son.' She walks towards me with a brave defiance that has me in awe. 'Every time he refused, they cut off a finger. He lost six before I told him to do it.' Her voice holds the slightest tremble as she speaks. I'm sure I only catch it due to my new and improved senses. She stands taller when she reaches me. 'He was forced to impregnate me. All the men here were forced.' She scoffs and shakes her head. 'Except for that bastard white coat who seemed all too happy to help.'

'Creepy guy with one blue eye and one green one?' I ask, thinking of his wandering hand as I lay feigning unconsciousness on the table. She nods. 'He's dead,' I tell her.

'Did it hurt?'

'Oh yeah.'

'Good. Now, if what you say is true, get your dead-arse back home and warn the others. We've got this place and the people inside in hand.'

'Listen. If we lose-'

'You really must be dead,' she scoffs, folding her arms across her chest and sneering at me. 'The Scarlett we all knew wouldn't even entertain the idea of losing. You can wear her Canary coat and hold her swords, but if you think for even a second that you'll lose, you're not Scarlett.'

I can't help the low growl that comes from deep inside my throat. I clear it, getting my animalistic response under control. 'Actually, I lost my coat. So you wanna know what I'm gonna do when I leave here? I'm gonna skin Noah Sands alive and make a new coat like no other.'

'Not so dead after all then.'

'But if we do lose The Haven, there's a place you can go. It was called a holiday village. There are houses made of brick and high walls and fences surrounding it. I expect Noah knows about it, Sky probably told him, but it will protect you for a while at least.'

I wait until she nods and then tell her exactly where to find it. I then turn on my heel and run outta there as fast as my legs can carry me.

I need to tell the others I'm alive.

Well, sort of.

But more importantly that Noah has a secret sodding bunker under his mansion with a man-made version of the virus which he plans on using on the army.

I run. Faster than I've ever run before.

Outside, it's dark and bitterly cold. I feel it on my skin but the temperature doesn't bother me one bit. I must be going three times faster than I ever could before I died. I leap over high metal gates that stand twice my size with ease and find the coast.

I run.

I don't tire.

I don't get out of breath because I don't need to breathe.

I just keep running, chasing the sunrise, all the way home.

CHAPTER THIRTEEN

Morning has arrived.

The sky in the distance is thick with dark clouds. They block the light which tries, with futility, to spread across the sand, as it rises across the ocean.

I've been running for hours but still feel full of energy.

I spot the wall in the distance and knowing that there will still be Grey Coats positioned all along the top of it, I divert towards the sea.

I dive in. The cold water makes my skin hum and the salt on my tongue is surprisingly pleasant. I see through the water for several feet before the murkiness becomes too dense. I swim hard. I swim fast. I swim beneath the waves without the need to emerge for air until the wall, covered in thick green algae, comes into view. I follow it, finding the end which is roughly half a mile out to sea and carry on. I swim further so that when I do emerge, I won't be seen by anyone up on the wall.

I drag myself along the seabed, clawing at it like an animal and then swim upwards.

Cautiously, I poke my head up from the surface and see nothing but the beach. No people. No soldiers. No Grey Coats.

I take the opportunity and emerge completely, running out of the breaking waves and onto the sand.

Pulling my hood up and tucking my white hair inside, I make my way towards Elder One's house.

When I get there, his home is swarming with Grey Coats who are in the process of searching it and tearing it apart.

No sign of Elder One though, so I carry on towards The Academy. I stick to the trees, following the Soldier's Road. The paths are all empty. Eerily so. Something's not right. What's worse, the further along the road I travel and the closer I get to the Military Village, the more I sense fear and anger. My stomach clenches again.

I push the sensation of starvation as far down as it will go and carry on, shaking my head and the thoughts of eating far from my mind.

As I run, I catch a scent drifting through the air.

I recognise it instantly. I've smelt it a hundred times before.

Cass.

But this time it's overwhelming. Not just a slight hint of his presence but an all-consuming sensation as if I were snuggled up beside him with my face buried in his neck.

I sprint towards him. My fingers grip the hilt of my sword as I get closer. Through the woodland I see him. He's with three others. Winder, Chilli and Loom. The four of them stand in a line, weapons drawn and their stance tell me that they're about to fight.

Then I see that blocking their path are three Grey Coats. One of them raises their sword and starts to charge the boys. The two others follow their lead.

Without stopping, I charge towards them all, emerging from the treeline and leaping clear over the boy's heads. I land between them, sword in hand and an unquenchable thirst for causing some pain.

With my hood up, the Grey Coats fail to see my face and turn their attack on me instead. They all come at me with everything they have.

I know instantly that they're like me.

I hear no heartbeat. Smell no fear. And feel their strength as they bring down their steel.

Our swords meet in almost a blur as all three attack. I dodge and counter each of their strikes, pivoting on my feet and delivering blow after blow. The three surround me and raise their swords before bringing them down on my head in one synchronised move. I catch two with my sword as I fall to my knees and lift my katana high above my head. The third blade I miss by lunging left. My back is almost parallel to the ground and my hood slips, revealing my face to the four boys watching in silent shock at the fierce spectacle before them.

Cass's eyes meet mine.

'Scarlett?' he whispers.

I have no time to explain. The Grey Coats have already pulled back their weapons and are preparing to attack.

I launch myself upright and return to my feet, spinning my blade wildly and skilfully, blocking and defending them at every turn. I duck and weave between their blows, dancing almost, as we battle. I see an opening with the one on my right and drive the tip of my blade up through his jaw. I retract it quickly, spin, and drive my sword clear through the neck of the Grey Coat beside him with a long sideways swipe. His head hurtles through the air before landing by the trees to watch with dead eyes as I turn to the final target. Our swords clash again and again as we cross blades. I force him back with my frenzied and focused onslaught of strikes until his feet meet the grass verge and his back touches the trunk of an oak tree. I pull back and plunge the tip of my sword into the very middle of his forehead. His stark blue eyes glaze over as his arms fall limp at his sides. When he drops his weapon, I retract my own and flick it clear of his blood. I notice that it's just as red as anyone else's, not black like the mindless monsters beyond the wall.

'S-Scarlett?'

Slowly, I turn.

My hood is back on my head and Cass is trying to peer beneath it. I see how red and puffy his eyes are. How grief has aged him in such a short amount of time. And also, how he clutches his haladie in one hand and my lost, second katana in his other.

'I-Is that you?' he asks, taking a step closer. Then another and another, until he stands before me. His hand reaches out and with his haladie still between his fingers, he lowers my hood. 'My God...' he whispers, looking at my pale skin and the veins I feel surging beneath my skin. 'You're... you're...' His face suddenly hardens and his voice turns cold. 'You're not Scarlett.'

He then proceeds to try and thrust his haladie through my temple.

I slam my palm into his chest, forcing him back so he lands by Winder's feet. Quickly, he scrambles up.

'Did you just try and bloody stab me?!' I snap. 'What the hell, Cassius?!'

'She's talking,' Winder says in a stunned murmur. 'How is she talking? She's dead. How-'

'I save your lives and you try to kill me?! You... You... YOU GIT!' I sniff. There's a scent in the air. One that I think I recognise. It's faint. In the distance. But I can smell it. I look quickly around me. 'Where's Tee?'

They all look at each other, not understanding what the hell is happening.

I sniff again and find the direction it's coming from.

'Where's Tee?!' I demand again. When I step towards them, they leap back.

'She said she needed to get something and ran off,' Winder tells me, his words tumbling from his mouth. 'She was furious at us for taking her away from you. We were running after her when the Grey Coats stopped us. Why? What's wrong?'

I sniff again and terror courses through me. 'I smell her.'

'You smell her?' he repeats.

'Winder... I smell her blood. I smell a lot of her blood!'

I run, leaving them behind me as I follow the scent of my sister.

I don't stop until I see the porch of my father's cottage.

The door is closed and there's no one in sight. I run up the steps. Inside, there's music playing. It's coming from the kitchen. The whole house reeks of Tee and in my panic, I struggle to sense where exactly it's coming from.

'TEE?' I bellow, rushing down the hallway.

I go to where the music is coming from but find it empty except for the old gramophone on the table with a record is playing.

'TEE?' I call out. I run back into the hall and really focus. The smell is coming from upstairs. I take them two at a time as I rush upwards. The gramophone starts to skip, playing the same melody over and over again. I reach the landing where my bedroom door is closed.

I kick it open.

The bedroom's been tidied and cleaned. The bed's been made. She's not in here but the smell has me covering my nose. I look to the left, to the closed bathroom door, knowing that that's where it's coming from.

I swallow a dry swallow. If my heart was beating, it would be in my throat. I reach and push it open.

I scream.

I scream so loud, my throat burns. I rush in and slip onto my side when my feet reach the deep pool of blood gathered around her. I crawl the rest of the way.

'Tee! TEE!' I grab the knife still in her hand and toss it away from her before clamping down on the two deep gashes across her wrists. 'TEE! TEE! PLEASE WAKE UP. OPEN YOUR EYES!' I just keep screaming. I shake her and shake her.

But she doesn't move.

She's so pale. Her eyes flicker open for the briefest second. Just long enough for me to see the lights in them go out.

'NO!' I know I'm screaming something. But I don't know what. I lie her down and start giving her compressions. Pushing down on her chest and breathing into her mouth, forcing air into her lungs and trying hard to get her heart going again. My tears spill down and land on her face.

Cass appears in the doorway, his haladie in his hand, ready to attack.

'GET AWAY FROM HER!'

'HELP ME!' I cry. 'CASS, PLEASE... HELP! SHE'S NOT BREATHING.'

'What?' He turns his attention from me, to Tee and the blood. 'Oh God. What has she done?' He drops his weapon, looking down at our beautiful girl, and rushes to her side. He grabs some towels and presses them against her wounds before resting his fingers to her neck, feeling for a pulse.

'I don't know if I have breath,' I sob, pushing on her chest again and again. 'You try!'

But he doesn't.

As I carry on trying to bring her back, he simply presses his fingers against her throat.

'Scarlett...'

'C'mon, Sweet girl,' I tell her, pressing down and breathing into her. 'Open your eyes.'

'Scarlett...'

'Just open your eyes. Take a breath. That's all ya gotta do.'

Winder slides to a stop in the doorway, panting and clasping his side.

'Who screamed? Scarlett? How... Tee?!' He looks at the blood coming from her open wrists and me trying with all my might to bring her back. 'Oh God. Tee... TEE!' He rushes to her side, falling to his knees beside me shaking his head. 'No. No. No no no no!'

He takes her face in his hands, brushing her blood-soaked hair from her face. 'No. No!'

I shove him away, taking back her face and resuming my attempts to bring her back to us.

Two breaths into her mouth and then thirty compressions. I have to hold back as I feel the fragility of her ribs beneath my palm.

Winder just sobs, watching in dismay.

And Cass does nothing but look at me, tears sliding down his face.

'WHY ARE YOU JUST SITTING THERE!' I sob at Cass furiously. 'HELP ME SAVE HER!'

'Scarlett... Scarlett look at me.' Cass takes my hands. 'Bloody hell,' he gasps. 'You're as cold as ice.' I shove him away. I have to save her. I can't stop. She just needs to open her eyes. That's all. I keep going. Compressions, breathing into her lungs, compressions.

But she won't wake up.

'JUST BREATHE, GOD DAMN IT!' I roar.

Cass grabs my hands. 'She's gone,' he says. I look at him, tears blurring my vision and a pain inside that's consuming me whole. 'Put her down. Give her to Winder. She's gone. She's lost too much blood and her heart has stopped. We can't bring her back.'

'No...' I shake my head but know the truth. I can't hear her heart anymore and she no longer smells alive. Yet my hands keep giving compressions. 'GET AWAY FROM US!' I scream, pushing him away. But the voice that came out of me isn't my own. It's demonic. He falls back looking frightened as I carry on. I keep trying to bring her home. 'WHERE WERE YOU?!' I scream at him. 'WHY WEREN'T YOU WITH HER?! YOU PROMISED YOU WOULD LOOK AFTER HER. YOU SWORE!' I look down at her still and pale form as I just keep trying. 'Wake up, Tee. WAKE UP!' Breathing into her, I pray to anyone who will listen. God, the Devil, I don't care. Someone, please just hear me!

'She can't be dead. Tee can't be...' Winder's struggling to talk or breathe. 'We were... I love her-'

'She's not dead,' I tell Winder, not stopping. 'She's not dead. She loves you too. She wouldn't do this! She's not dead.'

Chilli and Loom appear out of breath in the doorway.

'What-'

'Chilli, Loom, go get Elder One,' Cass says firmly.

'But... but...'

'Just get Elder One here now!'

'Cass, is Scar-'

'Please... just get Elder One before Noah turns up and kills us all!' he orders. The boys turn and leave at a sprint.

I have no idea what's going on. The whole house could be on fire and I wouldn't notice. I wouldn't care. All I care about is getting her breathing.

Why is no one helping me?

Why is Cass just sitting there?

I look up at him and I see it.

He's looking at Tee with grief. His hand covers his mouth as he sits on his knees with tears sliding down his face. My compressions slow because I see it in him. I see the truth in his eyes as I always have with everything I've ever been unsure of.

'She's dead... Cass... she's dead... isn't she?' I whisper. He nods and runs his hand through his hair. 'This can't be happening. This isn't possible.' I scoop her up in my arms, and I just hold her close. I stroke her hair and rock her back and forth. 'It's okay,' I tell her. 'You're okay, sweet girl. I'm here. Me, Winder and Cass are all here.'

I cry.

I cry so hard and so loud. My heart breaks right then and there. Tee. My Sweet girl.

My sister.

She's gone.

CHAPTER FOURTEEN

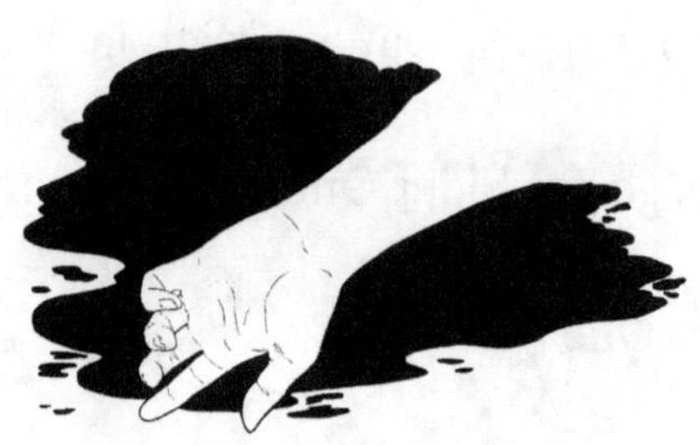

A hand rests on mine.

'Scarlett, can you look at me?'

I lift my head to see Elder One kneeling in front of me. I didn't hear him arrive. How long have I been here?

Winder and Cass are by the door. Winder's crying into his shoulder, mourning the loss of the woman he loves. Cass keeps his distrusting, miserable eyes on me. I look at Elder One. His face is softer than I've ever seen. He looks down at Tee and brushes a loose strand of hair from her face.

'I am so sorry, Scarlett. I am so so sorry.'

'She won't wake up,' I whisper, fighting through the sobs. 'I tried to get her to. But she won't wake up.'

'I know you tried, my dear.'

'How do I get her to wake up?'

'She's not going to wake up. You know that, don't you?' he says softly, giving me time to listen and answer. It kills me to nod and I cling to her even tighter. 'Now, I'm going to take Tee and give her to Winder. He'll place her on the bed and make sure she's comfortable. I know this is cruel, but we have to get out of here.

'I'm not leaving her.'

'Noah's coming. He's been looking for us and when no one turned up for work this morning, he gathered his Grey Coats-'

'I don't care.'

'The time will come to grieve. Now is *not* that time.' He reaches out but I hold her closer and shake my head. A low, animalistic growl comes from deep inside my chest, but I didn't mean it to. He retracts his hands. 'Alright. Okay. That's okay.' He looks at her hands which lie limp at her sides. Wrapped around them is my face scarf. She died holding it. Why does that small act make me hurt all that much more? He rests his hand on mine as if to comfort me.

'I don't have one,' I tell him as his fingers press not so subtly against my wrist. He drops the pretence and moves his fingers to my neck. Then he lowers his hand.

'No. You don't, do you,' he sighs.

'She doesn't have what?' Cass asks, sniffing and drying his face with his sleeve.

'A pulse, Cassius. Scarlett doesn't have a pulse,' Elder One replies, as simply as if talking about the weather, his eyes never leaving me. 'You should be dead. The wound Titan gave you should have killed you and by all accounts, you were left to be devoured. But here you are.' He returns his gaze to Tee lying lifeless in my arms. 'But that's not what matters right now.' Elder One holds out his hands once more. 'Let me take her.'

'No.' I shake my head and bury my face in her hair. 'No. You can't,' I sob.

'Scarlett, you have to give her to me.'

'I can't.'

The sound of footsteps coming slowly towards me are unbearable. The sound of Tee's blood as it squelches with every step is agony to hear.

'Please, Scar, let me take her?' Winder asks sadly.

I lift my gaze and see him kneeling beside me, his arms outstretched for his lost love. Her blood, soaked into his skin. His lip trembles as he looks me in the eye pleadingly.

'Please? Please let me hold her?'

Painfully, I nod and hand her as gently as possible to him. He whimpers when he takes her weight before cradling her to his chest and leaning down to kiss her cheek.

Elder One eases me to my feet and takes me through to the bedroom and then into the hall. Cass follows, leaving Winder to mourn in private. Once in the hall, I slump against the wall feeling lost in a sea of pain and despair.

'Listen. Noah's Grey Coats are searching for us. The others have sealed themselves in The Academy,' Elder One states. 'I know that right now your heart must be in pieces. That you're coming to terms with whatever has happened-'

'She's a target. She's dangerous,' Cass says darkly, snarling every word as he watches me.

'Does she look dangerous to you?' Elder One snaps. He turns and glares at him. 'Look at her. Her heart is broken. She needs you now.'

'She's a zombie. Look at her! Her hair... her eyes... you said it yourself, she has no pulse.' Cass looks at me with distrust and grief as more tears slide down his face. He's conflicted, just as I was when I saw my father turn in front of me.

Elder shakes his head. 'And yet she's talking. She's grieving. She's showing more emotion now than she did when she was breathing. She's not biting or-'

'You didn't hear her roar as I did a few moments ago,' Cass replies. 'I saw her, Elder. She was surrounded by Class Twos. No way she wasn't bitten. No way she survived-'

'Sky,' I reply, looking at the floor, hating the loathing I see in his eyes when I still love him so. 'Sky found me. She killed the targets and took me to where they're holding the missing people. Sky is the spy. She's infected too.'

I don't want to hear any more cruel words leave his lips. I get it. I'm not human anymore. I'm dead. My father is dead. My sister too. The man I love is looking at me like I'm a monster. All I have left is the mission and vengeance. So, I decide right here and right now, that that's all I will focus on. I return to my bedroom and start changing my clothes, peeling off the blood-soaked hoody and trousers that cling to my body and tossing them on the floor. As I change, Winder remains in the bathroom with Tee, sobbing.

Elder and Cass watch me cautiously as I tell them everything. I tell them about the human farming. That I was infected with a strain of the same virus that created the mindless monsters beyond the wall. That Sky is the spy. I tell them all I know of Noah's plans. I tell them about the boats being used to import more infected in order to keep us behind the wall, cowering in fear.

'Noah has a secret bunker under his house by the coast,' I tell them, pulling on a fresh vest. 'It's full of whatever serum Sky used to turn me. He has enough to turn the whole army at least. Maybe more.'

'Bloody hell...'

I sit on the bed and pull on my kicks. 'This is far bigger than just controlling us. He wants us all like this. This is his new world order.' I point to myself and get to my feet. 'But there's a hunger in me, Elder.' I turn to him as I admit, 'I don't need to eat but I feel the craving. It feels like I'm starving. When I smell fear or anger or...' I look to Cass. 'Hate. Love. It makes me ravenous.'

Cass firms his grip on the handle of his haladie as his eyes narrow.

'Will you bite?' Elder asks.

'I won't,' I promise. 'No matter what. I swear it.'

'Are you infectious?' Cass asks.

On the edge of the bed I see my mother's Canary coat and my empty back harness. I reach out and lay my hand flat on top of them.

'I said, are you-'

'Yeah,' I confess sadly. 'Yeah, I am. Back at the human-farm, some creep tried his luck when he thought I was unconscious. He kissed me and about fifteen minutes later, he turned.' I grab hold of my coat and slide it on before fixing my harness in place. 'But the others aren't. The guy that shoved his tongue in my mouth was really surprised when he turned. Happy, but he wasn't expecting it. I think, because I was bitten before Sky injected me with that serum, I think I'm something different.'

'Well, I guess that's a good thing.'

'Excuse me? What's good exactly?!' I snap.

'None of it really, but at least the others can't spread the infection with their teeth.' Elder takes a moment to think. 'The others are gathering everyone in the Main Hall. We need to go there now. Tell everyone what's happening.'

'I have a better idea.' I wipe my tears. 'You go. I'm gonna go kill Noah.' I head out onto the landing but he cuts me up as I reach the stairs and blocks my path.

'You can't!'

'I bloody can. Move aside, Elder.'

'The Grey Coats will kill you!'

'I have no intention of living past ripping Noah's head off. I don't wanna be this...' I gesture to myself in utter disgust. 'I'd kill myself now but I need to end this first. He needs to pay. Now move.'

'You're not going out there on a stupid suicide mission!' Elder One insists.

'I'm already dead!' I try to pass again. He blocks me.

'Scarlett, stop and think!' he says, stepping back as I try once more to pass, but he won't let me even though he's clearly a little frightened of me. 'If you, in your... condition... go out there and tear apart Grey Coats and try to kill Noah without explaining to the rest of the world why, nothing good will come of it. You either die and he comes after everyone you might have told. Or he dies and becomes a martyr. Someone else like him, one of his Grey Coats, will take his place. Maybe even Sky!'

'And it will be us and the word of a zombie against an angry mob,' Cass argues.

'Call me zombie one more time…' I step towards him, filling with anger. 'And we're gonna have a problem.' He stumbles back. 'Noah and Sky are the reason my sister is dead. Why my dad is dead. Why *I* am dead. They have to die. So move, or-'

'Or what? You'll kill me?' Cass argues. 'Is that what you are now? Am I right? You just a mindless human-eating monster now?'

'That psycho has destroyed my *LIFE*!' There's that voice again. They both flinch. 'I've lost everything. Absolutely everything. And now, so will he.'

'You haven't lost us,' Winder says, slowly stepping through the door and joining us on the landing. He dries his tears with the cuff of his sleeve. 'We're still here, Scar. And we need your help. Stop giving into that rage and take a second to think. This is it. This is the moment we can take control from Noah. But we have to stand as one and we have to be smart. I saw you kill three Grey Coats in a matter of minutes. We could really use your strength and your skill in this fight.' He glances over his shoulder where I see Tee's foot resting on the end of the bed. 'I've just lost the woman I love. You've just lost your sister. Help me kill the man responsible.'

'Winder. She can't be trusted!' Cass insists.

'SHUT YOUR MOUTH!' Winder bellows, slamming his forearm across Cass's chest and pinning him to the wall. 'The only girl I have ever loved is gone. The only woman you have ever loved is standing right there!' He points at me. 'She's right… there.'

'That's not Scarlett,' Cass snipes back, still pinned against his grip and not trying to break free. 'That's the monster that killed her. She's a goddamn corpse!'

'I'd take a walking, talking corpse over the lifeless and limp body currently lying on the bed beyond that door!' Winder snatches my katana from Cass's hand and tosses it to me. I catch it as he releases Cass. 'So what's the plan?'

'Okay then,' Elder One says gruffly. 'We tell the army what we know. Show them what Noah has done. Tell them about the boats. The breeding programmes.' He points to me. 'And what he plans for us all. That he intends to turn us all into Class Ones,' Elder says.

'I'm not a Class One,' I scoff. 'Do I look like a Class One to you? We all know the stories. Godzilla stuff.'

'A Class One is a lab rat. A label given to a target that's been made. Not bitten. You've been made. You're a Class One. The stories vary because the results varied,' Elder explains. 'After the outbreak, people and animals were experimented on. The government were looking for a cure. The effects were far from a cure. The subjects mutated into something terrible. Real monsters. Godzilla stuff, yeah. So they decided on making it a weapon instead. Create a creature that could kill the targets. They made some pretty damn effective killing machines. Turned people fast, strong and unstoppable. And for a day or two, they were fine. They were amazing at killing the targets.' Then he shakes his head. 'But then they weren't. They came after us instead. The hunger took hold. Their flesh started to rot. They couldn't speak. Some grew taller. Some mutated and grew extra limbs. Some even took on physical attributes of what they ate. Dog teeth. Cat claws. Snake fangs. By all accounts, it was horrendous.'

'How do you know this?'

'Elder Ten. He was a child but his father was involved in the units created to destroy them. He saw a few things he wished he hadn't.'

'Jesus!' Winder gasps. 'Is Scar going to change in a day or two?' *Oh God, am I?*

'I have no idea,' Elder shrugs. 'The whole programme was stopped more than fifty years ago because they couldn't fix the problem.'

'Someone should tell Noah that,' Cass says. 'Because it looks like he's still experimenting.'

'Well, as long as we don't get her saliva in our mouths, we should be safe. Probably best we steer clear of her blood too. We keep a close eye on her. The first sign that she's going towards target territory, we put her down. Agreed?'

'Agreed.' The boys reply without a moment's hesitation.

'And don't eat any animals,' Elder adds. 'Don't want you sprouting scales or wings.'

'That's not funny,' I huff.

'Wasn't meant to be.'

There's a loud bang on the door. We all fall silent. Whoever it is knocks again. We all peer down the stairs and look at the front door.

'You are ordered, in the name of The Verity, to open this door!' comes a booming voice from outside. We all stand in silence, watching as the handle wiggles. But it's locked-up tight. 'You have to the count of ten to surrender to us!'

It's the Grey Coat Commander. I recognise his voice.

'One.'

'What do we do?' Winder asks

'Two.'

'What's the plan?' Cass asks.

'Three.'

'You all go out the back. Climb out the bedroom window. Go to the Main Hall and spread the word. I'll deal with them and meet you after,' I tell them.

'You can't face them all. They will kill you!' Winder insists.

'Good job I'm already dead then, isn't it? The priority is the mission. Not a corpse.' I briefly look at Cass as I repeat his words. 'The Grey Coats out there might not even know what Noah and Sky have been up to. Maybe they're not infected. I'll talk to them. They could be on our side.'

'Highly unlikely,' Cass adds.

'But possible. Go to The Main Hall. Tell the soldiers everything. I'll deal with this and meet you there. Go!'

Winder and Elder One turn and disappear as I look down the stairs. It takes a moment to realise that Cass is still here.

We look at each other, both desperately wanting to hold the other and for everything to return to how it was.

'You need to go,' I tell him.

I see his hand twitch as he clutches his haladie.

'Do you really want to kill me?' I ask.

'You can't be her,' he says quietly. 'Scarlett, she's dead. You're-'

The front door explodes and two Grey Coats charge in. One of them lifts a dagger and hurtles it straight at Cass. I leap in front of him and take the weapon in the shoulder so he doesn't take it in the heart.

He catches me as I stumble back. I swiftly pull the dagger free and send it straight back to the Grey Coat. I'm a much better aim and it lands between his eyes. I look down at the wound amazed that, although it hurts, I can feel it already start to heal.

'You just saved my life,' Cass breathes.

'Run, Cass.'

'I'm not leaving you-'

I turn, knowing that the rage I feel has manifested in the thick black veins once more. He looks at them and steps back as I growl.

'I said, RUN!'

He turns on his heel towards the bedroom window, and I turn and charge the Grey Coats.

CHAPTER FIFTEEN

I pull up Tee's scarf which is still hanging around my neck and leap down the staircase coming face to face with the two Grey Coats, one of which lets loose an arrow. It hits my chest, less than half an inch from my heart.

'EVERYBODY STOP!' The Commander orders as his subordinates go to attack. They lower their weapons. 'Scarlett? Is that you? What are you doing here?'

'You're the ones breaking into my home and shooting me,' I snarl, pulling the arrow free. 'I think it's me that should be asking what you are doing here!'

'That arrow was not meant for you, I assure you. I wasn't expecting you to be here-'

'No. You were expecting my family. That's who you intended to kill with that arrow.' I point at him with the arrow's tip. 'Choose your next step carefully, Commander. I'm in a phenomenally bad mood.'

'Come with us. Lord Sands will be most thrilled-'

'You haven't said anything about my appearance. You just shot me with an arrow and I'm fine.' I look at them. They're not surprised at all. 'You know, don't you? Cass was right. I was being a hopeful fool to think for even a second that all of you Grey Coats aren't involved. You're in on it. You know exactly what Noah's done, don't you?'

'Someone's gotta load and unload those boats and make sure we don't run out of humans to turn.' He reaches up and pulls down his hood. The others follow his lead.

'Bloody hell...' I whisper. Their hair is ashen and their eyes a light blue. 'You're all infected.'

'Yes, mam. I'm sure you can understand that we don't want news about what we are getting out just yet. So I suggest you come with us quietly.'

'How long?' I ask.

'Excuse me?'

'How long have you all been infected?' He says nothing. 'Tell me and I promise you I'll come quietly and even surrender my swords. I'll talk to Noah and hear him out. But first, tell me how long you have been this way.'

After a moments pause, he answers. 'Personally? Me? Five years.'

I could laugh in relief. I'm not going to turn into a monster. Not anytime soon at least.

'Now, come with us as you swore you would.'

Now I laugh. 'No way. How can't you see it's all wrong? What he's doing is evil!'

The Commander turns and leave. With the briefest glance to the others behind him, he orders, 'Take her. We shall return her to her fiancé.'

They don't get a chance to follow his order before I'm on them. I kick one hard in the chest sending him flying backwards down the hall and clear off the porch. He soars through the air and slams into the path outside. I grab the archer by the scruff of his hood and hurl him even further. The Commander is on the porch. I head out to meet him, ensuring that by keeping them busy at the front of the house, the others can get away from here through the back unseen.

The Commander raises his sword. I dodge him easily, spinning on my feet and ducking out of the way of his blade. As his arms are raised, I ram my elbow into his ribs, hearing a satisfying crunch as I do. As he doubles over, I wrap my fingers around his throat and hurl him through the air so he lands in a heap with the other two. When I stand to face them, I see another three Grey Coats on the lawn, all with their hoods still up, ready to fight. Now on their feet, the archer readies another arrow and as the three behind hold their sword, axe, and even a mace and chain, their Commander gets to his feet.

'Lord Sands wants you by his side. He loves you and does not want you harmed. Saying that, he has given us orders to drag you to him in pieces if needs be.'

I draw my swords and spin them in my palm. 'You can try.'

The archer lets loose two arrows and the five men behind charge. I dodge the arrows easily enough and run to meet them. Leaping off the stoop, I jump into the air, clearing the archer and landing behind him with a skid. I swipe my katana. The swordsman I was aiming for lunges back and I miss. They're fast, like me. The axeman to my left brings his weapon down. I block him with my sword and kick him hard in the gut. He doubles over and while he's distracted, I go for the kill. But someone yanks me back by my hair and tosses me to the side. I slam hard into a tree. It groans and several branches fall with the impact. They are remarkably strong.

The mace-wielder is a girl. She yells as she swings her weapon high above her head and then brings it down with all her strength towards my chest. I narrowly manage to roll out of the way. She lifts it again, taking lumps of earth and stone with the spiked metal ball, and brings it down once more.

I dodge. Just.

I feel the cold metal brush against my cheek as she lifts it again. I slam the bottom of my feet into her knees with all my strength and hear a loud snap. She screams furiously and crumples, her legs bowed the wrong way. I leap up and block the attack coming from the swordsman. I counter every single move. As we fight, the clanging of our meeting blades echoes through the air, followed by my angry yell as I get an arrow in my rib and another in my forearm.

Screw this!

I throw in a little something his swordplay teacher wouldn't have shown him. But my dad certainly showed me. My foot slams into his crotch. He grabs his private area, yelling and dropping his sword. I kick the back of his knee. When he's down, I raise my sword and plunge it into his skull. He slumps and doesn't get up.

Headshot equals a kill. Just like any other zombie.

Good to know.

I ram my elbow into the mace-girl's nose. She staggers back dazed from the whack. The axeman is on me, swinging his weapon.

I lunge back so I'm horizontal but spring up with ease. Before he can return the swing, I thrust my sword into his gut.

He roars the same monstrous call I gave earlier.

He looks pissed!

He forces himself further up my blade and wraps his hand around my throat. He starts squeezing and I feel my bones grinding together. I let go of my embedded katana and yank out the arrow from my rib to jab it into his eye.

With a furious yell, he lets me go and pulls it out. I take my chance and retrieve my sword, as well as the arrow still in my forearm. I throw the arrow back at the archer and it lands right in the middle of his forehead. The tip pokes through the back of his skull. He looks at me stunned for a minute, then falls to the floor in a still and silent heap.

Two down, four to go.

'YOU'RE DEAD, BITCH!' hollers the axeman, bringing down the axe over and over as I dodge his every move.

'No shit,' I scoff.

I move, ducking and weaving every one of his raving attacks. He's angry and it's affecting his performance. That, and he's one eye down.

'Don't kill her!' The Commander orders. 'Lord Sands wants her alive!' As I duck from another of his attacks, he gets an arrow in the chest from the one who threw a dagger at Cass. He's picked up the dead archer's bow and tried to slow me down.

'Damn, you are an awful shot!' I scold before launching an attack of my own. Unlike him, I have 20/20 vision. I'm focused. And I have zero problems killing him completely. He does his best to fend me off. I relieve him of his axe-wielding hand by slicing clean through his wrist. It lands on the floor with a thud before I scoop his weapon up, hand included, and toss it at the pretend archer. It lands between his eyes and he slumps to the floor with his comrade. Their commander prises the axe from his skull and tosses it back to the axeman who looks, with shock, at his severed hand still clinging to the handle.

'DON'T JUST STAND THERE! DISARM HER!' demands the Commander. As the axeman attempts to prise his decapitated hand from his weapon, the mace-girl finishes breaking her legs back into the right position and stumbles to her feet. I hear them click and snap as she stands, slotting all the pieces back into place.

They surround me and the Commander unsheathes his sword before twirling it in his palm.

'You're a good fighter,' he snarls. 'I can see why he chose you.'

'You gonna fight me? Or are we just gonna flirt, Commander?'

'Scarlett?'

Everyone turns.

Oh crap.

Talk about bad timing.

Owl stands on the path and looks at me surrounded by Grey Coats.

'I-I thought you were dead. What's... why do you all look like that?'

'Owl... turn around and leave,' I tell her sternly. 'Get out of here.'

'Why is your hair white?' Owl can't seem to comprehend what she is seeing. 'And your eyes-'

The Commander returns his attention to me. 'Tyrion. Kill the little Green Coat,' he orders. The axeman nods, and turns.

'OWL! RUN!' I scream. 'RUN!' I go for the axeman but the Commander stands between us, shaking his head and smirking. He starts his attack on me. His sword moving swiftly as he strikes. I dodge and counter. He's much more capable than the others. Behind him, Owl's backing away from the axeman as he slowly descends on her.

'OWL, RUN!' But she keeps looking on, startled and stumbling away. 'OWL!!' I yell, blocking the Commanders attack and slicing at his chest. 'HEAD IN THE GAME, SOLDIER. RUN!!! THEY MEAN TO KILL YOU!'

He lifts his axe and with a scream, Owl barrels out the way. She pulls out her bow but he snatches it and tosses it to the floor before she can load it. So I do the only thing I can think of.

'OWL! HEADS UP!' I hurl her one of my Katanas and hope to hell she can use it. When she catches it and flips herself up to her feet with a near-perfect stance, I know that she can. So I return to dealing with the Commander, one blade down.

He lunges and forces me back.

'SCARLETT!' Owl yells, 'BEHIND YOU!'

I spin just in time to see a mace come flying at my face. I lean back and it misses me by a hair. Mace-girl retracts it and spins, twirling her weapon high above her head and building speed so she can come at me with a stronger attack. Behind me, the Commander is about to try and take out my legs. I kick up my feet and lower my upper body, spinning parallel to the floor so they both miss me. When their weapons have passed, I plant my feet on the ground, thrust my sword through her stomach, and use her as a shield between me and the Commander. But behind him, Owl's on the losing side of her fight. Even with one hand, the axe-man is stronger, quicker and isn't afraid of getting a sword in the gut. He elbows her in the face and she falls back, dropping my sword and looking dazed. He lifts his axe, ready to strike. So I retract my sword, punch mace-girl in the face with my knuckle dusters, and propel myself into the air, leaping over the Commander and landing with a surprising amount of grace. I sprint to the axeman whose hand is raised above his head, ready to bring down his weapon on Owl. I swipe. His axe and his remaining hand fall to the floor. As he hollers, I don't stop as I grab hold of her wrist and yank her up. She manages to scoop up my katana before I drag her away as fast as her legs will carry her into the woods.

'FOLLOW THEM!' The Commander shouts. 'DON'T LET THEM GET AWAY!'

They're hot on our heels. After a minute of solid running, I've put the slightest bit of distance between us. We're not gonna outrun them. Well, Owl isn't. I need to get her somewhere safe. I push her behind a large tree.

'What the hell is going on?' she whispers, panting and holding a stitch. 'What are they? What are *you*? They said you were killed!'

'You need to go to the Main Hall,' I tell her. 'It's where the others have gone. You need to find Elder One. Or Cass. Or Winder. Anyone we know who is on our side,' I tell her. 'You need to tell them that all the Grey Coats are infected.'

'Infected?'

'You tell them they're all like me. You tell them that they're in on the whole bloody thing. The boats. The human farming. Noah's new world order. All of it.'

'You're infected?!' She takes a few steps back. 'Like... a target?'

'I hear our attackers closing in. We don't have long. Thirty seconds maybe till they catch up. Owl, trust me. You have to go and tell them what I've just told you. They'll know what I mean and they'll explain it all to you. But if you don't go now, the Grey Coats will kill you.'

'Come with me!' she insists, taking my hand pleadingly. But I pull away.

'I'll hold them off. We won't both make it before they catch us. You go. Run as fast as you can and you don't stop for anyone or anything.'

'THERE THEY ARE!'

I shove her away from me, pressing my katana into her hand.

'Go. Run. Tell them exactly what I've just told you. I'll hold them off.'

'But-'

'GO!' I roar, making her yelp and turn on her heel. She disappears into the trees.

Sliding my fingers through the loops of my knuckle dusters and reaffirming my grip on the one and only sword I have left, I step out from behind the tree.

And get a mace straight to the chest and slam into the floor. Mace-girl leaps over me in hot pursuit of Owl. But despite the fact that I felt my ribs break and that I can taste whatever counts as my blood in my mouth, I still manage to grab her ankle and pull her down with me. She screams and rolls on top of me, slamming her fists into my face, my side, my ribs, anything and everything. Her frenzied attack doesn't distract me from her commander who is running full pelt after Owl. I lean up and slam my face into hers, followed by a metal-enhanced right hook to her nose. She roars as I roll her off me but she snatches my Katana and tosses it away. I have to choose. The sword, or stop the Commander.

Easy choice.

Especially as her mace is by my foot. I snatch it up, scramble to my feet, and run after the Commander, circling it above my head faster and faster and faster.

Then I let it go.

The mace soars through the air and hits him with a smack in the back of the neck. He lands face down. I can hear him growling so he's not dead. Well, no deader than he already is. I just need to keep them busy long enough for Owl to get to the others and tell them. I hear the familiar sound of metal slashing through air and turn to see mace-girl wielding my own weapon against me. I jump back but the tip of my sword catches me and cuts a centimetre or so into my stomach. It hurts. But not enough to make me stop. Not enough to slow me down.

She slashes at me again. This time aiming for my throat and then again at my chest. Each attack has such anger and strength behind it, I think she's forgotten about the not killing me rule. I leap back with each one. She's not giving me a chance to fight back. My constant dodging pisses her off and she pulls back my sword with a frustrated screech, the point aimed upward, ready to be driven through my jaw and skull. I lunge left. But not quick enough. I feel the edge of my sword slice my cheek. She draws it up, ready to hack off my head from the side.

'DO NOT KILL HER!' The Commander bellows angrily. 'LORD SANDS WANTS HER ALIVE!'

His yell distracts her and I lower myself, swinging my foot round and striking her ankles with a kick. She falls and as she does, I snatch my sword from her unworthy hand. Behind me, the Commander is back on his feet, mace in hand and sights set on where Owl is headed. As he takes off at a run, so do I.

Behind me, mace-girl is in pursuit. We're all running at full speed through the trees. I'm gaining on him. Getting closer and closer. When suddenly he stops, his feet skidding in the dirt as he turns, spinning the mace and driving it into the side of my face.

I go down.

My face is a mess of pain and when I reach up, my jaw's a good three inches out of socket and blood pours from my torn skin.

Pushing myself onto my hands and knees, I wiggle my jaw side to side. The bones grind and break as they force themselves right. More blood trickles down my face and they both stand beside me. I see their feet. I hear them laughing. The rattling of the chain is followed swiftly by the mace slamming into my back, forcing me facedown into the dirt. I reach out for my sword but his boot presses down onto my hand. He puts all his weight on it and I hear my fingers snapping.

I yell.

It's agony.

All this is agony!

I feel everything but the pain lasts for minutes only, then I start to heal. But right now... Christ! My face. My fingers. My back. So many broken bones. So much torn flesh.

He grinds his boot harder into my hand making me shout. Using my free hand, I grab his ankle and try to prise him off. But I can't.

'You put up a good fight,' the Commander says. 'But you're beat. Accept it. Just... come with us. Return to your betrothed.'

'Screw you.' I spit blood at his feet and look up at him. 'You'll have to take me back to him in pieces.'

He laughs and looks to the girl who stands beside him. 'Go fetch that little Green Coat,' he orders. 'Kill her before she can tell anyone what she's seen. I'll deal with this one.'

'Yes, Commander,' she replies, holding out her hand. He hands her back the mace and chain. As she steps away, I give up on trying to free my hand and latch onto her ankle instead. She tries to yank it free.

'Let her go,' he orders.

'No.' I tighten my already impossibly tight grip. 'I won't let you kill Owl. I won't.'

And then, all sense of control leaves him and he just attacks. He kicks. He punches. He slams his boot into my face. My ribs. My back. I can't get up. All I can do is curl up and try to protect myself. All the while, I don't let go of her ankle.

'I'll cut her hand off,' the girl says.

'No. Lord Sands won't want her permanently damaged. I'll kill the Green Coat. You, take this one back to the mansion.'

I reach out and wrap my fingers around *his* ankle. I'm still curled up in a ball. I just need to give Owl the time she needs to get to the others. That's all that matters.

He bends down. I watch as he picks up my katana.

He presses the tip of my sword into my side. Slowly, he starts driving it through. I scream out as I feel the steel slowly force its way through my body. He goes slow. It's beyond agony. Just as it was when Titan stabbed me.

'Let us go, Cadet,' he says calmly.

'That's Canary to you.'

He pushes it further in making me howl in pain.

'Let. Us. Go.'

'NO!'

He pushes it in harder. Deeper. Slowly and steadily. I feel every inch. Every bit of muscle that tears. Every organ that he ruptures. I feel it all.

'Let us go, Cadet!' he orders.

I look up at him. 'Kiss my arse.'

The girl lifts her mace and brings it down on me again and again. With each whack, I feel more of me breaking. They keep ordering me to release them. I just dig my nails deeper into their skin. I pour all my strength - everything I have - into gripping their ankles. Their bones start to snap and they yell out in fury and pain. They'll have to kill me or cut off my hands if they want out. My hands are like concrete.

'LET US GO!' he orders furiously, knowing full well that every second they're here with me is another second Owl gets closer to whoever I sent her to. He thrusts the sword down completely, driving the tip into the ground and pinning me in place. I cough and more blood forces its way up my throat.

'Never.' I get another hit from the mace and my fingers start to loosen.

'Cut her fingers off. I'm sure Lord Sands will understand.'

Whoosh.

Smack.

Thud.

Mace-girl slumps next to me in a lifeless heap with a haladie dagger between her eyes. Commander bellows furiously before an arrow goes into his temple. He stands there, swaying. A second arrow puts him down completely.

I can't move. I'm in too much pain. So many bones have been broken from the attack but even as I lay here, I can feel them fusing back together. They click and snap back in place, making me groan in agony. But what's even worse is the sword stuck through me. My body can't heal with it there. I feel blindly behind me for it when a pair of feet rush to my side.

'I got it,' Cass says. 'It's alright. Keep still.'

He yanks it out and I can't help the high-pitched scream that I produce, followed by a pathetic sob as I lay perfectly still with my face in the dirt.

Heal. Please, just hurry up and heal.

He rests his hands on me and tries to help me up.

'DON'T!' I bark. 'Don't touch me!'

'I'm so sorry. Did I hurt you?' he asks in a panic. 'Have I made it worse? What should I do?'

'I'm bleeding,' I tell him. 'Don't touch me, Cass. My blood is everywhere. I might infect you.'

'I'll be careful. Let me help-'

'Don't touch me! Get away!'

'Just-'

'GET AWAY!'

He steps back. We listen to my bones popping and snapping. I dig my fingernails into the ground and clench my teeth as I let my body do what it's gotta do. And as the sound of my mending bones begin to slow, I force myself up onto my knees.

Cass kneels in front of me.

'Is everyone okay?' I ask through the pain. 'Owl... is she alright? Did she find you?'

'Ask her yourself,' Cass says, nodding behind me.

I turn and see her. She's okay and has a bow in her hands. It was her that killed the Commander. But behind her are a dozen Black Coats, a few Green Coats, Elder Nine, Elder Ten and Elder One. All are armed and looking at the two Grey Coats with disbelief and anger. As I push myself slowly to my feet, a few ready their weapons. Winder runs out from beside Elder One and plants his feet between us, his arms up and his calm, easy-going smile.

'Easy, soldiers. She's one of us. Let's put those down.'

As I stand, I sway. Cass tries to steady me but I step away shaking my head. I won't let him touch me when I'm still bleeding.

'There's still one I can't be sure is dead,' I tell him. 'An Axe wielder minus two hands.'

'Big sod,' Owl agrees. 'He would have killed me if Scar hadn't have stopped him.' She points back to where we left him. 'He was up at the cottage, last I saw.'

Elder Nine turns to the Black Coats. 'You three, with me. We'll run back to the cottage. See if he's there.'

'If he's not, we have to assume he's returned to Noah,' I tell him, brushing off dirt and moving my body as it finishes putting its pieces back together. 'Which means he'll know that we know the truth. We must tell everyone else as soon as possible.'

The others gather as Elder Nine and his soldiers disappear into the trees. Faces I've known my whole life look at me with distrust but all that matters is the fight that's only just begun.

Cass and Winder stand firm by my side as the others get closer. Loom and Chilli, even Owl surround me. Their weapons all at the ready to protect me.

'They don't look like they trust me.'

'We don't,' says an older Red Coat. 'You're infected. But we believe you.' He looks down at the two very dead Grey Coats on the floor. 'Guess that explains why they wear those stupid hoods and why they're so selective on who gets to join. Guess they only want the insane.'

'You're on our side?' I ask them. 'You're willing to fight?'

'We all got a problem with Noah and his rules. We've all seen the strange catches in the pits. I killed a zombie wearing an Irish policeman's uniform last week. And three German soldiers a few months back.'

Another Black Coat nods. 'Yeah. And my girl got lashed two months ago because we were caught kissing. I got a telling off. The Grey Coats publicly lashed her. It ain't right.'

There are murmurings of agreement.

'And now this?' Another gestures to me. 'They're turning us? Infecting us? Farming us like cattle? Bringing more infected to our shores? Nah... that ain't happening. We have no intention of becoming zombies. None whatsoever. We've dedicated our lives to protecting humanity. To winning this country back. We're not giving it up to them without a fight.'

'Importing more infected...'

'Taking kids from their parents...'

'Kidnapping us...'

Elder One raises his hand and they all fall silent.

'So we all agree,' he says loudly. 'Noah and The Verity must be stopped.'

'What's the plan?' The Red Coat asks. I look to Elder One, ready for instruction. But he's looking at me. They all are.

'Scar...' Winder nudges me. 'What's the plan?'

'Me?' I whisper. 'Why me? I'm dead!'

'Cos... I dunno. You're the strongest and have seen more than us. They're all looking at you. Just... say something.'

I look out at all the faces waiting and watching. The Elders included.

'Right...' I exhale deeply and get to work. 'Where are the other soldiers?'

'At The Academy. Gathering in the Main Hall. When Owl came and told us you were under attack, we came to get you,' Cass explains.

'Much appreciated. The civilians need to get to the town hall. Tell them there's a breach. That it's not safe. And tell them that the Grey Coats are not to be trusted. We need to get the kids there too. And the little ones in the orphanage. Let's give the people back their children.'

'And then what?' Cass asks.

'We take the fight to Noah. All of us. One big hit. Take him down, destroy the infected Grey Coats and all traces of the infection so he can't turn anyone else.'

'I'll take a team to the civilians,' the Red Coat says, selecting a few others and heading away into the night. 'C'mon folks.'

'I'll get everyone back to The Main Hall and tell them what's going on,' Elder One says. 'C'mon you lot. Let's get to work.'

They all turn and leave.

All but Cass, Winder, Loom and Chilli. When the last back has turned, when only my friends remain, I can't hold it together any longer. I crumple to the floor and let myself feel the remainder of this physical pain. My muscles and skin are melding back together and the pain is easing. But it's still beyond anything I've experienced before. If I was human, it would have made me blackout. Apparently, I don't do that now. So I have to feel it.

'Are you alright?' Cass asks, kneeling down beside Winder. 'You're healing quick but your face was a right mess before. I can see it pulling itself back together. Does it hurt a lot?'

'I feel it all. Every injury,' I groan. 'Every break. Every cut.'

'Bloody hell...' Winder gasps. 'How are you conscious?'

'I'm not even sure I can be knocked out. I mean, you can't knock out a Class Two or Three.' I take a deep breath. 'I'll be fine. I just need a minute to let it heal.'

'Can we do anything?' Winder asks. 'I feel a bit useless.'

'Just, stay clear. Don't let my blood touch you. But, I do have good news. The Commander had been infected for five years. So I shouldn't turn on you all anytime soon.'

'That's something. Here,' Cass hands me back my sword which I gave Owl. 'I get the feeling you're gonna need this.'

CHAPTER SIXTEEN

There's pandemonium inside The Academy when we arrive. The hole where the revolving door used to be has been covered by a large sheet of thick and heavy wood. A group of the young cadets who are in the early years of their training are being herded into the lobby looking a mixture of scared, confused, and angry that they're not being allowed to fight. They're instead being ordered upstairs out of the way. Flash is on a stretcher being carried up the stairs. He's trying to get himself up so he can help, but Chilli reminds him that his face is so swollen, he can't bloody see!

Inside the Main Hall, the older cadets as well as the graduated soldiers, are in the middle of some kind of argument. Hundreds of voices all yell over each other as they try to be heard.

Elder One stands at the head of the room and says loudly, 'If you don't believe us, see for yourself!' He then gestures to me. Every head turns and there are gasps from almost every mouth before it goes eerily silent.

'How do we know she's infected?' someone yells.

I crouch and then push off with all my strength. I leap over the crowd and land beside Elder One with grace. I turn and see them all watching with mouths open. But there's no time for this.

'Noah plans to turn each and every soldier into whatever I am,' I say simply over the silence. 'I'm strong and I'm fast, yes. But I am also dead. Make no mistake. The day will come when I get hungry. The Grey Coats are all infected too and they are coming for all of you. To turn you or to kill you or to steal you away and force you to breed. Those are your only options in his "New world order". I look out at their faces. They're afraid. 'You are all that's left of humanity in this country. Maybe the world. If you don't stand and fight now, right now, everything we spent our lives fighting for will be for nothing! If you want to be turned and be the reason humanity dies, if you want to live under Noah and The Verity laws forever, if you want to live knowing that people are being bred like cattle and eaten alive then leave. Now. Go join Noah. No one will stop you. But if you want to live, if you want to breathe and love and have freedom, a family, hope... If you want to be human and win back our planet then stay and fight. Because the world out there is not dead. It's healing, it's alive and it's so beautiful. I've seen it and we can have it back, I promise you. So, what will it be?' I wait. They wait with me. They watch the people standing with them. Through the silence and anxious glances, no one moves. No one leaves.

'How can we trust you?' someone calls out. 'You're one of them. You're infected.'

'I didn't want this to happen to me. I don't want to be whatever it is that I am. Sky and Noah forced this on me. I pose no threat to you. And I swear, I will give you everything I have left to win for you.'

'And then what?' another demands. 'Like you said, you're gonna get hungry sooner or later. How can we start a fresh new life with an infected-'

'All I ask is for you to trust me long enough to see Noah and the Grey Coats dead. And then I am yours to do with as you please.'

'Well,' a female Black Coat folds her arms across her chest. 'I for one don't want a target living with us. You could turn against us.' There's a lot of agreeing from the crowd. She looks at them and then to me. 'So I'll follow you for now. But only if you give me your word that when this is done, you go quietly.'

'Meaning?' Cass asks from by the door.

'Meaning... Cass,' she replies. 'That if you want us to follow her lead, she has to agree to be put down when it's over.'

'Now hang on a sodding minute!' Elder One exclaims as the crowd agrees with her. But I raise my hand and shake my head.

'When this is done, when we win, all traces of the virus must be destroyed,' I tell her. 'That includes me. I agree to your terms.'

My friends all start yelling and arguing with the others.

Except for Cass who simply watches me with a furrowed brow. He makes no effort to come to my defence.

'It's the only rational thing to do. I'm infectious. I need to go. But after this battle is won. It's agreed,' I call out over the shouting. 'Boys, it's agreed. So, will you fight with me one last time?' I ask them all.

One by one, they rest their hands over their heart. The same gesture as they make at the lashing post. The same when a soldier passes. It's our universal sign for comradery. Respect. I look at the boys who all scowl at me. Slowly, each one does it too. The last one is Cass.

'Err, Scarlett?' calls out Owl who's peering through the window. 'We have company.'

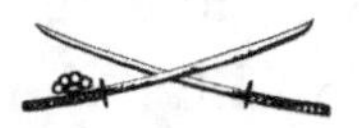

'That's a lot of Grey Coats,' Winder murmurs as he looks out the window beside me.

'They're around the back too,' Bowzer adds, joining us. They're all gathering. Their hoods up. Their weapons out and surrounding us completely.

'Close the doors,' I order. 'Seal the windows.'

Seconds later I hear the doors slam shut but the Grey Coats aren't making any effort at all to get in. They're just... waiting.

'Owl. Get as many archers as you can upstairs. If they start coming at us, open fire. Headshots only.'

'Got it,' she says, heading into the crowd behind me and taking several archers with her. Bowzer included.

'Are the young cadets up top?'

'Yes. All safe,' Winder reports back.

'Why are they just standing there?' Cass asks, standing beside me and Elder One. 'Why aren't they attacking?'

'Because they don't want to kill us,' Elder tells him. 'They want us turned or in the cages at Noah's human-farm.'

'There must be a hundred out there,' Cass whispers. He looks at me. 'You didn't mean what you said earlier, right? You're not gonna just-'

'Noah's here,' I tell him. The crowd outside parts and allows a Grey Coat through. His hood is up but beside him, skipping and smiling, is Sky. 'That traitorous little cow.'

Noah lowers his hood. His hair and eyes match mine.

'He's turned himself.'

'ELDER EIGHT...' Noah calls. 'SCARLETT. I REQUIRE A WORD WITH YOU.'

'Don't you dare,' Elder One warns.

'I'm dead,' I scoff. 'Not brain-dead. I ain't going out there.'

Noah waits and is met with nothing but silence.

'ONE MINUTE. THAT'S ALL I'M ASKING FOR. YOU HAVE MY WORD THAT NO HARM WILL COME TO YOU.' Another minute and he's starting to get angry. Sky starts biting her fingernails out of boredom. 'SCARLETT?' he calls out sternly. 'IF YOU DO NOT COME OUT HERE FOR ONE MINUTE OF CIVILISED CONVERSATION, MY MEN WILL COME IN TO FETCH YOU. YOU HAVE THREE SECONDS. ONE,'

'These arseholes like their countdowns,' I groan, straightening myself up and checking my harness is secure.

'You ain't going out there,' Cass laughs angrily. 'He'll kill you.'

'He already has killed me. If I don't make it back in, you know the mission. Destroy the virus. Kill the Grey C-' His fingers wrap tightly around my upper arm as I go to pass him. 'Think of it this way. If he kills me, it will save you a job.' Before he can stop me, I've snatched my arm free, leapt into the air and landed by the door. I walk out into the lobby and the Green Coats standing guard open the doors a fraction. Just big enough for me to fit through. When I'm outside, they're pulled closed with a bang. I'm alone and facing a hundred plus Class One zombies, Noah and that bitch, Sky.

She goes to follow as Noah heads to meet me but he orders her to stay put. With a pout, she does. Without a flicker of nerves, I stride down the stairs to meet him and he heads to meet me with just as much ease as he would when we were on one of his *"dates"*.

He stops at the base of the steps and watches me walk down them. As my foot reaches the bottom he sighs with contentment.

'You look beautiful,' he says, reaching out and twirling my ashen hair around his finger. 'I'm sorry I wasn't there to help you turn.' His eyes drift down and his thumb traces the edge of my lower lip.

'I suggest you remove your hand,' I tell him, looking unblinking into his eyes. 'Before I bite it off. Cos ya know, I do that now.'

Slowly, he retracts his hand and gives a small laugh. 'You most certainly do. It feels great, right? Being strong and powerful?'

'Oh yeah. Being dead is awesome. My favourite thing is smelling their fear.' I nod behind me.

'It's making me ravenous,' he smirks. 'Good job my men and I have the very best self-control.'

'I can hear some of your monsters licking their lips. It's disgusting.'

'It's an unfortunate side effect, yes. But they have their orders. No one is to be harmed. Unless...'

'Unless what? What do you want, Noah?'

'The same thing I've always wanted.'

I hear the door open behind me. He looks over my shoulder and his smile disappears. A look of hatred replaces it.

'Everything alright, my love?' Cass asks. I hear the smugness in his voice.

'All good,' I reply, ignoring the hole that swells in the place my heart should be beating. I know he only said that to annoy him. 'Noah's just getting to the point. So, what do you want?'

He drags his eyes away from Cass and settles them on me instead. 'You're not human anymore. You belong with us. With me.'

'I'll never be one of you.'

'I heard them,' he says darkly. 'They plan to execute you and you still stand with them? Fight with them?' he demands.

'Absolutely.'

'You agreed with me. For years we talked about my plans and you agreed that the way forward was with a strong army. With one clear, simple objective. To take back our country. To-'

'I'm gonna stop you there,' I tell him. 'Ya know, when we first met, you had such a vision. Such a beautiful, awe-inspiring vision. And I believed you. It's one of the main reasons I ever let you get as close to me as you did. In all other respects, you're a bit mad. The religious crap and such... I tolerated because of your vision, your drive, your goal, it was brilliant.'

'I have a plan that will-'

'You want to turn your chosen few into hybrid zombies while farming or eating the rest you deem unworthy. I know your plan and that's not a world I want to live in. And it's not what anyone in there wants either. Hence why they've boarded themselves inside. So why don't you take your freaks, turn around, and leave The Haven willingly? Before we tear you all limb from limb and burn your pieces along with all the other zombies we've spent our entire lives killing.'

'*You* are the future,' he says, jabbing me in the chest with his finger. 'Those people hiding in there? They have the potential to be great. To be perfection. With you by my side, we could rule a new breed of humanity. Ones that can't be killed. Ones that-'

I start to laugh. I giggle like a fool and shake my head.

'What's so funny?' he asks angrily.

'You.' I shrug, wiping a tear from my eye as I try to stop my hysteria. 'You are hilarious. The people in that building behind me have trained their whole life to kill what you made me into. Their dream isn't to live like this.'

'How can you not see how we are superior? We don't need to kill to survive,' he tells me, hoping that this will change my mind. 'We feel emotions. We can make love. We-'

'Can we have kids?'

'Well... no.'

'Will you free those you have taken?'

'I can't. I need to grow our numbers-'

'Can you assure me, without any doubt, that not a single one of these "superior" monsters won't lose control of their urges and eat someone?'

Silence.

'No. Because I know that they already have.'

'Mistakes happen.'

'So you turn us all into this. And then what? We just wander the earth? Remain in The Haven? What?'

'We live!'

'By your rules, right? They want love and family and hope. Things you and your rules have denied them for fifty years. They want you and your rules gone. They want to live, Noah. They want to be human.'

'You will live as royalty with me. You will want for nothing. I will worship you as the goddess I know you are. I love you, Scarlett. We're destined to be together. To rule together.'

I take a step closer to him. Our noses are almost touching. 'You're the reason my father and my sister are dead. I owe you pain, Noah. The only thing I'm destined for is being the one who kills you and your freaks. I'm destined to break Sky's neck and tear her head from her shoulders for betraying us. I'm destined to wipe every last bit of you and your memory from this world and I will do it all for those I love. For the man I love. The only thing you haven't taken from me are my feelings for him.'

'*I* am the man you love.' He points at Cass over my shoulder. 'NOT HIM!'

'Yes. Always him. It always has been and it always will be him. I will choose him, and them, over you any day. Noah, I would choose a steaming pile of shit as a husband over you.'

'What life could you ever hope to have with a human.'

'None. And I accept that. But at least I'll die with love in my heart. And not a speck of it will be for you.'

'This is your last chance,' he snarls, glancing at Cass behind me and removing the last bit of space between us. 'Apologise. Stand by my side. Convince them that my will is the only way forward. I love you. So much it aches. Our time together, you couldn't fake that. Our stolen moments. The way you kissed me.'

'You see that man behind me?' I look over my shoulder to Cass who has his arms folded across his chest and is watching us closely. 'Every time you touched me, I imagined it was him. Every kiss we shared, I thought of his lips.'

'I swear, if you say one more word,' Noah warns. 'I'll-'

'What? Kill me? You did that. Hurt those I love? You did that too. So I'm going to return the favour. I'm going to break your heart. Just like you did to me,' I tell him. 'No one will remember your name. No one will miss you when you're gone. No one will ever choose you. You're pathetic. A loser. A nothing and a nobody. That's your legacy. I'll make sure of it. I'm gonna tear everything you and your family built down to the ground and wipe you and The Verity out completely. That's *my* legacy. And yes, when they're done with me, I'll die. I would rather die than live in a world where Tee and my father are dead. Where I can't kiss the *only* man I love. Where every time I look in the mirror I see nothing but a walking, talking corpse. You turned Titan against us. Drove him mad. I don't know why or how yet, but I know that my father's death was your fault. I know that the hole we fell into was there because you wanted it there. You drove Tee to kill herself. You might as well have slit her wrists yourself-'

'Can you hurry this along?' he sneers. 'I'm getting bored.'

I unsheathe my Katana and drive it through his stomach.

'Still bored?'

He looks into my eyes and then down to where I've stabbed him. He pulls out my sword, wincing slightly as he does, then pulls back his head and slams his face into mine hard. Too hard. I land on my backside and watch as he turns his attention to The Academy and those within it.

'With me, there is no evil to fear. You will live forever. Unchanging. Impervious. I have found the cure. I have found the secret to everlasting life and I offer it to each and every one of you. Join me. Follow me and you will live as if you were divine. You will be blessed.'

That sounded a little convincing. I hope not too convincing.

An arrow shoots over my head and hits him in the shoulder.

'Piss off, you creepy Jesus-wannabe,' Owl calls out. 'We don't want your version of everlasting life and we will never join you, so just sod off!'

So, not too convincing.

He holds up his hand stopping the horde of Grey Coats that were about to charge. As I get to my feet, he pulls out the arrow.

'The people have spoken. They don't want you as their God,' I tell him. 'So just turn around and-'

'I'm going to kill you all,' he spits furiously, his nostrils flaring and eyes bulging. 'Forget you. I'll start over. I'll-'

'You'll fail. You'll die. That's all you'll do, Noah. Like I said... that's your destiny. And personally? I can't wait.'

'You ungrateful whore! I'm so glad I had your father killed. I only wish I was there to have seen it!' He tightens his grip on my sword and lifts it, the blade primed for my neck.

'SCARLETT!' Cass yells as Noah starts bringing it down. I duck and slam my fist hard into his chest, sending him flying backwards and crashing into his Grey Coats like a bowling ball hitting skittles. He's lifted to his feet as Cass joins me by my side. The doors behind me open and the Black Coats, Green Coats, Cadets and Elders pile out onto the stairway. They gather around Cass and me with their weapons in their hands and their masks around their faces. Winder, Loom and Chili stand front and centre with me.

A clear line has been drawn.

Us – versus - them.

'You!' he growls at Cass with hatred and anger in equal measure. 'You're the reason she-'

'Oh, just shut up!' Cass snaps. 'She doesn't love you, Noah. We don't want you here. And we won't take your answer to everlasting life.' He takes my hand in his, gripping it tightly. 'We will never let you win.'

'You think you have it all figured out. You have no idea. But you will.' Noah pulls out a black box and speaks into it. 'We're going to plan B. Repeat. Plan B.'

'Confirmed, my Lord,' A crackling voice replies. 'Now?'

'Now,' he agrees.

'What's plan B?' I ask.

But he simply grins, takes Sky by the hand, and turns to leave. A large portion of the Grey Coats follow him. But many stay behind and they have their sights on us.

'KEEP THEM BUSY!' Noah orders, raising my katana. 'Thanks for the keepsake, Cadet. It will give me something to remember you by.'

He disappears through the crowd.

'Death or glory,' Winder says, gripping his axe tightly as the Grey Coats ready themselves.

'Their death,' Cass adds, pulling out his haladie daggers.

'Our glory,' I reply, pulling out my last katana. 'I love you guys.' I give a final look to Cass. 'Very much.'

'Let's do this.'

CHAPTER SEVENTEEN

The remaining Grey coats start running at us and we run to meet them. It's two waves of steel and brute force colliding with each other.

We outnumber them.

But they're stronger and much harder to kill.

I swing my sword wildly. I leap from Grey Coat to Grey Coat, cutting and hacking as I go. Arrows fly down from above. The sound of screaming and shouting fill the air. The clang of metal on metal. The sound of the dying. The killing. The fear and the anger. It's deafening. I finish off a Grey Coat who was already on his knees and steal his sword. It's a heavy thing. Made with no skill whatsoever. But with two blades, I'm twice the killer. I look around me. I see them falling. See them dying. Our people and Noah's. I look to the doors and spot Melody on the floor. A Grey Coat towering over her. She plunges her sword upwards through his stomach. But it's not enough. I pick up an abandoned dagger from the ground and toss it at him. It lands in his neck, distracting him long enough for me to get to him. As I pull him off her, she retracts her sword and readies it for a fatal blow.

'Stop!' I order.

'You're a traitor!' she hisses. 'You protect them!' She raises her sword again, but this time to me.

'How about you stop trying to kill me and hold down his leg!' I bark back as I throw him to the floor. 'NOW! HACK IT OFF!'

She looks uncertain.

'We need to know what Plan B is! Cut it off!'

She does as she's told.

He lets out a furious roar as she brings down her blade, but it's barely audible over the din of the fight. I start dragging him away. A trail of his blood following us.

'Need a hand?' Cass asks, appearing by my side. 'Get back to the fight, Melody. We got this.' He takes an arm and pulls as she nods and runs off.

We take the Grey Coat round the back of the Academy and I use my stolen sword to pin him to the ground through his gut.

'Hurts, don't it?' I sneer.

Cass pulls down the Grey Coat's hood. Looking up at us, with deathly white skin and ice-blue eyes, is a man I recognise.

'Elder Two. Fancy seeing you here. This is the git that was happy to marry me to Noah while I was unconscious,' I tell Cass, who glowers at him with dark eyes before twisting the blade still embedded in his belly.

Elder Two goes to pull out the sword.

'If you try and pull that out,' Cass warns. 'I'll cut your hands off.'

'So, what's Plan B?' I ask. He doesn't reply. Cass twists the blade. 'I'll take you apart piece by piece, Elder. Tell us. What's Plan B?'

'The boat,' he says, not looking away from the blade. 'The boat's plan B.'

'What boat?'

'Noah's got a boat a few miles out. A boat full of Class Two and Threes. Plan B is for when it's clear the military population won't turn willingly. He's going to seal you all in the Haven then dock the boat on the beach by his house. He plans to unload the targets and wait for them to kill you or turn you. And when the civilians are in danger, he and his Grey Coats will step in and put every last one of you down.'

Well, that wasn't too difficult to get him to talk. Pathetic little coward.

'How many are on the boat?' I demand.

'T-t-thousand or so.'

'A thousand?' I gasp, shaking my head.

'They'll destroy us, and the civilians will think Noah's the hero because he'll save them all,' Cass mutters.

'And that's okay with you?' I ask appalled. 'Everything Noah's doing? You're okay with it?'

'I just want to live!' he says, as if that's some kind of justification. 'It's not too late. Join him! It's the logical thing to do. It's the only way we all survive!'

'How long till the boat docks?'

'If I tell you, will you let me live?'

I nod.

'It won't be long. Any minute. When the warning siren goes off it means the boat's here. We were told that when we hear the siren, we're to go to the wall and wait for the cargo to do what needs to be done, and then we intervene before they reach the civilians.'

'The wall? Where specifically.'

'Grey Coats will be posted at the mile markers to make sure no one escapes. But the majority of them, Noah included, will be at the gate. Now, please, let me up.' I shake my head. 'But... you promised! I can help you.'

'We all have our parts to play in this fight. Mine will end soon. And so will Noah's. But yours ends here. There's nothing else for you to help us with.'

'Please don't kill me,' he whispers terrified as a tear slides down his face. 'I'll join you. I'll do anything you ask. I'm sorry. I just... I don't want to die.'

'I know,' I tell him. 'Neither did I.' I pull out my sword and drive it through his skull.

He's beyond villainous.

He's cowardly.

And cowards can't be trusted.

As I stand, I reach out to pull Cass to his feet.

'Scarlett... I can talk to the others. I can try and change their minds about you.'

'I don't want you to.' I grasp both my swords and turn away. 'We need to stop that boat.' I walk past him and back towards the fight. 'It'll dock down by Noah's house. It's the only spot with a jetty and no one is watching it. We can try and sink it before it docks. C'MON!'

He follows me without another word.

As we rejoin the others, a loud and long siren bellows through the air. It's the warning alarm signaling a breach. In a swift move, the Grey Coats turn and flee towards the wall, just as Elder two said they would.

'We're too late. It's here,' I breathe. As the siren fades, I'm left looking at several dead soldiers on the floor and maybe five dead Grey Coats. Winder catches sight of us and heads over.

'What the hell's going on?'

Others turn to us too. We all try our best not to let the death of so many of our friends get to us. Not now. We know that we will get a chance to mourn. Or perhaps even join them in their endless sleep. But now is not the time to dwell.

We're soldiers first. Everything else second.

'We need to get to the beach. To the jetty. Noah's brought a boat full of targets in to dock there,' I tell them. 'He plans to set them loose. To wipe us out so he can swoop in and save the civilians. They will be locked up in the town hall by now.' I turn to Cass. 'Get the young cadets that are on the top floor of the Academy and any of the injured to them. Take Loom, Winder and Chilli too.'

'I'm not taking anyone anywhere. Someone else can. I'm staying to fight,' he argues.

'Damn straight!' Chilli demands. 'We ain't leaving you!'

'We need as many people as possible at the beach. But we need a team to help protect those who can't protect themselves in case we don't succeed. Get the vulnerable together and keep them safe. Make sure they know that Noah and the Grey Coats are not to be trusted. You tell them all what he's done. And if we fail, if there is no other choice, you leave the Haven. Take the tunnel behind Elder HQ and run.'

'We're good fighters! We're better off with you at the beach!' Loom argues.

'You're the best fighters which is why you need to protect the ones who need it. Now stop arguing with me and go! The rest of you, grab your horses and head to the beach. Kill anything in Grey and anything that bites.' They all turn and make for the stables, masks up and weapons drawn. As I turn, Cass grabs my arm and pulls me back. Behind him, the others watch us.

'I know why you're doing this.'

'Let me go.' I snatch back my arm. 'I gave you all orders. Move!' I turn, and head to the beach.

'You're going to die, Scarlett!' he calls after me. I stop and turn as he looks at me lost and defeated. 'Either by Noah's hand... or your own. You've given up. I can see you have. You want to die, don't you?'

'I already-'

'Stop saying that!' he snaps. 'Stop! You're not dead! You're right here!'

I walk towards him. All around us, soldiers rush around, paying no attention to us.

'I am dead, Cass. I've got nothing else to live for. But I have everything to die for.'

'I'm not leaving you!'

'I won't let you watch me die, Cass. Not again.'

He takes hold of my hands and steps closer, resting his forehead on mine. 'I- I don't want you to go,' he admits tearfully.

'You don't have a choice. Be happy. Just do that for me, okay?' I lean up and kiss the top of his head before stepping back and looking at each of them one last time. My friends. My family. 'Good luck.'

I turn and run towards the beach, leaving them behind.

'About bloody time!' Elder One bellows over the sound of screeching and hacking as he brings his sword down on the head of a Class Three. 'Get to it! These things aren't gonna kill themselves!'

The beach is a full-blown warzone. There are hundreds of Class Ones and Twos on the sand and hundreds of soldiers fighting them off with extreme skill and determination. At the end of the long jetty is a large boat with streams of dead clambering off, attracted to us by the bleeding and the noise. Class Twos leap over their slower counterparts and toss them out of the way as they charge towards us. All the emotions of the living has me clutching my belly. It suddenly feels like I haven't eaten in weeks.

'Get it under control,' I warn myself under my breath. 'I do not eat people!'

I spot Owl with her bow and run to her, killing and stabbing as I go. My arms move so fast, they're a blur. A Class Two leaps on her and she stabs it repeatedly in the head with a dagger she pulls out of her boot. I drag it off and get her swiftly to her feet.

'Get your archers on higher ground,' I order. 'You're no good down here!'

'We won't be able to tell the targets from humans.' She looks over my shoulder and readies her bow as I raise my sword. She lets loose an arrow and I drive the tip of my blade through a Class

Three's jaw before retrieving her arrow from the forehead of a Class Three behind me and handing it back.

'Then get them to the side of the fight and target the ones still coming off the boat. Focus your fire on them. We'll deal with the ones on the beach.' I grab a Brown Coat cadet as Owl runs off. 'Get a team together. You're on arrow reclaim. Make sure Owl and her archers don't run out. Got it?'

She nods and runs off, calling various names and being followed by several others as she goes.

I turn my weapons to the targets around me, cutting down anything that gets in reach. That's when I catch sight of Noah's house in the background, half a mile from the beach and surrounded by high walls.

I get an idea.

'BOWZER?' I shout. 'HAS ANYONE SEEN BOWZER?'

'He's over there!' shouts back a Green Coat who points to the water's edge before swiftly turning back to decapitate her Class Three.

I run to him. Swinging my sword at everything I can as I pass. I don't stop, just kill and run. Kill and run, until I reach him.

'Bowzer. Just the man.'

He wipes his forehead and lowers his mask when he sees me. He's out of breath and covered in dead-blood.

'What's up?' he pants.

'I wondered if perhaps you still had some of the explosives you enjoyed playing with so much when you were a Black Coat?'

'How did you know-'

'Do you have some?!'

'Yeah. Yeah, of course,' he shrugs. 'Unless it's gonna get me in trouble then no. No, I don't.'

'I got a job for ya. I want you to use everything ya got.'

'I mean... I have a lot! Are you sure-'

'Positive. You up for it?'

He grins at me. 'Oh yeah. What do you have in mind?'

'Something big.' I grin.

Owl and her team have taken a position to the west and are raining down arrow after arrow on the jetty.

And it's working.

The flow of incoming targets is slowing right down. A team of cadets, yet to graduate Brown Coats, are sprinting back and forth making sure they don't run out of arrows. Everyone else is just fighting with everything they have. Myself included. When I hear a familiar yell, I stop dead in my tracks and scour the area.

'ELDER ONE? WHERE ARE YOU?' I shout in a panic. I hear him yell again by the water's edge. He's fighting off two Class Twos. And he's not winning. 'ELDER ONE! I'M COMING!'

I won't lose anyone else. I won't! He takes down one with a deadly blow but he's exhausted and falls to his knees breathless. A Class Three staggers in front of me, its arms reaching out for the Green Coat to my left. He doesn't see it. I stop to drive the tip of my blade through its skull and carry on to Elder One who's forcing himself back to his feet. He barely has the strength to lift his sword. The Class Two is stalking towards him, it's mouth open and teeth chomping. An arrow lands in the sand behind him. Owl's trying to stop it but she's too far away. Elder raises his sword. The Class Two batters it out of his hand and sends Elder to the floor.

'YOU!' I shout at a Red Coat. He turns and sees me sprinting towards him. 'MAKE ME FLY!'

He drops to his knees with his hands cupped in front of him. He grabs my foot and gives me a boost into the air.

I fly.

High and long.

But not far enough. I drop my swords to get rid of some weight. I have to get to Elder One before it's too late. The Class Two is on top of him. Its mouth is wide and an inch from his neck. I land in the sand a few meters away and run to him. And as I reach it, something weird happens.

Something horrifying.

The urge to bite overwhelms me.

Completely!

It's a stronger drive than it was to breathe. I have to bite. My teeth need flesh. My stomach demands it! I roar. I sound like a monster. I feel like one.

'Scarlett! Stop!' Elder gasps as I lean down, my mouth wide and teeth barred, the dark veins tingling as they spread across my skin.

I wrap my arm around the Class Twos throat, pull it off him, and sink my teeth into its neck. My teeth pierce its rotted flesh and blood fills my mouth. The putrid liquid is as foul-tasting as it is smelling. It burns my tongue and makes me gag. I let go and drop it to the floor, spitting out its flesh and coagulated blood from my mouth. It falls from my mouth in a thick, dripping mess.

Elder looks up at me with revulsion.

'Did you just try and eat a zombie?' he asks quietly. 'Why?'

'I err... I dunno,' I reply, touching my lips with the tips of my fingers.

'You bit it?! Why the hell did you bite it?'

'It was just instinct. I had to bite it. My body just reacted.'

His brow furrows and he leans forward with curiosity. 'What was it like?'

'It was by far the most disgusting thing I've ever tasted in my entire life.' I grimace as I wipe my mouth with my sleeve, snapping out of the extreme confusion of my body's reaction. 'Eurghhh. Goddamn, bloody hell, Jesus almighty and holy Christ! That was gross!'

'Wasn't that great to watch either, if I'm honest.' He sneers as I pull him to his feet.

We both realise that the Class Two is still on the floor. It's not Dead. But it's not getting back up either. It's writhing and hurling its limbs around like it's having some kind of fit. It starts screeching like a wounded animal and judders like my dad did after he was bitten.

'What's it doing?' Elder One asks.

'I have no idea,' I reply, urging him back and standing between them.

It suddenly stops, snaps its head up and stares straight at me. Its eyes have gone bloodshot. It's foaming at the mouth and looks rabid. Even more than usual. It launches itself at us. I throw Elder One out the way but needlessly so as it jumps over our heads and grabs a Class Three instead.

And then it bites it before moving on to another Class Three. It grabs its arm and bites down on its shoulder, tearing its limb off completely. Then it leaves and jumps on a Class Two. It actually hurls a Green Coat out of the way to reach it and sinks its teeth into the Class Two's cheek. I watch as it seems compelled to bite! Just like I was a moment ago. It needs to! The bitten Class Two hurls it off and roars at it, but then starts to judder and screech itself. Its eyes start to turn red. The Class Threes too. All the ones that have been bitten roll around, twitching and spasming. Then they get up with red eyes and start attacking anything that moves that isn't human.

'They're not going for us!' Elder One says excitedly, whacking my arm and grinning. 'Look! It's like we're not even here!'

'Why?'

'Because you *are* a weapon! They did figure out the Class One Serum all those years ago. The virus Sky injected you with? It's made you their downfall! Look at what your bite has done! They're killing each other.' He gives me a shove. 'What the hell are you waiting for? Get in there! Get biting!'

'Eurgh,' I groan. 'But it's so gross.'

'Suck it up, Elder Eight,' he laughs, watching with joy as our enemies devour each other. 'Off you go.'

'Fine. Get everyone off the beach.'

I leap in and sink my teeth into as many as possible. I bite and move on. Bite and move on. I pull them away from soldiers and chomp while ordering the survivors to get away from the beach. They watch in stunned silence as I roar and snarl and tear at the dead. And soon, I can't see any without red eyes. After washing my mouth out with sea water, I head up to the others who watch in silence as the targets literally tear each other apart. The effect of my bite travels along the jetty and spreads into the boat. All we hear from the shore is screeching and the shredding of flesh.

'You infected them,' Elder says in a stunned whisper. With curious eyes, he looks me up and down. 'All those years ago they tried to make a creature that would kill the targets and they did it! It's gonna clear the beach in a matter of minutes.' He hands me my katana. 'Perhaps your bite will do something as wonderful to the Grey Coats up by the wall. Let's go.'

'Sir, you can't. You're done.'

'Humph. Done indeed.'

'You're tired,' I say firmly. 'Help gather the wounded and get them to the town hall where Cass and the others are. Protect the civilians. I'll head to the wall and see what my bite will do to the Grey Coats.'

'Not alone you won't,' a Red Coat says, coming to join us. 'The Black, Red and Green Coats will come and help you take out the Grey Coats up at the wall. The Cadets will go to the town hall with Elder One and help keep them secure.'

'See?' I smile at Elder. 'I have all the help I need. Go. We've got this.' I turn, but he wraps his fingers around my wrist. I look back at him.

'My name's Lisper,' he says as the others head off to prepare for another fight.

'Lisper?' I laugh.

'Yeah. Your father christened me with that name.'

'He did?' I ask, my smile slipping a little as I think of him. 'Why?'

'I lost my two front teeth cos of him back when we were kids. He punched me so hard they flew right out. He had to help me glue them back in. I couldn't say my S's or T's for months. I deserved it though. I teased him for how red he would go every time he spoke to this young girl cadet. Your mum. I understand that you share that very same trait. He said you would go crimson whenever Cass spoke to you as a young one.' He laughs before pulling me into a hug. 'He was so proud of you. You know that, right?'

'I know.' I sigh, patting his shoulder. 'I was proud of him too.'

He lets me go.

'What was his name?' I ask. 'My dad?'

'We called him Bash. Shortened from bashful, on account of the blushing.'

We have a gentle chuckle at that before I take a step back.

'See ya around, Lisper.'

'I hope so, Scarlett.'

'Oh, by the way. I'd get away from this beach if I were you.' I nod towards Noah's house. 'Bowzer's setting up a show. Probably best not to hang around.'

'Oh, bloody hell. Not that little pyromaniac,' he grumbles. 'RIGHT! EVERYONE, AWAY FROM THE BEACH. BROWN COATS, WITH ME. THE REST OF YOU, WITH ELDER EIGHT.'

I turn and face the gathering masses. Owl jogs up to me with her archers.

'We're heading to the wall,' I tell them. 'We need to get rid of the remaining Grey Coats. They're stationed all along the wall so no one can get out. In the centre, by the gate, is Noah. Here's the plan. We're gonna split up. One team will head west, to the first mile marker.' I point behind me to the back end of the wall. 'Another to the second. Another to the third and so on. Those who fight with a blade will climb the wall. Archers will stay on the ground. As the blades make their way along the top of the wall, archers will unleash arrows from below. Your job is to kill all the Grey Coats guarding the wall. I've been told there are Grey Coats at each marker. I want you to stop, one marker before you get to Noah. Understand? That's five markers to clear. After, you climb down and meet up. Head to the main gate on the ground. That's where we'll make our final stand.'

They all nod in agreement.

'Great. Owl, you and your team are with me. Red Coat?'

'Yeah,' he replies.

'You take the rest. We'll take East of the gate. You take the West.'

'What?' he scoffs. 'You're gonna go up the wall alone?'

'Yep. Owl, you'll need horses to keep up with me.'

'Sure thing, Scar.'

Where the stone wall meets the water, I say goodbye to Owl and her archers. I scramble up the wall like a spider. I'm not tired. I don't feel any physical pain at the moment. I just keep going. My feet hit the top of the wall, I pull on my own mask with the samurai face painted onto it and leave Tee's dangling around my neck before I start to run. The tail of my coat flaps behind me. My Nike kicks make me silent. I know that down below, hidden behind the trees, Owl and the others are following me. And soon, I smell blood. Human blood, and there's a lot of it.

I'm approaching the twelfth mile marker.

In the distance, I see two figures.

Grey Coats.

So much for their self-control. They're on their knees eating!

I crouch low and grip my sword. They hear me and turn. The one nearest to me draws his sword and gets to his feet. At the same time, a shower of arrows rains down on his comrade from below. He's hit by at least eight arrows, most of which find the upper part of his body. Two find his head and he slumps to the floor. The second Grey Coat doesn't get a chance to register where the arrows came from before I attack. I lift my right katana. He goes to block, not seeing that behind me I'm holding the sword I stole from the Grey Coat earlier. As our steel meets, I drive the hidden blade up through his jaw, the thick tip pokes out through the hood of his coat. When I pull it out, he slumps to the ground and I carry on to the eleventh mile marker.

I come to another dead Green Coat and two Grey Coats standing sentry. Another shower of arrows fall before I get there. The Grey Coats fall so I keep going. After a couple of minutes, I see a solitary Grey Coat peering over the edge of the wall. He's between the mile markers so I imagine there's another somewhere further down the line. I hold up my hand to those below, signaling them not to fire. The Grey Coat lifts his head just in time for me to body slam him down onto the ground and pull back his hood. I bite his neck. His blood spills into my mouth and tastes awful. Not as bad as the Class Two but still pretty damn terrible.

'Ahhh!' He head-butts me off and grabs at his neck to look at the blood. 'What the hell, man! You bit me? What's wrong with you?!'

I wait. But nothing. No signs that my bite affects him the same way it affects Class Ones or Twos whatsoever.

Damn.

He opens his mouth, ready to yell. I snap his neck and drive my sword through his temple before returning to my feet and running on. As expected, at the mile marker, another Grey Coat is standing guard. This one sees me coming. He pulls out an axe and charges. He's so fast, the arrows from below miss him.

I don't slow.

I go faster and just before we meet, I jump up onto the ridge of the wall, push off and somersault over him. My feet land before he can turn to face me and I drive my sword through his spine making his limbs fall limp.

He drops to the floor with me. I keep my blade firmly between his spine, making sure he can't move or heal.

He's paralysed.

'How many more of you are up here?' I ask in a whisper.

'Screw you.'

'Fine.' I take my other sword and rest it between his legs. 'You think it will grow back if I cut it off?'

'You wouldn't dare.'

'Try me.'

After giving him a few seconds to argue internally with himself, he begrudgingly tells me, 'Two at every mile marker. The rest are at the gate with Lord Sands.'

'Cool. Thanks.' I pull out the sword from his spine and drive it through his temple before getting back on my feet and running to the next marker.

Two more till we regroup.

I run at the two Grey Coats standing guard. They spot the arrows from Owl and her team below and duck down.

Not a single hit.

Bugger.

One has a club covered in spikes. The other, a bow. He kneels and starts firing arrows as the one with a club steams forwards.

He swings.

I duck, skidding across the floor on my leg beneath his heavy-swiping arm before hacking at his ankles. He's quick and jumps up, making me miss. The Grey Coat with the bow sends an arrow into my shoulder. Another catches my neck as I dodge out of the way. The club-man wraps his hands around my throat and squeezes. With his free hand, he grabs my wrist and snaps it back, breaking it so badly my bones poke through the skin, forcing me to drop my sword. I can't even yell he's got such a tight grip on my throat. From below, someone releases an arrow which lands slap bang in his temple.

With friends like these...

He lets me go and as he falls, I snap my wrist back, holding in the agony I want to scream out. I then turn to the archer who has an arrow aimed at my head. He's still ducked down and is out of sight of Owl and her team.

'You won't win against me,' I tell him. 'Not with a bow.'

'No. But I can kill your friends before I die.' He suddenly stands and turns his weapon down below before letting his arrow fly. I hear a yell from someone below as he readies another. He releases it as I charge. I hear another yell. He's hit two and just keeps reloading. He fires five arrows before I get to him. He doesn't even try to defend himself as I cut off his head. I grab the rope and quickly slide down to the ground before running to Owl and her team.

I can smell blood.

When I find them, they're all off their horses and gathered around three others. Two are dead. A third has an arrow embedded in her chest.

Owl.

She's still alive. Still conscious. But she's bleeding and wheezing. I kneel beside her and take a look, careful not to touch her or get too close as I'm covered in blood myself and don't want to infect her.

'It's punctured her lung. I can hear it. Get her back to the town hall as quickly as you can,' I order. 'They'll look after her there.' I show her a forced, *it's gonna be okay,* smile. 'You did good and you're gonna be fine.' I sure hope I ain't lying.

'Good luck, Scar,' she rasps. 'I'm rooting for ya.'

'I'll take her,' a guy states, getting to his feet and climbing onto his horse. The remaining three gently help her, careful not to move her too much. Once secured, they head back into town. The remaining Green Coats look to me for the next set of instructions.

'Last one,' I sigh, looking back up at the wall. My wrist is still threading itself back together and when I can move my fingers again, I look at them all in turn. 'Ready?'

'Ready,' they reply, climbing back onto their horses and readying their bows. They're even more pissed now they've lost people.

I take a deep breath and run back to the wall.

Once back up top, I sprint. I put everything I have into it. The worry I have for Owl. The heartbreak of knowing I'll never see my family again. The loss of Tee and my dad. And the fear that I'm going to let them all down and not be able to kill Noah. I'm reminded of when I used to run up here before I left. Every time it got too much, I'd just run and run till my legs couldn't carry me anymore. But now, I don't think I tire. I could run forever. With everything that's crushing me right now, I think I would.

The next marker's in sight. They see me coming long before I get there. One turns and runs away. Towards the gate. He sprints as fast as his little legs will carry him. To tell Noah I'm here. The team below start firing but he's too fast.

The second one comes at me with an axe.

He swings. I lunge back and watch the blade glide half an inch above me before I spring back upright. He brings it back down. I block it with my Katana and swipe at his gut with my left. He jumps back and I miss. His forehead smashes into my face, breaking my nose. As I stagger back, dazed and bloody, I see him raise his axe high above his head. My foot slams hard into his chest. I feel his ribs splinter as he stumbles back. I swipe at him with my left. He jumps back and I miss. I swipe with my right. Bastard dodges. He spins his weapon and jabs the end of the handle into my already broken nose. I fall back, coughing on my own blood. As I blink it out of my eyes, I watch him raise his axe once more, high above his head, and with a roar he brings it down. I ram my foot between his legs and he loses momentum. I grab his axe, pull, and as he tumbles down on top of me. I roll so I'm on top of him.

And then I bring his own weapon down on his skull.

I fall off him and pull down my mask. With my fingers, I feel the mess that was once my nose. With a low, pain-filled grunt, I straighten it out and give it a second to fix itself before heading to the rope. I sheathe my swords and slide down. But I should have made sure the coast was clear before I revealed myself. At least twenty Grey Coats are riding along the base of the wall on horseback and they're coming straight for me. I look into the trees. The archers linger. I hold out my hand and subtly gesture for them to leave. They hesitate but do as I have instructed and take off at a gallop. If I run away, the Grey Coats will follow me. I can't risk them going anywhere near the others. So, I just stand here and wait for them to reach me. Besides, there's only one other place I plan on going now. I watch for arrows. None come. I guess they don't want me dead just yet. They surround me completely creating a circular formation. Their swords, axes, hammers, daggers, every kind of weapon I could ever imagine, are all pointed straight at me.

A Grey Coat climbs down from her horse and saunters towards me. I know who it is even though the hood is up. No one else wears skirts on a battlefield.

'Sky...' I greet her.

She lowers her hood and beams at me, chewing her lower lip with glee.

'Hey, Scar.'

'Only my friends get to call me that.'

'We're certainly not friends. Not after all you have done to my God.' She giggles and bounces up and down on the balls of her feet. 'He wants to see you. I'm to take you to him now. I was so hoping that it would work out but I guess he'll have to find a new bride.' She swishes her hair over her shoulder. 'I'll make sure he's a very happy and satisfied husband. Much more than he could have ever been with you.'

'Two psychos perfectly matched.'

She smirks, chewing her lip. 'So, what *should* I call you now we're not friends?'

'You? You can call me the Devil,' I reply. Her smile turns to a sneer. 'Cos I'm the reason your God is gonna die.'

CHAPTER EIGHTEEN

With my hands tied behind my back, I'm taken to the gate.
It's swarming with Grey Coats. They all watch me as I pass.
So many of them. It's a sea of icy blue eyes and stark white hair.
They no longer have their hoods up as they no longer need to hide
their true appearance. They watch with smug smirks as I pass.
Both proud and delighted that I have been caught.

When we get to the base of the gate, I'm taken to the one and
only staircase the wall has. The steps are carved into the wall itself.
They're steep, so steep, you can barely fit the balls of your feet on
each one. It leads up to the mechanism that opens the gate.

'Up you come!' Sky orders as she starts climbing. 'Best not to
keep him waiting.'

I head up, followed closely by three others. She keeps talking.
On and on. She hasn't shut up the whole ride back.

'I don't know why you're all fighting this.' She shrugs and lets
out a long breath. 'It's inevitable that we're gonna win. We already
have. We won as soon as we became the strongest army in the
world.'

'Noah-'

'Lord Sands. Or God,' she barks back angrily. 'Have some respect.'

'I'm not calling a man who has had his tongue in my ear "God",' I scoff. 'He's not a God. There is no such thing. Everyone, including him, knows that, you crazy little psycho.'

'He's given birth to a new race. He's a God alright.' She glares back at me over her shoulder as we continue climbing the narrow stone steps.

'He's a vindictive, pathetic, egocentric psychopath. He will turn on anyone if it suits him. No matter how loyal they've been to him. He's nothing more than a tyrant.'

'Nothing you say will ever make me doubt him. My faith is unshakable.'

'Not trying to make you doubt him,' I reply. 'I just want you to know that when you realise that you're doomed and when you look to me for help, I'm gonna show you exactly how much of a vindictive psychopath *I* can be.' She reaches the top of the stairs and turns to look down at me. Her eyes are furrowed and there's a hateful grimace on her face. I simply smile sweetly up at her.

'I'm gonna enjoy watching what comes next,' she snipes.

'I'm gonna enjoy killing the pair of you slowly,' I reply.

'Now, now, ladies,' comes a familiar voice. 'Let's not fight. This is a most wondrous day after all.'

I'm shoved from behind and forced to carry on up the stairs. As I reach the top, there he is. The man himself, with his sword at his hip, one hand in his long black leather jacket pocket and my katana in his other. A self-assured grin is plastered across his face and he sighs happily when he sees me.

'Today is the very first day of our *"New world order".* It is a day of celebration and joy. Not catty outbursts and threats.'

'Today is the day you die,' I correct him, stopping a few feet from him with Sky's hand gripping my arm.

'I am very glad that you are still alive, Cadet.'

'Shame I can't say the same about you, psycho,' I reply. He just watches me. His eyes boring into mine. 'Why am I here? Why not kill me? I'm tied up and outnumbered.'

'I want to talk to you.'

'No.'

'You must see reason-'

'Nope.'

'This is the only-'

'Not. Interested,' I tell him, shaking my head and giving a shrug. 'Just shut up, you self-righteous prick.'

Sky pulls back her fist but Noah orders her to stand down.

'What the hell are *you* gonna do to me, Sky?' I laugh. 'Even when I was human, I could have kicked your ass with my hands tied behind my back. Despite you being a half-breed zombie. You've always been a half-rate fighter. What do you think I'll do to you now?'

'What if I made you a deal?' Noah interrupts before Sky can say a word in retaliation.

'A deal?'

'Look. You rallied them all together. I mean... you failed. The boat docked. They're probably nearly all dead by now.'

He doesn't know about my bite. That's good. He still thinks his plan to kill the defiant soldiers has worked.

'But you still managed to get them on your side even with their prejudices against your condition. You can do that for me. Convince the ones that are left, convince the civilians, that this is the right thing to do. Convince them that my cure *is* a cure.'

'And what do I get in return?' I ask.

'Well, with me you get to live. I won't execute you as they plan on doing. You get to live forever as royalty. You can rule with me. Fifty-fifty. We make all decisions together. I won't do anything you're unhappy with.'

'Anything I'm unhappy with? Like bringing in more infected when we've spent our whole life risking everything trying to kill them all?'

'It's complicated-'

'How about stealing babies and turning them into soldiers?'

'Ruling means making tough choices-'

'Or the new system of human farming? You gonna stop that?'

His steely silence tells me that no... he won't.

'Everything I have done has been for the greater good.'

'Like sabotaging the Canary missions?' I hold my head up and look into those cold eyes. 'Or how about killing my father? Was that for the greater good?'

'Technically...' Sky sings. 'I killed your daddy.'

Slowly, I turn and face her as she stands beside me.

'You?'

'Oh my. I've been killing Canaries for years!' she chuckles. 'We couldn't very well let them tell everyone that the country was healing the further north or south you travelled. The people may have started getting ideas!'

'Years?' I repeat.

'Sky was the very first,' Noah says. 'When my father and I found her, she was badly beaten and half-starved to death. Those boys... they did truly terrible things to her out there.' Noah looks at her with disingenuous sympathy. She fails to see he's laughing at her on the inside. 'My father and I were returning from inspecting the discovery of a military base when we came across Sky. Father was curious as to what this *"cure"* he had just found was capable of.' He takes the white strands of her hair in his fingers. 'So he told me to inject her with it. She writhed and juddered. She healed and became strong. But, as we would later discover when my father started experimenting with the serum on others, she hadn't received quite a high enough dose and wasn't entirely turned to her full potential. She is ageing slowly and her strength, although increased, is a fraction of what ours is.' He looks at me. 'Plus, she's still part human. Her heart beats and the targets would devour her just like any other human. There's a very specific quantity that needs to be taken to be perfect. And apparently, injecting an already infected host has certain side effects. The dose Sky here received was too low and so she failed to meet her full potential but you... you are very interesting. You're incredibly strong.'

'I was glad to be the first of your disciples, my Lord,' Sky adds, still looking at him wistfully. 'I am happy to serve, even as an inferior subject.'

He chuckles to himself at her pathetic grovelling before carrying on. 'Father lacked vision. Once he perfected the dose, he wanted to use the serum on only himself so he could live forever as ruler. He then planned on destroying it all. Well... I couldn't have that. It was my turn to rule after all. Besides, many of those who knew of the serum, his closest guards, they knew of its power. They were easy to recruit to my way of thinking once I promised them they would be blessed. They turned on my father and covered for me after I murdered him two years ago. I have been ruling ever since without anyone suspecting a thing.'

'Your father died less than a year ago.'

'I told everyone he died less than a year ago. Everyone believed he was a recluse. No one saw him and no one cared. Only when he was dead could I really get to work. Starting with making sure I didn't lose my flock. Increasing the target population was a necessary evil, it kept you all nice and safe behind the wall. I simply unloaded them nearby and let them find their way towards the only living people for miles. It discouraged those pesky Canary volunteers too. I just sentenced those I didn't want in my new world and sent them out as punishment.' He looks to Sky. 'With my disciple amongst them to ensure that they never returned.'

'The sole survivor... the one Canary that would return and report to Noah... that, was you?'

'Yep,' she says proudly. 'Twenty-two missions so far and I've been the only one to return every single time. Except for yours of course. I had to get you back in one piece, didn't I?'

'You killed all those Canaries?' I fight the urge to throw up as I think of all those who were lost out there, scared, alone, in pain. They trusted her. Hell, I trusted her.

She looks lovingly at Noah. 'Now that our great and wonderful Lord has created the reproduction facility, they no longer need to die. I just lead them there instead. Much less of a waste, breeding them, than simply letting them turn or just killing them.'

Noah reaches out and rests his hand on her cheek. She leans into it with closed eyes, letting out a wanton moan as she nuzzles his palm with her cheek.

'You really threw a spanner into the works by sneaking off and volunteering behind my back,' he adds to me. 'It was only by luck Sky discovered you leaving. She had no choice but to join your mission as a last-minute recruit.'

'I looked for you, my Lord. To tell you that she was leaving!' she insists, her eyes wide and in a panic. 'I tried to find you, I swear-'

'I know. You told me that, many times, and I have forgiven your failure, Sky.' He shows her a fatherly smile but I see annoyance in his eyes before they return to me with a roll. 'She told me how many times she tried to get you to return. But you have always been a stubborn creature, Scarlett. There was only ever going to be one way to bring you home.'

Sky giggles and looks at me as Noah lower his hand from her face.

'I sent a secret second message on one of the birds your daddy sent, telling my Lord of my plan. He sent a team to destroy the floor of the mortuary and placed the targets inside. And then I led you there, pretended to fall in and let nature take its course.'

'I could have been bitten. I could have been killed. There was no guarantee-'

'I had a dose of the serum the whole time,' she shrugs. 'Worst case scenario, I would have injected you. I would then have had to kill Chilli and Loom as well as your daddy, so they couldn't tell anyone, but I knew that if I did that you would never forgive me. But things didn't go according to plan. We hoped to make you believe that the other Elders were behind it all but then you started talking to Elder One behind my back and you discovered we were taking people. But my Lord...' She looks at him again with those puppy dog eyes. 'He never gave up hope that you would see the light. But I don't believe that you ever will.' She glowers at me with a nasty little pout. 'I think you're just a bad person, Scarlett.'

'There's still time for her to see the light, Sky,' Noah raises his brow to me. 'Submit now, beg for my forgiveness and I shall-'

'Listen closely, you piece of shit.' He twitches as I step closer and look him dead in the eye. 'Cos I'm getting sick of repeating myself. The answer is no. No. I don't want you. No. I won't betray them. No. I will never stop until they are safe from you. Even human, you were meaningless to me.'

'Shut up.'

'I would never love such a fool.'

'I'm warning you.'

'And I will never beg for anything from you. Never!'

'Quiet!'

'I will kill you, you pitiful, inadequate, crap kisser, slimy-'

'I SAID SHUT UP!' He thrusts my katana through my gut and pushes it in so the hilt meets my stomach. I gasp and stare at him with my mouth agape. 'Stop talking, Cadet. Stop.'

'Damn...' I groan, looking down at my own weapon currently skewering me. 'That's a sharp blade.'

'It sure is,' he agrees, twisting it making me scream. The Grey Coats step away. A look of utter hatred contorts Noah's otherwise handsome features. 'You think you won't beg?' He twists it again and I screech in agony. 'Beg me to stop,' he sneers. 'Beg me, Scarlett. BEG!'

'Please, Noah!' I sob. 'PLEASE...'

'Go on,' he encourages. 'More. Let me hear you.'

'Please...' I cry. 'Please...'

'Yes?'

I stop my pretend wailing and spit blood in his face. 'Go fuck yourself!'

He slams his fist into my face again and again and again as he bellows furiously.

'You ungrateful-' *Slam.* 'Bitch-' *Slam.*

As he keeps hitting and yelling, I laugh. I make a point of it. Despite the pain.

Wrapping his fingers in my hair, he pulls back my head so I have no choice but to look up at him.

'I'm keeping you. Even if you never see reason. I'm still keeping you and I'll have you in a way Cassius's never did.'

'Oh. He's had me, Noah. In every way a man can have a woman,' I hiss. 'And it was glorious!'

He roars angrily in my face as I continue to smirk. 'Your soldiers have died for *nothing*!'

'Oh yeah?' I wheeze as blood creeps up my throat.

'Yes,' he snarls. 'They had a chance to live forever and instead, they died pointlessly and with no dignity. Much like your daddy.'

He laughs as my face goes hard with hatred.

'I still have my facility up the coast. I have my first batch of children due any day. A whole new generation to mould in my image without any Elders to warp their minds with ideas of free will or individuality. They will grow up stronger and more disciplined than any of you or your friends ever could. They will jump at the chance to be blessed by me. I will have my choice of wife. And all the civilians here? We will farm them too. If they refuse to follow me then they will become cattle. I'm in no rush, Cadet. I have all the time in the world to build my new super-race, now I'm immortal.'

'I wouldn't be too sure about that.'

'Oh no? Tell me, what are *you* going to do to stop me?'

There's an enormous explosion and the wall itself shakes. He looks to the coast, where in the distance, a huge firebomb swirls in the air.

Good job, Bowzer.

'That's what *we're* gonna do to stop you,' I smirk.

'My Lord...' Sky gasps. 'That was your mansion! The bunker! The serum!'

'It sure was. There goes your virus.' I laugh like a maniacal, deranged psycho with blood between my teeth and more dripping down my chin. Behind me, I've been secretly using the blade protruding from my back to cut through the bindings on my hands. He's so shocked by the explosion and the loss of his serum that he doesn't notice.

Below, back on the ground, from behind the tree line, an army... *our* army, emerges. All mounted on their horses, their weapons ready. Hundreds of them. Brown Coats. Green Coats. Red and Black Coats. Elders. Hell, even the civilians have joined them, armed with swords, bats, pitchforks. Anything and everything. Upfront, Cass, Winder, Chilli, Loom and Elder One lead the way.

'How?' Noah mutters, looking below in confusion. 'How are they all still alive?'

Below, the Grey Coats turn to face them, their weapons ready. A solid line of bodies, shoulder to shoulder. They're making an impenetrable wall.

'My Lord,' Sky says, resting her palms on his chest and guiding him away from the edge. 'My Lord, I think it best we leave. You and me. We'll go to the facility and wait for the Grey Coats to dispose of these heathens. You and me.'

Noah glances at me.

She takes his face and guides his focus back to her.

'Forget her. We tried. We tried with everything we had to make her see the light. She is simply too far gone. Forget her.'

Still, despite the anger and hatred coursing through him, he looks longingly at me.

'You gonna run away?' I mock. 'Like the coward we all know you to be? Or are ya gonna actually get your hands dirty for a change?'

He shoves Sky out of the way and takes three purposeful strides towards me, stopping so his face is in mine.

'It doesn't matter how many of you try to stop us. One of us can kill twenty humans with ease.'

'My Lord,' Sky says in a nervous whimper. 'Look!'

She's pointing out beyond the wall. Past the safety of the gates to a large group of people appearing from the distance.

Her eyes widen when she realises. 'My Lord, it's the prisoners from the facility!'

'What?' Noah charges to the other side of the wall and looks for himself. 'That's not possible. That... That's...' Slowly, he looks at me over his shoulder and snarls, 'What did you do?'

'Oh, did I not tell you?' I say happily, my hands now free. 'I let them all go before I left. They said that they were going to burn your torture and rape facility to the ground before coming back here to help us kill you. It's all gone. As well as those monsters in white that ran it.'

He turns just in time to see me pull my katana from my gut.

'The people are free and they're coming for you. Your facility and your serum have been destroyed.' I spin the blade in my hand, point the tip at him and get ready to fight. 'And you're about to join them.'

The horse-mounted army below give an almighty yell as they charge.

In the arms of a Grey Coat is my confiscated back-harness and second katana. Noah snatches it free and gives it a twirl.

'Let's see what you got, Cadet.'

CHAPTER NINETEEN

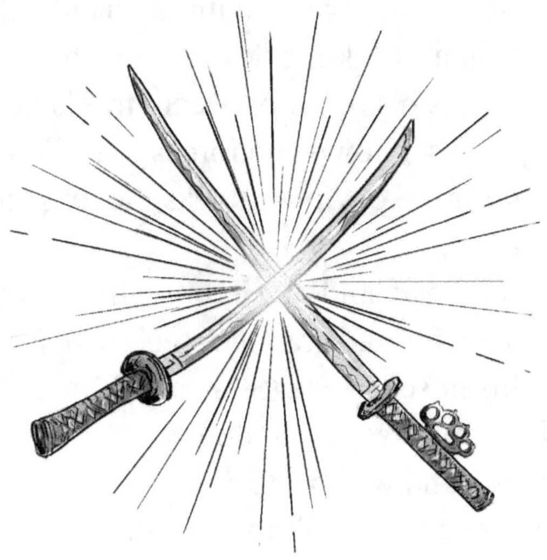

The clang of our metal rings through the air. Never before have my swords been against each other. Not once.

With the two blades crossed above our heads, he looks at me.

'You have never been able to beat me,' he boasts. 'In all those years I spent training you, not once have you bested me.'

'First time for everything.'

'Not today, Cadet.'

'How many times. It's Canary!'

He slams his head into my nose making me stagger back. While I blink blood free from my eyes, he lunges forwards. The tip of his blade aimed for my neck and both hands firmly on his hilt so he has the full force of his body strength behind his attack. I twist my steel around his and divert his strike. As he passes, I spin and we swap places. With his sword high, he attacks anew and we duel high up on the wall, our steel clashing and clanging loudly. He goes low, swiping at my ankles. I leap up and land on the ridge of the wall. He swipes for my knees before I launch myself up and land behind him. I pull my sword back and bring it down to his neck. He turns and blocks me. With his free arm, he knocks my sword away, grabs my wrist and twists. With his hand still gripping my stolen katana, he slams his knuckles into my nose and as my head flies back, he plunges his blade between my clavicle downwards to my ribs. He pushes it down and forces to my knees.

'You always go for the obvious attacks,' he tells me. 'That's why you'll never beat me.'

I point my sword down and ram it through his foot. As he yells, I toss my katana upwards and grab the steel so I can thrust the butt of the hilt into his nose. He staggers back with a bloody, broken nose, pulling his sword free as he does.

I withdraw mine, and we go again.

Our steel moves so fast it's almost a blur.

Finally, the threat the clouds have held breaks and snow starts to fall. It lands on my skin but fails to melt. It falls thick and fast, settling on the ground, making Noah and I slip as we battle. I attack high but he defends with perfection. He attacks low. I dodge and block with skill. And then we both make the exact same move and end up with each other's swords through our sides, right up to the hilt. He looks down at me, trying hard not to show any sign of pain but wincing nonetheless. Same as me.

Below us, the battle rages on. The fire at his home continues to burn and all I can think to say is...

'When you die, I'll never stop smiling.'

'You have something of the devil in you, girl.'

'You're the reason my father is dead. Why Tee took her own life. You've pissed off the Devil and now you're going to pay.'

He laughs a cruel laugh and shakes his head.

'Tee didn't take her own life, Cadet.' He leans in and whispers his next words into my ear and I hear malicious joy drip from every word he utters. 'I killed her. I held her down and carved open her wrists.' He leans back slightly and looks joyfully into my eyes. 'She only wanted to find your scarf so she had something of yours to remember you by.' He leans into my face with a horrid leer. 'She cried like a child as I forced her to watch herself bleed out.'

I feel the black veins spread and adrenaline surge throughout me at force. A savage and fierce urge to kill consumes me as a low guttural growl emanates from my throat. I grip my sword so tightly, I feel the steel warp around my fist. When he laughs, I lose it completely. A demonic, thunderous roar comes from deep within. From my very soul. His amusement slips and he flinches. Below, the crowd has fallen silent as they all look up at me. At the beast high up on the wall whose murderous and otherworldly scream sounds like it just came from the pits of hell.

'What was that,' he whispers. 'What are those lines? What the hell are you?'

I just let out another scream before we both pull back our swords and resume our fight.

I'm angry. Enraged with a murderous hatred that takes control. It spills from my hands straight down to the steel which I bring down over and over, hacking at him as if he were a tree I need to carve to pieces. Our swords clash again and again and he blocks me at every turn.

I'm pushing him back and I see a flicker of worry on his face.

But my rage is making me careless. I know I need to calm myself and focus on each and every blow, but I've lost control. All I can see is Noah murdering my sister!

Below, the fight has resumed. The momentary lapse of focus I caused has passed and they've returned to their battle.

Noah's feet hit the edge of the wall and he stumbles, losing his focus on my blade as he attempts to stop himself from going over the edge. I take my chance, pull back my sword and bring it down on his neck with a scream.

Sky tackles me to the ground from behind with one of her arrows in her hand. My sword skids across the snowy floor just beyond my reach as she flips me on my back. With a leg each side of my waist, she starts stabbing and stabbing, a high-pitched screeching coming from her mouth as she attacks. She doesn't stop and I feel every single blow. My lungs fill with blood. It spews from my mouth and splatters on the white snow around me each time she pulls her weapon free from my flesh, ready to bring it down again. Her hair flies wildly around her as she delivers blow after blow. My organs rip and tear. As soon as they start healing, she creates more.

'YOU'RE NOT WORTHY!' she shrieks. 'YOU HAVE NEVER BEEN WORTHY OF HIS LOVE! NOT LIKE I AM!'

I buck her off me. She rolls away and in a swift move leaps to her feet, placing herself between Noah and me, crouching low like an animal preparing to pounce. I, on the other hand, stagger to my feet grabbing my belly hoping my insides don't spill out on my feet. I feel my slick blood trickle through my fingers and hear it land on the ground with countless little *splats. Splats. Splats.*

I force myself up straight, my left leg suffering some kind of nerve damage which makes it refuse to bend or hold my weight. I groan quietly against the pain and look at the girl I almost died for many times over the past year.

'You won't touch him again,' she states, rolling the arrow threatening between her fingers. 'You're going to die here. But my Lord and me? We have a boat anchored just offshore ready to take us to any country we want. We'll travel the world together. We'll find more humans to breed. To turn. To eat.'

'You have no serum and you're not leaving this wall. You will both die here.'

'You want to kill him? You'll have to kill me first.'

'If you want to go first, that's fine by me!'

My skin seals back together and my leg can once again move. I glance over her shoulder, to Noah who still holds my stolen sword in his hand, and then to my lost katana lying in the snow between us. I lunge for it and get a kick in the face before I can reach it. As

I slide across the deepening snow, Sky snatches my sword up for herself. Quickly, I get back on my feet.

There's an explosion below. Bowzer cheers as he blows a hole in the gate. The soldiers from the facility are storming inside on horseback, their weapons raised and their battle cry echoing off the walls. The Grey Coats are falling one by one. Blood stains the snowy grass and blades are flying through the air with skill and without mercy. As I look down, I see Cass deliver a fatal blow to a girl in grey. He looks up to me, his haladie in hand and an anxious look in his beautiful eyes. He then resumes the fight, giving all he has to every attack.

Noah swallows hard when he sees that he's losing. That he's vastly outnumbered and completely unwanted. A few of the Grey Coats even turn and flee through the blasted-gate only to be showered with a bombardment of arrows from above. Archers have got themselves on the wall, the other side of the gate, and are shooting with skill.

'How...' Noah hisses. 'How have you done all this?'

'You forget,' I tell Noah. 'They were trained by the very best.'

'Why thank you,' he sneers.

'Not you.' I nod below. 'By us. By all of us you stole and forced to fight. By the families they made by choice and not by blood. All this time, this is what we were training for. To kill you and end your tyranny.'

As he opens his mouth to throw back a witty remark. An arrow lands in the head of the Grey Coat beside him, still holding my back harness. He slumps forwards and lands face down, my harness falling from his grip and skidding right back to me. I lean down and slide it on before turning to look at them both.

'I'll be taking my swords back now.'

Sky rushes me. She has my sword in one hand and a blood-soaked arrow in the other. She delivers her blows with force but also with anger. They miss me as I bend, turn, pivot and step around them. We're moving with speed. Faster than any human ever could. She may be a half-breed, but she's got some serious strength. I find myself regretting those swordplay skills I taught her.

I see my chance and take a brief opening, slamming my foot between her legs and as she doubles over, my fist delivers an uppercut to her jaw. She flies upwards into the air so high her feet pass me. With a thud, her spine lands on the very edge of the wall. Her hand grips the edge as she tumbles over. I see her fingers still holding on before her other hand takes hold too.

In my second of lapsed attention, Noah's readied my sword and is thrusting it forward, straight at my head. I fall back and feel the wind of its speed against my skin. As he pulls back, I stand straight.

'Nearly.'

'Just a matter of time, Lover.'

The army has got past the Grey Coats protecting the stone stairs carved into the wall and are making their way up to us. Dozens upon dozens of soldiers storm upwards. The Grey Coats by Noah's side turn and get ready to fight, creating a barrier between the incoming army and their master.

'You've lost,' I tell him. 'You'll never get what you want from us.'

'Not from you. But I will still get what I want. Believe me. My new world order will come to fruition, Cadet.' He wraps his hand around the back of my neck, pulls me in and lands me with a possessive kiss.

He slams me down onto the ground, raises my sword and brings the blade down on my neck.

With a yell, he's body-slammed by a blur. He and his attacker fall to the floor and in the surprise, Noah has dropped my sword. I snatch it up, my fingers sliding between the knuckle dusters perfectly, and get to my feet. Cass is hammering down punch after punch on Noah.

'GET THE FUCK OFF MY GIRL, NOAH!' Cass bellows furious-ly.

Sky has pulled herself back up on the wall and is running to Noah's aid. I'm on my feet and sprinting towards them too. Cass pulls out his haladie and raises it high. Sky reaches them and rests her hands on Cass's head, ready to snap his neck. I leap and land behind her, taking a fistful of her hair in my hand and tossing her away. She soars through the air, screaming furiously as she flies. Noah takes Cass by the scruff of his collar and pulls him down so he can thrust his forehead into his face. The hard knock from the inhuman monster dazes him. Noah goes to finish what Sky started and reaches out for Cass's head, to snap his neck as easy as snapping a twig. I throw Cass off Noah and slide him across the snowy ground towards the rest of our allies all busy fighting Grey Coats.

I turn to see Noah back on his feet, a murderous glint in his lifeless eyes as he looks at Cass.

The compulsion within Noah to stay and kill his competition tries desperately to win over his survival instinct. His death is coming. It's feet away. The army is hacking through the Grey Coats and getting closer. Cass has returned to his feet and stares back at Noah in equal malice.

Behind Cass, Sky is back up and borderline rabid. She goes for Cass who turns to face her. She has no weapon. Cass has both of his and they start their battle.

'RUN, MY LORD!' Sky hollers as she attempts to reach Cass through his deadly attacks. 'I WILL KILL HIM IN YOUR NAME. RUN! GET TO THE BOAT. I WILL MEET YOU THERE!'

Behind me, Noah has turned and started to flee.

'GO!' Cass yells at me. 'KILL HIM, SCARLETT! I'VE GOT THIS ONE. END IT!' He slams his foot into Sky's ribs sending her backwards onto the ground. He looks to me. 'And then you come back to me. You hear me? You come back to me alive.'

'I love you,' I tell him, backing up.

'I love you too,' he replies with a loving smile. A genuine smile with genuine devotion. The same as he held when I was alive. 'Go. I'll see you after we win.'

I turn and give chase.

Noah runs fast. The snow falls harder and harder. It's turned into a whiteout. It gets more difficult to see the wall's edges as the thick blanket of white gets deeper with every passing moment. I follow his tracks which pass one mile marker and then another and another. The sound of the battle starts to fade and the lapping of waves come into range.

Noah suddenly emerges from the thick snowfall and runs straight at me with my stolen sword over his shoulder. His eyes are on me like a hunter stalking its prey as he launches himself towards me. I stop his blade with my own and once again my swords are crashing into each other. The twangs of the steel echo around us again and again as we battle. Our feet slip in the snow as we both attack and defend against each other's immense skill. There's no yelling from him. Nor from me. We're focused, knowing that this is it. This is the fight where only one of us will walk away. As he spins, his coat whips behind him with a whoosh. My sword hisses as it cuts through the air. Snow crunches beneath our feet and the waves continue to break on the beach just up ahead as our steel meets over and over. He manages to backhand me across the face. I stumble and almost go over the edge of the wall. Below, fifty feet down, a group of targets have gathered, drawn to the noise and the smell of the battle. The scent of blood lingers in the air from our many fallen. Like me, they can smell it. The emotions spewing from the pores of the humans are drawing them in. The fear. The grief. The anger. It makes my stomach clench and my mouth salivate. The targets groan, gurgling their putrid bile as they sniff the air and feel that same hunger.

But I've been hungry my whole life. Not a day has passed when I have felt a full belly. I can control this. I'm not like them! I flick my head back and see Noah drawing back my stolen sword, ready to deliver a final and deadly blow. I'm not like him either. He has abandoned his followers. Left them to die for his cause while he flees like a coward to another shore.

Unlike him, I'm ready to die to save the people I love.

I'm ready to die to stop him!

He grabs my ankle and flips me off my feet. I land face down before spinning around. He drives my sword forwards, straight between my eyes. I drop my katana and slam my hands together, grabbing the blade in my palms before thrusting it backwards, driving the hilt into his nose. He staggers back, swearing and cursing me to hell. I'm back on my feet, sword in hand. Each blow I deliver drives him back as he tries to blink through the blood to see where I'm going to attack next. I kick him in the chest. His rib cage splinters and he staggers back further. His feet meet the edge of the wall and his footing fumbles. He's forced to drop the sword as his arms start circling wildly either side of him in a bid to regain his balance and not fall the fifty feet below. I raise my sword over my shoulder and prime it for a fatal blow.

Something rolls towards me through the snow and lands by my foot. A smell accompanies it that stops me dead in my tracks as I do a double-take.

Cass's haladie lies by my feet. His blood is soaking one of the blades. Slowly, I lift my gaze and find Sky standing there watching me with a smug smirk. Her face is bloody. She's a little out of breath and her clothing is torn from multiple cuts. But she stands confident as she gestures to the double-bladed dagger.

'He put up a good fight,' she says, cocking her head and swishing her hair over her shoulder. 'That man of yours... he *was* a challenge. I can see why you liked him. Feisty and rough.' She chews her lips and raises her eyebrows suggestively before shrugging. 'He still died like a dog though. Whimpering and whining.' She takes a purposeful stride towards me. Her eyes going darker. 'Bleeding and choking as his insides spewed outside.' Another step closer. 'His eyes all wide and bulging as he scrambled away, desperately trying to keep his guts from slipping between his fingers.'

'Y-you're lying...' My words come out in barely a whisper.

'It made me think of the time you and I caught those fish in that lake? When I gutted them before turning them into dinner? Remember that?'

Her cruel chuckle echoes all around me as I stand in stunned silence, looking at the red covered snow and the dagger dripping in Cass's blood, an unbearable lump growing in my throat.

'No...' I shake my head and try to get my scrambled mess of thoughts in order. 'No...'

Tears blur my vision. I feel dizzy. My limbs become lead.

'He c-can't be...'

Everything slows down. My sword slips between my fingers and lands with a dull thud in the snow beside me.

Slowly, painfully, I lean down and pick up his haladie. His blood is still warm and a painful groan forces its way up my throat. The groan carries on, turning into a pain-filled whine. I hold the dagger with the utmost care and land on my knees, shaking as grief swamps me.

Sky takes her chance to rush to Noah's aid. She has his face in her hands and looks up at him like a love-struck fool, caressing his cheek and beaming at finding him still alive. He bats her away, disinterested in anything but watching my pain and suffering.

I peer up through my lashes at them as they turn to face me. I can't stop the whine I'm producing. With no need to breathe, it just carries on and on. But seeing their smug faces. Seeing them look down at me with superiority and self-satisfaction, the whine turns to a growl. I grip the haladie in my hands, slicing open my palms, mixing my blood with his. Adrenaline surges once more. The black veins tingle as they spread. I feel them invade my eyes and my vision changes. It becomes sharper. Narrower. I see through the snow. Hell, I see the snow! Each flake as it falls to earth with a dance of grace and beauty.

But there is no beauty in the world any more. Everything I found beautiful is gone.

Because of them.

No dad.

No Tee.

No Cass.

No humanity.

No friends.

No place in the army.

I have nothing.

Because of them.

The growl turns to a roar. The same demonic roar that exploded from my soul when Noah told me he murdered my sister. Tears stream endlessly down my face and I shake with all the emotion consuming me. Their eyes widen and they flinch at the sheer volume of it.

I push myself with a leap high into the air. They watch me as I disappear into the heavy snowfall above.

'Where did she go?' Sky asks after a few seconds. 'Did you see that? She just flew-'

I land directly in front of her as silent as a mouse and as graceful as any of these falling snowflakes. In her eyes, I see my face reflected. The dark veins spread outwards from my eyes and mouth. As her eyes widen I see that the whites of mine are black.

My sights are set on nothing and no one but Sky. The bitch that murdered my father and the man I love. The heartless monster that spied on me, made me love her and trust her, only to turn me into a dead creature and then went on to destroy everything I ever cared about.

I drive the haladie into her gut so hard, my fist disappears inside her belly. Her mouth opens in a hollow O. I stare coldly into her horror-stricken face as I pull it back out. Then, with a spin and a low blow, I slice through her legs at the knees as far as the dagger will allow, turning her legs into something resembling a half chopped-down tree. I push her over the edge of the wall without a word. Her scream fades as she falls before it ends with a heavy thud on the ground.

But she's still alive.

She can't move. She's bleeding immensely. I can smell it. Not quite human but certainly not dead.

And I'm not the only one that catches the aroma.

The Class Threes that have gathered at the wall head straight for her.

'God...' she gurgles from down below, clutching her belly with one hand whilst using the other to drag herself away. Her two stumps spew copious amounts of blood creating a trail behind her. 'Save me! SAVE ME, LORD!'

The first Class Three sinks its teeth into her skin. The sound of tearing flesh and then chewing reaches my ears from all the way up here. Her desperate screams reach even further as she continues pleading for Noah to save her from being devoured alive. Their bites won't turn her into a target, as she's already infected with some form of the virus. Her body heals too, like mine does. So her death will not be fast. Nor will it be pleasant.

Good.

Numbly, I turn my head and face Noah. He's uneasy, watching me with uncertainty as to what the hell I'm capable of doing next. A silent tear slides down my cheek as I turn the rest of my body to face him. My fingers flex around the bloodied handle of my lost-lover's weapon and I lower my head, never letting my eyes leave Noah for a second. He's got both my swords in his hands.

'You won't defeat me,' he says. 'Not with that little dagger of yours.'

When the sound of the soldiers charging towards us reach our ears, his eyes flick briefly over my shoulder and his uncertainty increases. Below, Sky still screams and wails. The smell of her blood fills my nostrils and forces its way down my throat.

I take a step closer.

He takes one back.

'If you stay here, they will execute you,' he tells me, his hand fidgeting with the handle of my sword and his eyes glancing repeatedly over my shoulder. 'If we fight, we will both die here. Leaving is our only choice. Come with me! I have a boat ready.' He glances past my shoulder. 'They're getting closer. Scarlett! See reason! We're all that's left! If we stay and cross blades, we will both die here. Don't you see that?'

'You're right,' I tell him, relaxing my grip on Cass's haladie as my arms hang loose at my sides. The adrenaline fades as quickly as it came. The veins sink back beneath my skin and my body feels heavy and tired for the first time since I died. 'You're absolutely right, Noah. Staying means death. For both of us.' Below, Sky's cries have grown weaker. A minute or two and they will fall silent forever. I peer over the edge and see her surrounded and almost devoured completely. But her head remains undamaged and still attached so she's still awake and feeling it all. 'And I know that I will not defeat you with a blade.' I lift my head and we meet each other's gaze once more. 'But you're not leaving here. You're not running away. You don't get to live, Noah. Because we're already dead.'

'You'll have to catch me first, Cadet.'

He turns on his heel and sprints away from me and towards the ocean. I give chase, knowing that if he reaches the water's edge, we will never stop him. He will win. I know too, that if I fight him he may very well win. He may cut me down and leave my hacked-up corpse behind as he leaves these shores. Or the soldiers giving chase may catch us mid-fight and attempt to help. They will be killed. I see only one way.

I want... only one way.

I stretch out my fingers and take hold of the back of his coat. With a yank, I pull him back and wrap my arms around his waist, pinning myself to his chest. As I do, he plunges my sword upwards through my abdomen.

'I call that move the Titan special.' He twists the blade and I grunt against the pain, refusing to let out any further sign of the agony he's inflicting. 'I told you. You won't win against me, Cadet.'

'No. But they will.' I look past him to the soldiers heading our way. 'And I told ya, it's Canary.'

And then, I lunge backwards off the wall.

Taking him right along with me.

CHAPTER TWENTY

As I fall, it all seems to go in slow motion.

It feels like forever.

I look up at the sky and think of those I love. Of those I've lost. At least I'll be with them soon. Tee. Cass. Dad.

I hear Noah yell as we fall. His arms and legs flail violently as we plummet. The fury on his face brings a satisfied smile to my lips. I let the fall happen. Not that I could stop it even if I wanted to. He reaches out, clawing at nothing, desperately attempting to manoeuvre his body into a position that will mean less damage when he lands. Because he will land. His body will break. It will need time to mend. It may only be moments until it does but the soldiers will reach us by then and they will have him.

I close my eyes, feeling the wind whistle through my fingers and the snow chase me to the ground.

I'm coming, guys.

I'm coming.

Thud!

I feel my whole-body shatter.

Every bone.

Every organ.

I splutter blood into my mouth and blink up at the sky.

The sword Noah ran me through with has shifted, severing my spine completely.

As I lay on my back unable to move, my bones and organs start putting themselves slowly back together. I'm motionless. Submerged in pain.

Do you think that it's on fire?

Is what on fire?

The sky. And that it's ash falling?

I look up at the sky now and see it just as I did then. Delicate flakes of frozen water, each one unique, so my father used to say. Not a single one the same. They land on my skin slowly and so full of grace. They fall on my eyelashes and my lips.

Why must you look at something so beautiful and see only ash, Scarlett?

It looks like ash.

Only when it's falling. Look at it on the ground. It's beautiful. It reminds me of you.

Me?

Yeah. From far away, it can look scary. But close up, it's soft. Gentle. One of a kind.

I hear Cass's voice speak the words he said to me so many years ago as we laid together in the first flurry we ever experienced. Seven years old. Blisters on our hands from training. Black eyes and swollen bruises. Cuts that needed to be sewn back together and muscles that ached so bad we could barely walk. We laid, side by side on the beach, listening to the waves and letting the snow soothe our aches and slow down our swelling. I hear the waves now, lapping at the shore, just as I did back then.

On the day I realised I was in love with Cass.

A low, angry growl sounds beside me. Painfully and with extreme effort, I turn my head and see Noah forcing himself up. His right arm moves first as the rest of him lays face down. He lifts it high, snapping and twisting his mangled limb, realigning the bones that shattered. Then, his left arm. He grunts as he twists it and circles his wrist.

Snap. Crack. Click.

He slams his palms down flat and pushes his torso off the ground, whipping his head back and forcing his spine into a straight line. With a hideous grinding noise, he turns to face me, the bones in his neck creaking and breaking.

His focus and his wrath are on me completely.

I look at the sword protruding from my stomach. The blade is wedged in my spine and although my body is putting itself back together, it can't fix itself through the steel. I can't move. My fingers barely twitch.

Noah gets to his feet. His body is still a mangled mess. His legs are bent the wrong way. His arms are twisted and bones protrude through his flesh. His jaw hangs loose, the only thing keeping it from falling to the floor is his skin. He shakes his head, snapping it back into place with a loud click before rolling his head slowly in a circle. He lifts his dark and angry eyes and heads my way. His left leg drags behind him. Blood drips into the snow. His arms sway limply by his side and each step seems like agony.

He stops, standing over me with a sneer as I lay at his feet.

'You're gonna die knowing that everyone you ever loved is dead and that I'm the reason why.'

'As long as you die too, I don't care how I leave this world,' I reply with a smile.

The thunder of hooves is close. Very close.

'No way you get yourself back together quick enough to make it to the beach, Noah. Let alone swim to the boat you have moored offshore. They'll catch you. They'll tear you apart. They'll win.'

He sighs, looking out to the water. He barely keeps himself up as he staggers and stumbles on his mangled legs. He laughs and shakes his head before looking back down to me.

'You're right of course. I've lost. My serum is gone. My Grey Coats are dead. My facility is rubble and now, thanks to you, I can't even be a coward and run to save my own skin.' He looks at his body, weakly throwing his hands in the air and laughing to himself. 'But I tell you what. In *our* battle? Yours and mine? I've won.'

'In your dreams.'

'What hurts more, Cadet? The fact that all your friends died because of you? Because they got in the way of my pursuit of you? Or that you're about to die at my hand?'

He falls to his knees, sighing at the relief of not having to hold his weight any longer and gently, he brushes my hair from my bloody face. He leans down, his nose resting against mine as he lands a soft kiss on my lips. He reads me. Searching my eyes and seeing all my suffering. His fingers wrap around the hilt of the sword buried inside me.

'I've murdered all the people you have ever loved.' *Twist.* 'You friends.' *Twist.* 'Your sister.' *Twist.* 'Your daddy.' *Twist.* 'Your lover.' He twists it once more and I reach a point of pain my body just can't seem to process. I can't scream anymore. I can't move. I can't fight.

I don't want to.

I'm done.

My part in this fight has ended. He's been defeated. I have no army to belong to. No family left alive. No friends to see past my condition.

No Cass. No Tee. No dad.

I have nothing left. I lay as still as a marble statue and look into his malevolent eyes. The world around me falls silent. It fades away. And all that's left is us.

'I've even taken away your humanity,' he says. 'What have you got left... hmm?'

'Nothing,' I whisper. 'I have nothing left. But neither do you.' I look past him and back into the sky. I watch the snow fall in a flurry and find it beautiful. 'Kill me. I'm already dead anyway and I know that in less than a minute, the soldiers will be here and you will be dead too. I can die happily knowing that you have failed.'

He takes out the sword from my body and digs the tip of the blade into the frozen ground so he can use it to push himself up. He raises my katana high above his head.

'Goodbye, Cadet. I'll see you in hell.'

'I'll save you a seat.'

I close my eyes as he brings down the blade.

A high-pitched shriek rings through the air. It's so loud and filled with such rage I open my eyes and see Noah looking into the distance, the blade still coming down but his eyes wide in shock.

Slam.

He's attacked by a creature who claws and bites at him with a frenzy unlike anything I have ever seen. It's biting and scratching as it goes at his neck like a raving hell-beast. He tries to buck it off but it's too fierce. Too feral and savage. He falls back and tries to stop it tearing at his neck. His blood sprays everywhere and his screams are filled with terror as its teeth sink into his throat. His legs kick out. His body judders. And with the sound of one final rip, he falls still and silent.

His attacker stands and drops his severed head to the floor before slamming her boot down on his skull over and over, crushing it underfoot. She turns to me and kneels by my head, taking my face in her hands. Her long white hair falls over her face as she smiles the sweetest smile I have ever seen. Even with those vivid blue eyes and blood covering the lower half of her face, she looks angelic.

'Fancy that. Someone saving your arse for a change,' she chuckles.

I burst into tears of joy. 'Tee?'

CHAPTER TWENTY-ONE

Tee sits me up. I slump into her body and we embrace. I don't care how much every bit of movement hurts. I need to hold her. I need to make sure she's really here. We cling to each other just so relieved and happy that we can. My body's stitching itself back together. The clicking and grinding makes me twitch and groan. She just holds me as I go through it. Comforting me with her words.

'I've got you. It's okay. You're okay.'

I start to cry. My face is buried in her neck and I just cry like a heartbroken child.

'I'm sorry,' I whisper through my despair. 'I'm so sorry.'

'What for?' she asks, trying to lift my head. But I won't move.

'You're dead. Everyone's dead.'

'I'm not dead. Look at me! Scarlett, we're not dead!' I lift my head and meet her smile. 'I mean, we died. But we're still alive. Or you wouldn't be crying and I wouldn't have just literally torn a man's head off to save you, would I?'

'But... Cass...'

'What about him?' She shrugs, looking over my shoulder. 'He looks like hell, but he's okay!'

I turn and see several others making their way quickly towards us on horseback. Cass and Winder up front.

'He's alive?'

They all stop several feet away and Cass leaps off his horse before sprinting towards me. His hand clutches his side and there's blood seeping between his fingers. Tee gets to her feet and steps aside, letting him fall to the floor beside me and take me in his arms.

'I knew you'd be okay,' he says, burying his face in my hair and letting out a long sigh of relief. 'I knew it.'

I still can't believe it. I lift my arms and wrap them around his waist, scared that he'll fade into smoke and I'll realise that this was all a dream. But he's solid. I hold him tight and feel his heartbeat through his chest. 'Loosen your grip a tad, would ya?' he wheezes, chuckling as he leans back to see my face. 'You look like hell, baby.'

'Funny. I think I'm in heaven,' I whisper, looking at him stunned. 'Sky told me you were dead. She had your haladie. She... she...'

'The bitch stabbed me and took off with it.' He looks down and shows me the hole in his side. 'I'll be alright. It's not fatal.'

But it is! I scramble away from him shaking my head.

'I'm bleeding! Stay away, Cass. You could get infected!'

'Bloody hell!' Winder breathes, making his way towards us. His eyes glued to Tee and a look of disbelief on his face. 'You're... you're... alive?'

'In a manner of speaking,' she shrugs, a cheeky smile on her lips.

He rushes to her and pulls her into his chest.

'I thought I was never going to see you again,' he cries.

Cass attempts to help me to my feet but I refuse to let him get too close. As the other soldiers hang back, Cass and I step closer to Tee and Winder.

'She's dead,' Cass says. 'Like you, Scarlett.'

'I prefer respiratory challenged,' Tee grins, lifting her head from Winder's chest and looking up at us. '*Not* dead.'

'H-how?' Cass stammers, reaching out and stroking her white hair.

'Well, I went to the cottage to get Scarlett's mask. I just...' Her face falls as grief fills her eyes. 'After losing her like that, I needed something of hers with me. I just... I wasn't ready to lose her completely.'

I reach out and take her hand.

'Noah came to the cottage and grabbed me. He forced some kind of liquid into my mouth. I don't know what it was but I couldn't move. He dragged me upstairs and the last thing I remember is him putting me in the bathroom and cutting me!' She holds out her wrists that have no hint to the gashes he carved into her. With a look of disgust, she glances at Noah's body. 'Bloody prick. Anyway, I woke up like, ten minutes ago, with white hair and no pulse! I ran outside and I mean... I ran. Like super-fast. I bumped into Owl who had an arrow in her chest!' She looks at us all with wide eyes. 'A bloody arrow! Anyway, she filled me in on what was going on so I ran to help.'

'Was that you?' Cass asks, pointing in the direction they all just came from. 'We saw something shoot past us in almost a blur. Was that you?'

She nods, he mischievous grin growing. 'Cool, huh? Well, I saw Noah about to hack Scar's head off and I just lost it! It was like this undeniable urge just consumed me and I just attacked!'

'She tore his head off,' I correct her. 'Literally. With her teeth.'

Cass laughs a short sharp laugh, his mouth slack in awe.

'Scar gave you mouth to mouth for so long, she must have infected you. I'm so glad you're back,' Cass says, pulling her into an embrace. 'I can't believe you're both here.'

'Yeah, yeah,' Elder One bellows at us as he steps out from behind the rest of the soldiers. Cass lets her go and we all turn to face him. 'All very touching. But we have several injured that need tending to and a town to check for any stray targets or Grey Coats.' He points to Tee and me. 'You two, we need to talk.'

'About what?' Cass asks, standing between us protectively.

'Small matter of what comes next,' Elder says. 'C'mon, girls.'

'You can't let them do this to them,' Cass insists. 'We would have died without Scarlett, and Tee just killed Noah! They've earned their right to live. You can't let them execute them. You can't.'

'Execute?' Tee asks with a nervous laugh. 'We're being executed? Why? What did we do?'

Winder joins Cass as a human barrier. 'You ain't taking them,' he says sternly. 'No way. You'll have to kill us too. You're not taking them from us.'

Tee looks at me. 'What the hell is happening?'

'Winder? Cass? Take Tee. There's a boat moored just offshore ready to leave. Take her and go. Run-'

Elder One looks past them to me with his eyebrows raised.

'No need for that, Scarlett.'

'I was the one who made the deal, Elder,' I plead. 'Can you leave Tee out of it? I'll honour my word and you can execute me but she doesn't deserve to die! Let them go. They'll never return-'

'Over my dead body!' Cass warns, his fists clenched and shaking by his sides. 'You kill her, you better kill me too cos I swear, you'll regret it if you don't.'

Tee takes hold of my wrist and steps close, pressing her body into mine.

The soldiers behind Elder One withdraw their weapons. Archers aim their arrows.

'Oh for goodness sake,' Elder One groans. 'No one is being executed, alright? I think we've had enough death for a hundred lifetimes.' He points to Tee and me. 'I've got a job for ya. C'mon, girls. You're being reassigned. Follow me. And Cass?' He turns his finger to him instead. 'Get stitched up before ya bleed to death, would ya?' With that, he turns and walks back through the crowd of soldiers.

Cass turns to face me and I rest my palm against his cheek. He leans into my touch.

'I'll come with you. I'll–'

'You're going to go and get sewn up. He's right. You won't last long if you don't get that bleeding under control.'

He nods and steps closer, his hand still resting over mine.

'Just... don't go anywhere, okay?' he says. 'I keep finding you and then losing you. It's not fair.'

'Oh, Cass. You always had me,' I correct him. 'And you always will. Even if we do get separated. I'll always be your girl.' I stand on tiptoes and kiss his forehead. 'I love you.'

'C'mon!' Elder bellows. 'I ain't got all bloody day.'

I take Tee's hand and together, we follow Elder One.

CHAPTER TWENTY-TWO

My feet dangle over the edge of the wall and as the sun starts to set, I watch as the gathered Class Two and Threes finish devouring each other in the snow. Below, several soldiers are busy barricading the hole caused by Bowzer's explosives. Tee's holding my hand and sitting beside me, her feet swaying back and forth.

'So... that was gross, right?' she asks. I see her attempt to sound cheerful. To put on a smile. But I know inside she's just as miserable as I am. 'Biting the targets tasted disgusting. Do you think that the Grey Coats knew that our bite makes them crazy and turn on each other?'

I shrug. 'Maybe. Who knows. Good job it does or we'd both be dead... er.'

'I don't think we would,' she says. 'They wouldn't turn on us like that.'

'Humph. Kinda feels like they have.' I take the flask of water and wash my mouth out for the hundredth time, spitting the clear water over the side of the wall and over the remainder of the targets below. I don't want a single trace of their blood in my mouth. I know it's all gone but it keeps me busy I suppose.

'It makes sense. Their decision. You know it does,' she says with a squeeze of my hand.

I sigh, returning her affectionate grip. 'At least we won't be completely alone.'

'Yeah, we'll have each other,' she sighs. 'It'll be… fun.' She looks out at the setting sun, keeping the sadness in her eyes out of my view.

'I'm sorry.' I shift and face her. 'Do you wish that I hadn't tried to save you? That you weren't like this?'

She turns and glares at me. 'No!' she replies indignantly. 'I didn't want to die.'

'But what about Winder? Because I infected you, you could be just as contagious as I am. You can never kiss him. And we crave people, Tee! We're cannibals.'

'We're not them, Scar!' She points below. 'We have something called self-control and a soul. Being hungry is nothing new to either one of us and with our new job, we'll be far away from people anyway so their emotions won't give us the munchies.' I give a little laugh as she shrugs. 'The whole contagious thing sucks. And yeah, not being able to be with Winder sucks big time. The same with you and Cass. But we're alive. I thought we'd left you to be eaten alive and you thought I'd killed myself out of guilt. We're still here and our enemies are gone. Well…' She looks below. 'Some of them at least. We have each other and now we have a super important job to do. I see this as a gift.'

'A gift?' I scoff.

'Yeah. Look at what we can do!' She gestures once more below. 'We bit two targets half an hour ago. Their eyes went red and they turned on each other. Whatever we infected them with has spread. There were more than fifty and now look at them! They've almost destroyed each other.'

I peer down. She's right. There's three left. One has its lower half missing and is currently eating the remains of its own leg as another two lay beside each other eating. Each other!

Gross.

'Our bite turns them against each other and stops them craving human flesh. And then their bite passes the same effect along. Think of how many targets we can destroy by biting just a few.' She beams at me, proud of her new role in the war. 'I know there are like... seventy million or something. I know that it will take time to get them all but this is a good thing, Scar! Finally, humanity has a real weapon they can use against the targets.' She gestures between us. 'We're gonna save the world, Scar. You and me.'

From behind us, someone clears their throat. We turn to see Cass standing at the top of the stairs. He's not wearing his leather coat, but a black hoodie and pair of jeans instead. His hand holds his side and I smell the blood slowly seeping through his bandage. The snowfall has eased and is landing in his hair. His breath is thick in the air and he shivers a little against the cold.

It's all... very human.

Tee jumps down and pecks my cheek.

'I'll go and start packing,' she says.

'Okay.'

As she walks to the stairs, she rests her hand on Cass's arm and he gives her a peck on the cheek as she passes. I turn and get to my feet as he heads over.

I don't know what to say. What to do. I turn and look down at the carnage below and he stops by my side to look too.

'That bite of yours is pretty impressive.'

'Yeah. Suppose.'

'The targets on the beach are all dead. They killed each other.'

'I know. Elder One told me.'

The silence stretches on.

'When do you leave?' he asks finally.

'Tomorrow morning,' I reply. 'We've got one more night then we have to go. We're not even allowed to stay for the funerals of the fallen. It will take days to get them all ready and Elder won't let Tee and I stay that long.' That cuts pretty deep. Despite the rationality of Elder One's order, it still feels beyond shitty.

'I guess, with everyone so sad and their emotions so heightened, it's not particularly safe for you to stick around,' he adds. 'I understand that.'

'Feeling hunger for them as they mourn is about as inhumane as you can get,' I grumble, filling with shame and disgust. 'But he's letting me lay Dad to rest before I go. So that's... something. I guess.'

'How long will you be gone?' he asks, changing the subject as my eyes start to brim with tears.

'A couple of years. Probably more,' I sigh, wiping my eyes dry before the tears spill down my cheeks. 'I'm not really sure. The Elders want us to head to the rainforest dome to clear it and secure it with a wall. After that, we'll come back and escort a team there so they can start building the southern wall.'

'Southern wall?' he asks.

'Yeah. Down south. Land's End they used to call it. We're gonna build a wall right across the country. There's a five-mile stretch of land between St Ives Bay and a town called Marizion. If we build a wall there, it will seal off a good chunk of the country. After that, there's another chunk of land Elder One wants us to clear. And so on and so on. We're building more safe havens. We'll bite as many as we can along the way and in time, the targets should destroy themselves. But there's a hell of a lot of targets and only two of us so it will take years.' I lift my head and look at him sadly. 'Maybe decades.'

'Well, on the bright side, as of this morning there's no more Verity,' he offers. 'No more donation. The kids at the orphanage have been returned to their parents. The young cadets too. Anyone over sixteen can either stay in the army or go home. No more forced service. People can join the army if they want when they turn sixteen. Two years of training and then they can go out in the field. Not sure that's enough training if I'm honest.'

'Tee and I will be doing most of the fighting so they're just building walls and clearing up behind us mostly. Two years is plenty.'

'Your new job beats a death sentence,' he says. I feel him looking at me. His eyes burn into my face and I can't bring myself to look at him. 'Lisper said you wouldn't be allowed to live behind the walls with us after they're built. He says you craving human flesh is too dangerous. That you could lose control and turn on us.'

Now I look at him. 'That and we still don't know how permanent this serum is. I could eat a bird and grow wings or turn into a drooling Class Three.'

'A vegetarian zombie. Who'd have thought?' he laughs softly. 'Well, the Grey Coat Commander was five years old so you'll last that long at least.'

'Are you trying to make me feel better? Because you're really not.'

'I'm just teasing,' he tells me, nudging my shoulder with his. 'Lisper and I think you're different to the other Class Ones. None of the other Grey Coats had your speed or black veiny things. And they weren't contagious so we think you and Tee are something different altogether.'

'You spoke to him about us?'

'We did. We had something we needed to ask him.'

'*We?*' I ask. 'Who's *we?*'

But he simply smiles, avoiding my question. He then faces me and rests his hands on my hips. I sink into his chest. My ear pressing against his heart so I can listen to it thump. I miss my own heartbeat. I never even really noticed that I had one, but now it's gone, my body is so quiet.

'After I watched you ride away from me, the day you left as a Canary, I went to go get my horse to follow you,' he says sadly, his face buried into my hair. 'But Winder stopped me. He told me you'd already gone. That I'd just end up alone and lost. So I went to your room, curled up on your bed and cried harder than I'd ever cried before. I sobbed like a baby. I could hardly breathe.'

'I can't imagine you crying like that.' I hold him a little tighter. 'I'm sorry.'

'Well, up until then, I had no idea just how much I loved you. I couldn't face the idea of not seeing you every single day. Of not knowing if you were alive or dead. Of imagining you hurt and alone out there. And then I got you back only to lose you again. When you got stabbed and lay dying in my arms, I wanted so much to die with you. I was ready to. I would have if Loom hadn't knocked me out.'

I hear the utter conviction in his words. Just as I saw it in his eyes as he held me in his arms, my blood soaking into his skin. He was ready to die with me.

'I just...' He lets out a long breath. 'I didn't see a world worth living in if you weren't living in it with me.' He looks down and lifts my chin with his finger. 'I still don't.'

'You'll be fine,' I tell him. 'You'll find someone else and-'

'I need to confess something to you.'

'Yeah?'

'The letter wasn't the only thing your father left for me after you went with the Canaries.'

He puts his hand in his pocket and pulls out a closed fist. When he opens them, I see two silver rings. One of which holds a sparkling diamond.

'Your parents' wedding bands were in there too,' he tells me. 'And a note that simply said... *"look after each other. Love each other".*'

'Cass...'

'Now, I want to say that I want to look after you. To keep you safe. To protect you from anything that may cause you harm or sadness. But the truth is, you're the one that's kept me safe all these years. You protect me. You protect all of us. I just want to help you. Any way I can. I want to make you happy. I want to love you.' I drag my eyes away from the rings in his hand and meet the steely grey of his eyes. 'I want to marry you.'

'Cass...' I look between him and the rings with an open mouth and a sadness in my heart. 'We can't be together. I can't kiss you or make love to you. I can't give you a family like other girls can. I'm not even allowed to live inside the wall with you.' I close his fist and shake my head. 'I'm sorry. But no. You'd be wasting your life.' I walk past him towards the stairs. If I stay another second, my heart will break even more and I can't bear it.

'I don't want kids,' he says simply. I slow to a stop. 'I don't want a house. I don't want to stay here without you and I definitely don't want to be with someone else. I want us to travel the country and kill targets together. To see new places. I want to eat a banana in a jungle. To watch snow fall on a mountainside. To swim in the ocean. I want to do it all with you.' I turn and he's smiling at me, so sure that he knows what he wants. But he hasn't got a clue. He walks to me. 'I don't want to live a day without you. I want to kiss you. To make love to you. To live with you for as long as I possibly can.' He takes my face in his hands. 'I want you. Always have. Always will.'

Someone clears their throat behind us. 'Ready?' Elder One asks.

'Ready?' I ask desperately. 'I have a couple more hours! I'm not ready to leave yet! Elder... please!'

'You call me Lisper. Hear me? We're basically family.'

'Lisper...' I plead. 'I'm not ready to go yet.'

'I'm not asking if you're ready to leave, you daft mare.' Lisper chuckles, gesturing to us both. 'I'm talking about you two. If you're ready to get married, of course. You didn't turn him down, did you? Cos he was very persistent in getting my approval. Pain in the arse in fact.'

Cass grins excitedly and holds up my mother's wedding ring. 'What do ya say? Be my wife?'

'You can't be serious. What life can you possibly expect to have with me?'

'The one I always wanted. The one we were always destined for. One with adventure and freedom and each other. You always wanted to save the world. So let's go and save it!'

'I married your parents,' Lisper says. 'When Cass asked for my consent on his plan, to have my blessing for him to turn so he could be with you and help with your mission, I insisted I would be the one to marry you.'

'His plan? You want to turn? But... Cass... this is crazy!' But I'm smiling too. I'm laughing as I realise what he's planning to do. 'You'll be dead!'

'I think we've already established... some people are worth dying for. Now stop arguing and come here.'

He takes my hand and we face Lisper.

He clears his throat and begins.

'Do you, Cassius, take Scarlett to be your wedded wife'

'I do,' Cass grins back.

'To live together in marriage? To love her, comfort her, honour and keep her,for better or worse, for richer or poorer, in sickness and... err... in death... ish.'

Cass looks at me with a happy grin. 'I promise to do it all and more.'

'Will you forsake all others and be faithful only to her?'

'She'll kill me if I'm not,' he says with a wink. Then he nods and smiles warmly. 'Of course I will. So long as we both shall live. Or be dead. I dunno. Forever.'

Lisper turns to me. 'And do you, Scarlett-'

'Yes. To all of the above. I do. I do. I do!'

Cass chuckles at my eagerness as he slides my mother's diamond ring on the same finger his hand made band still sits.

'Then I pronounce you man and wife,' Lisper declares happily. 'Now, if you excuse me, I'll leave you to do the next bit alone. Congratulations you two.' He leans over and plants a kiss on my cheek. 'Your father would be proud.' He slams his hand on Cass's shoulder. 'He'd be proud of the pair of ya.'

He bows out and climbs down the stone steps.

'Are you sure about this?' I ask. 'Once it's done, there's-'

'Shut up and kiss me, wife.'

And with that, Cass pulls me in and kisses me hard. His tongue caresses mine and from that moment on, there's no turning back.

He dies, and together... we'll live.

My husband kisses my neck and runs his hands all over me as we walk up the porch steps of my cottage. We're a mess of giggles and kisses and so much touching. He pushes me against the door with some serious passion. It is our wedding night after all. I run my fingers through his stark white hair and peer into his vivid blue eyes.

'I love you, husband,' I breathe through his kisses as he presses my back against the door.

'I love you too, wife.' His hand fumbles blindly behind me for the door handle. But neither of us will let the other go to find it. When he eventually opens the door, we rush inside, still locked in a passionate embrace. I pull his hoodie off over his head as I kick off my Nikes.

'Upstairs?' he pants.

'Yes. Definitely!'

There's a smash from the kitchen and something heavy lands on the floor. When I hear Tee gasp, we let each other go and rush to make sure she's okay. I throw open the door.

'Tee, are you... OH BLOODY HELL!'

Winder and his almost completely naked body falls off the table in surprise as Tee sits bolt upright and covers her equally naked self with her hands.

'Scar! I thought you'd be gone for a few hours!' she gasps.

I slam my hands over my eyes as Cass locks his gaze and his enormous smirk onto the ceiling.

'On my kitchen table? Really? That's just unhygienic!' I peer through a small gap in my fingers as Cass tosses a tea towel to his best friend. Winder stands and uses it to cover himself. 'Wait... hold on...' I look between them and realise Winder's hair is white! 'Tee... you're contagious too? Hold on...' I turn to Cass. 'We? You said we. *We had something to ask him*'. You *both* asked Elder One to turn?' Cass simply grins. I look back to Tee who flashes me her wedding ring while using Winder as a barrier for her naked body. 'OH! OH, TEE!' I take a step to rush over and congratulate her, but quickly remember that she's a little bit too naked for that.

'Yeah... congrats all round. Now, guys?' Winder nods to the door, 'Do ya mind?'

Cass takes my hand. 'As you were,' he laughs, pulling me away as I beam at the ecstatic Tee.

Cass closes the door and looks at me with a beautiful, boyish grin.

'We're all going?' I ask joyfully. 'All of us? Out beyond the wall?'

'Yep.' He nods once. 'We're family after all. Now, get up those stairs.' He smiles, giving my backside a smack.

The next morning, I'm hurling my duvet off the bed and tossing pillows across the room, swearing under my breath as I search for my coat. I left it hanging on the bedroom door last night. I'm sure of it!

'Arggghh!' I grunt, throwing my hands up in the air and charging out into the landing. 'Can anyone see my coat?' I call down the stairs, leaning over the bannister. 'Lisper's gonna be here soon and I can't find my coat anywhere!'

Cass kisses my neck as he passes me on the landing. 'Calm down, will ya? Lisper's got the coats. He said he needed to fix them before we leave.' He heads down the stairs, his duffle bag over his shoulder and a big grin on his face. 'Now, finish your packing and meet us in the kitchen. We don't wanna be late.'

'Fix 'em?' I call after him. 'What's wrong with 'em?'

'I dunno,' he chuckles, peering up at me as his foot reaches the bottom step. 'Just get your stuff packed, will ya?'

'But... I hate packing. Can't you just do it for me?'

'I'm your husband. Not your slave. I'll be in the kitchen with the Tee and Winder. Who... by the way... *are* packed.'

'Tell those two they'd better have washed that table!' I shout down. I listen to him carry on laughing as he walks into the kitchen. 'Sodding packing,' I grumble, returning to my bedroom. 'I hate packing.'

The sound of all my friends laughing and joking is bliss. I walk into the kitchen and see them all. Winder has his arms wrapped around Tee. Chilli and Flash stand side by side, their fingers entwined for everyone to see as now, it's no longer forbidden to love whoever the hell you want. Loom is pouring whiskey into the many glasses laid on the table, and seeing us, he raises the bottle.

'Congratulations!' he cheers, heading over and giving me a hug. One I return happily. 'I didn't know what to get you guys as a wedding gift so I dug out some of your dad's whiskey. I mean... what do you get a bunch of zombies for a wedding gift?'

'I wouldn't call her a zombie when her teeth are near your neck, mate,' Winder warns with a smirk.

Loom chuckles and starts handing glasses to everyone. I pick up two and head to Chilli and Flash.

'I am so sorry I thought it was you two who were the traitors.' I hand them each a drink. 'I hope you can forgive me.'

'Forget about it,' Chilli tells me with sincerity.

'I think the whole, dying to save us all thing, definitely makes up for it,' Flash adds as they both lean in and hug me.

There's a knock at the door and I let them both go.

'I'll get it,' Cass says, passing me with a kiss.

When he returns, he's not alone. Lisper, Elder Ten, Bowzer and Owl are with him too. Owl's in a wheelchair and winces at every bit of movement. We take a moment to greet each other and Chilli makes sure there's a glass in everyone's hand.

'How are you feeling?' I ask Owl.

She rests her hand over her injury. 'Alright. Sore but alive. Thanks to you.'

'I never would have made it along the wall without you and your team.'

'Let's just agree we're all awesome,' Winder says, raising his glass before downing it in one. 'Top-up please,' he adds, sliding his glass to Chilli who promptly refills it. 'This being dead thing makes it really hard to get drunk and I need something to take the edge off.'

His eyes flicker to me briefly. I know what he means. Not only are we leaving our home behind for good in a few hours, but we are to lay my dad to rest before we go. Not sure any of us are really ready for that yet.

'So, how's it looking out there?' I ask Lisper. 'How many did we lose?'

'Too many,' he sighs, his eyes glazing over as he stares at the floor. 'Far too many. The funeral will be in a few days. We need time to find and identify everyone.' Lisper's voice cracks a little and he looks utterly devastated.

'We definitely destroyed the serum?' I ask.

'Noah's house is a crater,' Bowzer tells me proudly and giving Lisper a second to compose himself. 'There's no more virus.'

Lisper nods in agreement. 'I found a stray Grey Coat. After some persuading, he told us of a few Noah supporters we didn't know about and we rounded them up. He also told us where and when more boats loaded with targets are due in. There are still Grey Coats on them.'

'Do you need us to stay and help you to deal with them?' I offer.

'No. We'll be ready for them. Don't you worry,' Lisper assures us all. 'Next boat is due in three weeks time, a bit further up north than I'd like. But luckily, I know a gent who is rather skilled at making things go boom. Their feet won't reach dry land before we blow them all back to hell.' He pats my back and heads to the whiskey.

Everyone settles into an odd sort of chattering. Each of them attempting to add some lightheartedness and optimism to the sombre and heartbreaking aftermath of the battle. The moments pass and it becomes painfully clear that there really are no joyous words to share. Their words falter. Their smiles slip. Their eyes fill with sorrow and we all end up in silence.

Lisper stands, clearing his throat and making sure everyone's glass is full before he raises his own.

'To the fallen,' he says. We stand and gather around the table. 'For the brave men and woman who died fighting. Who gave their lives and saved so many others. To them.'

'To all those lost souls who believed Noah and lost their humanity along the way,' Elder Ten adds.

'To my dad,' I say sadly. 'Who died saving my life.'

Cass kisses the top of my head. 'To us all.'

'To us all,' we repeat together, our glasses high.

Everyone drinks.

'Right...' Lisper sighs, putting down his glass and picking up the package he brought with him. 'That's enough of that. Let's try and lighten the mood a little, hmm?' He unwraps the brown paper parcel and hands Tee, Winder, Cass and I, our coats. 'These are for you and your new unit, Captain.'

'Captain?' I ask, a single brow hitched.

'We thought Captain would be better than Elder. And no more numbers. Names only. Isn't that right... Handsy?' Lisper looks at Elder Ten who shrugs.

'We've all done it,' he insists.

'Not as much as you used to when we shared a room.' Lisper rolls his eyes before they land on me. He gestures to Elder Ten over his shoulder with his thumb. 'Like living with a horny dog, it was.'

I almost choke on my whiskey as everyone else sniggers.

'Here.' Lisper hands me my mother's black leather coat. 'I wanted to do your new unit proud. I wanted to do you all, as well as your father, proud. So, I created a new insignia for you. Something that inspires hope and light amongst all this loss and darkness. The Canary is just... well, it's all kinds of wrong. This. This is much more fitting.' He holds it out further, one hand resting on the top of the delicately folded garment.

I take the perfectly folded coat and examine the new symbol he's attached to it. No longer is there a little yellow bird, but instead there are two white doves mid-flight, their beaks touching.

'A Japanese god of war named Hachiman claimed the dove as a sacred symbol,' Lisper tells us. 'Amidst battles and conflict, the dove of Hachiman was worn to honour the peace that will follow the fight.' His hand settles on my shoulder, his fingers squeezing into my skin. 'Just like you and your team. You will bring peace. I know it.'

'How did you know about Hachiman and the doves?' I ask, astounded that he would know anything about Japanese history.

Lisper chuckles and steps back, sliding his hands into his pockets. 'Your dad told me after you insisted on reading him that Japanese history book you found several years back.'

I smile fondly at that memory. Of my father and me, sat at this kitchen table. He was still teaching me to read. I was getting good but he kept pushing me on and on. He said I was good. I needed to be brilliant. He'd found a load of books in an old library truck and snuck a few back in for me. It was the middle of the night and pouring with rain. Lightning kept streaming across the sky and the way the ground shook with thunder made it impossible for me to sleep. I climbed out my bedroom window back at The Academy and snuck to his cottage, anxiety twisting my insides at the force of the storm. I felt safe with him. Even when I thought the sky was falling to earth and the ground below was shattering. He let me in, wrapped me in a towel, and made me read to take my mind off the thunderstorm. I learnt about Hachiman and the doves that night and spent the following weeks doodling them over and over.

Lisper taps the badge. 'Much better than a Canary, don't you think?' he asks softly.

'I do,' I whisper, a sorrowful sob forcing its way up my throat. 'I really do.' Even now, he's still talking to me. He's still here. My dad.

'What is a Canary anyway?' Tee asks, watching me as my eyes brim with tears. 'I've never heard of them except in terms of the unit.'

'Long before the outbreak, people would dig deep into the ground for coal. They would take a Canary with them in a cage. If the Canary died, it meant there was poison in the air and they should leave,' Lisper tells her. 'About sums the Canaries up. Sending them into danger just to see if they ever come back.'

'You're not wrong,' I scoff.

I slide on my mother's coat and stroke the doves. My fingers softly glide over the delicate stitching and I feel a rush of emotion ripple through me, from the tips of my fingers to the ends of my toes. It's something I've never felt before. Not once in all my life. Not until this very moment.

It makes me tingle and warms my dead-heart. My head feels light and dizzy, and a bubbling sense of joy fills my chest causing a girlish grin to pull at my lips and a happy sob to sneak from my mouth.

It takes a moment to realise what it is that I am feeling.

Faith.

An absolute trust in an unknown force. In something that I cannot see. That I cannot hear and that I cannot prove.

But I know it, standing here with my friends, my family, my husband, my mother's coat resting on my shoulders and my father's locket dangling around my neck, and the destruction of the targets that plague this world coursing through my veins... I know!

Humanity will not just survive this. They will thrive. They will grow and they will love and they will be what I have always longed to be.

We all will. I know it!

Because now, I have faith!

I have faith in all of us.

We're going to live.

We're going to be free.

We are going to win!

'I much prefer this symbol,' I nod happily, smiling down at the insignia. 'By an absolute mile. It's perfect.' I lift my gaze to Lisper. 'Are you ready?' There's a hard strain in my voice as he looks down at me with glistening eyes. 'I think it's time. Don't you?'

'I do. C'mon. Let's go say goodbye.'

There are no words to describe how I feel, watching the flames flick up high into the sky as we stand on the beach out beyond the wall. My father's body has disappeared beneath the ravenous flames, fed by several bottles of his favourite whiskey of course.

Cass and Tee grip my hands as they stand by my side. Winder has hold of Tee's other hand and together, we stand in a line and watch my dad leave this world completely.

Tears stream down our faces.

Sobs tear at our throats.

My body shakes uncontrollably.

If they weren't here with me, I think I would leap into those flames and turn to ash right alongside my dad.

Beyond the pyre, the sea breaks gently on the sand. The snow continues to fall all around us, landing on our hair and skin, failing to melt on our cold bodies.

Behind us, countless men and women are standing tall. Hundreds of them. Their hands rested over their hearts in complete silence. Not just soldiers, but civilians too. Every one of them out here to say their final goodbye to my lovely dad.

Their grief and sorrow makes the air around me vibrate and my insides scream with hunger. I hate how I feel when I sense their raw humanity. I hate how heartbroken I am at watching my dad burn.

I see now that leaving is the best thing for all of us.

Both the living... and the dead.

I let go of Tee's hand and caress the locket around my neck, thinking of the photograph inside. I close my eyes and see my mum and dad looking happy as they hold me in their arms. I block out everything else and just hold onto that single memory.

And I promise him, I promise them both, that I will never ever let it go.

'Love you, Mum. Love you, Dad,' I whisper.

And in amongst the sound of the waves, the falling snow, and the fierce flames, I hear them whisper back.

'Love you too, Kiddo. We love you too. Now get out there and kick some zombie arse!'

CHAPTER TWENTY-THREE

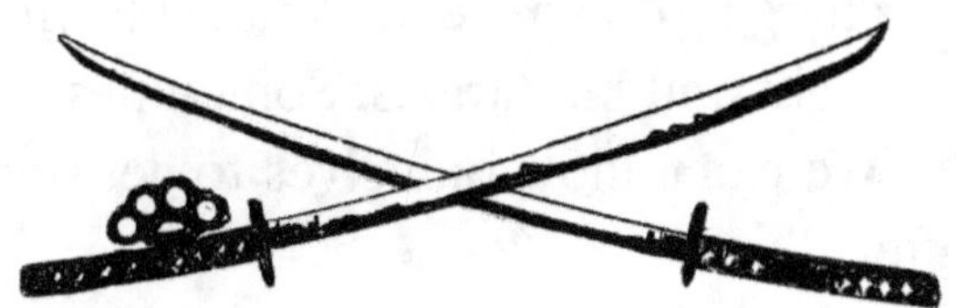

EPILOGUE

FREEDOM

The wind howls through my ears and whips my white hair across my face. I stand with my arms spread wide as I let it thrash around my body and chuckle as Cass whoops beside me, laughing heartily as he looks at the view below.

Well, a three-hundred-foot-high wind turbine in the heart of the Cornish countryside does offer one hell of a view!

'This is incredible!' he laughs, running his hands through his hair and twirling a full three-sixty. 'I can see the whole bloody world from up here!'

'It's pretty amazing, huh?' I turn to face him, loving his boyish excitement.

'These past two months have been heaven,' he sighs happily.

I agree. Watching Cass, Tee and Winder see the world in all its glory has been the best!

Racing through green fields. Camping in the recovering woodland. Playing in the abandoned theme parks and swimming in the sea. We have explored palaces and castles. Wondered at lost art hanging in museums. One of my personal favourites was the day we found a steam train filled with coal.

That was fun, charging down the tracks and blowing the whistle.

Every day we fight and kill targets. Sometimes we bite. Other times we fight. We can't allow ourselves to get sloppy with our battle skills, after all.

We do not need to eat, and we suffer no cravings for human flesh as there are no living people this far away from The Haven. But we *can* eat if we want. Food tastes even better now! Our sense of taste has heightened right along with all our other senses. Fruit and vegetables taste incredible and we discover food we have never seen before growing all over the place.

Cass wraps his arm around my waist and pulls me into his body so my back presses into his chest. He rests his chin on my shoulder and we look out to the distant ocean. The clouds are so low, we can almost touch them. We taste their moisture on our tongues. Salty and fresh. We smell the lakes and rivers where they have come from.

I hold Cass close, loving that he is here to share all this beauty with me.

Below, Tee and Winder lay in each other's arms, watching the snow fall from above. They wave up at us and we wave right back.

'How far away are we now?' Cass asks, planting a delicate trail of kisses along my neck.

'Another hundred miles or so. We're nearly there.'

'I can't wait to see it,' he says, his arms tightening around me a little. 'The way you and your unit talked about it... sounds like another world completely!'

'It is. My dad loved it. I know you will too. And so will the others back home. It will make a brilliant Haven.'

'I don't doubt it. Talking of Havens, I wonder how that island is looking now?' he ponders.

'Like a zombie massacre, I hope,' I reply, resting my cheek against his. 'We'll give it a few months and then head back to start burning the bodies.'

'I still haven't forgiven you, ya know?'

'For what?'

'For almost wetting yourself, laughing at me.'

'To be fair...' I lift my head and we gaze into each other's eyes, three hundred feet above the world. 'Watching you and Winder trying to sail us across to The Isle Of Wight was hilarious.'

'We got you there, didn't we?' he smirks, tucking my hair back over my shoulder and trailing his fingers gently down the length of my arm. 'When we go back in a few months, we'll burn the bodies and the people back home will have a whole island to themselves.'

'Won't that be something,' I whisper excitedly, turning to face him and to wrap my arms around his waist.

'It sure will.'

Cass and I race each other down the wind turbine's steps and rejoin Tee and Winder, who are entangled lovingly in each other, just lying on the snowy ground. Since the day we left, they have been utterly engrossed in each other. Even more so than Cass and me!

'Alright, love birds. Tongues back in your own mouths, please,' I call over, heading to the horses. 'Let's get a move on, shall we?'

'Yes, Boss,' Winder replies, his lips still pressed into hers. 'Just snogging the missus and then I'll be right with you.'

Tee giggles, kissing him back while trying to untangle his arms. After a few moments, we've mounted up and headed out, riding south.

'This looks so weird,' Tee says, looking up at the plastic dome and running her fingers across its sleek surface. 'What an odd structure.'

We pay no attention to the mass of un-dead currently slaughtering each other behind us and they pay absolutely no attention to us either.

'Wait until you see inside!' I tease, gesturing towards the large metal doors to the right which are still boarded up. 'Go wait over there. I'll let you in.'

'We can climb up with you,' Winder suggests, his arm draped over Tee's shoulders and his axe strapped to his back.

I shake my head and take hold of one of the thick vines. 'You'll appreciate it better this way,' I tell him. 'Trust me.'

Cass lands a kiss on my lips and heads to the doors with the others as I start my ascent.

It's a lot easier to climb up the side of the dome this time around than it was all those months ago, and soon enough, my feet land on the mossy ground inside.

I take in a deep breath, inhaling the scent of rotten vegetation and moist soil. As I walk, I see the little hut we used, still in the exact same condition we left it. The empty bottles of rum lie abandoned from our last night of drinking together. As I stand on the rickety steps of the hut, I see the ghostly image of my dad and me talking and laughing as we play cards. I smile fondly, knowing that even though he's no longer with me, he will never leave me. I will never forget him. I will never shy away from saying his name or talking about our time together. I pass the waterfall and see another ghost pass me. Dad's drenched through and he's storming off in a huff, his moustache is all wonky and lopsided from falling under the waterfall and I'm in a heap, hysterically laughing at him as he goes.

I chuckle softly to myself as I carry on to the sealed doors.

I prise them open and step back, throwing open my arms to welcome Cass, Tee and Winder inside.

'Welcome to the jungle, guys!'

They step through the door, their eyes like saucers and gasps coming from each and every one of them. As they enter, the doors close behind them, cutting off the sound of the targets tearing each other apart. Instead, the melody of birdsong, crickets and the tumbling waterfall fill our ears.

Cass wraps his arms around me, looking above us at the thick canopy of gigantic leaves and ripe bananas in absolute awe.

'This is incredible! Completely and utterly incredible!' He looks down at me, love and devotion emanating from him. 'I think I'm in heaven.'

'Well,' Winder laughs. 'We did die. We could be!'

'Who'd have thought,' Tee giggles, taking my hand. 'That dying would be so much fun. This is perfect!'

'Not yet. There's just one thing missing.' I clap my hands together. 'Now... as my dad would have said, where's the rum?'

The End?
No way.
This is the beginning!

Keep a lookout for more adventures as Scarlett and her family travel the country, and set about saving the world.

THANK YOU.

Thank you for reading The Verity: Duology.
I hope you enjoyed it!
Please take a moment to leave a review with your favourite retailer.
Reviews are so important to indie authors, and they are very much appreciated.
Amazon
Goodreads
If you would like to know about upcoming releases, please follow me on Facebook https://www.facebook.com/HelloMJLawrie/
Or sign up for my newsletter through my website: https://www.mjlawrie.com/

Also by

M.J.LAWRIE

The Last Witch Series

A dark, paranormal fantasy romance series.

The Verity Duology

A dystopian, romance, fantasy.

The Stolen Fae series

A dark, MFM, paranormal romance fantasy.

www.ingramcontent.com/pod-product-compliance
Lightning Source LLC
Chambersburg PA
CBHW072033190726
48294CB00005B/1243